Also by Tom Kirkbride

Gamadin Series

Book I - *Gamadin: Word of Honor*
Book II - *Gamadin: Mons*
Book III - *Gamadin: Distant Suns*
Book IV - *Gamadin:* Gazz

Short Stories

Stinky's Island
Surfing Roots

Book V

GAMADIN

CORE

Tom Kirkbride

WIGTON

Publishing

Published by Wigton Publishing Company
32857 Fox Lane, Cottage Grove, OR 97424

For ordering information or special discounts for bulk purchases, please contact:

Wigton Publishing Company, 32857 Fox Lane,
Cottage Grove, OR 97424 (541) 246-4135

Design and composition by Tom Kirkbride.

Publisher's Cataloging-In-Publication Data
(Prepared by The Donohue Group, Inc.)

Kirkbride, Tom (Thomas K.)
   Gamadin. Book 5, Core / Tom Kirkbride. -- 1st ed.

   p. : ill., maps; cm.

   ISBN: 978-0-9883633-1-1

1. Extraterrestrial beings--Fiction. 2. Space warfare--Fiction. 3. Surfers--California--Fiction. 4. Science fiction. 5. Fantasy fiction. I. Title.

PS3611.I75 G264 2015
813 / .6

Printed in USA

10 09 08 10 9 8 7 6 5 4 3 2 1
First Edition

For the San Diego City Lifeguards
For their Honor, Courage, & Dedication
The true Gamadin!

Who were the Gamadin?

Many, many thousands of years ago, when Hitt and Gibb were the cultural elite centers of the Omni quadrant, the Gamadin ruled the cosmos -- not in an authoritarian way, but as a protective force against the spreading Death of evil empires and their acts of conquest and domination. A wise and very ancient group of planets from the galactic core formed an alliance to create the most powerful police force the galaxy had ever seen. This force would be independent of any one state or planet. They were called "Gamadin."

Translated from the ancient scrolls of Amerloi, Gamadin means: "From the center, for all that is good." The sole mission of the Gamadin was to defend the freedom and happiness of peaceful planets everywhere, regardless of origin or wealth. It was said that a single Gamadin ship was so powerful, it could destroy an empire.

Unfortunately, after many centuries of peace, the Gamadin had performed their job too well. Few saw reason for such a powerful presence in their own backyard when the Death of war and the aggressive empire building were remnants of an ancient past. So what was left of the brave Gamadin simply withered away and was lost, never to be heard from again.

However, the ancient scrolls of Amerloi foretold of its resurrection:

"For it is written that one day the coming Death will lift its evil head and awaken the fearsome Gamadin of the galactic core. And the wrath of the Gamadin will be felt again throughout the stars, and lo, while some people trembled in despair, still more rejoiced; for the wrath of the Gamadin will cleanse the stars for all; and return peace to the heavens . . . ."

OMINI PRIME QUADRANT

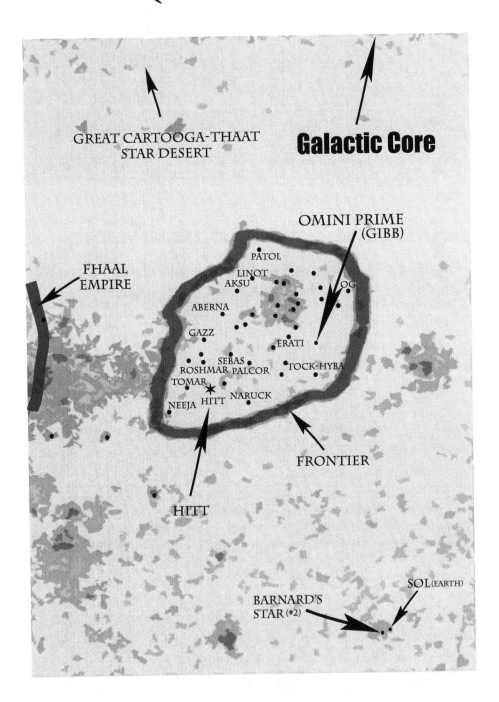

GREAT CARTOOGA-THAAT
STAR DESERT

Galactic Core

OMINI PRIME
(GIBB)

FHAAL
EMPIRE

PATOL

LINOT
AKSU

OG

ABERNA

GAZZ

ERATI

SEBAS
ROSHMAR PALCOR
TOMAR
NEEJA HITT NARUCK

TOCK-HYBA

FRONTIER

HITT

SOL (EARTH)

BARNARD'S
STAR (#2)

OUR GALAXY

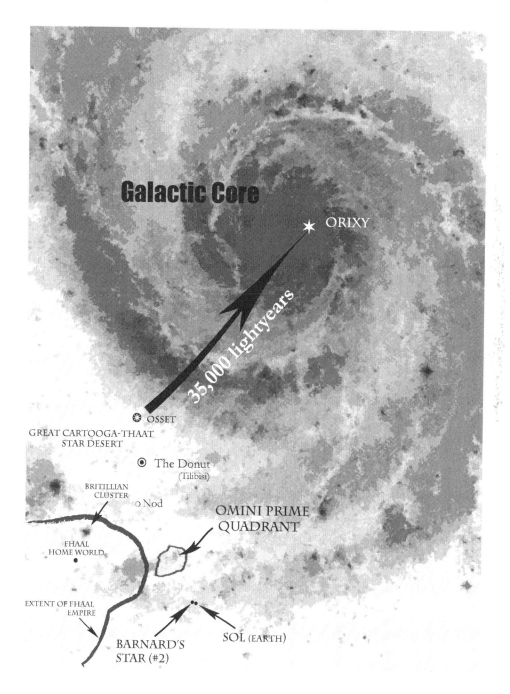

Galactic Core

ORIXY

35,000 lightyears

OSSET

GREAT CARTOOGA-THAAT
STAR DESERT

The Donut
(Tilibisi)

BRITILLIAN
CLUSTER

o Nod

OMINI PRIME
QUADRANT

FHAAL
HOME WORLD

EXTENT OF FHAAL
EMPIRE

BARNARD'S
STAR (#2)

SOL (EARTH)

"Even the longest journey must begin where you stand."

Lau-tzu, Chinese philosospher (604 BC – 531 BC)

1

Return to Hitt

All odysseys, whether it be across town or across the galaxy, begin somewhere. *Millawanda's* began at Amerloi as she drifted down through the acidic clouds of its toxic atmosphere. At a thousand feet above the planet's surface, she extended her long, golden landing struts as if she were stretching after a lengthy, cross-country drive. Upon touchdown, she kicked up a small amount of dust as her three landing pads settled among the weathered ruins of the dead city. Bathed in perpetual twilight from a dying primary star, the crumbled remains were all that was left of Hitt's once glorious past. The dark colors of desolation, the lifelessness, and the bitterly cold, minus 100 degree temperatures made a Bram Stoker novel seem cheery. What seemed out of place among the ruins were uncountable scores of dark mounds scattered far to the horizon. The planet may have been dark and soulless, but inside the forward observation room of the giant saucer, life went on. Captain Harlowe Pylott continued his recital for Leucadia Mars on the cobalt blue piano made from a rare jungle wood found on a remote planet a thousand lightyears from Earth. The piece he played for her was the melodic *Larghetto* second movement of Chopin's *Piano Concerto #2*. It was Leucadia's favorite. As she listened, she considered the mounds through the window with sadness. Although neither she nor Harlowe had ever been to Hitt, they knew what the mounds represented: death. They were all fallen soldiers left behind from a forgotten battle three-quarters of a century before. The air was so cold and dry on Amerloi, the remains would stay frozen in time for eons. It was an everlasting memorial to the madness that had brought the Neejian scientists to the planet where they made their remarkable discovery: They confirmed the existence of an ancient police force that had once fought for peace and justice throughout the known galaxy. With a single, incredibly powerful ship, perhaps the most formidable weapon in existence, these warriors kept the peace for a thousand passings. The Neejian scientists believed that if they found the secret of such infinite power, and some small part of that power had survived the millennia, then Neeja, their home planet, could survive the coming Fhaal invasion. The Neejian translation for this mythical police force was "Peacemakers." But according to the ancients, they were better known throughout the quadrants as Gamadin!

Leucadia's mother, Sook, and her squad of elite Triadian soldiers were sent to Hitt to escort the archeologists back to Neeja with their Gamadin artifacts. But before they could return with the discovery that would save their planet from invasion, Sook's elite team of rescuers was compromised. Fhaal attack squads swooped down and ambushed their landing party, killing everyone but Sook. It was only by sheer determination that she and her pet chinneroth, Mowgi, escaped with the Gamadin relics that were given to her by a dying scientist. The relics brought her to Earth, and after many decades, she sacrificed her life, and that of Leucadia's father, Harry, in the search for *Millawanda*, the last surviving ship of the ancient protectors of the galaxy called Gamadin.

Leucadia ran her fingers along the nearby dark blue lounge chair like she was touching something sacred. The spotless fabric was soft and plush and had the appearance of a furnishing bought at some high-end store in Beverly Hills. The carpet was equally as rich. It had the same qualities as the rest of the décor: lush, thick, and luxuriously deep blue. Her focus turned to the golden ceiling, the windows, and the rest of the handsomely appointed forward observation room. None of it was showy, extravagant, or overdone. The décor was simple and tasteful, like a European showroom. How something so old, 17,000 years old, could remain so beautiful was almost impossible to imagine.

But the journey to Hitt was a more pressing voyage for the young Gamadin crew than revisiting the place where Sook's quest had begun. *Millawanda* was dying. There was no other way to describe it, Ian and Leucadia had told

Harlowe two weeks ago as they left the planet Gazz for home. *Millawanda* had indeed survived her near-destruction while saving Gazz from a fatal gamma ray burst, but in doing so, it may have cost the ship her life. According to her system analysis, unlike the many times in the past where she performed her own self repairs, her systems were now shutting down little by little. She was slowly dying from within, as if some terminal disease had infected her body.

Harlowe had found it difficult to believe his powerful, beautiful ship was "sprouting wings," as he liked to say when speaking of the hereafter. "No way. Millie's fine," he argued. "She just needs time to heal. Give her a little sun and she'll be right as rain, right?"

"No, Captain," Ian countered respectfully. "Millie needs a complete top-to-bottom overhaul."

"Well then, let's blow back to #2." (Number 2 is the planet not far from Earth where the crew first landed on their long journey to save Neeja. It had become their favorite place to relax. The surf was perfect, the water warm, and best of all it was uninhabited.) "We'll put the clickers to work and get her fixed," Harlowe figured.

Ian glanced at Leucadia for support. The two of them had worked tirelessly for over a week to discover the real cause of *Millawanda's* slow degradation. "It's not that simple, babe," Leucadia said. During moments like these, while away from the bridge, official titles were often set aside as she went on: "Millie's really sick. She's beyond what the clickers can do for her."

To Harlowe, no explanation made sense. "I don't understand. She's tight. She running smooth on all cylinders. We just topped off her tank with a boatload of black thermo-grym. How far will that take her? I bet she goes another 5,000 years if we don't push her too hard." Harlowe said smiling big, trying to stay upbeat. But neither Leucadia nor Ian were amused.

Leucadia remained grim. "She's got about a month . . . maybe less, babe," she said with her bright green eyes remaining unshakable, even under Harlowe's hard stare for the truth.

Harlowe's mouth dropped open as wide as *Millawanda's* fifty-yard wide center hatchway. "A month?"

Leucadia projected a hologram onto the center of the table. The image was the giant blue crystal from Millie's power room. When they saved Gazz from the two gamma ray bursts, the surge of power she needed to produce to save the planet fried the only blue crystal they had. "If Millie would have been functioning normally, she could have handled the power surge easily. My guess is that this crystal was nearing the end of its lifespan. Millie gave all the power she had left to protect Gazz, babe."

"Why didn't we know that going in?" Harlowe asked. "We might have been able to make adjustments to protect her."

"Because we didn't know how deteriorated the crystal was until it happened," Ian replied. "I'm used to working on engines that run on gas not blue crystals."

"You mean she's been on E this whole time?" Harlowe asked.

Leucadia and Ian both nodded. Ian went on to explain, "That's right. Since the day we found her. When we blew out of the mesa in Utah, we assumed she was okay because she flew us to Las Vegas, Mars, and all around the solar system, to the Omni Quadrant and back without a hitch. She even fixed herself on #2, fed us, and kept us warm as we flew at light speeds across the galaxy, destroying the Fhaal Empire, the Consortium, and Anor Ran's corporate fleets. She was two thumbs up doing all that, Captain, but she did it all on fumes. She may be thousands of years old and still working, but she's not immortal. She has limits, pard. She's like the rest of us. She will die if we don't fix her."

Harlowe didn't answer right away or ask any more questions. He remained silent, as if he was shooting through all the possibilities on how to save her in his mind. "Then we find another blue crystal somewhere."

Ian wanted to scream. "It's not like they're just lying around, Captain. Unlike thermo-grym, they're not found in nature. They were manufactured by Gamadin engineers."

"The Gamadin call the blue crystal aara," Leucadia added. "Aara is rare. So rare we think the only place we can find another one is Orixy."

Harlowe's eyes flared open. He had never heard the word "Orixy" in his life. "What in the . . . is Orixy?"

"It's Millie's word for origin," Ian replied. "Lu and I think she needs to go home to find the aara she needs to live."

"Thermo-grym isn't good enough?"

"No," Leucadia replied, "it's like drinking kerosene when she needs high octane, formula-one, racing fuel."

"And we can't make any, I take it?"

Ian and Leucadia both shook their heads. "We believe only Millie's makers have that knowledge," Leucadia said.

"Orixy? Aara? Origin? How do you know that?" Harlowe questioned, like they were on trial and he was the prosecutor.

Ian admitted there were a lot of holes in their theory. "But that's how it translates to us."

"So you're guessing. Millie's life depends on your opinions?"

With tears in her eyes, she defended herself. "No, Harlowe, we're not guessing. That's all Millie could give us. Her systems seem okay, but when we ask her about her distant past, she remembers very little. Her long term memory has faded. She seems unable to remember something as simple as where she originated."

Ian added his own view. "My guess is home and and where she was made are the same, Captain. We find home, we find Orixy, we find another crystal."

Harlowe kept his questions direct. "That simple, huh?"

Leucadia sat up straight. Now was no time for being girlie, she thought. She needed to be strong for them all, and especially for *Millawanda*. She wiped her eyes and carried on without missing a beat. "It's the only logical answer. We need to find Orixy, and we need to find it yesterday! So, with all due respect, Captain, stop this denial. Millie is sick and she needs her medical team now! Find Millie's home, Harlowe, before it's too late!"

Harlowe was stunned by Leucadia's forcefulness. He figured after a few good surf days on Gazz, they were going home. Dodger would be in school, and maybe he could get back to that island in the South Pacific he was enjoying before Mowgi plucked him off his surfboard and the whole Gazzian mess began. Now, just as they were about to whiz past the Gall Moon, he was being told that all wasn't so cool after all. He thought his bad hair days had taken some time off. Apparently not. His ship was dying, and there was no way to fix her, except by finding her origin, a place called Orixy, wherever that was. If he had been a young man of lesser character, he might have drifted into some deep depression or drunk himself into a stupor, that is, if he had been old enough to drink. But that wasn't Harlowe's way. Like the problems he had met head-on the entire 18 years of his young life, the protecting Gazz from gamma ray bursts, or surviving life on Mars, and General Theodore Gunn's ruthless training, or putting an end to the Fhaal Empire. He had faced them all like he always did: Man up! Facing problems came with commanding the most powerful warbird in the galaxy. He was her Captain, and if she needed an overhaul to make her right again, by God he would do it or die trying.

"Okay, what are the options?" Harlowe asked, keeping his chin high. "Do we know where this Orixy place is?"

"From what my mother told me," Leucadia began, "the Gamadin originally came from the Galactic core, the center of our galaxy. So that's our direction."

Harlowe found Leucadia's answer wanting. "The center of the galaxy, huh? What are we talking about? A small center? A big center? Galaxy means big to me. What's it mean to you, Lu?"

"Billions of stars," Leucadia admitted.

Harlowe figured as much. "Yeah, that fits my definition. Next to finding babes for Riverstone and Rerun, I can think of nothing harder to find than a planet in a billion stars."

"What was her source of this info?" Ian asked. "Because I don't recall reading anything about the Gamadin coming from the galactic core."

"Children's fables," Leucadia replied.

"Children's fables?" Harlowe and Ian said together.

"How 'bout something a little more solid, Lu," Harlowe stated.

Leucadia darted an accusing glare at Harlowe and Ian. "My mother had that solid info before someone lost the star map."

Harlowe smiled sheepishly. He had lost the cloth map of the galaxy that Sook had brought with her when she came to Earth looking for *Millawanda*. The map was the only one of its kind. There was no other copy. "So what now?" he asked her.

Leucadia changed the crystal hologram to the pinwheel graphic of the Milky Way Galaxy. "We know about where it is." She pointed to a position just to the southeast corner of the galactic center. "Around here, give or take 500 lightyears."

Leucadia saw the long stare Harlowe was giving her. "Come on, Lu. Narrow it down a little," he pleaded. "That's still a ton of star systems to search. If Millie is as bad off as you and Wiz say she is, we'll be dragging her with ropes and chains to Orixy by the time we get there. We won't have the luxury to search the core. We'll need a specific place to go by then."

"Millie's memory has good intel as far as the planet Amerloi, but when we get into the Cartooga-Thaat star desert, she draws a blank. We're on our own from there. The good news, and our only real hope of finding Orixy, I believe, is the Gamadin had a system of bases throughout the galaxy. If we're lucky, we might find another map or chart to guide us to one of the outposts."

Harlowe stared at the galactic center where Leucadia had pointed earlier. "And how far is the core from here?"

Leucadia's eyes remained steady and frank. "Twenty-five thousand lightyears to the outer rings of the core, and then another five or ten thousand or so to the inner core." She then went from the galactic center to the opposite side of the pinwheel of stars. "But if Orixy is one hundred-and-eighty degrees on the opposite side of the galactic plane from us, that could be another 5k."

Harlowe tried not to act surprised by the distance, but he couldn't help himself. He let out a loud guffaw. "Thirty-five thou—" He almost choked on the number. "I hope that's a miscalculation."

Harlowe knew it wasn't. Leucadia didn't make miscalculations. When it came to precise measurements, she was never wrong. Her silence and solemn face told the story. The distance to the core was a solid number.

"So what's your plan, Lu?" Harlowe asked.

"We start with the ancient city of Hitt, located on the planet Amerloi, here," she said, pointing up at the holographic star map projected above the table, "and hope we find a clue to Millie's home. That's where the the Neeja scientists discovered the Gamadin relics that led my mother to Earth. That is where we should begin, Harlowe."

"Hitt, huh?" Harlowe asked.

"It's a start, Captain," Ian replied. "The Neejian scientists were looking for Millie, they weren't looking for Orixy. If Hitt was a Gamadin outpost, then it's possible a clue to Orixy's position in the galaxy is still there."

Harlowe shot a hopeful eye Ian's way with his second try at finding hope for a cache of aara lying around to be picked up.

Ian pressed his lips tight, shaking his head. "No way, Dog. The Gamadin wouldn't leave crystals just lying around for someone to pick up. They were too valuable. They would be kept under the tightest security possible. If the source of their power fell into the wrong hands, it could be used against them."

"Don't dismiss the idea so fast, Wiz." Harlowe cautioned. "Your dad's gas station had a ton of spare parts stored in the overhead racks so he didn't have to drive to the store every time he needed something."

"The outposts weren't gas stations, Harlowe. Gamadin ships didn't require fuel to make them go. Their fuel is everywhere."

Harlowe thought that didn't compute. "Didn't you just say Millie is running on E?"

"I did. But it's not like the thermo-grym fuel anyone else uses. Millie uses dark energy," Leucadia said.

"I thought energy was energy."

"It is," Ian agreed. "But the Gamadin went way beyond everyone else. To power their ships they needed a source of fuel that was limitless so they wouldn't have to stop and gas up for a very long time. Dark energy was the answer. It's the stuff left over from the Big Bang. It's everywhere."

"And it's called dark energy?"

"And the blue crystals suck it up like a vacuum?"

"That's right," Leucadia confirmed, and added, "it's an endless supply of power."

"Then if she has a good blue crystal, she'll be cool," Harlowe assumed.

Leucadia smiled at Harlowe like an approving teacher beams at her star pupil. "Very good, Captain."

Harlowe pinched his chin in thought. "So we're going to Hitt first, huh?"

Ian replied, "We have better sensors than the Neejian scientists. If there is something Gamadin they missed in the catacombs, we'll find it for sure."

Harlowe nodded his approval before turning to Leucadia with his next question. "If not, are there anymore children's fables we can draw on?"

Leucadia remained cool, despite the sarcasm. "No. If we don't find anything there, we will be flying blind after that."

Harlowe rose from his chair and went to the observation window. The dark side of the Gall Moon was beautifully purple and pitted with craters and cracks. The moon was the Gazzian crew's holiest symbol. For them, it brought stability and meaning to their lives. Maybe a little regard for the moon would give some stability and meaning to Millie as well, he hoped. It couldn't hurt. He made a small nod toward the Gall Moon before returning to Ian and Leucadia. "Sounds like this is a one way trip."

Their silence was again his answer. He turned back to the Gall Moon, thinking of his Gazzian crew, sailing back to their homes in their tall ship. He remembered the joy of the fresh ocean spray on his face, the flutter of the sails, the sway of the ship under his feet, and the sound of creaking timbers as the bow plowed through waves on the open sea. He closed his eyes wishing at times he was still their captain.

"Sorry, Dog," Ian said, knowing the pain he was suffering.

"Not your fault, Wiz. We'll get her fixed and have her back on the road, kicking bad guy's butts, in no time."

"Change course to Hitt, Captain?" Ian asked.

"No, Mr. Wizzixs. Stay the course for home."

"But Captain, we'll never make it past Cartooga-Thaat if we go home first. It's 300 lightyears in the wrong direction."

Harlowe's blue eyes remained unalterable. "If you think I'm taking my brother to the galactic core, your brain is twisted, Wiz. Our chances of getting there and back are zilch. Right?"

Ian and Leucadia both agreed the chances of survival were extremely low.

"Well, I won't put my mother through that kind of anguish . . . We'll just have to find more thermo-grym along the way." Harlowe leaned into Ian's space. "Or would you like to face Tinker in the hereafter with that kind of news, Wiz?"

Harlowe's mom was a former U.S. Marine D.I. who could turn a rose to stone with her stare alone. Harlowe had crossed her only once in his life. He forgot to take out the trash when she asked him. Big mistake. She tossed him through a window for his zen moment. He picked glass from his face and arms for a week and never neglected his chores again after that. So having grown up with Harlowe, Ian was well aware of Mrs. Pylott's bad side. He stared back at Harlowe, with the fear of God in his eyes, without answering the question. Harlowe answered for him. "Well, neither do I. Dodger is going home. That's final. Full speed ahead, Mr. Wizzixs. Let's get it over with and back on the road to Amerloi."

"Aye, Captain. What about Jester and Rerun? Should I call them back?" Ian asked, remembering that Harlowe had allowed the two of them to go on a weeklong surfing trip to the Lenor system in the souped-up grannywagon he had customized for their trip. The original plan was to swing by Lenor on their way home.

"Yeah, better get on it, Wiz, before they get out of range," Harlowe confirmed. "They'll want a little off-the-clock time at home, too, before we depart."

Harlowe sat back in his chair, looking up at the ceiling, trying to get his brain wrapped around where they were headed next. Twenty-five thousand lightyears from home, and that guesstimate was on the short side. Who knows how far it really was to Orixy? Regardless, he thought, whatever the distance and whatever the price, fixing Millie was worth the risk, however far they had to travel.

As Ian left the table for the ship's bridge, Jewels, Harlowe's robob servant, passed him on the way with a tray full of blue shakes, double-doubles, fries, and a Godiva chocolate smoothie for Leucadia. It was like the robob knew it was a Bluestuff moment without anyone telling him. Normally, Harlowe would have taken the first whiff of the SoCal delights and said, "You da man, Jewels!" But not this time. Harlowe could only see the tray with dull eyes. Thinking about *Millawanda's* condition gave him a bellyache. He couldn't eat a thing, not even a sip of his Bluestuff shake. He looked up at Leucadia, wondering what he could say to her. His wondering stopped the moment he saw the tears dripping off her smooth, flawless chin onto her food. Harlowe slid next to her in his chair and wrapped his strong arms around her. The meeting was over. It was okay to be girlie now. He almost wished he could join her with tears of his own. But he couldn't. He had a sick ship and half a galaxy to cross to make her well. Tears had no place in the plan.

A few minutes later, Ian came back into the cabin with more bad news. Harlowe was holding Leucadia like he never wanted to let her go. "I can't reach them, Capt—" Ian stopped in mid stride, knowing his timing was a little off. He looked to one side and said, "Sorry, Captain."

Harlowe only relaxed a little, still keeping her in his arms. "Go ahead, Wiz. Lay it on."

"Jester and Rerun must be out of range, Captain. They're dark."

"Dark, huh? Maybe they're too busy to pick up. Lenor's not that far away."

In Riverstone and Simon's defense, Leucadia raised a more plausible explanation. "Millie is conserving energy, Harlowe. Her com range is less than half of what it was only two days ago."

There was nothing Harlowe could do. He had to leave his crewmen behind for the time being. They would be angry they didn't have the chance to go home before the search for Orixy began. But it couldn't be helped. "All right. Leave them a note they can retrieve later. Tell them we'll pick them up on the return."

"Aye, Captain."

* * *

That was ten days ago when Harlowe brought Dodger back. He was now in school while Tinker's oldest son continued saving the galaxy from the bad guys. Harlowe said his goodbye, but Tinker knew from his hug that this was no ordinary mission. "This is one of these 'Mom, you don't want to know times,' right?"

With tears in his eyes and a crack in his voice, Harlowe answered, "Yeah."

She hugged him long before she said, "I love you, son, and I'm extremely proud of you. Whatever it is, I know you'll do it."

He nodded, wiping his eyes. "Thanks, Mom," he replied, turned and left her standing at the high security entrance to the White House with two U.S. Marines standing at attention next to her.

* * *

At any other time, Leucadia would have clapped and cried out "Bravo! Bravo!" at the end of Harlowe's recital. But not now. All she would allow herself to say was, "Wonderfully played, hon."

Hon was a name she rarely used for him. She would never call him that unless they were alone and off-the-clock.

Harlowe rose from the piano and stepped behind her, looking out the window as he gathered her in his arms. "Nice place," he said of the dark, cold, and lifeless planet.

Leucadia stiffened, not because of Harlowe's touch, but because of what she knew lay ahead.

"Our journey begins here, then," Harlowe stated.

"The first step . . ."

His eyes focused more closely on the crumbling archways, the broken avenues and what he thought was movement among the mounds. "What do you see?"

Leucadia's reply came with a long breath of sadness. "Death," she murmured.

2

Surfing Roots

"So what's this surf spot of yours called again?" First Mate Simon Bolt asked. When he wasn't a Gamadin, back on Earth he was an Oscar winning actor who played, Captain Julian Starr, commanding officer of the starship, *Distant Galaxy*. Simon often laughed that if his fans only knew that being a real-life star trooper was many times more perilous than the parts he played on screen, they would never believe it. On more than one occasion he tried telling the screenwriters what star travel was really like. At first they listened because he was, after all, an A-list actor now. But behind his back he knew they laughed and wrote what they wanted. During his early days as an actor he would have been upset by their attitude. But not now. Now he was much more than just an actor. He was a Gamadin, a proud member of a badass starship crew who actually lived and breathed what science fiction writers could only imagine.

He and First Officer Matt Riverstone had a whole week to themselves surfing in the Lenor system before their other shipmates rendezvoused with them at prearranged coordinates with *Millawanda*.

"I call it Roots. It's on the water moon of Lenor," Riverstone replied.

Simon checked the sensor on the console. A 3D graphic materialized above the dash, making it easy for them both to see the earth-sized, watery moon next to a larger planet with two other smaller moons.

"Looks cool," Simon offered. "Where do the babes hang?"

Riverstone shrugged, unconcerned. "It's uninhabited."

"Not a single doe on the entire moon? You're joking, right?"

"Nope."

Simon threw up his hands. "Then why am I even on this trip? You didn't say there were no babes."

Riverstone kept smiling. "You never asked."

"I never— Listen, that's always a given." Simon pointed a finger at Riverstone. "So, I don't care how good the surf is. What's the point of going on any vacation if there are no babes?"

Riverstone spun the image of the moon around until he found the location he was looking for.

"That's it. Right there. Just below that river delta. Nice, huh?"

Simon kept shaking his head, wondering why he had been so stupid as to go along on a vacation where there was no possible chance of scoring a date. He could have stayed on the medieval world of Gazz where the girls were tens, even though they had tails that could break his neck. At least they were babes, he thought.

"Is the water warm?" Simon asked, grudgingly.

"Yep. Like bath water," Riverstone replied.

"Sun?"

"Warm and yellow. Perfect for tanning that mug of yours. Just like SoCal in August. You'll feel right at home," Riverstone replied.

Simon turned his nose up. "At least SoCal has girls in August."

"Things have a way of working out. You'll see."

"How many times have you been there?" Simon asked.

"This is the first."

"How do you know there's surf? The place could be as flat as my koi pond."

"Pictures."

"Pictures?"

"Yeah, pictures. Prigg's been there. He showed me pictures."

Simon's eyes rolled. "Prigg's afraid of water. How would he know about waves?"

Riverstone touched an activator on the dash and a holo image of a tropical beach, tall palms, and glassy blue surf appeared beside the globe.

"Pretty sweet, huh?"

Simon pointed at the picture. "Are those tree roots sticking out of the surf?"

"That's why I call it Roots. We can surf right through them. It will be like shooting the pier at Huntington."

"Sweet. How big are those waves?" Simon asked, looking anxious.

"Oh, 20 feet, give or take."

Simon didn't look happy. "This is supposed to be a vacation, not a funeral."

Riverstone smiled. "No worries, brah. You'll be okay. We only have to be careful about one thing."

Simon didn't really care. He sat back with a sour look and waited for the other shoe to drop. For him, there was nothing worse than a vacation with no babes. So whatever Riverstone added was unimportant.

Riverstone continued: "The tides. It's a small detail, but once every twenty-three days when the three moons of Lenor align, the tide surges two-hundred feet."

Simon sat up. "That's not a small detail, Jester. How long do we have?"

"Not long. Ten to fifteen hours, tops. A whole day if you think about it."

"Ten? Let's pick another day when there isn't a surge."

"No worries," Riverstone replied. "We'll park the grannywagon on the bluff for the first night until the tide recedes. After that, we're home free for the rest of the week. It's a slam—"

"Don't say it! Last time you said something was a slam dunk the entire crew, *Millie,* and a planet almost ate the big one!"

Riverstone kept his upbeat smile. "You'll see. After this is over, you'll be thanking me."

Simon groaned. "That will never happen."

Riverstone touched a small gold medallion around his neck. "Got your SIBA?"

Simon lifted a similar medallion that was tucked inside the front of his flight suit. "Yeah, never leave home without it," he grumbled.

* * *

The watery moon was exactly how Riverstone had described it. The sky was cloudless and blue, and the air was warm from the yellow sun. It seemed a perfect start for a week of fun. As planned, they put down on the bluff overlooking the beach. Overhead, the blue-green fronds stuck straight up as if they were jolted with electricity. All of the strange plants they saw would have fascinated a botanist, but that was as far as it went. Offworld plant life was interesting but low on their list of wow-that's-cool. The surf was their priority, and just as Riverstone predicted, the waves were crankin', just like in Prigg's photo.

Riverstone retracted the craft's canopy and shut off the force field, allowing the soothing rays of the sun to soak their faces. "Look at those waves, Rerun! Who cares about babes with surf like this?"

Simon pointed at his chest. "I do. When I'm off-the-clock, that's what I care about."

"Don't be a toad. When you're out there, locked in a tube, you'll forget about everything but the ride."

They climbed out of the grannywagon and untied the hold-downs on their surfboards. Next, they stepped out of their flight suits and tossed them into the back seat with their weapons, utility belts, and a dull gold cylinder.

Simon pointed at the cylinder under Riverstone's flight suit. "You brought Alice?"

Riverstone smiled. "We're surfing, not roughing it. Who's going to make the double-doubles and fries?"

"Good point." Simon picked up his red board, and added, with a worried frown as he focused on the hundreds of trees projecting out of the surf up and down the coast, "I've never ripped through roots before."

"Watch me. It will be like sliding through pier pilings."

Wearing only board shorts and their SIBA medallions dangling around their necks, they made their way down the bluff to the wide-open beach. The sand was so beautifully white and squeaky clean, it was hard to imagine that in a few hours it would covered by a two hundred foot surge.

"How long do we have again? I don't want to be caught outside when the tide comes," Simon said as he felt the warm water of the shore break gurgle around his bare ankles.

"Sometime after dark. It will happen fast though. We should be back on the cliff by sunset to be safe," Riverstone warned. He then pointed at the small moon on the horizon. "The way Prigg explained it, once that little moon over there drifts in front of that big dude, the ocean will look like a tsunami on steroids. According to Prigg, it's loud, too, like a freight train rumbling in."

He nodded toward the trees growing out of the water with their massive arching root systems. "That's why the roots are so high. So the tide shift won't rip them out of the water."

"Smart."

"Eons of adaptation, no doubt."

Simon twirled his finger in the air. "Big deal. Who cares?"

They wasted no time in paddling out. The waves were perfect tubes of glassy 10 to 15-foot sets. Not quite the 20-footers Riverstone was hoping for, but plenty big for Simon.

When they paddled past the first tree, they marveled at its 200-foot trunk and its gnarled roots growing out of the water. The massive roots were like great arches that plunged into the clear water and clung like anchor cables to the sandy ocean floor. Looking into the clear water, they saw schools of colorful fish darting among the tangled tubers.

Simon's eyes flared with surprise when the slithery cables from the roots shot out and snared a fish swimming by. "Did you see that?" he cried out with alarm.

"Yeah, don't get too close or you'll be lunch," Riverstone cautioned as they watched the cables nab two more fish.

Riverstone took off first, cutting left and locking himself inside a tube twice his height. After a head dunk, he cut back, did a one-eighty, carving his way up and down the face, heading straight for a tree. He ducked under the first root, turned fast around the next and out its back side without a hitch. He then carved through two more trees before the wave folded, and he bailed out the backside, flying over the lip and yelling at the top of his lungs, "WOW! WHAT A RIDE! DID YOU SEE THAT, RERUN?"

But when Riverstone looked around for Simon, he was gone.

"RERUN?" Riverstone called out in a panic. "SIMON, WHERE ARE YOU?"

"Over here!" Simon's voice called out.

Riverstone let out a long sigh as he watched the movie star paddling back out.

Instead of going right, Simon had gone left, and was pushing his way through the sets as if he had done it a thousand times before. Riverstone hadn't thought much of Simon when it came to surfing, but from the looks of things, Simon could hold his own.

Riverstone caught up with him between sets and asked, "Where did you learn to surf like that?"

"My parents sent me to the Islands every summer," Simon explained.

Riverstone nodded, genuinely impressed.

"I wish my parents sent me to the Islands."

"Yeah, well, knowing my parents, I think they secretly hoped I would drown."

"You don't mean that."

Simon's forehead knotted tight. "I do mean that." He wasn't kidding.

"Is that why you became an actor?"

"It got me out of the house."

The next wave was about to break over their heads.

"Take the next one," Riverstone said, believing the wave had already crested too far.

"You take it. I've got this one," Simon countered, catching the fifteen-foot wall as it curled over. He dropped, sliding smoothly through the open tube before the wave buried him under its crushing power.

Riverstone smiled as he watched Simon's head bob up and down along the feathery crest as he cut up and down the wave, carving out turns like a pro. "Awesome!" he yelled to him.

Simon waved back as he peeked briefly over the lip of the wave. He then made a stunning three-sixty, catching air, before hitting the wall again and sliding back inside the tube. Riverstone was about to shout out at Simon for another fine ride when he heard the crack of a weapon and the simultaneous explosion out the backside of the wave. The wave thundered in a violent crash as Simon's red board launched high into the air above the boiling whitewater . . . without him.

3

Bushwacked!

It was a trained Gamadin reaction. Riverstone dove from his board a split nano second before a plas round drilled his brain. His board was the only protection he had as a burst of plas rounds thumped against the outer shell. If the board had been made of earthly board materials, he would have been toast. Instead, the rounds broke through the fiberglas outer casing but were stopped cold by the inner core of Gama-foam. His shield was short-lived, however. The next wave crashed down on top of him, ripping what little protection he had from his hands. As he struggled against the whitewater, he tried desperately to find his assailants. But he was in no position to see squat. He knew the moment he broke the surface again, he would be dead meat if he tried to take a breath. So he grabbed the medallion around his neck and activated his Self-contained, Individual Body Armor or "SIBA" for short. It was the only choice he had. In seconds, his body was engulfed by a fibrous, dura-fabric shell that was so tough, earthly bullets would bounce off. Searing lethal plas rounds, however, might, if they were powerful enough.

He dove deeper.

Almost instantly, Riverstone felt the fresh air pumping into his lungs and knew the SIBA was preparing his body for action. The sensors inside his watertight headgear switched on while his fly-like bugeyes lit up the underwater world with crystal clarity.

He found Simon two trees away, lashed to the underwater root by its tentacles. He remembered how the roots fed off the fish that swam too

18

close. To the tree, Simon must have been the catch of the year! He was struggling to break free but was no match for the strong cords that held him to the root like a straightjacket.

Quickly, Riverstone swam full tilt across the bottom for Simon as more plas rounds sizzled through the water above their heads. But 20 feet below, the rounds had little effect. Upon reaching Simon, the roots tried to snare him, too, and would have if he hadn't grabbed a small light torch, that was used for cutting through case-hardened spaceship hatchways, from his SIBA utility belt. The torch sliced through the root cables easily, even underwater. Each time a wiggly cord reached out, Riverstone cut it off at the end. After several swipes, the tentacles felt enough of its sting and backed off, letting him pass without harm.

By the time Riverstone reached Simon, his eyes were bulging from the constriction the cables had put upon his body. They were squeezing the life from him inch by inch like a bunch of tiny pythons. Leaking from between the cables were clouds of red from the plas wound he had suffered. Riverstone quickly activated Simon's SIBA and moved his inert body away from the root to the bottom of the sea bed, where his suit could do its magic. After several long minutes, Riverstone was relieved to find Simon among the living. His suit had done its job. His lungs were full of air, and his wound was patched.

When Simon reached out, touching Riverstone's bugeyes with his, his first words were, "What was that all about?" he asked through his SIBA communicator.

"This moon is off-limits to military. Whoever they are, they're breaking the treaty with Lenor," Riverstone figured.

"Got a plan?" Simon asked.

"Yeah. Climb a tree."

"Aye."

Together they swam to the surface, making sure a thick root was between them and the beach. At the waterline they discovered the root's food gathering mechanisms seemed to be isolated to life below the surf line.

Their SIBA claws clung fast to the bark. Riverstone went first, crawling up the arching branch like Spiderman until he came to the main trunk of the tree. Simon waited for the wave to break over him before he followed the same path. From there, they made their way up the trunk and disappeared into its leafy canopy. As their SIBAs automatically changed color to match the tree, to anyone on the beach, they were invisible.

Peering through the branches, they zeroed in on the object being towed away by the soldiers.

It was their grannywagon.

"They're taking our ride!" Simon exclaimed as they stared at the scores of soldiers in green camo scattered along the beach, towing away their shuttlecraft to some unknown destination. "Who are those guys? I don't recognize their uniforms."

"They're a mystery to me, but it doesn't matter who they are; they're not supposed to be here," Riverstone replied, more than a little surprised himself.

"No one told them that."

Riverstone patted the side of his utility belt. "Don't worry. I have the keys."

Simon studied their uniforms and their weapons. Unlike the medieval sword-carrying soldiers on Gazz, these troops had up-to-date military hardware. And the way they marched and worked together, they were well disciplined and lethal.

"Think they're from around here?" Simon asked.

When Riverstone was preoccupied with saving their lives, his replies were brief. "Doubt it."

"You're full of answers."

"Hey, I came in on the same boat you did," Riverstone snapped.

"I'm just a toad along for the ride. You're second in command. You're supposed to know all these things."

"I don't know squat."

Simon countered, "So wake up Alice and have her drive the grannywagon over here. Let's blow this place."

Alice was Riverstone's stick-like android that, when deactivated, collapsed to the gold baton-like object that was lying under Riverstone's flight suit in the back seat of the grannywagon. When called upon, she was able to perform many human-like tasks like cooking, cleaning, or in this case, driving the grannywagon to pick them up.

"Not yet. This could be big. I want to find out who these toads are first."

"We should call Harlowe to bring in the cavalry," Simon suggested.

"He's two days away, still surfing on Gazz before he picks us up on the way home. Knowing him and Lu, they're probably not answering the phone, anyway. Besides, we'll need the grannywagon's com to contact him. The SIBAs don't have that kind of range."

"What if there's more of them?"

Riverstone pointed at the soldiers picking up their boards after they had washed up on the beach. "I'm not leaving without my board."

"Millie can make you a thousand more just like it."

"I like that one." Riverstone said, keeping his focus on the troops as he took mental notes on their movements, their weapons, and the direction they were taking their ride.

Before Simon said another word, Riverstone raised a claw to silence any further discussion, which meant their vacation was on hold, and they were back on the clock. This was now a Gamadin matter. "I'll have Alice bring us our weapons, though."

Simon agreed. "I'm down with that."

4

Black Shadows

As Harlowe and Leucadia stepped around scores of frozen bodies scattered along the ancient road, he had no trouble recognizing who they were. He called them Daks. To the Gamadin crew, anyone big and ugly was a Dak. It was short for Dakadudes. So if a Gamadin ever called someone a Dak, it was no term of endearment. Harlowe had encountered them on the fortress planet of Og and in the box canyon in Utah back on Earth. If Riverstone were here, he would have recalled how the Daks killed Leucadia's mom and dad and tried to kill him and Monday on a Las Vegas golf course.

"They're Fhaal," Harlowe pointed out.

"I know," Leucadia said with a tone of bitterness in her that surfaced the moment she saw the first mound away from the ship.

Harlowe wanted to spit on the corpse, but his SIBA protected his lips from the instant death he would have suffered from the minus one hundred and fifty degree Celsius temperature outside his protective headgear. So he just grunted and said with distain, "They're scumbags."

Because of the perpetual darkness and the super-cold air, they were both dressed in full SIBA gear with utility belts, sidearms, extra plas clips, piton heads, five miles of dura-wire, and anything and everything they might need for exploring the vast underground world below Hitt. Even on lifeless worlds, Harlowe took no chances. Sensor sweeps had recorded no life signs. But danger, he knew, was always present. Although *Millawanda's* sensors hadn't picked up a single living thing, standard procedure was never assume there

22

wasn't any. Life seemed to exist in the most unthinkable places. Whenever they were away from the ship on some unknown world, that world was always considered hostile. Always! Having their SIBAs with them at all time was mandatory, and "enough ammo to fight the entire Mongolian Empire," as General Theodore Tecumseh Gunn often said.

A ways up the road they found another body lying by the road beside a pile of rocks. This body was different. It was a humanoid male. He was shriveled up like a dried plum, but his clothes were definitely Neejian. Harlowe was unable to read the name above his chest pocket, but Leucadia read the tag clearly. "This is Xancor. The lead Neejian archeologist who discovered the Gamadin relics."

"Sharlon's father?" Harlowe wondered out loud.

"I believe so." She looked around at the footprints and the impressions in the dust, remembering every word of her mother's story that she had told her about the rescue of the Neejian scientists, the betrayal of a fellow Triaidian, and the Fhaal commander who nearly killed her. She felt as if she were living that moment all over again as she knelt by Xancor and said, "This must be where he gave my mother the satchel." She touched his black hair, careful not to disturb him. "Rest easy, Xancor, your work was not in vain."

After speaking the words, the body crumbled to dust. Xancor could finally rest in peace.

"I'll have Monday send a couple of clickers to pick up the remains," Harlowe said.

Leucadia touched his arm. "Yes, Sharlon would like that."

Harlowe stood, his neck hairs feeling particularly prickly. He looked around at the collapsing temples, the black shadows, and the suffocating quiet. Mowgi's tall ears kept moving from side to side like radar, always vigilant for an unseen enemy. How the undog could stand the extreme cold and poison air was beyond him. But then, the shape-shifting alien pet had always been an enigma to him. "You been here before, huh, Mowg?"

Mowgi growled. He didn't like it then, and he didn't like it now.

The shadows were still, but Harlowe's gut never lied. He put a hand on his sidearm as he pulled Leucadia to her feet. "Keep moving, Lu. Which way?"

She took a com reading and pointed down the avenue that ran along an ancient riverbed. "That way."

* * *

It wasn't long before they stood before the colossal underground opening to the catacombs of the long dead city.

Leucadia shook. "How can anything live here?" Leucadia pointed out.

Harlowe looked down at Mowgi. "He does."

Leucadia had to admit that the undog was a freak of nature. "Yeah, he does."

"I know I saw something move when we landed," Harlowe said.

They both took another long moment to check the area all around them. Still, their sensors read no life forms.

Harlowe turned back to what was left of the portal entrance of the catacomb. A hundred thousand tons of stone and dirt blocked their way. "This is it, huh? The only way in?"

Leucadia rechecked her com. She didn't really need to. She had the way into the catacombs memorized to the inch, but just the same, she rechecked her stats. "The only way. There is a hundred yards of rock before it's clear." She pointed at the Gama-rifle slung around Harlowe's shoulder. "Are you sure that will work?"

Harlowe looked at the hole from the blast that had created the blockage. He removed the rifle that had blown off the top of the mountain in Utah, dusted a couple of Fhaal attack ships in deep space, and fried man-eating vines on Gazz like they were kindling. "I'm sure," he replied with confidence.

Leucadia stepped to one side. She was doubtful.

"We used it on low power for veggies. We'll click it up a notch for rocks," Harlowe said.

He turned the power up two clicks and aimed dead center. Just to be safe, Leucadia picked up Mowgi in her arms and switched on her personal force field. Harlowe glared at her for not trusting him, then fired. The brilliant flash tore through the rocks like a blue laser through metal, evaporating a path through the rock three feet in diameter.

Leucadia put Mowgi down and switched off her force field. "I'm impressed."

Harlowe pointed at the long barrel of the ancient Gamadin weapon. "You don't know the half of it. The only complaint I have is I wish it came in a smaller model like my dad's AR."

"Maybe Ian can make one for you," Leucadia suggested.

Harlowe shook his head. "He tried. No worky. For whatever reason, when he started doinking with the barrel, it wouldn't shoot. So we bagged the idea."

They stepped over to the newly formed entrance and looked in. The air was so cold, the heat from the blast dissipated quickly. Harlowe shined a powerful beam of light down the shaft. "It looks long enough."

"Can you make it wide enough to walk?" Leucadia asked.

Harlowe took two more carefully placed shots, making the shaft tall enough for three people to walk upright with ease. He bowed. "After you, dear."

Leucadia stepped into the shaft. "Thank you."

Harlowe was about to follow when Mowgi began to growl again. He looked back over his shoulder. There was no doubt this time. Several black shadows darted between the rocks, and they were coming their way fast on four legs.

Harlowe turned Leucadia around. Now she saw them. She removed her personal force field device from her belt and placed it just inside the entrance of the shaft. After everyone was inside, she switched it on. A half second later, a dozen creatures the size of grizzlies attacked the barrier. They were hairless and black with long, incisor fangs and large, red eyes that were beyond evil. They scratched and clawed at the barrier, but as hard they tried, they couldn't penetrate the small forcefield.

"Nice work," Harlowe said. They would worry about the creatures later when they returned to the ship. Until then, their focus was searching the catacombs for *Millawanda's* home.

5

Babes in a Cage

Riverstone and Simon didn't wait for darkness. The moment their sensors detected the soldiers had left the area, they swam ashore and followed their trail down the beach. After several miles, they came to a low-lying river delta where their attackers had taken Granny inland. Avoiding contact, they snaked their way along the river cliffs until they discovered the source of their attackers' encampment: a large spacecraft parked along the river, beside ancient stone buildings and crumbling monuments of a long ago dead city. Since they flew in low over the ocean, it was not surprising they had missed the ship coming in.

Looking down from the clifftop perch, the troops were busy setting up heavy equipment around a fascinating glass building that seemed out of place in the middle of the crumbling structures. Neither Riverstone or Simon had ever seen anything like it before. The building wasn't tall, perhaps two to three stories high, but it was wide and round and made of reflective glass and gold-colored beams. Curiously, there were no doors or entryways into the building, at least none they could see from their vantage point. At several locations around the structure, technicians were firing bright beam weapons at the outer walls, trying to gain entry, to no avail. A force field stopped any penetration cold. Back by the ship, the grannywagon was parked at the far end of the compound, where troops with powerful weapons were taking pot shots at her. Like the round building, their beam weapons had no apparent effect, either. Sensing an unauthorized entry, Granny would have

26

automatically switched on her force field to protect herself.

Riverstone snickered. "Good luck with that, suckwads."

Not far from the grannywagon, Simon's interest rose by a factor of ten the instant his bugeye opticals picked up six scantily-clothed females locked up in a cage just inside the compound. Judging from their hot looks, they were all candidates for the next Mrs. Simon Bolt "Out-of-This-World" contest.

"Jackpot!" Simon breathed.

A trooper brought a tray to the cage, and the tall blonde in the group grabbed it and slammed it back into the man's green face, spilling the tray's contents over his uniform and two other soldiers. The other girls joined in. They grabbed fallen containers from the ground and splashed the well-armed men standing nearby with the milky fluid and sticky food. When the containers were empty, they threw them at their captors, missing one and hitting the other in the head. The other girls stuck their legs between the bars and tried kicking any soldier that tried to get close.

"They're a handful," Riverstone commented.

"Who do we save first, the grannywagon or the babes?" Simon asked.

Without taking his eyes off the cage, Riverstone replied, "Millie can always make more grannywagons."

Simon grinned from behind his bugeyes. "I like your style," then said, "We'll need a diversion."

Riverstone nodded toward the ocean. "The tidal surge should do it. The morons put down in the middle of a delta. In a few hours a two-hundred-foot surge will clear the area of toads."

"What about the girls?"

"We'll have to be quick."

There was a faint clickity-clack sound that brought Riverstone's attention to the ground below the tree. "Alice is here," he announced.

They dropped 50 feet and landed like they had stepped off a high step. The power gravs in their SIBAs easily absorbed the shock as they hit the ground.

Alice handed them their pistol belts. She didn't talk or emit any sounds. Her triangular shaped head with its dim, blue-lighted rim just waited dutifully for her next command.

"How did she get by them without being seen?" Simon asked, strapping on his plas-charged Gama pistol. "The Invisible Man couldn't do that."

Riverstone checked his weapon. A tiny blue light glowed bright on its side, indicating it was fully charged. "I don't ask, and she doesn't tell."

6

Chamber of Columns

According to Leucadia's com, after more than an hour of walking, they had passed the 500-foot depth mark below the ancient city. They had left the shaft three miles back and were now walking through time among the catacombs. Harlowe didn't know what to expect wandering through the final resting place of over a billion beings, but it made his hairs stand on end if he thought about it too long.

"I wonder how Riverstone and Rerun are doing?" Harlowe asked to break the dreariness.

"Having fun, no doubt," Leucadia replied, as she read the glyphs on the ancient walls ahead of them. "Do you wish you were with them?"

"Right now, I do," Harlowe replied. He pointed to the corridors carved out of the bedrock. "What's in those openings? Should we look in there?"

Leucadia checked her com. "Bodies. Millions of bodies. Still want to go in there?"

"I'll pass." Harlowe pointed at the glyph writing above their heads they were about to pass under. "Can you read that?"

Without looking up from her com, she answered, "Not a word," as Mowgi yipped once. So focused on her work, Leucadia was oblivious to the undog's warning. Harlowe pulled her back before she tangled herself in a thick web. "Not so fast, babe."

"Where did that come from?" she wondered.

With his bugeyes at max, piercing the ink blackness of the room ahead of them, Harlowe petted Mowgi for his alertness and removed his pistol. "We need to check it out first before going in."

Mowgi also hesitated at the doorway. It wasn't like him to do that. Normally, if the way were all right, he would walk through like he owned the place. Harlowe learned long ago never to doubt the undog's keen sense of danger. If something was bothering him on the other side, he wasn't about to question him. His parabolics had stopped rotating and were now focused on a single area of the vast room. The room was the largest yet. Harlowe saw dozens of circular columns five feet thick rising clear to the three-story high ceiling, and they, too, were all covered with thick webs. According to Leucadia's readouts, the room was as big as a football field.

Suddenly, Mowgi took off, swelling to a beastly size as he charged forward. Harlowe didn't see the creature at first, but then from behind a column, something spindly and black crawled out into the open. The undog was in full dragon by the time he swooped up and caught his wings in its web. The web was strong, and the instant the creature saw Mowgi in its snare, it pounced. It tried to grab the undog's wing and wrap it with more sticky webbing, but just as it was about to sink its foot-long venomous fangs into Mowgi's hide, the undog grabbed it with a free claw. The loud screeches from the creature were deafening as Mowgi ripped him a new one, tearing apart its spindly legs from its pasty white, cretin hide. Buckets of nasty brown and yellow goo splattered onto the stone floor like spilled glow paint.

Harlowe wondered if the creature knew what hit him. Its life was thoroughly gone when the undog dropped its torn parts to the floor and tried to untangle himself from the web.

Harlowe was on his way to help Mowgi when Leucadia screamed. A web had snatched her, and she was being lifted toward the ceiling. Harlowe looked up, and not one, but three creatures were reeling her in. Harlowe shot all three through the head as he dove for Leucadia, grabbing her out of harm's way before the creatures dropped down on top of her.

Mowgi cried out again. He was still stuck in the web and getting more tangled the more he struggled to break free. Harlowe watched more black legs scamper across the ceiling as they went for the undog, now too tangled to defend himself.

Harlowe had to leave Leucadia to fend for herself. He leaped over dead carcasses, blasting creatures like they were targets in a computer game. Then, with pistol in one hand, he pulled out a cutter from his utility belt with the other and activated its beam. Suddenly, a plas shot cracked from behind. Landing not a foot away, a creature dropped from the ceiling. Harlowe didn't have to look to see who had his back. Re-holstering his weapon, he crawled up the side of the column with his claws and hacked Mowgi down from his restraints.

It was another twenty minutes before they were able to go on. Using the cutter like a hose, Harlowe cleaned their bodies of the sticky webs. Mowgi seemed in a bad mood after that. Harlowe figured the undog didn't like being tied up or walking around with splattered creature guts all over his fur. "Cheer up, Mowg. We'll be back to the ship soon, and Jewels will give you a bath."

The undog only growled at the thought.

Harlowe turned to Leucadia, slapping another mag into his pistol. "For nothing living on Amerloi, there's a lot of life here."

"They've adapted well," commented Leucadia.

"Big time. How do you explain that?"

"I can't. They don't even register as being alive."

"Great..." Harlowe mumbled.

"The next chamber is that way," she pointed.

They crossed the chamber of columns and into another large room, where more creatures were waiting. They quickly discovered, however, that a bright light worked as well as a force field in keeping the spindly beasties to the dark crevices of the chamber. They were left alone after that.

The successive rooms were of various sizes and seemed to go on and on and in different directions. On more than one occasion, they found themselves back in the same chamber. When that happened, they made a right turn instead of a left. The break came when they found a stairway down, and unlike other chambers they entered, the footprints they discovered this time weren't their own.

"Xancor's?" Harlowe speculated.

Leucadia knelt by them. "And others. Looks like they spent some time going up and down here." She peered down the long, curving staircase. "The com has this descending another three hundred feet before it drops into a void."

Harlowe noticed something else her com didn't tell them. "No webs."

The undog liked that so much he suddenly took flight down the steps, not waiting for anyone. As they watched him disappear to the depths in a slow glide, Harlowe quipped, "He acts like he's been here before."

Leucadia attached her com to her belt. "Let's see what he knows." She stepped to the edge of the stairway and followed the undog's lead, leaping outward and spreading her SIBA wings in a slow, controlled descent. Harlowe watched her with pride, as she turned gently from one side of the cavern to the other. Her gliding skills had improved greatly since the first time she nearly killed them both while attempting her rookie flight on Gazz. Dressed in a SIBA so no one knew it was her from a distance, she had traded places with Ian against Harlowe's strict orders. All was going well, until she was expected to leap off the side of a thousand foot cliff with SIBA wings. But with Harlowe, one should expect the unexpected. He was in a hurry, and without knowing it was her inside the SIBA, pushed her off the cliff, thinking she was Ian. Fortunately, after hearing her scream, Harlowe dove down the side of the cliff and caught her before they crashed into the rocks below. It was a lesson she never forgot. Harlowe instilled it in her further by tossing her into Millie's dark, rat-infested bilge for a week with bread and water for disobeying his orders.

Harlowe pushed off, watching her like a teacher proud of his pupil. She looked so skilled in her descent he made a mental note that when Simon and Riverstone returned from their surfing trip, they would dump a bucket of ice over her head to welcome her into their exclusive Mons Flying Club, which they began during their training days on Mars.

They had descended only a few hundred feet when Leucadia cried out, "Harlowe, the stairway's gone!"

Harlowe replied back. "Turn back!" He was a short distance behind and saw himself where the stairway ended. There was nothing beyond but empty space. Leucadia tried flapping her wings, but it was no help. She had already lost too much altitude to return, and wasn't going to make it.

Quickly, Harlowe dove, landing on the last step of the stairway. Retracting his wings, he pulled his weapon, attached a piton head to the muzzle, and fired into a step at his feet for an anchor. With his dura-line attached, he leaped into the void after her.

Leucadia saw what he was trying to do and flew into his outstretched arms. With wings dangling at their sides, they swayed in wide arcs until Harlowe was able to reel them back to the broken edge of the stairway.

Once they were stable at the edge of the stairway, they turned their attention back to the mission, never mentioning the close call they just survived. As for Mowgi, they figured the undog had continued on into the void. Unlike them, he could fly back to the stairway anytime he wanted.

Leucadia checked the edge of the stair with her com. "The break happened recently, Harlowe."

"How recent? Since Xancor's time?"

"Two weeks."

Harlowe didn't see that one coming. "Two weeks? Someone was here two weeks ago?" Harlowe looked at the com screen himself just to make sure. "You're right." He turned to the void, looking for the other end of the stairway. "I can see the other end. It's a ways."

"What were they trying to keep anyone from seeing?" Leucadia wondered out loud.

"Information," he answered, as he stepped to the edge of the void and peered down with his bugeyes at full power. What he saw blew him away.

"What is it, babe?" Leucadia asked, anxious to know why he had suddenly turned quiet.

Harlowe finally replied with a gasp. "A pyramid . . ."

7

Tidal Shift

Simon was the first to see the massive migration of jungle animals suddenly moving to higher ground. Riverstone glanced at his wrist chronometer. "It's the surge," he announced, scanning the ocean with his bugeyes and zooming in on a thin band of water across the horizon.

His sensor's calcs put the tidal wall at 10.2 miles out and closing fast toward the beach. From that distance, it was a small line of water no more than ten feet high. But as soon as the wall came within a mile of the shoreline, that would all change. The tidal wall would grow exponentially, crushing everything in its path.

A few soldiers stopped what they were doing the moment they felt the sudden quiet. Then the ground began to rumble beneath their feet. Searching mindlessly for danger everywhere but the coast, Riverstone wanted to shout, *You idiots, it's coming right at you!* But even if they had been able to hear him from the cliff, it was too late.

The silence had turned to a low roar as the crescendo built and the air became charged, turning quickly into a thunderous, unstoppable force as the tidal surge leaped upward the instant it hit the outer banks.

"Now?" Simon asked, eager to save the babes.

"NOW!" Riverstone yelled back.

Together they ran toward the edge of the cliff and jumped. Reaching out with their arms, they deployed the super-thin gossamer wings and took flight. Soaring like eagles, they glided silently down, touching the ground between the cage and the grannywagon. Dodging panicked soldiers who didn't seem to notice or care who the winged bugeyes were, Riverstone handed Simon the clip end of his dura-line and took off across the compound for the grannywagon while Simon went for the caged girls.

At the cage, Simon was greeted with a maelstrom of bottles and rocks, when the girls thought he was one of their alien abductors.

"Hold on! We're the good guys," Simon cried out, as he batted away the garbage thrown at his head.

"Who are you?" the tall blond asked, holding up a fist-sized rock like she could throw a 90-mile-an-hour fastball.

Her words went unheard. The roar of the tidal wall was deafening. The ground was shaking so hard it felt like it was going to split open and swallow them whole. All Simon could do was point at the hundred foot high wall of water, racing toward them up the delta valley. It would be on them in seconds.

The girls screamed in panic as they tried desperately to break out of the cage. Even if they could escape, they were trapped. There was no place to run.

Simon leaped on top of the cage and started to clip the thin dura-line end to the cage when plas rounds began whizzing past his head. With blinding speed, he drew his weapon and shot five soldiers charging his way. Behind him he took out four more entering the barricade. He nailed another two before they shot Riverstone in the back, running for Granny. Riverstone tumbled, found his legs again and caught a second round in the arm before he was able to dive through the force field and fire up the grannywagon.

With guns still blazing, Simon managed to clip the dura-wire to the top of the cage and yell, "GO! GO! GO!" in his com to Riverstone.

The massive wind ahead of the tidal wall blew Simon from the cage. It was only by sheer luck that he was able to crawl back and latch himself onto its bottom with his claw, just as the grannywagon took off, dragging the cage with it.

"HIGHER!" Simon shouted, holding on for dear life. The cage and his body were inside the wall as its power tried to swallow them all.

Then, as if the grannywagon suddenly shifted into overdrive, Simon and the cage went skyward, the wall slapping his backside the moment he was yanked from the wave's destructive path.

Looking down, Simon sighed with relief as he watched the crushing surge engulf everything in its wake. The compound, the alien ship, and its troops were erased in seconds.

8

The Place

The triangulation readouts inside Harlowe's bugeyes didn't lie. The largest stone structure on Earth was the Khufu pyramid at Giza. This structure was twice that size!

With Harlowe holding on to her utility belt, Leucadia leaned out over the steps, marveling at the underground structure. "Oh my gawd," she said, awed by its immense size. She had climbed Khufu herself several times. The resources to construct such a massive stone edifice were mind-boggling. Similarities to its earthly counterparts ended with its triangular shape. This polyhedron appeared new. Its outer casing stones, if they were stones, were still intact. The sole leftovers of the Seven Wonders of the World, the pyramids at Giza's casing stones were stolen thousands of years ago, exposing the inner limestone to wind, rain and sandstorms. After 4,600 years on the desert plateau, the pyramids were crumbling like the city of Hitt. Here, because of its location underground and away from the elements, the casing stones remained smooth and polished like new, making its actual age difficult to determine without closer investigation.

The other striking difference was its color. When Harlowe shot a flare into the room, filling the area with light, the Hittian pyramid shown like an immense jewel from a golden treasure.

"I think we found it, Lu," Harlowe gasped.

"We sure have, babe," Leucadia replied, out of breath.

"Think it's Gamadin?" he asked again.

She pointed to the golden ball sitting above the capstone and the slabs of gold casings covering the outer shell of the pyramid. "Does that look like Gamadin metal to you?"

Harlowe nodded. "It does."

"Let's see what we can find."

Gliding down to the structure was possible, but unlike Mowgi, it was a oneway trip for them. Harlowe's solution was simple. He shot a dura-line around the capstone golden ball and repelled down to the capstone. Once the line was secure, he motioned for Leucadia to follow him. He didn't worry about her screwing up like Monday had back on Mars. To this day his big first officer was still scared of heights. When Leucadia attached her pulley and rolled down the incline without a hitch, she made it look routine.

Harlowe reached out and grabbed her hand as she came beside him beneath the golden ball. "Nice work."

She touched heads with him. "Piece of cake."

"Let's find the front door," Harlowe said, looking down one of the steep sloping triangular sides.

Leucadia followed Harlowe's gaze. She saw no opening. If she picked the wrong side, they would be hours, even days, searching for a way into a structure this big, especially if it was a hidden door they were after. But when they heard barking from the opposite side, Harlowe zeroed in on the undog about a third of the way down, sitting on what remained of a wide bridge that had at one time stretched from the end of the stairway to what appeared to be an open portal on the side of the pyramid. The same beings responsible for the sabotage of the upper stairway had also blown away the bridge.

"Two yips. That's a yes," Harlowe said.

They repelled down the side together using the base of the ball as an anchor. By the time they reached Mowgi, a light from inside the opening was growing brighter.

They were being welcomed in.

"My mother never spoke of this place," Leucadia said.

"Maybe she never saw it. The lights would stay dark for Xancor or the dude who sacked the place," Harlowe said.

"Why would that make a difference?"

"Because they weren't Gamadin."

They dropped onto the broken section of the bridge and detached their lines. Stepping past broken stones from the bridge, Mowgi hopped along through the rubble ahead of them as they entered the structure. Inside, Harlowe touched the golden walls. It was like being inside *Millawanda*. The corridor was tall, perhaps twenty feet high, ten feet wide and arched at the ceiling, and like the long corridors aboard his ship, they seemed to go on forever. The end was undefined and obscure even with their bugeyes. After a short inspection, Harlowe announced, "Definitely Gamadin." His sensors showed the atmosphere rapidly becoming oxygen enriched with warm, sweet air. He retracted his headgear and sniffed the familiar aroma. "Yeah, definitely Gamadin."

Leucadia lowered her headgear as well, and shook her hair, letting the long blonde waves dangle below her shoulders. She then removed a Scrunchi from her utility belt and tied hair into a ponytail.

"Ready?" Harlowe asked, marveling at how a girl never went anywhere without her accessories, no matter what part of the universe she was in. She would forget her weapon before leaving her girlie things behind, he thought.

"Ready," she replied.

There was no Pharaoh's treasure to hide, so there was nothing trick about the corridor. No trap doors, no poison darts or massive stone balls that would crush them walking along the pathway. There were only broken stone and debris left over from the Neejian scientists searching their way toward the interior of the structure. Unfortunately, the carpet was covered with dust. Harlowe brushed aside a layer of dirt and was happy the familiar Gamadin blue fibers had not been sullied. This meant another thing to Harlowe: there were no clickers around to clean it up.

At various places along the way, they found the familiar round disks embedded in the floor. Harlowe's crew called them 'blinkers.' On board *Millawanda*, they allowed one to transport from one part of the ship to another in a blink. They would have saved a ton of time exploring the structure, but none worked. They had to do it the hard way...one chamber at a time.

The first room they came to was fifty feet across by nearly one hundred feet long, according to Leucadia's com measurements. The ceiling was high and arched like the corridors, but three times the height allowed a number of stairways they saw to reach the different levels. One thing was certain, the layout was more like an office building than a burial crypt.

"I believe this was a working headquarters for the Gamadin," Leucadia surmised.

Harlowe agreed. "Millie was underground when we found her. They seemed to like hiding themselves."

"But why? They were certainly powerful enough to go wherever they wanted."

Harlowe shrugged. "That is peculiar." The speculation ended when he turned his attention to the footprints he saw in the dust. The area was well tracked from the scientists, but the ones that caught his attention were fresh. There were four sets in all, two sets entering and two sets leaving. The shoe size of one set was quite large, twice Harlowe's size nineteen. The other set was average, about five sizes smaller than his and unusually narrow and pigeon-toed.

"Have you seen Mowgi?" Leucadia asked looking around. "He was right ahead of us."

Harlowe pointed to the floor at the small paw prints in the dust. "He's following those footprints." Harlowe looked toward the end of the long chamber where another corridor began. "He went that way."

Leucadia thought that logical. "Seems right," she said, then added, "whoever they were, they did their homework. They haven't strayed off course once. They knew exactly where they were going."

They went on, following the footprints, ignoring all the other corridors and doorways. Finally, they came to a small chamber about the size of an average bedroom. The undog was waiting for them, sitting patiently in front of a pedestal in the center of the room. Upon a quick inspection, the footprints ended here, as well, ignoring the other three exits.

The room was a mess. It was like someone had ransacked everything that wasn't tied down. All but one of the walls were vandalized. The reason it was undamaged appeared to be the removal of a large section of the wall. All that was left were remnants of a star map of the galaxy. The center portion, the one Leucadia had hope to find with Orixy's location, was gone.

"That's not good, is it?" Harlowe asked, pointing at the missing section.

"Like I said, the beings who came here ahead of us knew exactly what they were doing. It's like they are two steps ahead of us," Leucadia said.

As Harlowe continued scanning the room for clues, he made the astute observation, "They're looking for what we already have, aren't they? They want the golden ring," referring to J.R.R. Tolken's *Lord of the Rings* Trilogy where the ring was the ultimate power of Middle Earth.

Leucadia took Harlowe's hand. Her experience with the power elites on Earth ran deep. Her parents, Harry and Sook, owned the Mars Corporation, whose corporate enterprises were global. She understood the manipulations of markets, the back room deals, the unseen players and bankers who controlled the governments of the world. She knew them all personally on a first name basis. She was one of them. She played their game. She knew their thought processes, their lust for control, and why they would slaughter millions to achieve control of their world, their quadrant, or maybe even their galaxy! "That's the only explanation, babe," she replied. "By now everyone has heard what the Gamadin has done to bring peace and freedom to the Omni Quadrant. They've seen the power of *Millawanda*. The old guard is still out there. They want their power back, and they'll do anything to get it."

"And they'll use their governments to do it," Harlowe said with disgust.

"Government, money, collusion, war, plotting, genocide, any and all means imaginable to keep it," she added. She looked over the disheveled room. "So who would do this, Harlowe? Who do you know would have the means to know about Hitt and secrets she holds beneath her?"

Only one person who fit Leucadia's profile came to Harlowe's mind; Anor Ran, the owner of an entire planet and head of the Tomar Corporation, the most powerful business consortium in the Omni Quadrant. His company alone controlled the only known source of thermo-grym in the quadrant. If there was someone who had the means and desire to pull off such a costly operation, it was Anor Ran.

"Yeah, I know someone," Harlowe admitted.

Leucadia's face went straight into overdrive. "Who is it?"

"It's not him."

"You can't be sure."

"I'm sure."

"Harlowe…"

For reasons he didn't want her to know, about Quay, about the amount of water under the bridge, he felt knowing Anor's name served no purpose. "Look, I took care of the scumbag and his entire fleet. He's history. End of story. It's someone else."

"But—"

Harlowe's eyes went cold. "No buts. Forgettabout'im."

Leucadia took a breath to get back on track. It frightened her to think about the consequences if they didn't know who they were up against. "If they know Millie's hurting—"

Harlowe cut her off again. "Don't even go there, Lu. We're going to make her right again."

In frustration, Harlowe kicked a broke piece of dura-metal left on the floor by Xancor's research team. Leucadia picked up the small stick-like thing, eyeing its faceted sides and Gamadin symbols.

"Looks important," Harlowe said, touching several notches cut like a key at one end.

Leucadia stuffed it in her pack. "Could be. I'll save it for later."

Harlowe scanned the rest of the room. "There's nothing here that's going to help Millie. We need to find that toad who did this."

Leucadia sympathized with Harlowe's frustration, but the reality was, "They have two weeks on us, and we don't even know which direction they went."

Harlowe pointed at Mowgi, more to take his mind off the setbacks than anything. "What's he looking at?"

Leucadia stepped over to the pedestal. "He's been sitting there the whole time."

Harlowe joined her in the center of the room. "What is it?"

She ran her claw along the Gamadin glyphs. "Do you recognize any of these?" she asked.

"No, but Wiz might." Harlowe then called the ship.

"It's about time you checked in, Captain," Ian said. *"I was getting worried."*

"We've been busy," Harlowe said, and gave his chief science officer a rundown on their walk through the catacombs so far.

"Creatures? The sensors detected no creatures down there," Ian said concerned he had missed the life forms that could have killed them.

Harlowe explained their sensors missed them, too. "Lu and Mowg were almost spider meals."

Leucadia pointed the com at the pedestal. "Ian," she said, circling around the device, "can you read the symbols on the device here?"

"Yeah, that's easy," Ian replied. *"It's a calling beacon. I'm not sure what kind.*

Seems like some way to stay in touch with another Gamadin outpost. Try turning it on and see if it works," he suggested.

Harlowe glanced at Leucadia with a twisted face. "How does he do that?"

Leucadia shrugged an I-don't-know.

Harlowe went back to Ian and asked, "Where's the switch?"

"The blue button on the front of the panel should be it," Ian said.

Harlowe touched the button and nothing happened. "No go, Wiz."

"Press it harder, Captain."

"I did. No go," Harlowe affirmed.

"Maybe it's out of juice," Ian said.

Since the blinkers didn't work, it made sense that other devices that required power failed to function. However, the lights and environmental controls worked fine, which didn't make sense.

When no other suggestion was forthcoming, Harlowe figured a little fine adjustment was in order. He closed his claw and struck the top of the pedestal with a hard fist. Like an unconscious person coming back to life, the lights came on, dancing and blinking like Millie's back wall on the bridge.

"That worked," Harlowe said.

Leucadia kept recording while Harlowe looked for a way to make a connection to whatever or whoever the device was trying to call. Mowgi jumped up and down, yipping like he was about to catch a bone.

Monday broke in. *"Captain, Millie's communication panels are going nuts."*

Harlowe glanced at Leucadia. "Cool." Then to Monday he ordered, "Explain."

"I can't. I've never seen the panels act this way," Monday said.

Ian joined Monday. *"I'm looking at the panel now, Captain. It seems to be some kind of call to arms. The nearest explanation is what your dad would call an 'officer needs help' call."*

Prigg's voice came on next. *"Your Majesty, the overhead screen is displaying a number of points across this sector of the galaxy."*

"Freeze that screen, Mr. Prigg!" Leucadia called out in a near panic.

"Yes, Ms. Lu," Prigg answered. *"I've captured it."*

Leucadia sighed in relief as Ian directed Harlowe to adjust the glowing green slider above the blue button. As Harlowe followed his directions, Ian explained, *"That will expand the call, Captain. Maybe all the way to its Origin."*

But the moment Harlowe began sliding his claw along the bar, the pedestal went completely dark. Harlowe tried several times to bring the pedestal back, but nothing he tried worked. "I think we've blown a fuse, Wiz."

At Ian's suggestion, Harlowe was about to jerry-rig a SIBA power pack to inside the device when Mowgi took off through the door in a fit of anger. Harlowe and Leucadia dropped what they were doing and bolted through the doorway after him. The sounds of attacking carnivores combined with Mowgi's unmistakable earsplitting outcries drove Harlowe into a flat out run with Leucadia right behind him. Weapons drawn, they exploded into the chamber where Mowgi was in full dragon, biting off heads and ripping apart limbs and legs of large black beasts that were unlike the creatures they had seen earlier. These were more doglike with long saber teeth and yellow eyes that would frighten the dead souls of the catacombs.

Mowgi could handle the ten on him, but he couldn't handle the hundred in the pack clawing their way down the far corridor from the main entry.

9

The Pack

"Grogans!" Harlowe cried out, recognizing the beasts instantly. With precision, he quickly shot five of the black beasts clawing at Mowgi's backside. Mowgi tore away the face of one with a lethal swipe of his claw and snuffed the life of another, biting through the back of its neck with his bone-crushing jaws. Harlowe cringed. As many times as he had witnessed the undog's savagery, it still sent chills down his spine watching him. It was nothing short of disbelief as he thanked the gods the chinneroth was on his side.

The pack, however, was nearly inside the room. Leucadia shot the lead grogans, and briefly blocked the pack as they clawed and tore flesh to get past the fallen uglies. That allowed Harlowe to unsling his Gamadin rifle and blast a wide power bolt of blue plasma down the middle of the corridor, vaporizing the lot.

Leucadia came to Harlowe's side out of breath, her bright green eyes searching the exits for more grogans. "Where did they come from?"

"They live here," Harlowe reckoned.

More wild barking and terrifying shrieks of bloodthirsty grogans echoed through the structure, coming their way. This was no time to relax. Harlowe saw the squint of another round of kicking ass in Mowgi's yellow eyes as the undog was about to charge into another corridor to meet the next pack head on. Harlowe stepped in front of him. "No, Mowgi!"

43

Mowgi still had an inkling to rumble until Leucadia added her weight. "Mowgi, no! Do as Harlowe says!"

That was enough for the undog. He shook with an ear-piercing frustration, shrinking back from his dragon alter ego to dog size.

Together the three of them headed for the first stairway, away from the oncoming pack. Up they went, bounding twenty steps at a time in their SIBAs. In two steps Harlowe and Leucadia reached the top, bolting through the doorway into another corridor. They ran down that one and to another that led to yet another. Harlowe quickly piled up nearby furniture against the doorway in an effort to slow the grogans down. After tossing a heavy lounge chair onto the pile, he leaped across the room where Leucadia and Mowgi were waiting.

BOOM!

The pack blasted through the furniture like it was a pile of toothpicks.

Harlowe grabbed a thermite charge from his belt and tossed it at the pack. Leucadia scooped up Mowgi from the floor as Harlowe sheltered them both with his body forcefield. The blast blew them to the floor, but no one was hurt except the grogans.

They climbed to their feet and ran to an intersection. Right or left made no difference, but up was better than down. They raced for another stairway at the end of another room, and by chance, they entered a wide-open shaft that appeared to go straight to the top of the structure.

"A maintenance shaft," Harlowe figured.

Winding its way like a corkscrew was a stairway that would seem to take forever even in a SIBA. Three stories up, Leucadia eyed an elevator platform that made a lot more sense. If it worked, making it to the top would keep them far ahead of the pack. Harlowe attached a piton to his pistol and fired. The blast was deafening, but the result was worse. It ricocheted off the platform and fell back to the floor where they were standing.

Leucadia figured it out. The platform was made of the same super-tough dura-metal as the piton. It wouldn't penetrate even if Harlowe shot it at point-blank range. Their only alternative was to climb as the howling grogans had already found their scent.

Leucadia started for the stairway.

Harlowe leaped up and grabbed hold of the platform's vertical guide rail attached to the side of the wall. "This way, Lu!" and continued up the rail like a sticky-footed fly. Leucadia jumped across and started hand over hand right behind Harlowe, beating the pack by a split second, as the first grogans charged through the doorway. The lead grogan bounded high, and would have latched onto her leg if Mowgi hadn't snared the beast in midair. He bit off its head and jumped along a series of cables to the platform and waited for Harlowe and Leucadia to join him.

The grogans were quick, bursting through the doorway in big numbers. There seemed to be an endless supply, as they acted like army ants, swarming up the twenty-foot sections of stairway en mass.

While Leucadia searched for a way to start the platform, Harlowe kept plucking off grogans before they could get high enough to jump to the platform.

"Hurry, Lu!" Harlowe urged. He was worried less about running out of ammo but more about keeping Mowgi at bay. The undog's incessant lust for grogan blood was driving him nuts. No matter how many times Harlowe shouted him down, Mowgi quivered for action. Twice the undog nearly fell over the railing in his zeal for another grogan head.

"I got it!" Leucadia cried out as she borrowed from the Harlowe Pylott fix-it manual and slammed the control box with the heel of her boot. The panel came alive.

"You da babe!" Harlowe applauded the instant the platform started up. Grogans sprang from the stairway after them. Most fell short and crashed to floor far below, but two managed to claw the edge of the platform and hold on. Harlowe shot one through the brain as Mowgi tore the face off the second. By the time they reached the top of the structure, they were well ahead of the pack but the shaft had narrowed. It was only ten feet across. Below, the pack was still in hot pursuit, twisting its way up the steps with incredible speed.

Leucadia found the access door and tried to open it. "It's frozen shut!" she cried out with a heavy grunt. Harlowe shot two early arrivals before turning to the stubborn door. There was no way he was moving it. He shot three more grogans and attached a charge to the door as Leucadia grabbed Mowgi again, and squatted next to Harlowe. The thermite blew a hole wide enough to drive the grannywagon through.

Once outside the structure, Harlowe tossed Mowgi into the air. In a blink, the undog had sprouted wings, circling the capstone as he began making his way to the top of the cavern. Harlowe climbed out under the ball with Leucadia, but not before he left a care package behind for his pals. Once they attached themselves to the dura-line that had brought them down, Harlowe cut it loose from its capstone anchor and they swung out into the void. Moments later Harlowe's parting gift exploded. The resulting blast shot a superheated column of fire out the escape hole, vaporizing every grogan inside the shaft.

Harlowe called Monday as soon as they were within communicator range and ordered him to move *Millawanda's* perimeter rim over the catacomb portal. The thought of fighting their way through a thousand abiotic creatures didn't set well with him. For good measure, Monday detonated a controlled burn that swept the area of anything living or dead within a three mile radius of the portal. When Harlowe stepped on the blinker to the bridge, Jewels handed Leucadia a stack of Reese's Peanut Butter cups, her favorite, and Harlowe a shake, welcoming them back. Harlowe took one sip and about gagged. "Vanilla!" He cried out in pain. He held out the tall cup as if it were toxic waste. "What's up with that? No one drinks vanilla. Where's my double chocolate shake, Jewels?"

Ian came to the robob servant's defense. "That's all there is, Captain. Millie lost her latte function an hour ago."

Harlowe looked at Ian stunned. "No."

"Sorry, Captain."

Harlowe closed his eyes, trying to stifle the urge to toss his shake through the massive forward window. He took a long breath, slowly laid the cup on his control chair, and left the bridge, dragging his exhausted body toward a long, hot shower to rid himself of grogan stink.

10

Lock and Load

On the high bluff, overlooking the bay, the sun was setting on King Jowicht and Queen Sooty's majestic stone castle. All over the city and along the waterfront, bright banners and colorful flags waved in the soft, evening breeze. They had marked a week-long celebration of Princess Rhosyn's and her court's safe return to Lenor and honoring the two young men who had rescued them from mysterious alien forces that had invaded their largest moon.

As the gods of Lenor had promised, it had been a beautiful spring day. The glassy lines of surf glistened from the light of three small moons which hung low on the horizon. A fourth moon, Galbot, the largest of them all, lay above the castle like a giant street lamp, saying goodnight to the guests. On a nearby sandy berm, musicians were packing up their instruments as Riverstone and Simon came into shore, carrying their boards.

"I think we stoked the locals with a little Coldplay, Jester," Simon mentioned to Riverstone as they headed for the grannywagon parked on the beach.

"But you melted the ladies hearts with the Elvis tunes, brah. *Love Me Tender* brought tears to *my* eyes," Riverstone said, pointing at himself with his free hand. "Where did you learn to sing like that?"

Simon shrugged indifference. "It's a gift."

Riverstone kept extolling Simon's vocal talent until he caught sight of Princess Rhosyn in her white and pink string bikini. She was wet all over, strutting tall and lean out of the water. Riverstone and the Princess had hit it off big since the rescue. So had Simon with three of the Princess's ladies-in-waiting. The ladies had collectively eased the pain of his heartbreaking breakup with Sizzle. Since their return, the six of the them were inseparable; picnicking, surfing, cooking hot dogs on a stick by a beach fire, making s'mores with thick gooey chocolate, playing volleyball in the sand, touch football, tossing Frisbees and baseballs, and walking along the shore under the moons of Lenor.

Simon patted Riverstone on the shoulder. "Best vacation I ever had, brah. Thanks."

Riverstone winked back with a satisfied grin. "Wait till Harlowe hear's about the babes."

They looked ahead at the beautiful ladies giggling and sitting on their blanket in the sand. There was not a skank in the entire lot. Anyone with vision would have called them twelves on a scale of ten. But sadly, their off-the-clock leave was nearly up. Within the hour, Alice would be speeding them to their rendezvous with *Millawanda,* or Harlowe would have them cleaning Molly's and Rhud's catbox for a month.

"Do you think we could squeeze another day out of the Captain?" Simon asked, knowing it was a long shot.

"Not a chance, brah," Riverstone replied. "Something's up, big time. The way Lu looked at us as we were leaving has me worried. That's not like Lu."

"Yeah, I saw her. She wasn't happy. On Gazz she and Wiz were all work and no play. Not a good sign."

"I think it's Millie," Riverstone reckoned.

"Why do you say that?" Simon asked. "She saved Gazz, right?"

Riverstone wasn't so sure. "Maybe. Maybe not. She fried her crystal, remember?"

"That black thermo-grym seems to be working okay. We've been buzzing around the quadrant for a couple of weeks now with no problem."

Still, the worried faces among the brainiacs of their ship, made him believe something wasn't copacetic. "Why would Lu want Harlowe to take her to Hitt? That's no tropical island, Rerun. It's business."

"Listen, if it was that serious, why would Harlowe let us go surfing?" Simon wondered.

Riverstone thought it over. "Don't know."

Simon sighed heavily, refocusing his attention back to the ladies. "I really, really wish we had another day."

"I hear ya, pard, but if we don't meet Millie on time, Harlowe will take away our granny keys."

Simon's brow pinched tight. "He wouldn't!"

"You know he would."

"That means no Lenor and no Princess Rosy."

"And no Machee," Simon's favorite lady-in-waiting.

"We should get goin' then."

Princess Rhosyn broke away from the small group of male admirers the moment she spotted Riverstone. There was little doubt he was her main squeeze at the party. The males in military uniforms, however, weren't so happy by all the attention the ladies were giving them. They had given them sour looks since the day they arrived.

The Gamadin, however, ignored the soldiers as Simon waved at the ladies enjoying their SoCal treats of double-double burgers, fries, and a variety of tasty ice cream shakes Alice had whipped up special for the occasion. Like the Princess, they were all in skimpy bathing suits that left little to the imagination. But as Simon counted his hotties like a pirate tallies his treasure chest, his face suddenly lost its glow. His most prized jewel was missing from the group.

"Where is Machee?" Simon asked Riverstone, concerned. He could never leave Lenor without saying good-bye to his favorite lady-in-waiting.

Riverstone looked over Simon's gems. "She was with everyone before we paddled out."

Princess Rhosyn ran into Riverstone's arms. "Rivy! You were gone so long."

Riverstone caught her with on open arm while continuing to hang onto his board with the other. When they came up for air, he asked, "Have you seen Machee, Rosy?"

The Princess' dark brown eyes fixated on Riverstone. He was her hero. Worrying about one of her ladies-in-waiting was a distraction. "No, Rivy." She turned her playful eyes toward Simon. "Have you lost Machee, Sim-sim?"

Somewhere in the translation, the Princess had misinterpreted Simon's name on their way back to Lenor from Galbot. It came out Sim-sim, instead of Simon. Simon tried to correct her, but as he quickly learned, the Princess of Lenor was incapable of error. Riverstone didn't escape her tweak, either. Rivy was his new moniker. In an effort never to divulge their nicknames to Harlowe and the crew back at the ship for fear endless teasing, they made the Gamadin swear of 'what happens in Lenor, stays in Lenor' pact.

"Looks like it, Your Highness," Simon replied, disappointed. He looked everywhere, among the palms, down one side of the beach and the other, even behind the grannywagon in case she was playing hide-and-seek from him like Sizzle used to do.

No Machee.

Riverstone gently held the Princess away at arm's length and looked at her seriously. "This is serious, Rosy. Sim-sim wants to say goodbye to Machee properly, if you get my drift," he said with a wink. "You wouldn't want me to leave without saying good-bye to you, Rosy?"

The Princess turned sad. "I don't want you to leave ever, Rivy."

"We have to return to our ship, Rosy, or our Captain will have our heads."

"Poor Rivy."

"Help Sim-sim for me, okay?"

Rhosyn called to one of the soldiers and sent him on a mission to find her lost lady of the court.

"I am sure they will find her, Sim-sim," the Princess said. "In the meantime, let us all go for a walk and watch the sun leave us. Until you came along, Rivy, I had never believed our star could be so beautiful," she said, taking Riverstone's arm.

Riverstone guided them toward the grannywagon. From the looks of things, Alice was already packed and ready for takeoff. All she needed was the order to fly. After placing their boards inside the rear hatch, Simon told Riverstone and the Princess to go on ahead of him. "I'll stay here and wait for Machee."

"No, Sim-sim. I want you to sing for us again. I love Elvy. Sing another song for us, please, Sim-sim."

Simon was in no mood to sing unless Machee was there to hear him. Riverstone saw his funk and pulled the Princess away. "Let Sim-sim be, Rosy. When he finds Machee, he'll sing *Return to Sender*. Won't you, brah?"

"Yeah, sure."

The Princess clapped. "Oh, Sim-sim, that is my favorite." The Princess pointed at the rest of the soldiers and shooed them on their way to find Machee immediately. "Go now. Be off with you!" she ordered. "Find her quickly before I become angry."

"Yes, Your Highness," they said, and immediately ran off in different directions.

The soldiers were hardly enthused, but the Princess didn't care. She wanted Sim-sim to sing another Elvy song for her.

* * *

It was dark and Machee was still a no show. Simon couldn't wait any longer. He had to search for her himself before Riverstone and the Princess returned from their walk. He held onto his SIBA medallion for luck, hoping it would give him the energy to bring Machee to him. He was tired of making small talk with the other ladies when it was Machee he wanted to be with during his last minutes on Lenor. He decided to walk toward the castle in the hope of meeting her somewhere on the castle grounds. He put on a t-shirt from the grannywagon and headed in his trunks and flip-flops up the pathway that lead to the castle. He had just come over a sandy rise when he saw a group of Lenorian soldiers surrounding Machee. Three soldiers parted from the group the moment they saw Simon coming up the path and confronted him. Simon recognized the soldiers as the ones who were yuking it up with Princess Rhosyn earlier.

"Hey, what are you doing with her?" Simon said, confronting them all.

"They won't leave me alone—" Machee tried to say before a soldier struck her across the face.

All Simon saw after that was red. Fists flying, knee to the groin, heel kicks to the face and five soldiers were down. Simon grabbed Machee by the hand, and together they ran back to the beach.

Simon's head swirled with disbelief. From an honored guest of the Royal Court to having a run-in with the king's soldiers. *What's up with that?* Machee didn't know either. By the time they were back at the grannywagon, sirens were blaring from the castle.

"What's going on?" Riverstone's voice called out as he and Rosy ran towards them along the beach.

Simon was applying a little first aide to Machee's bloody lip with his shirt. "We've overextended our welcome."

Up the pathway from the castle, squads soldiers were coming fast with guns drawn. At this point no one fired for fear of hitting the Princess. Riverstone kissed Rosy on the lips. "Sorry, babe, got to go. It's been a slice."

"Will you come back, Rivy?" she asked, all dreamy-eyed.

"When the dust settles, Rosy."

At the same time, Simon gave Machee one last looong goodbye himself; then together they dove through the granny's side windows. Alice slammed the throttle forward, igniting Granny's blue pulse drive, and within seconds, they were streaking through the stratosphere headed for deep space at one quarter light speed and accelerating past Galbot.

"What was that all about?" Riverstone asked.

"The toads were hassling Machee," Simon replied.

Riverstone bolted straight up in his seat. "Why?"

"I don't know. They were roughing her up pretty bad."

"And you handled the situation?"

"Yeah, they're down for the count."

Riverstone slapped a high-five with Simon. "You da man, Rerun."

"Doesn't make sense at all, Jester."

Suddenly, the proximity alarm from Granny's sensors went off.

Riverstone jumped into the front seat along side Alice. "There's a squad of attack ships after us, and they just ramped up their weapons to full power."

Simon quickly blinked out of his malaise and headed for the rear cargo bays. "Can we out run them?"

"We won't make it to the rendezvous coordinates, if that's what you're asking," Riverstone said, hopping back to the cargo bay to help Simon retrieved the Gama rifles and ammo clips.

Yeah, that's right. A Gamadin never leaves home without packin'.

Snap, snap went the mags into their chambers. "Lock and load, brah," Riverstone said, watching the blue glow brightly.

"Ready!"

11

Na, Na, Na, Na

Harlowe stood at his quarters' observation window peering out at the vastness of space, dressed in his dark blue and gold trimmed one-piece uniform of the day. After a long hot shower to remove the vile stench of the creatures that wanted to eat him, his body felt whole again. His mind, however, was troubled beyond anything he had ever experienced in his life. His ship was dying, and there seemed little he could do to correct it. He was up against a wall he was unable to see through, around, or over to get past it. He wanted to blow it up. But with what? He had no thader or weapon powerful enough to bust through it. He had not spoken to anyone since Hitt, not even Leucadia. What would he say to his crew? How could he ask them to risk their lives on a one-way journey to the galactic core? He had no answers for them, little hope, and zero chance of survival to offer them. He should have known, he scolded himself. He should have been more careful on Gazz. If he had to save Gazz all over again, would he have gone about it differently? Should he have thought of a better way? After all, Millie was seventeen thousand years old. She was beyond ancient. Older than the pyramids, dork, and you're driving her around the galaxy like she's right off the show room floor!

Mowgi yipped once, snapping Harlowe out of his melancholy. He smirked helplessly at the undog sitting casually on the couch, gazing out at the stars with him. "Good work today, Mowg," he said, massaging one of his long parabolic ears. "You were absolutely badass."

Mowgi yipped twice. It was his way of saying, thanks.

Harlowe checked the undog's yellow, blood-streaked eyes, his cranberry colored fur, and his tall ears. After all that, no cuts or bruises. He peeled back his upper lip and gave his retracted incisors a once over. All checked out fine. There seemed to be no residual injuries or side effects from the the undetectable creatures. They were all lucky this time out. Pushing the putrid evil he saw today to some distant part of his brain, he couldn't get far away from the planet fast enough.

After two reassuring yips from Mowgi that he was indeed okay, Harlowe went back to the vastness. The luminous stars always appeared brighter than normal when *Millawanda* raced through space at hyper light speeds. As many times as he had seen their jewel-like brilliance, they always gave him a sense of wonder. During moments like these, he often recited a passage by Wordsworth that went: *"Continuous are the stars that shine, And twinkle on the milky way. Ten thousand saw I at a glance, Tossing their heads in sprightly dance."*

Harlowe closed his eyes, wanting to burst from the overload of what the future might bring if *Millawanda* died. *There was no future, toad! If she goes, everyone loses. Game, set, match!*

He quickly grabbed his hands. They were trembling. To steady his nerves, he called the bridge for a diversion. "How's our time, Mr. Platter?" he asked.

Monday replied, *"We're an hour behind, Captain. You want to step it up a little?"*

Harlowe hesitated before he answered. Leucadia had cautioned him on over-stressing *Millawanda's* hyperdrive. "We should keep at normal cruise speeds, babe," she reminded him. "No racing around the galaxy until we fix Millie." Which meant, no flank speed, or they would exhaust their supply of black thermo-grym before they found another source.

"No, keep her steady, Mr. Platter. Have we heard anything from our boys yet?" Harlowe inquired.

Prigg replied for Monday. *"No word yet, Your Majesty."*

Harlowe looked at the undog, acting as concerned as he was. "We should have heard something by now, don't you think? Are we still out of range, Mr. Prigg?"

"No, Your Majesty. We have been in contact range for the last twenty minutes."

Harlowe directed his next question to Ian. "What do you think, Wiz?"

"My guess?" Ian asked.

"Yeah, your guess."

"Jester and Rerun are sleeping in the back of the granny with the com on low volume, letting Alice do the driving."

Harlowe held his hand to his mouth in thought when a crease of worry crept across his brow. Yeah, he thought, that's probably what he would be doing after a week of surfing. He took a breath and said, "Okay, we'll give them a little leeway before I ring their bell."

"Aye, Captain," Ian replied.

The whisper sound of a sliding door meant someone had just stepped from the bridge into quarters. He knew who it was without looking. The flowery freshness that filled the room could only mean one person who would enter his private realm without knocking. With his gaze still on the stars, he said, "Just the good news first, Lu."

"There is no good news, babe," she said without a hint of happiness in her voice.

He turned to her as the door slid closed. Leucadia was dressed in an all business, dark blue jumpsuit that fit her tall model-like figure perfectly. In the split second that she stepped through the door, the stars of the heavens turned dire.

She continued walking toward him as his long, powerful arms gathered her in. "You finished the calcs?" he asked her.

"We did."

"Let's have it, then," Harlowe said, preferring to get the bad news behind him.

"We find Orixy," Leucadia said without a whimper. "without delay."

"How long?" Harlowe asked.

"I have no answer for that, babe," Leucadia replied. "Depends on how long Millie can survive without aara. My guess is not long."

"So we better hurry."

"Yes."

Harlowe petted Mowgi on the head before he led Leucadia to the large conference table on the other side of the quarters. Projected above the table was a holographic star map displaying Omni Quadrant with a little blue dot traveling toward the Lenor system. Another yellow dot indicated the rendezvous point where they would be picking up Riverstone and Simon in the granny wagon.

Harlowe asked, "Did you make any sense out of what we found at Hitt?"

Leucadia expanded the star map a tad. "We found some crumbs, babe. When we switched on the communications device inside the pyramid, it broadcast an emergency beacon to all outposts within a thousand lightyear radius."

Harlowe's eyes brightened. "Cool."

Leucadia pointed at the blue dots on the map. "As you can see, there are five outposts in the Omni Quadrant alone."

Harlowe studied the map with her. "And two more outside the quadrant on the way to the galactic core. Why are they brighter?"

"They're the only ones who responded to the call," Leucadia replied, "which seems to imply they're working."

"Maybe the others are dark for a reason," Harlowe suggested.

"Maybe," Leucadia said, "or maybe the entity that came to Hitt before us sabotaged them."

"How would they know where to find them?"

Leucadia had no answer for that. Not even a guess; she shrugged. "Somehow they found the information," she said.

"If these toads find the secret of the Gamadin," Harlowe asserted, perishing the thought.

"Or find another Millie parked at one of the outposts," she added.

Harlowe unlocked his arms around her and brought her to arm's length so he could see her bright green eyes up close. "You think that's possible, Lu?"

"We found Millie. Why not?"

"That's scary."

"We can't let that happen, babe," Leucadia said.

Harlowe turned grave. "We need to find them, then, before they do."

"We don't have the fuel for that right now," Leucadia said. "We have to stay focused on Orixy, or it's game over, Harlowe!"

"And if they find another Millie?"

"Pray that she's out of aara, as well."

"Back to plan A, huh?"

"There is no plan B, babe," she stated coldly.

Harlowe gritted his teeth. Leaving the quadrant without finding the entity responsible for taking out the Gamadin outposts burned his backside. But plan A only allowed for one thing: finding Orixy. There were no diversions.

No plan B, C, or D.

"All right!" Harlowe sighed. He felt like running twenty rimmers and scrubbing Millie's deck just to untie the knots in his gut. "But when Millie's running on all cylinders, the first thing we do is find those toads and dust them."

Leucadia moved back into Harlowe's open arms. "My mother trusted you, Harlowe, to take care of Millie. I trust you. You are the best, babe. If there is anyone in this whole wide universe who can save Millie, it's you."

Harlowe smiled confidently at her. "Thanks. But don't worry, Lu. That's exactly what I intend to do. I might bring her to Orixy on a shoestring, wrapped in duct tape to keep her together, but I have the best crew in the galaxy behind me. We'll do it."

"I know you will, babe," she said and stood on her toes to bring his lips closer to hers. They kissed for a long, passionate minute before Leucadia broke away, making Harlowe uneasy. "What's a matter? Something else is worrying you, right?"

"I want another promise from you."

He let her drop from his arms. "No, Lu. No more promises. I don't want to go there."

"Harlowe, you have to promise me…"

Harlowe covered his ears. "Na, na, na, na. I'm not listening. Na, na, na, na."

Leucadia pulled his hands down. "Harlowe, promise me if we somehow get separated, you'll go on without me."

"Na, na, na, na."

"Harlowe, I'm serious!"

Leucadia was tall, nearly six feet, but Harlowe was six-ten now and two-hundred-seventy pounds of solid muscle. He held her now like a giant looking down at her with his 5XL hands. "I know, I know you are."

She grabbed his chin and forced him to look at her. "Promise me."

"That's not going to happen, Lu. I'll promise you that."

"You can't promise something that's out your control."

"And leaving you behind is?"

"It's a long trip, babe. Anything can happen."

"A very long trip. So let's just leave it at that. That's an order."

"Don't pull rank on me, Harlowe."

"Then don't make me promise you something I will never do…again!"

"No!" Leucadia shot back.

"That's an order, Ms. Mars!"

Somewhere in the heat of the discussion Harlowe took her in his arms again and placed his lips over hers. He figured it was the only way to win the argument.

"That's not going to work," Leucadia said, her lips parted, taking a breath.

"It always has before."

"Not this time…Captain."

Harlowe turned to the star map, still holding her close. Maybe changing the subject would, he thought. The two brightest blue points of light on the holographic display interested him the most. "We should start with the outposts that called back, right?"

Leucadia glared at him to let him know the conversation over the promise wasn't over before she concurred. "At flank speed, babe, before they're taken out."

"I thought you said we have to take it easy. No more racing around the galaxy," Harlowe reminded her.

"I know. But we can't let them take out the other outposts. There may be something there we need, like a link to Orixy or another ship. If there is, we have to find it before they do."

Harlowe pointed at the map. "That outpost is near the center of the Thaat. According to your calcs, Millie will run out of thermo-grym before we're half way there."

The Thaat Harlowe referred to was Cartooga-Thaat, a vast star desert that stood in their way to the Milky Way's galactic core. Crossing the space void of stars would be difficult under the best conditions. Crossing with a limited supply of thermo-grym would be suicide.

Harlowe kissed her before he said, "All right, I put Prigg on scanning for any thermo-grym sources on our way to the star desert. We can't cross that until we top off Millie's tank." Then to Monday, Harlowe ordered. "Flank speed, Mr. Platter, and wake up our boys. I want them on the clock and ready to go the second they're back onboard."

"*Aye, Captain.*"

Ian turned around at his science station and asked Monday, who was now sitting in Harlowe's command chair in his absence, "Did the Captain say flank speed, Mr. Platter?"

Monday wasn't exactly sure, but "I think he did say that, Mr. Wizzixs." He then asked Prigg what he heard.

"His Majesty, indeed, said flank speed, Mr. Platter," Prigg replied.

Ian was worried. He knew Leucadia told Harlowe more than once after leaving Gazz to throttle back on the speed until *Millawanda* was right again.

"We should call him to make sure, Mr. Platter," Ian suggested.

Monday pressed the communicator and called for Harlowe to confirm his order.

No response.

After a long moment of silence, Monday said, "I think they're busy, Mr. Wizzixs."

"But we need to know if that's what he really meant."

Monday opened his palm toward the communicator. "Would you like to interrupt the Captain while he discussing important matters with Lu, Mr. Wizzixs?"

Ian felt Harlowe must have had good reason to order full throttle. He turned back to his science station. "Okay, Mr. Platter, flank speed, it is."

12

Outrunning the Posse

Another thermo-grym missile blazed past the grannywagon, the shock wave rattling Riverstone's and Simon's brains. Riverstone had taken over the driving from Alice. She was good at getting from point A to point B and making logical decisions about avoiding planets, asteroids, space junk, and other ships traveling across a star system, but outrunning attack ships that were chasing them took piloting skills that didn't think logically. *The enemy wouldn't!* Harlowe had reminded him of this before taking off on their surfing holiday.

Alice had her shortcomings as a fleeing-from-the-bad-guys chauffeur, but as a crack rifle shot, she had no peers. She could shoot the warhead off a thermo-grym missile ten miles away and do it without the scope! The problem was the Lenorians had fired so many missiles, they were ripping through their ammo fast. Considering the numbers of attack ships that were after them, more than a hundred strong, it was amazing that they had survived at all. For the last hour Riverstone's bobbing and weaving between asteroids, river valleys, and craters of moons was the only thing keeping them alive.

The Granny had a 10,000 klick lead when nine attack ships broke off from the main battle group.

Simon checked the dash sensors. "They're trying to cut us off!"

"I saw them. They'll hit us when we come out the back side of that moon," Riverstone said, turning the wheel hard right, a maneuver no attack ship could copy. After completing the roll, he headed Granny straight for the pack that had just split off. There was a large Jupiter-size gas planet behind them.

"You're not doing what I think you're doing?" Simon asked, worried that if they got too close, they would be crushed by the heavy atmosphere.

"I am. Let's see how their ships can handle a little gravity," Riverstone remarked, diving at the last moment under an attack fighter as they were about to cross paths.

"That was close," Simon cracked as a star-class warship materialized out of hyperspace.

"Alice!" Riverstone shouted to his robob. "Climb back to the front. I need you to handle the force field."

Simon couldn't believe the screen. He glanced behind them to see for himself, and his eyes went round with astonishment. The ship was every bit as big as a Fhaal class V battlecruiser. "Where's Harlowe? He should be here by now!"

"The rendezvous isn't for another thirty minutes," Riverstone replied as he pushed the throttle forward and dove down into the upper atmosphere of the gas giant.

"He could be early if he wanted," Simon muttered.

"That ship doesn't look Lenorian," Riverstone said.

Simon didn't care whose ship it was. "If that thing fires another missile at us, its engine wash will break us up."

"Think we can make the back side before he shoots?" Riverstone asked, but it was more of a wish.

Simon zoomed in on the starship's cannons. "Step on it! The outer turrets are lining us up."

"I need more time!" Riverstone shot back.

The starship fired. Following the heat signature of Granny's power drive, the missile ran straight and true. There was no escaping it. But before it struck, an amazing thing happened. The missile was cut in half by a powerful blue bolt and exploded in a bright ball of white light before it got halfway to its target. The shock wave shook Granny, but it was like riding through a mild turbulence. A half second later two beams of blue light cut off the port and starboard cannon bays of the starship like they were made of cheap metal. Their guardian angel hit the attack group next. Every ship was taken out by precision strikes to their main drives. In no time at all, the entire fleet was dead in space before Simon could tell Riverstone to brake. The gas giant had them. Its powerful gravity sucking their tiny transport into its crushing atmosphere.

"Their fleet is history, Jester," Simon shouted in his ear. "You can pull us out now!"

Riverstone tried desperately to bring Granny about. She flipped a 180, but she wasn't going forward; she was falling backwards into the gas giant. "She won't respond, Rerun! I can't bring her out of the dive!" he shouted, with every vein in his neck popping.

"WHAT?"

"Granny doesn't have the power to pull us out!"

A massive shadow appeared out of nowhere. Simon twisted around and fell against his seat looking up at the ship's massive hull.

"Jester, it's on us!" Simon cried out.

Riverstone was confused. "What's on us? You just said the fleet was wiped out." Then he saw it, too. "Oh, shiii . . ."

Granny was a tiny speck, as the monster opened its maw and swallowed her whole.

13

Mysterious Ship

The mysterious ship was from another galaxy. It was 50 miles long and half again its length in width. It was dark and unlit. It was built to stay hidden against the blackness of space. There were no markings on its superstructure or symbols that would indicate its origin.

Parked at a discreet half a lightyear away, the mysterious galaxy-class ship had observed the pursuit of the small craft with their powerful long-range sensors. The Lenorian flagship, along with its squadrons of small attack ships, had cornered the small shuttlecraft and could have destroyed it with ease, that is, until the craft's mothership suddenly appeared from hyperspace. What should have been a routine mission ended in a total rout of the Lenorian fleet. If the mysterious ship had not recorded the unimaginable event, they would have never believed such power could exist in the physical universe. The golden saucer's power readings were beyond measure. No measurement of this magnitude had ever been recorded...ever!

For the Mysterians it was a pivotal event, since they had found what they had traveled two million lightyears to capture. The golden mothership was their survival, and they would have her, her creators, and the technology that made her before returning home.

14

Welcome Back

Riverstone and Simon tumbled out of the grannywagon, helping each other like stiff, old men after a long road trip. Their legs were so weak from the chase to stay alive, together they stumbled onto the blue-carpeted floor and collapsed.

Riverstone rolled over on his back and asked Simon, "What happened? We headed for the gas giant and...and then what?"

"We got eaten," Simon replied, his chest slowly inhaling, absorbing every lungful of the sweet air, like enjoying the bouquet of fine wine.

"Where are we?" Riverstone asked, wiping the fog from his eyes.

Simon felt the blue fabric with his fingers, rolled over, and did a face plant in the soft, blue fibers. "Smells like Millie," he grunted into the carpet.

"Millie? Where did she come from?"

"She was early. You got your wish."

Riverstone tried to focus on something solid but could only make out a hazy image coming his way. "Millie, huh?"

A big raspy tongue began licking the side of Riverstone's face. One eye opened long enough to get a glimpse of the small freckles on the white snout. He pushed the black nose away. "Geez, Molly, give it a rest, will ya?"

A small paw clawed at Simon's head. "Oh my gawd! That breath! What have you been eating? Spoiled fish?" Simon rolled over in an effort to escape the gas. "Stop it, Mowgi!" He tried to shove the undog away, but the licks kept coming.

"What in the frickin' galaxy was that all about, Gentlemen?" Harlowe's voice growled.

"Hey, Captain. Thanks for the early pickup," Riverstone replied, looking straight up at a blurred silhouette with hands on his hips against the bright light of the cavernous foyer.

Simon repeated the gratitude. "Yeah, Skipper, like the calvary. Just in time."

Harlowe continued. "I let you go on a surf safari and you two bring a fleet of attack ships back with you! This better be good."

Riverstone nodded, holding Molly's face at bay. "It's a doozy, Dog."

"Give me the short version," Harlowe said.

"Okay, Skipper," Simon began. "It started out with some cool waves, got shot at, Granny was stolen, we got her back, dusted some mysterious bad guys, saved a few babes, and became heroes."

Harlowe's eyes narrowed. "Heroes, huh?"

"It went downhill quick after that," Riverstone added, picking up where Simon left off.

Riverstone was about to elaborate, but Harlowe already had heard enough. "On second thought, spare me the details." Two girl clickers, a short-haired brunette and a long-haired blond, appeared and helped the two Gamadin to their feet. With a stern, no-nonsense tone in his voice, Harlowe ordered, "Meet me in my cabin in twenty. God will want to hear how you out-did Him." He tapped the blond on her triangular head and headed toward the nearest blinker.

They understood that Harlowe's request had a deeper meaning. As tired as they were, they would not be late.

"Is he mad at us?" Simon asked, watching Harlowe step on the disk and blink away.

Riverstone found Harlowe's behavior odd, too. "He was a little edgy, wasn't he?"

15

Aara & Ynni

As ordered, and not a second late, Riverstone and Simon entered Harlowe's quarters off the bridge, dressed in clean, blue uniforms of the day. Being the highest ranking officer on the ship, Riverstone did most of the talking, while Simon added a few tidbits of information now and then, but mostly sipped on his 'vanilla' shake. In the middle of the table was a large platter of chips and bland salsa with little heat and no cilantro. Mowgi had a chair of his own and Molly and Rhud sat in their usual places: Molly on the couch and Rhud stretch out, licking his snow-white coat to a glistening shine.

"You're expecting us to believe all that?" Ian chuckled, shaking his head at their story.

Riverstone smirked at the question, as his gaze went from everyone at the table to Ian alone. It was almost as if he was taken aback by the idea that his lifelong friend would question his veracity. If their story had come from Simon, there may have been room for stretching the imagination. By nature, Simon was full of exaggeration. In his past life, he made a living at it. *But I'm not him! This is me, Wiz, your pard from as far back as we can remember!*

Riverstone put his blue shake aside and leaned forward directing his response at Ian's face. "Well, how 'bout this one, Wiz? There's this young surfer dude who rescues this half-alien babe at the Wedge, whose mother thought the surfer dude and his friends would make a great addition to her elite team of badass soldiers. So she sends them to an underground cave in Utah, where they find a 17,000 year-old spaceship named *Millawanda* that still

66

works. The ship takes these toads to Mars and turns them into these galactic warrior dudes so they can go be-bopping around faster-than-light protecting the neighborhood. Oh, and did I mention the Daks and the zillion different varieties of wild beasts that want to eat them for lunch? Or, how 'bout sailing around a 16ᵗʰ-century ocean with a boatload of tails and five moons in the sky? Would you believe that instead, *Mr. Wizzix?*"

Ian held up his hands. "Point taken, Mr. Riverstone. I apologize."

"Hey, I can't stop now. I was just getting started," Riverstone added. "I haven't recalled #2, and where Dog found Molly and Rhud and nearly got eaten by—"

Harlowe had enough payback and lowered the boom. "We get the point, Mr. Riverstone."

"I want to hear more, Captain," Leucadia glared at Harlowe, "especially, the eaten part."

Harlowe shot a hard glance at Riverstone for opening the can of what-happened-on-#2-stays-on-#2. "No, you don't."

It started as a small chuckle, then Monday couldn't hold it in any longer and neither could Simon. They began to laugh while Harlowe squirmed under Leucadia's accusing eye.

Finally, saving Harlowe from his significant other's grilling, Monday asked, "Yeah, who would believe any of it?"

Harlowe didn't squander his opportunity and rapped his knuckles on the table hard enough to get everyone's attention. "Okay, we need to get serious again," he commanded.

Leucadia gave in, but only for the time being. No one at the table believed Harlowe had escaped her curiosity. So she asked the table, "Would anyone like to hear my tall tale?"

The table suddenly went quiet. Without knowing what the subject was or what she was about to say, they all knew from the dire look on her face, they were back on the clock.

Harlowe sighed and said, "Go on, Lu. Lay it on them."

Riverstone's and Simon's faces transitioned from laughter to worry in less than a breath.

"We're not going to like it, are we?" Simon asked, hoping for some hint of positive feedback.

The expressions he saw from the table told Simon everything he wanted to know. "Sorry I asked." The grim faces also meant his next movie deal with Saul would be put on hold because *Millawanda* was not returning to Earth anytime soon.

Leucadia started from the beginning: From the time they found *Millawanda* in Utah, to the loss of her power on Gazz, the disintegration of the blue crystal in the power room, to their mission to Hitt, the pyramid, and its sabotage by an unknown force. Harlowe wanted everyone at the table, even those who had heard parts of her narrative before to be fully up to speed on *Millawanda's* condition. Their beautiful Gamadin ship was dying inside and would cease to function if they were unable to fix her.

"She's what?" Riverstone asked, almost choking on his words. "You're telling me after 17,000 years she's about to sprout wings?"

Harlowe faced his First Officer, like a father breaking the news to his son that their family pet had come down with a terminal disease. "That's right, Matthew."

Leucadia went all through the litany of questions and the what-ifs, like "Can't we just find a new crystal?" Riverstone, however, thought Millie was doing fine on the black thermo-grym.

"She's gagging on it, Matt. She's only using it because it keeps her alive. Millie's in survival mode. She can run on thermo-grym for a while, but without ynni or dark energy, her systems start to break down. It's like Simon's new Aston Martin Rapide running on regular gas, or something worse, kerosene!" Both Simon's and Ian's faces grimaced with revulsion at the thought of putting junk gasoline into a three hundred thousand dollar sports car, as Leucadia continued: "The Rapide will go for a while, but then instead of varooming off the start line, the engine begins to sputter because its fuel injectors are starting to clog from the bad fuel. If it is allowed to go on, the problem spreads to the other injectors. Then the valves are infected. The pistons after that, and so on. Everything in the engine is gummed up. On the outside the Rapide is still a beautiful machine you think will go forever, until one day she suddenly quits." She pointed at Simon. "Simon can call triple-A and tow his Rapide to his mechanic to get her fixed. We don't have that luxury. We have to find Millie's mechanic before it's too late."

"Ynni is what again?" Harlowe asked. This was the first time he heard of the word.

"It's the ancient word for dark power," Leucadia replied.

Harlowe could see his crew getting bleary-eyed as though they were listening to one of Professor Farnducky's lectures. Even Ian's mind was finding it hard to focus. "Slow down, Lu. For all us science challenged types," he said looking straight at Riverstone and Simon, "put it in simple terms that Chumlee could understand."

Leucadia nodded. "Of course." She touched the table in front of her, and a holograph of a giant double-double dripping with cheese appeared. Everyone's eyes came alive. They had no problem understanding what a thick, double-double cheeseburger looked like.

"Where are the fries?" Simon joked.

"Can it, Mr. Bolt. This is serious," Harlowe said firmly.

"Aye, Skipper."

Leucadia went on. "Pretend this juicy burger is the universe. If we take a small slice out of it, this represents all the lighted things we can see: things like stars, galaxies, novas, and planets."

"That's it?" Riverstone exclaimed surprised. He looked out at the bright starscape through Harlowe's wide cabin window. To him, and everyone else, the galaxy was crammed full of a billion, billion stars, and he was only looking through one window of the ship. "I thought all that was in between was zilch. You know, a vacuum."

"Hardly," Leucadia said, coming back to her hologram. "Like so many things in life, it's the things that we don't see that are the most important." She slid another slice out from the main burger about a tenth a wide as the first. "This section represents neutrinos, quarks, and other small particles of matter."

Next she pulled out a much bigger slice. Nearly double that of the first two slices combined. "This piece symbolizes all the dark matter in the universe."

Monday was amazed. "That's a lot of stuff, Ms. Lu. And there's still three-quarters of a double-double left."

"Seventy-seven percent to be exact, Mr. Platter," Leucadia affirmed.

Harlowe wanted to hurry things along. He waved his hand over the rest of the burger. "Enough with the slices, Lu. Let's jump to the ynni part."

Leucadia's bright green eyes became fixated on the large hunk of the remaining burger. "That's it, Captain. All that is left is ynni. Scientists call it dark energy. They know it's there. They just haven't found it yet."

Riverstone cooed with disbelief. "All that makes up three-quarters of the universe? Sweet…"

"Now can you see why Millie is so dependent on the aara. Without her aara, she can't produce the high test fuel she needs to exist."

"You mean like atom bombs?" Simon wondered.

"No, Rerun, like what our Sun does, only a million, million times more powerful," Ian explained.

"The power of ynni is for all practical purposes infinite, and it's everywhere. The Gamadin ship builders needed a way around the limitations of thermo-grym, fission, fusion, anti-matter. They needed a way to harness the actual building blocks of the universe itself. Ynni!"

"Okay, where do we find this aara, Lu? Will it be just lying around one of the Gamadin outposts?" Simon asked.

"That's what I thought, too, Mr. Bolt, but Lu and Wiz say there's no chance of picking up any aara at an outpost. So…" Harlowe touched the table, and the big double-double was replaced by a bright, three-dimensional holograph of a spiral galaxy. Twisted around a brilliant white center were spiral arms of a billion billion stars floating over the table like a massive pinwheel. He put his hand through the brightest part of the hub. "We go here, Mr. Bolt. The galactic core of our galaxy. To a place or planet called Orixy."

A deafening silence fell over the room.

* * *

After all the stunned faces regained their composure, Riverstone asked, "That's a long way, Captain?"

Harlowe understood his crew's shock. "No choice, Mr. Riverstone." But then, he followed up with another surprise. "Tell them the rest, Lu."

Leucadia hesitated, her eyes telegraphing to Harlowe whether it was the prudent thing to do at the moment or wait until they had more facts on the table.

"Go ahead. Tell them," Harlowe directed. "They have to know everything."

Leucadia nodded and went on: "We believe someone else is seeking Orixy."

Riverstone came back to Harlowe disturbed, "Why?"

Harlowe replied, "We don't know why for sure. Only that they beat us to

Hitt and took some important info that might lead them to Orixy. That's all we know about them so far."

"Who?"

"We don't know," Harlowe said straight out.

"I don't get it," Riverstone said.

Harlowe looked at Leucadia before he explained, "If they find Orixy and find another Gamadin ship, or find the technology to build one, then all bets are off. The galaxy is in big trouble if these guys are Daks."

"What if they're good guys like us?" Simon asked. "Maybe we could partner with them and everyone would live happily ever after."

Harlowe tapped the table again. "Not with pets like these." The new hologram depicted the scene of Harlowe and Leucadia being chased by a thousand black, dog-like beasts.

"Grogans?" Now Riverstone was really confused. "How did they survive? I thought Amerloi was cold as a witch's gunnels."

"It gets better," Harlowe replied. "Millie's sensors couldn't detect these scumbags either. They were out there by the thousands, and we couldn't see them until they were on us."

"How's that possible?" Riverstone wondered. "That's against nature. Anything that's alive can be tracked by Millie's sensors."

"That's right. But somehow these grogans were altered to evade our sensors. Now how would anyone know how to do that unless they have Gamadin technology? So, whoever they are, they left us a present, hoping we would find it," Harlowe surmised.

Leucadia changed the holo back to the star map of the quadrant. "This mysterious entity has struck here, here, here, and here," she began, pointing at the map. "They are all places we would search if we had the time, resources, and the ynni. There is no doubt about it, they're looking for another Gamadin ship, aara, or both. They do know about Gamadin technology. It really doesn't matter how much or how little they have. The problem is, they do have it, and we must stay ahead of them and find Orixy before they do, which means, going all the way to the galactic core."

Simon raised his hand like he was in school and Leucadia gave him the go ahead to ask his questions. "Do you know where these Mysterians came from?"

Leucadia looked at the star map. "No. We know nothing about them or where they came from."

"What if there's more of them? These Mysterians could be all over the place."

Leucadia agreed. "That's right. They could all be looking for Orixy. Although, this particular group seems to be following a search and destroy path across the quadrant, hitting all the Gamadin outposts in Omini Quadrant."

"Call me thickheaded, but I still don't get it," Riverstone thought out loud. "If we don't know the road to Orixy, where do we start? The core is a big place, Lu."

Leucadia pointed to bright light at the edge on the star map holograph above the table. "We begin here. It's the last outpost before Cartooga-Thaat that replied to the Hitt emergency beacon. It's still functioning."

Now it was Harlowe's turn. "And after that?"

Leucadia peered deep into the star map. "After that we cross Cartooga-Thaat."

"The star desert, My Lady?" Prigg asked, as his three eyes moved in separate directions.

"It is the only way, Mr. Prigg. If we try to go around Cartooga-Thaat, it will be a five thousand lightyear longer voyage."

"Can Millie make it across without refueling?" Monday asked Ian.

Ian glared at Harlowe as he spoke. "If we don't run into any bad guys and burn thermo-grym like there's no tomorrow, we should be fine. But if we make it that far, we will be on fumes," he warned.

Harlowe stood up. The chips were gone, the guac bowl was scoured clean, and he needed a refill on his shake. "Meeting is over. If we missed anything, we'll fill in the gaps along the way. Mr. Platter, you have our course?"

"Aye, Captain."

"All right, whatever planet that lighted dot is, get us there best possible speed."

"Aye, Captain."

As the others left the cabin, Riverstone lingered a moment longer to ask Harlowe and Leucadia, "If we don't find this Orixy, then this is a one way trip. Am I getting that right, pard?"

Sugarcoating the truth for convenience was not Harlowe's way. His deep blue eyes were tired and red from the many hours of troubled sleep he had since Hitt. This was his burden and his alone. "Yeah, one way."

Riverstone smiled easily. "If we flub this one up, we better hope for a nice beach somewhere."

Harlowe pressed his lips together in a slow nod as Jewels placed two more plain vanilla shakes on the table. His timing couldn't have been better. "That would be my worry."

16

Tofu

Leucadia was at her science station next to Ian when the outpost transmission suddenly went dark. "It was there, but now it's not," she told Harlowe. At their present speed, *Millawanda* was still a day away from their last stop before they would begin crossing the star desert, Cartooga-Thaat. "It's like someone turned off the lights, Captain," she added.

Harlowe looked out the front window of the bridge. Already the starscape was nothing but a few dim twinkles. Directly ahead was a single yellow star that stood out like a beacon against the black void. Beyond this star lay five hundred lightyears of empty space. "Anyone we need to worry about when we get there?" he asked.

"The planet appears older than Earth, but it doesn't seem as advanced. They're still using old style radio and television frequencies. My guess is they have no spaceships, only prop aircraft, or possibly jets. That's it," Ian replied.

"Did you get a lock on the outpost yet?"

"Nearly. We have an approximation within a few hundred square miles. If the beacon switches back on again, we'll have it for sure."

Harlowe rose from his command chair and stretched, looking over the star map and their position on the screen one more time. "I'm clocking out, Mr. Riverstone. You have the bridge."

Riverstone stood next to Harlowe, their six-foot-nine heights practically equal. "Aye, Captain. Date night?"

"It's Saturday isn't it?" Harlowe asked.

"That it is, Skipper," Simon agreed from his weapons station.

"Then that's where I'll be. With my date," Harlowe said, winking at Leucadia.

Riverstone took his place in the command chair. "What's on the menu, Captain?"

"A surprise."

"No double-doubles, Skipper?" Simon joked.

"Something your palate would appreciate, Mr. Bolt," Harlowe replied

Monday giggled. "Who's the lucky gal, Captain? Anyone we know?"

Harlowe stopped at his quarters as the doorway slid open. "You've seen her a few times. She's tall, hot, silky yellow hair, sweet smile, except when she's angry," he said, locking eyes with her. "Trust me; she can scare a grogan then," he groaned. He closed his eyes as though falling into an alluring vision of her. "To see her gorgeous eyes and her long neck in the moonlight and the way her eyes sparkle when she sees you coming...ah," he sighed, folding his right hand over his heart, "she would make your heart skip, Mr. Platter."

"Aye, Captain, an angel for sure."

"That she is. Carry on, gentlemen," he said, stepping through the doorway while continuing his date's long list of qualities to himself as the door shut behind him.

* * *

It was night inside Dodger's Jungle Room. A lone moon shared the celestial heaven in the sky dome overhead. Beside the pool was a small, white linen covered table with gold place settings for two. In the nearby lush jungle, tiny lights winked on and off, as they danced among the bushes and the trees. They gave the appearance of fireflies on a warm summer night. But there were no real insects in the vast room. Like the stars and moon, they were all romantic additions to the evening Harlowe had conjured up for his date night with Leucadia.

Somewhere not too far away, a large pig-faced hippo snorted and grunted between his deep fluttering breaths of sleep. In the opposite direction another pet with tall, parabolic ears curled up in the soft sand under a nearby fern. He made sleeping sounds that were even louder than the pig-faced hippo. Further away, at the edge of the pool, two great white tigers hardly made any sound as they yawned and growled playfully together in a pre-sleep ritual before settling down together.

"Kinda quiet around here tonight," Harlowe observed in jest.

Leucadia played along. "Yes, it's nice being alone for once."

They reached over the table and clicked their water glasses. Harlowe had had enough ice cream shakes for one day. "What shall we drink to?" Harlowe asked with a soft grin. "Privacy?"

Leucadia's green eyes glowed softly across the table. "No. We'll never have that it seems."

They laughed lightly, agreeing that their lives would always be different from any other couple in the universe.

Harlowe lifted his glass again. "Okay, how 'bout to finding a sandy white beach with perfect tubes, then?"

Leucadia thought that was too easy. "No, nothing with a beach or sand or waves, surfer boy," she replied.

Harlowe looked at her funny. "What else is there, Lu?"

She pointed her glass at him like it wouldn't take much to throw the contents in his face. "For a Gamadin captain, you have little imagination."

Harlowe cracked a sly smile and leaned across the table. He kissed her gently on the lips before saying, "I have my shortcomings."

"Ah, you admit it?"

"It's your night, dear."

"Good answer, Pylott."

She tasted his lips again. "But kissing isn't one of them."

The sound of clickity-clacking stepping through the jungle put their toast on hold. "Sounds like your dinner has arrived, Ms. Mars," Harlowe announced.

Leucadia sat up excitedly. "What are we having?"

"You'll like it," Harlowe said with a wink.

Leucadia pointed an accusing finger at him. "You know, my mother used to tell me that when she knew I wasn't going to like what she was serving."

"This time it's a slam dunk," Harlowe said confidently. "My mom's recipe."

Leucadia snickered. "Somehow I can't imagine you criticizing Tinker's cooking and living to tell about it."

"True. No one ever complained. Even when it was bad, it was good. Although, Dodger did say something critical once."

"And?"

"He learned a valuable lesson."

Jewels clickity-clacked out from the bushes carrying a wide tray of shiny, dura-metal covered plates. Harlowe and Leucadia sat back in the chairs as the robob servant skillfully held the tray with one mechanical hand while he placed the hot dinner plates on the table. Next, he took the bottle that was an exact copy of a rare vintage *Dom Perignon* and filled their glasses with chilled Bluestuff.

"Thank you, Jewels," Leucadia said.

The robob bowed to Leucadia and returned the stylish dark bottle to the golden ice bucket beside the table. Harlowe's personal android butler with the colorful bowtie then turned to him, awaiting further instructions. "Everything is perfect, Jewels. Thank you," dismissing the servant.

Jewels bowed with his usual panache, turned, and clickity-clacked away.

Leucadia chuckled, watching the robob servant disappear into the thick undergrowth. "Where do you think he goes, babe?"

Harlowe smiled. "I haven't a clue." He leaned forward slightly and motioned for her to come closer as he whispered a secret, "But if I had to guess, I think he has the hots for Alice."

"Riverstone's clicker? Nah…"

Harlowe sat back, putting his finger to his lips. "That's right. But don't tell anyone. It's the scuttlebutt among the crew."

Leucadia laughed. "Oh, my lips are sealed."

It made Harlowe happy to see Leucadia enjoying herself. Over the past few weeks he had worried about her a great deal. She had taken on too much of *Millawanda's* problems by herself. It had put a strain on their relationship, and he didn't quite know how to handle it except to let her know that the entire crew had her back. If they succeeded or if they failed, it would be on all of them together, not just her.

Harlowe raised his glass, coming back to the toast that he had yet to give. For him, it was as he so often said of the obvious, a "slamdunk." "To you, Leucadia Mars. I salute you. You are the bravest, smartest babe in this entire galaxy, and I'm honored to be sitting here with you this night. You da best," he said, clicking her glass of Bluestuff.

Tears welled up in her eyes. It was not the toast she was expecting. She swallowed the urge to let show her emotions at the table. With all the stress she had built up over *Millawanda's* survival since leaving Gazz, she allowed herself a few tears. It was just what the doctor ordered.

"Thank you, babe," she said, wiping her eyes with her napkin.

Harlowe leaned across the table and kissed her again. "You make it easy, Lu. I love you. You know that, right?"

She nodded, sniffling a little. "I know."

Sitting back in his chair, he said, "All right, then. Let's eat," and gave her the honor of removing the cover on their dinner first.

She wiped her eyes as she removed the cover. "I hope you like pecan and pepper crusted, garlic filet," Harlowe said, but the instant he saw the entrée, his shoulders dropped to the floor. "That's not what I ordered for tonight."

Leucadia stuck her fork in it. "Smells yummy."

"It's not meat," Harlowe growled.

"No, it's tofu."

"Tofu?"

"Come on. You'll like it," Leucadia quipped.

"How long have you known me?"

"Almost two years."

"Have I ever eaten tofu?"

"There's always a first time."

"I'm not eating tofu. I'm a Gamadin warrior, not some pencil-neck greenie."

"You're not going to try it?"

"No, I'm not going to try it. I want a steak, a big thick hamburger, roasted duck, chicken, anything but tofu."

"What Mother fixes isn't real meat anyway. You know that," Leucadia pointed out. "She synthesizes all your food to look like meat."

Harlowe kept his hand in place. He wouldn't let her raise the lid. "I don't care. It looks like it and tastes like it. That's all I care about. No tofu, Ms. Mars!"

Harlowe stared off into the jungle and called out, "Jewels! Bring me a steak, rare with blood dripping off the fat, a salad with a ton of goodies, smothered with bleu cheese, and a bowl of onion rings, animal style." He faced Leucadia. "Now that's a dinner to die for," he huffed, finally letting go of her hand.

Free of Harlowe's hand, she lifted the cover from the meal. "Fine, I'll eat it myself. Eat your silly steak!"

Both their eyes went round when they saw Harlowe's main course. The plate of food looked more like rotten eggs left out in the sun for a week than a fat, juicy fillet.

"No, thanks," Harlowe said, pushing the plate away. "I'll stick with my steak."

Leucadia stared at the plate as if probing for roaches. "That is really bad, Harlowe."

"Ya think?"

The familiar clickity-clack returned through the bushes. Jewels had another covered plate and set it down, removing the uneaten yuk from the table.

Harlowe dismissed Jewels again and lifted the lid off his dinner. Upon seeing another platter of unrecognizable food, he nearly lost it. He was about to recall Jewels again, and give him a piece of his mind when Leucadia stopped him.

"It's not Jewels' fault, Harlowe," she said, placing the cover over the vile food. "It's Millie. Her systems are failing and it's started with Mother . . ."

Harlowe wanted to cry.

17

Rhud's Panic

They got lucky. The unknown planet was the last source of thermo-grym before crossing the Thaat, as they now called the star desert. *Millawanda* put down on a small clearing inside a tall forest of thick green pines that was located at the northern end of a small pear-shaped continent the size of Australia. The planet was marked by a blue dot on the star map, which meant somewhere on the continent was a Gamadin outpost. Knowing the outpost was there was one thing... Finding it was another. The trick was to switch on the outpost's call beacon so they could home in on its location with no effort. For that, they needed the call sign for the outpost. But in Mille's condition, they were unable to pull the information from her memory. Without the beacon answering back, it could take weeks to locate it.

While Harlowe, Riverstone, and Simon went digging for the thermo-grym deposit in the nearby mountains, Leucadia and Ian set about looking for the workarounds to find the outpost.

The morning sun was pink and yellow on the horizon as the guys began breaking up the rock cliffs with well placed plas rounds from their Gama-rifles. Once the vein of thermo-grym was sliced out of the escarpment, a squad of robobs would break up the large hunks into manageable pieces and begin loading them onto the two grannys for Quincy and Alice to ferry back to the ship.

"It's not like the black stuff, but it's better than zilch," Harlowe commented to Simon as they stood around with their arms crossed like

Caltran supervisors watching the clickers shoveling the yellow crystals in a pile for the next load. All they were missing were the orange vests.

Mowgi was there, too, sitting on top of the nearest rock with his face absorbing the sun.

Higher on the slope, Riverstone steadied himself against a boulder as he blasted another slice out of the cliff. The clickers would be a few hours picking up the pieces after that one, he figured. It looked like it was going to be a long day shuttling grannies back and forth to fill the ship's thermo-grym storage room.

Walking topside on *Millawanda's* hull, Ian was making normal sensor sweeps of the area using a less powerful, but more reliable, handheld device. The beacons appeared connected to the Gamadin outposts and the blue dots, but his readings were different this time. These were like on and off switches. "What do you think it is, Lu?" Ian asked over his SIBA com.

"I'm not sure, Ian. It's definitely alien, though. A very high form of tachyon communication, so its origin couldn't be from this planet," Leucadia replied.

"You're certain?"

"Positive. My analysis indicates the intelligent life forms on the planet lack the necessary technology."

"That's whack. How can anyone be broadcasting on a tachyon frequency, then?" Ian questioned.

"Good question. That's my reading here, too," Leucadia replied.

"How far away?"

"Hold on, Ian," Leucadia came back. "I'll join you. With two recorders we can link them in a series for more power without disturbing the locals."

Ian put his com to the side and waited for Leucadia to join him. He let the sun's yellow rays caress his face, allowing the pungent pine scent of the trees to fill his senses. *Take your time and enjoy it, gomer. When we start across the Thaat, who knows when we'll see a sun again,* he mused.

Suddenly, something grabbed him by the back of his suit and pulled him back. When he opened his eyes again, he found himself about to fall off the edge of the ship. One more step and he would have taken a nose dive three hundred feet down to the forest floor.

"Watch it, Ian!" Leucadia cried out.

Embarrassed that he had been so careless, Ian stepped back. "Thanks."

"What were you doing?"

Ian turned to the forest below and the spectacular view of mountains and valleys, clouds, birds flying, the smell of pine and spruce, the quiet energy of the trees, the slight warm breeze on his face, and the feel of the sun. They were above it all, and nothing was in their way for hundreds of miles in all directions. "Taking it all in," he told her.

Leucadia paused to take in the sensory tour. "It is beautiful. I wish we could spend a week here."

"Another day wouldn't hurt, would it?" Ian hoped.

Leucadia put her arms around him. "Millie can't spare a minute, Ian."

Ian relaxed, savoring the short time he had in her grasp. Her freshness, her yellow hair flowing softly across his face, the warmth of her body touching him was unmatched by any view of beautiful landscapes. "What would Harlowe say if he saw us?"

Leucadia extended her arms, smiling widely as she held him closely and looked at him, touching noses. "He would say: "Hey, you two. Save the nookie for later. Back on the clock. We have work to do."

Ian blushed. "He never gets jealous, does he?"

"Harlowe doesn't have time, Ian. He has a ship to fix and a galaxy to protect," she pointed out.

They stood back from the edge at arm's length. "Do you think I'll ever find a girlfriend, Lu?" Ian asked.

"Are you kidding, Mr. Wizzixs? You are one hot dude. One day some lucky girl with find you, or you'll find her, and that, as Harlowe says, will be a done deal," she assured him.

"I hope she's just like you."

She kissed him on the forehead for the kind thought, and after one final hug, they reluctantly returned their focus to the problem at hand, linking their sensors together for greater sensitivity. Ian touched his screen with Leucadia's. It was a snap. The wireless connection worked flawlessly. The readouts were strong and downloading into the sensor memory banks when a loud roar from the forest stopped them. They instantly knew the beastly outcry. It was one of the cats, and it sounded serious. Before anyone left the ship's protective barrier, sensor sweeps of the area were made to detect any intelligent beings or large carnivores Molly and Rhud might tangle with in the forest. Finding nothing inherently dangerous, Harlowe had allowed them time to hunt for fresh meat. Until Mother's food production was solved, he had no choice but to let them feed on their own. The slop Mother had served up wasn't fit for a grogan. Harlowe began feeding them double-doubles, but he didn't know how long they could eat hamburger without getting sick. There was no substitute for fresh meat.

Ian's sharp eyes picked up a white, four-legged cat bounding fast through the trees first. "It's Rhud!" he said, recognizing the small freckles on the end of his snout. He pointed into the forest.

"I don't see Molly," Leucadia said worried.

"Me either. He's alone."

Rhud exploded into the clearing crying in loud, excruciating howls. They had never known him to act so terrified. They both quickly attached their dura-wires to the edge of the hull and repelled off the side of the ship to meet him.

Leucadia wasted no time calling Harlowe. "We have a problem, Captain. Rhud's in a panic. He's come back without Molly."

Harlowe's first question was, *"Where's Platter?"*

"He is busy overseeing the robobs unloading the thermo-grym," she replied, and looked at Ian as she spoke. He knew what she was thinking and nodded the go ahead. "Ian and I will take care of it, Captain."

Leucadia felt Harlowe's reluctance, but time was of the essence. If Molly was hurt or needed their help, she and Ian were the closest ones to the problem.

"All right, but you go nowhere until Mr. Platter gets you bad." And "bad" meant to get one fully armed and packed for war! Too many times in their recent past they were caught short with insufficient firepower to protect themselves. Now, Harlowe's standing orders were that everyone is bad, even for a stroll in the forest.

"Did you copy that, Mr. Platter?" Harlowe asked over the coms.

"Aye, Captain. Blinking down now," Monday responded. Since unloading bays were close to one of the utility rooms, all he had to do was jump from an unloading dock to a nearby weapons locker and load up. In no time at all, Monday blinked down to Ian and Leucadia with enough weapons and gama-belts to take on a small army.

"Thanks, Mr. Platter," Ian said, strapping on his pistol.

"Give us a call, pronto, understand?" Monday ordered, looking at them both.

Ian nodded. "Aye."

Leucadia kissed Monday the cheek. "Love you."

Ian was about to take off when Monday held him up. "Hold on." In his haste, Ian was about to leave without his headgear activated. It was like a soldier going into battle without his brain bucket. The big black man touched the side of his neck, encapsulating Ian's head with his SIBA bugeyes. "Now go!" he said, tapping him on his head and sending them both on their way.

18

Beleza

Imperator Muuk stepped from his cargo wagon and walked toward the captured beast. Strangely, the forest had suddenly become quiet of chatter. Birds, insects, animals large and small were still as stone. They feared her power, Muuk sensed. She looked at none of his soldiers, only him as he strode like the conqueror under the giant net that had snared her. As she swung slowly from side to side, she appeared to know he was the one responsible for her capture.

Staring in awe at her size, her pristine whiteness, and her striking blue eyes blazing down at him with obvious intelligence, Muuk wondered if she was actually real, or had she materialized from some childish fantasy. In all his life of hunting the wildest beasts on the planet Nod he had never seen such a beautiful creature. Her coat was flawless and seemed to glisten even in the darkening twilight. Unlike other beasts he had captured in the past, that struggled violently within the confines of the net, she remained calm. Why she stayed so composed was an enigma to him. No doubt she was conserving her energy for the right moment to escape, he figured.

"No, my beauty. I will not let you go. You are mine forever," he told her.

Muuk had been hunting the Haga Forest for the last five days. His objective was to snare the elusive haapffin bear to add to his keep inside his military compound. But this capture was far beyond his dreams. She was the desire of every hunter: to capture a species no one had ever seen before. His name would be famous across the planet as the Great Muuk who captured the beautiful white tigre of the Haga forest.

Her eyes were hypnotic and blue as the waters of Beleza. His heart leaped with joy. She was his prize, the one creature he had searched a lifetime to find. Yes, Beleza, he would call her; you are my beautiful one.

"Would you like to see your new home, Beleza?" Muuk asked her. He expected a defiant growl but got no response at all. She blinked slowly, as if knowing her captivity would be short-lived. "Does anything frightened you, Beleza?" He smiled at her while she stared impassively at him. "No, of course not," he answer for her. "You are the queen of all Nod." She watched his manner, his subtle moves, and searched for weaknesses as he continued the conversation. "Your intelligence equals your beauty, Beleza. Do you like your new name, Beleza? It means magnificent beauty."

Beleza remained still, for him her cunning was beyond all measure. She made no pretense about it, she would kill him or anyone else within striking distance of her powerful paws that were large as a mullie's head, if given the chance.

Muuk circled his prize one more time before he waved the capture vehicle to take her. Carefully his soldiers lowered Beleza into the armored body and swung the heavy latch over the locking mechanism. Muuk made one last inspection to assure the metal box was secure. Looking through the small portal, Beleza's haunting stare was all that he saw of her. He gasped, shaking from a sudden chill. Was she a demon? Should he release her now before something terrible happened? He turned away, breathing hard. He saw in the eyes of his soldiers that maybe she was better off left alone. The Haga Forest is a bad place, my Imperator, his keeper, Loomis, had said to him before the trip.

Muuk closed his eyes, purging the weakness from his mind. She was no warning of doom. She was his, and he was taking her, the conquest of a lifetime, from the Haga immediately. He climbed into his capture vehicle and motioned to his driver to hurry. Beleza's new home was waiting.

19

Crowded Skies

It was a foot race to find Molly. Ian and Leucadia had forgotten how far the cats could travel when hunting for food. Now they were deep into the forest, over five miles from *Millawanda* according to their sensors. As fast as they were able to hurtle over fallen trees, duck under prickly branches, and run flat out through the bushy undergrowth, they still found it impossible to keep up with Rhud, who tore his way through the dense forest like it was his own backyard. Without their SIBAs keeping a real-time track of their whereabouts, they could easily lose their way. The big cat, however, knew exactly where he was going. He had a natural GPS that worked no matter what planet he was on.

Another quarter mile into the rescue, Ian saw the dangling cables hidden in the thick branches of the trees. It was what they feared the most; a netted trap had captured Molly. Rhud bellowed, sending shock waves of terror throughout the forest. If any harm came to his sister, there would be hell to pay.

Leucadia and Ian searched the ground where the net had lain hidden. It was cleverly placed between a grove of trees where animals often wandered along a narrow path. Even so, it was hard to imagine Molly being so careless. She was always so cautious where she stepped, he thought. But going so long without fresh meat had obviously overtaken her prudence.

Ian bent down to pick up a tuft of white hairs. His sensor analysis gave him the answer they already knew. "It's Molly's," Ian said, dejected.

There was no sign of blood or anything that showed a struggle. Leucadia sighed, thankful that Molly was unharmed but probably had been captured and hauled away, as she pointed at the heavy transport tracks on the ground.

They had to hurry while the tracks leading away from the forest were still fresh. Around them, the forest was now black, but night or day, their bugeyes saw what they needed: a clear trail that could easily be followed.

Leucadia promptly called Harlowe when they had all their facts. "Molly's been captured, babe!" It was times like these when the mind was foggy with dread.

Harlowe returned her call instantly. *"What?"*

"Molly was trapped and was hauled away in some sort of transport."

Suddenly Prigg broke in, and there was a three-way conversation. *"Your Majesty, Millawanda has picked up incoming contacts headed our way."*

"What are they?" Harlowe asked.

"They appear to be fast moving aircraft, Your Majesty."

"How much time do we have?"

"Ten minutes, Your Majesty."

* * *

Harlowe shut down the thermo-grym operation and called everyone back to the granny, stat! Simon had already taken the second granny to the unloading docks only minutes before. All that was left to do was for Harlowe, Riverstone, and the robobs to jump in and head back to the ship. With only half a load of thermo-grym, Harlowe waited a split second longer for Riverstone to dive through the passenger side window before he slammed the throttle to the floor.

"What's the panic?" Riverstone asked, snapping into place his seat restraints. In an instant they were whizzing over rocks and scraping past thick trunks of two-hundred foot trees. Riverstone tried not to look. Since the first day Harlowe received his learner's permit, his driving habits were the same on or off the road...insane. Riverstone recalled his first solo day of driving. They were just two minutes from his house when Harlowe got his first moving violation. Somewhere in the Guinness archives that had to be a world record, he figured.

"Molly's been trapped!" Harlowe exclaimed.

"Trapped?"

"Yeah, and we have incoming aircraft charging down our throats,"

Harlowe added.

Riverstone grabbed the hand bar. "Step on it, Dog!"

* * *

The granny made a beeline up the ramp and made a sliding stop inside the ship's center foyer. Harlowe and Riverstone jumped onto the nearest blinker, and without even thinking, took the next step onto the bridge.

"Captain on the bridge!" Monday announced.

"Millie ready?" Harlowe asked, striding for his command chair.

"Yes, Your Majesty," Prigg answered calmly.

Harlowe vaulted into his chair like he was jumping into the driver's seat of a grannywagon. "How far out are they, Mr. Platter?"

Monday looked down at his console. "Thirty-seconds, Captain."

"Go, go, go!" Harlowe ordered.

Simon held his fingers steady over the lighted bars of his weapons array. "I have a lock on the incoming, Skipper."

"What are they?"

"Conventional jet propulsion aircraft, Captain," Simon replied.

"Can they hurt us, Mr. Platter?" Harlowe asked.

"Possible, Captain," Monday replied. "They have low yield nuclear missiles. Millie can take the hits but then—"

"Understood, Mr. Platter. We best slide out of here before they catch a glimpse of us. Set a course to the nearest moon, Mr. Prigg. We'll sit there a spell until we're good to come back and pick up Lu, Ian, and the cats," Harlowe ordered.

Through the windows, the forest fell away, and in a blink, the mountains disappeared below a layer of clouds. Moments after that *Millawanda* raced through the stratosphere, headed for a high parking orbit behind the nearest moon.

* * *

"Where are you now?" Harlowe asked Ian as the moon lay ahead through the forward window.

Ian answered from his SIBA com. *"We're following the truck tracks, Captain."* They could hear their labored breathing as they ran. *"It's moving pretty fast."*

Ian's view through his bugeyes was displayed on the overhead screen for everyone on the bridge. Rhud was charging through the forest ahead, with

Leucadia running right behind the big cat, leaping along in long, springy strides.

"Stay with it, Wiz. We can't help you right now. Millie needs to find a place to hide for a while," Harlowe explained.

"What happened, Harlowe?" Leucadia asked.

"We had company. A squad of jet fighters had us in their sights. We had to blow out of there or risk Millie."

"Understood," Leucadia replied.

"Are you bad, Wiz?" Harlowe asked.

"Mr. Platter set us right, Captain. There's even a couple of clickers in the bag."

Harlowe winked a right-on toward Monday. "Sweet."

"Don't worry, Captain. We'll get Molly back."

The jagged craters of the moon floated in front of the forward windows as they came around the back side. "I know you will, Wiz." Then as a small addition, Harlowe added, "And, Wiz?"

"Yeah, Captain?"

"Molly knows it, too."

Click, click.

Click, click.

Two clicks from each com was their way of saying "Message received. Over and out."

20

Ambush

A powerful rocket struck the forward vehicle in His Highness' convoy, killing the Royal Bodyguards inside and halting the line of ten vehicles traveling on a secret night mission through the black Haga forest. A second and third rocket streaked from between the trees with deadly accuracy and eliminated the two rear cars in the motorcade and their occupants. Upon seeing the destruction, the remaining cars broke away from the road and headed hastily into the forest. High-powered bullets ripped into the remaining cars as the Royal Guards forced open their doors and began defending themselves against their attackers. Bodies fell as they exited their cars. They didn't have a chance. The guards were ill-prepared for such a massive assault on their motorcade.

Bolting from behind the front fender, a brave young guard made his way back toward His Highness' car. Bullets whizzed by his head as he dove past one car, then another through a hail of bullets. Guards lucky enough to survive the initial attack were hunkered down behind fenders, engine blocks, and bumpers...anything that would give them cover. Others took to the woods in search of trees, bushes, animal holes in which to hide.

Amazingly, the young guard managed to stay alive through it all, making his way back to the royal car that was now riddled with bullet holes and shattered glass. A quick glance inside and the young guard saw the driver slumped over the steering wheel, bleeding from his wounds. The soldier next to him was still from the bullet hole to his brain, but the young man in the back seat was returning gunfire with the pistols he had taken from his dead guards. "My Prince, my Prince," the young guard called out, forcing open the door. "My Prince, you must come with me!"

"Where are my guards?" the Prince shouted over the exploding gun fire. "What has happened?"

A wave of bullets struck the car, sending them both below the open window for cover. The hardened doors protected the royal car from bullets, but it would not hold up against another rocket attack.

The young guard had been hit. It wasn't critical, yet. With gritting teeth, he reached out with his good arm and pulled the Prince from the backseat to the ground outside the royal car. "This way, my Prince," the young soldier urged. "We must get away from the convoy, or we will surely die."

The Prince yanked his arm away from his guardian and crawled to another body. He grabbed the sidearm from the dead soldier's hand and continued fighting for his life. The young guard glanced down both lines of cars. His fellow guards were all dead, lying in the road where they had huddled next to their cars. There was no one left to protect the Prince.

The young guard risked touching the Royal Person without consent. But he had no choice. The Prince would be dead if he remained by his car. He grabbed the Prince by the back of the collar and dragged His Highness into the forest. The Prince screamed he would have the young guard's head if he didn't release him. In that instant, as the young guard slammed the Prince behind the heavy trunk of a tree, rockets hit the royal car, exploding the vehicle into a million fiery shards. Upon feeling the searing heat from the explosion, the Prince stopped his tirade and allowed the young guard to lead him deeper into the forest without protest.

"Where will we go?" the Prince asked, following the young guard's lead.

"That is not important now, my Prince. It is important only that we stay alive," the young guard replied.

The Prince stopped his protector against a tree. "You're bleeding." The young guard's sleeve was wet with green fluid.

"It is nothing, my Prince."

Behind them, there was much movement in the dark forest. "They are still after us, my Prince. We must hurry while it is still dark."

Together, they slipped into a gully, rolling in the mud of the creek. Wet and cold, they helped each other to the far bank where the guard lifted the

Prince up the incline onto the bluff above.

"Now you," the Prince said, offering his hand to his young guard.

The guard took his Prince's hand just as a barrage of bullets exploded against the bank. Pulling with all that he had, the Prince lost his grip as the weight of the young guard yanked his hand from his grip. He watched helplessly as the young guard slid down the incline and into the watery creek and was still. More shots drove the Prince away from the bank. Unable to help the young guard, the Prince fired behind him as he dove behind a fallen tree. Bullets ripped at the bark. Peering through a small slit in the tree, dozens of black shadows were coming his way, with more behind them. He fired again, killing one, two, three more ambushers before a round struck his head, flinging him bodily into the dense undergrowth behind him.

21

No Choice

Harlowe stood at his observation window, staring down at the planet when Riverstone and Prigg entered his quarters together. Since leaving the planet forty-seven minutes ago, getting his crew back together was the only thing on his mind. But the bad news kept coming in.

"Something big is coming our way, Captain," Riverstone informed him..

"I thought the toads were incapable of space flight," Harlowe said.

Riverstone explained, "It's not coming from the planet. It's a ship . . . a very big and powerful ship, and it's coming fast right at us, Captain."

Harlowe looked at Prigg for his take. "I have never seen this craft before, Your Majesty."

Harlowe went to the conference table with his two crewmen. Prigg touched the table activators and a holograph of a huge galaxy-class vessel appeared. It measured over fifty miles in length and just short of two miles wide between its drive pods. It was long and slender and layered like sheets of metal fused together. The ship was indeed formidable. Its power readouts were impressive, even by Gamadin standards. It had over a hundred major weapons turrets and an uncountable number of minor close range weapons, along with dozens of torpedo launch tubes, fore and aft.

"A ship this size has traveled far, Your Majesty," Prigg stated. "Possibly from another galaxy."

Harlowe was impressed. "Cool."

"Yes, Your Majesty."

Harlowe studied the ship a long moment before he spoke. "I don't recognize it, either."

"I do," Riverstone said casually.

Harlowe stared at Riverstone like he had passed one of Farnducky's tests with an A. "You do?"

Riverstone recalled the ship that was crushed by the tidal shift on Lenor's watery moon when he and Simon were on their surfing vacation. "The one Rerun and I saw was tiny compared to this one. But it has the same look and feel as the one that ate it."

Harlowe put a star map of the Omni Quadrant to the edge of Cartooga-Thaat, where they were now. "If Prigg doesn't recognize them, then they're not from around here."

Prigg drew a line with a crooked finger indicating the starship's course. "Yet it came from the Lenor system, Your Majesty."

Harlowe suddenly became more concerned. His brow wrinkled between his intense blue eyes. "That doesn't make sense. They're obviously not Lenorian." Harlowe looked at Riverstone. "What were they up to on that moon?"

"We didn't get a chance to ask, Captain. You think they're the outpost destroyers?" Riverstone wondered.

Harlowe focused on the drive pods, thinking out loud to himself, "This is getting curiouser and curiouser." He pointed at the long star-drive pods and ordered Prigg to identify the mysterious ship's power signature.

The little Naruckian made a minor adjustment, and two wave length graphs rose from the table. "This is the signature from a Fhaal starcruiser. This is from this ship, Your Majesty."

"They almost match," Riverstone said surprised, and thinking that was peculiar, he wondered if the Fhaal and these toads were kissing cousins.

Harlowe thought that made sense. "Maybe," and pointed out they were using the same power supply, too…thermo-grym.

Riverstone saw the similarities. "But why are they ransacking old Gamadin stations?"

"Because maybe they're running low on fuel like the Fhaal," Harlowe replied.

"And they want our ynni?"

Harlowe nodded yes.

Riverstone stared back in a quandary. "They want Millie?"

"Bingo! What if you didn't have to go looking for thermo-grym anymore?"

"I would like that."

"Yeah, well, so would they. If you found an inexhaustible supply for your ships, wouldn't you want it?"

Riverstone answered for everyone. "Big time!"

Millawanda jolted. Outside Harlowe's cabin window bright streaks of yellow light shot across the deck.

"Incoming bandits!" Monday's voice exclaimed over the com.

* * *

"Captain on the bridge!" Monday called out.

For the second time in four hours, Harlowe entered his center command chair from the rear. "Status!"

"Twenty-three bandits, Captain," Monday replied, calm and professional.

"Controls to my chair, Mr. Prigg," Harlowe ordered.

"Aye, Your Majesty," Prigg countered.

Millawanda left orbit to put the moon between them and the Mysterian ship.

"We should have had better warning, Mr. Platter?" Harlowe said. His manner was authoritative, yet calm and unaccusing.

"They just appeared, Captain," Monday replied. "Sensors picked up the mothership but gave no warning on the attack group."

"Shields, Mr. Prigg?" Harlowe asked.

"Shields 100%, Your Majesty."

Riverstone had taken over Ian's science console in his absence. "Millie is slow in adjusting to their sensor blocks, Captain."

Harlowe addressed his bridge. "Hear that, everyone? Sensor readings will be sporadic at best from here on out. We'll need to rely more on our long-range visuals."

Harlowe directed his next inquiry to Simon. "Do we have a lock, Mr. Bolt?"

"On the first wave, Skipper. Long-range is iffy. The big guy is holding back," Simon explained.

Harlowe followed the tiny bandits the overhead screen. In close they were clear, but at a million miles out, a distance that should have been trouble-free for *Millawanda*, her sensors were erratic and fading. Simon needed more precision, or his shots would be wasted. "Very well, Mr. Bolt. Take them out when they're in range."

"Aye, Skipper."

At this point, Harlowe still had it in his mind that he could extract Leucadia and Ian from the planet. Leaving without the most important part of his crew was not an option. All he had to do was hold the Mysterians off long enough to put together a landing party and pick them up. A call to Leucadia, however, changed everything.

"We ran into a problem, Captain," Leucadia told him. *"Molly was airlifted out of the region."*

Harlowe was stunned. "That fast?"

Leucadia was heartbroken. *"It was a military operation. They had an aircraft waiting. There was nothing we could do to stop them. If we blew it out of the sky . . ."*

"Understood, Lu. Don't blame yourselves. You did the right thing. We have problems of our own. The Mysterians we talked about earlier are on us."

Leucadia came right back with dire instructions. *"Harlowe, you have to get out of there. You can't wait around for us. You have to cross Cartooga-Thaat before they do."*

"I'm not leaving you behind, Lu. Not again."

"You have to, babe. There is no other choice. It's Millie we're talking about, Harlowe. It's her survival, not ours."

"I know, I know."

"Look, you could save us but then what? That ship is way more powerful than Millie is now. Fix her, Harlowe! Ian, Rhud and I will be okay down here."

"But—"

Leucadia refused to let Harlowe finish. There were no buts, no alternate choices as she went on: *"We'll find Molly, babe, and be waiting for you when you get back. I know you will do it. I know you'll do it because you're the only one who can. Please, don't argue with me on this one, Harlowe. Get Millie out of there. No fighting, no last stand, just go! Promise me you'll do it. Promise me, babe! Promise me!"*

Tears welled up in Harlowe's eyes, as he spoke with a crack in his voice. "I love you, Lu."

"I know, babe. Bring back Millie whole again. Do that for us, okay?"

Riverstone turned to Harlowe in a panic. He needed Harlowe's full attention. Bandits were driving down their throats.

Kick butt, Pylott!" were the last words she said before her image went dark.

* * *

Harlowe reached out to touch her face, but she was already gone. "I love you, Lu," he said to her. With teary, red eyes, he said to Riverstone, "Blink down to the utility room, Matt. Lu and Wiz need a care package. You know what to do."

Riverstone shot up from his station and headed for the blinker. "Aye, Captain."

Harlowe glanced up at the overhead, watching the waves of attack ships coming straight for *Millawanda* at flank speed. "You have two minutes!" he called out to Riverstone before he blinked away.

The bridge suddenly became a morgue of solemn faces, knowing that leaving a crewman behind was the hardest decision any captain could make.

"How will we fix Millie without Lu and Wiz, Skipper?" Simon asked.

"Dittos on that, Captain. They know everything," Platter said.

With Leucadia off the ship, Prigg had replaced her as Harlowe's caution flag. "I concur with Ms. Lu, Your Majesty. We must avoid engaging the Mysterians at all costs. I have calculated the thermo-grym we have taken onboard." Prigg pointed at the vast Cartooga-Thaat void of star-less space. "We have a long crossing ahead. *Millawanda* will surely fall short if she expends her energy too soon."

Harlowe closed his eyes. If there was one being on his ship he never argued with, it was Prigg. The little Naruckian was loyal to a fault. The muscles in his jaws rippled tight with frustration. Nothing was going their way. If a 16 penny nail was placed between his teeth, he would have snapped it in two. He had never run from a fight in his life. But more importantly, there was his crew. How could he leave them behind? How would they find Orixy, or even the next Gamadin Station, without his two science officers?

His fist tightened, striking the arm of his center chair with a loud thump. He opened his eyes and addressed the distant enemy on the overhead screen. "Toad, this is your lucky day." Looking at the little Naruckinan, he said, "Thank you, Mr. Prigg, I get it." Like he was chewing steel wool, he turned to Simon and ordered, "Let the skanks go, Mr. Bolt."

Prigg breathed a long thank you.

Simon's mouth dropped open. He had them in his sights.

Harlowe felt his anguish. "I know, Mr. Bolt. Stand down." Then he directed Prigg to set a course for the tiny blue dot in the middle of the nothingness.

"Yes, Your Majesty."

"Best speed, Mr. Platter," Harlowe added, as he felt Simon's eyes still on him.

"The bandits, Skipper!" he said, his face fraught with pain. "We still have a lock!"

Harlowe mused for half a nano-second. He held up his hand, then brought is down. "Do it, Mr. Bolt."

"First wave are bye-bye, Skipper," Simon reported moments later.

Harlowe leaned over to Prigg. "The gauntlet's been thrown, Mr. Prigg," he said in reference to the way the Tails back on Gazz challenged someone to a fight. They would take off the spiked battle glove from the end of their tail and toss it at the feet of the being they wished to duel. Twice on Gazz Harlowe had been challenged by a thrown gauntlet.

"Course locked and ready for your order, Captain," Monday announced.

Harlowe held up his hand again. "Hold on, Mr. Platter." He looked over at Prigg's eyes twisting around in small circles. There wasn't time for explanations. "Mr. Riverstone! Is the package ready?"

"Two seconds, Captain," Riverstone countered.

"Tell Wiz and Lu," Harlowe hesitated searching for the words. The ache in his gut was agonizing. Words seemed meaningless. Leaving his girl, his life-long friend, and the cats behind was the hardest decision he ever had to make. "Tell them . . . tell them, God speed. We'll be back as soon as we can."

"I will, Captain."

"Now, Captain?" Monday asked, holding his fingers near the hyper-drive bars.

"The mothership has launched another wave, Skipper," Simon advised.

Harlowe kept his clenched fist up a little longer. He had to give Riverstone another moment before stepping on the gas. In the meantime, he wasn't quite through with the Mysterians yet.

"Mr. Bolt. Send Big Mama a parting gift from us. Let them know we still have plenty of sting in us," Harlowe ordered.

"He's out of sensor range, Skipper. I can't get a lock on the sucker," Simon said.

"Best guess, then."

Simon returned to his console, made his calculations and sent the gift on its way.

"It's sent, Skipper. Complete with a pretty bow and a card from us," Simon announced.

"Fantastic!" Harlowe acknowledged. "It won't stop them, but he'll think twice about coming too close next time."

With only seconds to spare, Riverstone called back to the bridge and announced, "It's done, Captain. One bad-ass package shipped FedEx!"

Harlowe went immediately to Monday. "Pedal to the metal, Mr. Platter!"

* * *

A short while later, when *Millawanda* was well on her way, running straight and true on her new course to the next blue dot deep inside Cartooga-Thaat, Prigg asked Harlowe, "Do you think we will see the mysterious ship again, Your Majesty?"

"Count on it, Mr. Prigg," Harlowe replied, leaving no doubt in his hard blue eyes. "They want Millie's power, and for that they'll follow us all the way to the galactic core to get it." Harlowe glanced over at Mowgi sitting on the edge of the couch. "And when Millie is right, they'll wish they've never heard of the Gamadin."

The undog yipped twice.

22

Four for the Road

The Prince awakened with a splitting headache. From a curled up sleeping position, he rolled over on his back, groaning that his head was about to explode. He felt the wet dew on his back, the chill of morning air, the scent of forest mixed with decaying wood. He was miserably cold, but the pain in his head overpowered his need to keep warm.

"Here, drink this," an easy voice said to him. A container of sweet fluid touched his lips. His pain was so intense and his mouth so dry, the Prince didn't question whether the drink was harmful to him or not. He blindly swallowed two big gulps before the container was taken away.

The Prince reached out and demanded more. A miracle, he thought. The throbbing stopped, and his head began to clear. "I want more!"

His hands were pushed away as the soft-spoken voice said, "Two swallows is all you need."

What insolence! "Who are you to tell me—" he tried to say, when he froze. Staring him in the face were two impossibly large blue eyes of a giant white head with beastly teeth that were nearly as long as his forearm. He pushed himself backwards with his heels, crawling over the dead leaves until a large fallen tree stopped his retreat.

"He won't hurt you," the soft voice assured him.

For the first time he saw the being behind the voice. It was no beast, but a dream looking at him with round green eyes that seemed to glow with a kindness and sympathy toward him. She was the most beautiful *puella* he had ever seen. She had lips the color of a pink morning. Her nose was small, turned up and delicately rounded at the end. Her hair was long and golden like his, but her strands were delicate and fine with the satiny glow of an Angelus. His hair was thick and dull and braided. She wore a uniform like nothing he had ever seen before. It covered her skin in a thin layer that seemed to blend with the colors of the forest. As she moved, the suit changed its hue to match the background, making it difficult to see her clearly. As she stood, she was taller than his tallest guard, yet nothing about her was out of proportion. Her curves were gentle, her legs long and slender, while her bearing was striking, like she was born of royalty. Her scent was as pure as a flower freshly picked from the palace gardens. Where had she come from, he asked of this Angelus.

He sighed and closed his eyes, praying she was no Angelus who would dissolve into a dream-like mist. When his vision returned, he sighed with relief. She was still there, as she touched the giant tigre on its head and kissed the massive beast, causing a throaty purr that sounded like an idling transport.

"Rhud won't hurt you. He is a lovable, big puddy-tat," she told him.

Keeping his eyes on the tigre, the Prince asked the puella, "I have never seen such a beast."

The puella nodded. "Yes, he is very rare."

"Are you Numeri?" the Prince asked.

The puella answered with a question of her own. "What is a Numeri?"

The Prince thought that strange. "You have never heard of the Numeri?"

"No. My friend and I come from far away," she replied. "We are unacquainted with your land and its customs."

The Prince then answered her question. "The Numeri are soldiers of Imperator Muuk. They killed my Royal Guards and tried to kill me."

The puella nodded like she knew his danger. "Then we must go immediately before more Numeri return," she told him.

The Prince pointed at her outer covering. "What is that?"

"Protection," a second being answered, catching the Prince by surprise. This being was a *mullie* and seemed to come out of nowhere.

The puella handed the mullie the container of blue fluid. He took one swallow from the container then clicked the top closed and attached it to an elaborate belt of devices and pouches around his waist. The Prince had never seen such an elaborate uniform before.

"What are those . . . those objects?" the Prince asked, staring at the articles.

"Stuff." The being replied bluntly and then asked, "Can you walk?"

The Prince moved his legs and twisted his body enough to know he was okay. "Yes."

"Then we need to go," the male being said, more like a command than a request.

The Prince was not used to being told to do anything. He came to his knees to reprimand the being for his disrespect when the puella interrupted him. "The boy said the soldiers were out to kill him," she replied.

"Daks?" the Prince asked.

"Bad people," the puella replied.

"You speak strangely," the Prince remarked.

The mullie was anxious to leave. "Look, dweeb. We can't talk anymore."

"Am I your prisoner?" the Prince asked.

The puella replied, "Of course not. You are free to go wherever you want."

The Prince stood, sticking his chest out proudly, yet only standing shoulder high to the tall mullie. "Then you don't know who I am."

"We don't care who you are," the mullie snapped.

"I'm Prince Maa Dev. Imperial Heir to the Throne of Dolmina. This is my kingdom," Dev boasted, spreading his arms out wide. "And this is my forest."

The male didn't care whose forest it was. "Cool. Now get your ass moving, or you'll be sleeping with the pine cones permanently, toad."

The puella touched his shoulder like his mother would before the bad times. "Nice to meet you, Dev. But Ian is right, if you stay, the Numeri will kill you."

"You may address me as 'Sire' or 'My Prince'."

The mullie called Ian made another affront to his Royal Highness by walking away without being dismissed.

"I could have your head for such behavior," the Prince threatened.

"I doubt it," Ian grunted, stepping away.

Dev stared at the puella's green eyes. "Your eyes. I have never seen ones with such color. Are they altered?" the Prince asked.

"No, Dev. They are all mine."

"No, Sire," Dev corrected.

In single file, the white tigre led the way between the trees, as Ian followed the beast. The Prince was next, with the puella continually watching behind them. When Ian unholstered the weapon attached to his leg. Dev was awed by the size. He had never seen a sidearm like that before. Oddly, it had no exit port, either, for the bullet to escape. He doubted that he could even hold the weapon with two hands, but Ian handled it like it was an extension of his arm.

The puella kept nudging the Prince forward, forcing him to walk faster. "Why do the Numeri want to kill you, Dev?" she asked. She had a weapon like Ian and wondered if she was as capable as he was with its use.

"I don't know. I was returning to the palace by a secret route when we were attacked," Dev replied.

Ian glanced back and said, "Someone scammed ya, Prince."

"Where are you going?" the Prince asked the puella. She was more pleasant to speak to than the mullie.

The puella replied, "We are searching for a friend."

The Prince's face turned irritated. "I demand that you call me by my proper titles. It is the law of the land that I must be addressed in such a manner!" The beings were treating him like a commoner. This could not be tolerated. Even though he was grateful for their kindness, they must respect his authority as Prince of Dolmina or great harm would come to them.

"Fuuggeddaboutit!" Ian said forcefully.

Maa Dev was so irritated he didn't see the obstacle in his path and tripped, falling flat on his face. The puella helped the Prince to his feet. When he looked to check out what he stumbled over, his eyes flew open at the sight of the dead body. "Numeri!" he exclaimed. When he looked up again, he saw dozens more scattered around the forest, still as fallen trees. "What happened here?" the Prince asked, alarmed at the number of dead bodies in the forest. An enemy of immeasurable power had surely struck them down with a mighty sword.

The puella stared at the bodies like it was regretful. "Keep moving, Dev," was her minimal response.

The tigre heard the sounds first. "They're on us," Ian said.

"The Numeri have returned, Dev," the puella said. She quickly touched the side of her neck, and by the gods, her head was swallow whole by a pliable fabric… her golden hair and all! She was now a giant insect with large bulbous eyes and no mouth. "We must run now, Dev," she said.

"How did you do that?" Dev asked.

The puella took his hand and urged him along. There was no time for explanations. "Hurry, Dev."

Dev grabbed the puella's arm. The uniform fabric was soft and forgiving, but underneath her muscle were hard and sinewy. "You must carry me," Dev demanded.

The tigre started to bolt toward the Numeri coming through the forest. "No, Rhud!" the puella said. "Leave them be."

The great beast stopped fast, growling his disappointment that he could not challenge the soldiers. The puella then guided the tigre back on the path away from the soldiers.

"Listen to me. I demand that you carry me," Dev ordered of the strange looking beings.

"Let him go, Lu," Ian commanded.

"He'll die alone out here," she said.

Ian hung his head with a relenting nod. "Yeah," and grabbed the Prince by the back of his outer garment and threw him forward as if he were a misbehaving child. "Run or die, dweeb. It's your choice."

23

The Enclosure

The enclosure was an impregnable arena attached to the main keep that contained over a hundred species of the rarest animals on the planet. The arena was one-hundred fifty feet across with thirty-foot high metal and concrete circular walls that supported a heavy, domed ceiling. The only window to the outside was a skylight centered ninety feet above the dirt floor of the enclosure. The only way in or out were two metal doors. One door was windowless and connected to the main keep. The second door had a large circular porthole made of inch-thick armor plate that led to the science laboratory, where experiments were performed on the captured animals that were kept in the adjoining keep.

Concerned over his recent capture, Imperator Muuk stood behind the safety of a stout metal door, looking through the portal with Loomis, his head animal keeper, admiring his beautiful white prize. His beloved Beleza was acting unlike any animal in his collection. From the time of her capture and her release into the enclosure, her only movement was to make herself comfortable in the soft dirt. She had not moved in two days or growled or roared or expressed in any way anxiety over her captivity. Her food and water went untouched. Her only activity seemed to be the constant grooming of her glistening white coat with her coarse, pink tongue. When she was not sleeping or preening herself, her head was upright and proud, as if she was queen of a Royal Court.

From the moment Muuk saw his Beleza he was smitten. If she were a puella, he would have swooned over her and offered her a kingdom. "So beautiful, Loomis. Have you ever seen such a gorgeous tigre as my Beleza?" he asked his keeper.

Loomis' assessment of the captured beast was more methodical and disciplined. His appraisal was based on evidence, not emotion. "No, Sire, and no one else has either."

"Look at her. She is powerful and confident, as if she were already plotting her escape." The Imperator chuckled. "A sign of remarkable intelligence I would say. Would you agree, Loomis?"

"This tigre is not from here, Sire," Loomis repeated.

Imperator Muuk remained fixated. "I have never seen such a magnificent creature in all my travels."

Loomis clarified his statement further. "This tigre is not from Nod, Sire."

Imperator Muuk blinked as he turned to Loomis. "Not from Nod?"

"Yes, Sire. I have studied Beleza's hair and spore. Her cell structure has elements not found in any animal from Nod."

Imperator Muuk went back to his prize with a new vision. "Are you certain?"

"Yes, Sire. My conclusions are absolute."

Imperator Muuk's eyes narrowed, as his mind deliberated on the meaning of Loomis' discovery. "Fascinating." He peered through the portal and asked, "What brings you to Nod, my Beleza?"

An assistant entered the laboratory and bowed apologetically for interrupting the Imperator and his head keeper.

"A Numeri officer has asked to see his Imperator, Ki Loomis," the assistant said.

Loomis was short with his assistant. "Not now. The Imperator is busy with more important matters."

The assistant bowed again. "He said it requires the Imperator's immediate attention. It concerns the Haga mission, Ki Loomis."

Muuk overheard the request and motioned for the soldier to come forward. "What is it, officer?"

The officer was hesitant to speak of military matters in front of Loomis and his assistant.

Muuk disregarded protocol. His thoughts were concerned solely with the recent off-worldly revelations over his Beleza. "Come, come. What of the Haga? Was the mission completed?"

The officer bowed respectfully. "No, Imperator. I must speak to you alone."

Muuk waved Loomis and his assistant out of the room. When his keepers had shut the door behind them, the Imperator allowed the officer to speak.

"The Prince's convoy was destroyed, Imperator, but his body has not been recovered," the officer explained.

"How is that possible, officer? The Numeri were well positioned for the ambush. I oversaw the planning myself."

"Sire, all went as planned. All Royal Guards were eliminated."

"Then what has happened to our Prince?"

"The Numeri tracked the Prince into the Haga, Sire, but after a short chase, they were brought down by an unknown force. The Numeri were wiped out, Sire."

"All my Numeri?"

"To the last soldier, Sire."

Muuk was stunned. His Numeri were the finest soldiers on the planet. How could any force wipe them out so decisively? As he went back to the portal, searching for answers, he saw only one answer that made sense. "Beleza . . ." he said to her. "Have you come to enslave us?"

The Imperator whirled around and instructed the officer to call out the milities. "I want a full division sent to the Haga immediately. Cut off all roads, bridges, and pathways in and out of the forest immediately." He shoved a commanding finger into the officer's chest. "Do this all before the sun rises."

The officer snapped to attention, eager to carry out his Imperator's orders. "What are we looking for, Sire?"

"The Prince, fool!" the Imperator shouted. "The Royal Heir must be found. Find him, and we will know that answer."

24

Jawbreaker

It was mid morning and they had been running since sun up. The sky was clear and blue-green above the treetops. The air had warmed considerably since the morning chill. It was good weather for a run through the forest, but not so good for descending the cliff ahead. The five thousand foot drop had halted their getaway. Without airlift vehicles, their run ended here.

"I command you to stop," Dev gasped. His chest burned as his lungs tried desperately to gulp enough air to express himself. But before he could wheeze another command, he bent over a nearby rock and heaved. He felt like he was going to die.

"We cannot stop, Dev. The Numeri are right behind us," said Lu. She spoke to him while Ian assessed the cliff ahead of them, looking down upon the deep river valley below.

Barely able to hold his head up, Dev wiped his mouth and said, "We have not seen the Numeri for some time."

Ian slapped the side of his leg. "Trust me, your friends are right behind us."

Dev heaved again before he said heatedly, "The Numeri are not my friends. They are traitors! They want to kill me! I shall see them all hung from the walls of Dolmina!"

Ian kept his focus on the valley. "Whatever."

"You dare mock the Royal Heir, init?" Dev challenged. He would have Ian's head when this was all over, but Lu, he would keep as his slave, for

109

she had been more kind than the mullie. "I will have you thrown into the dungeons of Vald. Or perhaps you would rather swing with the Numeri when they capture us?"

"Stop it, Dev. You're giving me a headache," Ian retorted.

The big tigre snarled at the Prince, causing him to back away from Ian and shut his mouth.

Ian stroked the giant tigre's white coat. "Keep it up and you'll be his royal lunch."

Suddenly, three Numeri appeared out of the trees but had yet to see them.

Dev crawled to the edge of the cliff. There was no way down but death. "We're trapped, in it. We have no escape."

Ian and Lu drew their weapons.

"The Numeri are out of range, init. You waste—"

Three blasts from Ian's weapon and all three Numeri dropped from sight. Lu whirled to their flank and fired four more rounds as more Numeri moved to cut off any escape along the cliff. Maa Dev had never witnessed such marksmanship. His question earlier as to whether she was as capable as Ian was answered decisively. They made impossible shots look routine.

"I know no one who shoots like that," said the Prince in awe.

"You should see my pards. I'm the worst shot of the bunch," Ian said.

"Dev needs a ride, Ian," Lu said, patting the tigre's back.

Before Dev could utter a word of protest, Ian grabbed the Prince by the back of his upper garment and bodily hoisted him onto the tigre's back. "Good idea."

Dev was shocked by Ian's nerve. Touching the Royal Person in such a way without permission was death.

"What are you doing?" Dev demanded.

Ian began strapping the Prince's hands and legs around the tigre's chest with strands of tough thin thread "I'm saving your puky hide," Ian replied, grudgingly.

Dev tried to struggle, but when Lu added her assistance, the battle was over before it had begun. The force of her grip was too powerful to fight. The Prince was quickly secured to the tigre's back and unable to move.

"Why are you doing this to me? You said I was not your prisoner."

Lu looked over the side of the cliff. "We're going down the cliff, Dev.

Our sensors show hundreds more Numeri approaching our position. Those first toads were only scouts. The main force will find them for sure and know we're here."

Dev's eyes went round with fear as he stared down the sheer wall of the cliff. "Are you mad? We have no rope. We will die!"

Ian checked the Prince's tie downs and said, "It's a jawbreaker all right. I would close my eyes if I were you. The ride will get narly."

"Close my eyes?" Dev wondered. "But what about you?"

Several shots hit the rocks around them. With blinding speed, Ian plucked off the two Numeri who fired at them.

"Ian and I will meet you at the bottom, Dev," Lu replied as she pointed at a wide river far down in the valley.

All the Prince saw was death. "I protest!"

Lu patted the white tigre, sending him on his way. "Go, Rhud."

* * *

With the Prince screaming at the top of his lungs, Rhud leaped off the side of the cliff and dropped fifty feet to the first rock ledge like he did it everyday before breakfast. It was not like he paused there to chew over his next outcropping. The big cat dropped down another thirty feet to the next ledge without a second thought, and continued bounding his way sideways to another protrusion and didn't stop. Leucadia nearly lost it when Rhud went into a long, hundred-foot free-fall. The big cat touched the thin slice of rock that was no wider than his paw, and continued his descent like a falling rock but never out of control. He kept bounding slightly this way and that but always down, using outcroppings as if they were simple stepping-stones. Ian and Leucadia watched in awe as Rhud's body grew smaller and smaller until he was out of sight under the cliff. Ian doubted seriously if mountain goats could match the cat's sure-footed deftness.

It was almost comical to watch the Prince's body flop around like a rag doll strapped to the great white cat. Ian allowed himself a small chuckle, wondering if the Prince had taken his advice and shut his eyes. But after hearing no sounds from His Highness after Rhud touched the first ledge, Ian figured it was more likely the Prince had checked out for the rest of the ride.

"You da man, Rhud," Ian said.

* * *

A fast moving object caught Leucadia's attention as it descended from the heavens and vanished into the forest valley below. Harlowe's care package, she thought. Matthew had relayed the news to them earlier that the package was on its way, and they were now on their own. An unknown ship had attacked *Millawanda,* and Harlowe had no choice but to break orbit and set course for the next Gamadin outpost. She wiped the tears from her eyes, knowing the heartache he was suffering at leaving them behind. How she wished she were there holding him, making sure he was okay. It would be difficult finding Orixy without them. Harlowe and his crew would have to reach deep into parts of their minds they never knew existed and learn new skills. They were used to fighting bad guys and defending the weak, but crunching numbers to make it all work wasn't part of their job description. Harlowe had Prigg, she thought, relieved. The little Naruckian was savvy in the ways of the cosmos. He would be a great help to them all. Regardless, it was an impossible journey even for a whole Gamadin crew. There was no turning back, no Plan B. Plan A had to work, or she would never see Harlowe again. She closed her eyes, savoring the last words he told her before she cut him off: I love you, Lu.

* * *

"Are you okay?" Ian asked Leucadia, noticing her shoulders bracing back and the stiff upper lip as she fought to regain her composure.

"I'm trying to be." She looked skyward with a small chuckle to mask her fear. "I'm worried there's no mother hen to watch over them."

"Yeah. But don't forget what Riverstone always says."

"What's that?"

"Harlowe doesn't lose."

She giggled again, thanking him for his encouragement. "Yeah, he is kinda like that, huh?"

"That's Harlowe. Always a winner." Ian put his arms around her to console them both. "Come on, Lu. Let's go find our girl."

* * *

The readouts from *Millawanda* suddenly went dark. All contact with the ship was gone. The way it winked out so fast meant only one thing; Millie had gone to hyperlight. There was nothing they could do to change that. They were now alone on a world they knew nothing about. A barrage of bullets whizzed past their heads, reminding them the cliff was no place to sulk. A few rounds sparked off their SIBAs as they leaped outward, clearing the edge easily and plummeting down another 500 feet before they deployed their wings and glided out over the valley. Ian twisted around and saluted the line of frustrated Numeri who no doubt were wondering what kind of enemy could dive off the side of a five thousand foot cliff and fly away like soaring eagles. It would be several hours before the Numeri could make the same descent. By that time, they planned to be a hundred miles away from the forest, the Numeri, and hopefully the monkey on Rhud's back, too.

25

Before Twynich

Imperator Muuk's headquarters was alive with incoming communiqués from his forces in the Haga Forest. Officers and orderlies busily crisscrossed the great underground bunker, handing off notes, passing along orders, and updating the giant wall map of the kingdom with minute by minute changes in the Imperial army's movements. The Prince of Dolmina and the two beings who aided his escape were still at large with no sign as to their whereabouts. The mission directive was straightforward: Find the Prince before the next twynich. (twi-nich) Twynich had no other spelling, pronunciation, or translation. To the inhabitants everywhere on Nod, twynich met only one thing: The period of darkness when all forms of electrical energy ceased to exist. The twynich did not afflict one town, region, or continent. Twynich applied to everyone on the planet. When the twynich struck, it imposed darkness worldwide, stopping all electromagnetic energy on the planet. "No one escapes the twynich" is an old saying on Nod. Flying aircraft, motorized vehicles, communications, television, resistors, capacitors, computers, hospitals, royal navies, palaces, and power stations are all treated equally. Nothing escapes the darkness. And because of this anomaly, Nod through the centuries has become a planet of two worlds; a modern world of illumination, electric motors, telecommunications, and powered conveniences, and a dark world of horse-drawn carriages, gas-filled air machines, and wood-fired machines.

The twynich's properties were no secret. The scientists had discovered the debilitating effects many centuries ago. But like a breaking dam releasing a crushing wall of water upon the valley below it, twynich was unstoppable. The planet's finest scientists had never solved the mystery of its crippling power. Lead shields or other exotic metals were all useless. Even mile-deep underground caverns provided no barrier against the twynich.

Two elements of the twynich made life within the darkness possible. First, it was never late. The twynich occurred exactly every seven days, 12 hours, 19 minutes, 8.7 seconds. Second, the duration of darkness was always the same, exactly one-half to the infinitesimal measurement of time of the length between the shutdowns: three days, 6 hours, 9 minutes, 57.25 seconds. Since the discovery of electromagnetism, the twynich had never missed a shutdown. However, the study of molecular polarity rocks two hundred twenty-three years ago found an interesting fact: the twynich was a recent phenomenon of Nodian geological history. Around seventeen thousand passings ago, it was theorized, the twynich did not exist. Now the Imperator himself was up against its obstructive force that he could not control. So he pushed his soldiers to locate the Prince before the next twynich or heads would literally… roll!

When Muuk entered the bunker, his highest ranking centurion reported an immediate update. "The fifth *vilites* had the Prince at the crest of the Margus cliffs, Sire, and lost them."

"Them? With the assistance of the same conspirators, I assume?" Muuk enquired as he understood the Prince would have needed help to escape his soldiers.

"Yes, Sire."

"Do we know who they were, Centurion, and where they came from?"

"No, Sire, but they felled many of our soldiers with their weapons."

Muuk was disturbed. He wondered if his Beleza was in anyway connected with the Prince's escape. He needed to know more. Recalling the terrain well, recently he had hunted the great haapffin beasts along that very same Margus cliff. The escarpment was treacherous and unscalable except by the skilled mountaineers. "Go on, Centurion. How did the Prince elude the vilites?" he asked.

The Centurion hesitated, knowing what he was about to say would seem farcical to the Imperator, but his duty to his Sire was supreme. He would fall on his rapier for him. The tall officer bowed, ashamed for what he was about to say. "Yes, Sire, but not exactly as one might imagine. It was not with the others but on the back of a white tigre, Sire. The tigre descended the great face of the Margus as if its paws were magnets attracted to metal."

To the Centurion's amazement, instead of ridicule and demotion, the Imperator's expression was delighted with the report. "Excellent, Centurion!"

"The report makes little sense, Imperator," the Centurion said. "I will interrogate my soldiers personally, Sire."

"No, Centurion. You will interrogate no one. Do I make myself clear?"

"Yes, Sire." The Centurion went back to the report in his hand. "The beings shot seven vilites at a distance of a thousand llath." He lowered the paper. "This must be in error, Sire. I will have these figures reconfirmed."

Impatient, Muuk wanted no more bits and pieces. He wanted the whole report immediately. "Read it, Centurion. Do not leave out any detail."

The Centurion bowed and went on. "Of course, Sire. The report says the beings jumped from the edge of the Margus and flew away with extended wings. Many vilites saw this, Sire. They also reported rifle projectiles struck the beings several times but had no effect, Sire."

"And what now, Centurion? Have the vilites given chase?"

"They have called in the vertical lifters, Sire, and they will transport the 5th squad to the base of the Margus within the hour."

The Imperator glanced at the time on the bunker wall. "The twynich begins before that, Centurion. The lifters must complete the transport before the darkness begins."

"I will inform the field commander of your order, Imperator."

"See that he gets all the equipment he needs. Have the transport animals and troop wagons brought to the valley. He will need them during the twynich."

"Yes, Sire."

"Is that it, Centurion?" the Imperator asked.

The Centurion nodded toward a subordinate who brought over a yellow crystalline rock and placed it on the table. "This rock was found in Haga Mountains, Sire. It may have nothing to do with the Prince. But operations chased a massive aircraft of unknown origin from the slide area. The Imperial attack force tried to pursue the aircraft, but its velocity was too great. The vessel left the atmosphere at a speed that was beyond our attack force capabilities, Sire." The Centurion looked up perplexed. "How can this be, Sire?"

Imperator Muuk smiled at the Centurion. "At ease, Centurion, you've done well. Gather all the papers and reports on the Prince and his conspirators, and bring them to my office, immediately."

The Centurion snapped his fist across his chest. "By your order, Sire."

"And Centurion. No one is to speak of this to anyone, under penalty of death."

"Yes, Sire!"

26

Care Package

Leucadia knelt beside the golden, delivery canister and retracted her SIBA headgear before she opened it and began accessing the supplies inside: three additional clicker cylinders, a hand sensor, extra SIBA power packs, a hundred mag clips that equaled two thousand rounds of ammo, five quart containers of Bluestuff, three personal shields, walnut-size thader explosives, two additional SIBA medallions for backups, spare clothes, and ten pounds each of nutrient bars. *Yuk!* She turned up her nose, remembering how bad they tasted every time Harlowe made her try one. Beneath it all were expandable backpacks to hold the supplies. It was all there. Everything they needed to make them "bad" and survive an extended stay on the unknown planet.

Under the packs were two carefully wrapped packages along with a hand written note from Riverstone that read: *For Molly and Rhud. Stay safe, Matthew.*

She unwrapped the first package and discovered a hunk of raw meat. No doubt, she figured, its synthesized molecular makeup was packed with enough nutrients, vitamins and minerals and special anti-disease formulas to last the big cat for weeks. She and Ian already had such protection. It was standard equipment that came with each SIBA.

Leucadia heaved the slab toward the big cat. "Here you go, Rhud. Dinner time." Rhud snatched the protein in front of Maa Dev's sickly face before it hit the ground.

"Who are you?" Dev asked them both. Ian had just returned from a short survey of the surrounding countryside with Rhud. Since the ride down the cliff, the Prince's ruddy face had turned white and miserable. His hands had to be pried open before Ian could remove him from Rhud's back. At the moment, the Prince was propped against a tree, holding his shaking hands while trying to keep what was left of his courage intact. "You appear no older than I am. Yet, you are able to do things I have never seen anyone do."

"We practice a lot," Ian replied.

Leucadia was concerned the Prince would pass out from lack of food, water, and more importantly, the residual shock he was suffering from his recent ride. She found a small portable heater and placed it on the ground beside the Prince. When she touched the activator, the radiant heat was almost instant.

"Like that," Dev said, eyeing the heater. "I have never seen a warmer like that."

"I told you before, we're not from around here," Leucadia said.

"You are called Ian?" Dev asked.

"That's right."

The Prince faced Leucadia. "And my friends call me Lu," she told the Prince.

Dev found that odd. "You have no titles, no ancestral connection to the ones who bore you?" he wondered.

"Nope. Just Ian and Lu."

"Who are you running from, Ian?"

"We're running from no one." Ian nodded toward Rhud. "We're hunting for his sister. Someone trapped her and took her away. We intend to find her."

"Why? She is obviously gone."

Ian snapped. "She's not gone, Dev! She is family. The Gamadin never leave anyone behind."

Dev examined the big cat more closely as he lay near him and began cleaning himself after his meal. "There is another tigre like this one?"

"Yes," Leucadia replied. "Someone has captured her, and we have come to find her."

"So your dad is the big cheese around here, huh?" Ian asked while he finished removing the final items form the canister and placing them in his pack.

"If you mean that he rules the kingdom of Dolmina, that is accurate," Dev replied.

"Why would someone want to kill you, Dev?" Ian asked.

Dev shrugged indifference as if it were common knowledge. "I am second in line to the throne. If my father dies, then my brother, Prince Nardo, will become king. And if Nardo dies, then I will be king."

Leucadia was familiar with the destructive nature of power. As sole heir to the Mars Corporation, one of the largest financial empires on Earth, she socialized on a first name basis with presidents, dictators, and royalty around the globe. She understood the ways of political deception, conspiracy, and murderous plots. "More importantly, who is in charge of the Numeri?"

Dev thought a moment. "The Imperator . . ." The Prince's voice trickled to silence as he realized the danger the Royal Family was in.

"What allies does your father have to counter this Imperator?" Leucadia asked.

The Prince found himself trying to think of things about which he had no experience. He had always been sheltered from the daily operations of the kingdom. "Allies? My father is king. The Imperator would do no harm to him for fear of execution."

Ian scoffed at the Prince's statement. "Our captain says rules are for people who lose fights. And Princey, dude, from what we can see, you're losing badly."

Leucadia was distressed by the Prince's innocence. "Ian is right. This Imperator has no fear of breaking the law, because he believes he is above the law. This is a common flaw of government. There is an old saying where we come from, Dev, 'Tyranny will come to your door in a uniform.' The uniform is the Numeri, and this Imperator is their leader. Is that right?"

With glassy eyes, the Prince looked at Leucadia. "That is correct, Lu. Is my kingdom in danger?"

"Maybe, maybe not. Our friends could help you one day," Leucadia suggested.

"Where are your friends, Lu?" Dev asked.

Ian looked skyward. "Far away by now, Dev. They are no help to us now."

Dev stared at Ian. His skin turned pinker as he spoke. The conversation seemed to calm his nerves. "They left you behind?"

"For a time," Leucadia replied, "and when they return, we will help you rid your county of this Imperator."

Rhud rolled over and scratched his back, staring at Leucadia upside down. He seemed impatient. Dev gazed at the great white tigre with a whole new respect. After riding him down the side of the cliff, the Prince still had the shakes, but his respect for the great white cat that had saved his life from the Numeri had grown. He wanted the tigre for his own protection.

"I would like to purchase your Rhud," the Prince said straight out.

Ian laughed absurdly and Leucadia smiled, as she stepped over to the great cat and caressed the top of his head. "We don't own him, Dev."

"He follows your commands," said the Prince.

"Sometimes."

"But I am prepared to offer you a great price for him."

Ian slipped his pack over his shoulders as he spoke. "This will be the last time I say it, Dev. He's not mine. Rhud is a free soul. He belongs to no one. That is a concept that seems to be in short supply around here."

"In your country, people are free?" Dev asked with naive innocence.

Ian and Leucadia traded doubtful glances, as Ian went on. "Well, it used to be a lot freer. Now the politicians have so many laws, you can't do anything without breaking a rule or having the government looking down your throat."

"And the people who follow the rules will lose their fight?"

Leucadia nodded. "Yes. If the people of our world continue down the road of compliance without responsibility, they will lose everything, including their freedom."

"I wish to know more about this thing you call freedom."

Leucadia lifted the Prince to his feet. "It is not a thing, Dev. It is untouchable. Freedom is an idea that is hard to maintain but easy to lose."

After cinching his pack, Ian bent down and pressed an activator on the side of the canister. The special delivery capsule turned a bright blue and then evaporated before their eyes.

Dev removed a timepiece from his pocket. He stared at the face in disbelief, shook the timepiece, then stared at it again. "The twynich is late. You should have never performed such an act."

"What are you babbling about now, Dev?" Ian asked.

"The twynich time is now. Power does not exist inside the darkness," the Prince explained, confused.

Ian looked up at the sky. It was late afternoon, but there was still plenty of sunlight left in the day. "Looks pretty bright out, Dev. No darkness."

"The twynich does not affect the sun. It affects Nod. No one on Nod has power. The twynich is like a switch. It turns off all power for days across the planet. No one escapes the darkness. How is it that you don't know this?"

Leucadia switched on the com device from her belt. The screen was bright, colorful, and normal. "It's working fine," she said, holding up the device for Dev to see.

Ian said, "The twynich must have missed us, Dev." He pointed at the heater. "See. There is plenty of heat coming from the warmer, too."

Dev went to his knees and stared at the heater. It was indeed working without interruption. So was Leucadia's device. The twynich had not stopped any of the beings' powered devices. "But how can that be? That is not possible," Dev said with alarm.

Ian picked up the heater, switched it off and reinserted it in a pouch on the backside of his utility belt.

"Come on, Lu." Then to Dev he said walking away, "See ya around, Dev." He hoped like the blazes the Prince was stupid enough to stay behind.

27

Finding Religion

Imperator Muuk tried to beat the twynich period back to his keep to check on his Beleza, but he was too late. Twynich had begun and travel back to his island compound off the coast became unbearably slow. His military caravan was forced to switch from motor-driven vehicles to $ci's$. On Earth they would be considered large, tailless wolves. A ci had a long toothy snout, perky ears, a huge barrel chest, thick powerful hindquarters, short nub tail, and a short but dense coat of dark grey, blue, and white fur. As terrifying as they appeared on the outside, they were gentle puppy dogs on the inside. Ci's were bred to do one thing: tow vehicles during twynich. Like Alaskan sled dogs, a ci's' endurance was legendary. A team of ci's could haul a three-ton car all day long without water, food, or rest. To Nodians, changing from motor-driven cars to ci's was like changing socks. It was a routine procedure when Nod passed into twynich. Muuk had anticipated the time of darkness and brought his strongest and fastest ci's for his return.

But as fast as his ci's were pulling the Imperator's long car, twynich had come at a horrible time. The shock at hearing the reports from the Haga campaign caused him extensive turmoil. The Prince's capture seemed almost secondary to the possibility of capturing the second Beleza and their masters. There was no doubt in his mind that the four of them were related and that he had stumbled onto beings from another world. The implications were far-reaching and powerful. If his theories were correct, capturing the Offworlders would be more significant than solving the mystery of the twynich!

* * *

Muuk met Loomis at the keep's heavy, vault door. "How is my Beleza, Loomis?"

Loomis' unemotional pink eyes blinked once before he replied, "She is as you left her, Sire."

They walked into the laboratory where lighted candles encased in dense, crystalline glass enhanced and magnified each flame, filling the room with a soft, warm light. The Imperator and his curator walked directly to the observation portal. Like the laboratory, candlelights had swiveled out on their pedestals and illuminated the arena in low, soft light. The Imperator sighed with relief upon seeing Beleza at her normal place, lying in the center of the grounds with her head up, seeming to glance up at the skylight, as she continued to take her captivity with abnormal calmness.

"Has she done anything in my absence, Loomis?" Muuk asked.

"No, Sire," Loomis replied. "As you can see, mostly she stares at the ceiling."

The Imperator looked up. "The window?"

"It seems to have captivated her, Sire," Loomis explained.

Muuk smiled arrogantly. "She is plotting her escape, Loomis."

Loomis thought that highly unlikely. "The window is too high and strong, Sire. She cannot reach it."

Muuk mused over the possibility. The arena was built to contain every animal on the planet. But Beleza is alien, he reminded himself. "Just the same, have the window reinforced and sealed with our strongest metal, Loomis."

"Yes, Sire, when the darkness ends."

Muuk understood that without power, fortifying the enclosure would be impossible. "Yes, the moment the darkness ends." Next his attention went to the uneaten bowls of food and water to one side. "Has she eaten?"

"No, Sire."

"The meat is fresh and untainted?" Muuk asked.

"Dressed within the hour, Sire, as per your orders," Loomis confirmed.

The Imperator pointed at the water bowls. "She ignored the drugged water."

Loomis was dumfounded. "The sedative has no taste or smell, Sire, yet she seems to know it will sedate her."

Muuk's probing, rose-colored eyes remained spellbound over his prize's high intelligence. "Yes, she knows, Loomis . . ."

"Sire?"

"She knows her water is drugged." Then as if he had been suddenly slapped back to reality, the Imperator turned to Loomis and ordered, "Release the haapffin!"

Loomis was shocked by the order. "But, Sire, Beleza will be killed."

"You will do as I say, Loomis. Release the haapffin."

"Of course, Sire." Clearly Loomis was against the release of the haapffin beast. He walked over to a dangling chain, hanging down from the ceiling and began pulling the weighty links. Through the viewing portal, a draw gate, many times larger than the laboratory door, lifted along the far wall, allowing a giant haapfin to enter the room.

With Muuk looking on with a curious amusement, the haapffin quickly made his presence felt. He roared loudly at Beleza, letting her know that he was the king of this domain. She would submit to him, or he would kill her and feast on her entrails.

Beleza remained motionless and calm as the haapffin circled her once, taunting her, challenging her to roll over on her back and submit to him.

Then suddenly, as if the haapffin had had enough, the bear-beast rose up on his powerful, tree stump legs, towering twenty feet in the air, and prepared to charge.

Fearless, Beleza came to her feet and answered with the most blooding curdling roar the world of Nod had ever heard. The affect on the haapffin was so chilling, the beast tumbled backwards onto its back. A second roar sent the whimpering creature back to his cage.

Beleza watched the haapffin leave before she turned and stepped calmly to the portal. Muuk and Loomis stepped back from the window as Beleza's blue eyes seemed to cover the entire viewing port. Her eyes glowed, even under the twynich spell, as she released a roar that shook the enclosure, the laboratory, and the ground beneath their feet. It was as if this deity of Nod put them on notice, that she was no life force to be trifled with, challenged, or tormented. That, if she were to remain any longer in this keep, there would be grave consequences for them all, including the kingdom.

Loomis stumbled back from the portal, shaking from her power, while Muuk had suddenly found religion.

28

Hog Heaven

Riverstone was the lone crewman on duty when Harlowe blinked onto the bridge. He found it unnerving to stare out the front windows and see nothing but black space. The-middle-of-nowhere was the only apt description for where they were headed. After days of travel inside Cartooga-Thaat, *Millawanda* had not passed a single star system or rogue planet. Nothing! It was a vast sea of emptiness.

Lying on the sunset side couch, Riverstone stopped playing *Mozart's Flute Concerto No. 1 in G major* the moment he heard the slight buzzing sound of the blinker energize. With his feet draped over the back, he kinked his head toward Harlowe and swung his feet around to the floor, knowing he was away from his duty station.

Harlowe held up his hand. "At ease, pard. The ride has been tough on us all."

Riverstone relaxed against the soft couch. "Yeah, I caught Rerun sound asleep the other night. Don't tell him I told you that. He'll think I ratted on him."

"It's our secret. Prigg was sawing a few logs himself on the morning shift."

They both laughed a little as Harlowe stared at the nothingness. Harlowe was out of uniform, bare chested in his shorts with a blue towel draped over his shoulders. He had just finished another workout with Quincy. Normally, he would blink directly to his quarters after a workout because he needed a

126

shower. Today he broke his routine and stopped by the bridge to check on things since the next watch was his.

Harlowe studied the overhead star map. "Almost there, huh?"

"Yeah . . . but I won't believe it until I see it," Riverstone replied dryly. He was done with the void and wanted to be through it yesterday.

"Have you seen Squid and Rerun?" Harlowe asked. "They've been hiding out the last few days. They do their duty time, then they're gone. I wonder what they're up to?"

"Rerun said they're working on something cool," Riverstone replied, and that was all that he knew.

Harlowe's mouth twisted unnaturally as he glanced at the ceiling. "Hmmm…" He looked around the empty bridge noticing how desolate it was without his crew. "Where's the Mowg?"

"Probably with Pigpo. Without the cats, he needs another soulmate to cuddle with, or he can't sleep."

"Mowg better watch out that Pig doesn't roll over on him," Harlowe quipped.

Riverstone laughed. "Kinda miss those big ears around the bridge."

Harlowe pinched his nose. It helped to relieve the sting he felt about his crew that was left behind. "Yeah," he said and tried to swallow away the lump in his throat.

Riverstone reassured Harlowe. "Lu and Wiz will get Molly back, Captain."

Harlowe only grunted. The heartbreak would never go away until they were all safe and sound on *Millawanda* again.

Riverstone held up his flute. "So you want to grab a violin, and we'll improvise a rock sonata from Hendrix or something?"

Before Harlowe could answer, the buzz from the bridge blinker went off. Simon was first, then Monday appeared next to him a half second later. Harlowe's and Riverstone's mouths dropped open as they admired the stylish new coats they were wearing that looked like *Sons of Anarchy* motorcycle jackets on steroids. The midnight blue hide was made of fine, satin leather. Gamadin gold snap buttons were at the lapel corners, cuffs and hand pockets. Along the front were three zippered front pockets with braided zipper pulls. Attached to the waistband of the jacket was a leather belt with a snapping buckle closure. Vertically opened at the front were more Gamadin gold, dura-metal zippers.

Simon stepped into the middle of the bridge with a wide grin and turned around, modeling his new creation. "Are we bad, Skipper? Are we bad or what?" Simon kept saying.

Harlowe was lost for words so Riverstone filled the gap. "Yeah, you bad, brah. You're very bad. When do I get mine?"

"We have the clickers working on them now," Monday replied, brushing his sleeve.

Harlowe couldn't help but laugh. "So where are your Hogs, Rerun?" as Harley-Davidson riders lovingly call their motorcycles. "We can't have jackets like these without bikes."

"This isn't a Hog jacket, Skipper. These will soon to be standard issue with our Gamadin uniform," Simon clarified. "That is, if it's okay with you, Skipper."

"We're soldiers, Rerun, not bikers," Harlowe reminded his weapons officer, referring to the popular Earth television series about motorcycle gangs.

"Before you make a judgment, Skipper," Simon offered in defense of his creation, "let me convince you how cool they are," He pulled the lower zipper on the front of his coat and removed a power pack. "We have three more in there, Skipper." He opened up his fully lined jacket and pointed to more pockets. "Here, here, and here are ammo clips. Twelve total for 240 rounds. Hidden behind the padding here, one small version of our pistols here and here. That's two Skipper." Simon removed one of the small pistols and handed it to Harlowe.

"Where did you find these?" Harlowe wondered, feeling the light weight of the weapon. He was impressed.

"In a small cabinet next to the rifles," Monday replied. "There was a whole drawer full of them."

Now Harlowe was along for the ride. "What else?"

Simon tapped his other front zippers. "Food packs here, Starbucks here. Small versions," he qualified, then pointed at his cuffs. "Knives here and dura-line here," he said, pointing at the waist belt of the coat.

Riverstone thought something was missing. "What about SIBAs? You got to have SIBAs, brah, or it's a no go."

Simon pointed at Monday. "Show them, Squidy."

Monday touched his cuff with his index finger. It didn't matter which side. Instantly, the jacket transformed into a fully operational SIBA.

Simon spread his legs and put his hands on his hips in front of Harlowe and Riverstone. "Now are we bad, Skipper, or what?"

Before Harlowe could answer Simon, Jewels blinked onto the bridge. In his claws he carried two more Gamadin jackets.

"Good man, Jewels, right on time," Simon said, and stepped aside to allow the robob servant to hand Harlowe and Riverstone their jackets. Harlowe's jacket had four hash marks on the collar, Riverstone's had three. Riverstone smelled the richness of the leather and admired the workmanship and the metal work before carefully sliding his arms into one sleeve and then the other. He reached down for the zipper and pulled it up and down flawlessly, without catching.

Harlowe simply put his on, admiring the fit.

"Do they come with instructions?" Riverstone asked, touching the supple leather with the back of his hand.

"Squid and I will show you everything, Mr. Riverstone," Simon replied.

"Well, Captain?" Monday asked. "Does it meet your approval?"

Harlowe stretched his arms out, touching the gold Gamadin insignias on his cuff, then the four hashmarks on his collar that indicated his rank, as he felt the butter soft fabric along his right sleeve. His head moved up and down slightly, as he pressed his lips together, and replied, "Hog heaven, Rerun." He turned to Monday. "Fine work, Mr. Platter. Congrats, to the both of you."

Simon and Monday bumped chests and high fived. There was no better compliment in the galaxy than one given by their captain.

"Did you make one for Lu and Wiz?" Harlowe asked.

"You bet, Skipper. Lu's is a nice, girlie blue. She would want to be different from us," Simon said.

Harlowe nodded in agreement. "No doubt."

Simon added, "Even Prigg has one."

Harlowe smiled. Somehow it was hard to imagine the little Narukian riding a Harley and wearing a motorcycle jacket. That was like oil and water.

"I put Lu's and Wiz's on their beds, Captain," Monday stated.

"They would like that," Harlowe said. He then removed the jacket and handed it to Jewels, as he and his servant left the bridge for his quarters. He wanted to clean up before his watch.

* * *

When Harlowe's doorway closed, Simon turned to Riverstone. "Do you think he really liked the jacket?"

Riverstone knew Harlowe had a lot on his plate. The jacket was just a crumb. "He said he did, didn't he?"

"Yeah."

He patted Simon on the back. "Trust me, he liked it a lot."

29

The Farmhouse

It had rained hard all day, and now it was night, and it was still raining. For Dev, who was wet, cold, and appeared to be coming down with a fever, the abandoned farmhouse they approached must have looked like one of his father's castles. Leucadia figured the Prince needed somewhere dry in a hurry, or the kingdom would have one less heir. Two hours before, Dev had collapsed along the trail. Ian had no choice but to lift the princeling onto Rhud's back, or he would have to be left somewhere back in the forest. But Ian gave the Prince credit. Since coming down the cliff, Dev had not complained once. Even his demands that he not be treated like one of his servants went silent for the time being. Still, the Prince was costing them valuable time. Without Dev, they could have covered a couple of hundred miles in a day, regardless of the weather. But babysitting a spoiled Prince cut that distance down to twenty. Leucadia made the decision for everyone. They would spend the night in the house and start out fresh in the morning after a good night's rest. Ian balked at first, knowing the soldiers were no doubt still behind them. Leucadia knew it too, but a few hours of down time was unavoidable.

Leucadia's green eyes pleaded for understanding. "Dev is done, Ian. We have to stop here."

They had already by-passed four other dwellings after leaving the forest. Like this farmhouse, they were deserted and ghostly looking in the dark. With unkept yards and vines growing up the sides of the structures, Ian

131

expected to see the Addams Family waving at them through the windows. Every pointy-roofed house was in disrepair, and the rich farmland their owners once tilled was overgrown with weeds and shrubs. It was apparent that no one had cultivated the properties for a multitude of seasons. In the fields, farm machinery lay rusted and broken as if the owners had merely stopped in the middle of what they were doing and walked away.

As they made their way up the porch, small rodents scurried out from under gaping holes in the foundation and the cracks in the siding. The steps leading to the front door were broken and splintered. Large sections of the roof were caved in. A dilapidated car that Ian thought resembled an early 1950's Hudson Hornet was left in the driveway with all four tires flat and peeling away from their rims. Plants grew wildly out of broken windows like the car was a large planter.

"What's going on here, Dev?" Ian asked, as the three of them stood dripping in the rain in front of the farmhouse. "This is the fifth farm we've passed, and they're all like this. Where'd the people go?"

Dev tried to open his eyes. He wasn't in the mood for talking. Farms and their inhabitants were hardly important when you are wet, hungry, and cold.

Ian had plenty more questions, but Leucadia turned him away. This wasn't the best time for a Q & A session. She stroked the top of Rhud's head as she spoke. "We need to find a way to transport ourselves."

"Dev was right. This twynich he talked about is real. Nothing works," Ian said.

Knowing how car savvy Ian was, she asked, "Any ideas on an alternative?"

Ian eyed the derelict car in the front yard. "A couple. I'll get the clickers working on something while you take care of Dev."

Leucadia lifted the Prince off the big cat's back. As she helped Dev toward the front door, Ian asked her, "Do you have a handle on what's causing this darkness Dev talked about?"

"I think so," she replied. "I'll confirm it when we're all settled."

She was about to go on with the Prince when Ian held them up. "Hold on. Let Rhud do a once over before we go in." It may have been twynich, but the Numeri were still looking for them; and even without transports, other soldiers could be inside waiting to cut them down. Ian had his bugeyes on max, and his sensors in his SIBA could detect beings beyond the horizon, but the big cat's built-in scanners were a hundred times more thorough than his, he figured.

"What's he looking for?" Dev asked as the big cat entered the farmhouse.

Ian watched the big cat in awe. "I have no idea. But until he says it's okay. We stay put."

Rhud went through the door in total darkness as if he had been swallowed by a bottle of ink. The cat's heavy body creaked along the floors in several places, but even with their super SIBA hearing, he was stealthy silent, like he was walking on air. Long moments went by before Rhud suddenly surprised them from behind.

Ian spun around, pulling his weapon. "Geez, Rhud, make a little noise, dude," he scolded the big cat.

Rhud growled his indifference, as he walked by and into the house, pushing open the front door with his nose as he entered a second time.

"I guess it's okay," Ian said, contritely.

A large sign was nailed over the front door. Leucadia tried to read it, but neither she nor Ian could make any sense of the script. Ian did what he often saw Harlowe and Riverstone do to signs telling them they couldn't swim in the ocean due to high surf warnings. He grabbed it with his claws and ripped it off the door.

"That is a Royal Decree, Ian," Dev said worriedly. "To deface a posting by the Authority is—"

"Is punishable by death," Ian said, cutting the Prince off. "Yeah, I get it, Dev."

"It is the law."

Ian flung the sign into the yard. "Bad law," and followed Rhud through the front door.

Leucadia held the eager Prince back until she made sure the way was safe. Unlike Dev, she could see clearly in the darkness. She wanted to made sure there were no holes in the floor or something the Prince might trip over and crack open his head. As they wandered into the front room, the farmers had left many things behind. There were couches, wood sitting chairs, a large overstuffed wing chair in the corner, tables, footstools, and a fireplace with plenty of wood by the hearth. Everywhere they looked, there was a thick layer of dust covering the area rugs. What surprised them the most was none of the furnishings were alien. If they didn't know they were on a planet hundreds of lightyears from Earth, they might have easily thought it was a typical Earthly living room. All Ian needed to see was his dad watching football on his five-foot wide flat screen TV, and he would feel right at home.

"I'm cold, Lu," the Prince complained.

Dev was shivering in his wet clothes and would have fainted if she weren't beside him to prop him up. When Ian came back into the main room, he quickly began making the room habitable by removing the clickers from his pack and popping them to life. Immediately, they began pushing obstacles into their proper places and sweeping up dust and debris. While Ian directed the clean up, Leucadia sat Dev on the nearest couch and began removing his wet clothes. When he was stripped bare, she wrapped him in a thin, foil sheet that captured his body heat and gave him a sip of Bluestuff. A short time later he was out like a light.

Making sure the windows were covered first, Ian pulled a small glow-ball from his utility belt and placed it on the mantel over the fireplace. Instantly, the room was filled with a soft white light. He eyed the wood near the fireplace and thought briefly about making a fire, but then decided against it, knowing it would send a beacon of smoke to the soldiers, giving away their location.

In no time at all, the farmhouse room was comfy and secure enough for them relax without their SIBAs.

* * *

After the clickers were stowed back in his pack, Ian sat in a cushiony chair near the fireplace and sipped on a bottle of Bluestuff. "Any readings on Molly?" he asked Leucadia.

Leucadia was sitting at the opposite end of the couch from the unconscious Prince, her sensor com in her lap, while Rhud lay quietly across from the front of the door, preening himself. "None. She is still out of range." Molly had no collar or locating device attached to her. All Leucadia and Ian had going for them in their search was their sensor com. Because Molly was from another planet, her genetic signature was different. Leucadia's sensor would find her, but she had to be within a fifty mile radius for her readouts to register.

"They airlifted her somewhere," Ian concluded.

"Yes, before the twynich," Leucadia added.

"We need to find wheels," Ian stated, knowing time was critical. The longer it took to locate Molly, the chances of finding her unhurt lessened, or much worse, stuffed in some wild animal hunter's trophy room. The second alternative was far too frightening to mention. Even with SIBAs, sensor coms, and Rhud, searching a planet on foot would take months. They needed a way to move quickly and efficiently, or Molly was lost.

"This twynich sounds like a giant EMP," Ian guessed, referring to an electro-magnetic pulse that disrupts all forms of electric fields, causing anything that uses electricity to suddenly stop functioning.

"The dark period is much more sophisticated than that," Leucadia went on to explain. "EMPs damage circuits and are over in seconds. The twynich lingers for days before it switches off and leaves circuits as they were before it began."

"Like *The Day the Earth Stood Still*?" remembering the old 50's movie of a space alien coming to Earth and switching off all the power on the planet to prove his power over the frightened Earthlings.

"Almost. In the movie, Klaatu, was selective. He left hospitals and airplanes alone so people were safe. Here there is no discerning. Everything shuts off."

Ian's nose wrinkled up with pain. "People in airplanes get 86'd, huh?"

"My guess is no. From what Dev tells me, the twynich has been going on for thousands of years. I'm sure everyone plans ahead of the shutdown."

"Thousands? Whoa! That's narly."

"Yeah, it happens like clockwork. Planes don't crash because no one flies during twynich. Hospitals, schools, important places switch to alternative resources like oil lamps, candles, and probably something like horses to get around. That's why we saw so many corrals along the way."

Ian pointed at her com and the light above the mantel. "Why does our stuff work?"

Leucadia turned her mouth up in a slight all-knowing grin. "Because it is Gamadin." She let that sink in a moment before she went on. "I believe this planet has been suffering from a Gamadin malfunction for thousands of years."

Leucadia's theory was so unexpected Ian completely forgot his trend of thought. "You're joking. A Gamadin malfunction?"

"That's the only way I can describe the twynich."

"What does Gamadin have to do with it?"

"Because the twynich has a distinct electromagnetic wave that only a

Gamadin power source can produce."

"Ynni?"

Leucadia held up her sensor com. Ian recognized the readouts. There was no mistake: the dark period everywhere was caused by a form of ynni that was canceling out all electrical activity on the planet.

Ian's mouth was stuck open as he went to a nearby closet and began rummaging through the clothes. "A Gamadin power signature doesn't make sense. Millie's charts showed no outpost anywhere near here," he said, tossing out several garments, a pair of goggles with brass frames, and three top hats.

"I know. But it should have been there."

"Something's not right, then. The Gamadin were smart. Why would they keep this outpost off the map?"

"Security?" Leucadia had no real answer. She would need to see the outpost to discover the reason. But she did have more to say about the malfunction. "The ynni completely turns itself off here. All the other outposts have a residual broadcast that Millie continues to receive. Here the broadcast only happens at certain times, and in such a big way, it shuts down all power globally."

Ian's brain was thinking beyond the dark period. While continuing the conversation, he tried on a pair of leather pants, thick leather belt, and dark vest that all seemed to fit with some minor adjustments. "If there's a Gamadin station here, then it could mean other possibilities for us."

Leucadia's face wasn't quite as perky. "Maybe. But if it is like Hitt, it won't help us or Harlowe."

Ian saw promise in the idea that if it was Gamadin, there was opportunity. "This on again off again has a purpose, Lu."

Leucadia agreed, but she was more practical. "Knowing how Millie was buried in an underground structure, and Hitt was also underground, if nothing else, the outpost could be somewhere to hold up until Harlowe returns for us."

Ian grabbed a long, dark duster from a clothes hook and shook the wrinkles out of the heavy waxed cloth as he looked at Rhud lying next to the couch between them. "Molly first, though."

"Molly first," Leucadia repeated, matching his intensity.

The duster was oversized, but like the other clothes, loosening straps, adjusting copper buckles, snapping metal buttons here and there, he was good to go. He picked up a black top hat from the pile off the floor and tossed it. It wasn't him. He grabbed the *akubra* with the wide brim instead, creased the rounded top just so, stretched the goggles around the headband, and adjusted it on his head. "How do I look? Like the *Wild, Wild West?*" he asked, turning around for inspection.

Leucadia chuckled. "Very Victorian, Ian. The goggles are a nice touch." Impressed by what she saw, she got up and went to the closet. "Anything for me in there?" she asked.

"Yeah, plenty. Best we look like Nodians from here on out."

Ian started for the front door in his new garb. "Where are you going? We just got here," Leucadia asked.

Ian picked up his pack. "I have work to do. I'll rest later."

"Need help?"

Ian eyed the sleeping Prince. His ruddy color had returned. He seemed to be on the mend and didn't want to risk a relapse. "No, I'm cool. You stay with him. I'll see you in the morning."

Before walking out the door, Ian turned back and asked again. "A Gamadin outpost, huh?"

Leucadia smiled, holding up a leather legging and a parasol. Ian nodded with a thumbs up. "Yeah, a thousand miles north of here."

"Cool." He opened the door, pulled his akubra down, and went out into the pouring rain with Rhud. He had work to do and little time to do it.

30

Mating Call

Loud clanking of metal against metal, thumping hammers, and various other disturbing noises awakened Maa Dev from his restful sleep. As soon as he could think, he began complaining how hungry he was. Leucadia went to the kitchen and came back with an assortment of canned food. The cans appeared in good shape, no dents, toxic bulges, or leakage. She opened the top of a can with the sharp point of her SIBA claw and smelled it. The contents had no foul odor, so she gave it to Dev with a fork-like eating utensil she found in an upper drawer. Dev took it gladly. He hadn't eaten in two days.

After consuming half the can, Dev offered Leucadia a bite.

Unless there was no other choice to stay alive, like the time she was marooned on the planet Gazz, she knew not to eat anything on an alien planet until her sensors had tested it first. But as good as it appeared, her readouts told her the organic matter had toxins unfit for her consumption. Regrettably, she had to stick with her icky tasting, nutrient cubes as her only source of nourishment. "No, thank you, Dev. I have my own."

Now that the Prince was warm, fed, and resting, Leucadia wanted to know more about the planet and its people. "What happened to the farmers in the valley, Dev?"

Dev's eyes had a vacant gaze to them. "They left."

"Why?"

Dev saw no problem. "There is nothing more to say, Lu. You can see no

138

one lives here anymore."

"Yes, but why, Dev? Was there disease, drought, a big storm that wiped them out? What happened here, Dev? As future heir to your father's throne, you should know why your kingdom is falling into decay."

"The Royal Authority owns the land now. That is all I know," Dev said unemotionally, as if the farmers and their problems were none of his concern.

"But the farms are going to waste, Dev. To be productive, the land needs farmers to produce the crops and feed your people."

Dev shrugged again. "I was told the cultivators were charging too much for their crops. The Authority had to do something," Dev explained.

"That makes no sense, Dev. Farmers only can charge what the market allows them to charge. If a farmer asks too much for his crop, his buyers will go elsewhere where there is a market that is cheaper."

Dev thought back. "I believe there was a drought, Lu. Yes, it destroyed much of the cultivator's harvest."

"Well, that's the reason, then. They had to charge more because there was less of it. In order to make ends meet, the farmers needed more money for their crops. That is only natural, Dev."

Dev saw the world differently. "The cultivators must charge what the Royal Authority says they can charge, Lu. That has always been the way since my father became king."

"Your father is wrong, Dev."

"My father is king. The king is never wrong, Lu. That is the law," the Prince said, as though to question or doubt the King of Dolmina was even against the laws of nature. "Do you have an Authority where you come from?" he asked her.

Leucadia answered. "Yes, and they never get it right, either. The more our authorities try to fix things, the more problems they cause for everyone."

The Prince grew weary of talking of farmers and their lack of production. He wanted to know more about her. "Where do you come from, Lu?" the Prince asked as he ate from his can of food.

"Far away from here," Leucadia replied.

"You look Nodian," Dev said, then added, "but I've never known a Nodian who had eyes like yours."

"They are genetic defects." She lied.

"Is Ian your mate?" he asked her.

"No. He is a friend."

"Friend?"

"A person who I am very close to but who is not a mate."

The Prince understood the concept. "We call them amicus in Dolmina. Do you have a mate, Lu?"

A sudden ache struck Leucadia's heart. It was nothing a spoiled Prince would see or understand. It was an unimaginable piece of her existence. It was so large that if she lost it, it was like a dying flower losing its petals. She would wither away and die.

"Yes, I have a mate, Dev," she answered. That is all she would say. To talk more about Harlowe, and feel more pain than she already had, was pointless. There was too much to do, too many responsibilities to others, to allow self-pity.

"Where is he?" Dev asked.

"Far away."

"Is he a warrior like Ian?"

"Yes. A great and powerful warrior."

Dev's skinny body stood with the thin blanket wrapped around his waist. "I will challenge this warrior for your hand, Lu."

Leucadia tried to keep from laughing too loudly as she handed the Prince some dry clothes she found in the closet. "Put these on, Dev."

"You mock me, Lu. I could order you to be my mate," Dev threatened.

Leucadia stood a head taller than the Prince and stared into his big dark eyes with her compassionate green lights on max. "I apologize, my Prince. It was wrong of me to express amusement over your bravery. But try to understand, I cannot be yours when my heart is with another."

"If I order it, you must obey me, Lu."

Leucadia guessed there had to be a million reasons why Dev was clueless about farms, friendship, and the freedom to choose one's mate. As the Royal Heir stood looking proud, while at the same time looking pitiful and frail compared to a Gamadin, she felt sadness for him but even more pity for Dolmina's people. To have a future king with such ignorance was disheartening.

The racket outside the farmhouse finally made Leucadia curious enough to walk to the window and see for herself what was going on. She excused herself as the Prince took the clothes and began to dress. When she pulled back the window covering, she was stunned to see the gold-colored clickers working like a team of busy tinker toys. One was tearing apart the vehicle left in the driveway and tossing away the plants growing inside the cab. Another robob had removed its wheels and was tossing them away, while a third clicker was cutting away sections of the metal body. A fourth robob held open the hood while two other clickers pulled out the motor and tossed it to the side.

Dressed in a combination of Nodian leathers, heavy cotton shirts, and pair of dark blue, Nike running shoes, the Prince asked of the robotic stickmen, "What are they?"

The strength of the tubular beings was mind-boggling to the Prince. He watched two more clickers haul a rusty cultivating machine in from the field with Ian at the wheel.

"They are little helpers," Leucadia replied. She opened the front door and stepped out onto the porch with the Prince to survey the incredible scene more closely. Rhud was lying in the grass, lazily absorbing the morning sun.

"What are you doing, Ian?" Dev asked.

Ian replied from the cab of the tractor, "I'm making our ride."

"Ride?" the Prince questioned. Ian's speech was peculiar. Half the time he didn't know what he was saying. It was like he spoke some foreign language.

Leucadia pointed at the robobs dragging more metal parts from the barn to the center of the front yard. "Clickers are scavenging parts from around the farm to build us a car, Dev. We'll be able to make better time that way."

"Lu, vehicles have no power during twynich," Dev said.

Leucadia surveyed all the goings on with confidence. "This ride will function. Ian is a master at putting parts together from nothing and making them work. You'll see."

31

Nardo & Aboka

It was early morning when the Numeri officer entered the room and announced, "The Royal carriages have arrived, Sire."

Imperator Muuk was in a foul mood. The tywnich had slowed his search for the Royal Heir to a standstill. His troops were forced to go it on foot or ride pack animals. With communications down, the fastest link between the Imperator and his forces was a series of ci transport carriages that shuffled dispatches back and forth from the field outposts to headquarters. The last sighting of the Prince was four days ago. His soldiers had scoured every square gradus of the Haga Forest from the Nos River to the Conolac Valley and beyond. They found no trace of the Prince.

The problem he faced now was about to come through his doorway. Muuk could hear the Royal ci's howling and barking in the compound. The rumbling of carriages and the voices of the Royal security guards barking orders to his troops turned his face blue. His dislike for Prince Nardo and his sister Princess Aboka ran deep. The Royal duo had abused the Numeri resources too many times. When the day was right, he had plans for them all.

And that day was soon.

The heavily armed guards in deep royal red uniforms slammed their way into his office as if his keep was a low-ranking milities barracks. Six guards entered with weapons drawn and ready, and quickly confirmed the office was secure for the Royal Couple's presence. As the Royals entered, their Royal Guard announced, "The Royal Highnesses Prince Nardo and Princess

Aboka!"

Prince Nardo strode in first, followed immediately by Princess Aboka. They both took over the room as if they were gods. Unlike his brother Maa Dev, Prince Nardo was short. He wore no crown or head covering. His hair was dark and always trimmed and neat. He smiled easily, but his eyes were humorless and calculating. Now that his father was dead and his brother, the second in line to the throne, was presumed dead, he wore the golden vest of authority by decree. The Princess Aboka, on the other hand, was tall. Her beauty was renowned throughout the kingdom: long black hair to her waist, a long pointed nose, and dark eyes that could freeze fire with a single look. Of the two, there was no doubt in Muuk's mind that Princess Aboka was the mastermind behind the overthrow of the throne. The Prince, like his worthless younger brother, had the imagination of a haapffin. The day the king drew his final breath, Muuk knew, was the day Aboka launched her dream of total control of the empire.

Muuk knelt to the floor and kissed the large red and gold, jeweled rings that signified the ultimate Dolomina authority of the empire as bequeathed by the ancients many thousands of annos ago.

"Your Highnesses, welcome to Numeri headquarters," Muuk said, keeping his eyes to the floor.

Prince Nardo started the interrogation immediately. "Where is my brother's body, Imperator?" the Prince demanded. "You promised me I would be rid of him days ago."

The Imperator bowed deeper in shame. "My Lord, the Prince has escaped during the twynich."

"But how, Imperator?" Nardo asked with closed fists on his hips. "One boy against an army of Numeri? How is that possible?"

Before the Imperator could reply, Aboka continued, staring accusingly with her cold eyes. "The reports were that Maa Dev's motorcade was ambushed, and no one survived. Yet, the body is missing. What is your explanation, Imperator?"

"Prince Maa Dev had help, Your Highness," Muuk replied.

"Help, Imperator? Who has the means to save the Prince but you, Imperator?" Aboka asked accusingly.

"Your Highness, it was not I, I assure you. My security agents have uncovered a plot against the realm. Terrorists have entered the kingdom,

Your Highness. They are the ones who are assisting Prince Maa Dev," Muuk replied defensively.

"And when were we to hear of this plot, Imperator?" Aboka asked, still questioning the Imperator's voracity.

"It was confirmed only this morning, Your Highness."

"How convenient, Imperator."

Prince Nardo lifted Muuk's chin to look him straight in the eyes. "You must find my brother, Imperator, and these so-called anarchists, or it will be your head that will take their place, I assure you."

Princess Aboka sat on the side of the desk, crossing her arms casually in front of her. It was clear from her manner she had more on her mind than the missing Prince. "Imperator, we have intelligence reports that you possess a white beast of incredible beauty. Is that true?" she asked callously.

Muuk was stunned. How had she learned of his Beleza so quickly? His face turned ashen. He should have realized her royal spies were everywhere. If he denied it, she would have him executed immediately as the Royal Guards leveled their weapons on him. A wrong answer now would end his life.

Muuk bowed his head graciously. "Many pardons, Your Highness. I was preparing the beast as a surprise for you, Your Highness."

Finally, Muuk gave an answer that pleased the Princess.

"A gift for me?" Aboka asked.

Muuk forced a generous smile. He had to stay alive for his plan to work. If he was forced to give up his Beleza for the time being, so be it. He would get her back eventually. It was a small sacrifice to make in order to complete his plan. "Yes, Your Highness. A special gift for your life day."

"My sources say she terrified a haapffin," Aboka said, delighted by the prospect of seeing the beast her spies had told her was incredibly beautiful by all accounts.

"What is it?" Nardo asked.

"A tigre, Your Highness. The most beautiful tigre one could imagine," Muuk replied.

The Princess was overjoyed with anticipation. "I want to see my tigre at once, Imperator!" she commanded.

Muuk bowed and extended his arm toward Beleza's enclosure. "Yes, Your Highness. She is this way."

Suddenly, one of Loomis' servants begged the guards to let him see the Imperator immediately. It concerned the tigre.

Muuk summoned his servant the instant he heard Beleza's name. "What is it? Has something happened to my Beleza?"

The servant crawled along the floor with his head down, never looking up. He said, sobbing like a infant. "The great tigre, Sire. She has escaped!"

32

"The Ride"

What Maa Dev witnessed, by all the science he understood and studied, should not be. Ian's "The Ride," as he called it, was built in a single day from the discarded parts the mechanical beings had scrounged from around the farm. The Prince had never seen anything made so fast and with such precision. Especially not from what anyone with common sense would call trash! *The Ride* had four large wheels as tall as him attached to a large black cylinder. Welded to the top of the cylinder was the wheelless body of the vehicle found in the front yard. An extension of the body was added on to the back for a purpose Dev had yet to determine. Its size seemed illogical considering there were only three beings. Growing out and down from the front end of the contrivance were polished brass and copper pipes that attached to the lower cylinder like thick vines as big around as his legs. Thinner polished pipes curled back to another long metal box inside the passenger cabin. Sticking out the top of it all was a single dark pipe, where, he was told, hot vapors would soon vent to the sky in great puffy clouds.

When asked why the transport was so large, Ian's answer was simple, "Rhud. And when we find Molly, we'll need the extra room for her, too."

"Rhud will travel in the vehicle with us?" Dev asked aghast. He had never heard of such a thing. Transporting an animal the size of the tigre was well . . . highly improper.

The stare in Ian's blue eyes was chilling. "Don't even go there, Dev, or you'll be the one walking, toad."

146

The Ride

He and Dev were about to get into it more when Leucadia walked out
the front door and froze all conversation. Decked out in her Nodian clothes,
she was screaming hot. Dev had never seen a *puella* so stunningly beautiful
in all his life. All Ian could utter was, "Wow..." From the limited clothes
she had found in the farmhouse, she had fashioned an outfit that would
make Dolce & Gabbana, Versace, Chanel, and Christian Dior feel envious.
She started with a short red corset that pushed her breasts up and out with
lots of cleavage. Below her bare stomach, her glossy black leather pants
were low on her hips and skin tight. Ian couldn't remember if she ever wore
anything that wasn't. A large brass buckle hung loosely from the belt around
her waist. The wide band held her pistol at an angle, making it easy for her to
draw if necessary. Her shoes were also leather with more brass and copper
snaps along the sides. An outer long-sleeved jacket, fluffy cuffs, opened at
the front and cut slightly below the waist, finished the look. Like her pants,
it was mostly leather with some metal shoulder coverings that clanked a little
as she walked.

She had a sultry smile as she stepped with purpose down the steps. She
wiggled her fingers through the wrist cuffs, touched the dog collar adorned
with dangling gold trinkets around her neck as she placed the black driver's
hat on her head, and asked, "What do you think, boys?"

Dev couldn't speak a word. There was nothing in his vocabulary that
would adequately describe what he saw. Ian, on the other hand, had plenty to
say, but there wasn't time to go through all the accolades that were rushing
through his mind. "The gods of Nod are all breaking out in cold sweat over
you, Lu."

She hugged them both as she went wide-eyed with astonishment upon
discovering Ian's new ride. "She is so beautiful, Ian. I would never have
dream of something so . . . so . . ."

"Practical," Ian joked as he gathered the robob cylinders from the
ground.

"No, no. Magnificent!" She clapped with pride at a job well done. "It's
exactly what we needed." She kissed him on the side of the cheek. "I am so
proud of you, Ian."

Ian blushed as he was placing the robob cylinders back in his pack.
"Thanks, but they did all the heavy lifting," he said holding up a cylinder.

"But it was your dream, Ian. Your vision made it happen. When will my carriage be ready?"she asked.

"This machine cannot work during twynich," Dev said.

Ian ignored the Prince's pessimism and bowed to Leucadia. "My Lady, your carriage awaits you, forthwith."

Leucadia took his hand and climbed the ten foot ladder to the entry door of the cab. It was a big ride.

The Prince kept protesting the idea that transports were useless during the twynich without ci's to pull them. But Ian and Leucadia paid no attention to his doubts and went about preparing *The Ride* for departure. Ian rechecked the rear holding tank where he had poured a large quantity of water through a funnel. After capping the filling hole, he climbed up the ladder, folded his duster under his legs, and sat in the driver's seat next to Leucadia.

"Get in, Dev. This Ride is leaving the station," Ian said to the Prince, who was still standing on the ground with his arms folded defiantly in front of him. He wasn't about to climb into any cab that was going nowhere during twynich.

Ian closed the door. "Suit yourself. It's a long walk to the palace, dweeb." After twisting open a brass valve on the floor beside his seat, he lifted a small metal door on the top of what he called a dash and placed a small cube from his Gama-belt into the jar-sized chamber. He shut the door again.

"Isn't that a power module for your SIBA?" Leucadia asked.

"Yep. We have a whole bunch more in the care package Jester sent."

"What will it do?"

Ian pointed down. "Power the boiler chamber."

"For steam?"

Ian grinned. "Excited?"

"Yes!" she replied clapping with eagerness. "How fast can we go?"

Ian smiled mischievously. "I don't build anything slow."

He checked the readouts on the large dials above the dash and said to the Prince, "Hasta la bye-bye, Dev."

"Bye-bye?" Dev questioned. Ian's vehicle was going nowhere.

"Please, Dev, you can sit next to me," Leucadia offered, looking down at him through a side window.

The Prince reconsidered. How could he refuse such an offer? Sitting next to his future queen excited him. He was about to run around to her side of *The Ride* when Rhud leaped into the cab ahead of him from the large, rear opening of the vehicle.

Ian twisted around to the Prince. "Too late, Dev. Your seat is taken, bro."

"I shall have you arrested you for your insolence. That is my seat," Dev threatened.

Ian shrugged indifference. "Whatever, Dev." He turned a valve wide open on the dash and waited for the long hiss to equalize before he pulled a lever below his seat from down to up, allowing water to gurgle into an empty chamber. When the reservoir was full, he touched a blue button on a device he had mounted on the side of the steering wheel. There was a short delay before a cloud of white exhaust puffed from the top of the cylinder stack. Soon after that, hot white vapor hissed sideways from the massive boiler, which caused Dev to jump back or be scalded.

With one hand on the steering wheel, Ian put his other hand over a golden ball that was attached to a long rod between the seats and said to the Prince one last time, "TTFN, brah," and carefully pushed the ball forward. Incredibly the vehicle began to inch forward. Dev stood with his mouth agape as the heavy sections of metal rods, gears, pistons, flywheels, and hissing valves applied force to the four large cultivator wheels.

Poo shee, poo shee, poo shee went Ian's Ride as it began to move away from the farmhouse toward the gravel road. Looking out the rear of the cab, Rhud's blue eyes smiled back at the Prince.

Suddenly, the shock of Ian's creation hit home. The contraption really did work! It defied the twynich. The darkness had no effect on *The Ride*! Ian's vehicle was moving on without him, and he was taking his future mate with him. If he stayed behind, he might never see her again. His life, therefore, came down to two unavoidable choices: either run and catch up or lose his future queen!

Dev ran!

33

Elimination

Imperator Muuk ran through the driving rain back to his keep inside his compound. There was no time to wait for his carriage. Soaking wet, out of breath, and clutching his chest, he went straight through, passing the laboratory and into the open vault door to the area where Beleza was kept.

"How is this possible, Loomis?" Muuk cried out. He was shaking with fear over losing his prize. Loomis stood helpless in the middle of the arena looking disheveled and confused.

Following moments later, Princess Aboka entered the compound. She was as wet as Muuk. Her Royal Guards were unable to protect her from the rain. The Princess wanted answers to her gift's disappearance, as well.

Loomis dropped to his knees the instant he saw the Royal Princess. "Your Highness," Loomis said cowering before her.

"Answer your Imperator, Keeper," Aboka demanded. "What has happened to my tigre?"

Never lifting his eyes once, Loomis answered, "I do not know, Your Majesty. Beleza was here. I heard her last night, and I saw her sitting—"

Muuk interrupted. "Where was she sitting, Loomis?"

Loomis pointed to the center of the arena where the tigre had lain since the first moment she was brought to the enclosure. The impression of where she laid in the sand was still there. Aboka was awed by its size.

The Princess searched the arena along with Muuk. A guard moved inside the vault door and was quickly hushed by the Princess. "No one move. I

151

want no sound from anyone," she demanded.

The search continued; the only sound was the drops of rain hitting the floor in the center of the arena.

"Beleza is powerful, Your Highness, but she could not have vanished like a puff of smoke," Muuk said.

The Princess stepped to the center of the arena, studying the wet ground as she stepped on the shards of broken glass. She bent down and picked up a piece of the thick glass, careful not to cut herself as she showed it to Muuk, looking up. "Your skylight is damaged, Imperator."

Muuk followed her gaze as he walked under the droplets of rain hitting his face. The skylight dome, a hundred pedes above their heads, was blown wide open. "Impossible," he said with a gasp.

"This tigre is capable of such power, Imperator?" Aboka asked in awe.

"Beleza frightened my haapffin back to its cage, Your Highness. Yes, she is the most powerful beast I have ever seen."

The Princess gazed at the Imperator with a changed expression. For the first time, there was actually a hint of admiration for him. "And you captured her?"

Muuk's bewilderment could not break away from the ceiling. "Yes, Your Highness, in the Haga."

Princess Aboka kept looking at the skylight with Muuk. Even she, who was no huntress, understood how extraordinary the creature must have been.

"She is not from this world, Your Highness," Muuk muttered, unaware of his slip of the tongue.

Princess Aboka turned to Muuk in stunned wonder. "Not from this world? Did I hear you correctly?"

Muuk blinked himself back into the moment, realizing his secret was no longer his.

"Explain yourself, Imperator." Princess Aboka charged accusingly. "I will have your head for your treachery."

Muuk signaled to one of his guards standing at the vault doorway. An instant later shots rang outside the arena and all around the keep. Aboka's guards ran toward the door, but only made a few steps before they were cut down. Muuk lifted Loomis off the ground and sent him scurrying out the vault door.

The Princess stomped her feet. "What are you doing, Imperator?" she growled, standing angrily in the center of the arena.

Muuk smiled briefly then went slack-faced as he replied coldly, "I'm leaving you here, Your Highness."

The vault door closed with a heavy clank. The two-inch thick bolt slid into its locked position as another bolt on the opposite side of the enclosure opened. The order to release the haapffin had been given.

34

The Donut

Ela looked up at the night, confused. "The stars are gone, Matthew." The gleaming specks of light were gone as if someone had come along and plucked them out of the heavens.

Riverstone came from behind and put his arms around her thin waist. He was unconcerned about the blackness. He knew they were still there. He had seen them before, many times. But Ela had never seen a star, or a white fluffy cloud, or felt the warmth of a sunny day on her face. One day he would show her all the beautiful wonders of the world above ground. But for now, all he wanted to do was hold her. His cheek lay against her soft short hair. She smelled clean and fresh, like she had just bathed in the little pond that was near their modest nest inside the cavern. "The stars are there, Ela," Riverstone assured her. "When Harlowe finds us with our great ship, I will show them to you; I promise. There will be so many millions and millions of twinkly lights across the sky, it will look like a river of silver glitter."

Ela's pink eyes remained puzzled. "What is glitter, Matthew?"

Riverstone tried to explain. "It's these very, very tiny dots." He searched the rocks around him and reached down, pinching a small amount of yellow thermo-grym dust crystals between his fingers. "They're like this," he showed her, rubbing the specks between his fingers. From the light of a small candle, the specks twinkled like tiny lights.

"It's so . . . so? What is the word you call me, Matthew?"

"Beautiful . . ." He kissed her. "Like you, Ela, you are beautiful."

Suddenly, Ela grabbed his arms and began shaking him. "Matthew, wake up. Rest period is over. Dagger will be mad if we are late."

"Forget him, Ela. The toad can't harm you anymore. I'm here now."

"No, Matthew, you must wake up."

Ela was becoming violent. She wouldn't stop shaking him.

"Okay, I'm awake. Stop it, Ela." He was starting to get ticked at her unrelenting insistence. "Come on, Ela, chill. Stop shaking me. I'm awake!"

Riverstone's eyes shot open. Falling asleep on duty was common. Even Harlowe admitted that staring out at a heaven full of nothing was whack. Still, nearly kissing the rim of a large, triangular shaped head with a blue-lighted rim was beyond embarrassing. It was sick!

"Alice! What the...?" Riverstone questioned. He had his hands around the girl-bob's tubular torso. When he realized what he was doing, he let her go and fell backwards in shock.

He picked himself off the floor, gazing around the empty bridge in an effort to hide his humiliation. Once he had himself together, he stared out the forward window. The black void of Cartooga-Thaat had not gone away. Riverstone thought to himself: "The stars are still gone." Now he realized where he was. He wasn't inside the cave, after all. Worse, he wasn't with Ela, the girl who helped him survive the most torturous captivity he had ever been through in his life. Captured by Ra-loc and sold into slavery miles below the surface on the mining planet of Erati is where he met her. She had saved his life and would not let him die. Her kindness, her caring, her loving soul, gave him the reason to live. But sadly, only days after Harlowe had rescued them from the vast depths of the mine, she passed away on the beach as he held her in his arms looking up at the stars she had never seen before then. He recalled her asking him, "Is that a cloud, Matthew?" And he replied, "Yes, Ela, that is a cloud. And behind it are the stars I told you about." "I have never seen anything so beautiful, Matthew." He held her in his arms, rocking her back and forth, praying to keep her alive as they lay next to each other on the beach. "They are, Ela. You are as beautiful as the stars and the clouds."

He buried her on a sandy hill overlooking a tranquil ocean and named the unknown planet after her. He sighed heavily, knowing the dagger in his heart would never leave him.

He wiped a tear from his face. He was wide awake now. He walked to the bridge console and checked the ship's chronometer. It was 0500, ship time. He had another hour to go on his shift. After a heavy breath, he turned to the girl-bob standing by his chair, and asked, "What's up, Alice?"

Alice pointed at the overhead screen, and his mouth dropped open. *Millawanda* had made an unscheduled drop out of hyper-light. At this point, they were a little over halfway across the Thaat, with many more days to go before they reached the first inhabitable star system on the other side.

As per protocol, whenever something unusual happened this unexpected, Harlowe was awakened, no matter what time of day it was.

Harlowe yawned. "Yeah, Mr. Riverstone."

Riverstone didn't know why *Millawanda* had suddenly reduced her speed, but when the forward sensors spotted something directly ahead, he notified Harlowe immediately. "You better check this out, Captain."

"A planet?"

Riverstone stared at the overhead. Normally, from a billion miles away, *Millawanda's* optical arrays could focus on an object the size of a football field with crystal clarity. But with her diminished capacity, the object in question appeared vague like a pixilated digital photograph.

"No, not a planet. More like a donut," Riverstone described.

"A donut, huh?"

"Yeah, two of them. One inside the other."

Harlowe thought a moment before he ordered, "Better get everyone to the bridge. Millie wouldn't be making a pitstop unless she had a reason."

"Aye."

* * *

The Donut was, as Riverstone described it, a huge torus circle surrounding a smaller inner circle. Up to this point, Palcor was the biggest space structure Harlowe had ever seen. The emerald green space city, owned by the Tomar Corporation, that Harlowe had visited in search of his missing friends, could fit inside the smallest torus circle of the Donut. Each torus turned in opposition to each other. The inner circle rotated clockwise, while the more massive outer ring, turned counterclockwise. It was made of some type of dirty brown and grey metal. The outer ring had entryways to the interior at several locations, whereas the inner ring had none. The outer ring also had various towers, platforms, attached structures, and parabolic defense stations at strategic locations around the torus. The inner torus was smooth, with just a single dark band around its perimeter.

"What is it?" Simon asked from his weapons station.

Riverstone wrinkled his nose as he made his comment, "Whatever it was, it's kaput now. Without sensors, we could have run right into it." He pointed out the forward window. "It's right in front of us, and I can't see a thing."

Prigg had been studying the structure since blinking onto the bridge. Within minutes he made his best guess. "I believe it is a way station, gentlemen," the little Naruckian stated.

"A way station, Mr. Prigg?" Harlowe asked.

"Yes, Your Majesty, a place where travelers crossing Cartooga-Thaat stopped to refuel their ships and rested before continuing their journey."

Although the space structure looked innocent enough, Harlowe put everyone on high alert just to be safe. "Is there anything alive in there, Mr. Prigg?"

"No, Your Majesty, the structure is as Mr. Riverstone described it, kaput. No life signs or power signatures detected."

"Is this a blue dot stop?" Harlowe asked looking at Prigg for additional info.

Prigg checked over his console screens, "No, Your Majesty, *Millawanda* has made the stop on her own," he replied.

Harlowe stood up to study the massive structure that now took up the entire window. "Millie may be sick, but she didn't stop here on a whim. We could have flown right by the Donut in a blink and never known it was here. Something's going on," Harlowe suspected.

"Does that mean we're having a look-see?" Riverstone asked.

Harlowe put out a thumbs up. "It does, Mr. Riverstone."

Riverstone made an observation. "Prigg's suggestion made me think about our road trips to Las Vegas. Remember? We'd stop in Baker to fill up and grab a burger and fries at Bun Boy."

Harlowe wet his lips. "Yeah, and they had narly chocolate shakes, too."

"But it went out of business," Simon commented with a forced grin.

Riverstone made his point clearer, nodding at the space structure. "That's my point. Like the Bun Boy, this one horse donut town is a pit stop for everyone. Maybe Millie's stopping here because that's what she normally did when it was a happening place."

Harlowe stared at Riverstone, then to Prigg, who concurred. "Yes, Your

Majesty, that would be logical."

Harlowe went back to his center chair. "Makes sense to me, too. I'm willing to bet the farm Millie didn't stop for a hamburger, though. She came for a night on the town. I'd say more like Las Vegas than Baker, Mr. Riverstone."

"Worth a look, Captain," Riverstone said, returning to his own chair to the right of Harlowe.

Monday, however, was more practical. "Maybe there is something we can scavenge for Millie, Captain?"

Harlowe traded an approving smile with Monday. "Good idea, Mr. Platter. Exactly my thoughts. Instead of a Happy Meal for Millie, we might find her a double-double cheese and some fries." He turned to Riverstone. "You, too, Mr. Riverstone. Outstanding work." Then to everyone, he said, "So let's have a look inside."

"Take her in with caution, Mr. Platter, if you please," Harlowe ordered.

"Aye, Captain.

Harlowe recalled the time *Millawanda* was approaching a crashed spaceship on a desolate moon. It was the ship where he found Quay a half breath away from death. When they tried to land near the burned out hull, several gun turrets were still alive and would have caused great damage to *Millawanda*, had they not had the shields on at full power.

"You, too, Mr. Bolt. On your toes, in case someone has left us a surprise."

"Aye, Skipper. Weapons and shields at full power."

35

The City

It was daybreak, and the weather was thick with fog and rain when *The Ride* rumbled into their first Nodian city. Ian had driven all night following the path set by Rhud. A various times, when the road split, Ian would stop *The Ride* long enough for the big cat to sense which direction to turn. Rhud's hard focused stare was all that he needed, and they were rolling again. According to Leucadia's com, they were heading straight for the coast. The road mainly followed the terrain, rolling up and down small hills and gullies. Now and then they passed a few ci-drawn vehicles, but mostly there was no concern for opposing traffic. The jaw-dropping looks on the Nodian faces as they drove by created a few humorous moments for an otherwise monotonous drive. When darkness came, the roads were deserted of vehicles and beings. No one traveled at night during twynich. The few villages they passed through were dark as well. Maa Dev said Dolminian people stayed in their dwellings, or the roving gangs would harm them.

"Where's the police?" Ian asked, steering *The Ride* with one hand as he eased back in his seat with his other arm out the window. The engine with its constant hissing and chugging poo-chee, poo-chee was noisy. They had to speak loudly to hear one another over the constant churning of gases.

"Police?" Maa Dev questioned.

Leucadia explained. "The guards who protect the people from the gangs, Dev."

"Oh, the Milities?"

159

"The Milities, yeah, where are they?"

"I don't know, Lu. They are military. Imperator Muuk is in charge of the Milities. You would need to ask him," Dev replied.

Ian wanted to slap the Prince across the face. "I thought your family runs the country?"

"The King rules everywhere."

"Then have him fix the problem, Dev. Get the gangs under control. Stop the madness. Your people have a right to live free without being hassled by gangs," Ian said forcefully.

The Prince was clueless. "You and Lu speak of this freedom often, Ian. What is this word?"

"It means the individual has the power to live as he chooses. You know, do your own thing without someone telling you what to do or how to do it, Dev. You are responsible for your own life, not some government. If you want to be a baker, you can. If you want to be a farmer, you can. Truck driver, teacher, rock star. Whatever. Whatever you want to be is up to you. You make your own choices in life instead of some Royal Decree."

The Prince leaned forward from his seat in the back row. "No one can farm unless the Authority approves this, Ian."

"That's my point. Your people don't need an Authority to make a good life. Let them be free to make their decisions on their own."

"I'm afraid that's not possible, Ian. My people cannot survive without the Royal Authority. That is the way it has always been."

Ian closed his eyes and began slowly counting to ten, the way his mother taught him to do when he became so frustrated and angry over nonsensical dweebs that he wanted to explode. She would lay a warm arm around Ian's shoulders and walk with him. "Not everyone can see like you, Ian. It is frustrating sometimes when you know things are so clear in that wonderful mind of yours, when others see only haze."

"No haze, Mom, a block wall," he said aloud to himself.

Dev had no answers as to why there was no one to protect against the roving gangs of his country. "You have no ruler, Lu?"

"We have rulers, Dev, just like you. But where people have the most freedom is where people are the most prosperous and happy because they make their own choices," Leucadia said.

The Prince laughed. "I've never heard of such a system. How can your people survive without a king?"

"A lot better than your people, toad. We tossed out our king with his soup bowl a long time ago, and for the most part, it's worked better than any other system in history. My country is called the USA, and we have the best hamburgers, cars, and baseball players on our planet."

Ian shifted gears and pulled back on the throttle to slow *The Ride* as they entered the outskirts of the city. Through the mist, the city could have been like any small town in Midwest America. Except here, the buildings and offices were run down and decaying. Shops were boarded up and unoccupied. Vehicles parked on the streets were empty shells left to rust in the same way as the car from the farmhouse's front yard.

"Look at this town, Dev. It's a mess," Ian said, in disbelief.

"I was told times were better before I was born," Dev replied defensively.

Leucadia saw the ruined structures of a collapsing nation where the producers of the nation were replaced by the takers, and everyone lived in constant fear of suppressive rules and uncaring authority.

"My people were prosperous under my grandfather's rule," Dev added.

"When did this Authority you speak of begin?" Ian asked.

The Prince thought back with sadness. "It was after my grandfather passed away," and then suddenly began connecting the dots with his own observation. "After he left us, the Authority came into being."

"So your people were freer and more prosperous before the Authority, Dev?" Ian asked.

"I guess they were." He turned to Leucadia. "Is that called freedom, Lu?"

"Yes it is, Dev."

Ian and Leucadia traded all-knowing glances. "Makes sense," Ian said, but *The Ride's* noisiness made the comment unheard. He went on much louder. "You're the Prince of Dolminia, Dev. You can make it happen. You can give your people freedom again by ridding your country of this Authority. If you're going to rule this land someday, get your act together or you will have no country to rule. Some other country will eat you alive, and when that happens, you will be the one in the streets begging for scraps," Ian warned.

Dev glared Ian. "What you speak is treason, Ian! I owe you my life, but I will not allow anyone to speak in such a manner, or you will be turned over to the Authority. Dissent against the crown is death!"

"Dissent comes from corruption and poor leadership, Dev," Leucadia said calmly. "Ian is right. It will take someone of strong character and leadership to bring your country back to what it once was . . . a prosperous land of happy and free people."

Ian applied the brakes again as he approached and turned the corner. The way was clear, but the buildings bordering the street were suspicious. For the first time since entering the city, he saw what can only be described as hundreds of bullet holes in the walls. Before he could pull up and turn off to another street, heavily armed beings pushed a large transport in front of *The Ride*, blocking their way. Ian stopped. Reversing *The Ride* was not like driving Leucadia's Ferrari or even Harlowe's old Volkswagen bug, Baby. It was built to run straight ahead, and that was it. When a second pile of junk was shoved behind them, the thought of turning around was only a dream.

The Ride was trapped!

36

This is the Place

Millawanda drifted silently through the large access hole in the side of the hull, and into a lightless world of total darkness. The silence, the blackness, and the absolute creepiness of flying inside a structure made everyone on the bridge uneasy. Riverstone half expected a body to thump against the forward window at any moment. Ahead, sensors displayed a frozen interior of tall skyscrapers, secondary buildings, streets, fields, and frozen lakes along the outer regions of the structure that went on for miles.

"Captain?" Monday said, feeling queasy, like Riverstone, about the blackness. All anyone could see out the forward windows was the dim blue shimmer of the shields. Beyond that, it was all black.

"Right," Harlowe replied with understanding. He ordered the launch of an ion flare that quickly turned the black to day, bathing the interior ring with light.

"Thank you, Captain," the crew said collectively.

* * *

They put down beside a frozen, kidney-shaped lake near one of many cities. Harlowe, Riverstone, and Monday wasted no time in blinking to the perimeter edge of their ship for a look-see. From three hundred feet above the ground, the view was magnificent. They stood in full SIBA gear, because the temperature was near absolute zero with no atmosphere. Across the lake cities buildings loomed high overhead. Still parked along the streets were cars and transports where the city dwellers had left them presumably thousands of years before. Everywhere there was silence. Riverstone thought he could have heard a flea burp on the other side of the torus. In order to survey the rest of the interior that went for miles in each direction, they wore small jet packs to get the job done fast in the zero gravity. Even though *Millawanda's* sensors had found no lifeforms, Harlowe learned on Hitt that mutated creatures could exist anywhere. Besides extra mags and the Gama-rifles Harlowe and Riverstone carried, Monday packed his weapon of choice; the flame thrower-like device he used on Gazz to fry the man-eating vines.

"Look at those billboards and marquees," Riverstone waved with excitement. "That main drag over there with all those Harry's Places. How cool is that?"

"What happened to everyone?" Monday asked, clutching his fire-breathing weapon.

"Something scared them," Harlowe replied without a hint of doubt. He stared at the large open egress and ingress port they had come through, wondering himself what had caused the abandonment of such a massive enterprise.

Riverstone was still thinking about the glitz. He pointed at the buildings to his right. "Look at the architecture and all the fine metal work, sculptures, glass fountains, wide streets, and this lake. Wow, what kept the water in?" he wondered, looking down at the frozen water.

Harlowe nodded at the torus. "Gravity. When the Donut turns, it makes gravity."

Riverstone floated away from the edge of the ship to make his point. "What gravity?"

"It has to move, dumb-dumb. When the power was cut off, the torus's rotation faded over time." Harlowe pointed up at the ceiling. "It's still turning, but too slow to be felt. It takes over one year to make a single rotation. One day it will drift with no spin at all."

Riverstone discovered a wide-open space that interested him. It was away from the city buildings with nothing built on it. "That seems wasted."

"Could be a landing area," Harlowe guessed.

Riverstone thought it made sense. "Yeah, it's big enough for three Millie's, that's for sure."

Prigg added more precisely from the bridge, *"Seven and a half Millie's, Your Majesty."*

While he was on the line, Harlowe asked the Naruckian, "How much time do we have, Mr. Prigg?"

"Three hours, twenty-two minutes, Your Majesty," Prigg replied over their coms.

Harlowe signed off. "Understood."

Riverstone asked, "I thought we had longer than that?"

Monday answered. "That would cut it too close, Captain. We have two hours before the Mysterians arrive. We don't want to engage anyone with the fuel remaining."

Harlowe grumbled. He hated having both feet and hands tied behind his back. He stepped over the perimeter rim and joined Riverstone, floating effortlessly away from the hull. "Let's move out, gentlemen. We have a lot of Donut to cover."

They rocketed off. With no air resistance to hold them back, their micro jets shot them across the lake in a seventy-mile-per hour cruising speed in seconds. With no earthquakes to worry about, some of the structures they flew by were high as three hundred story buildings back on Earth.

Flying five-hundred feet off the deck as they turned up the first long avenue they came to, Riverstone asked, "What are we looking for?"

"We'll know it when we see it," was Harlowe short reply. Then, contacting the ship, he asked, "Anything I should know from your readouts, Mr. Prigg?"

"The residual radiation count and the rotation slowdown places the Donut destruction over a thousand years ago, Your Majesty."

Riverstone whistled in surprise. "Wow, except for that big hole in the ceiling, they could have left yesterday."

* * *

The three Gamadin circled the Donut in a little over two hours. They discovered several more cities with the same m.o.: tall buildings, abandoned vehicles, shops, frozen lakes, trees, and many amusement parks, all deserted, all silent and ghostly. But in all the miles they covered, they found no particular reason why *Millawanda* would have dropped out of hyperspace to stop here. They had little time to spare before the Mysterians arrived. If they didn't find something...and quick...their questions would go unanswered.

Harlowe led Riverstone and Monday to the top of *Millawanda's* dome. At slightly over three hundred twenty-eight feet from the ground, they stood at the apex of the golden ship with an unencumbered, breathtaking view of the entire arching Donut structure that circled them.

"What are we missing, gentlemen?" Harlowe asked as their SIBA optics scanned at full power, searching for his we'll-know-it-when-we-see-it thing that he thought for sure was right in front of their noses.

"Could we have flown past it?" Riverstone asked, staring across the lake and beyond for the umpteenth time. As the two focused on deciphering the Donut's riddle, Monday kept an eye out for anything that moved.

"Maybe," Harlowe replied, opened to any possibility.

Monday pointed off the sunset side of the ship behind them both. "Was that there before, Captain?"

They turned toward the empty space Harlowe had pointed to earlier when they first stepped outside the ship. What was there now, was not there before. It was a large, circular shaped gold building made of mostly of glass. The flat roof structure was sitting plain as day in the middle of the empty space. Even more odd, at least from their perspective, they observed no windows or doors.

"I don't think so, Mr. Platter," Harlowe replied cautiously.

"How did we miss that?" Monday asked.

"We didn't," Harlowe answered. "It wasn't there before."

"Are you sure?"

"Positive. It popped out of the ground."

"I have seen it before," Riverstone said out of the blue.

Harlowe and Monday both turned to the First Officer.

"What?" Harlowe asked.

"Yeah, I have seen this building, or one like it, before," Riverstone explained. "On Lenor's moon where Rerun and I went surfing. Those Mysterian dudes were trying to crack it open when the   tidal wave hit and snuffed them."

Together they turned back to the structure with a different take on its meaning when Simon announced over the com, *"The neighborhood is getting crowded, Skipper."*

Harlowe glanced at the countdown inside his bugeyes readouts. "They're way early."

"It's not the Mysterians, Your Majesty. It's something else entirely. They're coming our way in a hurry. Twenty-nine minutes, eleven seconds, Your Majesty," Prigg calculated.

Harlowe pushed off the dome taking Riverstone with him. "We have to check it out. Mr. Platter, stay with the ship. I want you there if things go south while we're away.

"Aye, Captain."

"Lock and load, Mr. Bolt," Harlowe ordered.

"Aye, Skipper. Powering up."

* * *

The gold beam and glass structure was a lot bigger than it looked from *Millawanda's* dome. They circled it once, looking for the front door but found no entrance, not even a small crack in the wall. Harlowe made a wild guess, believing like all the other buildings in the area, the front would be facing the lake.

"This thing's as big as Millie, Captain," Riverstone observed, as they touched down a football field away.

"It looks Gamadin," Harlowe reflected, kinking his head up at the reflective glass wall.

Beneath their feet was once real grass. But like the pool, the blades were frozen solid and felt like they were stepping on Shredded Wheat as they walked.

"Good guess, Captain. You're right," Riverstone concurred, confirming Harlowe's assessment. He had landed away from Harlowe to get a better view of the structure.

From a hundred yards away across the frozen lawn, Riverstone looked tiny, but with a quick zoom, he was life-size again. "How do you know that?" Harlowe asked.

Riverstone pointed at the top of the structure. "Because it says so."

Curious, Harlowe had to see for himself. He powered over to Riverstone's side and stared up, mouth agape. There was no doubt about it, the hundred foot wide insignia was Gamadin. It was the same starburst symbol that emblazoned the front of *Millawanda's* dome below the bridge windows.

"Another station?" Riverstone wondered.

Harlowe hit his jets and headed for the front door. "No doubt."

"Prigg is registering a power surge, Captain," Monday said from the ship. *"I think whatever it is, it knows we're here."*

37

No God

Leucadia quickly switched on the force field to protect everyone inside before the first rounds of gunfire struck *The Ride*. From all sides, bullets mushed against the blue shimmering protective shield and dropped to the pavement like dead gnats. When the bullets were nearly expended, Ian calmly stepped out of the cab and aimed the Gama-rifle at the transport. One squeeze later, the transport was history. Those who were behind the transport, or next to it, were turned to subatomic dust. Dev sat back in his seat in awe, stunned by the supreme power of the Gamadin weapon.

With Ian's focus forward, Leucadia turned to the gang members on the second transport behind *The Ride*. The Gama-rifle didn't scare them as much as Rhud leaping out the backside of *The Ride* and roaring like he was about to eat them all. Bodies scattered, wildly screaming as they dropped their weapons and fled for the back alleys and doorways like scared mice.

Ian called for Rhud to step back before he finished the destruction of the second transport with another blast. For Dev, it seemed no hour passed when his saviors displayed an even greater power than he had seen before.

Ian lowered his rifle, keeping a close eye on the streets, while Leucadia gave Rhud a big hug around the neck. "Thank you, Rhuddy."

Ian went around *The Ride* to inspect for any possible damage. He found a few bullet nicks to the front-end boiler tank but nothing serious. The force field had not only covered them, but its protective umbrella had protected all her vital parts, as well.

168

Ian was about to return to *The Ride* when he heard movement and moaning from behind one of the barriers. A few makeshift blockades along the street had survived the Gamadin blast, but anyone close to the impact zone was still toast. Whoever had survived the discharge was lucky to be alive.

While Leucadia covered his back, Ian jumped over the wooden crates the gang had used to make their barrier. Lying beneath the debris were two bodies, a guy and a girl about his age. Both were alive but unconscious and bleeding. He thought briefly about leaving them where they lay. After all, they tried to kill him first. But the guilt he felt wouldn't let him do that. His mother was hovering behind him with *that* look in her eyes. Take care of those kids, Ian, or there will be a price to pay. Unlike Harlowe's mom, Tinker, Betty Wizzixs was never physical with him. She was petite, pretty, kind, a great cook, and so soft spoken that one had to listen hard to hear her. Her eyes, however, were her strength. They were as powerful as a Mrs. Pylott left hook. If he left the two wounded gang members to die without helping them, his mom's eyes would haunt him for an eternity.

Ian yielded without protest. "Alright, Mom," he sighed, and wondered if he was ever going to find Molly again with all the sidebars he was taking. He picked up the girl first and laid her in the back of the platform with Rhud. "Nicktoe," he called out, and by the time he returned with the male, the clickers were busily cleaning the girl's head wounds and applying their special gel-like bandages to the injuries along her arms, neck, and face.

Dev watched the entire scene from the backseat of *The Ride*. He appeared in a daze and had remained silent from the moment Ian's shot blasted the transport from the street. When the robobs were done with their emergency patchwork, they lifted the two injured bodies into the cab and returned to their cylindrical form next to Ian's pack.

It wasn't long before Ian had the boiler at full steam again and *The Ride* moving through the streets unmolested. It was as if the word spread like wildfire that *The Ride* was a rolling death that defied the Darkness.

An hour out of town and making good speed, cruising along the open road again toward the coast, the Prince finally spoke. "What happened back there, Ian?" he asked, his voice trembling as he spoke.

Ian understood the Prince's fear. He stared at his own hands on the steering wheel. As one-sided as the battle was, he was still shaking. When someone pumps hundreds of bullets at your head, it doesn't matter how powerful the force field is, it's scary to be on the receiving end. Harlowe and Riverstone faced those kinds of problems all the time. Harlowe said he never got used to it. He told Ian right up front that after the gunfight with Sar on the planet Og, his hands didn't stop shaking for a week. Ian doubted the story was true, because he had never seen Harlowe that way in his whole life. But to this day, nearly a year afterward, Harlowe insists he still wakes up in the middle of the night with cold sweats thinking about it.

After sucking in a long breath to calm himself, Ian replied, "That was their call, Dev."

Dev's eyes were unblinking and filled with outright fear. "That's not what I meant, Ian. I saw you do things that no one can do but the gods!"

Ian forced a small grin to hide his embarrassment. "Trust me, Dev, I am no god. Just ask Lu."

Dev found no humor in Ian's reply.

Ian tried again. "Look, Dev, Lu and I are just looking for Rhud's sister. That's it! Read no more into it than that. And when we find her, you'll never see me or Lu again."

Ian faced Leucadia. "Right, Lu?"

"That's right, Dev. We are only here to find the second white tigre. Then we are leaving," Leucadia explained.

"Where will you go?" the Prince asked worriedly. He pointed at the clouds. "Back to the heavens?"

The logical answer would be, yeah, that's exactly where I'm going, Ian thought. But how were they going to accomplish that without Millie? "Something like that, Dev."

"Then you are a god."

Leucadia weighed in with her diplomatic charm. "Dev, we aren't gods. We come from a place, far away, where our technology is allowed to grow."

"Freedom again," Dev said, becoming weary of hearing the term over and over again.

"Yes...freedom. Where we can live, think, and produce things which make our lives better without someone looking over our shoulder telling us what to do."

"How does destroying a vehicle with such power make your life better?"

Leucadia had an answer. "That vehicle was a symbol. It was put there to stop our freedom. They would have taken our freedom away to find our lost friend if we didn't protect it."

Dev turned back to Ian. The idea of freedom was still hard for him to imagine. It required a subjective concept he wasn't quite ready for. But the unbelievable feats he had seen from Ian were quite real, and yet were just as unimaginable as defying the Authority. "I have seen you fly without machines. I have seen you defeat scores of the Imperator's finest soldiers as if they were children. I have seen you shoot with incredible accuracy at unimaginable distances. You made a transport from farm trash," He held up a robob cylinder, "and bring to life a piece of metal with a spoken word. And now I have seen you wipe out a street gang to the man by two rounds from this weapon," he said, pointing at the Gama-rifle in the back seat. "I know for a fact, Ian, that no one on Nod can do such things. No one on Nod has control of the twynich. But you do, Ian. No one has that kind of power except a god," Dev argued. "You must be a god! That is the only explanation I understand."

Ian understood how the feats he performed would seem godly to any Nodian. This was why the Gamadin were always careful about using their 54th century weapons and devices on less developed worlds. On the 16th century planet of Gazz, Harlowe made exceptions to save his ship, his crew, Lu, himself, and the planet. His Gazzian crew had witnessed many amazing devices like the clickers with their strength and agility to rebuild a broken ship, the weapons that shot many rounds without reloading, and the cannons that wiped out an entire fortress with a single broadside. But when it was all over, and the pirate galleon was returned to it's Gazzian crew, Leucadia corrected the problem by erasing their short term memories of their voyage and the 54th century captain and his toys.

Ian could only look ahead. There was no turning back the clock, no logical explanation that Dev would understand without a visit from Bolt's therapist. He clasped his shaking hands around the steering wheel and repeated, "I'm no god, Dev," because that was his only answer.

38

Bigbob

"Where's the door?" Riverstone asked bewildered as they stood in front of the newly discovered Gamadin Outpost. The curving wall was solid. They saw no entry anywhere around the entire structure.

Harlowe touched the side of Riverstone's head. "Turn on your sensors."

When he did, like a fairy had touched him with a magic wand, the reflective glass transformed into a structure of transparent glass windows, recessed balconies, and tall doors.

"Sweet," Riverstone gasped, relieved that he didn't need to blast his way in.

Harlowe drew his sidearm and went through first. There was no door that required opening in the normal sense. The entry was more like a portal. It seemed as long as he wore a SIBA he was clear to pass freely through any entry point. With their bugeyes lighting the way, they stepped through the portal and moved between the dust covered chairs, desks, and tables. Like the furnishings aboard *Millawanda*, they were simple, comfortable and . . . grey? The carpet was grey as well. None of the furnishings had their normal blue color until Riverstone touched one of the chairs, brushing away a thick layer of dust. Under the muck was the familiar blue color they were used to seeing. "Apparently the clickers had been on strike," Harlowe quipped.

Riverstone then asked the obvious question again. "What are we looking for?"

"Same as before."

Together they said, "We'll know it when we see it."

Harlowe took the lead, moving carefully farther into the building of high-arched ceilings and partially opened sliding doors. If the floors were clean and the lights on, they could have easily thought they were aboard *Millawanda*. Except for the fact that nothing worked, it was chilling in its sameness. Although the place was obviously empty of life, they kept their weapons ready for Freddy Kruger or anything unimaginable that might jump out and attack them. Riverstone hand signaled that he wanted to explore the first room off the corridor. Harlowe nodded his okay and watched his First Officer slip quietly through the open doorway.

"Captain," Monday said, breaking in. *"twenty-two minutes, tops."*

"Understood, Mr. Platter. Keep me advised," Harlowe replied with calm.

"Captain," Riverstone's voice echoed from inside the small room. "I think I found something."

A moment later they met in front of the room. Riverstone had in his hand what was obvious to them; a robob cylinder. Only it was three times the size of any cylinder they had seen pop out of *Millawanda's* walls.

"Think it works?" Riverstone asked, handing it over to Harlowe for his appraisal.

Harlowe shook cylinder and tapped on it lightly with the end of his pistol. "Seems okay."

"It doesn't look damaged," Riverstone said.

"Find anything else?"

Riverstone handed Harlowe what appeared to be a stick of clear Juicy Fruit gum. It was flat like gum, about the same size but was translucent like crystal. "I found it in a trash can."

Harlowe eyed it once and handed it back. "Give it to Prigg for his take." He then turned his attention back to the cylinder and said to it, "Nicktoe."

Riverstone cocked his head like Harlowe was smoking something hallucinogenic. "How would it know our code word?"

"I don't know. It might," Harlowe defended.

The cylinder, however, remained unchanged.

"Apparently, this one didn't get the memo," Riverstone cracked.

Harlowe returned the cylinder to Riverstone. "Here, you try."

Riverstone held the cylinder in front of him and said simply, "Help us."

Harlowe grunted. "That's imaginative."

A full three seconds went by before the cylinder began to shake in Riverstone's claw.

Harlowe mumbled his approval as Riverstone laid the cylinder on the floor and stepped aside. Together they watched the cylinder do its thing. A normal clicker on the ship expands almost instantly. At times, a clicker will pop to life so fast it's fully transformed before it hits the floor. If you blink, you can easily miss the conversion. This cylinder was was like Rip Van Winkle waking from a long sleep. Riverstone bent down and helped it untangle its extremities.

"Seventeen minutes," Monday called out, reminding Harlowe to make it quick.

Thirty seconds later, with Riverstone's assistance, the robob finished his transformation and stood up, towering over them both.

"He's a big one, Dog," Riverstone commented.

Harlowe added, "He's taller than Squid," who was the tallest crewman on the ship at seven feet two-inches.

The big robob stayed still as they inspected the biggest clicker they had ever seen. It was a good three feet taller than Jewels, who was the tallest robob on their ship.

"His rim looks a little dim," Harlowe pointed out.

"He probably could use a shot of Bluestuff," Riverstone said, scanning it with his switched on SIBA sensors. "It's running at less than twenty percent."

"Millie will give Bigbob something to eat later. Time's a wastin'," Harlowe said.

"You're taking him with us?" Riverstone asked, surprised that Harlowe would take someone on board their ship without testing it for viruses or any mechanical bug that could infect the entire ship.

Harlowe patted Bigbob on the round ball of his shoulder. "Yep," but cautioned, "we'll put him in isolation until Prigg gives him the okay."

Riverstone found that acceptable. "Now where?"

Harlowe checked his sensors. "We look for a power source. I have a reading, but it seems to be below us."

"I haven't seen any stairways, but then, this is a big place," Riverstone said, turning around.

"We don't have the time to search for one either," Harlowe added and faced the tall clicker. "Where's the main power source, Bigbob?"

Stiffly, Bigbob reacted obediently and headed down the corridor like he knew exactly where he was going.

Harlowe pointed at the big clicker, whose foot sounds were more like a clunk than a click. "Let's follow the big guy. If he works, maybe other things do too."

They walked for another ten minutes until Riverstone stopped long enough to pick up a few items he found interesting on the floor.

"What are they?" Harlowe asked as he watched him place the items in a small belt pouch.

"They look like memory crystals like the ones we use on Millie."

"Grab 'em. You never know," Harlowe said. When he looked up, the tall clicker was nowhere to be seen. "Where'd Bigbob go?"

Riverstone pointed his pistol at an open doorway ahead. "I think he went in there, Captain."

Harlowe followed him into the room. Bigbob was waiting beside a blinker on the floor.

"He wants us to follow him," Riverstone assumed.

"*Seven minutes, Captain,*" Monday called out. There was an unmistakable hurry-up edge to his tone.

"Understood, Mr. Platter," Harlowe answered. "We're onto something here."

"*Make it fast, Captain; they'll be on us soon,*" Monday countered.

Time was short, but it couldn't be helped. If they found a power supply or even another blue crystal, it was worth the risk. Like Ian said a week ago, "Aara is rare, Captain. You won't find it lying around anywhere but Orixy. That is our only source."

Riverstone pointed his sensors at the blinker. "It's got juice, Captain."

"Wait here," Harlowe said, as he stepped on the blinker with tall clicker.

"What if it's a trap, Dog?" Riverstone cautioned.

"We'll know soon enough. Stay put," he ordered.

Before Riverstone could say 'be careful,' Harlowe and Bigbob had already blinked to who-knows-where.

39

Cheesa & Tweto

Everyone needed a rest. The sun was nearly below the horizon, and Leucadia figured it was time to hold up for the night. The first opportunity she found, she pulled *The Ride* off the main road and continued on through the dark shadows beneath a canopy of trees. For nearly five hundred miles they had traveled night and day, stopping only long enough to stretch their legs and fill *The Ride*'s reservoirs with water. Now they were only an hour's drive from the coast where, according to Dev, the road Rhud was leading them was on a direct route to Imperator Muuk's coastal headquarters. It was time to regroup and plan their next move before going any farther.

Dev was scared. "The Imperator will kill me."

Leucadia assured the Prince that wouldn't happen. "We will take care of you, Dev."

"With your weapons?"

"If we have to."

That settled Dev only a little. To take his mind off of the Imperator's camp, the Prince wondered how it was even possible to track the other tigre. "Your tigre does not talk."

"He knows the way and will let us know if we make a wrong turn," Ian replied.

"Rhud can find his sister anywhere on Nod?" Dev asked.

"Anywhere," Ian replied firmly.

Dev stared at the big cat's bright blue eyes, almost waiting for something magical to happen. "But how does he do that without instruments?"

Leucadia explained: "Animals have senses we don't understand. There was a flood on our planet a short time ago that killed thousands of people, but no animals were found among the dead. It was as if they sensed the danger long before the ocean flooded the land. How Rhud knows where his sister is, I have no exact answer, Dev. His senses are far more acute than ours. A twynich period or other electronic disturbance cannot trick his senses. Ian and I just know he is right. He will lead us to his sister far better than any of our instruments."

* * *

A short way from the road, Leucadia parked *The Ride* along a clear stream lined with shady, broadleafed trees. The gurgling river, the birds chirping and fluttering between the branches, and the setting orange-green sun slowly sinking below the foothills were all images that reminded one of a wilderness magazine cover. Leucadia sighed, lamenting she was unable to enjoy it.

Ian released the pressure from the boiler tank and capped the stack so white residual steam that floated between the treetops wouldn't expose their position to any military patrols. Before the wheels had stopped, Rhud had jumped off back to fish in the nearby stream. While Ian finished shutting down, Leucadia instructed Dev to find firewood. The Prince was exhausted. All he wanted to do was lie down somewhere warm and go to sleep. His droopy eyes gazed outward, unblinking and distant as he watched Rhud meander to the side of the river, and in a blink of an eye, grab a large fish with his claw and swallow it whole. He wished life for him was that simple.

Leucadia was on her way to check on her two patients when they jumped out in front of her will long sticks they had found on the ground. It was easy to see why they were frightened. Until now, they had been asleep and unable to know why someone had transported them out of the city. They were also dirty and disheveled, and from the way they looked bony, thin, and pale, nearly falling over where they stood. They hadn't had a square meal in a long while.

Leucadia held up her hands. "We mean you no harm."

The young male took a step closer, holding his stick higher. At that moment, Rhud walked up behind Leucadia and growled. She patted the big cat's head and asked them, "Think those will hurt him?"

The two froze. They had never seen a beast so terrifying. Ian walked behind them. "Put the sticks down, and he won't harm you."

The gang members were too frightened to move so he carefully removed the sticks from their hands without protest; their eyes remained fixated on the big cat.

Like they were manikins, Ian led them to a fallen tree that made a good place to sit. "Stay here while we make a fire."

The dried wood in the area was plentiful. It wasn't long before Dev returned with an armful and put it down in front of them. Leucadia guided the Prince to the side as Ian lit the wood with a low discharge from his sidearm. In no time at all, hot flames were crackling brightly, spreading warmth to everyone around the campfire.

The girl, who was thin, of medium height, with reddish, curly hair, and cute hazel eyes that smacked of defiance asked, "Where are we?"

Ian replied as he tended to the fire. "I don't know what it's called but we're a few miles west of the coast."

"That is impossible to travel this far during twynich," the young male stated emphatically.

Ian pointed at *The Ride*. "Not with that."

"I remember your transport. It came into our domain," the young man said. "What happened to us?"

"Your transport was not harmed?" the girl asked confused.

Ian thought it pointless to discuss how he had blown their barrier way. Instead he explained there was an explosion, and they managed to escape. "You were hurt, so we brought you here to save your lives."

"The Militie fired upon us?" the young man asked.

Leucadia thought that was a good explanation. So she went with it. "Yes, it was the Milities."

"We escaped the Militie?" the young man asked surprised. "We knew they were close, but the twynich keeps them from entering our domains without their transports for protection," he added.

"Yeah, we got lucky," Ian replied.

"We are not prisoners of the Milities?" the girl asked.

"No," Leucadia answered. "You are not prisoners of anyone."

"Who are you then?" the young man asked.

Ian walked back to *The Ride* and returned with two cans of food. He opened them up and handed them each a can. "Someone who wishes you no harm," he told them.

Like ravenous animals, the girl and the young man ate every bite, licking their utensils and sticking their tongues as far as they could inside the cans. A slight breeze blew their body odor in Ian's direction. It was rank and vile, like they both lived in a sewer.

Ian tried to hide his disgust as he asked, "What are your names?"

They didn't answer. They seemed scared of divulging their identities, so Ian led by saying his name first. They still would not say their names until Ian fetched more cans.

He held out one can. The girl reached to grab it, but before she could take it, Ian pulled it back. "Your names." He thought she had promise behind the dirt. If her face was clean, she might even he cute, he thought.

"I am Cheesa," the girl finally said, staring with ravenous pink eyes at the can in Ian's hand.

"I am Tweto," the young man said, looking equally starved.

Ian held out the cans for both of them, and like before, they devoured the contents in seconds, not wasting a single morsel.

Behind them, coming into the campfire light, Dev tried to introduce himself, "And I am—" But before the Prince could complete his introduction, Ian cut him off with a slight tap to his midsection.

"Dev," Leucadia said, finishing the Prince's intro for him. The hit was slight enough to go unnoticed by the Cheesa and Tweto, but to Dev, the pain was excruciating.

"He's been a little sick lately, and sometimes he has trouble talking," Ian explained in helping the gasping Royal to a place away from the fire.

Tweto turned his attention to Rhud who had returned to his place near the river. In the dark his white coat shimmered from the reflection of starlight while his blue eyes glowed hauntingly as he came closer. "What is that beast?"

"Our pet," Ian replied.

"A tigre?" Cheesa asked.

"Yes. A tigre," Leucadia answered, going with the flow again.

"I have only seen images of them. I never realized they were so enormous," Cheesa said.

"He eats his Wheaties every day," Ian joked.

No one found the joke humorous. Ian felt like he was talking to beings who never experienced anything fun in their lives. More importantly, he wondered if they had ever taken a bath. Sadly, he thought they probably hadn't.

"Where are you going?" Cheesa asked.

"To the coast," Ian replied.

"That is the Numeri stronghold," Tweto said, then asked in the same breath, "Why?"

"We are looking for a friend."

"The Numeri has taken your friend?" Cheesa asked.

"Yes," Ian replied.

"You will never get your friend back. You must consider him dead," Tweto said glumly.

"She is not dead," Ian stated calmly. Then more forcefully he added, "And we will find her and we will get her back."

"The twynich will be over by this night. When the *ferol* returns, the Authority will once again spread terror across the empire," Cheesa said with a sense of futility in her voice as if she had fought the Authority all her life. "If you defy the Authority, you will never find her. You must wait for the next twynich or you will not succeed. Even then it is doubtful."

Ian spoke with a clear edge of defiance. "We cannot wait. We must find her now."

"Then you will die," Tweto said as if it were a given.

"So be it," Ian stated, his eyes locking with both gang members.

"Where are you from? You cannot be from Dolmina," Cheesa said perceptively. "You speak strangely. I have never heard a Dolminian talk like you."

Leucadia had a plausible storyline already in her mind. "Our aircraft crashed in the mountains." She looked at Dev, whose face was recovering slowly. "We managed to escape, but our friend, Molly, was captured by the Numeri."

"If you defy the Numeri, we will help you," Cheesa volunteered.

Leucadia would not allow it. "Thank you, Cheesa, but where we go tomorrow, we must go alone."

"You will leave us here?" Cheesa asked.

"It is safer for you that way. From here you can find your way home. If, as you say, the twynich ends tonight, you can hitch a ride in a transport back to your city," Ian replied.

"Ian is right, Cheesa. We must find our way back from here," Tweto said.

"No, Tweto, we will go with Ian and Lu. They are not Dolminian. We must help them find their friend, Molly. We owe them for saving our lives.," Cheesa argued.

Another whiff of foul odor wafted by Ian's face. He tried to cover his nose, but the smell made his eyes water. He tried moving to one side, hoping the smoke from the fire would mask the stench.

No luck!

He was doomed. There was no escape. What was it about the beings on this planet? Was there a Royal Decree against bathing?

Tweto pointed accusingly at the Prince. "But he is Dolminian. Who is he?"

This time, before Ian or Leucadia could stop him, Dev stuck out his chest and boasted, "Prince Maa Dev. Imperial Heir to the Throne of Dolmina."

"You are Prince Maa Dev?" Cheesa asked with great surprise.

"Yes, I am Prince Maa Dev," he repeated with pride.

Tweto's face suddenly changed to hate. "If what you say is true, you are no longer the Prince but the King!"

Ian didn't know what to say. The last thing he wanted was to get involved in Domina's politics.

Dev challenged Tweto. "You dare speak blasphemy of the King? I will have your head for this!"

Cheesa spoke up, defending Tweto's statement. "The King is dead, Prince. This is true. It happened six days ago. The King, Princess Aboka, and Prince Nardo were all assassinated. Imperator Muuk is in complete control, Your Highness."

Ian held the Prince from behind him as Leucadia straight armed Tweto, holding him in check. Things were going south fast. This wasn't the plan. He wanted a simple capture. The soldiers would take them to wherever they were holding Molly. With his small squad of clickers, they would break her out and be happily on their way back to the forest, hang out a while, and then find the source of the Gamadin power signature. Maybe there was hope there. But now things were complicated. If the Authority were indeed in charge of the country and had assassinated the Royal Family, then Dev would be lucky to see tomorrow. Their plans required more thought. First, they had to find Molly; then he and Leucadia could think about saving the royal heir's neck.

"He should die now for what the King and his Authority have done to our people," Tweto said, seething with disgust. From the look of Cheesa's cold stare, she felt the same.

Ian kept holding the Prince for his own safety. "No one is going to harm, Dev. He's under my protection."

The Prince tried to break free. "I don't need your protection, Ian. I can take care of this *proditor* on my own."

Tweto fought against Leucadia's vise-like grip. "Stop it, Tweto!"

Ian added: "The Prince may be a toad, but he's our toad, Tweto. If you or anyone else tries to harm him, then you have to go through Rhud first," he said pointing at the big cat.

Ian tossed Dev aside and took Tweto from Leucadia, slamming him against *The Ride* to drive his point home. "Understand Tweto! He's under my protection." Ian went nose to nose with both gang members. "He dies, you die. That's the way it works around here."

Tweto didn't care. He would sacrifice his own life to kill the Prince. Ian saw that and turned to Cheesa. "Tell him, Cheesa, or we'll have it out right now."

Cheesa fought with herself. Her whole life revolved around the destruction of the Royal Family and the Authority. She was being told to throw down her hate for someone she wanted to kill with her bare hands, now standing only three feet away.

"Ian, you do not know what you are asking," Cheesa cried.

Neither Tweto or Cheesa would listen to reason. Ian had no choice. The rank odors were driving him crazy. To their astonishment, he picked them both up by the back of their pants and dragged them kicking and screaming down to the river.

"What are you doing, Ian?" Cheesa screamed.

"Time to cool off, suckwads," Ian replied, and tossed them into the river with all their clothes. There was no way he was taking Cheesa and Tweto with them smelling the way they were. Dev was already a drag on their mission and had delayed them several days. He made up his mind they were all staying behind, the Prince included! In the morning he would tie them all to a tree and leave them to find their own way back home, wherever that may be.

As expected, neither Cheesa nor Tweto could swim a stroke. Ian watched them flail around in the water. When he figured enough of the foulness had washed away, he waded into the river and dunked Cheesa's head under the surface several times. She fought wildly. Tweto tried to take a swing but a small thump to the side of the head, and he was out cold. To keep from drowning, Ian laid him at the river's edge while he finished up with Cheesa. She fought so hard against more head dunks, that Ian had no choice but to say, "Lights out, Cheesa," and finished her bath looking like a sopping wet, rag doll.

Afterwards, and with Leucadia's help, they dragged them both back to the fire to dry out. When Dev tried to take aim at Tweto's unconscious body, it was lights out for the Prince, too. Ian had had enough babysitting for the day. Leucadia sat down near the fire, as Ian took the first watch. It wasn't long before everyone was sleeping soundly, including Leucadia. Ian looked over at Rhud by the river. He wasn't sleeping. He was moaning and pacing back and forth along the riverbank. The big cat didn't care about anything but getting Molly back.

40

The Hive

"**C**APTAIN!!" Monday cried out. *"Incoming bandits are on us!"*

Harlowe blinked back to the room with Bigbob where Riverstone was jumping up and down like he had to go to the bathroom. Together the three of them ran for the front door exit.

"I hope it was worth it," Riverstone said as they charged down the corridor.

"The power room was trashed. Nothing's left down there to pick," Harlowe said. "Worse, it looked like sabotage."

"Why would someone destroy the power supply?" Riverstone wondered aloud.

They made their way outside and ignited their jet packs.

Harlowe grabbed one of Bigbob's metal hands, and Riverstone latched onto the other. "Don't know. At least we didn't come away empty-handed."

They lifted the big robob off the deck and headed for *Millawanda* as fast as their jets would take them. In zero gravity, pulling Bigbob was like pulling a feather. He had no weight. Once the big clicker was flying, his body went slack.

The instant they touched down on the hull of the ship, they blinked directly to the bridge, leaving Bigbob standing alone at the back of the room while they went directly to their stations. They deactivated their SIBAs and tossed their sidearms to Jewels as they strode for their command chairs.

"What is it, Mr. Bolt?" Harlowe asked, placing himself in the chair.

On the overhead screen, thousands of dots were swarming toward the Donut.

"It looks like a swarm of bees," Simon commented.

Monday had only one opinion. "They're not friendly, Captain."

Harlowe asked, "Do you still have our weapons up, Mr. Bolt?"

"Locked and loaded, Skipper," Simon replied, eager for a fight.

Prigg twisted around in his chair. "Your Majesty, our power reserve is critical. If we expend it now, we will fail to cross Cartooga-Thaat," he warned.

"Suggestion," Harlowe asked. If it made sense, he would do it. All he was concerned with was protecting his ship.

Prigg replied quickly, already having a plan. "Pods up, Mr. Platter. Guide Millie to the Gamadin Outpost, and set her down on the top surface, if you please."

Monday looked out across the vast lawn. "It's not there again, Captain."

"It's there, Mr. Platter," Prigg said. "It is hidden again."

"A cloak?" Harlowe asked.

"I think so, Your Majesty."

Then back to Monday, Harlowe directed, "Follow Prigg's directions, Mr. Platter. Park Millie on top of the station, smartly."

As ordered, Monday guided the saucer over the top of the station, putting her down exactly in the middle of the outpost. When the maneuver was complete, he announced, *Millawanda* is down, Captain."

"Make her dark, Mr. Prigg," Harlowe ordered, then to Simon he added quickly, "That includes weapons, Mr. Bolt."

Simon discharged all weapons' batteries, down to the smallest micro cannon. Moments later, the wall of lights winked out behind them, and the bridge went dark. The only light remaining came from the residual afterglow of the Donut structure coming through the forward windows. The light had turned spooky with a purplish tint, like a moonless graveyard at night, when the bee-like drones swarmed around the Donut like feeding locusts.

"Shut down, complete, Captain," Riverstone announced from Wiz's science console.

Prigg had more to do. He continued to toil frantically at his station, sliding activators and adjusting power levels, fighting against time. In frustration, he turned to Harlowe and said, "The station will not add Millie to its cloak, Your Majesty."

Riverstone added more bad news. "A section of the swarm broke away, Captain, and they're coming our way."

Watching the tiny metallic specks whizzing through the opening like mad bees, Harlowe pointed at Prigg's console station. "Make it work, Bigbob. Raise the station's protective shields over the saucer."

Bigbob reacted instantly as Prigg moved aside, giving the tall clicker full access to his workstation. The tall robob began inputting code to the activators and screens at amazing speed. Before a single bee had flown by the forward window, the cloak was extended over the perimeter rim and above the bridge dome, hopefully cutting off the ship's power signature from the hive's sensors.

Riverstone leaned over to Harlowe and asked quietly, "Think it worked, Captain?"

Harlowe shrugged. "It had better." He didn't really know. From the *Millawanda's* bridge everything looked the same. The view through the massive windows was unchanged. It was what others saw from the outside that counted. All they could do now was sit tight and wait as hundreds of copper-colored drones buzzed around them like vampires searching for blood. Throughout the city, thousands more of the tiny, ten-foot long ships darted between the buildings, combing every nook and cranny for whatever had alerted them in the first place. As they whizzed past the forward windows, the crew caught a glimpse of the bullet-shaped ships that shined like new copper pennies. Attached to their fronts were three, whip-like antennas that seemed to taste everything they came upon, and no doubt send all their information back to the queen bee.

Five feet away two bee-drones hovered over the forward window for a good amount of time.

"No one move," Harlowe said in a low whisper.

Three more drones joined in. They darted up and down and around in short spurts, appearing to avoid crashing into each other at the last possible instant. A few times they came so close to one another, their antennae sparked when they touched. The dance went on for five whole minutes before they became bored and burst away in different directions.

Prigg's eyes went crazy the entire time they were being scanned. "That was close, Your Majesty."

Then, at the very top of the window, a massive ship bigger than the

Donut moved across the portal in the superstructure. The queen bee was too large for them to see much of it, but it was the same copper color as her worker drones. It had millions of long antennae waving in space behind it like a giant Medusa jellyfish. Surrounding the strange craft, thousands more drones darted between the long filaments, like they were in some kind of symbiotic ritual.

"What in the…?" Simon tried to ask as he stared in awe.

"Stay cool, everyone," Harlowe said calmly, studying the massive creature.

"Looks deadly," Riverstone commented, then added, "My money is on that having something to do with the Donut going belly up."

Harlowe thought so, too. "Yeah, that's what I'm thinking."

"How long do we wait here?" Simon asked, acting like a fidgety kid sitting in the backseat of the car with nothing to do.

"Until it leaves," was Harlowe's soft-spoken answer.

41

Dear John

The Gamadin crew didn't have to wait long. The bee drones started leaving the Donut in a mass exodus like Mowgi had just pooted inside the torus.

"Was it something we said?" Simon joked with a cheesy grin.

Prigg had the answer after Harlowe ordered the power back on line. "The Mysterians are within a parsec of the Donut, Your Majesty." He brought the overhead star map on line, as the Hive and bee-drones charged toward the single bright blip on the screen.

Harlowe saw the opportunity and ordered, "Set a course for the next outpost, Mr. Platter. Let's put some distance between us and our pals."

"Aye, Captain."

Simon caught a few leftovers at the side windows. "Looks like a few bees got left behind, Skipper."

In front of the Donut opening, three small bee drones moved into position, blocking the exit.

"You know what to do, Mr. Bolt," Harlowe said.

Giddy at finally being able to retaliate, Simon recharged his weapons array. "Aye, Skipper."

There were times Harlowe thought Simon was a little too trigger-happy. Idle hands are the devil's tools, he remembered reading somewhere. He made a mental note to find Simon more responsibility during his down time... when he wasn't blowing up the universe.

Before Prigg nagged him about wasting precious fuel again, Harlowe, adding a little caution of his own said, "Make each shot count, Mr. Bolt," which got an approving third eye from Prigg.

"Aye, Skipper."

Three short bursts later, Simon gave a happy thumbs up. "Three shots, three kills, Skipper."

Harlowe nodded his appreciation. "Nice shooting, Mr. Bolt."

Now that the way was clear, *Millawanda* could exit the Donut without a hitch.

"Course, Captain?" Monday asked.

Riverstone interrupted Harlowe's reply. "Hold on, Mr. Platter, if you please."

Harlowe wondered what was important enough to hold up his orders.

Riverstone held up one of the memory crystals he found in the Donut outpost. "This, Captain." He placed it inside the console slot, and instantly glyphs appeared on the overhead screen. "I didn't recognize the writing at first. It's been a while since we've seen these glyphs." Harlowe's face perked up, recognizing the symbols. Riverstone continued: "It's the same writing we saw when we first found Millie. It's Gamadin."

Harlowe called to the screen. "Translate the writing for us, Millie, if you please."

Because *Millawanda* wasn't her usual self, it took way longer than normal before anything appeared on the screen. What they saw was not a complete rendition. There were several missing parts to the document.

With a hand gesture, Harlowe ordered Monday to take *Millawanda* out of the Donut. He wanted maneuvering room in case the Hive returned. As they blasted through the exit hole, Harlowe twirled a hurry-up finger toward Riverstone. "Give us the short version, Mr. Riverstone."

"We got lucky, Captain. It's a history of the Donut city," Riverstone said proudly. "It tells of a rich and prosperous space port called Gal...," He stopped and made adjustments but couldn't decipher the name. "Sorry, Captain."

"Continue, Mr. Riverstone. We'll work on it later," Harlowe said.

"Well, it was built by a race of beings called the Illearsi. It looks like their own star went nova some time ago, but long before it exploded, they built the Donut to house their population."

"Does it say why they ended up in the middle of nowhere?" Harlowe enquired.

Riverstone let out a small chuckle. "The short version is they ran out of gas."

Harlowe couldn't believe it. "They what?"

"The inner circle is what's left of their star drive. Can you believe it?"

Harlowe twirled his index finger to hurry it along. He didn't much care about their star drive. Riverstone went on: "They miscalculated their fuel consumption and found themselves stuck here."

Jewels clickity-clacked from Harlowe's quarters and handed him a tall cup. Harlowe winced with distaste, finding the vanilla shake at room temperature. "So how did they survive without power?" he asked, giving the shake back to Jewels without taking a sip.

Riverstone connected with every eye on the bridge before he replied, "The Gamadin."

"The Gamadin?" Simon blurted out. The thought of the Gamadin rescuing the Donut people never occurred to anyone.

Harlowe's eyes brightened. "We saved the day, huh?"

Riverstone had a few more surprises. "It gets better. Guess where their final destination was?"

"Og?" Simon replied, thinking the worst possible place he could think of that still had a breathable atmosphere.

"No, toadhead. Earth!"

Simon's mouth dropped in his lap. "You're joking?"

"No, I found an image of the planet they were headed for. Check it out."

The image on the screen was a watery blue world with white fluffy clouds and a single bright moon. The planet's land masses, however, seemed off, and there were great sheets of ice covering the northern and southern hemispheres.

"That's not the Earth I know," Harlowe said, pointing out the problem areas he saw.

"It's Earth, alright, during one of its ice ages. From what it looks like, they sent an advance research team there, but they never came back. It was a one-way trip for them. They were supposed to set up house and wait until the rest of their people showed up in the Donut," Riverstone explained.

Monday's brain kicked in at the thought. "You mean we could be descendants of these guys?"

"Ain't that a kick?" Simon said.

"Small galaxy," Harlowe observed. Without taking his eyes off the overhead, he reached behind, and Jewels placed a bottle of Bluestuff in his hand. After a quick slurp, Harlowe motioned for Riverstone to go on with his narrative.

"They made a deal with the Gamadin. The Gamadin needed a way station in the middle of the Thaat, and the Illeari needed protection. It was an opportunity for them both. They would set up house here, and the Gamadin would get their outpost in the Thaat. Once they established themselves, they were able to carry on like before. The Illeari were great traders and entertainers. A place the history speaks of often is a place called...?"

Harlowe answered without hesitation. "Gibb."

Riverstone eyebrows rose in surprise. "Very good, Captain."

Harlowe took a second sip. "Finish it, Mr. Riverstone. We've got beasties out there that don't care about the Donut that time forgot. So get on with it."

Riverstone blinked. "Aye, Captain. As I was saying, the Donut became a way station in a sea of nothing for interstellar travelers going to the Omni Quadrant. The Donut was the Las Vegas of the Thaat for thousands of years. Mr. Prigg found these images as I was reading." Everyone was stunned. The city pictured on the overhead was like nothing they just left. This Donut city was full of bright lights, amusement parks, space docks, tall buildings, and transports scurrying everywhere throughout the torus.

Harlowe found the knowledge fascinating, but how did it help them now? "So what happened to everyone? Does it say why the Donut people left town in a hurry?"

"It does," Riverstone confirmed. "It wasn't that long ago, either. Ten centuries perhaps, according to Mr. Prigg's calculations."

"The Gamadin were already gone by then," Harlowe pointed out.

"That's right. Long before that. By then the Illeari had their own defenses, but nothing like the Gamadin. Their station was all that was left. When the Gamadin departed, the building faded away. The people thought it was an omen, and the day the Gamadin returned, the outpost would return with the Gamadin."

Riverstone and Harlowe traded sober glances. "I guess it did," Riverstone said.

"Yeah, it came back if only briefly," Harlowe said.

"Then what?" Simon asked, eager to hear more about the high-rolling city.

"The Zabits found them," Riverstone replied.

"Zabits? The dorky little gnats Rerun blasted?" Harlowe described.

"It was bad, Captain. The Illeari were wiped out. Power in the Thaat is like water in a desert. The Zabits found the Donut and sucked it dry. They killed everyone, and that's why they were after us. They detected Millie, and if we hadn't cloaked, her we might have ended up like the Illeari, too."

Harlowe leaned forward in his chair. "This is why we haven't gone to hyperlight yet?"

Riverstone held up the little crystalline piece Monday found in the trash. "This is a letter to a Gamadin officer from his girlfriend." Before Harlowe gave him one of those why-are-you-wasting-our-time looks, he said quickly. "It's important, Captain."

"Read it, then," Harlowe directed.

Riverstone displayed the letter on the overhead screen as he read the short letter. "It's from a girl named Darce who wrote a letter to a Gamadin soldier named Mannisca.

> *My Mannisca, my brave and wonderful Mannisca. Know I will always cherish our warm walks together under the moons of Lamille. Today they are as blue as the aara you gave me. I envy your call, brave soldier of the heavens. My soul is with you out there, somewhere protecting us. I know not where our future lies. Who does, Mannisca? But I know yours lies with the stars. That is unavoidable. For your duty belongs to a greater calling. So farewell, Mannisca. I will miss hearing your voice and having your arms around me as the water speaks to us. There is no greater mission than yours, my Gamadin. Farewell, my Mannisca, my brave soldier of the stars. I will always love you.*
>
> *Darce*

Riverstone went on in his own words. "She's heartbroken that Mannisca hasn't returned to her and that she must go on with her life. She misses the warm summer nights they shared on Lamille."

"Maybe he had a babe in every port," Simon figured.

"Maybe she was his wife," Monday added.

Harlowe's face saddened. The banter between his two crewmen suddenly hit home. Darce's letter to Mannisca was as if she were writing to him. Only it wasn't Darce he was thinking of, it was Leucadia. By now, she was hundreds of lightyears away on a planet he may never return to again. He took a deep breath, fighting off the urge to cry like a baby. Leaving her and Wiz behind crushed his heart like Rex had just stomped on it with his three-ton claw. At the moment, he was no brave soldier of the stars. He was a helpless, pathetic toad for leaving her and his pard behind.

Harlowe had to swallow the knot in his throat before he could say, "The Gamadin didn't have wives."

"How do you know that?" Riverstone asked.

Harlowe glared at Riverstone. "It's obvious, isn't it? Zipping around the galaxy and putting out fires is no place for girlfriends, wives, or lovers."

Riverstone saw the look in Harlowe's eyes. He knew the pain. He had seen it when he lost Lu the first time. Then Quay came into his life and he lost her, too. Lu returned, but only for a short while. So many heartbreaks, and no time to heal. He had been there himself with Ela. He buried her on that unknown planet. Prigg left his wife and kids behind on Earth. And now, Simon saying goodbye to Sizzle on Gazz. Everyone except Monday had their heartbreaks, their Ocea in some form or another. That was their lot in life. The monkey on their back. The jealous mistress who would never allow another being before Her.

"I'm sorry, pard," Riverstone said to Harlowe.

Harlowe knew what he meant. They all did. He wrinkled his nose, fighting the sting. There was nothing else to say. It was just a fact. A Gamadin would never have but one family, and he was looking at them all right now.

Harlowe turned to Prigg and asked, "What do we have on Lamille, Mr. Prigg?"

Prigg checked the database of star systems and inhabitable planets. "The name is not listed, Your Majesty."

"Maybe it's not a planet," Riverstone speculated. "Who would say: I miss the warm summer nights on Earth, babe? Or I miss holding your body on the warm sand at 42nd Street?"

Simon rolled his eyes. "Yeah, right. How romantic."

"Whatever," Riverstone scoffed. "The point is Lamille is not a planet but a location on one. Millie should know where this place is."

Harlowe thought Riverstone had something. He went to Prigg and directed him to recheck the database for anything on Lamille in the hopes the name was still in *Millawanda's* memory.

Prigg recheck the database. "No listing, Your Majesty."

Harlowe pointed at the screen. "Mr. Prigg, you once found a planet by the language they spoke. Try that."

Prigg plugged in the info and read Millie's interpretation. "Osset is the only planet listed, Your Majesty."

Harlowe only wanted to know one thing: "Can we make it?"

"Osset is not the next outpost on the list, Your Majesty," Prigg said.

"I don't care. Can we make it?"

Prigg made the calculations. His results had to be dead on. Even a small error would cost them big time. If they dropped out of hyperdrive too soon or went beyond their intended target, they might find themselves a full lightyear from any habitable planet. That didn't seem like much in the hundreds of lightyears they had already traveled, but for a ship drifting in space without fuel, it was forever. If they were lucky, they might make contact with another inhabitable planet in the next 10,000 years!

"It is too risky, Your Majesty," Prigg stated, after putting his calculations on the overhead for everyone to see.

Riverstone had his own take. "We'll be way past "E" if we make it there at all, Captain."

Harlowe studied the results like everyone else and then made a command decision that brought wide-eyes to everyone. "Change of plan. We're skipping the next station."

After a long silence, Simon spoke out loud of the elephant in the room. "You mean we're risking everything on a Dear John letter?"

Harlowe twisted around to his weapons officer with a forced smile. "Ain't love grand, Mr. Bolt?"

"Captain," Monday said with alarm. "Sorry to interrupt, but the swarm has returned."

Monday was right. The swarm had broken off their pursuit of the Mysterians and was changing course back to the Donut.

"Do we have a course for Osset, Mr. Platter?" Harlowe asked.

"Aye, Captain."

"Pedal to the metal, then. Before the neighborhood goes south."

42

Down with the Authority

Rhud's muffled growl awakened Ian in the early morning. He had spent the night stretched out on the front seats of *The Ride*. When he sat up, it was still dark under the trees, but on the eastern horizon the pink light of dawn and the fluffy yellow clouds were showing above the low-lying hills. The Nodian star wasn't far behind.

Still, something wasn't quite right. The gurgling river still flowed tranquilly along the banks, but the cheery sounds of life that usually greeted the dawn were silent. Another growl brought his attention back to the river, where Rhud was standing with Leucadia at the water's edge. She held the big cat like she was hugging him goodbye. She spoke to him for several moments as his bright blue eyes stared keenly across the river. Ian found that odd. If there were a problem, why would he be so focused on the other side of the river? Trouble, it would come from the road, not on the river, he thought.

After one last squeeze, Leucadia let the big cat go. Rhud splashed across the water in two great bounds before he disappeared through the dense thicket on the far side of the river.

Ian quickly climbed out of the cab and met Leucadia returning to the campsite. With wet, swollen eyes she said, "Rhud had to leave us."

"Why?" Ian wondered.

She wiped her face with the back of her hand. "The Numeri…"

Ian was confused.

"Muuk's forces have found us, Ian."

195

Ian activated his SIBA bugeyes. His sensors indicated hundreds of beings had surrounded them and were approaching their encampment through the trees. There was little doubt it was the Numeri military.

"I couldn't let them take Rhud, too," she explained tearfully.

Ian agreed. "Yeah, he might even find Molly before we do." He lowered his bugeyes again and asked her, "Do we fight? We could take them, you know."

Leucadia put her arms around Ian and spoke softly to him. "You are so brave, Ian. But we cannot engage the soldiers." She pulled back and looked down at Maa Dev, Cheesa, and Tweto sleeping peacefully around the smoldering coals of the campfire. They were all wrapped in thin, Gamadin blankets to keep them warm during the night. "We are not warriors like Harlowe or Matthew. Can we guarantee their safety against so many? If the Prince dies, then what of the kingdom? Will they ever find freedom without him?"

As much as he wanted to resist, Leucadia was right. Their personal forcefields and weapons could protect them from any force on the planet but not the other Nodians with them.

"If we surrender, they'll kill them anyway," Ian said glumly.

She laid her hand on *The Ride*. "We have something to bargain with."

"*The Ride?*"

"What price do you think they'll put on a vehicle that is immune to the twynich?"

Ian saw her point. "A lot."

"We should make ourselves ready, then. The soldiers are almost upon us," Leucadia said.

* * *

Ian raised his hands as the soldiers emerged from the trees. "We will come with you peacefully—"

"No!" Tweto cried out. The young rebel would have committed suicide if Ian hadn't grabbed him by the back of his shirt and pressed him to the ground before the soldiers shot him. Tweto had no intention of surrendering to anyone. His arms and legs fought to break free of Ian's much more powerful grip. "Let me up, Ian. I will kill them all! Down with the Authority! Down with the Royals! Down with all who want to suppress us! Down with—"

Ian thought that Tweto had said enough and lowered the boom, knocking him into Never, Never Land before he could blurt out another treasonous outcry.

Cheesa went to Tweto's side believing Ian might have killed him.

"He's okay, Cheesa," Ian assured her. She looked up at him tearfully, knowing he had done the right thing.

The soldiers were dressed in camouflaged, sock hats with dark painted faces. The intent in their eyes was to take no prisoners. The officer pointed his weapon at the Prince first.

Leucadia stepped in front of his line of fire. "No. If you harm the Prince or anyone else, your Imperator will not know you destroyed the vehicle that moves during the darkness," she told them, pointing at *The Ride*.

The lead soldier quickly changed the subject. "The tigre? Where is she?" he demanded.

"She?" Leucadia said, glancing quickly at Ian.

"Yes, where is the Imperator's tigre?"

"I assure you we have no tigre with us," Leucadia said.

The soldier pointed at the ground. "The tracks. They tell a different story."

The officer moved to put a bullet in Tweto's head when Leucadia boldly challenged him. "If you try to harm anyone, you will never find your tigre. We can work this out if—"

"No arrangements," the officer spat. "Where are your weapons?"

"We have no weapons," Ian replied.

The officer scoffed and pointed at *The Ride*. "Search the transport."

Ian backed away and allowed the soldiers to make their search. They found nothing.

"Where did you hide your weapons?" the officer demanded.

"I told you. We have no weapons or tigres," Ian repeated in their language.

A soldier came up from behind and tried to hit Ian with the butt of his rifle. Ian grabbed the weapon and brought the soldier in front of him as a shield. As hard as he tried to break way from Ian's grip, he remained frozen in place. "We want to come peacefully," Ian said.

The officer shot the soldier in Ian's hands. "Your weapons, alien," the officer demanded.

Leucadia's dropped her hood, revealing her eyes and hair to the soldiers. The officer knew instantly he had found another prize for his Imperator.

Her eyes were green like the sky and appeared to glow like a *virdis* flower. He backed away in awe, staring at her long yellow hair as it glistened softly in the morning light.

"What are you?" the soldier asked.

Leucadia saw his dismay. "A woman."

"But you are not from Nod," he stated.

Leucadia glanced at *The Ride*. "We travel from beyond the twynich."

"Nothing escapes the twynich!" another soldier scoffed.

Leucadia stared at the officer coldly. "We did."

The officer studied the vehicle. It was massive. The large tank was rusty and old, but the bright copper and brass pipes were polished, as were the valves, levers, and wheels. He stepped over to the side of the main boiler tank and touched the holding tank. His fingers snapped back from the hot surface. "Impossible," he muttered in disbelief.

"Like we said, our transport defies the twynich," Ian said defiantly.

The soldier stewed over anything breaking the twynich. He whirled and now pointed his weapon at the Prince. Leucadia moved in the line of fire again to protect him. "Harm the Prince, and the secret dies." She held up her com. "Try anything, and I will blow up the vehicle and you and all your soldiers with this device."

"You are bluffing," the officer challenged.

Leucadia stood her ground. "Is it worth such a risk when we have offered to come with you peacefully?"

The soldier tried to gun butt Leucadia across the face. She grabbed the stock and had him in a neck lock so fast the others had no way to stop her. Pointing the weapon at the officer's head, she said, "Peace or death? The choice is yours."

"You are the one who is dead, alien," the officer gasped.

"Alien? We are not aliens, sir," Ian said defensively.

"You are not Dolminian," another soldier said.

"I said we are from the land beyond the darkness," Leucadia said.

The officer tried to laugh. "Twynich is over," he gasped.

"They'll be another one in five days." Ian said. "If our ride fails, you can kill us then."

Leucadia held up the com. "Deal?"

The soldier accepted the offer.

43

Junk Yard

It was mid-day, dark and overcast, with spitting rain hitting the forward windshield as *The Ride* steamed through the two foot-thick, grey metal gates of the Imperator's vast, fortified military base along the coast. From the size and number of living quarters, Leucadia estimated the troop strength at well over a hundred thousand strong. A hundred-foot-high, reinforced steel wall enclosed the installation and stretched for miles, all the way to the sea. When the gates shut behind *The Ride*, it felt like they were enclosed inside a vault. Neither Ian nor Leucadia had anticipated such an immense stronghold. In the back seat, Cheesa and Tweto were awake, sitting up, and manacled. Their vacant stares told of their fate. For them all was lost. Maa Dev was no different. He laid still on the floor with his head covered, his hands and feet in chains. It appeared all hope had been drained from their bodies. Ian, too, had his doubts. If he weren't needed to operate *The Ride*, he would have been chained like the others. Ian was sick with self-blame that the Nodians he had tried to save were now hopelessly caught in an inescapable trap. He reached over and took Leucadia's hand. She was the only one of their group allowed to go unshackled. As they drove along, he marveled at the lines of jet aircraft, tanks, field artillery, troop transports, and curious gas-filled propeller-driven airships swaying in the wind as they floated off the ground anchored to their moorings. Beneath their grey dirigible air sacs, wicked muzzles stuck out of the many gun ports on all sides of their gondolas. The Numeri had built an armada that could only be for one purpose: Offensive power!

Their escort of a thousand Numeri troops motored on for several more miles, steering clear of the main structures of the base, no doubt for security reasons. After Leucadia's threat to blow up *The Ride*, the "powers that be" were taking no chances. The convoy finally came to a stop near the ocean in front of an immense hangar where piles of aircraft junk lay rusted and broken from the salty mist. Not long after their arrival, another motorcade of several more military transports rolled to a stop in front of *The Ride*. The entire brigade of fifteen hundred troops suddenly snapped their boots together as a lone officer in a simple grey uniform emerged from the center vehicle. "Imperator Muuk, we salute you!" the soldiers shouted as their hands slapped at their sides with a loud clap.

Ian and Leucadia climbed down from *The Ride* and waited for the Imperator. Their wait was short. The Imperator had no real interest in the officer who made the capture. After making a small gesture of accomplishment toward the officer, his focus went immediately to Leucadia the instant he saw her blond hair blowing wistfully in the ocean breeze.

* * *

Muuk was speechless. The alien mullie was taller than he was by two heads and physically strong. "Astonishing," Imperator Muuk said, catching his breath to speak. "Such a wonderful specimen. She is like my Beleza," he uttered to himself. He slowly stepped around the alien, continuing to study her striking beauty. Even in the ocean air, she smelled fresh and clean as a royal garden. But her eyes. They were bright and jewel-like under the darkest clouds. He glanced at the alien mare next. His height and stature were even taller than the mullie. A legion of soldiers like him would be invincible. And like the mullie, his alien eyes were different. They were not pink but blue. Nowhere on Nod had he seen such a color. "You are so young," he said to them both. "From the reports, I was expecting beings much older."

The alien mare spoke first. "Believe me, I've aged a lot in the last year," he said in perfect DOmnian.

The Imperator was taken aback. "You know our language?"

"A little."

"No, no. You speak clearly. How long have you been on Nod?"

The alien mare shrugged. "Too long."

The Imperator was indeed impressed. "A translating device perhaps?"

"Perhaps," the mullie answered.

"With soldiers like you I could conqueror Nod," Muuk boasted with an evil tone in his voice. He then asked the mullie, "Do you have a name?"

"Leucadia."

And to the mare he asked the same question. "Dude," was Ian's answer.

A soldier handed the Imperator the alien's pack and showed him the contents. "This was found with their possessions, Imperator." He examined them briefly. He found them quite intriguing. "What are these items?"

Dude looked inside the bag. "Some junk I found on a farm."

"I think not. The craftsmanship is not Nodian, and you would not have made the effort to carry them if they did not have value to you."

"I like junk."

As Muuk spoke to Dude, his sight never left Leucadia for long. "I understand you are an excellent marksman, Dude."

Dude held out his hand. "Give me your pistol, and I'll show you."

Muuk smiled as he removed a cylinder from the pack. "What is this?" the Imperator asked.

"A nut cracker," Dude replied.

The Imperator didn't get the joke. He handed the alien's items to a subordinate and ordered, "Give these to Loomis for examination."

The Imperator turned his attention next to the alien vehicle. He circled it once, eyeing everything, missing nothing. "It runs on steam. How charming. You made this?" he asked Dude.

Dude crossed his arms in front of him and nodded. "I did."

"By yourself?"

Ian nodded at the sack. "Me and the clickers."

"Who are clickers?"

"My friends who helped me?"

The Imperator addressed the officer who brought the aliens in. "Were there any more beings?"

The office saluted and replied, "No, Imperator. There were only the four."

Muuk began to understand that Dude's answers were less than truthful. He tried to touch one of the alien machine's brightly polished copper pipes, but Dude grabbed his hand. The instant he did, twenty rifles pointed at his head.

"It's hot, sir. The pipes will burn you," Dude warned, defending his actions. He reached into a nearby bucket of water hanging from the side of the vehicle and flung wet drops at the bright yellow pipes. The water droplets crackled to hot steam the instant they struck the pipes.

Muuk had his guards stand down as he thanked Dude for his caution. "What is your combustion source?"

Dude winked with a grin. "An old family secret."

Muuk smiled back. He understood the humor this time. "And it moves during the twynich?"

"No problem."

It was Muuk's turn at humor this time. As he had been all along, he spoke with an arrogant confidence of someone knowing he had all the power in the world at his disposal. "My officers are very good at persuasion."

"I'm sure they are," Leucadia said, joining the conversation.

"You don't fear that?" Muuk asked, then answered his own question. "No, of course not." He took a moment to look around. "You don't feel threatened at all. Why is that?"

Leucadia turned to the alien vehicle. "Because we have something you desire."

"And what would that be?" Muuk asked.

"The ability to transport your armies during the darkness," Leucadia replied as if the answer was obvious.

"I can transport them now."

"In a limited way, Imperator. Without animals to pull your transports, the main body of your army remains immobile, and your ships cannot leave their moorings." She pointed to the fleet of ships tied to their docks in the distance."

"Very perceptive," Muuk admitted. "How do you know such things?"

"I observe, Imperator," Leucadia replied.

"Walk with me, Leucadia," Muuk directed. "Why do you want to help me?"

"To gain our freedom," was Leucadia's simple answer.

"And you believe what you have to offer is worth such a price?"

Leucadia stopped and faced Muuk. "Is it worth the conquest of Nod, Imperator?"

"And what of the Prince?"

"He lives."

Muuk found that impossible, and spoke casually on the matter as if it were a mere formality that he must die. "With him ends the Royal lineage forever."

Leucadia had another suggestion. "If the Prince becomes king, it will allow you to rule Nod uncontested. Let the people believe you have discovered the killers of the Royal Family, and you are protecting the Prince, the last heir to the throne. The people need a figurehead, Imperator. They understand tradition. They want security. Give them the security of their monarch, and you will have the masses behind your quest for global domination."

Muuk thought briefly, appearing to seriously consider Leucadia's scheme, when he ignored it altogether and slowly turned toward her with cold pink eyes and asked, "Where is my tigre, Leucadia? Where is my Beleza?"

* * *

Neither Leucadia nor Ian understood the importance of Molly and Rhud to the Imperator until now. Did conquering Nod or their twynich-defying vehicle have no value to him? Above all else this despot wanted the answer to this question. Until now, she assumed the Prince, *The Ride*, and knowledge of aliens from another world were the main focus of the Numeri hunt. Now the game had suddenly changed. The Prince may have been at the heart of the Imperator's scheme in the beginning, and obviously he was still important but not the total focus of the Imperator's resources. The heir to the Royal throne was now merely a secondary objective. Molly had become his sole mission in life. She was his quest. From his line of questioning and from the officer who captured them, Molly was the only tigre he knew about. He had no knowledge of the second tigre. Unless the Imperator was given the answer he was looking for, Leucadia saw Death in his eyes, and there was no negotiation.

"We set her free," Leucadia replied.

The Imperator's facial muscles went rigid. "You know where she is." It was not a question but a direct statement of fact.

Leucadia hesitated. In that short time, no more than a second, Muuk pulled his sidearm from his holster and shot Tweto through the heart.

"You *know* where she is!" he repeated. The Imperator was not about to stop with Tweto. He cocked his sidearm again and pointed it at Cheesa.

Still handcuffed, Ian tried hobbling to Tweto's aide but was held back by a horde of Numeri soldiers who began hitting him with the butts of their rifles.

"NO!" Leucadia cried out. "Don't shoot her. I will help you find the tigre."

44

The Arena

Ian, the Prince, and Cheesa were thrown into a wide-open, circular enclosure, and a vault door shut behind them. The arena was roomy but inescapable. The walls were three stories high and smooth as glass. The dome-shaped roof over the arena sealed anyone inside like a giant cell. Even if he could scale the wall, making it to the center skylight was impossible for him with his hands shackled behind his back. He rolled in the dirt over to the wall and sat up with his back it. Maa Dev followed Ian's example but found a mouthful of dirt for his effort. Cheesa remained still. The shock over Tweto's death was still raw. She didn't seem to care what happened to her next.

The Prince spat out a mouthful of gritty sand, wrinkling his nose at the odor of blood and animal waste. "Why didn't we fight, Ian?" His tone accusing, blaming Ian for their predicament.

Ian didn't like the guilt trip. "Maybe we should have left you back in the forest."

"Maybe you should have. I would not be eating animal waste there."

"No, you would be dead."

"We are trapped like animals."

Ian ignored the statement with a grunt. This was no time to play the blame game when there was much work to be done. He continued his scan. Besides the vault door they entered, there were only two other hatchways around the perimeter.

"What is this place?" Dev wondered aloud.

"A place for the slaughter of animals," Ian replied, confident of his answer.

"How do you know that?"

Ian nodded toward the dirt floor. "The footprints, the bones, and the stink I've smelled before on a planet far from here. I know Death when I see it, Dev."

Dev stared at one paw print that was at least a foot across and swallowed hard as Cheesa finally spoke. "That's why we're here, Prince. We are meat for the Imperator's beasts."

"No. I'm the Prince. I am not meat."

Cheesa turned away. "You are a naive aristocrat, and soon you will be a dead one, like us all."

Dev turned to Ian. "Is she right, Ian?"

"Yeah, Dev, we're dinner if we don't find a way out of here." Ian pointed to the dirt. "Look at the claws. Those are predator paw prints."

"How long do we have?"

"Until Leucadia returns."

"Will she do that?"

Ian shrugged. He didn't really know. "Maybe, maybe not. The cats will only be found if they want to be found."

"If they are unwilling to be located, then what?"

Ian kept looking over the compound as he spoke. "We're Happy Meals."

"I find that answer wanting, Ian."

"You know what I know, Dev. This Imperator will keep us alive until he has what he wants; then he will dispose of us."

Using it for support, Ian scooted up the side of the wall and stood upright. He stepped over to Cheesa and looked at her face. She had big welts along the side of her face. One eye was swollen shut. "How are you doing?" he asked her.

"It doesn't matter," she replied with a caustic edge.

He couldn't blame her. Better to have died with dignity, he thought, than to be eaten.

He left her alone with her hate. There was nothing he could say or do that would change it, so he made himself useful. He walked around the perimeter and carefully examined each doorway, rapping on each one, testing their makeup. They were all made of the same heavy, vault-like materials as the main door. Completing his inspection, he returned to the Prince and Cheesa.

"What now, Ian?" Dev asked.

Ian sat against the wall. "We rest."

The Prince thought that unproductive. They should be doing more to escape. After all, his life was on the line. "Rest?"

Ian kinked his head up at the skylight. It appeared to have been recently repaired. Heavy crossbars were welded over the window from the inside. Looking below it, he saw the glint of broken glass in the dirt.

"Just chill, Dev, and let me think," Ian explained with an even tone.

"Are you going to get us out of here, Ian?" Cheesa asked.

"I'm working on it."

"How?" the Prince asked.

"I'm not sure yet."

"By resting?" Dev asked.

"We rest now because we won't have the option later," Ian explained.

"How can we rest when we are about to be eaten?"

Ian thought about the Prince's question. Right now they were safe. He figured as long as the Imperator was away, they would all be kept alive because he would want the gratification of slaying the last heir to the throne himself.

Focusing on Loomis looking through one of the vault doors, he needed a diversion to take his mind from the Prince while he thought of a plan.

Ian strode straight to the window and said forcefully, "Where is the tigre, Loomis?"

Loomis grinned with a caustic smirk. "The Imperator will find her."

Ian smiled back. "Did you know she was pregnant?"

Loomis quickly lost his malicious smirk.

45

The Search

Imperator Muuk's flagship was impressive by any military standard. It was the largest, most heavily armed dirigible in the fleet. It was as long as an Earth-type nuclear aircraft carrier, with seventy-three gun ports on two levels below the bridge. Each level consisted of twelve cannons, twenty-four total on each side. There were three more cannons, and three small caliber machine guns aft and six cannons and two large caliber machine guns forward. Its electronic sensor and optical arrays were state of the art. Bright CRT screens, large 3D overhead terrain maps, sweeping radar displays, ground and air infrared sensors, communication stations, and transparent plotting boards lit up the bridge's command center. Besides the Imperator's plush, aft cabin, there was a galley. Above deck, there were sleeping quarters for a hundred Numeri soldiers who ran the ongoing operations of the ship. Below decks were accommodations for a thousand soldiers. The airship could stay aloft for weeks without refueling, even during the darkness. Not that the Imperator's flagship's systems were immune to twynich, they weren't. But its ten propellers and hydraulic steerage could fly at reduced speed for two days on compressed air, if necessary. Escorting the giant dirigible were thirty smaller versions of the flagship. They carried another two hundred troops each along with all their supplies and transport vehicles.

As she was led up the ramp of the flagship in chains, Leucadia wondered why the Imperator had suddenly lost his cool. Something had turned him frantic in his search for the tigre. At first she thought Muuk had discovered there were two white tigers, not one. But the way he kept calling Molly his Beleza lead her to believe Muuk had no idea there was a second white running around Nod. Somehow, Molly had escaped, she figured, but he had already known that before their capture. No, it was something even more profound that was bothering the Imperator. Something that was beyond losing his Beleza, and it had occurred only moments ago. If it wasn't Rhud, then what could it be? What was so important that Muuk was taking no chances by leading this mission himself?

Leucadia could not even speculate. But as she thought through their chances of survival, she was clear about one thing. Whether they found Molly or not, Muuk had no intention of keeping them alive for long. The Prince would go first. The moment Muuk returned, his attention would be focused on Dev, and he would be executed immediately, thus erasing the Royal Line from Dolmina forever. Cheesa meant nothing to Muuk, other than the fact that he knew the girl meant something to the aliens. Unlike Tweto, if she kept her head, she might survive for a while longer. Ian was important because he knew the secret to the vehicle that defied the darkness. But once Muuk had what he wanted, his Beleza back, even she was doomed. Muuk cared only about two things: his Beleza and absolute power over Dolmina, in the that order.

By the end of the first day of the hunt there was still no trace of Molly. The last paw prints were found along the riverbank where the soldiers had captured the aliens. But that was all they found. There were no more signs of either cat after that. It was as if both Molly and Rhud had vanished from the planet completely.

The longer Muuk stood in front of his giant screen, the more he became visibly agitated. The number of negative reports had finally snapped his coolness and sent him into a rage. He thundered his way to the rear of the bridge where Leucadia prepared for his assault. "Where is she?" Muuk demanded. "Where is my Beleza?" he shouted in her face, spitting hate at her for defying him.

She was right. Muuk had no clue of Rhud. "I am as surprised as you, Imperator."

Muuk leaned heavily into her face. "You know where she is; I want her."

Leucadia played innocent. "The female is not in your possession?"

Muuk's jaws went ridged as his face transformed into a venomous embarrassment. He snapped at her. "She escaped!"

Leucadia remained motionless. *Nice one, girl. Muuk fooled you once, but he couldn't keep you, could he, girl?* She wanted to burst out laughing but kept her cool. Muuk was self-destructing without her help. "When?" she asked.

Muuk couldn't look her in the eye. He was too humiliated at his failure to keep her. "Three days ago during the darkness," he replied. "But then you knew that."

"How would I know? It was twynich."

"Like your vehicle. You defied the darkness."

"I defied nothing. We were looking for her ourselves. I was hundreds of miles from your base at the time. You know that."

"Beleza is my property," Muuk said to her.

"She is no one's property, Imperator. She is a wild animal. Neither you nor I have any more control over her than we do the stars. Her capture was pure chance. She will not let that happen again."

"I will find her," Muuk said confidently, "or no one will have her."

"You would kill such beautiful animal? Are you mad?"

Muuk struck her with the back of his hand. "I want my Beleza! Where is she?"

Leucadia went down hard. The way she collapsed, it was obvious she was unconscious. A communications officer handed Muuk a radio dispatch and reported, "Two tigres have been spotted, Imperator."

Muuk stared at the officer in shock. "Two?"

The officer glanced at the communiqué to verify the dispatch. "Yes, Imperator. Two white tigres were reported entering the Haga by several sources, Sire."

Muuk looked down at the still mullie. He didn't care if she was dead. He strode back to the bridge, where his communications officer put details to the sighting.

"Where are they exactly!" Muuk cried out.

The officer went to the lighted map in the center of his station. He pointed to the sighting far north of their present position. "The tigres have skirted the Haga, Imperator. They are continuing on a northerly path. Soon they will enter this valley which leads directly to the black land, Sire."

Muuk knew the region. It was called Du Tir. It was where the twynich never ended. Over the years he had never ventured into the black land itself. Those who did never returned. On the few occasions he hunted along the ridge line of the Du Tir, he recalled seeing a single, cone-shaped mountain in the distance. It seemed harmless enough. The mountain was small compared to the mountains between the Haga and the Du Tir. Using telescopic glasses, he had studied the mountain that rose from the plain of tall grass and sparse trees from a safe distance. Strange animals roamed there. Some ate beings that ventured too close to it. He had seen their tracks going and coming from black land, seemingly at will. Migrating fowl, however, stayed clear. Twice he tried leading an expedition into the Du Tir to fully explore its boundaries of the perpetual darkness. He was convinced that if he found the source of the twynich he could rule Nod with impunity. But each expedition met with failure. Within a day of entering the Du Tir, the death toll on his soldiers was too great, and he was forced to abandoned his expedition. To this day, the Du Tir remained unexplored. His thoughts turned worrisome. If the tigres passed through the Du Tir boundary before he could capture them, they were lost to him.

Muuk pointed to the top of the map where he believed the tigres were vulnerable. "By skirting the Haga, this narrow pass through the valley is the only way open to them," Muuk told his officers standing behind him. "Flank speed, Commander. We must arrive ahead of them to set our traps before they enter the pass."

"There is a powerful storm approaching from the east, Imperator. I highly advise the fleet take refuge here," he pointed on the map, "at the base of the Haga and allow the storm to pass."

"No, flank speed as ordered, Commander."

"The 5th corps is only a hundred *pasies* from that position. I can have them there before our arrival, Imperator. That will allow time for the storm to pass, Sire," the Commander explained.

Muuk wanted desperately to be in on the capture, but his air fleet was still too far from the pass, and the tigres were traveling at incredible speed. To make matters worse, the airships couldn't fly in bad weather. If they were to capture the tigres at all, they had to do it before the storm entered the valley. Still, Muuk marveled at the distance the tigres had already traveled. It would take his flagship a day of flying at flank speed just to get there. Grudgingly, he relented and gave the order to deploy the 5th Corps to the valley.

Feeling that he had regained control of the situation, he returned to the aft section of the bridge to check on the condition of his mullie prisoner. He had something to boast about now, regaining his lost face.

Returning aft, Muuk found the area unusually dark. The bulkhead lights were out. Even in the muted light, he quickly saw his two guards lying flat on the deck, still as corpses. Beside them lay the mullie's chains.

She was gone.

46

Captain Starr

"Osset, Your Majesty," Prigg announced as *Millawanda* eased into a stationary orbit 1200 miles above the planet's surface. It could have been Earth, Harlowe thought, as he looked down upon the thick atmosphere of swirling weather fronts, fluffy white clouds, wide swaths of thick green forests, blue-green oceans, three major continents, polar white caps, mountain ranges, deserts, lakes, long winding rivers, and wide grassy plains. Time-wise, he and his crew were still newbies at traveling around the cosmos, but the one thing that he marveled over every time they came upon new, inhabitable worlds, was the number of Earth-like planets they had seen. Planets circling their primary stars were abundant, and unlike what Farnducky's science class had taught him, Earth-like planets were common. One would find the galaxy a very populated place if they had a ship like *Millawanda* to buzz around the cosmos in.

Riverstone's head nearly dropped in his lap after learning Cartooga-Thaat was behind them. "Finally," he said exhaustively.

As predicted, their arrival had come at a cost. Prigg's calculations were dead on. *Millawanda* was running on fumes. The last thermo-grym crystals were thrown into the energy converter, and that, as they say, was all she wrote. There was nothing left in the hold. So when they burned through that, it was lights out. Riding on 'E' had taken on a whole new meaning for the Gamadin crew. 'E' now stood for the "End-of-the-Line" unless they found a new source of thermo-grym or some other substitute on this planet.

212

Otherwise, Osset was their new home . . . permanently!

Prigg's wayward eyes kept shifting around as Harlowe asked the little Naruckian, "That bad, huh?"

"We have another problem, too, Your Majesty. We have no weapons. If we run into trouble, all we have are pistols and rifles." Prigg explained.

Destroying hostile spacecraft with Gama-rifles was nothing new to Harlowe and Riverstone. They had plucked off a few Fhaal attack ships on their rookie flight away from Earth. *Millawanda* had been weaponless then, too and flying on a prayer. Her shields were toast. She had suffered black battle scars up and down her hull as a result of the many hits she had taken during the conflict. There was no way she could defend herself back then either. Riverstone came up with the only plan left to them. He snagged an old Gama-rifle from the utility room and went hunting for Daks. A fully charged Gama-rifle has incredible power, that is, if one is capable of shooting it. But both Harlowe and Riverstone were in the same sad shape as *Millawanda*. Harlowe had a broken arm and swollen face from the header he had taken against the forward console. His eyes were so puffy he could barely see past his nose. Riverstone's leg was no better than Harlowe's arm. He had to use the Gama-rifle as a crutch just to get around. To say Riverstone's shooting of the Fhaal attack ships was miraculous was an understatement. To this day Riverstone swears his marksmanship was the reason the attack ships went kaablewy. But Harlowe wasn't so sure. He had no contradictory proof since he was blind in both eyes and saw nothing. Thinking back, he did feel what he thought was the ship lurching backwards the instant Riverstone pulled the trigger. Did Millie have a hand in the destruction of the Fhaal attack ships or was it Riverstone's inconceivable aim that really saved the day?

Harlowe kept his thoughts to himself and just let sleeping dogs lie.

Riverstone turned to Harlowe and said, "Let's hope Osset's a friendly place."

As if they were being overheard, Monday declared, "We have company, Captain."

On the overhead projection screen a squad of attack fighters rose from the planet's surface and was headed their way at a fast clip.

"I bet their weapons work," Simon quipped.

"Shield status, Mr. Platter?" Harlowe asked.

"Millie can handle it, Captain," Monday replied.

"But nothing sustained, Your Majesty," Prigg added with each of his three eyes following their own tactical path over his readouts.

Harlowe acknowledged his caution. "Understood, Mr. Prigg."

"Incoming contact, Captain," Monday announced.

Harlowe gave a dubious nod to Riverstone before he gave Monday the go-ahead. "Put it on, Mr. Platter."

At first there was nothing but unintelligible language until Monday switched on the universal translators. "Stop your vessel and prepare to be boarded by the Ossetian Central Command."

Riverstone found the demand upsetting. "We just flew fifteen hundred lightyears of star desert. Whatever happened to 'Welcome, Star Traveler, can we offer you a Slurpee?'"

Harlowe looked over at Simon, who appeared bored with weapons station dark. "What would Captain Starr say, Mr. Bolt?"

Like a light switched on, Simon took his cue. It was show time. In an over-the-top theatrical posture, he stood stick-straight, chest out beside his chair with a commanding high chin as he clasped his uniform by imaginary lapels and began as if he had rehearsed this role for a life-time. "I am Captain Starr of the Federated Galactic—"

Harlowe stopped his weapons officer in mid sentence. There was no time for a lengthy audition. "Bravo, Mr. Bolt. You got the part. Have Jewels pick out something appropriate, and get back up here pronto, Captain Starr."

*   *   *

A short time later, Simon stepped onto the bridge looking like the Duke of Wellington about to lead his battalions against Napoleon at Waterloo. The dangling medals, bright brass buckles, crimson jacket, and black pants with gold trim down the sides made for a few laughs, but no one thought he should tone it down at all.

Riverstone started the compliments with, "You da dude, Captain Starr!"

Followed by, "You look incredibly handsome, Mr. Bolt," Prigg commented.

Mentally, Simon was already in his role the moment he blinked onto the bridge. Majestically, he stepped forward, eyeing his fellow Gamadin like General Gunn looking up and down their uniforms for microscopic dust particles.

Harlowe was impressed. Simon's get-up was better than he envisioned. "There is no one better for the role, Mr. Bolt. You're on," he said, marveling at his acting prowess as he rose from his command chair and added with aplomb, "The bridge is yours, Captain Starr."

In a flawless stride, and knowing each of his crewmen was behind him, Simon bowed with a slight head nod and said with a distinguished, deep voice, "Thank you, sir," and relieved Harlowe of his chair. Keeping his laughter in check, Harlowe took his place at the left of the center command chair. When all was ready, he gave Prigg the go-ahead to re-establish contact with the Osset commander.

Captain Starr wasted no time in letting the officer know he was no second-string bench warmer. "To whom am I speaking, sir?" Simon asked, looking straight at the Osset commander with well-practiced, hardened eyes.

"I am Commander Gerb. Your vessel will be boarded—" the commander tried to say before Simon cut him off at the knees.

"How dare you treat my visit to Osset like we are mere rank and file pedestrians. This is an insult! We have come to your planet on a mission of grave importance, Commander. The high council of Zadeon will hear of this insolence," Simon barked as he freely used lines from his movie scripts on the fly.

Immediately, there was a crack in Commander Gerb's tone as he viewed Simon's aggressive posture. "I apologize, sir, but we have orders—"

"Nonsense! This is the star-class Federation vessel, *Millawanda*, sir! We have risked life and limb in crossing Cartooga-Thaat on a top-secret mission for your planet and the quadrant."

"That is not possible. No vessel crosses Cartooga-Thaat and survives," Commander Gerb countered.

Before Simon found himself trying to explain how *Millawanda* could cross the star desert, Prigg interjected, "Many pardons, Captain Starr, but if the Commander would simply scan *Millawanda's* tacyhon hyperlight course, his sensors should verify our direction of travel for 10 plylubian cycles out."

Simon turned to the Commander. "Do you have such capabilities, Commander, or must we interpret them for you?"

Commander Gerb appeared apologetic at his ship's lack of sensor ability. "Our sensors can only verify to three plylubian cycles, Captain Starr."

Simon applied a pathetic frown. "Three?"

"That is all, Captain Starr."

"Pity. Still, even a rather primitive array such as yours should establish our course as coming from the Cartooga-Thaat region of the galaxy, Commander."

A moment later, a young subordinate handed the cycle verification to Commander Gerb. The expression on Gerb's face was enough for Simon to proceed without knowing the exact contents.

"The Zabits are spreading their power beyond the Thaat, and you want to play games?" Captain Starr stated forcefully.

Suddenly there was fear in Commander Gerb's eyes. Simon had definitely struck a nerve. "Zabits?"

"Yes. Zabits. And they're spreading."

"The Zabits had never crossed the Cartooga-Thaat frontier before."

"Does Osset want to take that chance?" Simon asked, and then leaned forward, "If Osset continues to treat us like grogan waste, then Osset will suffer the consequences alone. Take us to your leaders now, Commander. That is no request."

Commander Gerb snapped to attention, saluting Captain Starr. "Landing coordinates will be sent to your navigation officer immediately, sir!"

Harlowe nodded toward Prigg to shut down the communication the instant they received their landing coodinates.

* * *

Harlowe congratulated Simon on his performance. "Nice touch with the Zabits, Mr. Bolt. What movie did you pull that name from?"

"No movie, Skipper. That one's real," Simon explained. He looked at the Naruckian. "Prigg told me about them yesterday at breakfast."

"Those metallic fleas were Zabits?" Harlowe asked Prigg.

"Yes, Your Majesty. The Donut memory sticks described them in great detail. No one knows where they come from but the memory sticks recorded a nest of them coming from an unknown source inside the Thaat."

"Looks like they've branched out a little since then." Back to Simon, Harlowe said, "Good work, Mr. Bolt."

"Indeed, an Oscar worthy performance, Mr. Bolt," Monday said proudly.

Riverstone's thoughts were more down-to-earth. "You got us in the front door, Captain Starr. Let's see if they invite us to dinner."

Simon stepped out of the command chair, giving it back to Harlowe.

"What are we after, Skipper?" he asked.

"Anything that will get Millie to the next gas station, Mr. Bolt." Harlowe went to the crew with additional instructions. "Our survival here depends on us making them believe we're here to help them. If they think they're about to be invaded by a hostile force of Zabits, they'll be more willing to help us with our search. The ancients kept the Zabits away, and we're here to help them keep it that way. All we need is their help to find Lamille. The Zabits are our ticket to ride."

Harlowe went back to Prigg and asked him if he had found anything yet to put into the gas tank.

Prigg checked the surface readouts with Millie's limited sensor range. "Uranium and several minor derivates. Petroleum is plentiful but no thermo-grym as yet, Your Majesty."

Riverstone wondered jokingly. "Any blue crystals lying around?"

If Harlowe had only one wish, that would be it. Instead, he tossed up a prayer. "How about Gamadin signatures, Mr. Prigg?"

Prigg's wayward eyes frowned at the question. After long consideration, he replied to Harlowe, "There was something, Your Majesty. But it was too brief to capture. The way *Millawanda* has been acting lately, that may have been an echo from her. I will recheck the source."

"Not from Lamille, huh?" Harlowe asked.

"That appears unlikely, Your Majesty," was Prigg's brief answer.

47

Escape

Muuk sounded the ship-wide alarm: Shoot the alien mullie on sight. He took a squad of armed guards with him as he charged through the open hatchway that led aft to the galley and the crew's sleeping quarters. Others would be coming at her from the lower decks. The alien mullie was trapped. His flagship was 10,000 *pessas* above the planet. There was simply no place for her to hide. If she tried to enter the lower levels, two hundred armed soldiers would catch her exiting the hatchways.

By the time Muuk reached the galley, a squad of guards was already there, picking up the pieces. The mullie had taken out a half dozen galley crew who tried to stop her. The soldiers entering the galley from below had not seen her. After a quick search, a crewman found an open doorway leading to the outer hull of the gondola.

The decks suddenly jolted, making Muuk painfully aware that his flagship was approaching the storm as a crewman pointed at the open hatch. With his sidearm cocked and ready, Muuk led his crew through the hatchway onto an outside gangway that led to the upper roof of the gondola. Once outside, he and his crew struggled against the buffeting winds and pouring rain as they pulled themselves along the catwalk ropes toward the top of the gondola. Two crewmen perished when a gust of wind blew them off the catwalk. With no safety harnesses, the soldiers tumbled over the side and were lost, screaming as they fell through the clouds below.

Muuk kept on. He had no time for pity.

Halfway out on the walkway, a crewman spotted the mullie climbing the netted side of the dirigible. She appeared tiny against the flagship's massive gas-filled blimp. Even more astonishing than the mullie was the mechanical being climbing beside her. Muuk figured the gold, stick-like creature had assisted her escape. But where had it come from, he wondered? His cargos were checked thoroughly before liftoff. Suddenly, the thought of the gold cylinder that he had brought aboard his ship came to mind. Somehow the alien mullie had transformed the cylinder into a sentient being.

Two soldiers raised their weapons and were about to shoot the mullie from the side of the balloon when Muuk saw the danger and cried out, "Don't shoot! If you strike the balloon, we will all perish!" But over the howling wind, no one heard the warning. A soldier fired his weapon, missing the mullie but hitting the mechanical being next to her. The bullet didn't harm the being but the bullet's ricochet off its triangular shaped head sent sparks flying, puncturing the outer air sack of the balloon. The escaping gases blew the mullie and mechanical being off the netting. Muuk and his crew watched the two disappear in the swirling clouds and rain like the two soldiers before them. Their concern now was their own survival as the rip in the balloon's fabric grew. Muuk's flagship was dropping, and their was no way to stop it.

48

Ian's Plan

Through the small porthole in the vault door, Ian watched with interest as Loomis and his assistants used various acids, hammers, drill bits, and torches on the golden cylinders. Every experiment failed to leave a single mark on their dull surfaces. Several times during the day, Loomis asked Ian what his cylinder's purpose were, and each time the answer was the same: "Eat my shorts, toad," or something equally uninformative.

Loomis didn't find the answers amusing. "I will enjoy seeing you die slowly, alien. Tell me what their purpose is, and your death will be quick and painless."

"The truth, huh?"

"Yes."

"Okay. The cylinders are little dudes that turn into five-foot tall mechanical beings called robobs. I plan to use them to escape this rat hole." Ian wiggled his little finger from behind his back. "Pinky swear. That's the truth, butthead."

The conversation ended with another promise of a slow and agonizing death. Ian stared back, unemotional. "Whatever . . ."

After a long frustrating day, Loomis and his assistants finally called it a night. When lights went out in the laboratory, Ian made his move. A clicker opened the vault door from the lab and came into the compound as if it was the plan all along. After the clicker cut the shackles from his hands and feet, Ian took the com from the clicker and placed it on the ground next to Dev.

220

"What are you doing, Ian?" Dev asked, red-eyed and depressed after the long, uneventful day. For security reasons, low-level lights inside the arena kept the grounds well lit at night. Although it had been two days since their capture, a sound sleep had eluded the Prince, who knew his life, at this point, was worthless.

The astonished Prince stared at the mechanical droid standing with Ian. "How did the clicker get here?"

Ian pointed at the open door. "From the lab."

Dev sat up straight. "We're escaping?"

Ian gently, but forcefully, pushed the eager Prince back to the ground. "Not yet. You have to stay here a while longer."

The Prince, however, wouldn't stay down. "I want to go now."

"No. I need you to stay put in case toad face comes back," Ian said.

Dev looked around. "All right, but where are you going?"

"Outside," Ian replied.

The Prince was even more disturbed at being left alone with Cheesa. "You are leaving us?"

"For a short time. I need to check on some things," Ian answered calmly.

Dev rolled over wanting his shackles cut, too. "Take me with you, Ian."

Ian slammed his body against the wall. It was the only thing that brought him back to his senses. "Stop it, Dev. I need you to stay here quietly like nothing has changed. Is that clear? Quietly," Ian explained forcibly.

"The guards will see that you have left the compound."

Ian lowered the Prince back to the ground. "I've got that covered," and pointed at a holographic image of himself still manacled and sleeping against the wall.

The image was so real Dev nearly jumped out of his skin. "That's you!"

Time was short, and Ian had run out of nice. A well placed blow to the jaw put the Prince down for the time being. He carefully laid the Prince beside his projection and apologized. "Sorry, Dev. Sweet dreams."

Ian was about to walk away when he realized Cheesa had watched the entire exchange. "Do you understand why you have to stay here?" he asked her.

She was obviously frightened. "I think so."

"Good."

"Are you leaving us here?"

"No."

"You have a plan?"

"Yes. I'm working on it."

"For us all?"

Ian put a calming hand on her shoulder. She was obviously terrified about being left alone with the unconscious Prince. "Yes, for us all."

"I am confused, Ian."

"I know. I would be, too." He put a container of Bluestuff to her lips and let her drink. "Sip this. It will make you feel better."

"What is it?"

"Nourishment."

"How did you—"

"Cheesa, I must go now. I'll explain later."

He gave her another sip before he twisted the cap back on. "I'll be back, Cheesa," he reassured her. "Soon." And went through the heavy door with the clicker.

*   *   *

Loomis never left the compound. He started to leave, but the nagging premonition stopped him at the compound gates. He walked around the grounds instead of retreating to his billet to reenergize his troubled mind. The night air was crisp and clear. He looked up at the stars, bright and glimmering down upon him, wondering which heavenly speck of light the aliens had come from. He knew, of course, the alien called Dude was less than truthful with him. When the Imperator returned, he would ask his permission to dissect him and the mullie to learn more about their species. Until then, he would continue to work on the alien artifacts to find what secrets they held. The Imperator had given strict orders that no one was to know the outcome of his work. When he returned with his Beleza, he wanted a complete report on how the devices would benefit his new Empire.

A clickity-clack noise from the lab's direction alarmed Loomis. After Beleza's unbelievable escape, he was taking no chances. This time there was an entire squad of armed soldiers patrolling compound's perimeter. Loomis felt confident no one could enter or leave the compound without being seen. Yet, he felt that way with Beleza, too, and she had escaped. Feeling uneasy, he returned to the lab to satisfy himself that his prisoners were indeed still inside the arena.

Loomis quickly switched on the lights and went directly to the arena viewing port. With a combination of surprise and relief, the alien was asleep next to the Prince. Nothing seemed wrong. Yet, it was all too quiet, he thought. There *was* something wrong. What had he missed? He peered through the arena port again, even wiping his eyes for an extra bit of clarity. Nothing changed. The scene was unchanged and utterly quiet, as it should be. Every prisoner was accounted for.

Still apprehensive, he turned his focus back to his lab. It took only a moment for him to realize the alien artifacts were missing . . . all of them!

Before he could sound the alarm, a strange looking being with long spindly arms and legs leaped across the room with amazing agility. Loomis tried to turn and run, but the being was too quick. The thing touched his shoulder with a glowing ball of blue light. And that was all he remembered.

* * *

Maa Dev felt something push him. Swinging wildly, he tried to fight off his attacker until he was grabbed by the shoulders and a voice said,"Dev, wake up."

The Prince opened his eyes, a little groggy from the blow that had put him down in the first place. Two large hands lifted him to his feet and steadied him until he was able to stand on his own.

"Can you walk?" Ian asked.

"I think so," Dev said. He took one step, but his legs were too wobbly to walk without help. Ian handed him off to a clicker and told him to hang on.

"Where are we going, Ian?" Cheesa asked, coming beside him.

Ian opened the door to the arena and the three of them and the clickers walked out into the night. The Prince searched the compound for guards. There was no one in sight.

"We're leaving," Ian answered.

"But how—" the Prince tried to say before Ian covered his mouth to silence him.

"Do not speak. Your voice carries a long way in the dark." He turned to Cheesa and asked with his eyes, did she understand? Cheesa nodded. She was cool.

Calmly, but at a steady pace, Ian led them away from the compound toward a row of box-shaped bungalows. By the time their small group arrived at the rear of the first building, the Prince was able to walk on his own. Twice they stopped in the shadows to allow security vehicles to pass. Once clear, they strode across an open field toward an enormous black structure a mile away. It was the same hangar where the Imperator had left *The Ride* to be turned into scrap. Ian ushered through an unlocked door like he was familiar with the layout. Once inside, it was so dark, Dev couldn't see his hand in front of his face.

"Where are we, Ian?" Cheesa asked, reaching out as if she were blind.

Ian didn't have time to explain. "We must hurry. It is almost morning," he told them.

"I can't see," Dev complained.

"I can. Don't worry. Just hang on to my hand," he said.

"Where are we going, Ian?" Dev asked.

Ian's thoughts were elsewhere as he answered, "You'll see."

They walked for a long way, deeper into the building. Minutes passed before Ian stopped them, followed by the metallic sound of a door opening.

He took their hands and placed them on bars. "I need you both to start climbing the ladder."

"It feels like *The Ride's* ladder," Cheesa noted.

"It is."

It was at that point that sirens began to blare loudly across military base. This wasn't part of the plan.

"Hurry!" Ian shouted. "Start climbing, or we're dead!"

49

Genpok Xatz

The Ossetians were taking no chances. *Millawanda* was escorted to a landing site in the middle latitudes of the second largest continent, 150 miles inland from the capital city of Cornicen along the coast. Scores of gunships and thousands of ground forces surrounded the great Gamadin saucer as she put down on a wide-open plain inside a vast military installation. The Osset forces had the same look and feel as the U.S. government forces which tried to do the same thing with his ship north of Las Vegas.

Harlowe wasted no time. His landing party of Simon, Monday, and Mowgi. He left Riverstone and Prigg behind to hold down the fort. Stepping down the outer ramp, Mowgi led the way, strutting out front of the garish Captain Starr. Harlowe and Platter trailed behind, looking like they just stepped off the *Sons of Anarchy* set. They were dressed in dark blue jeans, black boots, designer sunglasses, and their new, midnight blue, Gamadin leather jackets that Simon had designed for them. For appearance, they wore no Gama-pistols on the outside of their clothes, but they had protection. Inside the lining of their jackets was an undetectable arsenal of weapons and protective hardware just in case.

"Why didn't we just blink down, Captain?" Monday asked Harlowe as they marched along.

Harlowe grabbed Monday's arm to stress his point. "Don't call me Captain, Squid. Rerun's the Captain now."

Monday apologized. "Aye, ah… What are you, Dog? First Officer?"

"Close enough."

They were met at the bottom of the ramp by an armored escort, who led them to a waiting transport. After rising straight up, the transport took off on a northwesterly course. Out their viewing ports the wide open plain quickly turned to a forested range of mountains. All they saw the entire way was one major road, which, unlike the crowded Southern California freeways, was deserted of normal traffic like personal cars and commercial trucks carrying products to markets. Instead, there were military convoys, troop transports, and supply trucks headed south en masse toward *Millawanda*.

The sight of so many armed forces made Harlowe uncomfortable. He was having second thoughts about leaving his weakened ship in the middle of an armed camp. Without additional power, Millie was helpless. All she had left was nominal flight capabilities, life support, and shields but not much else. She couldn't leave the planet if she wanted to. When Prigg said they would be arriving on fumes, he wasn't kidding. The yellow Ossetian sun would help stretch her power reserve somewhat, but with her shields demanding more power than the sun could produce, she had nineteen days left before she was bone dry.

*   *   *

It was a short thirty-minute flight to Cornicen. They put down on the tallest skyscraper in the city center. Upon exiting the transport, they had a panoramic view of a modern, metropolitan city bordered by the coastal mountains and green forest to the west and a beautiful green ocean with long, sandy white beaches to the east. The lines of perfect rights made Harlowe yearn for just one ride to get his face wet. How long had it been since he rode a wave, he wondered? Way too long was all he could remember.

As Captain Starr sucked in a huge lungful of the sea air, Harlowe thought he would pop several of his twenty medals off his chest. "Nothing like an ocean to clear your head, huh, gentlemen?" Simon breathed.

"Nothing like it, Captain Starr," Harlowe agreed, closing his eyes and allowing himself a brief moment to savor every salty molecule. It really did smell like heaven.

The tallest structures had no right angles. They were built with curiously rounded corners on all sides. Capping them were bulbous, onion-shaped domes that were painted gold and silver and green like brightly colored Christmas ornaments. Darting along the avenues, transports whizzed between the buildings in a stop and go fashion at various levels, depositing their passengers at corner terminals.

A cool eye from Harlowe brought their attentions back to the business at hand. Armed guards were everywhere. "Make this quick, Captain Starr," Harlowe whispered to Simon as they all surveyed the scores of gun-toting soldiers watching them carefully.

"Aye," was their respective replies. There was something about the military reception that didn't set well with anyone. Harlowe called Riverstone on the bridge to ease his worry over his ship using a word code between them. "How's things at the ranch?" he asked.

Riverstone stayed with the theme. *"We have a lot of skittish cattle around us, Dog."*

"Keep your eye on the herd, Jester."

"Cattle rustlers are thick as flies here, pard."

"They're around us like roadkill here, too," Harlowe added.

Two clicks of confirmation was the reply. If things went south, Harlowe was confident Riverstone and Prigg knew how to protect against any aggression toward the ship.

Their armed escort led them into the building through a sliding glass doorway. Once inside, they passed through a security check that scanned each of them for weapons. They found nothing. Captain Starr and his crew then went directly to an open platform. Once the Gamadin and their ten armed escorts were aboard, the platform floated down a wide open area of hanging gardens with small birds that flew around playfully like it was one big tropical aviary. For such a large military presence, Harlowe thought the building's interiors were out of place. Birds and jungles didn't seem to fit the style of the military presence until Monday made the observation that it was all made up.

Harlowe turned to Monday like he was speaking Chinese. "Say what?"

"It's not real, Dog," he whispered, and pointed to one of the birds flying toward the window. "Watch." As the bird was about to crash head first into the window, it disappeared, then reappeared again in another place as it came back into the aviary.

"How do they do that?" Simon wondered.

"Must be some elaborate hologram," Harlowe said. Come to think of it, once they entered the building, he didn't smelled live plants or feel the heavy humidity like Dodger's Place that was full of lush, aromatic plants and trees surrounding the giant pool inside *Millawanda*. The only thing that was real seemed to be the people and the superstructure.

"It's all fake," Monday concluded. "Everything. Even the building is made up."

"That's good to know," Harlowe observed, tucking the factoid into the back of his mind. He added, "No construction, no resources to manufacture, no waste. Design what you want in an instant."

"Presto. Sim City," Simon quipped.

Harlowe's thoughts were more pragmatic. "Something keeps it together."

"Power?" Monday murmured.

Harlowe agreed. "And a lot of it."

"What do they use?" Monday asked, looking at everything in a whole new way.

"It's not nuclear or thermo-grym," Harlowe replied. "Or Prigg would have picked it up on his scans."

The group stepped off the platform and proceeded down a long, arched corridor. Once they reached the bottom of the structure, they stepped out onto a long passageway where great wall banners hung along the entire length of a giant hallway that was twice the size of one of *Millawanda's* main corridors. The banners were obviously symbolic. The bold red, black, and grey colors depicted the Osset beings happily tolling in the fields, working the mines, and harvesting the crops as they rode their machines and waved to their paternalistic leaders, who watched stoically from afar from their grand palaces. Maybe they were unable to read the words printed in tall block letters, but their slogans were universal. Here on Osset, the state ruled with an iron hand.

At the end of the hallway they came to an enormous chamber filled with military, diplomatic types, dignitaries, and high-ranking officials. It seems Osset's elite had come to greet the travelers from across the star desert. Like the hallway, even taller and broader draping banners hung with their same red, black, grey socialistic slogans. A hush preceded them as they moved across the room. They talked to no one, but the Cornicenians eyed their guests with great interest. Finally, they came to the head of the chamber where five bigwigs sat peering over everyone from an elevated bench. Behind the platform, overlooking them all was an enormous portrait of what can only be described as a crusty old lady. The bigwig's uniforms continued with the red, black, and grey color scheme. Their oversized chest medals and silly, taffeta hats, however made Captain Starr's gaudy outfit look like last year's fashion. No wonder Rerun's uni seemed unimpressive to them, Harlowe thought. These clown outfits had already cornered the market on stupid.

Curiously, one chair in the middle of the VIPs was left unoccupied. It was soon apparent who it belong to when a tall and anemically thin old woman entered the room from a side door.

Simon leaned over and commented in Harlowe's ear, "Imagine waking up to that in the morning."

Harlowe's face twisted with revulsion as he glanced at her portrait then back to the real thing. "She redefines ugly," he whispered back.

The walk to her seat was a slow process. She needed assistance. Like many of the Ossetians, she had large pale eyes and was dressed in a dark scarlet pantsuit that had no medals, decorations or insignias indicating her rank or title. The moment she appeared on the stage, the room came to stick-straight attention and saluted her. "Genpok Xatz, the Clarity salutes you!"

Harlowe recalled his grandma Pylott had the same affect on everyone around their dinner table. When she spoke, it didn't matter who was speaking at the time, or what the conversation was, even God stopped to listen to her. Harlowe didn't need to be told where the power resided on this planet. The crusty old lady was at the top of the food chain.

"Greetings, Travelers," the old lady began from behind the bench. It was the first actual acknowledgement of their arrival. Her voice was weak but calm, even, and to the point. "It is our understanding that you have come to Osset from across the great star desert. Is this true?" she asked.

Harlowe marveled at Simon's poise as he stood before the tribunal like Julius Caesar addressing the Roman Senate. It was showtime, and Simon never failed to answer his curtain call. "That is correct, ah . . . I'm sorry, ma'am, but to whom am I speaking?"

Very good, Rerun. You da man! Harlowe would never have thought about being so polite. He would have simply stated his case and damn the protocol.

"I am Genpok Xatz, supreme leader of Osset. And who are you, Traveler. Your vessel is unfamiliar to us. Where is your source?" she asked, but the tone was more coarse than before, less respectful.

Simon bowed cordially but did not bend at the hip. He wanted to give the impression he and his crew were on equal footing with the tribunal, not subservient. "I am Captain Julian Starr of the Grand Semper Fi Federation. Greetings from the planet, Gama," he told her.

A casual wink from Harlowe let Simon know he was doing an outstanding job of covering their tracks.

"Your vessel must be quite powerful to travel such distances and survive the Zabits," Genpok Xatz said.

"I am afraid our vessel is more fortunate than powerful, Genpok Xatz. We were one of a hundred and three vessels that embarked on our mission to Osset. My ship is all that is left," Simon explained.

A deep concern spread across the table as Genpok Xatz conferred with others on the bench before she went on. "How do we know what you are telling us is true, Captain? Your fleet may be ready to attack Osset as we speak."

"It is not my fleet that is headed this way, Genpok Xatz. It is the Zabits. Have your Osset resources not heard of the Fhaal Empire's total destruction?" Simon asked.

"Indeed, word has recently reached us of their annihilation. But as yet, this tale has not been confirmed."

"I confirm it now, Genpok Xatz. The Fhaal Empire is no more. The Zabits have destroyed them, and if you do not heed our warning, Osset will fall with them."

"Osset will fall?"

"Yes, that is exactly what I am telling you, Genpok Xatz. The Zabits are real, and they are expanding their domain beyond the great star desert."

The talking among the crowd grew loud. Even among the bigwigs the discussion continued for several minutes until Genpok Xatz raised her hand to silence the room.

"Go on, Captain. You have Osset's attention," Genpok Xatz directed. "Surely, you have not come this far to offer only a warning."

Simon bowed slightly again. "This is true. The Semper Fi believe Osset has the answer to not only its own survival but to Gama's and the quadrants surrounding Cartooga-Thaat, Genpok Xatz."

The old lady leaned forward. "Tell us, Captain? If it is our property you seek, Osset will not give up resources which we may need to fight our enemies."

Simon opened his arms to the table. "I must apologize. Apparently, I have not made myself clear. We have no interest in Osset's resources, Genpok Xatz. We have come for information."

This surprised her. "Information?"

"Yes, Genpok Xatz, information. We are on a quest to find a place that was once called Lamille. Our records are scant. But it is all that we have. Our ancestors once came to this planet many thousands of passings ago in search of the Gamadin protectors who guarded the trading routes through Cartooga-Thaat from the Zabits. We hope to locate these protectors of the galaxy once again for the good of us all, Genpok Xatz."

After conferring with the bigwigs again, Genpok Xatz came back to Captain Starr and explained, "No one knows of such a place on Osset, Captain. And as for the Gamadin," she smiled, "the mighty protectors of the galaxy are nothing more than children's fables. They have never existed. So it seems this place called Lamille, Captain, never existed on Osset."

Simon stayed persistent. "That is understandable, Genpok Xatz. Time has a way of extinguishing a planet's past. But our resources are quite reliable. The Gamadin did indeed exist, ma'am."

"What proof do you have, Captain?" Genpok Xatz demanded.

Simon held up a clear memory stick they had found at the Donut for everyone to see. "Here, Genpok. Within this device are the records of a Gamadin soldier who was stationed here at Osset many thousands of passings ago. I assure you, it has been validated by our scientists to be true."

Genpok Xatz was stunned by the revelation and asked, "At Lamille?"

"Yes. According to the Gamadin logs, Lamille was a coastal city of Osset somewhere in the southern equatorial region of the planet."

"The region you speak of is the land of the Surwags. It is forbidden to enter there lest you face certain death." She held up her shaky hand. "But allow us a moment, Captain. We have a specialist that may assist you in your search."

Simon bowed his head. "Excellent, Genpok Xatz. That would indeed be helpful. Thank you."

A runner bolted for the exit, and a short while later he returned, accompanied by a tall, strikingly beautiful girl with large dark eyes and long black hair. Simon practically stuck Harlowe with one of his chest medals when he breathed lustfully in his ear, "Whatta babe!"

Harlowe had to admit the girl was definitely hot. "Easy, Captain Starr," he cautioned, pushing Simon's medals away from his new coat. Fortunately, the leather was tougher than the medal points and didn't puncture the fabric.

When the girl walked up to Simon, her looks and delicate perfume caused some uneasy adjustments to Captain Starr's composure.

"Captain Starr," Genpok Xatz said, trying to get Simon's attention.

Harlowe had to elbow Simon to bring him back into focus.

Simon coughed to cover his brain fart. "Ah, yes, Genpok Xatz. Forgive me. You were saying."

Genpok Xatz continued: "This is Naree. She is our curator of antiquities. She will assist you in your search for this place you call Lamille. Because you are still unknown to Osset, a military escort will continue their protection of you at all times during your investigations. Is that clear?"

Harlowe whispered in Simon's ear. "Close your mouth, Captain Starr, before you drool on the floor. The Genpok is still talking to you."

Simon almost said, Yes Skipper, but caught himself before he blundered.

"Is that clear, Captain?" Genpok Xatz asked more forcefully.

Another shot to the ribs made Simon blink. He closed his gawky mouth and put his mind back into his role. "Yes, thank you, Genpok Xatz. That is most generous of you. I am sure Naree will be quite helpful in our search."

"And Captain," Genpok Xatz added, "you and your entourage will abide by all the laws of Cornicen. You have no immunity here. The punishment of any crime committed by your crew will be as though you were citizens of the city."

The long stare from Genpok Xatz meant only one thing: don't even breath wrong, or you will be arrested. Harlowe understood quite clearly that even though they were here under the pretext of helping the planet, they were unwelcome guests. As far as he was concerned, the sooner they finished their business, the better.

Two armed guards stepped briskly in front of Harlowe and Monday. "What is the meaning of this?" Simon asked Naree.

"They will guide your officers to their quarters," Naree replied.

"I want them with me," Simon demanded.

"I am afraid that is impossible. The Hall of Antiquities is a high security zone. The Clarity cannot allow unauthorized personnel to enter," Naree explained.

"But they are with me," Simon protested.

"Yes, but only you are authorized to enter, Captain Starr."

Simon looked helplessly at Harlowe and Monday. "Sorry, Gentlemen. Looks like it's out of my hands." But Simon wasn't fooling his officers one bit. He was eager for a little one on one with the curator.

Harlowe glared at Simon. "Take the Mowg with you." It wasn't a request.

Simon pointed his finger up. "Ah, good idea, Officer Dog."

Since Genpok Xatz's decision was final, it was time to move on to other matters. The old lady summarily dismissed Naree and Captain Starr from the chamber. It appeared to Harlowe the fate of her planet was low on her priority list, or more to the point, their Gamadin-Zabit act was about as convincing as a politician's speech. Judging from the way the Osset military had mobilized around *Millawanda*, it didn't matter what storyline they had given them. Their ship's capture was the ultimate goal.

Nothing earthshaking about that, Harlowe thought. Millie has always been the grand prize. No matter where they traveled, whether it be Earth or any star system or quadrant in the galaxy, the powers that be had always envisioned the Gamadin ship as their way to eternal, god-like authority over their people. It was the monkey on their back. Osset would continue assisting them in their search only as long as Genpok Xatz felt it was in her best interest to keep them alive. The moment she got what she wanted or became weary of the game, Harlowe hoped he had what he came for before their welcome mat was withdrawn.

Their escort was leading them away from the great chamber when the loud roar of a combustion engine brought the chamber to a standstill. Through the large, ground level windows, a black behemoth of a vehicle rolled to a screeching stop outside the building, breaking trees and crushing other vehicles with complete disregard for anyone's property. The black, heavily ribbed tires were tall as a two-story building. The tank-like monster body was dark metal, sewn together by heavy rivets. It reminded Harlowe of the monster trucks his dad had taken Dodger and him to see at the Pomona Fairgrounds outside of LA. Only this Osset vehicle made anything he saw then seem like a model toy. This humongous vehicle was weaponized up the wazoo with plas cannons fore, aft, and along the sides of its hulking body.

"What the ..." Simon stuttered before he pointed and asked, "What is that, Naree?"

Naree's face revolted like she wanted to spit. "That is Darkn's gerbid. He is the Margrave of the southern provinces and leader of the Tappers. We need to leave the chamber immediately or the Margrave's ilodudds will kill your animal, I can assure you."

Mowgi's snout peeled back, displaying the ends of his sizable incisors. He could already smell the vile creatures before they even left their truck. Harlowe bent down and patted the undog's side. "Settle down, Mowg. You'll get your chance." Harlowe held Simon's arm. He wanted to see more. "Hold on a sec, Captain. The Wiz, when he returns, will want a report on Darkn's ride."

Simon felt the vise-like grip of Harlowe's hand and knew this also was no request. "Ah...you are quite right, Officer Dog. The Wiz will find the vehicle quite fascinating." He turned back to Naree. "The Magrave's gerbid is quite fascinating. It looks lethal. What's it used for?"

"Collections," Naree replied. "Darkn is a ruthless collector of the empire's tributes. That is all I can tell you. Please, we must leave before the ilodudds are set loose."

It was clear Naree wanted no part of Darkn's show. She urged everyone to leave the room before he entered the chamber with the three ilodudds barking loudly as they tugged at their restraints.

The pets were sizable and ugly as grogans. Harlowe thought they were probably kissin' cousins at one time. They were barrel chested, had dark, short fir, and looked as mean as any grogan, but that was where the similarities ended. They had short legs and no tails, and their faces were black and punched in like a bulldog's. Long razored teeth protruded upward from their lower jaws in a severe under bite. If that were not enough, wet drool dripped from their mouths and splattered like vile waste onto the floor as the beasts charged through the outer doorway, scattering the occupants to the far corners of the chamber. The owner of a pair of white cats didn't move fast enough. Darkn's lead ilodudd gobbled them both up whole without breaking stride.

Darkn seemed like the two-legged version of his pets. His face was flat like it had been run over by his monster truck. His under bite was greater than his ilodudds, and had small, yellow, pointy teeth. Harlowe thought his jawbone would make a wonderful hatrack.

"Man, that's one ugly being," Monday said in a whisper to anyone within range.

Around his heavily boned and scared head was Darkn's strange skullcap, made from the bleached bones of his victims. His garb was skins and belted leather. His pants were bright red and tight like stretch pants. More bones were attached to the sides of his heavy boots, and they clanked loudly as he strode into the room with his beasts. As fearsome as Dankn was, Genpok Xatz gave no indication she was riled by the giant Tapper's surprise visit. Quite the opposite. The instant she saw him, her face changed to one of endearment. The reason soon became clear.

"Welcome, my son," Genpok Xatz said with motherly pride.

Simon nearly lost it. "Really…"

Harlowe added without a second thought. "A freak of nature."

"More like, Nature's reject," Simon countered.

The ilodudds were still hungry and quickly set their sights on their next meal…Mowgi. The undog wasn't the least bit frightened of the ghoulish creatures and stood his ground. He was going nowhere. Harlowe saw the long knives peeking out of the jaw line. If he let Mowgi do his thing, there would be blood in the streets. This was no time to slaughter the local pets and make friends. Harlowe scooped up the undog in his arms as Naree led Captain Starr toward another open doorway.

"Hurry!" Naree urged, waving the Gamadin from the chamber to an adjoining hallway.

But ilodudds had no intention of letting their meal escape. They charged across the room in a feasting frenzy. The beasts were already airborne, coming down on top of Harlowe holding Mowgi, when Naree produced a small device from a hidden pocket and pressed the activator. Incredibly, as Harlowe dropped Mowgi to pull his hidden weapon, a solid wall of molecular energy formed in front of the charging ilodudds, sealing the hallway off from the chamber. The ilodudd's bodies slammed against the materialized surface with a crashing thud. With howls and beastly screams, they scratched and clawed at the wall, but not one beast could break through the solid barrier of molecular density.

Monday breathed a collective sigh for everyone. "That was close."

Mowgi laid his parabolics down in disappointment. He wanted to play.

50

Ride II

When Ian switched on a light, Maa Dev and Cheesa stood in awe the instant they saw *The Ride's* new look. Outside, *Ride II's* body had been radically altered. The big tractor wheels were gone. In their place were three long landing struts, tipped with round pads. Attached beneath the cabin was the discarded fuselage of a jet aircraft, wings and all. At the aft end, extending upward, was a single, massive propeller connected to a steam-driven rotor in an intricate system of cables and pulleys that were in turn connected to the drive gears powered by the steam boiler. Even more amazing were the three giant air bags fastened with thick cables to the roof. They watched aghast as two more clickers climbed the roof to guide one of rubberized bags into position while a third and fourth robob held onto the pipe, filling it with helium gas. As the hissing continued, more gears turned, causing a chain reaction that made *Ride II* bounce and shudder as if it were about to explode.

"Hurry!" Ian shouted above the clattering and hissing noise. "Get in!"

Hesitate at first, Dev and Cheesa followed orders and climbed into the cabin where they discovered the interior had been completely gutted. In place of the original bench seats were four high-backed, aircraft seats firmly attached to the floor. Two seats faced the forward dash of instruments and steering wheel while two more were right behind them. Each contoured seat was heavily padded and came with buckled, shoulder harnesses that dangled along the top of the seats.

Dev touched a buckled strap. "What are these for?"

236

Ian sat in his forward command chair facing the steering wheel to demonstrate. He put his arms through the straps and snapped the buckles together with a metallic click. "To keep you from being tossed around when we take off. Things could get a little bumpy from here on out, so keep these harnesses tight against your bodies at all times."

Cheesa's face went slack. "Take off?"

"Yeah, we're flying outta here."

"Flying?" Cheesa figured he had lost his mind.

Ian opened the energy hatch, checked the tiny blue crystal, closed the door, and initiated the start up sequence.

"What are you doing, Ian?" Dev asked in alarm. "How can we move without wheels?"

"I told you, we're taking off!" Ian exclaimed over the loud blast of expanding gases. A spindly clicker dropped down from the roof and sat next to him and began pulling flow levers that opened valves, adding more water to the holding tanks. Then suddenly, the force of *Ride II's* floor began to push against the bottom of their seats. Unable to fight it, both Dev and Cheesa grabbed the arms of their chairs and held on for their lives.

"Cheesa, Dev!" Ian shouted again. "Buckle your harnesses like I showed you!"

Cheesa grabbed her shoulder harness and after several tries finally clicked them into place. The Prince had trouble finding his and couldn't hold on. He bounced from his chair and fell spread-eagle onto the floor. Somehow in all the commotion, she managed to grab the back of his shirt and return him to his chair. She grunted, forcing the Prince's belts together when the vibrations suddenly stopped. Overhead, the building's roof split open with a loud CRACK! Metal beams twisted and broke from their fasteners. It seemed the entire hangar was collapsing all around them. Through it all, the falling roof didn't stop them from rising. Miraculously, *Ride II* continued upward, defying the force of gravity.

When the entire cabin was clear of the building, Ian called to a clicker, "Open the rotor valves, if you please!" The robob swung a lever down along a shiny bright pipe and instantly *Ride II* lurched forward. Now, instead of being pushed down in their seats, Dev and Cheesa were thrust backward.

Dev stared at the outside as the ground fell from view. "Ian the ground! It's…it's leaving us!"

Ride II

Ian looked back with a prideful smile. "Yeah, Dev. We're flying!"

Ian's grin quickly vanished when ricocheting bullets struck the sides of the boiler. He reached for the device on the dash that switched on the force field. Instantly, the blue shimmer of the barrier stopped the bullets and *Ride II* flew on, climbing higher and higher into the morning sky.

Their troubles weren't over yet. Behind them, jet aircraft with their fully, loaded automatic weapons had taxied out onto the runway. Ian's shield was meant for personal use. It wasn't meant to cover a hundred-foot high sac of air and boiler at the same time. If a bullet or missile struck a balloon sac, they would be headed down in a hurry. Without the balloons for lift, *Ride II* was dead weight.

Ian rummaged through his pack and removed a small cube. "This should do it," he said, finding what he was after. He took the cube and went aft. He delicately touched the cube and watched it glow blue. He made several adjustments before tossing it out the window. When it hit the runway, the aircraft that were about to takeoff magically stopped in their places. Every squadron on the ground was paralyzed.

"What was that?" Cheesa asked.

Ian returned to his command chair. "Think of it as a mini twynich. Everything electrical within a 50-mile radius will be dead in the water for at least a day."

"Then what?" the Prince asked.

"Then we better be long gone."

"Where are we going, Ian?" Cheesa wondered.

Ian went back to his instruments and continued making adjustments to levers and valves as he replied, "We're going to find Lu and the cats."

"How will you know where to find them?" she asked.

Ian tapped a small box he had placed on the dash. A tiny light expanded over the box then quickly turned into an image of Leucadia's head and shoulders. She was drenched. She looked like she had just stepped out of a pool of water. *"Are you airborne yet?"* the image asked, wiping her soaking wet face with her driver's hat.

"It's Lu," Dev cried out in amazement.

"No, it's her image. We've been communicating since she bailed out of Muuk's flagship," Ian explained. He went back to Leucadia's holograph and answered her question. "Yeah, we're up and flying north by northwest and heading your way.

"Be careful, Ian. There is a big storm here. I will make my way east, away from the storm center," Leucadia said.

"Do you have a fix on Molly and Rhud?" Ian asked.

Leucadia shook her head. *"Not yet, but Muuk's forces have located them heading north. The report was that there were two white tigers running together."*

Ian found that surprising. "North? Why north? I figured for sure they would head west to the Haga Forest where they last saw Millie."

"I'm as surprised as you. It appears they are skirting the forest and headed toward a range of mountains."

Dev spoke up. "They call it Du Tir, the Black Land."

Leucadia's image turned large as life as she came away from the dash and stood in the middle of the cabin looking at the Prince. *"That's right, Dev. That's what Muuk called it. What can you tell us about this place?"*

Dev reached out and tried to touch Leucadia with his hand. His fingers went right through her image as if she were a *draugar*.

Ian shouted at the Prince to snap out of his stupor. "Dev, answer Lu. She's just an image. She's not really there. She's far away from here."

"It is . . . it is a place of perpetual darkness," he stuttered a moment, before he grew comfortable talking to the ghost. Then he settled down, talking to her like she was standing next to him in person. He warned her, "No one has gone beyond the mountains and returned, Lu. Those who have tried do not come back. The Imperator led an expedition to Du Tir and lost his entire brigade of Numeri. It was said monsters ate them. He was fortunate to have escaped alive and has never gone to the Black Land since."

Water dripping from her face, Leucadia looked skyward. *"This storm is delaying Muuk. He's sending a battalion ahead of his arrival to set traps for Molly and Rhud before they get through the pass that leads to this Black Land."*

"That still leaves the question of why Molly and Rhud are running north instead of toward the Haga," Ian pondered. "What is it that's leading them there? They know nothing of the Du Tir."

"Perhaps they know more of Nod than you know," Cheesa commented innocently.

Leucadia's green eyes brightened as she considered Cheesa's observation. *"What do you see, Cheesa?"*

Cheesa squirmed in her chair, feeling that she was intruding where she had no right to be.

Ian helped her along. "Go on, Cheesa. Tell us what you know. At this point your opinion is as good as ours."

Leucadia added kindly. *"Yes, Cheesa, your thoughts are very important to us. Please go on. I know your heart is for their safety."*

Cheesa nodded. "I believe if they were running from fear of being caught, they would have returned to where they began."

"The Haga," Ian stated.

"Yes, the Haga. But they are shunning the Haga and its safety for some higher meaning to them. That requires logic. Molly and Rhud must know the route through the valley is not safe, yet they travel through it anyway. If we know what lies beyond the mountains, within the Du Tir, then we will know what drives them there."

Leucadia and Ian conferred visually. It was an idea that neither had thought about: the cats thinking logically. They both knew the cats were incredibly smart, but having some ulterior motive othe than their own survival hadn't crossed their minds. They had always gone on the assumption that Molly and Rhud were normal animals following their basic instincts. Now it seemed, from Cheesa's perspective anyway, there was more to their travel northward than survival...or was it? Was survival somehow different for them?

"Now I'm confused," Leucadia admitted.

Ian shrugged, no less baffled himself. "One thing is for sure, it's Molly's doing because she was on that path before Rhud caught up with her."

"I believe you are right, Cheesa, they indeed know more about the forces on Nod than we do," Leucadia mused deeply.

"Set course for Du Tir, then?" Ian asked Leucadia, already knowing the answer.

"Aye," Leucadia replied with a head bow of thankfulness toward Cheesa. *"Set course for Du Tir. Best speed."*

"What about you?" Ian asked. "How will we find you, Lu?"

"The storm is too intense for you to fly. Veer to the east, away from the storm. Once it passes, I will join you along the way," Leucadia explained.

Ian frowned at the idea. "Negative. That's not a good plan, Lu. I'm not leaving you behind for Muuk's toads."

"He is not looking for me. He believes I fell to my death, Ian. Steer east; I'll find you."

"Promise?"

Leucadia raised two fingers. *"Girl Scout's hon—"* Before she finished her reply, she vanished in a cloud of static when a thick bolt of jagged yellow light shot down from the heavens and exploded.

51

Three Alarmer

Their accommodations were low rent. Harlowe had to pee so bad his back teeth were floating. There were no bathrooms anywhere in the room. "Even a jail cell has a toilet," Monday complained with disgust. The room did have chairs, couches, and tables, but they were all a colorless grey and uncomfortably hard. Apparently, the Ossetians believed their stay would be too short to warrant necessities, which would have suited Harlowe just fine if he didn't have to go so badly.

Looking out at the ocean didn't help matters either. He was starting to dance from the pain of holding it as he stared at the biggest bathroom on the planet a short walk away...the ocean!

The waves were small, but to Harlowe it didn't matter. It was a toilet, and he desperately needed it, or he would burst at the seams. He and Monday had done nothing but sit in the room and watch the perfect rights peel off without him while they waited for Simon and Naree to return from the Museum of Antiquities.

Monday wiggled his hind end around, searching for a comfortable position on the couch. "For something fake, it sure feels real, Dog."

Harlowe kept looking up at the tall structures along the coastline to keep his mind off his bladder. "Did you notice anything odd about the city?"

"Not really. Tall buildings and cool architecture. Kinda looked Russian."

"There were some parts that were incomplete."

The couch's cushions felt solid as wood. Monday tried to stretch out but nearly rolled off the end trying to get comfortable. "I thought it was part of their urban renewal projects."

"I thought so too, but then you pointed out they were all phony. That got me thinking." Monday shrugged. He was more concerned with his own comfort and eyed the floor as a possible alternative as Harlowe continued: "The closer we came to the city's center, the more the power increased on the com. So why is the power concentrated here? Why isn't it even throughout the city? And why isn't there a bathroom in this whole frickin' place?"

"A one alarmer?" Monday asked.

Harlowe held up three fingers.

Monday sympathized. "That bad, huh?"

Harlowe held his crotch tighter, gritting his teeth. "That bad."

Monday tried keeping Harlowe's mind off 'Nature calling.' "Maybe they're running out of power," he said at the very moment the edge of the couch broke off. He hit the floor with a thump. When he looked back, the section of couch miraculously healed itself and returned to normal.

Harlowe reached down and helped Monday off the floor. "That's awkward."

Harlowe's orders were to keep Millie on full alert. He had spoken to Riverstone several times over the last few hours and was not surprised to hear the Ossetian military had already surrounded *Millawanda* with everything they had, along with another few thousand troops. So far they had made no attempt to penetrate the force field, but it was only a matter of time, Riverstone figured. Genpok Xatz had the military behind her, but he didn't recall seeing many happy faces along the way. The population seemed rather suppressed. He saw no one walking the streets either, or driving their cars, or shopping in department stores. They were not engaged in any of the everyday things a population does to simply exist. And what about the unfinished structures, he wondered again? So many buildings were sitting empty. *What's up with that?* From the looks of things, Cornicen had no real population. Was it even a real city? If so, where was everyone? To all of these questions and more, Harlowe wanted answers, but his ship came first. Millie needed energy, and where to find it was the only question he wanted answered. The idea of spending the rest of his life in a city held together by phony molecules didn't sit well with him, especially when he was about to explode!

"Do you ever worry about Lu, Captain?" Monday asked out of the blue.

"Now, Platter? Really?" Harlowe asked, wondering what drawer he pulled that question out of. "You want to know about Lu and me?" Had their time really come down to that, talking about his relationship with Lu? Well, why not, he figured. That would keep any shrink occupied for hours.

Harlowe turned to Monday with a forced grin. "All the time."

"You think she's okay?"

"I worry more about the guy who gets in her way," Harlowe replied in all seriousness.

"Yeah, but—"

"Listen, there's one thing I've learned about Lu: She can take care of herself just fine, thank you very much."

Monday didn't know it, but he had accidentally struck a nerve with Harlowe. "So don't start feeling protective of Ms. Lu. Remember on Gazz? She went down in the Tomarian Flagship with all hands on board and survived. Pirates then looted her encampment on the beach and took everyone with them as slaves. A week later guess who's running the show? Leucadia Mars, dude!" Harlowe smiled from ear to ear. "I wish I had been a fly on the wall when that Captain tried crawling in her bed. Poor guy probably thought he had a chenner by the tail," Harlowe said, petting Mowgi. "She's a live one, I tell ya. Taking care of Leucadia Mars is in her genes."

"Yeah, but—"

"Platter, her mother was a badass Triadian soldier, remember? She's got survival training up the wahzoo. Did I ever tell you the story about the time we were kidnapped?"

"You and Lu? No way."

"Yes way."

"I heard about that FBI Agent Scott's little daughter who you and Jester rescued from the dudes in the Nevada desert," Monday recalled, "but I never heard about you and Lu getting kidnapped."

Harlowe wagged a finger at Monday. "I should have said almost kidnapped. Ms. Mars nixed their plans but good. Talk about cool under fire; she's it, Squid!"

Monday's black face reared back in astonishment. "How come it never made the papers?"

Harlowe snickered. "Because it was over before it started. It was never news. No one knew about it except me, her, and the bad guys that ate the big one." He looked at Monday with his intense blue eyes. "You know, Mr. Platter, that was the second red flag I should have seen. Three days after rescuing her from Bolt's sinking yacht, I'm part of a world plot."

"No way."

"Yes, way."

Harlowe shook his head, wondering how he could have been so stupid not to see trouble with a capital T from the start. "Oh, well. Here we are in a room with no bathroom and who knows where she is. But trust me, if you want to worry about something, worry about finding a place to take a leak. I'm dying here!"

Harlowe's focus went back to the ocean.

"Don't leave me hanging, Captain. Finish the story. What happened to you and Lu? Did the kidnappers have guns?" Monday had to know almost as bad as Harlowe had to pee.

Harlowe's head drooped. "Okay. Guns? Let me tell ya. They were packin' all kinds of heat. A sawed-off shotgun, 9mm Glocks, and two Uzi's under their towels. I should have seen it coming," Harlowe said regretfully. "But she was two steps ahead of me wearing a bathing suit you could stuff in a Band-Aid box. Now who's going see bad guys when you're focused on that?"

Monday pointed at the undog. "Where was the Mowg? Wasn't he with you guys?" he asked.

Harlowe glanced at the undog as his mind sighed, retreating back from the thought of Leucadia in a skimpy blue bikini. "Mrs. M had taken him to get a pedicure."

"A pedicure? Mowgi?"

Harlowe laughed as he raised an open hand. "I swear. Gamadin honor. Right, Mowg?"

Monday looked to the undog to confirm. Mowgi yipped twice. His lingo for yes. "Go on," Monday urged.

"There's nothing more to tell. The dudes were waiting for us on the beach when we walked by."

"That's when they pulled their guns?"

Harlowe nodded. "Yeah, big mistake for them. Before I knew what happened, the Daks were doing face plants in the sand with Lu shoving the dude's own Uzi up his nose."

"Wow…"

"That's right. Wow. Nailed them. The toads were down for the count before they knew what hit them."

"Why would they put the hit on Lu?" Monday wondered. "She would never hurt anybody."

Harlowe smiled like an all-knowing guru who understood the real game of power. "She's a Mars, Squid. They want what she has gobs of."

"Money?"

"No. Not even close. They want her access, influence, and most of all her power."

"Why not money?"

"It's never about money, Squid. I used to think that way, too, but after a week with Ms. Mars, you become enlightened on the way the elite think. Money is nothing to them…power is. You can have all the money in the world, but if you don't have power, you have nothing. It's why Anor and the Fhaal wanted Millie. They didn't care about us. They wanted Millie, because with her they could rule without opposition. She's Frodo's golden ring, Squid. That little knob foot didn't have money, either, but he had the ring, right? 'The one ring to rule them all'… Millie is the ultimate ring, and all the Gallums in a galaxy want her." Harlowe bent down to Monday's level and continued. "Listen, the power brokers on Earth have had the Mars family in their crosshairs for a long time because they don't play by the rules . . . their rules anyway. They have control of the banks, the media, and the governments of the world, but try as hard as they could, they could never control Harry and Mrs. M. The Mars family was the one thing they were missing in their new world order. The Mars Corporation was always ten steps ahead of them, and that ticked them off to no end. If Harry and Mrs. M weren't so engaged in finding Millie, they might have put the power brokers out of business. But Millie was their priority. So they let the elites play their little power games while they searched for the biggest ring of all. *Millawanda,* the most powerful weapon in the galaxy!"

Monday seemed to be connecting the dots. "They're still there, Captain, manipulating stock markets, buying up politicians, and starting wars. What happens when President Delmonte's term ends?"

Harlowe didn't seem too concerned. He shrugged and replied simply, "We get someone else."

Monday wasn't sure that was cool. "Rig the election? That's not right,

Captain."

"The elites do it all the time, Squid. Elections are rigged. It's a given. We don't really cheat. But it may seem like it because we make sure the election stays honest, like when Rerun won his Oscar. He really won it, you know, but if we hadn't kept it honest, he would have lost to the toads that tried to stuff the ballots."

"What if the people pick the wrong guy?"

"They won't. When the people know the truth, they always do the right thing. So that's our job, to get the truth out."

Monday grinned proudly, knowing he had been a part of the change. "The people sure love President Delmonte. No one has ever been as popular, not even Reagan."

"It's amazing what freedom does for a planet, Squid. Get the governments out of the way," Harlowe waved his right hand like he had a magic wand, "and presto! The people win every time. It's a no brainer. The people always know what's best, given the freedom to choose their own path," he added proudly.

Harlowe walked over to the window and stared out at the long white beach. "You know what else, Squid?" Monday kept quiet, knowing Harlowe wasn't finished. "I don't care where we go in this galaxy, whenever we see unhappy faces and poverty, it's always the toads with the power behind the killing and the loss of freedom...always!"

Monday nodded in agreement. "You're right, Captain. The Consortium, the Fhaal, Sanborn, Bugabu, they were all power brokers. Even Anor, right?"

Harlowe pressed his lips as he thought of Quay's father. "Yeah, he was the biggest broker of them all. He owned not only the governments of the planets but the quadrant! I can't even imagine something that big."

"But he never got Millie."

"No, he never got Millie. He never got the Ring," Harlowe chuckled as he went back to the problem at hand. "Let's hope Rerun is on the clock."

Monday sighed, knowing Simon's propensity to enjoy his work a little too much when it came to a pretty face. "Aye, Captain."

Harlowe stretched the kink from his neck. He'd had enough waiting around for things to happen. He needed a bathroom, and at this point, he didn't care where he found one. "Let's go for a swim."

"Naree said we should stay in our room," Monday said.

Harlowe picked up the small device Naree had given them. She called it a disruptor. It worked like a small flashlight. All one had to do was point it at any part of the wall and a dull green light would dissolve a hole large enough to walk through for ten seconds before it returned to its solid state again. Harlowe had already tried it twice. It performed as advertised. Why Naree had found it necessary to give him such a device, he wasn't quite sure. Her motives seemed genuine, though. The look of fear in her eyes, however, made him believe there was plenty more she wanted to tell him but couldn't. Harlowe was familiar with fear. Fear from the Clarity bigwigs that if she said anything more than she was told, there was a price to pay. Probably her life, he suspected. Nevertheless, she had the cajones to pass him a device that he was forbidden to have. That took courage. Maybe it was the romantic in him that hoped it had more to do with Simon's charm than he realized.

Harlowe removed his clothes down to his underwear and switched on the beam. "I won't be long. Are you coming?" he asked, placing his clothes to the side.

Monday kept his clothes on as Harlowe zapped the wall with the green beam.

"I'll keep an eye on things here, if you don't mind, Captain."

"Suit yourself." Harlowe stepped through the portal and lit out like Genpok Xatz was after him for a kiss.

52

First Lesson

The Osset Museum of Antiquities wasn't as large as Simon feared, only half the size of a Costco warehouse, he guessed. If there was something about Lamille here, he should be able to find it in a few hours…tops! A small pain in his heart reminded him of the time he and Leucadia spent a month together hobnobbing across Europe, wandering the corridors of the Louvre, the Prado, and the Rijksmuseum. She was enthralled with the past, while truthfully, Simon didn't care about the bygone days as much as he cared about being with her. He would have searched garbage if she wanted him to. But that was all in the past. The day she met Harlowe was the day his dream ended. Somewhere inside him he wished for those days again. He knew that dull pain in his heart would never really go away. "Forever love," his shrink called it. For him she would always be his first love. The unobtainable love he always hope for but never found.

Simon sighed away his wish back to that part of his mind where he kept things safe from prying eyes, and he turned to Naree. She was no Leucadia Mars, but what the hey, Captain Starr, she was the hottest babe he had met on this world. Looking on the brighter side, Riverstone wasn't around to horn in on his action so who knew how things might turn out by the end of the day!

As Simon and Naree entered the museum a few steps ahead of the six armed guard babysitters, Naree asked, "What can you tell me about the place you seek, Captain?"

Simon tried to keep his mind focused, but her hot body made concentrating on Lamille difficult. If Naree had been a frumpy book type, the search would be a no brainer. Every time he got a whiff of her fresh scent, gazed into those beautiful eyes or noticed that perfectly shaped, upturned nose, it took all of his willpower not to take her in his arms and try out those tasty, red lips. After being recently jilted by Sizzle, his last heartbreak relationship, how was he supposed to keep his mind straight?

A glance at the stoic faces around them helped keep his pheromones in check. At least they had some usefulness, he thought, as no doubt a babe like Naree probably had an army of boyfriends calling night and day.

So what's the point of getting all heated up, Captain Starr?

Simon pulled out the love letter Prigg printed out for him and showed it to Naree. "This is the only thing we have to go on."

Naree studied the letter with great care. She felt the paper, turned it around in her hand, and briefly held it up to the light. "How did you come by this document?"

"We found it at The Donut," Simon replied as if the name was a common one that everyone would know. "This is a print out from the memory stick I showed the old hag, I mean the Genpok. Sorry," apologizing half-heartedly.

Naree's eyes narrowed, as she touched the letter to her cute chin. "The Donut?"

Simon didn't know what else to call it. Nobody did. The place was not on any of Millie's maps. "It's this place in the middle of Cartooga-Thaat. We don't know its real name, but it's out there in the nothingness, big and round like a donut. You know . . . round." He tried showing her with circular finger twirl of what a donut looked like. She still didn't understand what a donut was, but she did understand the concept.

"A torus ring?" she offered as a guess.

Simon had no idea what a torus was, either, but did know what a ring was, and that was close enough for him. "Yeah, something like that. My science officer believes the place was a rest area for travelers crossing the Thaat."

Naree multi-tasked as she read the letter again and continued with a brief history of the Donut. "Yes, Tabilisi." To her it seemed common knowledge. "You are correct, Captain Starr, in assuming the Donut, as you call it, was a rest station. But no one has occupied Tabilisi since the time of the Zabits."

Simon was surprised by Naree's casual reply. "You know of the Zabits?"

"Yes, of course. Osset has known of the Zabits for many thousands of passings."

Naree led Simon to a display not too far from where they entered the building. She showed him a large glass enclosure of clay pottery and very old jewelry that looked like it was made of gold, rubies, and diamonds. At the bottom of the case was a stone mural that depicted people running from what looked a like a hive of bees buzzing down on them from the clouds. Only the bees weren't really bees, they were shaped like the same bug-like creatures that invaded the Donut.

"Zabits . . ." Simon uttered like he was about to throw up.

"Yes, Zabits. You have seen them then?" Naree asked.

"Yeah, we saw them all right. They nearly fried our ship."

For the first time Simon thought he caught a glimpse of emotion from Naree, but it was quite subtle. "How did you escape, Captain Starr? No one escapes the Zabits."

Simon gently took her hand. "Please, Naree, call me Julian."

Naree looked at him like a deer in the headlights. "Julian?" She pronounced it more like "ah-le-an." But he wasn't complaining. Her accent was disarming, but holding her hand was like holding a dead fish. It felt cold and unresponsive to his touch. He wondered if any of her boyfriends felt the same way.

"That's my first name," Simon explained. "It's what my friends call me. Don't you have a name your friends call you?"

"My name is Naree. That is my only name. Is there a reason to have a second name?"

Briefly, they came almost too close, about to touch lips. Then one of the guards lowered his weapon, and it clanked against a stone sculpture. Whether it was done on purpose, or it was just an innocent misstep, it chilled the moment. They separated and refocused on their search.

Simon cleared his throat and answered her question as they strolled along. "No, no. Not at all. One name is enough. Makes it easier for everyone."

"Is there a specific period of history you are seeking?" Naree asked.

"Something about 17,000 thousand years ago should work."

"Are you speaking of revolutions?"

Simon nodded, reminding himself to keep it simple. Every planet the

Gamadin had visited had a different name for what they called a "year." On Gibb it was called a passing. In German it was call a *jahr*. The Irish called it a *bliain*. However, one thing was common to all, whatever they called a year, it was all equal to one revolution around the planet's primary star. He twirled his finger as if he were winding a toy. "Yeah, way back in time."

Naree pointed at a narrow hallway at the far end of the building. "Our oldest relics are through there."

The space was hardly bigger than his dining room at home. He was expecting something at least as big as the building they were in.

"That's it?"

"I am afraid there is very little before the Clarity began. The Genpok Xatz believes all that went before is unimportant," Naree explained.

"Is that what you believe, Naree?" Simon asked.

"It is the Clarity edict which we must obey, Captain."

Simon didn't need his therapist to understand that dissent was unhealthy on Osset. From what he had seen so far, everyone lived in a social straightjacket. Naree would not cross the line against the Genpok's decree, nor would he ask her to with the Genpok's armed thugs watching every move they made. For the moment, he left the pre-Clarity questions in the air as they entered the small room. So as not to alarm their escorts, he activated the com in his pocket and began readings of the items in the room as Prigg suggested.

Naree kept looking with interest at the letter. "What is a love letter, Ahlian?"

Simon bumped into a display table and caught the glass jar before it hit the floor. "Clumsy me," he said with a disarming grin at the guard behind him. He placed the jar carefully back on its display and said to the guard, "No harm, no foul, hey, pard?"

The guard was not amused. The lead guard motioned with the muzzle of his weapon to hurry it along. Simon retained his cheap smile as he explained what a love letter was to Naree. "It's a communication between two people who have deep feelings for each other."

Naree had no trouble stepping past the antiquities without hitting anything. "What are feelings, Ahlian?"

Simon thought he was making progress. He placed his hand over his stomach. "Feelings are something warm that comes to you when you're with someone you care about, Naree."

"Can you show me this, Ahlian? I would like to know more about feelings," Naree asked innocently.

Simon couldn't help himself. His smile grew wider like he had just drawn his fourth ace. "Sure, I can do that."

"Are you a master of this practice?"

With all the confidence of a master, he replied, "I am."

"Then you must be well disciplined in the subject."

"I've had a lot of practice," he admitted.

"Excellent. I will be in good hands."

"Yes, you will."

"Will I need any special equipment?"

Simon looked her up and down like Mowgi eyeing a steak. "No. You have all the requirements necessary and then some, Naree." He glanced back at the guards following them. "But for best results, the lessons do require some privacy," he said, tipping his head at their escort.

She glanced at the guards and then at Simon. "I understand. I will see we are not disturbed." She walked toward another doorway on the far end of the room. "If you would follow me, Captain."

As the group continued along, their footsteps echoed off the black marbled floors. Walking by more displays, Simon found nothing that interested him: Broken pieces of pottery, a necklace made of a dull metal, glass beads in a tray, several small statuettes in various conditions. A multi-faceted amulet did catch his attention. It was carved from blue crystal that he found intriguing because across its face was a gold inlay of a starburst. There was little doubt in his mind that the inlay had Gamadin origins. Simon licked his dry lips as he stared at the ornament like he just struck the Mother Lode. Glancing back at the guards, who were watching every movement they made, he wondered how he was going to lift the jewel without being caught. Thankfully, Naree solved that problem for him.

"Does the abordar cartouche interest you, Captain?" she asked.

"Yes, it does, Naree." He picked up the brooch and examined it closer. It was heavier than it looked. The blue crystal seemed to also glow brighter in his hand. "This writing on the back looks very familiar."

"Are you able to read it?"

"No, but I believe my science officer can."

"Then you may borrow it. Just return it when you have finished your investigation," she told him.

Simon's mouth hung open like he was going to swallow the abordar whole. "Thank you, Naree. That is very generous of you," he said, putting it in his uniform pocket.

Naree turned to a large stone carving on the wall. "This may also interest you. According to our records, this wall stone was found with the abordar. We believe it is from the same time period. Would you care to take that, too?" she asked.

The wall carving seemed trivial compared to the amulet. The ages had not been kind to it. Its surface was weather-worn like the headstones he and Leucadia had seen while meandering through the graveyards next to the ancient churches in France. The wiggly lines and markings were hardly visible. It was also four feet tall and twice that in length. The three-inch thick stone could easily weigh a ton, he figured. There was no way to transport it back to the ship, but he had another idea. "May I scan it?" he asked her.

Naree was surprised since she had not seen a device in Simon's possession. "You have such a device?"

Simon pulled out his com and showed it to her. "Yes, I can take an image of it for my science officer."

Naree stepped out of the way. "Of course, Captain, take your image."

After scanning the stone, there seemed nothing else in the room that was worth his time. The rest of the relics were stacked in piles with little care. None of them had descriptions or labeling. It was like he was a picker rummaging around an old storehouse full of old junk. He shooed away the dust from his nose and sneezed. Nobody would buy this trash, he thought.

Teary eyed and still sneezing, Simon scanned everything in the room with his com anyway. He figured Prigg could make some sense from the garbage even if he couldn't. Besides, it was more to show Harlowe that he wasn't wasting his time lusting for the babe.

"Is this all there is, Naree?" Simon asked.

"This is all that anyone is allowed to see," Naree replied.

"You mean there's more?" Simon asked.

"Yes, but the Clarity has forbidden the Vetus Vault to the unauthorized."

Simon saw an opportunity. "This Vetus Vault is very private then?"

Naree quickly caught on. "Why yes, it is, Captain." She turned to the lead guard and directed him to, "Open the Vetus Vault, Number One."

"The Vetus Vault is secure property of the Clarity, Naree," Number One reminded her in a curt, authoritative tone.

Naree stood her ground, which surprised Simon. Up to this point she had been soft-spoken and accommodating. He had not expected her to be so assertive. "I will determine that, Number One. Do as I say," she ordered in a cool but quite authoritative tone of her own.

Number One snapped to attention, clicking boots together. With a disruptor like the one Naree had used earlier, the guard pointed the device at the wall and created a large, door-sized portal into the vault. Lights on the other side automatically switched on, revealing an incredible storehouse that was a hundred times the size of the Clarity room.

Naree led Simon into the Vetus room where a huge quantity of antiquities lay dusty on the shelves, piled high inside boxes and wooden crates as far as his eyes could see. Stone sculptures, some whole, but mostly broken, were lying on their sides. Plates, pottery, and stonework, looking as though it was scooped up by front loader, were dumped in large square crates. Urns filled with who-knows-what were lined up like soldiers along one far wall. It appeared to Simon whatever the Clarity found was brought here and piled into heaps with no intent of ever cataloguing or organizing any of it systematically. The Clarity obviously had no interest in the past. As Naree stated earlier, Osset's history began the day the Clarity began and not a day sooner.

Ugh, Simon cringed. He hoped his com's memory had enough room to cram everything into its tiny storage banks. But a little of something was a whole lot better than nothing, he figured. Regardless, he needed to get crackin' and finish scanning everything so he could get on with Naree's lessons.

"Does the Vetus room meet with your approval, Captain? We have our privacy now," Naree said.

Simon was ecstatic that they were on the same page. "Perfect," he replied, taking hold of her hands. She felt a little stiff so he kept it simple and didn't try to rush her. "Do you trust me?" he asked her.

Naree nodded hesitantly as her dark eyes appeared to search his thoughts. "Of course."

"Close your eyes."

She was a willing student. She closed her eyes as he gave her more instructions. He said softly, "Keep your lips slightly parted, Naree."

Her lips separated. "Like this, Captain?"

"You're doing great. Now take a deep breath and relax, letting it out slowly. We're alone, so there is no hurry, Naree."

She blinked, opening her eyes briefly making sure he was still there, and then closed them again.

There were no more instructions as they touched lips ever so gently. "Was that okay?" he asked her.

She opened her eyes, looking at him like she was unsure. "Again, if you would," she requested and closed her eyes, waiting for him to touch her. Her breath was warm and fresh as they made contact again. He felt her lips softening as her hands relaxed, letting him guide her through the lesson. She trusted him.

Suddenly, the static discharge of the portal opening interrupted their session. They quickly separated as Number One stepped through the portal apologizing for the interruption. Before Naree could reprimand the guard, Number One said, "There is a problem, Naree. The Captain's crew has been arrested for high crimes against the Clarity."

Simon closed his eyes in disbelief. "You've got to be kidding." The lesson was over.

53

Jaws of Death

The storm hit *Ride II* like a hard slap in the face. Ian had to go farther east than he wanted, but it wasn't enough to avoid the turbulence of the storm. They had traveled through the night without a hitch, following Leucadia's advice to steer away from the high winds. By morning, the tempest had plans of its own. A second mass of low pressure had split off the main front and had found them sneaking around the back side. A narly black cloud had them in its sights, ready to eat them.

Ian didn't know if he could outrun the cloud or not. Lightening bolts fired jagged swords of charged light at them, missing the balloon by a fraction.

A second jolt strained everyone's harnesses. Cheesa grunted as the air was forced from her lungs. Dev's head slammed backwards, and he went limp. The robobs were the only ones able to hold themselves to the floor. Ian was grateful for that because he needed all the help he could get.

He yanked the steering wheel hard over while a robob twisted open a valve for more steam. *Ride II* lunged forward, not like one of Leucadia's Ferraris, but like a slow moving tortoise trying to make a getaway. "Come on, Baby," he said to his airship. "Gitty-up. That cloud is right on our tail."

The rain was so bad, Ian could see little out the forward windows. For all practical purposes he was flying blind. If it wasn't for the com on the dash, he wouldn't know if he was flying up or down, north, south, east, or west. The com was the only thing keeping him from crashing into a mountain.

Another hard bump and the com went flying off the dash. Ian tried to snatch it, but it tumbled off his fingers and clanked onto the metal floor near Cheesa.

"Stay where you are, Chee!" Ian called out. "Let the clicker get it!"

Too late!

Reaching out, Cheesa managed to unbuckled her harness and was stretching for the com when . . .

WHAM!

The cabin lifted, sending her to the floor like a hundred pound sack of concrete hit her in the back. Ian knew the reverse slam was next. Instead of the floor, she would hit the ceiling with the same counter force. Only this time, her neck would break against the ceiling. Ian had no choice but to unbuckle himself and dive for her. The robobs had their claws full adjusting valves and fixing bursting pipes. They couldn't move from their positions without something breaking.

Ian was the only one who could help her. In a single bound he reached out and grabbed her legs the instant the slam struck.

CRACK!

They both hit the ceiling together. Ian didn't know if he saved her life, but in doing so, he knocked himself unconscious. Dev awakened with no one manning the steerage wheel. Behind him, Cheesa and Ian were out cold on the floor. Two robobs were attending the valves, feverishly trying to keep *Ride II* from flipping on its side while a third clicker was opening a porthole. Dev thought that was a bad idea when there was no one at the wheel.

"Stop! You're letting in the storm," he shouted at the robob. But no amount of yelling would stop the stickman from opening the door. The storm blasted in as the black cloud opened its jaws, engulfing them with its jagged bolts. The next thing he knew the world was vertical. *Ride II* parts went flying as hot gases shot from fractured pipes that blew their gaskets.

That was all Dev remembered.

54

Conehead

Riverstone fired a hundred and fifty mile an hour fastball at Bigbob, low on the outside corner of the plate. The robob caught it easily and tossed it back without too much heat. The first time he and Bigbob played catch together, the big clicker nearly shattered Riverstone's hand with a two hundred mile an hour bb. If it wasn't for Riverstone's tough dura-leather mitt, his hand would have been history. Even so, his hand required a quick trip to the nearest med unit to mend the cracked metacarpals. Once the feeling was restored in his hand, he toned down Bigbob's fastball a mite before they returned to the ball field under the ship.

Improvising a ball field was no different on Osset than other worlds. Depending on the protection they needed from the atmosphere, the bases and home plate were either inside or outside the barrier. On #2 the diamond was set up outside on the beach because, as everyone knows, baseball is best played in the sun. On Olympus Mons, however, the outside temperature hovered around minus 150 degrees Fahrenheit. That was way too cold for any sport except Mons diving. But on Osset, the weather was perfect and the ground was wide, flat, and grassy, perfect for hitting grounders and running the bases. An aggressive Osset military made playing outside the barrier a problem, though, so Riverstone was forced to keep his robob ballplayers behind the barrier. As play continued under the hull, outside the barrier the soldiers had set up their cannons, tanks, lasers, drills, and various explosive devices of all shapes and sizes in a futile effort to breach the force field.

Millawanda's shields, of course, were impregnable. Nothing they tried even came close to poking through the shimmering blue light.

Overseeing all the activity, an Osset officer strolled along the perimeter between explosions, investigating the results of each failure. Riverstone guessed he was some high-ranking officer by the number of guards watching over him. He wore a drab green, camouflage uniform that was perfectly creased and ironed. His boots were black and polished, and each time he returned from inspecting the results, the dust that he picked up on his boots was wiped cleaned by his orderlies. Strapped to his waist was a black webbed belt that supported his sidearm. Riverstone wondered if it was as deadly as the Gamadin pistol he had strapped to his own leg. Rounding out the officer's uniform was a comical looking cone hat with small flaps sticking out the sides that distinguished him from the other regulars. No other soldier wore anything like it. Interestingly, the officer walked with a noticeable limp that he managed with stiff authority. The way Conehead, as Riverstone began to call him, used his ornately engraved crutch gave Riverstone the impression the hobble was no recent injury but a permanent handicap.

From the general concern on his bodyguards' faces, Conehead's inspections so close to the barrier were worrisome. They got really torqued when he stopped and began watching Riverstone and Bigbob playing catch. They cocked and pointed their weapons right at Riverstone's head.

Riverstone took another toss from Bigbob and threw it back before he asked the Conehead, "Do you play?"

Conehead looked up with concern at the shimmering forcefield.

"It's harmless," Riverstone said.

A security guard cautioned Conehead about going near the barrier, but he ignored the warning and hobbled closer. "Play?" Conehead asked.

Riverstone caught the ball again and held up the threads for Conehead to see. "Do you play baseball?"

"I am afraid I have never heard of base. . .ball," Conehead replied.

"Baseball. It's a game we play on our planet," Riverstone explained.

Conehead forced his lips together like Riverstone. "Basssseball," and repeated the word several times. When he was comfortable pronouncing the new word, he asked Riverstone, "You speak our language?"

Riverstone felt underdressed for an official meet and greet. His dark blue Nike's, the old red baggy, Billabong shorts he liked to play around in, and a grass-stained, white Lakewood High football jersey that Alice, his robob servant, had fashioned for him with "JESTER" and the number 7 printed in bright red letters on the back was hardly formal wear. But he was on a roll and didn't want to seem unfriendly even though the officer wanted to capture his ship. "I speak many languages." Maybe they were tired of wasting ammo and drilling gear on Millie, he thought, as he held up the baseball again. "Would you like to toss one?"

Conehead pointed at the barrier.

"No problem," Riverstone said. "Get your hands ready." Conehead rested his cane against his good leg and opened up his hand. Riverstone made a gentle toss. The baseball went through the barrier without a hitch, hitting Conehead's hand dead center. He was so startled by the ball actually passing through the barrier, he neglected to grab it when it hit his hand.

The ball dropped to the grass with a thump.

This sent his bodyguards into a tizzy. The instant the ball traveled through the barrier, one might have thought a bomb was about to explode. Fearing the worst, a half-dozen guards covered Conehead with their bodies while one brave guard grabbed the baseball and threw it to an open area, out of harm's way. A heavily armored vehicle then quickly rolled over the white sphere and waited for the blast.

Nothing happened.

Conehead pushed his guards aside in an angry fit. After dusting himself off, he straightened his uniform and limped over to the armored car that had covered the sphere. He barked a series of loud orders, waving his arms and cane violently for the vehicle to move. Another guard quickly retrieved the baseball and brought it back to him.

When Conehead returned to the barrier, he held up the crushed baseball and asked Riverstone, "Can we try that again?"

Riverstone produced another baseball from his mitt. "Sure," and tossed it to Conehead who caught the ball easily this time. "Good. Now toss it back."

"The barrier," Conehead said, pointing at the barrier.

Riverstone motioned to throw the ball. "Go on. It's okay."

Conehead tossed the ball, and it sailed right through the barrier like it wasn't there. The toss, however, went a little wide, but Bigbob snared the ball before it touched the ground. Bigbob lobbed it back to Riverstone, who in turn threw it back to Conehead, and said, "Not bad for your first pitch. Better than a lot of politicians I know."

The next time Riverstone tossed it back, Conehead picked the baseball out of the air like a third baseman stabbing a line drive.

"You learn fast," Riverstone said amazed.

Conehead examined the baseball looking for some hidden code in the stitches. After finding nothing obvious, he handed it off to one of his subordinates with orders.

"Hey, that was my baseball," Riverstone objected.

"It now belongs to the Clarity," Conehead said.

Riverstone had two dozen more in a bucket and could have a million more made if he wanted, but it was the principle: Like thou shall not steal or take things that don't belong to you. Riverstone knew why Conehead kept the baseball. For him it was the key to city. *Sorry, Toad. You're SOL.* "It's just a baseball. Nothing trick."

Conehead offered a deal. "If you discharge the barrier, you can have the baseball back."

Smiling thinly, Riverstone said, "Not happening, brah."

"My forces will eventually find a way through the barrier."

Riverstone scanned the perimeter outside the barrier. Debris was spread all along the barrier from the failed attempts. "I doubt it."

"The Clarity has commanded me to seize your ship," Conehead said. "This will be done, or I will have it destroyed."

Riverstone figured it was a pointless argument. The Clarity could try whatever they wanted. In the end, it would be a waste of time. So he kept the kept the conversation cordial and never mentioned once that, if push came to shove, *Millawanda* could wipe out his army in a blink.

"What's your name, Sir?" Riverstone asked.

"I am Legatus Fiv," Fiv replied. Then in a casual, modest manner, he added, "Commanding Geffredinol of the Osset military and all that you see around you."

Geffredinol, Riverstone thought, must mean he's the top brass like General Gunn. This surprised him. He expected someone much older and ugly like Gunn to be the top dog. Fiv was boyishly handsome and looked closer to Simon's age, mid twenties tops. But then how many times had others thought of Harlowe as being far too young to captain such a powerful ship as *Millawanda*?

All the time, Riverstone snickered.

"Impressive," Riverstone said to Fiv, then saluted him casually and added, "First Officer Matt Riverstone. A pleasure to meet you, Geffredinol Fiv."

Fiv eyed Riverstone carefully, accepting his role as spokesman for the captured ship. "You are in charge while your Captain has business with the Genpok?"

Riverstone had no idea who the Genpok was, but he figured it was Fiv's boss. "I am."

"Your ship is impressive. We have nothing like it," Fiv said, genuinely awed.

"She's one of a kind."

"How far have you traveled?"

"Far."

Riverstone figured Fiv already knew they had crossed Cartooga-Thaat and so kept his answers minimal.

"A thousand light passings is indeed far."

Riverstone was right. Fiv did know more than he let on.

"And you survived the Zabits?"

"We did."

"Impossible. No one survives a Zabit assault."

"We did."

Fiv reared back on his metal cane and stared at the saucer with a different eye. Now that it was near darkness, Millie was even more stunning in her shimming blue dress. To see her at her best, however, one needed to stand a mile away to grasp the full extent of her beauty.

Fiv hobbled closer to the barrier, side-stepping spent shell fragments. "This allowed your ship to survive?" he asked, touching the barrier with his cane.

"It helped," Riverstone replied without giving away any family secrets.

"I see no weapons."

"Trust me, they're there."

"You carry one in the open," Fiv said with a glance toward Riverstone's sidearm.

"Habit."

"Are you fast?"

"Faster than you."

Fiv returned a small smirk. He didn't seem the type that would test anyone unless he was assured of winning.

"You have not used your weapons against my forces. Why?" Fiv asked.

"Our visit here is peaceful. We only came to warn you of the Zabits and gather information about our ancestors. When we have completed our research, we will leave your planet just like we came…in peace."

"The Clarity demands you drop the barrier for inspection of your ship," Fiv said directly.

"Demand all you want. That's not going to happen, Fiv. The barrier stays." Riverstone was beginning to wonder how many ways he could say "no" in the Osset language.

"But I order you to," Fiv said again.

"Yeah, so order all you want. The barrier stays," Riverstone replied calmly but forcefully. As Harlowe often pointed out, once you have survived three months with General Theodore Tehcumsa Gunn, no one frightens you, not even a toad face like Sar, and now Conehead.

"Your ship will never leave Osset intact, like your Captain's subordinates," Fiv said.

Riverstone dropped his mitt on the grass. "Come again?"

"Are you aware of the fate of your subordinates?"

"Talk straight, Fiv. What's happened to our crewmen?" Riverstone demanded.

"I assure you, your Captain has broken no laws, Officer Riverstone, only his subordinates. Their sentence will be carried out at first light."

Riverstone kept his cool, staying unemotional. The idea of Harlowe and Monday breaking any laws was absurd. Harlowe would never do anything to jeopardize the mission. "The subordinates? What laws have they broken?"

"They have killed Keenishas and decimated a Follish Pimar. They are protected species around Cornicen. They must pay for their infraction, Officer Riverstone."

Riverstone motioned for Bigbob to join him as he approached the barrier to discuss the matter further. "Keenisha and Follish Pimar, huh? What are they?"

Fiv bent down and picked up a tiny crab-like creature from between the grass. The tiny legs of the crustacean wiggled between his fingers as Legatus explained, "This is a Keenisha. It lives in the grass here." Next he pointed to a nearby clump of red and yellow flowers that were no bigger than the tip of Riverstone's pinky finger. "Those are Follish Pimars," said Fiv.

"That's what they killed?"

"Yes. Two Keenishas and ten Follish Pimars."

"Two?" Riverstone couldn't believe what he was hearing. "But you're stepping all over them. You've killed a hundred standing here talking to me. The shells you fired at my ship probably killed millions more. And if I checked the grass, I bet your tanks smashed a zillion more Follish Pimars driving your ass here this morning. Looks like you've broken the law yourself. When's your execution?"

"This field is a Clarity Military base, and as such, that law does not apply. The Keenisha and the Follish Pimar are only protected along the Cornicen shoreline where your crewmen committed the crime against the State. Additional crimes were also committed by entering the Clarity-protected waters."

Riverstone closed his eyes briefly to visualize Harlowe drooling over the waves as he unknowingly stepped on a crab on his way to the beach. "Swimming in the ocean is forbidden?"

"That is the law, Officer Riverstone."

"So what's the fine?"

"There is no fine, Officer Riverstone. The subordinates will be put to death at sunrise."

"WHAT?" Riverstone snapped. "Punishable by death?"

"That is the law, Officer Riverstone."

"They're not from this planet. How would they know they were breaking the law?"

"The Clarity decision is final."

Fiv was beginning to sound like a broken CD. Riverstone reached down and picked up his mitt. "Fiv, we came to your planet to help you and now you've taken my crew and prosecuted them like criminals. This is no way to make friends. If anything happens to my crew, there will be a price to pay, and it won't be pretty," Riverstone warned.

Fiv motioned, and several armed guards sprang to life, closing in around the Officer with their automatic weapons. "Are you threatening the commander of the Clarity military, Officer Riverstone?" Fiv asked directly.

The game suddenly changed from catch to war.

Riverstone relieved Bigbob of his glove as he kept a cold eye on Fiv. "That's right, Conehead. Make no mistake about it. I...am...threatening... you, Toad," he said very slowly and clearly. He was done playing nice. "Any harm comes to my crew and the Keenishas will be the highest form of life left on this field."

"Fire!" Fiv cried out, but before one soldier fired his weapon, all six of his guards dropped beside the Geffredinol. Fiv was stunned. He had never seen anyone draw so fast.

Riverstone waved his pistol. "Grab Conehead, Bigbob."

The tall clicker exploded through the barrier, snatched Fiv, and deposited him on Riverstone's side of the barrier before his troops could react.

"I protes—" Fiv tried to say before Riverstone lowered the boom.

Wham!

"Welcome to our clarity, brah," Riverstone said, reaching down to pick up Fiv's walking cane and comical hat. Bigbob lifted Fiv's conscious body from the ground and followed Riverstone to the nearest blinker. Along the way Riverstone marveled at the cane's blue stone and intricate scrollwork, which seemed totally out of character for a Clarity-made object.

Fageddaboutit, Riverstone thought, crushing a Follish Pimar under his foot. He had his hostage.

55

My Crewmen!

"I protest, Naree!" Simon shouted. "Take me to the Genpok. I insist!"

Naree stepped in front of Simon to explain that it was against Clarity law to enter the great chamber without permission.

"I'm having words with that nag!" he told Naree in no uncertain terms. "My crewmen are being unjustly prosecuted for some stupid law that no one in their right mind would have known about! Take me to her, or I will find her myself, Naree!"

"If you persist, Captain, the Genpok Xatz will dispose of you, too," Naree pleaded, clearly in fear of his life. "No one can demand anything of the Genpok Xatz," she warned him.

Simon glared down at her. "I can, and I will!"

"You cannot go there, Captain. You will be shot if you try."

"We'll see about that."

Simon turned to walk out the museum door, only to be blocked by the security guards. "Listen to Naree, Captain. You must stay where the Clarity orders," Number One guard said.

"Get out of my way, Butthead," Simon ordered, "before I rip your face off."

The security guards pulled their weapons but before a single guard could stop him, Simon nailed Number One with a hard right. He delivered a forearm shiver to another guard. After more fists and high kicks, the other guards were laid out on the floor, out cold. It wasn't pretty, but it was fast and decisive. Naree stared at the unconscious guards in shock.

"What have you done?" Naree asked stunned.

"What I had to," Simon replied coolly, then added, "My crewmen, Naree. Take me to them."

Simon had to shake Naree to bring her out of her trauma. "Naree, please. Take me to my crewmen."

Naree began slowly. "They would be at the Clarity detention building."

Simon pulled her along, side-stepping the fallen guards. "Show me."

"They will kill you if you try to leave the building."

Simon removed a hidden pistol from his sleeve. "Let me worry about that."

56

Jailbirds

Harlowe and Monday didn't resist their arrest. Why should they? This was an innocent mistake that would soon be straightened out by Captain Starr when he heard about their imprisonment. There was no sense jeopardizing the mission either, since they had done nothing wrong. He and Monday were taken to the Clarity prison in the center of the city and led several levels below ground to a small cell with thick bars. It wasn't until they were told that swimming in the ocean and stepping on tiny crabs and flowers was a capital offense, and they would be executed in the morning that Harlowe decided enough was enough.

Monday stared at the guards sitting at a table down at the far end of the hallway. "They gave us back our clothes. That's odd. You'd think they would give us prison uni's or something."

Harlowe stretched out on the floor and used his jacket for a pillow against the barren wall of their cell while they waited. "We're the only ones in this joint. That's even odder. The whole place doesn't make sense. No swimming, no stepping on the flowers, no bathrooms... What's up with that? Don't these people ever have to pee?"

"Yeah, I could use a toilet now," Monday said, sounding urgent. He then asked, "How long do we wait?"

Harlowe yawned and closed his eyes. "Until Captain Starr checks in with the info we need."

"That could be a while. Did you take care of things?"

270

"First thing."

Uncomfortable, Monday danced a little.

"You feelin' a little tight, Squid?" Harlowe asked, peeking out of one eye.

"I might not make it until then," Monday replied in pain. "Rerun better hurry."

A tiny ring went off in their ears from their hidden communicators. "That's him now." A second unique ring meant Riverstone was checking in at the same time. Harlowe put them all on a conference call.

"Dog, you okay? I just heard," Riverstone asked first.

"Squid has to tinkle, but yeah, we're good," Harlowe replied.

"Do you know what's coming down, Dog?"

"We know."

"Where are you?"

"Somewhere underground."

"They're in the Clarity jail," Simon's voice broke in. *"Naree and I are on our way there now to get you out."*

Harlowe jumped to his feet, barking orders. "Oh, no you're not," he said, slipping on his jacket. "You're staying with plan A, Captain Starr. Have you found anything yet?"

"Plenty, Skipper."

"What did you find?"

Simon sounded like he was running as he spoke. His breathing was heavy and choppy. *"Some good stuff, Captain. I found a blue brooch with a Gamadin logo carved on it."*

Harlowe found that hard to believe. "Really?"

"This thing is cool, Skipper. You gotta see it."

"All right. Get back to the ship with it, pronto. What else?"

"A bunch of things, but I don't know what it all means. Could be nothing, Dog."

Harlowe motioned for Monday to get himself ready. When the conversation ended, they were breaking out. "Let Prigg worry about that. Find someplace safe and upload what you have to him ASAP. Then scoot back to the ship with the blue thing. Squid and I can handle things here. We'll be making a lot of noise. While they're worried about us, you get your buns home. Got that? Get out of town in a hurry. Stay away from the main highway, and keep your head down."

If what Simon described was true, the jewel was a big find. It was way more than he expected. Harlowe just hoped Simon could make it back to the ship without getting nailed by the Clarity thugs. He had confidence in him knowing he had his SIBA, his weapons, and plenty of ammo clips. He was also Gamadin. It would take a major effort by the Clarity to stop him. Just the same, he wouldn't breathe easy until Simon walked through the barrier.

"Aye, Skipper," Simon confirmed.

"And Rerun," Harlowe said, having one last thing to add.

"Yeah, Skipper."

"Good work, Gamadin."

"Thanks, Skipper."

Harlowe signed off and addressed Riverstone. "Okay, you heard what I told Rerun?"

"Every word, Captain," Riverstone replied.

"The same goes for you. We stick with Plan A. Don't get ideas about coming here to help us. Millie stays put, and that's an order. We'll make it there. Count on it."

"Captain, they have thousands of soldiers and tanks surrounding the ship," Riverstone warned.

"Understood. We'll be careful. Just stick with Plan A."

"Aye, Captain. Plan A. Riverstone out!"

Monday looked at Harlowe as he removed his SIBA medallion from a hidden pocket. "Now, Captain?"

Harlowe did the same. He removed his SIBA medallion from its hidden pocket and replied, "Now, Squid." Within two-heartbeats they were encapsulated in Gamadin armor. Harlowe found his mini torch and went to work on the bars. He pointed the searing flame at the bar and cut through easily, only to discover that the flame didn't work on the faux metal. The bar healed itself the instant it passed through the bar. The same thing happened when he tried to shoot the bar with his pistol. The plas round went straight through the metal but then reconstructed itself like it had with the torch.

Monday tried grabbing the bars with his SIBA claws and pulling them apart. They didn't budge. The bars were as solid as the real thing.

Harlowe looked at Monday frustrated and confused. "How do they do that?"

Monday was beside himself. He grabbed his crotch and said, "Think of something, Captain."

57

Goodbye, Ahlian

Simon and Naree ducked down the first deserted street they found. Once he was certain the area was clear, Simon uploaded all that he could back to the ship from his com. When he was finished, he turned to Naree with a long face and told her, "I have to go, Naree."

"Your ship is far away, Ahlian. How will you make it without a transport?" Naree asked. "By now the Clarity knows you have broken the law by leaving the Museum. They will be after you."

He put his com in the pocket with the amulet and took her in his arms. "I'll make it okay. Don't worry." He kissed her, once, twice, three times before he pleaded with her. "Come with me, Naree. This Clarity stuff isn't for you."

Naree looked at him sadly. "I can't, Ahlian. I must stay here. It is where I must be."

"No, Naree. You don't belong here. You belong with me. Come with me, you'll see. You'll see what freedom is really like. It's life, Naree. Really living. Not like here where everyone fears that old witch!" He tugged on her arm to go with him. "Come on, Naree. Come with me."

Suddenly, the sirens began to blare loudly all over the city.

Naree pushed Simon away. "Go, Ahlian, before it is too late. I will stay here and lead them away from you."

"They will hurt you, Naree," Simon said, taking her hand. "I can't let that happen."

She pushed him away and ran off down the sidewalk. At the corner, she turned back and shouted, "Save your world, Ahlian. Save your freedom." She touched her quivering lips as heavy tears fell down her soft, pink cheeks and waved goodbye.

Losing hot babes seemed to be his lot in life.

58

Escape

The explosion rocked the cellblock, flooding the corridors with guards. Voices barked out orders through the smoke and fire. "Get the prisoners!" The smoke was so thick the guards had to feel along the wall to make their way to the prisoners' cell.

"I can't see them!" a guard cried out.

"Unlock the cell," a commanding voice shouted. "Get them out before they suffocate."

"Yes, sir!" the guard replied. The guard quickly removed his disruptor device and de-energized the prisoners' cell bars. Before they could enter the cell, they were struck so hard by a heavy blunt instrument that they slammed against the back wall of the corridor, out cold.

Harlowe snagged the guard's disruptor off the floor. "This might come in handy."

Monday led the way, stepping over the downed guards in the corridor and running toward the elevator in full SIBA gear. "How did you know they would follow your orders, Captain," Monday asked Harlowe as they ran.

"The toads know nothing about security. They gave us back our clothes, didn't they?" Harlowe reasoned. "Who does that? They follow orders like robots."

"They give me the creeps." Then as an afterthought, Monday asked, "Do you think Bolt's blue thing means anything?"

They came to the elevator without a fight. "Sounds like it. We could use

275

a break," Harlowe said, testing the doors. It was no surprise the power to the elevator was shutdown from the explosion. Sirens screamed throughout the levels as more guards were heard coming from the opposite direction. Monday shot a wide burst of plas rounds, but no one went down. The guards didn't seem affected at all, and they began to fire back. Their SIBAs protected them against the Osset projectiles, but Harlowe wasn't sure how they would hold up against something heavier, like a 50 caliber faux bullet. He didn't want to wait around to see.

"Shoot the head," Harlowe suggested as he forced open the elevator doors with his claws. The open shaft below was like looking into a black hole. He couldn't see the bottom even with his bugeyes. Three levels above them, though, was the elevator car blocking their way to the surface.

While Harlowe studied the cables running vertically inside the shaft, Monday focused on targeting the guards' heads. His very first shot made all the difference. "That works!"

Harlowe took out the disruptor he had taken from the guard and focused the beam on the cables. "Did you copy that, Rerun? Use head shots on these toads."

Simon broke in. *"Roger that, Skipper. Thanks!"*

The elevator car dropped like a dead weight. Harlowe jerked his head back before he was decapitated. The shaft was so deep, the car only made a slight puffing sound when it finally struck the bottom.

Looking back up the shaft, the way was now clear. Monday continued head shots while holding onto Harlowe's belt as he leaned in and fired a piton head straight up the shaft. They prayed that whatever it hit, faux metal or something else, that it would stick. The dura-line played out for nearly two thousand feet before the explosive head thankfully sank into something solid. More guard reinforcements were making their way down from the upper levels as Monday snapped in a full mag and urged Harlowe to hurry.

Harlowe grabbed Monday's arm and pulled him to the shaft where he clicked his belt pulley to the line. "I'm right behind you."

"Aye, Captain."

Monday swung out into the shaft and went up like a shot, just like they had done a thousand times on Mars scaling the 15,000-foot vertical cliffs of Olympus Mons. Harlowe attached his pulley to the line next. Before heading up, he tossed a couple of thaders down each side of the corridor.

The resulting explosions followed Harlowe up the shaft, but his SIBA kept him from getting his butt hairs singed as the flames blew right past him on his ascent.

Before reaching the top, two guards on an upper level poked their heads into the shaft. Shocked at seeing Monday rising on an invisible line, they quickly drew their weapons, but before they could fire a single round, Monday grabbed them as he flew by and yanked them into the shaft.

"Look out below, Captain!" Monday yelled.

Harlowe swung to the side and allowed the two guards to scream by unobstructed.

At the top of the shaft, Monday pointed the disruptor at the wall, and a flood of sunlight poured through the open portal. He swung himself out, landing on the rooftop of the building. Two seconds later Harlowe joined him; a half second later the portal slammed shut.

"Where are we?" Harlowe asked, going straight to the edge of the building. Flying all around the building were air patrol cars searching the lower levels for the escaped prisoners. As yet, no one believed they could have made it to the roof so fast on foot.

"Are we jumping?" Monday asked.

Harlowe knew Monday didn't like SIBA flying if he could help it. Looking down the couple hundred stories, he spotted divisions of military convoys headed toward their skyscraper. Monday rejoined him after canvasing the opposite side. "Double that number coming behind us, Captain."

Harlowe leaned over the edge like he was searching for something. "Stay put, Squid." Then, without explanation, Harlowe dove off the side of the building and yelled back, "I'll be right back!"

From a second and third hatchway, security forces exploded onto the roof. Apparently the word was out that the escapees were trapped there on the roof. Monday had his hands full piling up bodies with head shots, reloading twice in the process. He had no cover. When the air patrol cars finally saw him, he would be outflanked. He felt his jacket pocket where he kept his supply of mags. He would be out of ammo in a hurry if Harlowe didn't return soon with the cavalry.

A patrol car suddenly popped over the far ledge and headed straight at him. Monday was about to shoot the driver when Harlowe's voice shouted, *"It's me, Squid!"* into his SIBA communicator.

The patrol car turned sideways and slammed into the side of a rooftop tower. Harlowe opened the door. "I'm still getting the hang of it."

"Our ride, Captain?" Monday asked, smiling.

"Yeah, picked it up on the cheap," Harlowe replied, waving him into the cab. "Get in!"

There wasn't time for finesse. Harlowe pushed the lifters forward, taking out two of the building's exhaust vents in the process. Intending go left, he swung hard right into another tower before he finally got control and was airborne, headed back to *Millawanda*. That was the good news. The bad news was they were almost home when the patrol car began to sputter and lose altitude. Harlowe slapped the fuel gauge. It didn't change. They were out of fuel.

59

Need a Lift, Lady?

Naree saw Number One standing defiantly at the top of the museum steps, waiting for her to appear before him. He would ask questions, and she would tell them she was forced to go with Ahlian. She corrected herself. She meant to say Captain Starr. She had to keep his name right, otherwise Number One would suspect that she helped the Offworlder to escape. She would tell them she had escaped and that the aliens were headed north; when in reality Ahlian's true course was south.

Captain Starr! She kept telling herself. She had to remember his name, or they would know she was lying. They would hurt Al—, Captain Starr, and his mission to help his people would fail. The Clarity would take his freedom away and kill him if he were caught like his crewmen. She touched her lips, knowing she couldn't allow that to happen.

Number One met her at the foot of the stairs with his weapon pointed at her like he was going to shoot her.

"Put down your enforcer, Number One," she demanded. "I am not a criminal."

"You will come with me, Naree. We have orders to absorb you immediately," Number One told her.

"By whose authority?"

"Genpok Xatz. The prisoners have escaped, Naree. We know you have assisted in giving the Captain Clarity national secrets. You have committed high treason against the State, which is punishable by immediate absorption."

"How did I accomplish this act of treason, Number One? I am here. I have returned to the museum. I am not with Ahlian. I have given him no secrets. Check the manifests. All national antiquities are still with the Vetus Vaults," Naree argued in her defense. She then realized she had called the Captain, Ahlian, and hoped Number One had lost sight of her error as well.

"The Vetus abordar. You gave it to the Captain."

"I did...I did, yes," she said, stuttering slightly. "You were there. You know that. It was loaned to him to assist his people against the Zabits."

"That is Darkn's personal treasure. He has given order that all that were in on the theft shall be absorbed. Now where is it? Is it with the Captain you so fondly call Ahlian?" Number One demanded to know.

Naree looked for a place to run, but the guards surrounded her, quickly cutting off any escape she might have entertained.

Naree turned hard. "If you absorb me, you will never find Darkn's abordar, Number One."

That wasn't Number One's problem. He would absorb her no matter what she said. "The Captain's direction of travel, Naree. Where has he run?"

"Why should I tell you?"

"Because once you are absorbed, your form will never be as it was. You will be reprogrammed with a new identity. Tell us now, and it may be possible to have your identity remain as it is, Naree."

Naree had only to think a moment before she answered. "South. Ahlian has headed south."

Number One quickly turned to his closest subordinate. "Communicate to Darkn; the alien in question has headed north."

"I told you south, Number One."

"I know. You lied to protect him by telling me his common name, not his official calling."

Number One waved his weapon at Naree as two soldiers grabbed her arms and led her to the wall.

"What are you doing, Number One? You promised me I would have my identity."

"My orders are explicit, Naree. You will be dissolved."

"Not absorbed?"

Number One holstered his weapon and took out his disruptor, dialing it to full power.

"You can't do this, Number One."

"Darkn's orders, Naree. No choice."

Once the disruptor was fully charged, Number One pointed it at Naree. But before he could press the activator, a sizzling blue round blew though his head as a military transport drove to a screeching stop in front of the museum steps. Leaning from the side window, Ahlian dropped the remaining guards before they could fire a single round in their defense.

Ahlian casually stepped from the vehicle's side door with his sidearm in hand, and asked Naree with a smirky grin, "Need a lift, Lady?"

60

End of The Ride

Ian shouted orders, flailing his arms wildly as he pointed. "Release that valve! Open that spigot to the aft lines! I need more revolutions to the starboard rotors!" He continued shouting commands, while fighting off an unseen force that was trying to destroy his airship. "More steam! I need steerage!" *Ride II* had to change direction fast, or the vortex would consume them. But something powerful had his wrists. Try as he could, he couldn't get to the steering wheel to save his ship.

"Stop! Let me go!" Ian cried out. "The vortex! We have to turn to starboard before it's too late!"

A girl's soft voice kept saying, "Wake up, Ian, wake up."

When Ian opened his eyes, he found himself face to face with Cheesa's worried face. Above his head, two mechanical hands held his wrists, keeping him from doing harm to himself or anyone else around him. After a few calming breaths, he suddenly realized that he wasn't aboard his airship anymore. He was lying on the grass and not inside the cabin at all. He had no clue where he was or how long he had been unconscious.

With Cheesa's help, he sat up against a fallen tree and tried to comprehend the new world around him. The rain was coming down hard, pelting the makeshift shelter over his head.

A rush of disaster filled his head. "My Ride!" he cried out. Suddenly, he remembered his creation being caught in the jaws of the storm. The black cloud was breaking them apart, and they were going down.

282

A loud explosion startled him, bringing his attention to a billowing plume of black smoke rising through the treetops. Between the tall evergreens, his once beautiful machine lay broken and mangled on the forest floor. Its rotors were bent and torn from their mounts. The cabin that he had fashioned from an abandoned car was crushed, and the boiler was horrendously dented and hissing white steam along a crack in its seam. Yellow brass and copper manifold pipes lay twisted on the ground all around. There was no use even thinking about repair. *Ride II* was history! Borrowing a line from a childhood nursery rhyme, Ian said to himself, *All the King's horses and all the King's men can't put my Ride back together again.*

"What happened?" Ian asked.

"Lu saved us, Ian," Cheesa said empathically, knowing Ian's loss was heartbreaking to them all.

Ian turned slightly to his right. Leucadia's arms were around Dev's rain soaked body, keeping him from collapsing face down in the mud.

Ian's head was still groggy. He lay under the tent wondering how he had made it from point A to point B, not understanding why he was looking at Leucadia at all until Cheesa explained, "Somehow Lu climbed into the cabin and brought us down here."

Ian looked at her warmly. Just like Harlowe, she was beyond amazing. He didn't care how she did it, he was just happy to see her and everyone else alive. She appeared weary and mentally frazzled. Ian was certain the SIBA would shut her down if she didn't find a way to rest. "Thanks, Lu," he said to her.

"I was a little late to help, Ian. I'm so sorry," Leucadia said, feeling terrible as they watched the contrived vehicle that had brought them so far, die a fiery death.

Ian rolled onto his knees, and with Cheesa's assistance, he was able to stand. His legs felt wobbly at first, but as his SIBA kicked in, repairing his body and injecting him with the nutrients he needed; his strength returned. A couple of deep knee bends, and he was able to put his arms around Leucadia. All he wanted to do was hold her. "I'm so happy you're okay," he said, surrounding her and the Prince with his arms. When he finally let go, he carefully brushed back the long, blonde ends off her wet face so he could see her green eyes and asked, "Molly and Rhud, have you heard anything?"

Leucadia stared into the rain. "Muuk's forces are heading north."

"Then they're still headed for the Du Tir," Ian determined as if it was a given.

"Yes, his airships will be heading our way at flank speed. We must hurry."

"You need some rest, Lu," Ian said concerned.

"I can't, Ian; we have to keep moving."

Ian led her and the Prince under the shelter. "Your body is on 'E', Lu. If you don't rest, the SIBA will do it for you." They had a long distance to cover. Without Gamadin assistance, they would never make it through the forest on foot to the Du Tir, so Leucadia agreed to some down time.

While they rested, Ian went through *Ride II's* wreckage one last time. Inside the cab, he retrieved the small blue energy capsule from the boiler chamber. He unscrewed a brass valve lever for a keepsake and put it in his a pouch, along with the boilermaker's medallion he pried loose from the front of the tank. It was slightly larger than his SIBA coin. It was scratched and charred and a little bent from the crash, but it was a part of his creation he would keep forever. He stuffed it in his utility pouch and patted a wheel one last time. "Thank you," he said to her one last time.

He then joined the others. It was time to go.

61

To Die For

Legatus Fiv awakened in the most comfortable bed he had ever slept in, with a tubular and ball jointed mechanical being standing over him. The thin-tubed droid, that was holding a tray with a glass of blue water, had long pale hair attached to the back of its simple, triangular shaped head. Upon seeing Fiv alert, the droid bent over and offered him the glass of blue liquid along with some sweet smelling wedges covered with a gooey amber liquid. Scattered around the plate were fatty, red and tan strips beside the wedges with tiny, deep purple spheres. No item on the plate was familiar to Fiv. If Officer Riverstone wished to poison him, he figured he could have done him in easily while he slept. He doubted the nourishment would harm him, since it was more likely he would be kept alive to exchange him for Officer Riverstone's superior. Still, the aroma of the plate was tempting and made his stomach growl.

No, Fiv thought to himself. He must stay disciplined for the Clarity and keep his mind clear; for quite possibly the nourishment was laced with mind controlling drugs.

He sat up, taking into account that he was naked under the covers except for dark blue shorts. Looking around the room, he found his prison cell more comfortable than his own quarters. The space was far bigger and the finely appointed floor coverings, soft chairs, and golden tables next to his bed were like nothing he had ever seen.

Fiv suddenly felt odd but not in a bad way. For the first time in many revolutions, his legs seemed free of pain. It was strange how he thought he could even wiggle his toes again. Peering under his silky covering, he was astonished to find his right leg lying straight like his good left leg. He wiggled his toes to convince himself the leg really belonged to him. The crooked bones he had suffered during an explosion long ago had miraculously reshaped back to normal.

Excited to test his leg, he swung it over the edge and placed both feet on the thick, cushy floor. Would his foot take the pressure without his cane? He had to try. He wiggled his toes again, making sure he wasn't imagining that his foot really was normal. He breathed deeply and cautiously stood, holding onto the table by the bed. He was fine so far. He took a step forward. It was painless. He took two more, then three and four steps in succession. It was as if he had never suffered the crippling injury. He would never need his cane again!

"How does it feel, brah?" a voice asked.

Fiv turned and saw Riverstone standing in the doorway. "How ... Why?" he stuttered, sliding his hand down the side of his repaired leg. Why would anyone do such a thing to an enemy, Fiv wondered? Was there something sinister in his kindness?

Riverstone smiled, knowing the reason was obvious. "It needed fixing, didn't it?"

"Yes, but— You have such capabilities?"

Riverstone waved his hand in an off-handed manner. "Millie fixes everything. You should see what she did for Lu. Gave her a new ticker without her knowing it. To this day, she's still torqued about it, but she keeps humming along, good as new, like your leg. You like it?" he asked, pointing at Fiv's foot.

"It feels like it was never injured," Fiv admitted. "There is no pain."

"Sweet. Another happy camper."

Riverstone walked over to the untouched plate of edibles. "The food's not to your liking, Fiv?" He picked up a wedge coated with the amber fluid and swallowed it whole. "Pretty tasty," he said, smacking his lips. "Mother makes the best French toast and bacon this side of the Thaat."

"I wasn't sure ..."

"If we wigged it out or something?"

Fiv had never heard the phrase. "Wigged it out?"

Riverstone translated for him. "Poisoned."

"Ah, yes. The thought had crossed my mind."

Riverstone sipped the blue fluid and popped a few purple spheres in his mouth. "Man, the blueberries are to die for. You should try 'em." He pointed a playful finger at Fiv's nose. "Don't tell the EPA, though. They have no sense of humor. They're organic."

"What is EPA?" Fiv asked.

"The Clarity on steroids," Riverstone replied, heading for the door. "When you're ready, you'll find clothes in there," he said, pointing to a door across the room. "The head is through there. If you have any questions about how things work, ask Alice here," tapping the droid with the long, pale, shoulder-length hair. "She'll show you everything you need to know. Right, Alice?"

Alice's blue-lighted head nodded up and down.

"There, you see. She's at your disposal. Enjoy the accommodations, Fiv." Riverstone started to leave.

"Where are you going?" Fiv asked.

"I'll be on the bridge. When you're dressed, Alice will show you the way."

"Am I a prisoner?"

"Well, kinda. But no worries. We do things a little differently around here," Riverstone explained. "You're cool, though. Give your new leg a test run down the corridors. They're nice and long. Plenty of room to stretch it out."

"You are not concerned I might escape?" Fiv asked.

Riverstone chuckled. "Where would you go? Your best minds couldn't break in, so how are you going to break out?" He waved going out the sliding doorway. "TTFN, Fiv."

Fiv stood in disbelief as he watched the young officer go. Never in his life had he heard of a prisoner being treated in such a manner. His captor even left the door open behind him. Fiv found the alien system unnerving. This would never be the Clarity's way, he told himself. His captor did have a good point. Even if he knew the way out of the ship, how would he escape when his best military minds were unable to break its code?

Walking around on *two* good legs made Fiv hungry. He reached for a wedge of amber coated nourishment and took his first bite of the alien's offering. The instant he tasted the sweet liquid, his eyes closed. He had never tasted anything so wonderful in his life. He savored every moment of sweetness as he repeated Riverstone's words to himself. "Died and gone to heaven . . ."

62

The Exchange

Harlowe's air transport ran out of fuel a mile short of *Millawanda*. He had only enough fuel to land on the military landing strip where a thousand soldiers were pointing every weapon imaginable at them. The thought of taking their chances by leaping for the barrier was doable. With their personal force fields and their SIBAs at full power, they could easily cover the distance to the barrier if they had to. But Riverstone informed Harlowe he had a hostage to trade, so making a dash for it, wasn't necessary.

"Did you hear from Rerun yet?" Harlowe asked Riverstone over his com. "He has that blue thing he says is Gamadin."

"Not a peep, Dog. Think he's in trouble?"

"He's with a babe."

"Yeah, he's in trouble."

"No doubt, but keep trying to reach him while I take care of these toads. Captain out," Harlowe said, signing off.

After the landing, an officer broke from the line of troops and came strutting toward them. From the way the officer walked with his armed escort, he intended taking them both by force if necessary. To help speed up things, Harlowe and Monday met the official group halfway.

"Do you understand me?" the officer asked. They all wore dark green fatigues, pointy felt hats, black boots, and sidearms, belt high on their hips.

"I do," Harlowe replied cooly, tugging on the bottom of his leather jacket.

The officer minced few words. "You are under arrest."

"Sorry," Harlowe pointed at *Millawanda*. "We're going back to our ship."

The officer stood firm. "You have broken Clarity laws. You will be dealt with accordingly."

"Not so fast, brah," a familiar voice said as Riverstone's projection materialized a few steps away. Harlowe's second in command was dressed in an impressive, dark Gamadin blue uniform. Riverstone's image stepped forward and continued. "My crew are returning to our ship, unharmed and unescorted, sir."

"They will be shot if they resist arrest."

"Try that and all your soldiers will perish before your eyes. But first I'll start with Legatus Fiv," Riverstone said without a quiver of hesitation in his voice.

The officer suddenly lost his hubris. "You're bluffing."

Riverstone pointed at the ship's barrier, shimmering in the morning sunlight. "Sight in with your optics, sir, and tell me what you see at the base of the ramp."

A soldier quickly brought the officer a pair of optics. It wasn't long before he had his answer. Riverstone wasn't through. He pointed at a line of heavy cannons miles away that had shelled the alien ship for three days to no avail. "Now, Mr. Prigg, if you please," Riverstone ordered.

From the alien ship's perimeter, a searing bolt of blue light streaked across the plains, and in an instant, a row of cannons vaporized to subatomic dust before their eyes.

"Do you wish to continue, sir, or would you like to see more?" Riverstone asked. "I'm just getting started. With another wave of my hand, I will lay waste your entire command. Shall I proceed, Officer?"

"Please, do not harm the Legatus," the officer pleaded.

"When my crew is safely across the barrier, Legatus Fiv will go free," Riverstone assured the officer.

The officer motioned to his soldiers. "Allow the aliens to pass." As Harlowe walked by the ghostly image, Riverstone whispered, "Welcome back, Captain."

"Nice work, Mr. Riverstone."

* * *

Harlowe and Monday had less than a few hundred yards to go when Darkn's monstrous four-wheeled land tank roared onto the plains from out of nowhere. The massive vehicle was so reckless, its two-story high wheels crushed soldiers who were slow to get out of its path, along with a number of smaller tanks, jeeps, and other transports that were also flattened. Strangely, the military did nothing to stop the killing or the destruction of their vehicles and equipment. It didn't take a rocket scientist to figure out the bright orange and black beast was headed straight for them.

"Move!" Harlowe shouted as Monday emptied a twenty round clip into the monster's front end. But it wasn't enough. His plas holes had no effect in stopping it. "Matt, take that thing out!" Harlowe cried out, running in twenty foot hops for the blue wall.

"We can't, Captain," Riverstone said in their coms. *"Millie shot her wad on the demo. If we reenergized, we'd lose our shields."*

Harlowe felt the heat of the monster behind them as they leaped with every ounce of strength left in the SIBAs. "JUMP, SQUID!"

63

Gray & Red Wheels

Simon slammed the throttle forward, pushing the stolen transport to its limits, which was anything but impressive. Top speed was a paltry 30 mph, but from the look on Naree's face, one would have thought they were racing along at hyperlight.

"Why are you nervous, Naree?" Simon asked.

"I've never been in a transport, Ahlian," she replied, holding on to anything she could grab to keep herself inside the doorless vehicle.

Simon found that hard to believe and thought, how sad never to have ridden in a car. How was that possible? Was she imprisoned in the museum her entire life? That was outrageous, especially for someone who globe-trotted around his own planet, Earth, with ease. He was never in one place too long before he had to fly, drive, or take a train to somewhere. He looked at her stunned and asked, "How old are you, Naree?" He knew it was a forbidden question no one should ever ask a woman, but under the circumstances it was one that needed to be asked.

"Old?" she asked.

Simon thought the question was straightforward enough. "Yeah, you know, how many years ago were you born?"

Naree's expression remained unchanged. It was like he was speaking Icelandic to her. She didn't understand the concept of age at all. He tapped the back of his ear thinking that his universal translator might have malfunctioned. It hadn't. She did not understand the concept of age. After a couple of more birthday tries fell short, he tried a different tack. "How many winters can you remember?"

"Winters?"

"Cold. Snow. The white stuff that falls from the sky. That happens here doesn't it?"

"Yes," Naree replied, never taking her eyes off the road as they drove by frontage stores and shops filled with products, goods, and services. Strangely, the most important element of all was missing from every store... shoppers! People were walking along the sidewalks, but no one was inside the stores browsing or buying anything that he could see. *What's up with that?* "I can remember 2,121 times the frozen water fell upon Cornicen," she said, believing that was a reasonable guess.

"WHAT?" Simon exclaimed, nearly driving off the road. After regaining control, he turned to her with a follow up, but two gray and red transports, Cornicen security colors, had turned the corner and began pursuing them down the avenue. Telling Naree to hang on was unnecessary. Her hands were white-knuckle tight around the grab-bar already. At the next intersection, Simon made a casual left to see if the two patrol transports followed. They did and accelerated past the 30 mph limit to catch them.

Simon knew he couldn't outrun them so he pulled his transport curbside and waited for the gray and reds to catch up. He told Naree to stay put until he called her. "When I wave, come running to me in a hurry, Naree," he instructed, getting out of the car.

With his hands up, Simon began walking toward the patrol transports which stopped right behind them. From the look on their faces, they were in no mood to discuss surrender or give him his Miranda rights. They had only one thing in mind...eliminate the threat. With weapons drawn, they threw open their doors with a vengeance. Simon knew the drill. In his last movie, his leading lady, Phoebe Marlee, was about to be kidnapped by black-suited aliens when Captain Julian Starr saved the day by taking out the reptilian thugs before they could abduct her to their planet and dissect her.

Two shots later, two heads exploded outside the patrol transport. Simon re-holstered his sidearm and waved for Naree to join him. She bolted to his side and froze. "You shot them!" she exclaimed in disbelief.

"They were going to shoot me first," Simon said, defending his actions.

"But they are Clarity guards."

"Not any more." Simon dragged an exploded head out of the shotgun side of the gray and red transport. Oddly, there was no blood or splattered brains anywhere. When their heads burst, the bodies collapsed in place, never twitching or jerking like a normal body might after being shot. No blood, no fuss, just pull them to the side and get in.

"What are you doing?"

After he pulled the second body away from the transport, Simon hopped in the driver's seat and motioned, "Their ride is better than ours. Let's go."

Pushing the drive lever forward, they took off down the street, and in no time at all they were past 30mph and headed for 50. Simon was ecstatic. "This is more like it." A 20 mph increase made all the difference in the world. They would be out of Cornicen in no time now. As an added benefit, he quickly discovered no one bothered to notice who was driving. At the only road block they came to before leaving the city, guards just waved them through without checking their ID's.

"Cool," Simon said, smiling and waving at the guard as they headed south out of the city.

64

Return My Abordar!

Harlowe almost made it clean through the barrier. But before the front end of Darkn's beastly tank smashed into the barrier, it clipped Harlowe's foot, spinning him like a top as he passed through. He tumbled headfirst, bounced back into the air, his body continuing to twist as he made two more forward flips, bouncing off his shoulder and coming to a tangled stop, spread-eagle on the grass. Monday wasn't so lucky. The tank's grille caught him with a full body slam. When the tank struck the barrier, his momentum carried him through the blue veil like a human cannonball. Before he smashed into the nearest landing strut, an invisible hand caught him mid-flight and suspended him above the ground like some magician's trick. Darkn's front end was totaled, but it didn't stop him from backing up and taking another hit at the barrier. Six more times the massive wheels churned, killing billions of poor Follish Pimirs as his wheels spun backwards, then, forward again, ramming the barrier repeatedly until the engine coughed and exploded into a ball of flames. A vault-like hatch suddenly flew open on the side of the tank and out stomped the repulsive being they had met when they first arrived in Cornicen. Darkn seemed twice as ugly in the daylight. His oversized head and thick browed features jutting out between his haunting eyes; large mouth with long, yellow incisors; and long dark hair made Freddie Kruger look like a Miss America finalist. Darkn stomped down the ramp, firing a huge pistol at the barrier with no effect. Roaring hate, he dragged his weapon close to the ground and began kicking the veil of blue light with his heavy, square-toed boots.

"Return my abordar, you thieves!" Darkn shouted at Harlowe as he repeatedly pounded the force field with his weapon and fists.

Harlowe paid no attention to the ogre. He dusted himself off the grass and ran to Monday as the tractor beam lowered him to the ground. "You okay, Squid?" he asked, releasing his headgear.

Monday's eyes darted from side to side, trying to focus. "I felt like I was hit with a granny wagon," he grunted.

Harlowe found no broken bones, but just to make sure, he called the robob medics to fetch Monday stat! Two robobs materialized from a nearby blinker, holding a stretcher. The mechanical medics picked Monday up, all 300 pounds of him, like he was a hollow mannequin and carried him away. The instant the robobs and Monday were gone, Harlowe turned back to Darkn, giving the ugly dakadude his full attention.

The last time Harlowe felt this kind of rage was when he met Sar in a gun duel. The end result wasn't pretty. Harlowe sliced up the Fhaal commander like a butcher carving meat. After that, he destroyed his entire fleet in a single day. This was that kind of moment.

Without a word from Harlowe, Jewels materialized from the same blinker the robobs had taken Monday and tossed him a fully charged Gamadin rifle. Harlowe snagged the weapon out of the air, racked the plas rounds into the magazine chamber, and began shooting from the hip, blowing away the top Darkn's tank with the first round. The dozens of crewmen inside jumped from the open hatch, scrambling for their lives. When the tank was clear, Harlowe opened up and didn't stop. He blew car-sized holes through its body, lifting the chassis in the air, tumbling it backwards away from the barrier. It then crashed against the remains of searing hot metal away from the ship as it exploded into smaller and smaller pieces of twisted, insignificant hunks of metal, spread over miles of open plain.

With crazed eyes, Harlowe came after Darkn next. The hideous giant made no attempt to flee. All he wanted was his abordar returned. "I want my abordar! Give it back, or you will die a thousand deaths!"

Harlowe stepped to the barrier, pointed the barrel at Darkn's head, "We don't have your stinkin' abordar, Toad," and pulled the trigger.

Click!

Nothing happened.

Darkn shut his eyes in relief.

"You are a very fortunate being, Butthead," Harlowe seethed, keeping the barrel of the rifle pointed at Darkn's brain. "Pray that nothing happens to my crewman, Toad, or I will come looking for you personally with a full mag."

"Do that, alien. I will enjoy eating you when I tear your limbs from their sockets."

Harlowe's eyes didn't flinch as he spat at Darkn's feet, turned, and tossed the rifle back to Jewels, who caught the weapon effortlessly on the fly with his pincers. Harlowe didn't look back. He went straight to the blinker and winked away. Everyone knew where he would be. It was a given. They would find him sitting at Monday's side day and night until his crewman was out of danger.

* * *

Riverstone walked up to Fiv, who had seen everything from a safe distance, and said, "It's over, Fiv. You're free to go."

Fiv was clearly shocked by what he had just witnessed. "He is your commander?" Fiv asked, gulping air.

"In the flesh," Riverstone replied, proudly.

"He is powerful."

"And then some."

"I would not like to face him in battle."

"He doesn't lose."

"By nightfall, all my siege forces will depart the plains."

"A wise decision, Fiv."

"You could have destroyed my army at any time," Fiv admitted.

"Like I said, we came in peace. We will leave that way. We are Gamadin. We are about freedom, not about destruction or conquest."

"This idea called freedom. I must know more about it."

A girlbob with blond hair clickity-clacked forward with a rolled up document in her pincers. Riverstone took the document from the clicker and said, "Thanks, Alice." The girlbob flung her hair to the side and returned to the blinker and winked away.

Riverstone handed Fiv the *Declaration of Independence* and said, "We're spreading the word. Think of it as our gift to you."

"Will I understand its meaning?"

"Freedom is simple. It's keeping that's hard."

"Where will you go now?" Fiv asked.

"We're not done here yet. We must find an ancient city called Lamille. Have you heard of it?"

Fiv thought a moment. "No, it must be old."

"It is. We believe it existed here on Osset sometime in the distant past."

"If I hear of anything, I will send word."

Riverstone thanked Fiv as they stopped at the barrier.

"How will I pass through?" Fiv asked, pushing his hand against the blue force.

Riverstone reached out and touched Fiv's shoulder. "You can go now."

Fiv closed his eyes and went through without resistance. On the other side, he turned back, his stride never once displaying that he had ever been a cripple. "It seems so simple," speaking of the barrier. "Yet, it's impregnable."

"Don't feel bad. It's a common complaint."

Fiv saluted with the document in his hand. He was about to turn and walk away when Riverstone called out, "Wait!" as he held the Osset officer's intricately adorned cane in the air. "You forgot your walking stick!"

"My gift to you," Fiv said smiling. He tapped the side of his leg. "I no longer need it." He walked a short distance, then turned abruptly, recalling something he forgot to ask Riverstone. "What was that last sustenance we had, Riverstone?"

Riverstone winked with a grin. "A double-double cheeseburger."

Fiv smiled gratefully. "To die for!" he yelled back.

Riverstone saluted, and they both turned and went their respective ways.

65

Yes, Dear

It was night when they arrived at the top of the ridge where the Du Tir boundary crossed into the Black Land, where twynich never ended. The stars were bright and abundant, except for a region in the northwest quadrant of the sky. It was void of stars like it had been swept clean of glitter. This must be the Thaat, Ian surmised, where Harlowe had taken Millie. He prayed that he had made it to the other side of the great nothingness by now. The two moons on the horizon were as large as Earth's moon. Their pockmarked yellow and rose-colored faces looked down upon them like big streetlights, peeking through the trees. Leucadia had to practically carry Dev the last mile. Cheesa had gutted it out, but she could not go further without collapsing. They all needed to rest. While the Prince and Cheesa slept under the trees, Leucadia and Ian surveyed the down side of the ridge with their SIBA optics. It didn't look black to them. Surrounded by a range of mountains, the land beyond was a beautiful valley of green hills, meadows, and meandering streams. In the middle of the valley was an extinct volcano that seemed out of place in the peaceful basin. It was like the valley had grown a wart. There were no trees or bushes, no plant life at all growing along its steep sides. The basalt spikes around its caldera reminded Ian of Mowgi's teeth.

After making a few adjusts with her SIBA sensors, Leucadia concluded, "This is the source of the darkness, Ian."

"The cone?" he asked.

"Yes."

298

"Gamadin?"

"A perfect match," she assured him.

"Morning then," Ian said with a yawn. Even Gamadin need some down time.

They came back to where Cheesa and Dev were sleeping and found their own places to rest. It wasn't long before a warm body scooted next to him. "May I join you?" Cheesa asked, touching him softly on the shoulder.

Ian rolled toward her and smiled. "Sure." He detached his canteen from his belt and offered her a drink. It was cool water from the creeks along the trail. He had run out of Bluestuff miles back.

Leucadia sat by the Prince, who was awakened from an exhaustive sleep by her presence. She handed him a drink from her canteen and asked, "You say Muuk lost many of his men here, Dev?"

"An entire regiment," Dev replied after taking a refreshing drink. "They say something ate them."

She admired the vista across the horizon. "The valley looks so peaceful. It is difficult to imagine what could have happened to them."

"From here on, no one has ever ventured beyond the Du Tir boundary and returned," Dev mumbled, wanting to sleep.

Leucadia continued studying her readouts. She pointed her com toward the valley and moved the sensor beacon along its entire length. There was no one living there but, there was plenty of life.

"Animals?" Dev asked.

Leucadia nodded. "Yes, they don't seem to be affected by the twynich."

"Your tigres, too?" Dev asked.

"Yes, they came this way," Cheesa said, overhearing their conversation.

"How do you know that?" Ian asked.

Cheesa pointed at the ground a few feet away. "She left a mark for us."

Leucadia went to where Cheesa pointed. "That's Molly's print, all right."

Suddenly, a wild beast screamed in the forest behind them startling Cheesa as she returned Ian's canteen to him.

"The animal frightens you, Cheesa?" Ian asked, concerned with her abrupt mood change.

"That was a haapflin, and it is near," Cheesa said, standing.

"How do you know that, city girl?" Dev asked.

Cheesa stood and pointed at another huge footprint in the dirt. It wasn't a cat's.

Ian grinned. "Not bad for a city girl, huh, Dev?"

Dev swallowed hard just as a loud roar thundered and shook the forest.

"My sensors put the source several miles away," Leucadia said. She activated two robobs as sentrys. "But just to be safe, we should post the clickers."

Ian removed two cylinders from his pack. "Good idea."

"Better hope the cats don't run into one of them," Dev cautioned.

Ian turned to the Prince with an easy smile. "Where Molly and Rhud come from, Dev, they eat haapflins for breakfast."

Dev found that hard to believe.

"Harlowe and Quay saw their mother nearly kill a full grown T-rex," Ian said.

"What is a T-rex?" Dev asked.

"A beast twice the size of a haapflin, brah."

Dev yawned. He wasn't buying it. He curled up against the tree and and closed his eyes. Ian thought the Prince had the right idea.

"What are you doing, Ian?" Cheesa asked, alarmed. "The haapflin?"

Ian pointed at the clickers standing silently alert on both sides of the clearing where they were bedded down. "They'll take care of anything that tries to harm us, Cheesa. Go to sleep."

Cheesa wasn't buying that, either. She knew what a haapflin could do to a person, and she had never heard of a T-Rex. She nudged closer to Ian. After a while, when the screams seemed to subside, she asked him, "Are the heavens different where you come from, Ian?"

Ian wondered about that. Was he seeing the same stars, only from a different angle? Or had they traveled so many lightyears from Earth that the stars in this heaven here were not his at all. "We only have one moon from where I come from, Cheesa."

"Did someone steal your moons?" she asked innocently.

Ian smiled. "No. My planet only came with one."

"What about the stars, Ian? Are you as blessed as Nod?"

"Stars? Oh, yes, you would be very impressed by our stars." He pointed to the empty darkness to the north. "We live far away from the star desert, so we have many more stars that fill our nights."

Cheesa snuggled closer. Ian didn't pull back, but he was a little nervous. Unlike Riverstone and Simon, he was a little slow in the "getting-to-know-you" department. She felt so comfortable and warm next to him. He had wanted to do that from the moment he met her.

"Will you share your heaven with me someday, Ian?" Cheesa asked, looking up at him with the twin moons reflecting in her eyes. She had grown more beautiful every day they were together. Now he was beginning to understand why girls were so important to the other guys.

He was about to answer her with a kiss but a loud scream of an animal in pain broke them apart. Ian stood quickly and was joined by Leucadia. Another outcry, and Ian ordered the two Nodians to, "Stay here."

Dev was now wide awake and scared to be left alone. "Don't leave us, Lu."

The two robobs waited for Leucadia's commands. "Protect Dev and Cheesa," she ordered.

In perfect sync, both robobs stood straight, instantly acknowledging her commands.

"What if you don't come back. How will we survive?" Dev asked, afraid of being left behind.

Ian pointed to the robobs. "Do as they say!"

"They are mutes!" Dev shot back.

Cheesa came beside Ian and grabbed his arm. "I want to go with you."

"No. You'll just be in the way."

Cheesa snapped her hands back. "I will not be in the way! You will be in my way!"

Ian was at a loss. What happened? They were getting along so smoothly a second ago. Was this why there was always tension between Harlowe and Lu? Did girlfriends always have problems following orders, he wondered?

Dev tried to take Cheesa's hand. "Touch me, Prince, and I swear I will cut it off."

There was no doubt in Ian's mind that Cheesa would do it, too. He pulled her aside and said, "We don't have time for this, Chee," he scolded with the shortened name he had started to call her. "Please, stay with Dev. Lu and I will be right back. I promise."

Her shoulders were rigid in his hands. He glanced at the moons. Maybe he would take Harlowe's advice after one of his discussions with Lu: "Stay smart, Wiz, don't get involved with babes...ever!" He couldn't recall which time it was when he and Leucadia had their differences. There seemed so many. One thing he did remember clearly, however; every time they had one of their heated chats, Harlowe would always say, "Yes, dear," to Lu, and that seemed to smooth things over until the next time.

Man, this was all too complicated, he thought. With no time to figure it out now, he turned back to the Prince and said, "Just don't let her out of your sight."

Before Cheesa could object again, Ian motioned to Leucadia to lead on, and together they took off through the trees in search of the beastly outcry. Every step away from the campsite, he felt Cheesa's daggers sticking him in the back. He would make it up to her later, he promised, and said to her as he ran, "Yes, dear."

66

Photoshopped

With his feet dangling over the perimeter side of his ship, Harlowe sat in a funk. Dressed in faded jeans, gray workout shirt, blue Nike knockoffs, and the leather jacket Simon had created for him, he had no one to blame but himself for the mission's dismal failure to find Lamille. Somehow he had to get the mojo back, but the morning was cloudy, like his brain. The sun tried a few times to peek through the overcast, but at this point, the day sucked so bad no amount of sunshine would help it. He hadn't a clue what his next move would be. The information Simon sent back was worthless. God only knew why he scanned the things he did. There were plenty of Naree images, though. Harlowe reckoned if she had a map of the planet tattooed on her lips, they would have found Lamille in a heartbeat.

Harlowe lay back on his elbows wondering how in the universe he was going to get his ship off the planet, let alone the 30,000 lightyears to Orixy that Prigg had figured.

"Not lookin' good there, Pylott," he said to himself.

From his position, nearly 300 feet from the ground, he watched with indifference the divisions of Cornicen soldiers, tanks, and military hardware packing up and leaving the plains. They had never really been a threat to *Millawanda*. They were just another somber reminder that no matter where they landed in the vast galaxy, the powers that be would always be the monkey on their backs.

"Working on a plan?" Riverstone asked, tapping the tip of the cane Fiv had given him on the hull.

"One or two," Harlowe replied, keeping his eyes forward.

"Are they better than the last one?"

Harlowe squinted at Riverstone sitting down beside him. "They're full of possibilities."

"Care to share?" Riverstone asked, toying with his decorative staff.

"I'm working out the kinks."

Riverstone looked across the plain at all the activity going on below. "How long have you been out here?"

"All night." Harlowe eyed Riverstone's gift. "That's cool. Where'd you get it?"

Riverstone pointed the tip of his cane at the soldiers. "The head dude gave it to me after Millie fixed his leg. He's a double-double convert."

"Was he real or faux?"

Riverstone stared at Harlowe puzzled. "Faux? What do you mean?"

Harlowe waved at the retreating army. "Those dudes out there aren't real. They're synthetic beings, like a holograph but solid."

"How do you know that?"

"Because when I shot one, he didn't bleed. He repaired himself like the cop in *Terminator 2*. The buildings are the same way. All made up. Nothing's real, even the people. I can't wait to blow this place."

Riverstone thought that was amazing. "How did you get away?"

"Shot them in the head and they exploded like grapes," Harlowe explained and then asked, "So the head dude liked burgers, huh? That sounds real enough."

"Yeah, big time, and he walked with a limp before Millie fixed him."

Harlowe mulled over that information. "Some of them must be real then."

"How would you know? Shoot them in the head?" Riverstone suggested.

"It works every time it's tried," Harlowe quipped.

"The missiles they fired at Millie were real enough. So how do they do it?"

Harlowe didn't know exactly, but he had ideas. "They have devices that disrupt their structures, some kind of power phase keeps it all together somehow."

Riverstone went on: "And that monster tank was history after you finished with it. It didn't repair itself, either."

Harlowe was hard pressed to understand any of it. "Good point."

"So what if they conjure up a Godzilla that sits on Millie and won't let her get up, then what?" He stared hard at the troops. "They might look like they're retreating, but that general wasn't stupid. If he could find a way to capture or destroy Millie, he would do it, you know. I don't care how many double-doubles I give him."

"Yeah, we can't stay here," Harlowe admitted. He touched intricate symbols on Riverstone's cane. "That scroll work looks familiar."

"Prigg's working on it." Riverstone then informed Harlowe that Monday was back on the bridge.

That didn't sit well with Harlowe. "I told him to stay put for a day or two."

"He said he was tired of clickers hovering over him like they wanted to replace something."

"Any word from Bolt?"

"Yeah, he and Naree made it out of Cornicen okay."

Harlowe found that remarkable. "On foot?"

Riverstone snickered. "No, he hijacked one of their police transports. He said the toads never bothered looking inside to see who was driving. So they're parked in the forest about 30 miles out of the city, waiting for the troops to pass before they headed this way."

"No doubt he's teaching her the finer points of making out."

"It would pass the time."

Harlowe scanned the plains. "Was Naree eating?"

Riverstone eye's narrowed. "Now that's a question I should have asked him considering our predicament here."

"No. Really. Was she eating anything?"

"You think she's faux?"

"Don't know. She helped us escape. Could be his charm even works on the fake babes."

"Wow, her pictures were hot. Hard to imagine that. Think he knows?"

Harlowe felt a little sympathy for his crewman. "I doubt Captain Starr saw past her gunnels." Harlowe faced Riverstone directly. "Would you?"

Riverstone bowed his head with a sly smirk. "I like gunnels."

Harlowe stood up and stretched. "What's Prigg found? Anything helpful?"

Riverstone pointed at his staff. "This interests him a lot. He can't wait to get his hands on Rerun's brooch. What did that big toad call it?"

"An abordar."

"Yeah, well, Priggy thinks my stick and the Dear John from the Donut could be linked somehow."

Harlowe's mouth dropped open. "How long were you going to keep talking until you told me this?"

Riverstone stood with him and replied, "Until you asked."

Harlowe stomped off in a huff across the hull toward the open hatchway to his quarters.

"Was I supposed to read your mind?" Riverstone asked, running to catch up.

*   *   *

By the time Harlowe and Riverstone reached his quarters, Prigg and Monday were already talking with Simon and Naree's holographic images above the conference table. From the background behind them, the two were sitting inside a car-like vehicle with rain pouring down around them.

"I wish I could have found something more for Millie," Simon apologized, still unhappy with himself for not finding the smoking gun that would lead them to Lamille.

"Where was this picture taken, Mr. Bolt?" the little Naruckian asked.

"That's the junk room, Mr. Prigg."

Prigg's eyes drifted around the room until his lower left eye focused on the wall stone. He enlarged the holograph and zeroed in on the slab's unusual markings. Along the left side of the slab was a ragged line that seemed more like a crack in the stone than anything important. Harlowe saw nothing unusual about the stone. It was weathered and broken in several places. To him it looked like a hunk of rock, nothing more.

"It is called a kort," Naree replied, sitting next to Simon. Outside, the wind was howling so loudly they had to almost yell to be understood. *"We believe they were hung on walls for decoration."* But Riverstone's cane was more intriguing to her than the slab. *"Where did you find that scepter? The markings are curious."*

"From General Fiv?" Riverstone replied. "I think his first name was . . ."

"Legatus," Naree answered for him.

"Yeah, Legatus. He was Fiv to me."

"He is the supreme commander of the Clarity ground forces."

"Yeah, that's him," Riverstone said.

"And he gave this scepter to you?" Naree asked.

"As a gift. He didn't need it anymore."

Naree examined the cane more closely as Riverstone held it up for her to see. *"The writing is ancient."*

Harlowe broke in: "Mr. Prigg, here, believes it is from the same time period as the abordar and the letter Captain Starr has with him."

"Alhian?" she corrected.

Harlowe glared at Simon as Riverstone and Monday both let go small chuckles. "Yeah, Alhian. Do you agree, Naree? Are they from the same period?"

"Yes, definitely," she concurred.

Simon opened the letter and compared the writing. The letters were different, but the style was the same. *"She's right."*

"There's also the symbol," Naree said, studying the cane like a jeweler.

"The symbol?" Prigg questioned.

Naree pointed at the top of the cane. *"Yes, the symbol represents the power given to the city for its protection."*

"You call that a scepter. Why?" Harlowe wondered. "Riverstone's pal used it as a cane."

"Yes, but that was not the original purpose. The possessor of the scepter had great social prestige in the city-state from which it came," Naree explained, pointing again to the symbol at the top of the staff.

Harlowe picked up the scepter and examined the staff himself. After going over the markings from one end to the other, he kept coming back to the symbol at the top.

Tapping the symbol, he asked Naree, "Could the Gamadin symbols mean this city was under their protection?"

"That would be my conclusion, Captain," Naree replied.

Harlowe felt like he was onto something. "So, now we have a city or a region that was protected by someone, perhaps Gamadin. But we don't know if this is Lamille."

"Why does it matter, Captain?" Riverstone wondered with a shrug. "If it was Gamadin protected, that's all that matters. Just call it Lamille, and get it over with. The problem is, if it's Lamille or not, we still have no idea where this place is."

"This is no scepter, Your Majesty," Prigg suddenly stated.

All eyes went to the little Naruckian waiting for the other shoe to drop.

"It's not?" Harlowe asked. "Naree is wrong? It's not for protection?"

"No, Your Majesty," Prigg replied, taking the staff from Riverstone. "She is quite correct. The device is for protection, but it is not a ceremonial staff. It is an instrument used in conjunction with a communications array."

Riverstone leaned over to Harlowe. "Are you following him?"

Harlowe took the staff from Prigg and examined the bottom end more closely. "Now it all makes sense." He got up from the table and handed the device back to Prigg. "Nobody move. I'll be right back," he said, going to a blinker near his desk and winking away.

*   *   *

Harlowe hadn't been in Leucadia's room since he left her, Ian, and Rhud on the unknown planet to find Molly. It was too heartbreaking to walk among her memories, smell her essence, and be among her things like the selfie on her desk of the two of them walking the streets of Montevideo. Or the picture she took of him walking out of the water, dripping wet, tall and muscular, carrying his long, black fins. And his favorite, a black and white of them kissing on a London bridge with Big Ben in the background.

He sighed, catching his breath, feeling the tightness in his chest as he turned to her bed, perfectly made. The robobs never left a wrinkle in her bedsheets without smoothing it out. Lying on her pillow was the jacket Simon had made for her, all folded and nice, waiting for her to try it on. Harlowe wouldn't let the clickers touch it. It would stay right where it was until she returned.

Next to the bed was the nightstand where he knew she kept some personnel items. He tapped the sliding drawer and found the broken stick he was after. They had found it in the room inside the underground pyramid at Hitt. He held it firmly and started for the exit. The door slide open. He stopped at the threshold but didn't look back. He wanted to. He wanted to see the memories one more time...but couldn't. One last deep breath of her was all he could take. He touched the pain in his nose as he leaned against the doorway, lingered briefly, then went back to his quarters.

Harlowe stepped off the blinker and handed Prigg his stick. "Lu and I found this at Hitt," he told those at the table.

Prigg examined it with all three of his eyes traveling back and forth in all different directions. "Yes, I believe this was a common instrument given to an entity for protecting by the Gamadin, Your Majesty." Prigg took the unbroken staff, and after touching the top of the staff, placed it upright in the middle of the table as the top of the staff lit up like a Christmas tree. Curiously, it remained perfectly straight and did not fall over.

Monday rushed into the room a few seconds later wondering what was going on inside Harlowe's quarters because the dancing lights at the back of the bridge were going crazy.

"It's all right, Mr. Platter," Harlowe said calmly, "It's a little experiment, is all."

"It set off all the emergency systems, Captain."

"Understood." Harlowe tapped the device again, shutting it off. "What's it look like now, Mr. Platter."

Monday poked his head out of the doorway. "Back to normal, Captain."

"Thank you, Mr. Platter. Carry on," Harlowe said.

"Aye, Captain," and Monday left the room.

"So we have a warning beacon soo…." Riverstone began, "What's the point? It's not like we have a lot of time before Millie goes dark. If we don't find that city, we're screwed, right?"

Harlowe wanted to know that answer, too. "How long do we have, Mr. Prigg?"

Prigg had the answer already figured. "Fifteen days, twelve point seven hours, Your Majesty."

Harlowe turned his attention back to the stone slab on the wall. "Remember that experiment Farnducky had with that old painting?" he asked Riverstone.

"The Rembrandt?" Riverstone recalled, straight out.

Harlowe was stunned by Riverstone's quick response and stared at his First Officer as if he was an imposter. "You always slept during Farnducky's lectures. How would you remember that?"

"I was awake that day."

"Okay, then tell me what he said about Rembrandt, brain?" Harlowe asked, dubious of Riverstone's memory.

"I remember a lot. He showed us how x-rays or ultra-violet waves, whatever, could see behind the layers of paint. In some cases there were two or three paintings underneath the top painting."

Harlowe was impressed. "Good work, Mr. Riverstone." He faced Prigg. "Do it, Mr. Prigg. Run a spectral analysis on the slab and let's see what we get."

"Aye, Your Majesty."

Unfortunately, after several attempts at analyzing the stone with ultra-violet, infrared, gamma rays, x-rays, and green, blue, and red lasers, it was becoming obvious the slab was giving up none of its secrets.

Simon then made an off-the-cuff suggestion that seemed to come out of left field. *"Photoshop it, Skipper."*

"Photoshop?" Harlowe repeated, wondering if he heard the word right. His crew was full of surprises. Often many of their ideas, including his own, were way out, but somehow, some way, their combined imaginations, more often than not, found a workaround. He had heard of the software program before. Wiz used to talk about photoshopping the digital photos of Harry's cars for his bedroom wall. It always amazed him how he could take a dull picture from his digital camera and turn it into a cool work of art.

"Yeah, Skipper. Photos have different levels that reflect light. Using the sliders, you can see things you might not normally make out by adjusting the contrast levels."

Harlowe was open to any ideas that made sense. "All right, Mr. Prigg, contrast the slab. Let's see if Mr. Bolt is onto something."

The adjustments didn't take long. They worked like Photoshop on steroids. Within moments, Prigg had jaws dropping around the table with his fine-tuning.

Riverstone responded with a loud, "Whoa!"

"Niiicce," Simon followed.

Harlowe gawked at the stone in disbelief. "It's a map!" he exclaimed, laughing at the revelation. "A wall map."

"Yes, Captain," Naree said, looking at the wall stone with interest, *"A kort is very common to preserve documents in this way."*

"Maybe so, Naree, but this kort is no ordinary slab when it comes to that symbol," Harlowe said, pointing at the symbol displayed along the coastline of a long neck of land that jutted out into the ocean. The symbol was an exact copy of the Gamadin protected city-state on the scepter.

Riverstone smiled. "Our Lamille, Captain?"

Harlowe grinned back. "Like you said, close enough, Mr. Riverstone. Close enough." He looked at Simon with a big congratulatory smile. "You da man, Mr. Bolt."

"Thank you, Skipper."

Mowgi yipped twice.

Naree was less elated. She seemed almost fearful. *"Surwags . . ."* she said, barely audible.

Harlowe caught the dread in her eyes. "You know this place, Naree?"

"Yes, Captain."

Harlowe activated the Osset globe over the table. He pulled the holographic image down and placed it in front of her. "Show us, Naree."

As she gave instructions on how to manipulate the planet, Harlowe turned the globe around, flipped it poles to her satisfaction and found the continent she wanted. *"You are here, Captain. The Surwags are here,"* she said, and pointed at the lower portion of the globe.

The good news was that Lamille, or the city they would call Lamille, was on the same continent. The bad news...it was over 1500 clicks to the south of their position.

Suddenly, *Millawanda* shook like she was hit with a sledgehammer. The crew went to the observation window and looked out. What they saw was unbelievable. Overnight, the Ossetian army had erected a giant ramp two miles long and a thousand feet high. Coming straight at them again was a metal ball that reminded Harlowe of the shiny steel balls from a pinball game. By the time the wrecking ball reached the barrier, it was traveling in excess of a hundred miles per hour.

"Hold on!" Riverstone cried out.

Millawanda shook again. Harlowe thought his eyeballs would fall out unless they stopped the ramming. How long they could withstand the hits was anyone's guess. More importantly, how long could Millie's shields absorb the punishment? Harlowe's conclusion was simple. "Move her now!" or be crushed if the barrier suddenly lost power.

"Is that your buddy, Fiv's idea," Harlowe asked Riverstone.

"No, it is Darkn," Naree corrected. *"The Tappers see revenue for the Clarity in your vessel. They devise many ways to extract the wealth from our people. Their reach is extensive,"* she explained.

"Why do you work for the Clarity, Naree?" Harlowe asked.

"To survive. If you don't work for the Clarity, you are insignificant."

"Then you are a slave," Riverstone whispered to himself, having been there himself not that long ago. As a slave miner, deep in the mines of Erati, a planet far from Osset, he had survived the long, torturous labor as a digger. He had escaped, one of the very few who had. But the love of his life, Ela, was not so fortunate. She died from the torture and beatings by her captors.

Riverstone looked up with a tear in his eye. *At least she had seen the stars.* The lump in his throat returned, remembering their last night together lying on the beach. They were all alone on the small towel, he and Ela, watching the clouds overhead. She had never seen a cloud before, or the twinkling bits of light that were far away places that he promised he would take her one day. She passed away in his arms. *At least she had seen the stars*, he mumbled to himself over and over and over.

Monday sounded the alert this time. "Hold on!"

67

Mama Haapffin

It was pitch dark, and Ian and Leucadia were over a mile down the ridge, deep in the forest when they found the source of the frightful scream. It was a baby haapffin stuck in a trap and hanging from a tree. A similar one had captured Molly in the same way weeks ago. Below the cub was a worried mother, trying desperately to reach her four hundred pound infant. But she could do nothing to save her cub. Her best effort was a good body length short of where she needed to go.

Ian pointed to the trap's tie-downs that were secured to the tree. "Cover me," he said, softly to Leucadia. "She might think I'm going to hurt her kid."

Leucadia readied her sidearm, ratcheting the power down to stun. A being the size of a human would drop like a chopped tree from her weapon's discharge. The mother haapffin, nearly twice the size of an American Grizzly, would only feel a sharp sting. She didn't want to kill her. She was just doing what any mother would do to save her offspring. But if it were the mother or Ian, she would not hesitate to put her down.

Leucadia gave Ian the go ahead as he moved slowly toward the tie-downs. "Careful, Ian," she cautioned.

The moment the mother saw Ian moving toward the tree, she stopped her moaning and put all four paws on the ground, facing him. Any provocative move toward her cub, and he was dead meat. Her bright orange eyes followed him as he eased his way across the small, open space to the anchoring tree.

"Easy, mama," he told her softly. "I'm here to help you."

313

"That's it, Ian," Leucadia said through her com into Ian's ear. "She's listening to you. Keep talking to her."

When he reached the tie-down, he discovered to his dismay that it was no simple untie-the-rope-and-be-done-with-it. It was a chain with links as thick as his thumb. He could cut through it with a shot from his pistol, but there was no way he could ease the cage down. With the mother directly under the heavy metal cage, it would crush her when he made the cut.

He spoke back to Leucadia in a whisper. "You have to get her from under the cage, Lu."

"Roger that," she whispered.

As Leucadia began making her way toward the opposite side of the clearing, branches snapped, turning the quiet of the clearing into Grand Central Station.

Cheesa and Maa Dev crashed the underbrush, completely unaware of what they were walking into. The instant they saw the mother haapffin, they froze. At that point they knew they were somewhere they didn't belong. The mother charged. But it was only a bluff. It was her way of telling the newcomers to back off. Ian saw the opening he needed and took advantage of the moment. In one fast motion, he unholstered his weapon and sliced through the chain. The cage crashed down, startling the mother and jolting the cub inside.

Ian kept his weapon ready as he moved ever so carefully toward the cage to unlatch the door. The mother was now focused on him. She snorted, growled, and began to charge him. But he held his ground, pointing the muzzle of his pistol right at her nose. "No, mama! Back off!" he shouted at her.

Ian wanted to jump out of his SIBA, but he kept his cool. Once he was at the cage, he grabbed the latch with his free hand and threw it back. When the door was free, he pushed it open with all his might. He thought the door was going to slam back down, but the cub was so frightened, he leaped out before it closed and got smacked on the hind end. He yipped, but he wasn't hurt. The cub was too frightened to care about anything but his freedom. Both mother and cub bolted into the forest and quickly disappeared into the night.

Ian exhaled a heavy breath of relief as he waved good-bye. "You're welcome." He turned back to the clearing, his face changing instantly to anger at Cheesa and Dev for disobeying his orders. He took one step and realized the danger wasn't over. Two of the largest, orange eyes he had ever seen were moving stealthily toward Cheesa and Dev. It was papa haapffin about to pounce.

"Lu!" Ian said in hushed voice of urgency. "Daddy's behind Cheesa and Dev."

Dev heard the bushes snap and grabbed Cheesa. But as they tried to run, they moved in front of Leucadia's line of fire. Ian's angle was no better. The giant haapffin was about to slice their heads off with with one swipe of his powerful forepaws, when out of the bushes leaped a giant white flash of glistening fur. Rhud's charge was so powerful, he bowled over the mammoth beast, pinning him to ground before he knew what hit him. He would have ripped pappa's throat out, but Ian screamed, "NO, RHUD!"

The pappa haapffin tried to fight back, but Rhud's hold was vise hard. With each effort to break fee, Rhud's twelve-inch incisors clamped down harder on the haapffin's throat. If that wasn't enough to stop the struggle, Molly leaped out of the night and faced the pappa haapffin maw for maw as she expelled the most bone-chilling roar Ian had ever heard. Pappa haapffin wasn't stupid. His ears pinned back in full submission, squealing for mercy.

Leucadia holstered her weapon and came to Molly's side, taking hold of her mane. "It's okay, hon. Let him go, girl."

Molly did as she was told as Ian put a calming arm around Rhud's neck. "It's okay, big guy. Release him." There was some bright yellow blood where Rhud's knife-like incisors had broken through the skin, but it didn't appear life threatening. Rhud lifted his head, sliding his teeth from its neck and allowed papa haapfin to gather his senses. But to make sure papa knew who the king of this jungle was, Rhud's roar shook the forest. For many eons to come, the creatures of the Haga would remember this night.

The giant beast then rolled over and stumbled forward on his paws to join his family.

Ian patted both cats on their heads. "Where have you two been?" he asked them. "Wait until I tell Harlowe what pranksters you are," he said, wagging a finger at Rhud's nose. Rhud growled happily while Molly purred like a lawnmower on idle, huddled in Leucadia's arms.

"Sorry, Ian," Cheesa said.

Ian glared at her disapprovingly. "You ever disobey an order again, and

I'll leave you for the haapffins."

Cheesa lowered her head with a protruding, lower lip. "Yes, sir. You would be in your right to leave me."

Ian could only be a hardass for so long. Her puppy-dog look of contrition drained his anger in less than two seconds. He walked over to her and put his arms around her. "I'm just glad you're okay." He turned her chin up to his and was about to kiss her when the sound of whirling rotors broke the silence.

Leucadia pointed south in the night. "Airships!"

Ian grabbed Cheesa's hand. "Muuk's forces can't be too far away." He hoisted her onto Rhud's back and added, "Hold tight to his mane," he directed. She followed instructions, clenching her fingers through his thick fur.

Dev stepped toward Molly, gritting his teeth. He knew the drill. Molly went down on her haunches, and Dev climbed aboard. Cheesa looked dubious. She had never ridden a tigre before.

"Take my advice, Cheesa," Dev warned, "keep your eyes closed."

When everyone was snug and ready, Leucadia came to Molly. "You know where to go, don't you, girl?"

Molly answered with a small roar. She did.

"Take us there. Lead the way, hon," Leucadia urged.

Molly sprang toward the Du Tir, leaping out ten body lengths with Cheesa tied securely to her back. Before Molly had taken her second jump, Cheesa had taken Dev's warning to heart and closed her eyes tightly. Rhud followed next. Now that Cheesa and Dev had rides, Leucadia and Ian were free to speed ahead, their SIBAs powering them along with superhuman strides.

68

Creature From the Black Lagoon

It was night, and only the stars were out. Both Osset moons had vanished from the heavens. Monday and Riverstone clasped arms and touched heads. "Remember what I told ya, Squid. Flare your wings a hundred feet before you hit the deck, or . . ."

"Yeah, I got it. Or I'll lose my Mons Jumping privileges," Monday kidded, adding a high-five slap of thanks for the flying tips.

Riverstone pointed a finger between Monday's bugeyes as they stepped through Harlowe's hatchway onto the upper hull deck. "That's right, Lunkhead."

Monday had heard Riverstone's instructions a hundred times since beginning his solo jumps on Mars. Leaping off three-mile high cliffs had never been his strong point. The act of gliding by his SIBA wings was unnatural and frightening to him. He left those kinds of things to Mowgi and the birds, he liked to tell everyone. But through sheer grit and persistence and Riverstone's patience, he had now become a member in good standing in their very exclusive Mons Flying Club. It was an honor he proudly displayed by the patch on the right shoulder of his SIBA. And if the truth be told, it was also his most prized possession in the world.

"Come back safe, Gamadin," Riverside added with a pat on the shoulder.

Mowgi sprang through the hatchway next, just ahead of Bigbob. Riverstone, the doorman, tapped the tall clicker on his ball shoulder and said, "Do us proud, big guy." As Harlowe came through, he added, "Bringing

317

your first string along, I see."

Harlowe had his game-face on. He was in no mood for loose talk. "Do or die." In passing, he went nose to nose with Riverstone. "Take care of my girl, Mr. Riverstone."

"Count on it."

Riverstone held him up briefly, checking his packs and utility belt, making sure he was properly geared up. There was really no worry about Harlowe leaving anything to chance. His mind had turned into a checklist of don't-forgets since Gunn left them hanging without food or power packs a thousand miles from *Millawanda* at Schiaparelli Crater on Mars. They were all thorough as his mother Tinker's inspections. "You're cool, Pard," Riverstone proclaimed. "You have enough ammo to fight a war."

Harlowe looked out across the hull at the mass of military encampments surrounding the ship. "It could get nasty out there," he grunted sourly.

The plan was risky. After lifting a few hundred feet off the ground, enough to put them above the treetops, *Millawanda* would skim below Clarity radar toward the coast. At a prearranged moment, Harlowe and Monday would push off a split-second before Riverstone micro burst the saucer over the ocean to dive her below the surface before the Osset military had a chance to track her. She would then rest on the bottom until Harlowe called with what they prayed was enough aara to blow the planet and head to the next Gamadin outpost, wherever that might be. They didn't figure much beyond that because they didn't want to jinx this mission by looking too far ahead. Until they had a way off the planet, Harlowe wanted everyone's focus on the here and now, believing it was a waste of time to think otherwise.

Once they hit the coastline, Harlowe and Monday would glide down to the beach and head south where Prigg and Naree had matched up the stone map with an ancient city they hoped was Lamille or something equally rewarding. Of course, the kort that was carved out thousands of years ago wasn't an exact match with the coastline of today. Erosion, earthquakes, and tidal shifting had done a number on the beaches of any land mass over the centuries. Who knew what they would find when they got there. But in Harlowe's mind, like horseshoes and hand-grenades, close was good enough. "Mark it, Prigg. That's where we're going," Harlowe ordered.

Harlowe wasn't kidding when he said, "Do or Die." It was the elephant in the room that nobody wanted to talk about. If they didn't find any blue crystals there, Millie's last flight was to the bottom of the ocean. They had to scrounge power from every source they could find just to lift off the ground and go the short distance to the ocean.

The grannywagon was the first to be tapped. Then came the med units, utility rooms, Dodger's Pool, everything was shut down. Even the bridge was put on minimal survival power. Besides air, water, and heat, the only thing left on was the open channel of communications to the Gamadin on the ground, waiting for their call.

The countdown was eight days. They had that long to find a source of energy before a complete environmental failure occurred aboard the ship. *Millawanda* could survive the five hundred foot depths without shields, but the crew inside her would succumb to the bitter cold. Speed was essential. There would be no rest for Harlowe and Monday until they found the aara, or they were dead. It was that simple.

Harlowe adjusted his pistols solidly on his hip and asked, "Is Rerun up to speed?"

"I spoke with him five minutes ago. He had to bug out of his holding area. The patrols were closing in, but he knows the plan. He and Naree are headed for the coast and will wait for you there," Riverstone replied.

"Did you tell him to drive like Sebastian Vettel and get his buns there in a hurry?"

"I told him to forget about Naree's gunnels until he's back here."

Harlowe tapped Riverstone in the chest. "Good point."

"Just make sure you bring us a bucket of fries. I'm starved for real food," Riverstone said, tightening the straps on Harlowe's pack.

Harlowe matched concern with Riverstone. "I will," he uttered confidently.

Millawanda's interior lights suddenly went blue.

"Incoming ball, Your Majesty," Prigg announced over the ship's com.

Harlowe and Riverstone grabbed the hatchway jamb to steady themselves. "Mag up, Squid!" Harlowe called to Monday, who was too far away to find a hold on to anything. *Millawanda's* hull was smooth as glass and offered nothing to grip when the shock of the steel ball hit the ship. Mowgi and Bigbob took the jolt in stride. Mowgi winged up and let the shake pass before his paws touched down again. Bigbob magged up along with Monday. Only with the big robob, it was all automatic.

Monday snapped his SIBA gravs to on and his feet stuck to the hull. When the hull shook violently, he wished he had followed the undog's lead.

Wham!

"Enough of that noise," Riverstone barked angrily. For the last several hours, until they had figured out their plan, every nineteen minutes, twenty-seven seconds like clockwork, a massive steel ball hit the side of the ship with the force of a bunker-buster bomb.

"Get her out of here, Matt!" Harlowe ordered, his insides sick that his ship had suffered through so much punishment.

"Aye, Captain," Riverstone said, ducking back through the hatchway. As the hatch slid shut, Harlowe tapped Her one last time for good luck and leaped down the hull toward the perimeter, linking up with Monday, Mowgi, and Bigbob along the way.

*   *   *

The four reached the perimeter edge of the ship just as *Millawanda* lifted off. Bigbob collapsed into a large cylinder, allowing Harlowe to slip him inside a special sleeve in Monday's pack until he was needed later. Mowgi, of course, had his own means of travel. Once on the ground he would either wing-it or bounce along on all fours, trotting along side Harlowe and Monday like the old cartoon character, Pepé Le Pew.

It was no surprise when *Millawanda's* landing pods began to retract that the Osset ground forces began opening up everything they had. They seemed upset that their alien guests were leaving their designated parking place without permission.

Millawanda had too little power left in her to do anything trick. She reached an altitude of 300 feet, turned on her axis, then slid silently across the treetops on her hundred mile journey east to the coast. There were no tall mountain ranges or valleys to navigate. It was a straight shot to the ocean over a few low hills and a tall, yellow forest. According to Prigg's calculations, she would make it to the coastline and a little more without losing altitude. The "little more" Harlowe was hoping for would get her past the shallow continental shelf and into deep water; they figured she would be out of reach of anyone trying to find her.

Ten minutes after lift off, Harlowe, Monday, and Mowgi dropped off the trailing side of the saucer's rim and took flight. As they glided down, they watched *Millawanda* skip the surface of the ocean three times, extending her distance from the coast by several miles, a trick Harlowe had learned crash landing on the planet Gazz. By the time the Gamadin landing party had touched down, *Millawanda* had settled on the surface.

With his bugeyes on high, Harlowe swallowed the lump in his throat as he watched the golden dome slip below the surface. The melancholy over his ship was short lived. Monday neglected to flare his wings like Riverstone told him to and hit the beach like a sick duck. The only thing that saved him was the shore break. Harlowe leaped to his side and gave him a hand, pulling him out of the watery froth. His face was covered with seaweed and wet, oozy sand, making him look like the *Creature from the Black Lagoon*.

Monday's only worry as he brushed away the mess was, "Don't tell Riverstone, Dog, please. He'll take away my Jumping patch."

Harlowe pulled the kelp from his back. "No worries, Squid, your secret's safe."

Relieved that his Mons Jumping patch was secure, Monday washed off in the surf as Mowgi landed and returned to his normal, big-eared self again. In a land of no dragons, Harlowe thought a medieval beast flying around would attract far too much attention

Suddenly, Monday came out of the surf in a panic. "I lost Bigbob!"

Harlowe handed the oversized cylinder to Monday. "You're cool. It was lying in the sand over there."

Monday sighed, taking the cylinder and placing it back in its sleeve with an extra knot around the top for good measure.

"Thanks, Captain."

Harlowe faced south. "Let's get 'er done, Mr. Platter." He led the way with Monday right along side, matching him stride for twenty-foot stride. Mowgi bebopping along without breaking a sweat as they headed for the city that a Dear John letter they found a hundred lightyears away said was there.

Good luck!

69

TTFN!

All through the night and well into the following day, Molly led them deep into the Black Land. There were no trails or roads into the Du Tir. The meandering river that flowed from east to west was the least resistant pathway through the valley. By the middle of the first day, it was apparent to everyone that Molly was guiding them toward the ancient volcano that lay straight ahead. They only stopped for brief catnaps and a bite to eat. Leucadia doubted Muuk would have stopped at the Du Tir boundary. Like them, he would have to contend with no roads. His animals would also pick up their scents and know which direction they were headed. It was now a race. Ian and Leucadia could only guess as to why Molly was leading to the mountain. Their journey was full of unanswered questions. But the fact that the com's readouts appeared to be of Gamadin origin was enough for them to believe more was there than they could perceive.

It was the morning of the second day, and the sun was still behind the mountains to the east, when they arrived at the base of the extinct volcano. Upon closer inspection, the shape of the cone was nearly perfect, rising in a 60-degree angle a thousand feet to the flat caldera above the forest floor where they were standing. Covering its slopes were green grasses and bushes, but strangely, out of the forest of trees they had just come through, not one tree grew anywhere along its slopes.

"A little too perfect," Ian commented, leaning backward, studying the incline.

Leucadia agreed. There seemed to be nothing special about the mountain except that it looked even more out of place up close than it did from the ridgeline.

"Why have you brought us here, Molly?" Leucadia asked, not really expecting an answer.

Molly growled, staring at them both as if to say, "Isn't it obvious?"

"I guess it's up to us to figure it out from here," Ian said. He was about to suggest climbing the cone when he looked at Cheesa and Maa Dev already fast asleep beside Rhud on a soft, grassy spot next to the river. It had been a grueling, two day run for everyone, including the cats.

"We should make camp here," Leucadia suggested.

Ian's curiosity was too hyped up to rest now. "I want to see what's up there," he said, pointing up at the caldera.

Leucadia turned back, looking up the river valley. "Look for Muuk when you get there."

"I will."

"Any idea what this place is?" Leucadia asked, turning to study the cone.

Ian had nothing positive to add. "I haven't a clue. I'll be back in a couple of hours, though," he said, bounding up the side of the slope with Molly beside him.

"You don't have to go, girl," Ian said, his legs springing from one rock outcropping to the next.

It was like Molly didn't hear a word he said. She bounded up the incline, stride for stride like she was racing with him to the top. Back and forth they went, trading leads. The last two hundred feet his legs chugged up the side of the mountain like Harlowe and Riverstone did during the summer football workouts, charging up and down the stadium bleachers at Lakewood High. Once they reached the caldera rim, he took a moment to catch his breath. As powerful a runner as his SIBA made him, it was still an exhaustive climb. He looked at Molly staring at him with her big, blue eyes. She was hardly panting at all, appearing fresh as if she were walking on a point five gravity planet.

Ian patted her affectionately over her powerful, white shoulders. "I let you win, you know," he said, using her for support.

Molly snapped at him with a roar.

"Hey, lighten up. I was only kidding."

He turned to the river and was stunned by Muuk's forces pouring down the the valley. The Imperator's massive half-tracks carried a company of soldiers each as they carved a wide swath through the forest, breaking tall, old growth trees, two feet thick like they were twigs. He estimated the advanced forces would be here by morning, sooner if they drove through the night.

Ian contacted Leucadia and informed her of the situation. For whatever reason Molly had brought them here, they had to find it fast. Ian attached a small optical transmitter to a rock face before heading down into the caldera. Like a GoPro on steroids, the device allowed Leucadia to pan, zoom, and take stills of Muuk's assault on their position day or night.

With the monitoring station in place, he and Molly went on into the caldera. As they made their way over the lip, Molly stopped. Ian wasn't so cautious, and the rock ledge he stepped on crumbled under his feet. He nearly fell off the thousand-foot vertical drop that encircled the cauldron. He reached back, grabbing the ledge with his claw and avoided the fall and severe headache, not to mention death.

He chided himself for not being more careful. He knew better. He took a couple of deep breaths to calm himself as he focused on the lava dome inside the caldera. Unlike the sides of the volcano where grass grew, there were no plants, grass, or trees anywhere. The readouts indicated the Gamadin power source lay somewhere under the dome. Like it or not, he would have to climb down to continue his search.

There was no easy way down, either. No steps or rocky trails. The sides of the caldron were vertical cliffs. Harlowe and Riverstone would have glided down with their wings, but he wasn't a member of the Mons Jumping Club, yet and didn't particularly care to be, either. He would shimmy down using a dura-line and be done with it.

He removed a piton head from his belt and secured it along with the dura line to a sturdy rock. When he was comfortable with the setup, he hugged Molly and told her there was no pathway down for her. Molly's dejected eyes were heartbreaking. "Stop that. You go back to Lu, and don't worry about me. I won't be long."

Molly wouldn't leave.

Ian figured it was senseless trying argue with a cat that was determined to watch over him until the end of time. "All right. Stay there, you thick-headed puddy-tat." Climbing over the edge, he eased his way over the ledge and rappelled down, pushing off the rock face and dropping fifty to a hundred feet with each bounce. In no time his feet touched the base on solid ground. He looked up at Molly's small head peering over the side, still watching him like a worried mother. He pointed at her again. "Go back, Molly!"

She might as well have been deaf. She wouldn't leave. "Fagettaboutitthen!" he yelled up at her and returned to his exploration of the caldera dome.

The lava dome was much larger than it looked from the lip of the cauldron, at least three stories high and twice that length across. Out the side of his bugeyes, he saw something slithering among the rocks. He checked his line and thought briefly about going back up. "Nah," he grimaced. He had to stick it out. With Muuk's forces breathing down their necks, retreating was not an option. One hand on his sidearm, Ian checked the rocks and according to his sensors, there wasn't anything there. However, it did pick up a network of tunnels below the surface that led to a deep, underground cavern. He tried calling Leucadia to get her opinion but was unable to raise her. His only logical explanation was that the cauldron around him had cut them off. But how, he wondered? Their SIBAs should not be affected by ordinary rocks.

You'll have to make do, Wiz, Harlowe's voice said to him from far away.

"I wish you were here, pard," Ian said to the voice, then he asked, staring at his choices, "What would you do, Dog? Which path should I take?"

Harlowe said with assurance. *Just pick one, Wiz. Whichever you choose, it will be the right one.*

He started to walk along the slabs of magma with no real direction in mind. "How do you know that?"

Because I trust your judgment.

Ian dropped his shoulders and exhaled. "All right. I choose this way."

Perfect. Now do it!

He went for the open gap in the magma vent on the far side of the dome. It seemed the most logical entry to him because it was big enough for him to walk to the large chamber that was several hundred feet below the surface.

He bounced along the slabs of hard rock until he came to the opening. Unlike the small portal they found in Utah leading to *Millawanda*, this breach in the cauldron could fit three grannywagons side by side through the opening. At the edge of the opening a draft of heated air blew steadily up from the cavity. For a moment Ian thought of the second *Star Wars* movie where the

Millennium Falcon was nearly eaten by a giant space slug. His common sense told him he was crazy for thinking such stupid thoughts, but just to put his mind at ease, he unholstered his sidearm and fired a round at the rock floor of the cavern.

No tremors.

He sighed. *Thank God, no worm!*

Satisfied the path ahead was safe, he made his way into the cavern with his heart thumping like a bass drum. Remembering he had almost bought it at the edge of the cliff, he continued slowly for about fifty yards when he had the sudden urge to look back. Hovering above the entrance of the cavern was a giant serpentine creature with yellow eyes and a black tongue that slithered out of its open maw in a whip-like manner. Ian swallowed hard. *Maybe space worms really do live here.*

Ian didn't know whether to run or shoot it. Fortunately for him, the creature made no advance toward him. For whatever reason, the serpent bobbed and weaved over the entrance but would not follow him farther into the cavern. Just the same, he kept his weapon ready with the hope that he would somehow find his way back to Leucadia along this alternate path.

Wary of the path ahead, he jumped, rappelled, and sprang across wide cracks in the magma that over the centuries had become crumbly and unstable. Even with all the hurdles, he was making good time, until he came to a broad underground, waterfall that drained into a magma vent, its bottom undetectable even with his bugeyes. On the opposite side the pathway continued. But to use it, he had to get there. Looking around, he discovered intelligent construction where a bridge had once spanned the falls a long time ago.

A lot of good that does me now.

Even so, it was the first sign that he was on the right path. If someone had built the bridge here, then the cavern must have served a purpose. To find the answer, he had to make it to the other side. He thought of leaping, but it was too far. Harlowe and Riverstone would have made it with ease, but he was neither of them. The chances of him making the gap were fifty-fifty. No way was he trying that when Leucadia was counting on him returning in one piece.

His next choice was the rock ceiling overhead where he could shoot a piton and swing across. He was about to put his plan to work when his SIBA proximity alarm went off in his head. He whirled around just as the giant serpent he met coming in slithered toward him with its tongue whipping around like a bullwhip. Ian had no time to take a running start. With all his might together with every added boost his SIBA would give him, he launched himself from a standing position, flying high, waving his arms in desperation for the far ledge. Somehow, by sheer luck, his claws found a piece of something hard and dug in. It wasn't much. If the rock gave way, he was history, down the magma hole. Behind him, the slithering creature reached out, and if it hadn't hesitated for a split second, it might have made it across the gap and had a great meal. Instead, it was like the creature suddenly got cold feet halfway across. That was its undoing. The slithering thing fell short, clipping Ian's heel as it disappeared into the bottomless cavity.

TTFN!

Ian's problems didn't end there. His claws were slipping and the waterfall was slapping against his suit, trying to dislodge him from his perch. If he couldn't move away from the splashing water, he would be joining the serpent.

70

Stoking the Locals

After running two hundred miles and some change along the coast, Harlowe and Monday found the river delta they were looking for. They had two more hours of daylight left, and Harlowe wanted to make the most of it before their SIBAs put the brakes on their bodies. From their suit readouts, they were already pushing the limit, so they continued due west, going upstream, following a red and orange sunset strafed with dark purples and greens until they found a good place to bed down for the night. From wherever that point was, they would rise before dawn and follow the river to a pre-determined point, one hundred and three miles inland, then cut south across a mountain pass, and back toward the coast again. Cutting across the peninsula in this way would save a thousand foot miles, and then according to their best estimates, Lamille would then be the first shallow bay they came to on the opposite coast. If they were lucky, they should see it from the ridge line coming over the backside of the coastal mountain range.

Not far from the coast, they came across the first city in their travels. It was nothing to write home about. The buildings were broken and dilapidated. Storefront windows and doors were missing. Rusty cars were parked along streets, and vegetation everywhere broke through cracks, crawling up the sides of buildings and overtaking it all.

"What happened to this place?" Monday wondered aloud, as they slowed their pace.

Harlowe shrugged indifference. He had no opinion. His focus was on the mission, his ship, his crew at the bottom of the ocean, Leucadia Mars, and Wiz. Not a single moment went by that he didn't think of their well-being.

The safe route would have been around the city, but that was a waste of time and energy. Instead, they walked straight down the middle of town, taking a wide boulevard that had once been energetic and noisy with traffic and beings carrying on with their daily lives.

Monday saw the locals first and drew his pistol. "Ten o-clock," he informed Harlowe.

Harlowe eyed more stalkers to their right. "One o'clock." He didn't feel the need to unholster his sidearm just yet.

"They don't look like they want to chitchat," Monday observed.

Harlowe agreed and bent down to the undog with instructions. "Time to stoke the locals, Mowg," and let the chenneroth scamper ahead. Back to Monday, he said, "When Mowg does his thing, we bounce out of here like Rerun chasing a virgin."

Monday grinned behind his bugeyes. "That will wake the neighborhood."

"I'm counting on it."

Moments later Mowgi exploded, growing as tall as a two story house, his wings flapping, red-laced yellow eyes blazing hot, and jaws open wide, drooling sticky spit from eighteen inch incisors while screaming like he was Gigantis about to consume entire city. The locals got the message and scattered to the farthest ends of the city. It was almost too simple.

Harlowe watched the show in amazement. "I swear, I know he's on our side, and I still feel like running."

"He does make a statement, Captain," Monday added, as astounded as Harlowe at how fast the undog turned the streets into a ghost town.

After that, they casually trotted on without seeing a single local the rest of the way through the city. They ran for another twenty miles before their SIBAs pulled their plugs.

Crossing a small stream, Harlowe made the mistake of not watching where he was going and ended up in a deep pool up to his neck. He climbed out of the underwater hole dripping wet. Monday reached out and gave him a hand up the embankment. "Find a pothole, Captain?"

Harlowe looked around, deactivating his bugeyes. "Embarrassing."

The forest was quiet and peaceful. The gurgling brook Harlowe tried to cross sounded soothing and restful. Mowgi made his mark on a nearby tree, confirming their campsite for the night along the water's edge. "We'll park here, Squid."

"Aye, Captain."

*   *   *

Early the next morning, Mowgi nudged Harlowe's face with his cold nose. "Do you mind?" he cringed, wiping the wet from his cheek.

The undog's parabolic ears turned in several directions like he was honing in on something urgent.

"What's with him?" Monday asked, watching Mowgi's focused movements. They both stood and strapped on their packs. The undog's early warning signs were never taken lightly.

"We'll find out soon enough," Harlowe said as he checked the magazine of his sidearm. Monday did the same. Seconds of quiet passed before a mixture of gunshots and plas fire overwhelmed the tranquility of the gurgling brook.

71

The Structure

Ian awakened from an exhaustive sleep. Worried that he had been out for days, he checked his SIBA chronometer and was dismayed that it was only twenty-seven minutes later. Relieved that his snooze was short, he crawled to his feet and checked his body condition with his SIBA. According to the readouts, he was good to go. A little shaken up, but nothing a little spelunking wouldn't cure, he told himself. That is, unless he met more slithery creatures along the way.

He located his com, thankful that he hadn't dropped it in his escape, and unholstered his sidearm. He would be ready this time. The readouts showed him moving in the right direction and not far from the Gamadin power source. The path seemed to level out on this side of the waterfall and became more like a sidewalk an intelligent being would construct. It was was graded and smooth with no more large gaps or waterfalls to cross. There was an occasional rockfall in his way, but it was nothing that impeded his progress. The path was mostly clear and wide enough for the grannywagon to drive along without scraping the sides of the rock walls. Strolling along, he found it curious that the tunnel began to look like one of *Millawanda's* corridors the way the ceiling arched overhead. At any moment he half expected the lights to come on automatically and feel the cushiony blue carpet beneath his feet.

As much as he wished for that to be so, Harlowe was always close by to keep him focused. *Quit dreamin', pard. Stay focused on your mission.*

Ian saluted as he went on down the pathway. "Aye, aye, Captain."

* * *

Continuing a short ways, he arrived at a dusty, old, arched doorway that was built into the rock like a vault. It also appeared locked solid and unopened for a very long time. Excited about his discovery, Ian tried raising Leucadia on the com to tell her but got no response. It was strange to him how the communication between them was still malfunctioning, and according to his self-checks, there was nothing wrong with his end. His gear was functioning properly.

Going back to the door, there seemed no other way around it. The thought of retracing his way back across the waterfall and meeting another toothy serpent made him ill. He would find some way of getting past the door even if he had to blast the thing open. Thinking all doors, even vault doors in banks, had some way to open them, he brushed back the curtains of cobwebs and stepped closer to inspect the doorway. To his amazement, the door began to open all on its own as if he was the key to entry.

Sweet, he thought, grateful for small favors.

What was even more reassuring was the fact that the characters written on the inside of the foot-thick framework around the door were familiar Gamadin cuneiform letters. "Cool." Now there was no doubt he was in the right place.

Passing through the entryway, he was awed by the power and grandeur of the underground structure. Lights began to brighten automatically, welcoming him in.

"See Captain, it doesn't hurt to wish for some things," he teased Harlowe as he walked along a pathway that turned to dura-metal after he passed through the doorway. The arched corridors were massive. It took his breath away to be walking inside something he knew to be thousands of years old, yet, like *Millawanda*, still functioning like it had been made yesterday.

But what was it, he kept asking himself over and over. What was its purpose? This was not a ship like *Millawanda* buried inside a Utah mesa. Of that he was certain. It was a Gamadin installation of some type that was causing the twynich periods that had plagued Nod for so many centuries. There was no other explanation.

Ian checked his com. Now that he had entered the structure, the readings were off the scale. He had unknowingly activated the twynich. Nod would be experiencing an unexpected, global-wide power outage, and he apologized to the planet. "Sorry about that." The fact that the people of the planet were accustomed to living with the twynich, on or off, gave him some solace knowing that there wouldn't be too much damage. The good news, he thought, was that Muuk's forces wouldn't be counting on the shift. His vehicles would be stopped cold in their tracks. They would be forced to carry themselves and their supplies the rest of the way into the Du Tir on foot. It seemed Ian had inadvertently bought some time.

After closing the vault door behind him to keep out any unwanted slithery things, Ian continued down the corridor, passing more arched doorways that he wanted desperately to investigate but couldn't. He had to find the others and let them know of his discovery. But first he had to find a way out of the underground structure. If his hunch was correct, they would be safe inside of it. No one on the planet, not even Muuk, had the resources to crack open anything Gamadin.

When he came to the end of the corridor and looked over a catwalk railing, he made another startling discovery. Where he stood now, at the edge of a circular walkway around the structure, was not the bottom of the structure as he thought, but near the top of a vast, underground network more incalculable than he had imagined. The openness was over a half-mile across and thousands upon thousands of feet of levels below that were switched on level by level, coming alive with power.

Ian was so overwhelmed, he stumbled backwards from his light-headedness. He found a wall to steady himself, taking a moment to gather his wits. How would he find any way out of this place, he wondered? It was all so immense. Where would he begin? Which level was the first floor? Where was the elevator between the levels. He checked the floor for blinkers as he walked. But even if he found one, where would he blink to? He took a deep breath and kept walking, trying to keep his head in check.

He wanted Harlowe's input really bad. "Any ideas, pard?"

Keep walkin', Wiz. That's the best way. Knowing Lu, she'll find you, before you find her.

Ian looked skyward trying to digest his discovery. "In this place? I can't even find me, Dog."

A muffled sound came from behind. He turned, but not fast enough to catch a glimpse of the attacker. Something beastly slammed him to the floor, and the world went instantly dark.

72

Lessons

Two days of parking in the woods with a beautiful doe had its limits, even for Simon. It had begun innocently enough. While sitting in the car waiting for the endless convoys of troop transports, armored vehicles, and tanks to pass their hideout in the forest, Simon asked Naree what everyone did for fun when they weren't running from the Clarity.

Naree stared at Simon like she had never heard the word in her life. "Fun?" she asked, looking mystified by the term.

They had no games to pass the time in the car, no books to read, no radio listen to, or movies to play on a car dash DVD. They had nothing to do but talk to each other, so Simon, being who he was, thought there was no better time than now to make his move. "Yeah, what do you do when you're not working? Do you go to the beach, go dancing with your girlfriends, paint, draw, read books? You know, fun things."

Naree shifted around in her car seat and pointed back to Cornicen. "I am always at the museum. That is what I do for the Clarity."

"That's it? Just work for the Clarity?" He took her hand and recited on old verse with a slight twist. "All work and no play, makes Naree a dull lady."

"I am dull?"

Simon forced a grin realizing he might have said the wrong thing. "No, no. You're anything but dull, Naree. I meant when your not working for the Clarity what do you do with your time?"

"I rest like everyone does."

334

At times Simon felt like he was talking without a translator in his ear. Asking a simple question was proving to be more difficult than he thought. He had to choose his words more carefully or be lost in a tangled game of charades. "Even in your spare time?" Simon asked.

"We are devoted to the Clarity. There is no idle time for what you call fun, Ahlian," she replied and then asked Simon what he did for fun.

"I make movies, surf when I can, drive my car along the beach, and hang out with my friends at a cool restaurant in Venice Beach," Simon replied.

"Then you are not always a captain?"

"No, Harlowe is captain. I was only pretending."

"Harlowe is like Genpok Xatz?"

Simon laughed. "No. Not even close. He's loved and respected by his crew, not hated like that witch."

Her cleavage made him squirm in his seat. His heart raced, and the collar around his neck grew tight. He tried unbuttoning his tunic, but it only helped a little. He fought for self-control, but being cooped up in a car with a goddess was testing his willpower to the max. A saint didn't have that kind of control, he thought.

"You speak so strangely, Ahlian," Naree went on. "It is often hard to understand your meanings." She then wanted to know more about this concept called fun, "Is it like the love of your Captain?"

Simon laughed again. "Oh, no. There are different kinds of love."

"Explain," she directed.

Simon saw his explanations were going nowhere fast. He thought maybe a hands-on approach would be more useful. "Let me teach you."

"You will be my teacher again?" she asked eagerly.

"Exactly."

"This will require a lot of training?"

Simon's face became instantly hot. *Bingo!* "Well, yes," he pointed out. "we'll need many hours of practice."

* * *

That was two days ago and now Simon figured it was time to leave their little love nest and head for the coast. Outside on the highway, the military procession had all but passed. There were only a few scattered convoys here and there, so figuring no time was better than the present, he threw caution to the wind and joined the motorcades. When a convoy of red and grays drove by going their direction, he was in. He shifted into gear and linked up with the line of transports traveling south. Naree huddled close to him wanting the lessons to continue while he drove.

Simon fixed his collar with one hand while doing his best to keep the car from wobbling all over the highway as they raced to catch up with the others. "Come on, Naree. I have to concentrate on the road."

"The lessons are over?" she asked, nibbling his ear.

Simon sucked in deep breaths trying to hold his own. "Don't you ever sleep?"

"I don't require rest until the moons of Mis have turned," Naree said.

Simon wiped his eyes, doing his best to clear away the effects of two sleepless nights. "How many hours is that?"

"Not hours, Ahlian. It is twenty-one turns before rest is required," Naree made clear, smiling with desire, that the lessons would continue until then.

Simon closed his eyes. At that rate he wouldn't make it till noon before his SIBA shut his body down, even with a fresh power pack.

73

Fyn

The loud blasts of gunfire had intensified by the time Harlowe and Monday reached the wide-open meadow where the shots were coming from. At the far side of the meadow a thatched-roofed house was beautifully set under giant trees with thick, dark branches full of glittering green and yellow leafy leaves. Windows were broken, but the structure's heavy timbered sides still held up under the intense assault. A river flowed between it and a barn-like outbuilding that had caught fire, shooting flames high in the sky along the back wall. To the side of the outbuilding, a high-fenced corral had also caught fire. A heavy wooded bridge connected the ranch house with the outbuilding. Scattered about the property was a tractor, watering troughs, and other tools necessary for a working ranch to function. Parked on the opposite side of the meadow was a massive six-wheeled monster that was similar to the one Darkn had crashed into *Millawanda*. Troops in dark camo scurried about, taking offensive positions and unpacking heavier weapons to use on the ranch house.

With bullets mixed with bright orange plas rounds flying in all directions, no side was backing down. But with old-fashioned lead bullets against modern plas weapons, the Tapper's firepower would eventually destroy the ranch house. Even so, the beings inside the house were far more deadly with their weapons than the Tappers. If a Tapper lifted his head too high or exposed himself a little bit, he was plucked off like owls in a shooting arcade.

"Those guys," meaning the ranchers, "are very good, Dog," Monday noticed.

The side door from the ranch house suddenly opened and two females ran out. They were young and tall with long dark hair pulled back in thick braids down their backs. Through a hail of plas rounds, they dashed across the wooden bridge toward the outbuilding, returning fire as they ran. Like trained soldiers, before coming to the corral, they hit the ground, rolled under the fence railing, and when they were clear, sprang back on their feet, diving through the partially open barn door. More shots rang out inside the barn. Then a moment later, to Harlowe's astonishment, a boy not much older than Dodger, came out of the door with guns blazing. Behind him the females appeared leading a half-dozen beautiful horned creatures from the burning building. The creatures were unlike any horses Harlowe or Monday had ever seen. They were taller by several feet than Earthly horses. Their large, majestic heads were crowned by two giant horns that swept back over their long, wavy manes. Instead of hooves, the beasts had padded feet with retractable claws attached to long, graceful legs that rippled with sinewy, powerful muscles.

Harlowe had seen enough. He and Monday drew their weapons and bounded out across the meadows, plucking off Tappers as they went. Monday broke off for the monster tank, taking Mowgi with him while Harlowe made a beeline for the barn.

*   *   *

Fyn knew he was finished. He looked around the room. Two of his hands were down, probably dead. They were motionless and green blood was dripping from both bodies onto the wood floor. A third hand had taken a plas round through the head. There was little doubt of his condition. It appeared Fyn was alone holding the house. He checked the chamber of his pistol. Three shells left. That was all he had to defend his property. Peeking through a gun port, he watched Isara and Oea climb their *ceffyls* and lead his stock away from the burning building.

"Nice work girls," he said to them. "Now ride away. Don't let the Tappers take our beauties."

He fired two quick rounds to cover them and fell back. He didn't remember seeing Muis. "Where is that boy?" he said aloud.

The clanking and banging of metal against metal meant the Tappers had positioned their large weapons on the house. It didn't matter, he thought, disheartened by what he knew was the end. Regardless, he was taking as many Tappers with him as possible until his ancestors yanked him from the planet to the heavens above. Before that happened, he prayed mightily they would give him the power to cover his children long enough so they could escape with the ceffyls to the high country besfore the Tappers found them. He lifted up and fired his last rounds. A Tapper dropped crossing the bridge but still no Muis. Where are you, son? A plas round grazed his shoulder when he took too long to cover himself. "No matter, it will take more than a Tapper to put old Fyn down," he cursed.

He heard Muis shouting. "Pappa!"

"My son!" he called out, grabbing a long blade off the floor. He lifted himself to the portal and watched three black uniforms fall crossing the bridge. "Great shooting, Muis!" And there he was. His son charging through the plas fire as he charged toward the house. His orders were to go with Isara and Oea. "Zalezzabob, boy! Leave me be! Don't come back here. Save yourself!" he gutted out in a desperate breath.

Muis heard nothing. The boy kept running and shouting "Pappa! Pappa!" Once, twice, then a third plas round struck his son in the leg, arm, and hip. Muis spun from the impact, tumbling on the bridge. Spitting green blood, he tried to get up but fell flat again.

"Zalezaa! Stay down, Muis!" Fyn screamed.

Muis continued crawling toward the house, reaching for his weapon. "Pappa!" he cringed in pain. Unable to hold is pistol upright, he fired it sideways until it was useless. Like Fyn, he was out of ammo.

Fyn grabbed his wide-blade knife and charged for the door. If he were going to die, he would be with his boy. He flung open the door to the sound of unfamiliar explosions happening all at once. By the time he stepped out onto the porch, the shots of plas fire were reduced to one or two volleys followed by complete silence upon the meadow.

His head filled with the fog of battle, Fyn limped farther onto the deck, expecting a hail of plas rounds to cut through his body at any moment. But strangely, not a shot was fired. The eerie quiet made no sense. What made even less sense was the being he saw walking toward the house with an odd looking pet with tall ears, bouncing along beside him. Over by the bridge, a second being dressed like the first, was picking Muis up in its arms. Fyn's stunned eyes looked around around the meadow. The massive Tapper transport was still parked at the edge of the woods, but not a single Tapper was around it. He scanned the forest and the bushes. Every Tapper was lying on the ground, still as death.

The tall being carrying Muis brought him to the front of the house where the first one joined him. "He'll live if you'll allow us to help him, sir," the second being said, holding Muis.

Stunned by the suddenness of it all, Fyn nodded his permission to bring Muis inside the house. What choice did he have? From what he saw of their power, these beings could have shot him anyway if they had wanted him dead. Yet, here they were asking to save his son.

Quickly, the second being removed a cylinder from the first's rucksack and laid it on the floor. What followed was the most remarkable transformation Fyn had ever seen. The cylinder came to life, becoming a tall, tubular, mechanical being with a lighted blue band around its triangle-shaped head. The second being spoke words to the android, and immediately it went to work slicing away Muis' bloodied clothes and attending his wounds with devices Fyn had never seen before. As the android attended to Muis, the first being went to the other bodies in the house, turning them over and checking their vital signs. "This one is dead, Captain," he informed the second being, "the other two have lost a lot of blood, but they're alive," he reported.

"Take care of them, Squid," the second said, without taking his eyes away from Muis.

"Aye, Captain."

Then, like the android, the first being obediently removed more strange instruments from his belt and began working on the wounded. All Fyn could do was watch and pray that whatever these extraordinary saviors were doing was going to save everyone's lives.

Suddenly, Isara and Oea came crashing through the front door with guns pointed at the beings. Fyn quickly met them with his hands outstretched. "No, Isara! They helped us defeat the Tappers!"

The strange pet stood between the two girls, bearing its incredibly large incisors from its expanding open maw.

"Back off, Mowgi," the second being ordered. The being then looked at Isara with its large bulbous insect eyes and said, "Please, let us work."

"What are you?"

"Friends," the being said.

"How do I know you are not killing my brother? Tell me what you are," Isara insisted.

The being tapped the side of his head, retracting the cover over his head. The large eyes dissolved away, revealing an almost normal being. "I'm like you. Now let us care for the boy," he demanded.

Isara was not fooled. He was not like them. He was fair skinned with light colored eyes like a Tapper. But when the first being lowered his mask, he *was* like them, dark skinned like the black wood trees of the forest.

Isara and Oea carefully lowered their weapons.

74

Just Lying Around

Ian was shaken but unhurt. The first thing he faced coming out of his funk were two enormous, blue eyes. "Molly?" he questioned. "What in the— What are you doing here?" he asked the massive, white head staring down at him with her wide, pink tongue.

"She couldn't wait to find you," Leucadia said, giggling next to the big cat. She thought the joke on Ian was funny. She reached down and gave him a hand. "Surprised?"

"Yeah," Ian replied, straightening himself out. "How did you get in?" he asked, sorely.

Leucadia went over to the rail and pointed across the vast, open shaft. "Through the front door."

"What? You found a front door?"

"Molly did," Leucadia replied, giving the feline a warm hug around her thick, white neck. She then explained, "We didn't understand it either. She came down off the mountain top all wound up, fretting and growling like something was wrong. We thought you were in trouble at first. But when she led us away from the slope, we figured she had something else in mind. Appears she was playing a game to beat you coming in the back door."

Ian glared at the big cat. "Just a game, huh?"

Molly purred knowing she had won.

"Not funny, girl," Ian said sourly.

"Oh, don't be mad at her," Leucadia defended. "She was only playing."

Ian frowned at Leucadia. "You don't know what I went through to get here."

Leucadia saw his anguish. "Tough going, huh?"

Ian turned away. "You could say that. How far away was the door?"

"A few hundred feet from where you climbed," Leucadia replied.

That hurt even more, as he shook his head, thinking of all the hassles he went through.

Leucadia glanced in the direction Ian had come from. "Anything back there of interest?"

Ian retracted his bugeyes. "Nothing but a bunch of passageways." He came back to Leucadia and asked, "Where are Cheesa and Dev?"

"I left them at the front door with Rhud," she replied, and added as a precaution. "I told them not to go exploring without one of us."

Ian agreed that was wise. There was no telling what dangers were lurking in a place that had not been visited by any intelligent beings for thousands of years. "We should go find them."

"You look troubled, Ian. Muuk can't enter the Gamadin outpost. Its fortifications are too well-built."

"That's what you think it is, too, huh? An outpost like Hitt?" Ian wondered.

She ran her fingers through her long, yellow hair as she spoke. "Yes, it is vast and well-hidden just like Hitt. Have you found anything alive, yet? Like spiders?"

Ian looked at her straight. "No spiders. Try big snakes."

She looked around the vastness. "Snakes?"

"Big ones outside the vault door back there," he said pointing with his thumb.

"We should stay alert."

"You got that right." Ian shot back. "This place gives me the creeps."

They started walking. He had to find Cheesa and Dev before something unexpected happened. The more he thought about it, the more fearful he became. Muuk was just one of their problems. They may have been wearing a SIBA, but it wouldn't protect them from being swallowed. Rhud could take care of one or two slithering beasts, but what if there were a whole nest of them? He hurried his pace as they continued their catch-up conversation.

Worried, Leucadia glanced back. "It was big, huh?"

"Yeah, like in one of those anaconda movies but bigger. It had teeth, too, like Mowgi unchained."

Leucadia knew Ian was not prone to over exaggeration like Riverstone or Simon. "I thought we would be safe in here."

They stepped up the pace to ten-foot strides with Molly loping beside them.

"How far is the front door?"

"Down three levels."

Ian pointed. "Molly go!" He leaped over the side of the rail and took flight, his SIBA wings gathering air. "Too far." Leucadia followed. Neither gave falling a hundred stories down a second thought. They landed side-by-side, raising their legs over the lower guardrail as they touched down on the pathway leading to the front door.

This level was quite different from the one coming in from the caldera. The ceiling was much higher with ten story double doors as wide as *Millawanda's* main foyer at the top of her center ramp.

"What's this for?" Ian wondered. "The Gamadin didn't build this to play football in."

"It's not large enough for Millie either," Leucadia pointed out.

"Yeah, not even close." Ian nodded at the large doors. "How did you get through those?"

Leucadia led him over to the side of the giant cavity. "The entry door is over here."

"Sweet. But where did Cheesa and Dev go?" he asked, searching the area. "They're not here."

Leucadia tried looking for footprints, but incredibly, there was no dust on the floor to disturb. It was clean like it was mopped yesterday. They both switched on their SIBA headgear and dialed up the infrared. The footprints were still there and leading off in the direction of an open doorway on the opposite side of the main floor. Molly joined them halfway across as they came to the door.

They were about to enter the room when Dev surprised them, running out of the room with a big grin on his face. "I think I found something, Lu! Ian, where have you been?"

"Where's Cheesa?" Ian asked, looking past the Prince. "Is she with you?"

"No." Dev pointed down. "She wanted to check the lower levels."

"I told you two to stay here, Dev," Leucadia scolded.

Dev looked at her helplessly. "If she didn't listen to you, you think she would listen to me?" He pointed at himself. "And I'm the Prince."

Ian took off running with Molly in the direction Dev pointed. "Stay with Dev, Lu!"

"Turn on your com, Ian!" Leucadia yelled back.

Ian tapped the side of his SIBA headgear, giving her a big thumbs up as he leaped away in big strides toward the opposite end of the great room. He heard the scream before he reached the second level down. Her footprints were still fresh through the infrared optics, although with Molly along, he didn't need them. He knew exactly where to find Cheesa and Rhud. Ian drew his weapon as Molly tore off ahead him. As fast as he was in a SIBA, she was faster. His springy steps followed her as best he could, but in no time, she was a good hundred yards ahead him, as he watched her charge into another tall doorway. More screams came from the room, along with a mixture of tiger roars and hissing beasts. Ian leaped as fast as his legs would take him and then dove headfirst into the room with weapon locked and loaded. He slid along the floor and came up eyes popping with disbelief. There were two of the largest, toothy anacondas he had seen yet, making his belief in multiple serpents come to life. These two were adults compared to the juvenile he had dealt with earlier. Ian couldn't get a clear shot yet. Rhud was attached to the one's neck, biting and clawing deep chunks of flesh from its shinny, slick hide. Just as the second slithering beast was about to stick Rhud, Molly launched herself with ten-inch claws, burying them into its face and eyes. The beast jolted up, writhing in pain. Sweeping back and forth, both anacondas whipped their heads back and forth in a desperate struggle to dislodge the cats. But neither cat would let go. They kept up the battle, gouging and scratching, tearing flesh in massive hunks that hit the floor in dull splats. The gooey, green globs splattered Cheesa who was huddled in a niche against the wall.

Ian ran to her side and pulled her out of the recess. Cheesa pointed. "Rhud, Ian!" A third anaconda had suddenly emerged out of nowhere with jaws wide, headed for Rhud. Before the beast struck, Ian riddled it with a dozen rounds. The beast slammed to the floor with a heavy thump, dead as stone. Soon after that, the other two beasts fell, their brains and eyes, literally torn from their heads.

Ian yelled at the cats to back off. Once they were clear, he finished the kill with more plas rounds to each head. He was leaving nothing to chance.

Cheesa was a green mess, but Ian didn't care if she came from a sewer pit when she threw her arms around him, kissing him passionately on the lips. He would have liked the moment to last, but their concern for Molly and Rhud outweighed their enthusiasm for each other. They separated and went to the cats, who were, like Cheesa, covered with green blood and hunks of gangly flesh. Ian checked them over thoroughly. He pulled the stringy pieces from their fur and hugged them both. He found scrapes and minor cuts but nothing that wouldn't heal quickly.

"Why were you down here, Cheesa?" Ian asked, continuing the clean up of the cats with Cheesa.

Before Cheesa could answer, they were interrupted by Leucadia and Dev excitedly rushing into the room. But when they saw the cats, and the gore of green blood and the bodies of the giant dead beasts lying on the floor, their jovial expressions turned to instant dread.

"Oh, my gawd! Why didn't you call me?" Leucadia trembled, going to Rhud first to check him over.

"There wasn't time. It just happened," Ian answered, suddenly feeling the exhaustion from the battle.

She went to Molly next. "Are they okay?" She turned to him, shaking from what might have happened as she glanced at the dead beasts. "Cheesa?"

"I'm all right, Lu," Cheesa said as they came together in a relieved hug.

Dev was dumbstruck by the amount of destruction. "Molly and Rhud did this?" he stuttered.

Ian nodded.

Dev looked at the dead serpents and back to the tigres in total disbelief. Since the first time he met the great, white tigres, he had become more and more awed by their feats. He was now staring at them like they were great, white gods.

In tears, Leucadia let go of Cheesa. "Thank God you're okay . . ." Her voice trailed at the end.

Ian turned to her, wondering why she had suddenly drifted back from them, looking up at the ceiling. "What's a matter, Lu?" he asked.

Leucadia took a breath. "Do you know what this is?"

Ian turned to look up. "What is?" He followed her gaze toward the ceiling and his mouth dropped open like he had seen another slithering beast come through the door. But it wasn't a beast this time; it was the perimeter edge of a Gamadin saucer just fifty feet above their heads. Both of their mouths could have swallowed the ship whole.

"This is what I was trying to tell you, Ian," Cheesa said, putting her arms around him again. "This is your ship, like the one you told me about."

"It's a Gamadin ship, alright," Ian said, gawking up at every last detail from the three landing pods that curved down touching the floor, to its perfectly round, sleek, golden skin.

"But she's much smaller, Chee," Leucadia said, sizing up the ship.

"She's probably a shuttlecraft of some kind," Ian guessed.

Leucadia wasn't so sure. "I think it is too large for short distances, Ian. I think it goes farther," she speculated.

Ian looked at Leucadia with hope in his eyes. "Interstellar?"

"That's my feeling. Only for small missions."

"You think she still works like Millie?"

Leucadia sighed at the thought. "She appears in good shape. It's possible."

For the first time in a long while, Ian cracked an optimistic smile. "Wouldn't that be cool?"

Cheesa looked at Ian uneasyly. "What are you saying, Ian?"

Ian put his arm around her shoulders as he continued about what could be. "What Lu is saying, Cheesa, is that if this ship still works, we can leave Nod."

Now Cheesa was beginning to tear up. "You would leave me, Ian?"

Ian was stunned by the question. There was never any doubt that one day he would say goodbye to Nod. At the very worst, he and Leucadia would be stuck on the planet until Harlowe returned to pick them up. But if there was a way to escape Nod without waiting for Harlowe to return… Wow, he was in! Where would they go? Back to Earth? How far could she travel, and at what speed? Would it explode the instant he switched on the power drives? Would he subject Cheesa to such an uncertain fate? The answer, of course, was no. For Leucadia and him it was a risk they had to take. But to ask Cheesa or Dev to incur the same risk was out of the question. He cared too much for her to endanger her life on a journey that had such little hope of succeeding.

He gathered her in his arms, brushing away some green goo from her neck. "When our journey is done, Cheesa, I'll be back for you; I promise."

Cheesa pushed him away. "You're not coming back. You are leaving me," she challenged.

"Cheesa, I can't take you. I won't risk your life. You don't know the danger if you come with us," he explained.

She pointed angrily at the dead beasts on the floor. "Is it more dangerour than this, Ian Wizzixs? Or being shot by the Imperator or eaten by a haapffin?" she asked, shooting daggers with her eyes. "Tell me which one is less deadly than going with you? Tell me, Ian!"

Ian thought hard to remember a day Death had taken a holiday since meeting her. His mind froze. There were too many of those near-death moments he wanted to forget, including today! Drawing a total blank, he turned to Leucadia for help. There was sympathy in her eyes as she said, "Now you know how Harlowe feels."

"I don't like it."

"Neither does he." She took his arm and went on to say, "Without Cheesa's help we might never have found Molly and Rhud, Ian. Think about that."

"You're supposed to be on my side," Ian told her.

"I am." She stepped to Cheesa and put her arm around her. "Like it or not, she's part of our team."

"What am I?" Dev asked, as if he was being left behind with no say. He pointed at the blood all over the floor. "Green goo?"

"You're a pain in the ass, Prince . . ." Ian began, but Leucadia stopped him short. She had other ideas about Dev's future.

"He may have saved us all, Ian," she said.

"You're kidding, aren't you?" Ian asked, searching her every facial movement and flicker of green in her eyes for any sign of jest. She wasn't kidding. Ian's eyes shot skyward. "Luuuuu..." he groaned in pain.

Leucadia motioned with her index finger. "Let Dev show you what he found; then you can make your decision if he goes or stays."

Ian looked around for any sympathetic eyes to join his side. Even the cats were sitting this one out. He shook his head in defeat. "All right, Dev, lay it on me. What did you find?"

* * *

Ian stepped in the room back up on the main level with the double doors and went immediately into a state of total shock. If the little Millie ship had jolted him, what he saw before him now was so completely overwhelming, his SIBA supports were powerless to keep him standing. He collapsed to the floor with his face turning from an absolute, jaw-dropping astonishment to a sick, almost psychotic laughter as he rolled over on the floor.

"They're just lying around," Ian babbled incoherently. He was so close to a nervous breakdown, one of Simon's shrinks couldn't have helped him. "It's just like Riverstone said. They're lying around on the floor, waiting for us to pick them up."

Ian crawled on his hands and knees and ran his fingers along the first foot-thick, six-foot long, faceted blue aara crystal he came to. As immense as it was, it was one of the smaller Gamadin crystals out of the many dozens in the room.

"Is this a treasure beyond all dreams or what, Ian?" Leucadia asked with her eyes gleaming a happy smile.

"So sweet, Lu. So, so sweet." His face turned sad as he looked up from the floor and asked, "But how will we get one to Harlowe?"

Leucadia went quickly somber. There was no question about it, finding the aara was the easy part. Getting one to him would be impossible if they were stuck on the planet. But before she could answer the how question, loud explosions roared from outside the outpost, shaking the floor beneath them.

"Muuk!" Leucadia announced. "He's here."

75

Ceffyls

It was the morning after the battle at Fyn's ranch. The sky was light green above and pink to the east, and the air was moist with dew. The fresh scent of the forest had yet to replace the stench from the pile of dead Tappers in the meadow. Bigbob had worked through the night, finishing the reconstruction of the barn and corral as Harlowe stood alone at the fence, admiring the most remarkable animals he had ever seen. At home in Lakewood, this would have been the quiet time before the freeways were jam-packed with commuters going to work. But here, on a working ranch, Fyn and his family had risen before dawn, cleaned up the Tappers' mess, and carried on with ranch chores that never ended. Monday gave Oea a hand pitching hay for the ceffyls while Muis, as injured as he was, carried water from the river and dumped it into their drinking buckets. Harlowe only looked idle. Earlier, he and Isara had dragged the dead Tappers from the bushes and stacked them where Fyn wanted them. He said he would take care of them later. What that meant, Harlowe could only guess. It was a filthy job, but someone had to do it. Finding a little time, he meandered back to the corral to admire the creatures he had only seen from a distance. Horse-like in appearance, they were tall, magnificent creatures with giant horns and dark flowing manes, bulbous eyes, that glistened with intelligence, perky ears, long heads, and proud tails held high like the famous Austrian Lipizzaners he and Leucadia rode once on their trip to Vienna. Yet, as common as their features were to Earthly horses, they were not horses at all, but a special breed of creature not found anywhere but here in the mountain foothills of what Fyn called the Ozans. For one, their size was immense, a third taller than any horse the Mars family had roaming their vast spread in Texas.

"You didn't sleep," a woman's voice said softly.

Harlowe smiled without looking. He knew who it was. He had heard her coming from a distance. Gamadin never took their surroundings for granted. It was their training. He pointed at the sleeve of his SIBA. "My garment replenishes my body," he told her. "We only need a few hours' rest to function."

"Muis is better. He is nearly healed," Isara informed him. "Thank you."

Harlowe looked toward the boy returning to the river for another pail. "He's very brave. I have a brother about his age. He reminds me of him."

"You miss him."

"Yes, very much." Thinking of home, his mother, and Dodger made him homesick. The fear of never seeing them and Leucadia or Wiz made the lump in his throat a little tighter with each day he was away from them. He needed to keep his mind occupied with the mission. "What are they, Isara?" Harlowe asked, "I've never seen such beautiful animals like them anywhere in my travels."

Isara came beside Harlowe as together they watched the creatures munching hay in their troughs. "They are called ceffyls. For thousands of passings, they have run wild in the Ozans. Darkn and his Tappers have hunted them for horns over the passings and now there are only a few left in our valley."

Isara was nearly as tall as he was. She smelled of ranch and pine sap, together with a hint of grass and soil of the corral, and salty sweat from the morning's chores. Nothing at all was disagreeable. There was something earned and honorable in her aroma. Her skin was smooth and dark like Monday's, her eyes large, round, and intelligent. Her braided hair was long and black and swayed like a thick rope down her strong back. To look at her sinewy smooth arms, wide shoulders in her homemade leathers, the poised and confident way she carried herself standing near him, Harlowe knew straight out she was no helpless babe. She was as beautiful as her ceffyls, but also like them, physically powerful and disciplined. Harlowe thought of one word to describe her: "courageous," like the whole family he had come to know and admire in the few hours since coming to the ranch.

Ceffyl

"Shameful," Harlowe said of the dwindling number of ceffyls left on the planet. "Why were you attacked? You seem isolated here from the Tappers."

"For many passings Fyn paid Darkn's tariffs. Now that is not enough. He wants what he cannot have, the rest of Pappa's ceffyls. Pappa will die before he gives them up," Isara explained.

"I have met Darkn. His Tappers will return until they get what they want," Harlowe cautioned.

Isara understood their plight. She had lived it since she was born. "We know."

"Can you hide?" Harlowe asked with concern.

"No. Pappa will not leave the valley."

Harlowe stared back. "Darkn has thousands more than what we faced yesterday. You have no defense against them."

Isara was insistent. "Pappa will not leave. His Pappa and his Pappa before him and on and on for generations have been the ceffyls' protectors. If we leave, the ceffyls will cease to exist. It is our duty to defend them with our lives. Once they are gone, there will be no reason for my family to be . . ." She stopped briefly to gather herself. "We will defend our herd to our last breath, Harlowe."

"That is suicide."

"That is our way."

In many ways, Harlowe and Fyn were alike. They each had a calling to protect all life from the madness. Fyn's duty was to his creatures. Harlowe's was the planets. Their calling was no less important than the other. It was only a matter of degree. He wished more than anything to help Fyn. If he had known their problem, he could have brought them the 54th century weapons he needed to defend the ranch until he found the aara and returned with *Millawanda*. But for now, he could do nothing. Without his ship, Fyn's ranch, his family, and his ceffyls were all sitting ducks.

"Can you stay a while longer?" Isara asked, as they started back to the ranch house.

"I also have a duty," he told her. "But if you can hold out a while longer, I promise you Isara, I will keep your ranch safe for a very long time."

"Who are you, Harlowe? I saw how you handled the Tappers. They were no match against you and Squid." She reached down and stroked Mowgi's parabolics. "And this one. He is not what he seems."

Harlowe knelt beside the undog, scratching his back. "No, he's special, alright."

"A ruthless warrior," she noted.

Harlowe wouldn't argue the point. There were times the undog was a merciless killer, and there was no way to reform him. "He does have a bad side," he admitted. He stood, thankful the chinner was on his side.

"You did not answer my question, Harlowe," Isara insisted. "Why are you here? You are not from here."

He would not lie to her, but to tell her everything would serve no purpose. "No. We're from far away." He pointed to the mountains looming high on the horizon. Even from this distance, a hundred miles away, they appeared large and uncrossable. Harlowe wondered if following the coastline might have been better after all. "We're headed through a pass that leads to the coast."

"Yes, I know it. It goes through the Surwag land."

Harlowe surveyed the tall, snow-capped peaks. Their sheer vertical faces reminded him of the Swiss Alps he had seen on one of his holidays with Leucadia when they had climbed to the top of the Matterhorn. "Surwag land?"

"A deadly race of beings," Isara said fearful at saying the name. "Even Darkn will not venture through Surwag ground."

"It's a journey we must make, Isara. We have no choice."

"You will never make it on foot," she advised him.

"We've come this far. We will make it. We have to."

"With ceffyls it is possible."

"Thank you, Isara, but Squid and I must make our journey alone."

"I assure you, without ceffyls you will die. They can shorten your journey by many days."

"I will not risk them, Isara. If it is as dangerous as you say, they could be killed. I don't want that on my conscience. I'm sorry."

"We owe you our lives, our ranch, and our ceffyls, Harlowe. It is a debt of eternity. We are your servants. Our family must aid your journey or lose face. That is *our* way."

Harlowe confronted the same argument on Gazz when he rescued Shortstop from the jaws of a giant traa. It seemed no matter where he went in the galaxy, saving one's life meant gratitude forever. If Isara was half as thickheaded as Shortstop, which she was in spades, then he had already lost the argument.

Still, he had to try. "You owe us nothing, Isara. It is the duty of every Gamadin to protect those who are preyed upon by the madness," Harlowe said.

Isara's eyes drifted to one side. She found Harlowe's answer wanting. "Gamadin? The ancient protectors?"

Harlowe was surprised by her question. "You know of the Gamadin?" he asked, showing her the starburst insignia on his cuff. "This is our symbol."

"Yes, I have seen such a symbol," she admitted.

"Really? You have seen this symbol before?"

"Yes, the Monuments have such symbols engraved in their structures. It is said they were carved by the gods who came from the stars to fight the wazimu. If you are Gamadin, then you are from the stars, Harlowe." Her posture turned straight and direct while her expression remained still. There was no doubt in Harlowe's mind: Isara's statement was no guess but a rational truth.

Harlowe tried hiding the fact that he was an alien spaceman. Did she know about starships and travelers from the stars? Seeing Bigbob, a mechanical being, had little effect on her or her family. Even a big, yellow-eyed dragon seemed unordinary to them. He wondered why. If their roles were reversed, would he be so accepting of dragons and robobs?

Staying with the truth had always worked well for Harlowe in the past. "Yes, Squid and I are from far beyond your planet, Isara," he began. "We came here in a spaceship looking for a city called Lamille. Our ship is crippled. We must find this city along the coast to save her."

"Lamille? I have never heard of such a city now or in the past."

"Even if Lamille no longer exists, we have instruments that will help locate the things we hope to find for our ship."

It appeared to Harlowe that Isara wanted desperately to lend a hand, but she knew only of ceffyls and life on a ranch, not starships and ancient warriors from the stars.

"This place you call Monuments," Harlowe inquired. "Can you take me there? The symbols you speak of could be helpful."

Isara took his hand. "Come with me, Harlowe," and led him toward the house. "We will help you find your city." When they stepped through the door and into the main room, Fyn was the only one sitting at the big table. Bigbob was serving him breakfast. Fyn's huge dark hand waved Harlowe and Isara to sit next to him.

"Your droid has fixed a hearty meal and works like twenty of my best hands, Harlowe. May I purchase him from you? I will be generous."

Harlowe smiled gratefully. "I'm afraid he is not for sale at any price, Fyn."

"Pity. I will then make the most of him while I can."

Harlowe tapped Bigbob on the shoulder. "Do that."

"Harlowe must leave now, Pappa," Isara said before Harlowe could say another word. "He is on a long journey through the Ozans. But first he must visit the Monuments."

Fyn kinked his head oddly at Harlowe. "The Monuments? That is Baago's land. They will not treat you kindly if you enter without permission."

"I only wish to look, Fyn. That's all. I will not harm the Monuments," Harlowe promised.

Fyn pointed at Harlowe's sidearm, hung low and strapped to his leg. "Are you fast with your weapon?"

"Very."

"Good, because Baago's son, Nath, will want to challenge you to a contest. If you win, you will be allowed to pass. If you fail . . . Well, do not fail if you wish to see the Monuments, Harlowe."

"I'll keep that in mind. How far are is it?" Harlowe asked.

"A day's ride," Isara replied.

"A day," Harlowe repeated, grateful it wasn't far. He wanted to be on his way as soon as possible. "We will run there."

"Nonsense. A ceffyl will have you to the Monuments before the sun sets," Fyn bragged.

Saying no to anyone in Fyn's family was proving tougher than winning an argument with Lu. He didn't want to infringe on Fyn's hospitality any more than he already had. But was "no" part of their vocabulary? He remembered the time he went with his dad and told him about Mr. John wanting to pay him for mowing his lawn when he was sick with the flu. Harlowe didn't want the money, but Mr. John insisted. His dad said, "Take the money, son. It will make Mr. John very happy. You don't have to spend it. Give it away if you want. But allow Mr. John to show his thanks. It will make his day."

Fyn chambered three rounds in his rifle as Isara said, "Allow me to choose a ride for you, Harlowe."

Harlowe had no idea what one ceffyl was from another. To him they were all incredible creatures. He had ridden quarter horses in Texas, a Lipizzaner in Austria, giant Traas on Gazz, and Mowgi's back many times, but never a ceffyl! He wondered if Monday felt like him. Scared! Harlowe swallowed hard. "Yeah, sure. Pick one."

Isara pulled Harlowe out of his chair, and together they ran out the door and across the river bridge to the corral. She didn't bother to open the gate. She slipped through the cross boards and disappeared into the barn. After a short wait, she came galloping out of the barn on a ceffyl of her own, leading a beautiful, jet black mount by its reins, fully saddled and ready to ride. Trailing behind her were Oea and Monday. Monday rode a rich auburn mount like he was born in a saddle. Harlowe was already panicked enough at the sight of Isara's choice when the black, and all three riders, leaped over the ten-foot high corral fence like it was a low hurdle in the road.

"Why even bother with a corral, Isara?" Harlowe asked as he watched the three leap across the twenty-foot wide river in the same, easy manner.

"It's for the younger ones. We rarely open it," Isara said.

As the trio rode up, Harlowe asked Monday, "Where did you learn to ride, Squid?"

"My Uncle Earl had a cutting horse ranch in Georgia. I worked there in the summers cleaning the stalls. As I got older I was allowed to exercise them," Monday replied while guiding his ceffyl in small circles, then backing up and going forward again in perfect control.

Harlowe sneered at Monday. "Showoff." He wondered how to mount his ceffyl since it was taller than the others. A smaller one would have suited him just fine.

Fyn took the reins of the black from Isara and came to Harlowe with some fatherly advice. "You have chosen a treacherous path, my son. To cross the Ozans without ceffyls is sure death," Fyn said.

Harlowe looked up at his mount. The great horned head pranced and dipped as its braided mane glistened from the morning light. The ceffyl was anxious to run like the wind. Like Millie, he was fast and true. "This is the way, huh?"

"If you are to survive."

Muis then asked, "Will you show me how to shoot your weapon, Harlowe, when you return?"

Harlowe bent down to Muis. "Yes, but promise me, you'll stay well until then. Leave the Tappers to us."

"I will, Harlowe. By the gods, I will."

Harlowe patted Muis on the back as he came back to Fyn with advice of his own. "Darkn will miss his gerbid. They will come looking for it and his missing Tappers."

"I have places. They will not find it soon."

"The girls. They will stay with you," Harlowe said.

"No. They are your guides," Fyn said directly. "They will travel with you to Lamille."

Harlowe tried to look stern, but the counter from Fyn was disarming. He swore Fyn had learned that look from Shortstop. "Fyn, this isn't your battle. The girls must stay with you."

"This is not negotiable, Harlowe. The honor is ours to serve the Gamadin."

Harlowe had lost control. This was not his ship where he was the captain. This was Fyn's place, and by helping to save his ranch, Fyn, like Shortstop, would sacrifice all that he had to help Harlowe and his mission.

Harlowe grabbed Fyn by the arm, clutching him like a brother. He had only known him for a few short hours, but already he felt like he had known him a lifetime. "Be here when I return, or I'll kick your butt, Pappa," Harlowe growled into Fyn's ear.

Fyn smiled and handed Harlowe the reins. "Off with you now. Find your city, and return so we may enjoy each other's company again."

Harlowe gave a grateful wink as he looked up at the black, wondering how he was going to reach the saddle. "I will Fyn. Count on it."

"Just do it, Captain," Monday directed, "and hold on."

Harlowe took a deep breath and leaped for the saddle. He wanted to be as cool as Indiana Jones, landing on the saddle and galloping after the Ark of the Covenant. Instead, he got nothing but air, flying over the saddle and landing flat on his back. "That was smooth, Captain," Monday quipped as Harlowe sprang to his feet and dusted himself off. The good news was that his black mount had remained in place and had not run off.

Harlowe came back around and faced the black. "Thanks for staying put, big guy." This time he reached up and took hold of the leather tie on the front of the saddle. There was no horn like Western saddles he was used to. The tie would be the only thing that would save him from over-shooting his saddle this time. Then with one kick up, he swung his leg over while gripping the tie like his life depended on it.

Flop!

It wasn't a stylish landing like Indy would make, but nevertheless, he was sitting tall in the saddle and feeling proud of his accomplishment. Being fifteen feet above the ground gave the world a whole, new perspective. The horizon had expanded five fold.

Harlowe glanced over at Monday. "Sweet. How do I look, Squid?"

"Studly, Captain."

After a trot around the grounds, Harlowe felt like he was getting the hang of it. The smell of leather, the pull of the reins holding the raw power of the black prancing about felt exhilarating. He wanted to go to the next level as he watched Isara and Oea lead the way. "Come on, Mowg," Harlowe waved. He didn't want the undog displaying his finer qualities just yet. Although Mowgi could easily fly, or even be-bop along as fast as any ceffyl, Harlowe thought it best to keep things normal for the present.

Mowgi showed his usual deftness and leaped up the side of the tall ceffyl like he could do it in his sleep. He stuck to the front of the saddle as Harlowe called over to Monday. "What now?"

"Let her rip, Dog!" Monday cried out as his red charged forward, following the girls.

Harlowe hated eating anyone's dust. He pointed his black at the three bounding away in unbelievable jumps, touching down, then leaping again, matching each other stride for stride. Harlowe's heart jumped to his throat as the black launched skyward on his first thirty-foot vault. From then on, it was all Harlowe could do to stay in the saddle, holding on for dear life with his knuckles white from squeezing the leather and the long hair in his hands.

76

Just Ask

Muuk's forces continued shelling the outpost. The Imperator had over a thousand soldiers in the valley and all the military hardware needed to explode his way into the mountain outpost. The force field that normally protected all outposts from attack had not snapped on, making Ian believe it was either switched off or broken. Maybe there was a switch they needed to throw, but there was no time to look for it. Without it, it was only a matter of time before the first Numeri were bursting through to the main level. As Harlowe would say, "That's a given." Ian counted on the heavy doors staying intact long enough for them to gather some aara, find a way into the ship, and fly away.

If you're going to dream, dream big, a voice said to him.

Knowing *Millawanda's* little sister was their only hope for staying alive, Ian snapped out of his daze and quickly organized a detail to gather up all the crystals they could carry and head back down to the abandoned saucer. The largest crystals were too heavy for humans to carry, but when a clicker touched one of the big boys, some kind of anti-gravity force took over, enabling them to pick up a two-ton hunk of aara with ease.

Back at the ship, Maa Dev stood with the cats and the others gawking up at the underside of the saucer, and asked, "How old is this ship?"

"It's previously owned," Ian confessed, figuring the less the Prince knew about her actual age the better.

The answer didn't sit well with Dev. "You believe this…this… Whatever this is can help us?" he questioned, dubious that anything that was this large, round, and had no visible means of entry or propulsion was useful against Muuk?

"I do," Ian replied, walking away.

Cheesa trailed after him when another explosion shook the outpost. "How, Ian?"

There was no time for Q & A. Ian left that to Leucadia who told them, "This is a transport ship that is made to travel great distances. Farther than you can imagine. If she works, she will take us away from here…count on it!"

Dev kicked a loose crystal back onto the pile. "Why have we brought these here? It was a waste of time. We should be looking for a way out of the outpost."

"Give Ian time, Dev," Leucadia said. "He knows what he is doing."

Cheesa wanted to know why the crystals were so important. "Wouldn't one be enough?" she asked.

Dev held up a sack of small ones. "And these? They're so little."

"They're for our friends. They need them," she explained.

The explosions continued, making Dev more anxious than he already was. "We should be looking for a place to hide. The Imperator's forces will be here soon. We are wasting time with this, Lu."

Ian had enough. He needed to think, and he couldn't do it with all the meaningless chatter going on around him. "Dev. Zip it! That's all you need to know."

"But—" Dev tried to say before Ian covered his mouth.

"We're done talking, Prince." Ian pushed him down onto a large crystal and, in no uncertain terms, ordered him to stay put. Taking orders from a commoner, even one who had saved his life a number of times, was still difficult for His Royal Highness to understand.

Dev bounced back up. "But if you can't—"

Boom!

Even Ian's usual cool had reached its limit as Dev became a quiet addition to the pile. Ian whirled back around to the others. "Anyone else have a question?" The cats hid behind a landing pod while Leucadia and Cheesa both shook their heads. "Good. Let's find a way in, shall we?"

Ian began by searching each landing pod while Leucadia and Cheesa scanned the underside of the ship.

"It shouldn't be complicated," Leucadia said to Cheesa, who had never seen a spaceship before and certainly nothing that flew without an engine. "The Gamadin were very straightforward."

"I see no access door, Lu," Cheesa said, looking for any hint of an entryway.

"It's there. We just need to let her know we're here, and she'll reveal the way in for us," Leucadia said.

Ian found nothing along the smooth landing pod to suggest any kind of access panel existed. He glanced at the other two pods, making a quick scan of each. He saw nothing there either.

Viewing the saucer from the upper level was like looking down at a small *Millawanda*. But her size was relative. Compared to other Earth-made aircraft, she was nearly twice the size of two 747's put together, end to end, and ten times their volume. Where *Millawanda* was over three hundred feet from the ground to the top of her dome, the little saucer was no taller than five stories high. Like *Millawanda*, she was a flawless, golden saucer with three landing pods but had only one large observation window in the front of her center dome. Yeah, a lit'l Millie, Ian thought. So cool. But did she have an interstellar star drive, he wondered? He shuddered to think if she didn't. Dogging along at anything below hyperlight to the power of ten would take years to travel where they needed to go. One look at the bridge and he would know if she was a light duty transport or a little Millie with kickass weapons and speed to match. He grew excited the instant he touched her satiny skin along her pod. "Feel that, Lu?"

Leucadia touched the surface, following Ian's example, and as she did, her green eyes grew brighter and rounder. "Yes!"

Cheesa wanted to know why they were so excited. The only thing she felt that was unusual was that, "It's warm," she observed.

"Exactly! She's warm," Ian exclaimed. "She's alive, Chee. If she had no power, she would be cold as death."

"Why doesn't she open up, then?" Cheesa asked.

Ian looked up. He had no answer. "I don't know."

Another explosion sent a tremor through the outpost. They were getting louder and more frequent now.

Leucadia leaned against a nearby pod. "There is a way, Ian. We're just not seeing it," she said with confidence.

Cheesa pointed at the robobs waiting patiently with their heavy crystals for someone to order them to board the ship with their load of aara. "Why don't you just ask one of them?" she suggested.

From fifty feet between them, Leucadia and Ian traded why-didn't-we-think-of-that faces. It was a light bulb moment.

Leucadia said, "I think she's got it, Ian."

Ian led the charge back to the pod where the clickers were silently killing time. "Take the aara to the power room," he ordered the first robob in line.

Its head grew brighter. There was nothing to touch or gesture to make. The clicker simply stepped forward as the sounds of life came from within the ship. That was all that it took. The act was so straightforward Ian believed if his SIBA was activated, he would have had the same response. The wide ramp appeared immediately, extending down from the center of the ship to meet the robobs as they climbed the incline like disciplined little soldiers.

Ian kissed Cheesa fully on the lips. "Way to go, babe!" He then charged up the ramp, ahead of the robobs. "Stay there!" Along the way, he drew his weapon and activated his SIBA, headgear and all.

Molly was about to leap ahead, but Ian stopped her short. "No, girl. Not yet." The great cat growled her displeasure but remained at the top of the ramp as ordered.

Cheesa turned to Leucadia. "Why must we wait, Lu?"

Leucadia activated her SIBA at the same moment Ian went hot. Holding her weapon ready, she explained to Cheesa, "The ship has been dormant for a very long time. There could be a number of dangers inside. This is his ship now. He wants to make sure it is safe for us before we board."

"His ship?" she asked.

"Yes, Ian is our captain now. We must follow his commands at all times from here on out. That is our way."

After a short absence, Ian reappeared at the hatchway and waved them up the ramp. Behind him the lights inside the ship had already turned bright, welcoming them in. "We're good to go," he announced as the robobs passed him on their way down the ramp for more aara. One clicker picked up Dev from the pile just as a slithering monster flopped onto the floor next to them.

77

First Kiss

Harlowe, Monday, Isara, and Oea rode the 200 miles in a little over five hours with only brief stops to water their ceffyls and eat some special food the girls had brought along in their saddlebags. For the girls and Monday, it was a brisk ride through the forest and across a flat plain to the foothills of the Ozans, but for Harlowe it was sheer torture. Without his SIBA constantly battling saddle sores, blisters, and butt aches, Harlowe would never have made it past the first mile. Even SIBAs had their limits. When they finally stopped for the day, Harlowe was a chocolate mess. He had never been this sore in his life. Not even 20 miles of rimmers during his Mars recruit training gave him this much pain.

"That bad, huh, Dog?" Monday said, helping his captain to a nearby boulder to lean on. Harlowe couldn't sit. When he tried, he felt he would die. If they were off-the-clock, Monday might have been laughing at Harlowe's expense. Riverstone would for sure, on or off the clock. But the pain on Harlowe's face was so heartbreaking, Monday felt no humor in his suffering.

Harlowe propped himself against the rock with his rear sticking out like he was waiting for someone to kick him. "Yeah, it's really bad," he gutted out. "Not a word to Riverstone," he added, breathing in heaves to fight the agony.

"Aye, Captain, not a word," Monday promised. The list of secrets between them and Riverstone was growing longer by the day.

They had stopped at the edge of a grassy bank along a fast and furious river that roared out of the mountain pass they were about to enter. Behind them was the thick forest of tall, yellow pines they had spent the last hour riding through. Except for their color, a turmeric orange and yellow, the pines were practically identical to their earthly cousins with prickly needles and pointed cones dangling from their branches. On the opposite side of the river, a quarter mile away, were the ruins of an ancient city. From what they could see, the city had once been a thriving metropolis. The crumbled streets and structures stretched as far as the eye could see along the base of the mountains and on both sides of the pass. It appeared to Harlowe, the way it was leveled, it had been destroyed by war.

Although grateful they were setting up camp, Harlowe asked Isara why they were making camp now when there was still a few more hours of good sun left in the day.

"We must wait for Baago's blessing to enter his land," she replied, as she began feeding her ceffyl handfuls of a pasty, oat-like gruel. Monday had already started helping Oea to care for their mounts. Harlowe felt guilty that he was unable to help with the camp chores, but until his SIBA kicked in, he was a basket case. Fortunately, everyone understood, so he was allowed to suffer in peace.

"Baago is the head dude here, huh?" Harlowe asked, leaning against a tree while trying really hard not to act like a rookie. Having no luck finding relief for his backside, he stared at the river, thinking if he dipped his hind end in the cool water, it would help douse the flames.

Isara asked Harlowe what he meant by "head dude" as she helped him grit his way down to the river's edge. "Baago is the lord of Ragoss, if that's what you mean, Harlowe."

Grunting out words his mother would slap him for saying in the house, he stepped into a shallow eddy and lowered himself into the water. "Ahh, ahh, ahhhhhhhhh… That's exactly what I mean." Once settled in the pool of water, away from the current, he added, "If you only knew how good this feels, Isara."

Isara kept looking at Harlowe thinking he needed more rest than her ceffyls. "You are no rider, Harlowe?" she asked as if surprised that a soldier like him had no riding ability.

"Not yet," he oohed and ahhed.

"Yet, you rode a hundred leagues today."

"I should have run it," Harlowe said in retrospect.

Isara snickered. "You would have fallen far behind."

"Maybe."

"No animal on Osset can outrun a ceffyl," she boasted.

Harlowe watched the ceffyls graze, awed by their seemingly inexhaustible endurance. To come so far in a single day, and yet look as though they could go another hundred leagues was beyond belief. "No doubt."

Harlowe touched his cuff allowing his SIBA to dissolve away from his body, leaving his blue t-shirt and denims exposed.

"Your suit gives you strength?" she asked.

"Among other things." He kept waving the cool water toward the sorest parts of his body.

"The water helps?"

"Big time." He wondered out loud about the ruins. "What happened here, Isara? Ragoss is the second messed up city I've seen so far, and I've only seen two. What's up with that? Was there a war here or something?" Harlowe asked.

Isara's face turned ugly. "The Clarity's work." She explained that in the beginning, the Clarity movement was a great help to their people. Osset prospered. Ceffyls roamed freely in great herds. Then gradually the Clarity wanted more control over everything. There was never enough revenue. They wanted more blood from them. When the people revolted, the Clarity created the Tappers to ensure the flow of resources continued to fill their treasury.

Isara stared at the destruction across the river with distain. "The Clarity is the reason for the destruction of our once proud land, Harlowe."

Isara mistook Harlowe's clenched teeth for a humorous smirk and slammed him for his insensitivity. "I assure you, Harlowe, the Clarity is no laughing matter," she seethed, glaring at him with suddenly hardened eyes. "They are evil tyrants that have killed countless millions of my people over the centuries to solidify their power. The Clarity killed Ragoss, killed the Ozans, our way of life, our happiness, and my mother!"

Harlowe sobered. He was unaware the hurt that his innocent smirk had caused. He rose from the water, fighting off the intense agony and came to her side. Enraged, she pushed him away, nearly knocking him back into the river.

"That wasn't laughter, Isara. It was disgust," he pleaded, coming toward her again, slowly and carefully. "Your story is common. My crew and I have fought against injustice and corruption everywhere we travel, every government we meet. Every battle we fight is against the madness. Believe me, your land is not unique; sadly, it is the norm. Freedom is in short supply no matter where we go. Someday, when there is time, I will tell you more about our mission to eliminate this evil."

"You come from a planet that is free?" Isara asked.

"Nearly," he replied. "There are problems on my planet, too. A wise man once said, 'Freedom is always on guard against oppression.' It is a battle that never ends, I'm afraid."

Isara's eyes turned sad. "Our freedom ended long ago, Harlowe."

He made a wrong move, and the pain shot up his spine with a vengeance. "We'll help you get it back," he cringed, forcing the words with great difficulty.

Isara guided him back to the water. "Enough talk, Harlowe. You must sit where you are comfortable," she directed, appearing to have lost her ire.

"I will be good as new in an hour or so; I promise."

"Is your armor malfunctioning?"

"No, but it is working overtime."

"How long will it take?"

"Not soon enough," Harlowe replied, resigned that looking like a pathetic moron in a pool of water was about as uncool as he could be. But on the good side, sitting in a river surrounded by beautiful trees had its pluses. He might even have Mowgi do a little fishing out of sight of the girls for their evening meal. He would say he caught them, of course, he mused.

While Monday helped Oea make camp, Isara wandered off into the woods. She wasn't gone long before she came back with the largest black and red bee Harlowe had ever seen. His eyes wide with caution, and one hand near his sidearm in case the bug got away, he asked her, "What are you going to do with that?"

Isara stepped in the river with the bee. Its stinger stuck out like one of Mowgi's fangs. "The bo-chee is for you, Harlowe."

The stinger looked as lethal as the black thermo-grym knife that he took from the pirates on Gazz and now carried on his utility belt. "No thanks," Harlowe replied, warily edging his way from the buzzing giant and its dripping stinger. "I have other plans for dinner."

"The bo-chee is not for eating, Harlowe. It is for your pain," Isara explained. She was quite serious that the insect was the cure for his problem.

Harlowe backed away farther. "It works. I feel better already."

"Don't be frightened, Harlowe, the bo-chee is known for its healing powers."

"Did I say I was hurting? My mistake. Let it go on sucking flowers."

"Hold out your arm," she told him.

Before Harlowe could fend off her *goodwill*, Monday and Oea walked up, curious what was going on between them.

"What's with the bug, Dog?" Monday asked as he eyed the giant bee with the same uneasiness.

"It's her remedy for my ass," Harlowe replied with his backside up against the rocks along the riverbank.

Oea stepped forward, looking not at all alarmed. "The bo-chee is a common remedy for pain. You would be wise to let Isara care for you if you wish to get better, Harlowe."

"Really?"

"How do you do it?" Monday asked, believing the sisters were sincere.

Isara removed a yellow sac from the side of the bo-chee's leg. "Swallow this," she said holding the sac for all to see. "It is the pollen gathered from the flowers. The effect is immediate."

Monday turned to Harlowe with on okay nod. "Can't hurt, Dog."

Harlowe sighed. "I thought it was going in my arm."

Everyone laughed. "No, Harlowe, the sting would have killed you," Isara said as she took the yellow bo-chee sac and squeezed it into Harlowe's mouth. To his amazement it was sweet like honey. He looked at Monday with a smile. "Wiz would trade a case of Goobers for this stuff, Squid."

She handed him the rest of the pouch and said, "Swallow it all, Harlowe." Isara then released the bo-chee into the air, reviving its short wings like a model airplane as it got its bearings.

Harlowe happily downed the remains of the sack. It tasted so good, he wished he had thought to pluck off the bo-chee's other sack. "It won't die from your knife?" Harlowe asked, watching the scary insect dart away into the forest.

"No. I was careful to put the blade where it only stuns it. It will live," she said.

"Cool."

And like Isara said, the bo-chee potion was fast working. Unbelievably, Harlowe felt the pain leave his body like he had just swallowed a quart of Bluestuff. It was a miracle!

Feeling like he had tossed out his old body for a new one, Harlowe stood up, dripping wet and thanked Isara with a big kiss on the lips. "Thank you. You da woman, Isara!"

Isara blushed green through her dark skin. From the startled look on her face, Harlowe wondered if she had ever been kissed before.

"I'm sorry, Isara. I didn't mean to… well, you know…" Harlowe said, trying to appologize, believing he may have crossed a boundary with his actions.

She touched her lips. "This is called?" she asked.

"A kiss," Harlowe replied.

"And it is a way of showing thankfulness?"

"I got carried away. Sorry."

Isara moved closer again. "Thank me more, Harlowe."

Isara reminded him of Becky Martin, his tenth grade heart throb, whose cat never got enough attention once you petted it. Harlowe knew, traveling that road was dangerous,. Like his taste for bo-chee pollen, Isara wanted more. He knew the look because he had experienced it himself. As as a star athlete growing up in Southern California, by the time Harlowe was fifteen, he had had his share of kisses. He still remembered his first kiss like it was yesterday. He was seven, and Ashleigh Pedigrew, who was the hottest doe he had ever seen at that point in his young life, was eleven and lived on Hersholt, two streets over from his parents' house on Autry. He and Riverstone were walking home from school when Ashleigh and her friend, Martha, crossed the street, ignoring Ricky Buttman and two of his ruffian toads, Casey Gates and Bo Mathis. The dudes were seventh grade bullies, a head taller and a good forty pounds heavier than either Harlowe or Riverstone. Even at that age, Harlowe seemed to have a knack for finding trouble. "Where are you going?" Riverstone asked, already knowing that they were about to rock and roll when the dudes spilled Ashleigh's bookbag on the sidewalk and tore Martha's sleeve.

"Those girls need help," Harlowe said it like it was a given. Never mind the odds of being better than good, he would get his head handed to him on a platter.

Riverstone pleaded for their survival. "They're way bigger, Stupid. Can't you see that?"

To Harlowe, size didn't matter when it came to doing the right thing. "We can't let the bad guys win, pard," he answered, leaving Riverstone shaking his head at what an idiot dork he was for marching into Death's stronghold alone.

Harlowe didn't bother with formality or even try to introduce himself to Ricky and his friends. He hit Buttman so hard, he went tumbling over the nearby bus bench and didn't get up. He explained later, "There was no point in talking. I know what he was going to say." Casey tried to blindside Harlowe with Ashleigh's book bag, but Riverstone put a fist to his stomach. Casey doubled up and collapsed to his knees, yelling he couldn't breathe and was going to die. Bo must have thought twice about taking on the little beasties, because he left his pals in the dust, running down Del Amo toward Woodruff and never looking back.

As Harlowe, Riverstone, and the girls stepped away from the hurt bodies, Harlowe picked up Ashleigh's book bag and gave it back to her. "Are you all right?" he asked her, his blue eyes dazed with the fog of love.

He couldn't recall if Ashleigh said anything or not. She probably did, but his recollection went haywire the moment she pulled him to her face and laid a big wet one on him. It was no ordinary canoodle, either. They locked lips for what seemed like an eternity. He thought he was going to choke when her tongue wiggled half way down his throat.

Wow, that was a kiss . . . he recalled, still feeling heat produced by that first encounter.

Harlowe's head remained in a daze for a week, and Riverstone's was stuck in the clouds as well. Comparing notes, Ashleigh's girlfriend, Martha, had thanked him, too, with the same tongue action. All both of them could remember was the girls' sweet breath, wet tongues, grateful eyes, and their heads filled with the fog of marrying them when they turned eighteen.

From time to time they would see the girls around Lakewood at a shopping mall, in a car with boys who could drive or having a burger at In-N-Out on Bellflower and South Street. They were always nice to them. The girls called Harlowe and Riverstone their little heroes. But that was it. No more kissing, no more tongues, not even a peck for old time's sake. They were too young for them. It wouldn't be cool for hot babes like them to be seen with dorky kids who were shorter than than they were and had no wheels.

Knowing how special that first kiss was for him, Harlowe puckered up and waited for Isara to come to him. He wouldn't disappoint her, and well, she was hot. It wasn't like he was stepping out on Lu. She would understand… Well, when pigs fly maybe, but it was all in the line of duty, their mission, and *Millawanda*, right?

Mowgi yipped once followed by a low, snarly growl. It broke the spell between them and put the Gamadin on full alert. At first blush, no one heard or saw anything unusual, but doubting the undog's warnings was never a good idea. Isara and Oea felt the tension, too, when the ceffyls' heads bolted upright from their grazing.

"The animals feel trouble," Oea observed.

Harlowe confirmed her observation. "Something's spooked them."

Isara pointed across the river. "The Fagans have come to greet us. Look!" Galloping away from the city ruins, a posse of two dozen heavily armed horsemen came riding their way. Their horse-like mounts were far less majestic than the ceffyls. They were short muzzled and had no horns. They looked like normal Earth horses, except their feet were like the ceffyls, heavily padded with large claws protruding from their toes. It began to look like hooves weren't in style on Osset.

The riders were moon-faced and, like their mounts, short-legged and stout. From the way they handled their reins, they were skilled horseman. They wore animal hides, leather boots, and furry hats with long flaps on the sides that waved in the wind as they rode. Harlowe wondered if they had enough speed if they would fly like Dumbo the Elephant. One thing was sure, they were far better horsemen than he was. They rode like they were permanently attached to their mounts.

Without slowing down, a rider removed a long weapon from the side of the saddle and waved it at Oea and Isara, shouting a greeting from across the river. Just when it looked as though the entire posse was going to plunge right in, the riders came to a skidding stop at the river's edge, impressing Harlowe and Monday even more by their horsemanship.

"Can you do that?" Harlowe asked Monday.

"Not even," Monday replied.

"The river is too high for the Fagans to cross," Oea said.

"Look, Oea. Nath sees you," Isara said pointing at the leader in front waving at them.

Oea turned up her nose.

"He is looking right at you, sister. I think he still has passion for you," Isara kidded.

"Stop it, Isara!" Oea snapped. "Fagans do not bathe. They sleep with their animals, and they have many wives. It is not a way of life I accept."

"Baago has many tangas (Which is the Ossetian word for the horse-like animals the posse rode.)," Isara reminded her.

"But no ceffyls. Only our father has ceffyls. And I will not disgrace him by mating with a filthy Fagan.

Harlowe came back to Mowgi. To him the posse seemed like a non-event. He wasn't looking at the flappy-hatted riders at all but away from the pack and farther downstream. "That can't be good," Harlowe muttered to himself. Isara was about to continue her teasing when Harlowe stopped her. "Everyone, to your mounts," he ordered.

Oea said, "It is all right, Harlowe. Baago's people are friends."

"It's not them I'm concerned with, Oea. It's what's coming," Harlowe said, looking down river.

Both girls searched where Harlowe was pointing. They saw nothing. The posse didn't care either. Nath had Oea in his sights, and that's all he cared to see.

Harlowe pulled rank. "Don't argue. To your mounts," he ordered. As he was about to run for his, Oea let out a loud whistle, and all four ceffyls came charging toward them in great leaps as the roar of powerful engines broke through the yellow forest in the direction Harlowe had pointed.

"Tappers!" Oea screamed.

78

Forty-Four

Ian drew his sidearm and blasted the toothy snake with three shots to the head, dropping the beast beside the aara pile. Leucadia shot two more coming at them from the side. Another three heads popped over the banister from the lower levels as Ian shoved Cheesa inside and pointed at the foyer wall. "When Dev's in, press that activator," Ian ordered.

Leucadia and Ian continued firing at heads coming at them, while the clicker carrying Dev and the other two robobs with the aara trotted up the ramp. When everyone was safely inside the foyer, Ian yelled, "Now, Cheesa!" and watched the portal close, leaving behind half the pile of aara still on the floor.

Leucadia saw the disappointment in Ian's face as they re-holstered their sidearms. "It will keep," she told him. They turned their attention to the foyer and the corridors leading from it. Like *Millawanda,* the foyer was the main ingress of the ship. Although not nearly as vast as Millie's, the entrance was large enough to play a full court game of basketball with room to spare. The plush blue carpet added an extra touch of familiarity. When Ian entered the ship for the first time, the air had smelled stale and musty, but it was breathable. In the few minutes they were aboard, the environmental systems had already replaced the unpleasant odors with the sweet, fresh air they were used to. After lying parked for what had to be thousands of years, he reckoned there were many unknowns about the ship and its operation that should have been checked out first. The possibility that something harmful was lurking in the corridors and rooms after all this time was real. To do a thorough inspection, though, would have taken days, so he counted on Molly and Rhud to flush out any unwanted guests. Since Muuk's forces were on them, the only question Ian needed to know was whether the Gamadin ship still had enough juice in her to fly? Any other concerns he or Leucadia had about the ship, they would learn on the go.

While Cheesa stayed with the sleeping Prince, Ian and Leucadia quickly searched for the passageway leading to the bridge. They counted five possibilities in all. To Leucadia Ian said: "Start with that one, Lu. I'll take the one next to it. If it's like Millie, it won't be far. If we're wrong, we run back here and go to the next corridor until we find it."

They hadn't taken two steps when Molly emerged from the corridor behind them, urging them to follow her. "I think she found it," Leucadia said.

Ian didn't argue. They both took off after the cat. Sure enough, it was the corridor they were looking for. The big cat had already blinked away by the time they came to the disk on the floor.

Ian took Leucadia's hand, and together they were instantly transported to the bridge. Molly and Rhud had already staked out their places beneath the large forward window, ready for takeoff.

Like the rest of the ship, everything was downsized including the bridge. It was more like a small room than a grand stage of consoles, science stations, and massive wraparound observation windows. There was only one control chair instead of three and just four console stations instead of the twelve on *Millawanda*.

Ian took immediate charge. "Take the command chair, Lu; I'll take the front stations."

"You need to be here, Ian," Leucadia said, knowing Ian was the captain of the ship, not her.

Ian touched the console panels with his hand. As he did, the panels came alive with color and power. "Forget the formalities, Lu. I know how to work these. You steer."

Leucadia nodded affirmatively. "Aye, Captain," acknowledging Ian's authority.

For a split second, Ian felt a pang of discomfort being addressed as Captain. That had always been Harlowe's place: captain of the baseball team, captain of the football team, captain of practically every group, crew, or team he had ever been associated with. But for Ian, it felt unnatural. He had never been captain of anything, not even his after-school chess team. He was used to taking orders, not giving them. But, like it or not, as the senior officer aboard a Gamadin ship, he was, by default, her captain.

Ian returned a confident lets-do-it wink as he ran his fingers over the lighted bars, preparing the ship's power drives for ignition. Leucadia seated herself in the command chair, touched the activators that adjusted the seat to her body and said, "Ready here, Captain."

Ian faced her with his right hand on an activator. "When I press this, we'll know if there's life in *Forty-four*."

Leucadia grinned, looking at him whimsically. "*Forty-four?*" she asked.

"Yeah, that's what I'm calling her."

Leucadia wondered if she heard Ian right. "You're calling our new ship, *Forty-four?* Why?"

"My Aunt Doris had a pistol she kept by her bed. She called it her Big Stick."

Leucadia found it difficult to picture a little old, lady with a pistol that size. "She had a 44 magnum?"

"No, she had a 38 special. But after her house was broken into twice, she didn't feel safe until she saw *Dirty Harry*."

"The movie?"

"That's right. The next day she went out and bought herself 'the world's most powerful handgun.'" Ian laughed. "My Aunt Doris was raised on a Wyoming ranch. She had to deal with wolves, grizzlies, and coyotes killing their cattle. Trust me. She could handle a forty-four as well as Harry." He chuckled again. "I've seen her put a three-round group in a bullseye at 20 feet."

Leucadia remembered a recent article she read on the *Drudge Report*. "Was she the same little, old lady that put down the three bank robbers at Lakewood Savings and Loan two years ago?"

Ian smiled from ear to ear. "That's her."

"Wow! That was national news for a week."

"And guess who taught Harlowe how to play poker?"

"Aunt Doris?"

"Bingo."

"No way."

"Yes, way. No one messed with her. She was as badass as Mowgi. And no one, I mean absolutely no one, beat her at cards, not even Harlowe." Ian went on with great pride how his aunt still drives a 30-year old Mercedes diesel like it was a sports car.

Leucadia laughed approvingly. Ian had made his case. "All right, *Forty-four* it is!" Her green eyes went bright with optimism. "Do it, Captain. With a name like that, we're invincible!"

Substituting a high-five slap for a bottle of champagne struck on the side of the hull, Leucadia did the honors, christening *Forty-four* with a soft pat on the arm of her chair. Ian then slid his hand over the activator to begin her maiden voyage by energizing the main drives. A long silence passed, and nothing happened. Figuring he had made an error, he swiped his hand over the controls again. Still nothing. "Come on, *Forty-four*. Don't let your namesake down. Do her proud." Two more times he waved his hand over the bars, and two more times the drives remained silent.

"What's wrong?" Leucadia asked, her confidence switching to concern.

Ian rescanned all the readouts. "I don't know." He pointed at bright blue power indicators on the screen. "She's powered up. She should work."

"What did we miss?" Leucadia wondered.

Ian was at a loss. He had done everything by the book. Even with explosions outside rocking the outpost and the ship, Ian kept his cool, knowing whatever he did in the next few moments, meant their survival.

"Hurry, Captain. If Muuk can't break in, he will try to seal us in."

Knowing his drive activators were inline on his consoles, Ian went to Leucadia and the command chair. "Harlowe always deactivated the drive overrides before Millie could start. Most of the time, he did it automatically when he shut her down." He thought through the shutdown procedures again before coming to a conclusion. "*Forty-four* might require the same deactivation before she starts." After careful thought, he instructed her to run her fingers over the blue bar on the left side of the chair. "One time should do it, Lu," he told her.

When she did, the unmistakeable whir of Gamadin energy coming to life was felt throughout the ship.

Leucadia clapped. "That's it!"

Molly added a roar of relief while Rhud panted like there was nothing to cheer about until they were off the ground.

Then out of nowhere a giant worm flopped onto the upper hull. The massive head looked around as if to say, "You're going nowhere, humans." The serpent weaved from side to side then struck the window with a massive thump, rocking *Forty-four* before she could deal the cards.

"The window is holding, but I don't know how many of those she can take," Leucadia said, feeling the pounding through her teeth.

Ian jumped over two stations and activated another screen.

"Landing struts retracting, Captain," Leucadia announced as the worm continued knocking its head against the window. "Do we have shields?"

At the same station, Ian touched another lighted bar. "We do." He touched the screen once. "Shields on now," he called out. When the familiar blue shimmer snapped on, the worm turned instantly to subatomic dust. Ian came to Leucadia, wide-eyed with disbelief. "I've never seen it do that before."

"Good to know though," Leucadia said.

"Aye."

Leucadia kept her eyes forward as she rotated *Forty-four* on her axis and slid her sideways over the railing and into the inner shaft of the outpost. Once clear, the saucer slowly rose toward the main level and the outer doors. Anticipating a *Millawanda*-like escape, exploding their way out of the mountain, Ian located the weapon's array and brought them on line to full power.

"Look, Ian," Leucadia called out. "I'm sorry, Captain," she corrected, "the doors are opening on their own," she observed.

Ian watched with relief as the doors began to slide apart. By the time they retracted fully with room to spare, hundreds of slimy monsters had made their way to the entrance. The doorway looked like a disturbed hornet's nest as they slithered all over each other trying to escape. Fearing their window of opportunity might collapse at any moment, Leucadia guided *Forty-four* forward through the portal. The snakes that tried biting her as she moved past them were instantly fried upon contact.

Outside the outpost it was a feeding frenzy. Muuk's soldiers were being gobbled up by the mouthfuls. There was no time to check whether Muuk himself was on the menu, but one could only hope.

When *Forty-four* glided over the Haga Forest, 5,000 feet from where they had first landed on Nod, Leucadia tilted her incline, and like a bird of prey released back into the wild, *Forty-four* shot skyward, breaking her gravitational chains as she headed for deep space.

79

Raid on Ragoss

The first blast from the plas cannons blew away a third of the posse before they understood what hit them. The riders that were left managed to save their mounts and themselves behind whatever cover they could find before the next blast hit. Exploding into view, two Tapper monster trucks roared out of the forest, their two-story high wheels crushing trees like twigs while their cannons continued pounding the riverbanks.

Harlowe and Monday had SIBA-upped and headed down river for the two hundred foot bluff before the smoke had cleared. To the jaw-dropping awe of Isara and Oea, the two Gamadin charged up the bluff in twenty-foot strides and dove off the cliff, extending their wings as they took flight. Appearing out of nowhere, a dragon-like beast spread its wings and joined them as they crossed the raging waters and touched down on the opposite side of the river. The dragon hovered over the bug-eyed Gamadin who continued in great leaps toward the giant tanks. Because of the rocky terrain, the Tapper trucks found it slow going. Their cannons, however, kept blasting their way up the valley round after round.

"My god they're huge, Dog," Monday said to Harlowe through his com. *"How do we stop them with pistols?"* he asked, watching the massive turrets grinding from side to side, spitting rounds of death at Ragoss.

Harlowe pointed at the top of the lead battlewagon. "Go for their drivers, Squid!" he ordered. Projecting from the front of the truck, the drivers were protected behind a heavy glass dome just below the turrets. This allowed the driver and the command personnel on the bridge a sweeping, panoramic view of the battlefield. It was a great observation point, but it was also a weakness. With a weapon powerful enough to blast through the armor plated windshield, the driver was an easy target.

At five hundred yards from the Tapper trucks, Harlowe split off from Monday. There was no specific plan except to stop the Tapper battlewagons before they killed any more Fagans.

Harlowe took the lead truck, while Monday made a beeline for the second. Because of their SIBAs' near invisibility, as the tanks rolled on, they were able to approach their flanks undetected.

At eighty yards out from the lead battlewagon, Harlowe took up a position at the top of a large boulder. At that distance it was like shooting dancing targets on the pistol range back on Mars. He could do that in his sleep.

A single shot exploded through the forward window, and the Tapper driver was history. His head jerked backward first before dipping forward and landing with a dead-cat bounce against the joystick steering control. Monday's aim was less clean. He held his sidearm up in what General Gunn called the Weaver stance. He placed his feet shoulder-width apart with his strong-side leg slightly back like a boxer. With knees bent and his body weight slightly forward, he grasped his gun with both hands, keeping his elbows bent slightly downward for support, and fired. Five shots later, the result was the same, but the driver's station was a bloody mess. Besides the driver, two unlucky Tappers became collateral damage from Monday's shot spray. Driverless, the battlewagons swerved off track from their line of travel up the valley. Monday's truck rolled a few hundred feet farther before it came to a thumping halt in a wide ditch. Harlowe's truck continued on with Tappers whooping and screaming in panic. Before they could replace the driver, Harlowe found opportunity in the confusion. He leaped around to the backside and attached a thader to the engine housing. Harlowe hid behind a boulder and five seconds later…BALEWWWY! The whole back end of the truck exploded like it had been hit by one of its own cannons. The great truck stopped dead in its tracks without so much as a sputter. In that instant, the heavy hatch at the side of the truck blew open. Before the ramp fully deployed, Tappers charged outside with their weapons blazing. They shot high and low and at anything that moved. Harlowe felt like the safest place to be was in front of them. When he had seen enough, he lowered the boom. Bodies piled at the bottom of the ramp until the last of the Tappers refused to exit.

"Toss your weapons, and step out with your hands above your heads!" Harlowe shouted from his rocky perch.

No one took him up on his offer as they waited for him to come closer.

A Tapper poked his weapon out the side of the hatchway less than an inch, just enough for Harlowe to blow him away with a sizzling shot through the side of the armor plated door.

The body dropped out of the doorway like a fallen statue.

"You're trying my patience, Toads," Harlowe said to them.

No takers.

"If you don't come out now, I will incinerate your tank with you in it," Harlowe warned.

Again, no takers.

Harlowe removed a thader from his utility belt and set the charge to low for more smoke and less death. He then tossed it inside the hatch and let it do its thing. A half-second later, the explosion sent a billowing blast of dark smoke out of the open hatch. Nine Tappers tossed their weapons as they ran out with their hands above their heads. Harlowe waved them to the ground. With the fear of instant death, the Tapper crew dropped like their legs had been cut out from under them. Harlowe radioed Monday. "You clear over there, Squid?"

"*Yeah, all clear, Captain,*" Monday replied.

"I have nine toads. You?" Harlowe asked.

"*Ah . . .*" Monday seemed a little hesitant. "*None, Captain.*"

Harlowe was taken aback. He expected a number close to his. "None?"

"*Mowg got a little carried away when someone tried to shoot him. There are a lot of missing heads here, Captain. Sorry.*"

Harlowe's face twisted like he had ingested a shot of vinegar. He was about to sign off when Monday made an observation. "*Riders coming our way, Captain.*"

What Harlowe saw emerging from the smoke and fire of Ragoss wasn't a posse, but a thousand moon-faced Fagan riders galloping flat out toward the burning battlewagons. But that was the least of Harlowe's worries. Something big and dark growled thirstily as he jumped down from his boulder to meet

Monday. Apparently, the thader hadn't cleared out every Tapper. Something else was still inside. The deep-throated growl sounded less than human as it stepped from the darkness with its two heavy calibered sidearms pointed right at Harlowe's head. Harlowe checked his own sidearms for ammo. No blue light. He had shot his wad. Both pistols were empty.

80

Yes, Captain

After entering a stable orbit and making sure *Forty-four* was functioning properly after her 17,000 year layover, Ian felt comfortable enough to leave the bridge to Leucadia and return to the foyer, where he found Dev and Cheesa in a heated discussion.

"Problem, Dev?" Ian said, confronting the two of them.

Dev was clearly irritated by his treatment. "Why did you strike me, Ian?"

"You were out of line, Dev, and we were in a hurry."

"Me? For what? Believing you were wrong?"

Ian pulled Cheesa aside and got in the Prince's face. "I wasn't wrong. This discussion ends now, or I'll put you down a second time."

Cheesa stepped between both of them. "Stop it. The both of you," she yelled at them. "There is no sense in this. We've come too far to be enemies," shoving them apart.

After expelling a long breath, Dev asked Ian, "Where have you been?" as he looked around. "Where are we? Cheesa says you went somewhere to lift off. What does that mean?"

"That's right. We lifted off," Ian confirmed.

Dev gazed at the floor. "Where is the portal? I don't see it."

"It's there. Trust me."

Dev glared at them in disbelief, when Cheesa said, "It is true, Prince. Ian has closed the hatchway."

Dev let the information settle before pointing at the aara by the wall.

"Where are the rest of the crystals you had us carry down here?"

"We had to take off before all the crystals were inside," Ian replied. "It's all right, though. We have more than enough for our mother ship," he explained.

"And the robobs?" Dev snapped, angry that Ian didn't seem to care about his mechanical servants. "Were they left behind, too?"

Ian nodded at the three cylinders lying at the far side of the foyer floor. "No, they're still with us, Dev."

"That is really them?"

"Yes, they turn that way when they are reenergizing."

"You said 'lift-off'. What do you mean by that?" Dev asked, questioning the phrase he heard earlier.

Ian motioned for Dev and Cheesa to follow him. "Come. Let me show you. We're flying now."

"Flying?" Dev questioned. "Wouldn't we be feeling something? I felt no lift-off like when we left the hangar." He looked around the foyer as they made their way to the bridge corridor. "The explosions. They are gone," he said, listening for any sound of detonations outside the ship. "Has the Imperator given up?"

"In a way, he has," Ian replied before he went on about the ship's inertia dampeners. "The reason you didn't feel anything, Dev, is because this ship is equipped with devices that keep you from being torn to bits when we accelerate too fast. If we didn't have the dampeners, we would be slammed against a wall and break every bone in our bodies."

"We would die without them?" Cheesa asked, unable to grasp the concept of the physics behind when a body at rest accelerates to thousands of miles per hour and far beyond that in a matter of seconds.

"Instantly," Ian replied.

"That's impossible," Dev stated, believing Ian was out of his mind.

Ian guided them to the blinker on the floor. "You're going to find many impossible things on this ship, Dev. Lu and I will explain as we go along. But for the time being . . ." He guided them onto the blinker and... *Poof!* They were on the bridge. "Enjoy the view."

The planet, Nod, filled the entire front window. When Dev and Cheesa stepped off the blinker, they were dumfounded by what they were actually looking at. Neither Nodian had ever seen their planet or pictures of it from a high orbit in their lives. The view was breathtaking.

Ian pointed to a large land mass at the lower right of the window. "That is Dolmina there, Dev. The circle of mountains over there to the left is the Du Tir, and beyond that coming into darkness now is the Haga Forest," he explained.

Dev turned to Ian, his face expressing shock and awe over what he saw. "You really are from another world."

"That's right Dev," Ian admitted. "And now we must hurry. We have a long voyage ahead of us. After a few more preliminary inspections, we'll take you home."

The Prince suddenly became angry again. "To what, Ian? To Muuk? He will kill us both. He has already killed my family and my guards. I'm all alone now. I am the only one left to ascend the throne, and now you want to take me to a certain death?"

Leucadia entered the conversation for the first time. "Dev is right, Ian. He can't go home, nor can Cheesa. They have no allies, no power to back them up. Muuk has eliminated everyone that would stand in his way of absolute rule."

"This is their home, Lu. We may never come back to Nod again," Ian said, solemnly.

Cheesa stepped forward. "We want to go with you, Ian. Nod is not our home any more. Our home is now with you," she said, coming to his side.

Ian was still unwilling to take on two more beings he cared a great deal for, even loved. He knew the dangers that lay ahead, and they were formidable. At least on Nod, Dev and Cheesa knew how to survive. Cheesa had fought the Authority and lived. In space, every world they came to would have a new Authority. Muuk had destroyed cities and killed thousands, but forces like the Fhaal Empire and the Consortium destroyed worlds! Ian felt like he would be leading his flock to the slaughterhouse if he let them stay.

Cheesa saw the doubt in Ian's long face. "It is my choice, Ian. When I joined the resistance, I knew each day could be my last. But aren't we fighting for the same thing? From what you have told me, you also fight for freedom, knowing full well that each day death is with you. Yet here you are. You have survived another world, and you still may never see your friends or home again."

"Cheesa . . . you don't understand," Ian pleaded. "It is a million times more dangerous out there than back on Nod."

Cheesa removed her sidearm from her hip and held it out to Ian. "Then kill me now. For that is what it will take to remove me from your ship." She shook the weapon at Ian. "Go on. Kill me. I would rather die here, at your hand, than return to Nod and be killed by Muuk."

Ian looked over at Leucadia like he couldn't believe what he was hearing. Her green eyes spoke volumes. *It's your call, Captain*, they told him. His mouth twisted with indecision. What would Harlowe do, he asked himself. Would he let her come along? Or was it something more? Something inside him he couldn't come to terms with and admit. For a moment, he saw Harlowe behind Cheesa with that all-knowing grin staring right through him. *She's your responsibility now, pard, he said. You know that's what you want. Look at her. She's a hot babe. Smart, courageous, and way too cute for you, Wiz. The reason you're having a problem is simple. You don't want something to happen to her. Come on, admit it. If she came along, you would be thinking of how to keep her safe from all the bad guys. But if you dropped her off, she'd be on her own, and you'll be a thousand lightyears from Nod. If something happened to her then, you would never know. You'd be off the hook, pard. So, man up. She's part of your crew now whether you like it or not. At least with you, she'll have a fighting chance. On Nod, she has no chance, and you know it. You would be condemning her and Dev to a certain death. You can't allow that to happen. You're the Captain now. So act like one.*

Ian sighed, letting the weight of the entire galaxy expel from his lungs. "Aye . . ." he said, caving imperceptibly to Harlowe.

"What was that, Ian?" Cheesa asked.

Ian perked up, taking in a full breath of courage he found in Harlowe's confident wink that was looking over her shoulder. "I said, aye, you're right. You have to stay here."

Cheesa put her weapon to the side and ran into Ian's arms, kissing him on the lips. "Thank you, Ian."

Ian had to push her away. "Cheesa. This is the bridge. We can't do that here."

"Why not?"

"Because the bridge is a sacred place."

Cheesa looked at him, saddened by the news. "No kissing?"

Ian shook his head as he gave her hand back. "No, Cheesa. No kissing. The bridge is all business, all the time."

"Yes, Ian."

"Captain," he corrected her. "Here I am called Captain."

Cheesa smiled proudly and saluted across her chest, "Yes, my captain."

Ian then turned to the Prince to make sure he understood the new rules. "And you, Dev, what say you? The decision you make now can't be taken back. It's forever."

Dev thought a moment. The look in his eyes lacked the cheerfulness of Cheesa's. Dolmina was still in plain view but growing rapidly smaller as they drifted away from the planet. His sacrifice was greater than hers. The Prince had a lot more to give up. He had a kingdom to toss away. But as he looked out the window, a thought came to him; what good was a kingdom when you are a dead Prince?

"I will stay, too, Ian," Dev conceded.

"Captain," Ian corrected. "On this ship, I am King. I am the ruler over everyone. Remember that. That is a law that cannot be broken. You must understand this, or I will leave you now on Nod."

Dev knelt down in front of Ian, bowing his head. "Yes, Captain. I am yours to command."

That was a little too capitulating for Ian. He glanced at Leucadia who tried her best to hold her laughter. Ian lifted Dev up and said, straightening his shirt as he spoke, "Respect yes, but as a member of my crew, you must never kneel to anyone, not even me. Is that clear, Dev?"

Eyes wide with surprise, Dev replied, "Yes . . .yes, Captain."

* * *

Once clear of the Nodian moons, Ian gave the go-ahead for Leucadia to punch it. "Light speed, if you please, Ms. Mars."

"Our course, Captain?" Leucadia asked.

Ian switched on the overhead screen. On it was a star chart of this section of space, a hundred parsecs out. "We follow Harlowe," he replied, and entered the course. "That way!"

"Harlowe never does anything by the book," Leucadia mentioned. "He could have gone almost anywhere."

The side of Ian's mouth turned up in a casual, all-knowing smile. "Yeah, but he always leaves a trail of crumbs."

Leucadia smiled back. "Good point, Captain. That he does," and engaged the star-drive that brought *Forty-four* into hyper light speed.

81

Gnarr

The brutish giant ducked below the eight-foot hatch. "Who are you?" the deep, brooding voice asked, stepping loudly onto the ramp. His head was huge and covered by a puffy, wheat-colored mane. The eyes were pure evil, dark, lifeless things that stared straight through Harlowe. Except for his hair, and the missing electrodes on the side of his neck, the Dak was a true Frankenstein monster in his black, oversized clothes and heavy boots. The yellowed, vampire teeth protruding from a severe overbite, chomped up and down, drooling gooey spit from its hairy mouth, making Harlowe believe he wanted him for his next meal. As big as the ogre was, he was only slightly shorter than Darkn. To Harlowe, the two beings were cut from the same mold. They had the same fiendish disposition.

Harlowe filed the observation for recall later and then answered the question. "I'm Death with a smile, Toad. Who are you, ugly?" To make nice with a Dak was never one of Harlowe's strong points.

"I am Gnarr, and these are my gerbids that you have destroyed."

Harlowe pretended to look behind Gnarr. "Any more back there in the woods? I'll destroy them, too."

"You will die a slow death for this."

Harlowe only nodded. At this point he saw no reason in discussing his fate.

Gnarr pointed his weapon at Harlowe's head. "You are out of ammunition, and my weapons are full."

Again, Gnarr spoke the obvious. "A minor glitch," Harlowe noted, unfazed by his lack of ammo.

"I could kill you now and be done with you," Gnarr threatened.

"What? And miss the fun of killing me slowly?"

Gnarr smiled thirstily.

"Listen, Gnarr," Harlowe continued. "I came to this valley in peace. These people have done you no harm, and yet you have killed them and caused them a lot of ill-will here. Your crew has given up. Your trucks are toast. Call it even and go home, or I promise with tears in my eyes, I will destroy you and anyone else who does harm to these people."

"Why do you care about these Fagans?"

"I care about all people, Gnarr. I would even care about your ugly face if you weren't such a dirtball." Harlowe sighed and scratched his head with the tip of his gun. "But you are a dirtball, and there is no chance of reforming you. So, I'll just have to kill you, I guess."

Gnarr laughed heartily as a large cat-like beast rumbled to his side. It was nearly as large as Rhud with heavy shoulders tapering down to its crouching hindquarters. Its panting maw of long, curving teeth was large enough to swallow him whole with little effort.

"My pet," Gnarr bragged, petting the top of its head. "He hasn't feasted today."

As if right on cue, Mowgi trotted out from the shadows to Harlowe's side, rubbing against his leg for attention. He didn't seem to care at all about the goings-on around him. Harlowe brushed the undog's parabolics with his pistol. "This is my pet," Harlowe boasted with a forced grin of clean, white teeth. "He's feasted on a few of your guys today, but he's never one to turn down a meal. Right, Mowg?"

The undog yipped twice with his thin, green tongue panting like he was waiting for a treat to be tossed his way.

Gnarr laughed again, shaking the ramp.

"My offer still stands, Gnarr. If you wish to drop your weapons now, I'll let both you and your pet live," Harlowe said kindly.

Gnarr's pet tried to force his way free, but the giant Tapper was having too much fun toying with Harlowe to let him go just yet. Like a cat that captured a mouse, Gnarr wanted to play a little longer with his prey before becoming bored and killing him.

In the middle of Gnarr's decision, Monday stepped from around the back of the gerbid like he was just taking a Sunday stroll on the beach. "Sorry, Dog, did I interrupt the party?" he asked.

"This is Gnarr, Squid. We totaled his gerbytes—"

"Gerbids," Gnarr corrected.

"He wants damages," Harlowe added.

Monday didn't care for the bantering and went right to the point. "Are you going to kill him?"

Harlowe shrugged unsure. "I'm trying not to, but if he insists on being a butthead, I'll have no choice."

"He's out of ammunition," Gnarr said, laughing. Now the lion-being had a pistol pointed at Monday's head.

"You told him that was a minor glitch, I assume?" Monday asked.

"Yeah, my exact words."

"He looks narly. I would be careful."

"I'm doing my best."

Monday shook his head as he looked around at all the the prisoners lying facedown on the ground. Figuring this was Harlowe's problem, not his, he leaned on a nearby rock and relaxed. "Well, I guess you better get on with it, then. We're wasting time. The Fagans will be here shortly," he said, pointing at all the torches coming their way.

Harlowe turned and faced Gnarr. "Yeah."

Gnarr suddenly lost his mirth. "Enough!" he bellowed, and released his pet. In one bound the beast launched in a long diving arc for Harlowe and Mowgi. There was nowhere to run, no escape possible as the beast's ear-splitting scream ripped the air. Its razored fangs and outstretched claws stuck outward like steel knives as they were about to tear into the flesh and limbs. Harlowe had witnessed Mowgi's transition from undog to a cold-blooded killer many times since the first time he watched him bite the head off of a grogan in Utah. He shivered just thinking about it. The result was always the same: he showed no quarter, no leniency, no compassion, ever, toward evil. Mowgi didn't play with his opponents like Harlowe, he decimated them, ruthlessly and without remorse. Watching the chenner was no spectator sport. It was chilling and brutal in its swiftness. The beast stopped mid flight like it hit a foot-thick wall of lead. To Gnarr's stunned eyes, the headless body of his pet dropped at the bottom of the ramp with a deathly thud. Its carcass continued twitching and spurting blood out of its headless neck. The undog flapped his wings, tilted his head back and swallowed the skull whole like he had just gulped down a large plum, pit and all.

Gnarr roared with revenge. He wanted payback, and raised both barrels turning toward Harlowe's head. But before he had time to squeeze the trigger, Harlowe had reloaded his sidearm and put a sizzling round of hot plasma between Gnarr's enraged eyes. Like his pet before him, Gnarr fell like a slab of meat, tumbling down the ramp with a loud bang, landing between the other dead members of his crew.

Monday stood, stretching his neck like it was all in a day's work. "You were polite," he admitted to Harlowe and asked him what they were going to do with the prisoners."

"We let them go," Harlowe replied.

"They'll tell their friends," Monday cautioned.

Harlowe figured as much. "That's the idea. I want them to tell Darkn what happened here today."

"He'll bring a division of gerbytes next time," Monday counter, intentionally mispronouncing the gerbid name as Harlowe had done.

Harlowe's gaze went to Gnarr, the dead Tappers, and the smoking gerbid stuck in the ditch. "One can only hope."

Monday saw the plan. "You're sucking Darkn in like you did the Fhaal at Og, aren't you, Captain?"

"That's one plan."

"Is that wise, Captain? We have no ship to fight with. Darkn will kill the Fagans first chance he gets."

Harlowe looked Monday in the eyes. "These people aren't safe, Squid, until Darkn's bye-bye. When he comes here with both barrels blazing, we'll be here to turn his Tappers into sub-atomic dust."

"What if we don't find Lamille?" Monday asked.

Harlowe turned from the carnage. "That's not part of the plan," he said, and stepped away quickly to meet up with Isara and Oea, who were riding hard with their ceffyls in tow. The look on their faces was not like they had seen victory, or that they had witnessed a heroic achievement by the Gamadin pros from across the Thaat. It was more like they were frightened by the consequences of the result. The hundreds of round faces with their torches lighting the area around the gerbid, had the same expression of fear.

This was a reaction that caught Harlowe off guard. He expected faces of victory from the Fagans, but instead he found horror.

Isara handed him the reins of his black. In front of the gathering crowd, he leaped onto his saddle without overshooting his seat. The soreness was gone. Between the bo-chee bee and his SIBA's injections, long rides would never bother him again. The fear in Isara's eyes, however, was unsettling. "What's the matter, Isara?" he asked concerned. "Why is everyone so troubled?"

"You killed Gnarr," she stated as if he were the villain.

Harlowe tried to defend his actions. "Yeah, I tried not to. Ask Squid."

"Gnarr is Darkn's brother, leader of the Tappers."

Harlowe glanced over at Gnarr's still form. The back of his thick mane was covered with green blood from the exit wound. "I know the family tree."

"You do not understand, Harlowe; Darkn will seek revenge."

Harlowe waved his hand at the Fagans surrounding them. "I should have let Gnarr slaughter them with his gerbids?"

She found it hard to answer his question, mumbling something to herself, she replied contritely, "No. Of course not."

Harlowe thrust his finger at the ground. "The Tapper reign of terror must end, Isara. Their destruction begins today!"

With tears in her eyes, Isara pleaded her case. "They will come with an even larger force many more times than what you have destroyed here. They will come with flying ships and many thousands to find you and kill you, Harlowe. You will never find your lost city."

"Then we must hurry and find Lamille before Darkn gathers his forces."

"Darkn is too powerful. You cannot win this battle."

"I've fought worse. I will take care of him, Isara."

"How Harlowe?" Isara wondered frightfully. "I've seen you do impossible feats today, but to fight Darkn is beyond even what you are capable of."

"I am a Gamadin, Isara. The word failure does not exist." Thinking he might have hurt her feelings, Harlowe leaned over from his saddle and put his hand on hers. "Isara, lead us to Lamille, and I promise you, the Tappers will cease to exist after my crew is done with them."

Out of desperation, Isara repeated her warning, her tears displaying the fear of losing Harlowe. "Darkn is forever. He will crush us all when he discovers his brother is dead."

He squeezed her hand with great confidence. "Darkn is not forever. He is mortal like you and I. Look there," he said, motioning toward Gnarr's corpse, "his brother isn't getting up. Darkn is no different. You have to trust me, Isara. We find Lamille, and Darkn, and his toads will never hurt you, your family, or the Fagans again. They'll end up like Darkn's butthead brother over there."

Harlowe was about to lead Isara away from the crowd, now beginning to eye the gerbids as something to scavenge, when what was left of the posse came slowly walking through the crowd with their mounts.

82

SoCal

Out of uniform and wrapped in her satiny, blue kimono she fashioned from the ship's stores, Leucadia continued drying her long, blond hair with a towel when she stepped onto the bridge to answer Ian's summons. "What is so urgent, Captain?" she asked as Molly appeared right after her. Her big, blue eyes barely awake, she yawned and continued on across the bridge, flopping down next to Rhud, who was still asleep at this early hour. It was still forty-seven minutes before the morning shift change. Neither Ma Dev or Cheesa had the experience or understanding of a spaceship's operation to be left alone on the bridge without supervision. That left Ian and Leucadia to run things in six-hour on-off shifts.

With his eyes still on the overhead screen, he replied, "We're stopping."

Coming forward, she draped her towel over her shoulder. "Why? Is there something wrong with *Forty-Four*?"

"She took herself out of hyperlight on her own." Ian pointed out the pulsing, blue dot on the star map. "She seems to be headed for that object there."

"What is it?"

"Can't tell from here. We'll get a better look when we come into viewing range," he replied.

They both squinted to find the object through the large observation window. But even with Ian's super sharp, Gamadin eyes and Leucadia's nearly as keen, half-alien eyes, there was nothing definable yet. That was hardly

393

surprising. With the scarcity of ambient light within the star desert, any object, even a large planet, would be undetectable until they were practically upon it.

Cheesa, who was Ian's shift mate, scanned ahead with a pair of Gamadin binoculars. "I see no object, Captain."

"Try searching five degrees to port, Chee," Leucadia directed after looking at the sensor readouts.

Cheesa turned to Ian for help. She was still getting used to ship's terminology. Ian smiled and pointed her slightly to the left. "Try that."

She refocused her optics on the new heading and found the object almost immediately. "Yes, I see it now."

"Can you tell what it is?" Ian asked.

"I have never seen anything like it." She lowered her binos with a puzzled frown toward Leucadia. "It looks dead, Lu."

Leucadia brought the object into focus with the ship's long range optics. "It's a spaceship," she declared. "And from the size and shape, it looks like a cargo transport."

Ian gave his take. "Cheesa is right. It appears dead in the water."

Cheesa pointed out that was not how she described the object. There was no water around the ship at all. He was changing her meaning. A quick "that's okay" wink from Leucadia, however, told her not to worry. It was another one of those descriptive phrases Ian often made that made no no sense at all to her. This wasn't the first time. Early on in the voyage she had asked Leucadia why Ian spoke in such a manner. Leucadia laughed as she placed a warm arm around her shoulders and explained to her, "It's something you just get used to, Cheesa. From where they come, a place called SoCal, there are many times I wish I had a translator to understand what the boys were saying."

Cheesa's face turned even more confused. "Boys?"

"Harlowe and Matthew."

"Ian's friends? They speak that way, too?" Cheesa asked quite seriously. "How does anyone communicate with them?"

Leucadia looked off briefly, feeling a tinge of pain a galaxy away. After a short heartfelt breath she replied, "It is challenging." She pointed below her right ear. "Even our translators have difficulty interpreting SoCal."

"That's the name of their language?"

"Kinda," and held her hand. "Listen, if you have a problem again, come see me. We will work it out together. After being with Harlowe this long, I think I'm getting the hang of it."

Cheesa's mouth twisted with confusion again. "Hang of it?"

Leucadia bit her bottom lip as they stepped toward the bridge blinker. "Oh, my gawd, I've been around Harlowe too long. SoCal has overtaken me at last."

* * *

When everyone had run out of guesses as to why the ship had suddenly stopped on her own, Leucadia asked the only entity that knew why they had suddenly stopped in the middle of Cartooga-Thaat. "Why are we stopping, *Forty-four?*"

LIFE was her response.

83

Bodies in the Hold

They had no choice. *Forty-four's* auto controls had taken over. It wasn't until they came within a quarter mile of the object that she returned the controls back to the bridge. "We have the helm again, Captain," Leucadia announced.

Except for her short answer of 'LIFE', there was no clear reason why she had brought them to the unknown object. Ian, who was now firmly in place at his command chair, ordered a full analysis of the object before going any closer.

Maa Dev, who was also called back to the bridge, reported from his weapons station, "Ready here, Captain." Shortly after leaving Nod, Ian had tested *Forty-four's* weapons array as they traveled across the star desert. As far as he and Leucadia could tell, she may have lacked the robust offensive systems of *Millawanda*, but after a few bursts of her main plas cannons, she was a dog that could hunt. Her weapons array was formidable. Ian was more than satisfied as he tapped the control console, pleased. "Sweet."

* * *

Sensors indicated the unknown ship was well over a hundred times *Forty-four's* mass, far smaller than *Millawanda*, but nevertheless, quite sizable compared to their ship. Its long, heavy, dark metal superstructure and thick struts connecting its power drives to the main hull gave Ian reason to believe that Cheesa's first thoughts were correct. The object was dead.

"It's so dark," Cheesa noted.

Leucadia reached across the console beside Dev and switched on the flood lights that lit up the object's hull like a small sun. Instantly, everyone was blown away by the hundreds of scorch marks, blackened holes, and long, ragged rips in the hull plating that blighted the ship from bow to stern.

"What happened?" Dev wondered, coming to his feet to look more closely.

"Someone tried to kill them," Ian replied, studying the damage. He had seen many battle-scared ships in his travels as a Gamadin, but this was really bad. He was amazed that it was still intact. "Any internal readings yet?" he asked.

Leucadia glanced at her readouts. "Registering some power, but it's quite low and deteriorating fast."

"Weapons?"

"No power."

"Fuel?"

Leucadia shook her head negatively. "Empty."

Ian cautiously guided *Forty-four* to the back of the ship, being careful to keep the shields at full power in case something inside the derelict triggered a self-destruct. They found even larger blast holes along the port side drive pods.

"How did they make it this far?" Cheesa asked, observing the starboard drive strut dangling by a thread.

Ian shrugged. He had no idea why a ship with no power and no fuel was in the middle of Cartooga-Thaat? "What were they thinking?" he wondered aloud, and went to Leucadia for her observation. "Life signs, Lu?"

Leucadia turned to him. "More than a hundred and fifty, Captain."

"Their condition can't be good," Ian stated with concern.

Leucadia ran her long fingers along a slide bar to focus the sensor to a narrower range. "They are alive, but without going aboard, their condition is questionable. They have only a few hours before the ship goes completely dark, Captain."

"Then that's the answer, isn't it?" Ian concluded. "Life. That's why *Forty-four* stopped here. She's following the Gamadin directive to save life where she finds it."

"Appears so," Leucadia agreed.

* * *

A once-around tour of the derelict ship revealed there was too much damage entering the ship through the main hatch at the bottom of the hull. Ian wanted a safer way in before he would risk any lives. They continued their search around the ship when Cheesa saw an opportunity.

"Can we enter there, Captain?" she wondered, pointing to a small portal she found using her binoculars. It was near the bow of the ship and a good way from where the bulk of the lifeforms were located, but it appeared to be their best option.

Ian reached over and touched her on the shoulder. "Nice work, Chee."

* * *

Once *Forty-four* was in position, the forcefield extended over the hatch, allowing them to open it without a perfect seal. Leucadia volunteered first. "I should go, Captain."

Ian thanked her, but he wanted her on the sensors looking out for him.

"Take Dev with you then," Leucadia said. From the tone of her voice, it wasn't a suggestion. At moments like this Ian understood why Harlowe always said to her, "Yes dear." It was his catch all reply to a no win situation. Ian knew the dangers of exploring a derelict ship. This away mission was only slightly different from the time they found another derelict transport Riverstone called, Shipzilla. On that ship there were supposedly no lifeforms. But when Riverstone and Harlowe entered that ship, they found plenty of trouble. The undetectable cyborg security force came out of nowhere and nearly ended their short space careers. Fortunately for them, before the robots overwhelmed them, Prigg had found a way to shut them down before they were toast.

Ian nodded his okay. "You're with me, Dev." Dev jumped at the chance. As the Prince dashed to his quarters to get his things, Ian added, "If you see any movement . . . Anything! Don't waste time thinking. Holler."

"Aye," Leucadia countered, glancing Cheesa's way. "We'll have your back, Captain."

Ian gave her a thumbs up as he turned to the cats. Their tails wagged in whip-like fashion, eagerly anticipating their walk. After being cooped up in the ship for days, it was hard not to say no. "Can they handle it in there?" he asked, concerned with the low oxygen levels and plunging temperatures inside the ship.

"It's cold, but they can handle it," Leucadia replied.

Ian was relieved. He liked the idea of having his big guns along for protection, especially ones that could sense danger far better than his SIBA. Ian waved Molly and Rhud toward the blinker. Happy as dogs, the cats leaped onto the transport pad and winked away. Ian turned to Leucadia and asked, "What if I had said no?"

Leucadia chuckled. "There would have been mutiny."

*   *   *

Locked and loaded, and standing by the cats in full SIBA gear, Ian and Dev looked through the hatch into a dark, empty passageway. It gave Ian the chills. Unable to see Dev's face behind his bugeyes, he could only guess how the Prince felt. The locking mechanisms were nothing complicated. Four touch levers and the pressure latches released. Opening the hatch door, though, needed persuading. Ian and Dev pushed with their bodies, but the door wouldn't budge until Rhud pushed it open with one slap of his powerful forepaw.

Ian patted the big cat going in, "Thanks, Rhuddy."

Not the least bit shy, the cats led the way, leaping through the doorway. Two armed robobs went next, followed by Ian and Dev. A third robob trailed them all, while the fourth stickman stayed behind, preventing anyone from locking them in.

"I can't see a thing," Dev complained as they went clomping along the metal floor.

Ian reached over and tapped a side activator on Dev's bulbous eyes. "How's that?"

"Wow! Bright...like day."

"Can you hear okay?"

"I can hear the clickers walking. Is that good enough?"

"Good enough," Ian concurred, removing his sidearm from his holster.

"Are you scared as I am, Captain?" Dev asked

Ian thought through his reply. Since this was his first mission as captain, he had to set the example or lose face. Should he be macho, or understanding, or comforting, or should he just pat him on the back and say, "That's okay, Dev; we all feel that way before we rock and roll." He had a lot of captains to choose from for advice; Captains Kirk, Picard, Malcolm Reynolds, Janeway, and the one he looked up to the most, a real life captain, Harlowe Pylott. Each had his own style of leadership. Each had buckets of courage, honor, and the 'right stuff.' And they all worked best under stress. They faced certain death often and somehow managed to survive the greatest hardships and evils confronting them. Who would he be like? In the final analysis he chose to stay in his own skin rather than follow someone else's path. "I'm shaking in my boots," he coolly told Dev.

Ian heard a long, heavy breath from Dev's com. "Thank you, Captain."

Ian pushed the barrel of Dev's pistol away from his chest. "But keep that end pointed away from me, or I won't be captain long."

"Sorry, Captain."

They hadn't gone far when the narrow passage ended, and they were switching back and forth down stairs that led them to the lower levels of the ship. By the time they made it to the lowest level, Molly and Rhud had vanished.

"Where did they go?" Dev asked, looking down another long passageway.

Ian stared a little stressed. "That's not like them." He called Leucadia for assistance. "Molly and Rhud took off. Do you have a location on them?"

Leucadia responded almost immediately. "*They're moving fast, toward the back of the ship, Captain. What happened?*"

"I don't know. They just took off."

"*Be careful, Ian,*" Leucadia added.

"Roger that," Then he asked, "Where does this passageway go?"

"*Transferring the ship's layout to you now. You should see their tracks with your infrareds.*"

Ian adjusted his bugeyes, following Leucadia's suggestion. "I see them."

"*They're moving fast, like they know where they're going, Captain,*" Leucadia said.

Dev had trouble activating his infrared optics, so he just followed Ian. He didn't want to be left behind, especially when they came upon their first bodies.

"They look dead," Dev said with a touch of unease in his voice.

Ian's sensor readouts were dark. "They are," Ian answered.

"*Molly and Rhud went directly to the main hold, Captain,*" Leucadia directed.

"Have they stopped?" Ian asked.

"*Yes. Looks like they're hovering around something or someone. Whoever it is, it is close to death along with the hundred or so other bodies around them. It seems like the hold was their last refuge.*"

"These bodies didn't freeze, Lu; they were starved. They're nothing but skin and bones," Ian noticed.

"Ian, they're running out of time. Oxygen levels are critical, and the temperature is dropping past freezing. You must find their environmental controls or whoever is left alive in the ship will die."

Ian understood the urgency. "Copy that. Can you direct me to the control panels?"

"There's a system control up three decks. You'll have to retrace your steps back to the level above you."

Ian and Dev took off clanking back down the passageway. "On our way, Lu!" Ian exclaimed.

For every five steps Ian climbed, Dev took two. Once they found the control center, Ian located the power banks and quickly discovered the environmental panels were fried. He had only one solution: "Send a clicker down with a crystal, Lu. I'll put the others to rebuilding the circuits. If we cut in the power slowly to handle the surge, it just might work."

"Detach the reduction coil on your left."

"I see it."

"The clickers can install it in the new panel. It should diminish the surge," Leucadia suggested.

"Roger that."

A short time later, a robob appeared with a small hunk of aara in its claws. Ian stepped aside and let the clicker do its thing, tearing into the panel, fixing wires, redirecting circuits, and welding new capacitors and transformers that would handle the power from the aara. Finally, the robob took the reduction coil from Ian and put it into place. Watching the clicker work was like watching a magician perform slight-of-hand tricks. Its claws worked so fast, the panel was rebuilt from scratch in no time at all. The only thing left to do was pop the thumb-sized crystal into place and flip the switch.

When the clicker nodded he was ready, Ian gave the thumbs up and ordered, "Do it!"

The robob affixed the aara inside the brackets and pulled the lever down. The reaction was instantaneous. Like powering up a Christmas tree, the room came alive with all kinds of brightly colored lights of energy.

"We have juice, Lu!" Ian cried out. He turned to Dev, trying to give him a high five. But the Prince ducked under the open hand, thinking Ian was about to hit him. Ian didn't have time to explain it was a gesture of success.

He pushed Dev out the door and together they strode off down the stairway toward the main hold again. Along the way Ian offered a small prayer for those still alive in the hold.

* * *

As the sea of bodies met their eyes, Ian and Dev froze at the doorway. For Ian, it was the horror of Erati all over again as he stared at the suffering mass of cold bodies a breath away from death. Surrounded by a mire of filth and vermin, skeletal forms of men, women, and children were huddled together for warmth, fighting for their lives.

"What happened here?" Dev asked, aghast by the deep intensity of the suffering.

"It's called Hell, Dev," Ian murmured, understanding at that moment that he and his crew would be the only ones who could bring them out alive from so terrible a place. From the cursory readouts of his SIBA, many had already lost their battle to hold on.

Sloshing their way through the slop and dying bodies, Ian couldn't even imagine the putrid smells and disease that were brewing in the muck. It was a place unfit for beings of any kind. He quickly ordered Leucadia and Cheesa to ready *Forty-four's* holds for all the bodies the robobs would be transporting back to the ship.

Ian's voice cracked as he spoke. "Do it now, Lu! Don't think about anything else but getting these bodies off this ship!"

"Aye, Captain."

At the far end of the room, Ian found Molly and Rhud hovering over a sickly, thin body of a young, dark-haired girl. For some strange reason the cats were nervously moaning, lying beside her in the ooze in their effort to keep her warm. Sensors showed the massive room rapidly heating up as the overhead lights grew brighter. Thank God, he thought, and prayed he could save the ones who were still alive. The task would be difficult, and *Forty-four* would need to produce hundreds of gallons of Bluestuff for days to meet their nourishment needs. After so many thousands of years lying dormant, he wondered if she was up to the task. Even as he thought, could-she-do-it?, a score of robob medical teams had entered the hold and were picking up bodies from the floor to take back to the ship. The question was moot after that. *Forty-four* would use every last resource she had to save the living.

Ian kept his eye on the dark haired female as she struggled to lift her arm to feed a small child. She had barely the strength in her to stay alive, yet she was doing whatever she could for the children around her to keep them alive. Molly never stopped licking her legs while Rhud laid down beside her, licking her body to clean her. The pitiful look in both cats' eyes made Ian believe the cats were crying in despair. Tears were actually flowing down their furry, white cheeks, something Ian had never thought possible for a cat to do. But when Molly nudged the girl with her nose to turn her over, that's when Ian lost it.

His nose burned, his throat squeezed shut in a sudden convulsion as tears poured uncontrollably from his eyes. Unable to stand, his entire body trembled in fear when he collapsed to his knees beside the female. All he could say in a raspy voice choking of dread was, "Oh no…Quay…"

84

Hercules

It was a night of celebration with whooping and hollering, singing, dancing, music, drums, and striking anything that made a noise. The Fagans had little to share, but what they had, they gave willingly and generously to their heroes, Harlowe and Monday. They may have been poor, but to Harlowe they were the kindest, most hospitable, "our house is your house" beings he had met this side of the Thaat. Most Fagans lived in makeshift homes that were made from abandoned buildings and whatever scraps they found around the dilapidated city. Living conditions were deplorable. They had no light except from the campfires at night, no sanitation, no running water, no fresh food, no gardens, and no markets from which to buy the simplest things in life like a toothbrush, toilet paper, or pans to cook what little food they did have. Whatever they had was scrounged from the land around them. Doctors and medicines to help the sick or injured were nonexistent. The grand city that had once been Ragoss was sucked dry years ago by the Tapper collectors. Yet as poor as they were, Harlowe and Monday felt like honored guests. By last count Harlowe was betrothed to no less than five young, moon-faced Fagan girls, and all were beautiful by anyone's standards. Monday was treated like a rock star. He had twice that number. His dark skin attracted young ladies like a magnet. A Fagan marriage was unusual by Earth standards. It was not one male and one female joined together in a nuptial agreement. It was as many mates as one wanted to partner with. Monday thought the concept had promise. The custom had worked well for the

Fagans. He saw no jealousy, no envy, no resentment among the groupings. Harlowe, on the other hand, believed one girlfriend was plenty. Imagining a second or third Leucadia Mars never crossed his mind. Even if that were possible, would Leucadia be willing to share him with another female or two? Harlowe laughed out loud at the thought.

When pigs fly!

It broke Harlowe's heart to leave Ragoss, but leave they must. He had a broken ship to repair and a galaxy to cross to fix her, so before dawn the following day, when everyone was still asleep from a night of celebration, Harlowe, Monday, Isara, and Oea saddled up their ceffyls and headed out to find the trail that would take them over the pass to the coast. Not far from where they began, they quickly realized, however, they were lost in the labyrinth of dead-end streets, fallen structures, and vine-clogged avenues. Neither Isara or Oea had ever been farther than the river before. To their relief, Nath, and half a dozen sleepy-eyed and hungover Fagans found them in the maze and offered to be their guides. Oea protested straight out. She did not want Nath along for any reason. Isara, however, countered her disapproval. "Do you know the way, sister, like our Fagan friends?"

Oea took issue with calling Nath a "friend."

"Oea, please," Isara snarled back. "Now is not the time to bring up an old pain."

"I have no pain for the likes of him, sister."

Harlowe leaned over to Isara and asked, "Pain? Nath seems like a good guy."

Isara made clear the following point. "Nath wants to marry Oea."

Harlowe eyed Oea. "Can't say I blame him."

Isara added: "And she wants no part of it. She would become his seventh wife."

Harlowe's face twisted around to the Fagan leader in disbelief. "Really, Nath. Six wives?"

Nath saw nothing wrong with multiple mates. "A Fagan has many wives to survive." He answered quiet innocently. "We are a poor people, Harlowe. Our wives give us strength. The more we have, the stronger we are."

"They should call you Hercules, then, instead of Nath," Monday suggested from his eavesdropping.

Nath inquired innocently. "Who is Hercules?"

Harlowe laughed. "A strong dude, Nath. A god from where we come."

Nath thought that was cool. He stuck his chest out. "Yes, I am a god! And with Oea I will be an even bigger god."

Everyone laughed but Oea. "You are weak like a *pinthit*," she said insultingly.

Neither Harlowe nor Monday knew what a pinthit was but from the look on Isara's face, trying to stifle her giggle, to Nath's embarrassment, Oea's stab had its desired affect.

Trying to stop the ticking thader from exploding, Harlowe turned to Oea and asked, "If Nath promises not to marry you, will that be all right, Oea?"

Oea grunted her distain. She wanted no part of any compromise. She whirled her ceffyl from the group and rode away.

"I think that's a no," Harlowe said.

Isara turned to Nath and said, "My sister has spoken, Nath. We welcome you and your riders, but Oea will not marry you when we return."

Nath grudgingly accepted the terms, but his eyes never left Oea. He smiled, knowing Oea would eventually marry him because he was, after all... Hercules!

* * *

"Ha, ha, ha. Only Nath knows the path," Nath said, looking toward the Ozans to the west. Their escort mounts appeared small next to the much loftier ceffyls, but the way the Fagans rode with strong, powerful legs close to the ground, their size was not at all a disadvantage. Harlowe was grateful to have the locals lead the way. Oea joined them, too, but preferred to stay well behind the group.

Once they were out of the city, their pace quickened up an inclined path that paralleled the fast moving river on the left and the sheer granite cliffs on their right. Finally, by late afternoon, the small band of riders made it to the base of a massive metal gate that blocked their way further up the canyon.

Isara pointed to the sign that hung from the gate. "It's a Tapper warning. To go beyond this point is death," she translated.

Harlowe turned to Nath, asking him if his people had ever ventured beyond the warning.

"Yes," Nath replied, sheepishly. "To hunt."

"Really..." Harlowe said, studying the sign. "I like your style, pard."

Then, drawing his sidearm, he blew away the sign with three clicks of his trigger.

Nath and his riders cheered. "Down with Tappers!" Harlowe's stock had just exploded to the upside.

Harlowe urged his black forward, crushing the Tapper warning as he galloped up the pass. Nath looked at Monday and said, "I think he is also a god."

Monday watched Harlowe speed away with Isara. "No, but gods do fear him," he said, charging after his captain.

* * *

Another mile or so up the trail, the party came to a vast concrete and steel dam that covered the entire width of the gorge. Harlowe looked up the side of the cliffs with his bugeyes on full. There appeared no way a mount could climb the nearly vertical face of the rock wall.

The roar of great white arcs of water blowing from the bottom of the dam was deafening. "A power station, Captain!" Monday shouted, referring to the building off the side of the dam.

Harlowe pointed at the towers nearby. "Power lines?"

"What are they for?" Oea asked. The girls had never seen a dam before.

Harlowe rode to her side so she could hear him. "This holds back the river to make electricity," he said, pointing again at the power house.

"Electricity?" Oea asked again. From the look on her face, and the others who were listening, the concept was unfamiliar to them.

"Energy. It makes things go," Harlowe explained. He pulled a flashlight from his utility belt to demonstrate and switched on the beam. (A Gamadin flashlight is way more sophisticated than its Earthly cousin. It doesn't use electricity at all but instead uses a form of dark energy that would last a lifetime before it needs recharging. On several occasions, Harlowe had used to it like a cutting torch to cut through metal bars. But for this demo, the concept was the same.) To everyone's amazement, Harlowe's device lit up the face of the dam like it was daylight. "Electricity inside this device powers a gizmo that makes the light."

"And why do they need this power?"

"To run their cities."

"Ragoss could use such power," Nath said.

"My guess is that this dam once powered your city, Nath." Harlowe pointed along the edges of the dam. There was clearly a difference between the real structure that was old and cracking to the new, faux construction that was held together like Cornicen's tall skyscrapers. As long as the electricity continued flowing, the dam held the water back like a real barrier of concrete and steel. But if the power failed, the Clarity's cities would also fail, which made Harlowe wonder why there was no security surrounding the dam? This obviously wasn't the only Clarity power station, but even so, to not have guards watching over such an important installation seemed irresponsible.

Monday saw it, too. "No security, Captain?"

"Yeah, stay alert. It's here, we just can't see it."

"Aye."

"Ragoss had lights like your device?" Nath asked, interrupting Harlowe's discussion with Monday.

Oea didn't wait for the answer. She rode off before Harlowe answered the Fagan leader. "Yes. A river like this could light up all of Ragoss with plenty left over."

Nath struggled with the visual of his city with many suns. But after mulling over the concept, he grew angry like someone had stolen his favorite saddle. "Ragoss must have her power back!" Nath demanded.

"It will one day, Nath. I assure you," Harlowe promised.

"Elrish Dag!" Nath cried out. "Darkn has taken the power there."

Harlowe followed the power lines up the side of the gorge until they disappeared over the far ridge line. "Elrish Dag, huh?"

Nath waved his hairy hand ninety degrees away from their line of travel. "Many days' ride to the north."

Harlowe turned back to the cliffs. There was nothing he could do for Nath and his city now. One day, when *Millawanda* was her old self again, he would keep his promise to Nath and return the power to Ragoss so it could once again be the beautiful city by the river. But for now, the cliffs were the problem. It seemed this was the end of the line for Isara, Oea, Nath, and their mounts. The cliffs that supported the dam were nearly a mile high. Impossible for their mounts to climb, but for them, they were a piece of cake. They could scamper up these rock walls in minutes.

Harlowe looked at Isara with disappointment. "We must leave you here, Isara."

Isara was having none of that. "You have not found Lamille yet,

Harlowe."

"I know, but as you can see, the trail ends here," he tried to tell her.

Isara's jaw set. "No, Harlowe. The trail does not end here." She urged her ceffyl forward and headed straight for the cliff. Harlowe and Monday watched awestruck as Isara and her ceffyl leaped up the side of the rock cliff like its feet wore SIBA claws.

Oea went next without a second thought, following behind her sister in a race to the top. Up, up, up they went as though trotting along a horizontal road.

With his mouth agape, Monday said in awe, "That's impressive, Captain."

Harlowe could barely control his black. He pranced about impatiently, eager to follow the other ceffyls. "That it is, Mr. Platter," he admitted, wide-eyed with disbelief.

Monday made an observation. "I think we'll slow them up if we do it our way, Captain," he said, watching the girls climb.

Harlowe tightened his reins with a vise-like grip and gave the black his head. "I think you're right, Mr. Platter. Let's not keep the ladies waiting." With Monday at his tail, Harlowe charged up the vertical path set by Isara and Oea. After several teeth-clenching bounds, the Gamadin were stunned by their rate of climb. Not once did their ceffyls hesitate or slip on a loose rock. Their climb was steady and always up, ascending the 5,000 foot escarpment like it was part of their daily exercise. Before the sun had set, all four riders were over the top of the precipice, staring at the most remarkable find yet on their quest for Lamille. Nestled between the tall coniferous trees were structures that Harlowe believed could only being be made by Gamadin engineers!

85

A Kindship

For three days, Leucadia commanded *Forty-four* on her own. It wasn't like Ian to concern himself with just one being out of so many. Yet, after returning to the ship with the girl he found in the hold, he had never left the medical unit where he brought her. The care of the remaining survivors and the day to day operations of the ship were left to her. With Dev, Cheesa, and a dozen robobs assisting her, the task of doing it all without him was possible but exhausting. She found little time to sleep, grabbing a catnap between her shifts on the bridge and helping with the survivors who were kept in the makeshift wards created for them in *Forty-four*'s empty spaces. The survivors who had made it through the initial forty-eight hours of care had a good chance of survival. Those who hadn't were wrapped in cloth and were allowed to drift in space forever. Some might say it was a heartless way to dispose of the dead, but under the circumstances, it was the best they could do.

Leucadia didn't believe in miracles. Miracles were found in fairy tales and saintly stories. But now, after caring for a spaceship full of starving, half-living beings, each life she saw come back from the brink of death made her question those beliefs.

"How else would you describe it, Lu?" Cheesa asked her. The Tels, as they were called, had no food, no air, and no sanitary facilities that functioned. No fuel to run their ship. No water to drink. No power for warmth. In less than an hour they would have frozen to death. "Every one of them would have perished if not for us," she argued.

Leucadia admitted the survivors were extremely fortunate, as she handed the bridge over to Cheesa.

"Where are you going?" she asked.

Leucadia's exhausted eyes appeared as though she were about to collapsed. "To check on Ian."

"You should rest, Ms. Lu."

She saw the concern in Cheesa's face as she rose from the command chair. "I will…after I see him."

When she stepped into the medical room, she found Ian slumped over, at the foot of the girl's med table, out cold. Lying above him, the girl was still and quiet and dressed in a long, powder blue sleeping garment. A thin, dark blue blanket covered her chest, arms and legs. Judging by her weight and color, she was by far stronger than the others. She had already recovered nearly fifty percent of her original body mass. As the girl lay peacefully asleep, Leucadia was struck by her incredible beauty. Her hair was long and dark. Her skin flawless and youthful. She was not a Tel, she figured. They were dark and yellow, and some were a mixture of both. This girl was fair and taller by a foot than any other survivor. Taller in fact than her by several inches, she guessed.

Rhud greeted her as she entered, rubbing against her and yawning widely. The cats had not slept either, she knew, acting like guardian sentinels over the girl. After hugging Molly, she had two clickers lift Ian off the floor and lay him on the other med table next to the girl.

Next, she scanned the wall of holographic screens, studying the spectrum of colored 3D displays of the young girl's condition. Ian's efforts had paid off. Her vital signs were greatly improved from three days ago.

Turning her attention back to the girl, Leucadia wondered why she was so important to Ian and to the cats. Their actions were more than just attentive. They were dutiful and reverent. The way they slept by her every hour of the day was like they were watching over Harlowe. Out of the eighty-two survivors left, she was the only one they were so passionate about. Why?

Even their course change made no sense. When the robobs had completed the transfer of the survivors to *Forty-four*, she went directly to hyperlight on her own. Instead of skirting the star desert like they had originally planned, the new course was taking them deeper into Cartooga-Thaat. Was it divine intervention or a helping hand? It was no miracle; of that, she was certain.

With far more questions than answers, Leucadia found herself drawn back to the girl. "Who are you?" she whispered.

From out of nowhere a trembling warmth came over her. It caught her off guard. She closed her eyes, trying to think it all through. The emotion ran deep and primal as if there was some kind of connection with the girl she couldn't explain. How was that possible? She had never met this girl in her life.

Exhausted and needing sleep, she decided to take Cheesa up on her concern and get some rest. She started for the doorway, and as the door slid back in its usual, quiet manner, a soft voice spoke to her: "Please, don't go."

86

The Arrow Points the Way

Simon yawned so wide he looked like Pigpo before he settled down for the night. Fighting his urge to sleep, he reached into his pocket and pulled out candy from the breast pocket of his Julian Starr uniform jacket. "We're almost to the place where my ship was parked, Naree," he informed her. They had traveled incognito with the convoy for over two days. Several times along the highway they had come upon road stations where the Clarity was stopping vehicles to search for the aliens who had escaped. But since they were attached to a convoy, they were neither searched nor stopped by the check points. They were waved through with the others in the convoy without incident. Simon found that an unbelievable stroke of luck.

He ripped open the orange and yellow wrapping with his teeth while keeping one hand on the wheel. "Care for a peanut butter cup?" he asked Naree.

She looked at the chocolate covered sweet with disgust. "No, thank you."

"What woman doesn't like chocolate?"

"I prefer not."

"You haven't eaten for days." As a matter of fact, he couldn't remember Naree having eaten anything since he met her. "You need something to eat, or you'll get sick."

"Please, no," she said as she twisted around and looked back. "More transports have joined our line, Ahlian. If we leave the highway, they will know we are not one of them."

413

"We can't say on the road forever, Naree. It's turning south."

"Yes, the road goes to Elrish Dag. Darkn's fortress."

"Yeah, I'm sure he would love to see us there," he said with a snide twist to his mouth. He held up the abordar, and added, "My pals need this, Naree. Harlowe believes it is important. He thinks it might help him find Lamille, so we need to go east toward those hills over there. That is where my ship will find us," he explained, ending with a long yawn as he forced his eyes to stay open a while longer.

More than anything, Simon needed sleep. Naree always looked fresh, like she had just stepped out of a shower. How she kept herself so alert without food was beyond him. He tried several times to teach her how to drive so he could grab a quick nap, but each time she got behind the wheel they nearly crashed. Other than Harlowe, she was by far the worst driver he had ever met. Now his fatigue was so bad his SIBA was giving him the first warning signs that it was about to shutdown his suit if he didn't get some rest soon. An hour was all he needed, and he and his SIBA would be square for another twelve. It he didn't find a place to rest, his suit would find it for him.

"There are no roads to take us east, Ahlian," Naree pointed out.

As luck would have it, the many roads that had once branched off from the highway to the coast were long gone. Only the scant remnants of ancient roadbeds remained. The winds of time had erased them from the landscape eons ago. The only useable road left was the one the Clarity maintained between Cornicen and Elrish Dag. Any road to the coast would be his own creation.

Simon glanced east, looking out over the plains where *Millawanda* had parked. For some distance, the off roading would be easy going to the coastal hills, where they needed to cross. With his bugeyes on high, he made out the three impressions where millions of *Follish Pimars* were flattened like tiny pancakes from Millie's landing pods. The way the dents were positioned, they were like an arrow pointing the way through the hills. He would steer for the pass it directed him to and hope for the best. "Thank you, Millie," he said, saluting her prints.

A short distance later he picked a spot and veered off the road. It didn't matter where. The grasslands were smooth all the way to the foothills. "This is it, Naree," he yawned sleepily. He tried to stay awake, but he was fading fast. "We're getting off here and tearing up a few billion *Follish Pimars* along the way for Dog and Squid."

Naree grabbed hold of the seat handle next to her. "I am with you, Ahlian."

Simon forced a sleepy smile. "That's my girl."

Five miles from the highway, he took a heading off *Millawanda's* last impression when his right foot slipped off the pedal. Their transport came to a slow stop in the middle of the plains as his face rested against the steering wheel and didn't move.

87

Introductions

Leucadia came back into the room. The girl's eyes pleaded for her to stay. She spoke again. "Please—"

"Of course."

The girl looked around the room. "My people?"

"Being cared for."

"How many?"

"As of this morning, eighty-one."

The girl closed her eyes in sorrow. When she opened them again, she asked with a trembling voice, "And the children?"

Leucadia came to her side. "They all lived."

"Thank you. Thank you."

"They were stronger than the others. You gave them the last of your food and water, didn't you?"

The girl lay back on the table as she stuttered, "Yes..."

"It worked. They live today because of your sacrifice."

The girl stared at Leucadia curiously. "You are Nejian?"

Surprised how anyone could know her linage, she replied, "My mother was Nejian. How do know that?"

"My mother is also Nejian."

"You are Nejian?"

"My father is Tamarian."

"We must talk when you are stronger."

"Yes, I would like that." The girl kept studying the room, going from one wall to the next. "*Millawanda?* But how?"

"No. This is *Forty-four.*"

"Not *Millawanda?*"

"No."

"But Gamadin? The displays and markings are all old like the Gamadin."

"Yes, *Forty-four* is Gamadin."

"My Captain is here?"

Leucadia wasn't sure what she meant by "my" Captain as the girl continued to pet the cats obviously excited at seeing her Captain. "Molly and Rhud are here. My Captain must be also."

Leucadia found it curious how the cats were so affectionate toward her, purring loudly in her presence. She had only seen them act that way with Harlowe, never with her or with any other members of the crew and especially not with strangers. That the girl was not in the least intimated by them was odd. She caressed them lovingly like a mother. The girl's familiarity with the ship and the cats indicated they were all old friends. But how? How could someone they just picked up in the middle of a star desert know so much about them? She nodded at the table next to her. "Our captain is lying next to you. He has not slept in days, watching over your recovery."

"Ian…" she said warmly, but it was apparent he was not the captain she was hoping to see.

"They know you." It was not a question, but an observation of a true and deep devotion the cats had toward the girl.

"They have grown so much."

"When did you see them last?"

"When they were babies."

"How?" Leucadia asked, amazed that anyone other than a Gamadin would know Molly and Rhud so intimately.

"When my Captain and I found them after their mother was killed."

Like a sledgehammer hitting her squarely between the eyes, she realized who the girl had to be. From every detail of Harlowe's physical description of her, how they first met, her rescue from the Consortium, entering the Omni Quadrant, her mother Sharlon, her father Anor Ran, and the message she had left Harlowe, telling him that she had a mission to complete that did not include him, she knew all about her and the story of how they found

Molly and Rhud after their mother had been killed by a T-rex. This was Sizzle's older sister. They were all Neijian like her mother, Sook. Leucadia had always considered Sizzle her sister. And now she knew why she felt that certain bond between them. She was Quay.

Quay touched her head as she tried to sit up. Light-headed and very weak, she nearly tumbled off the table. Leucadia caught her in time and laid her carefully back down. "You should rest, Quay."

Quay seemed confused. "Have we met?"

"I am Leucadia."

Quay passed into a state of awe. "My Captain's other," she said. "You are even more beautiful and gracious than I imagined. I am honored."

Leucadia didn't quite know what to say. She had heard so much about her, especially from Matthew and Simon, when they described how unimaginably hot she was. She was that and more. She was intelligent, courageous, and caring. From the short time she had been with her, Leucadia saw how selfless her devotion was to her people. She swallowed hard. "It is I who am honored. I welcome you and your people to our ship and all that we have."

She seemed to find strength in her reassurance. "My Captain did not bring me here?"

"Captain Wizzixs brought you here," she replied, nodding toward the sleeping body on the table next to her.

"Ian is captain?"

Leucadia forced a grin. "It's complicated."

Quay closed her eyes. They seemed heavy as she fought to stay awake. When she came around again, she understood what Leucadia meant. "Yes, complicated," she repeated, her eyes settling on the view screens as she tried to rise from the table. "My people! You said they are being cared for."

"By robobs in our dispensary."

"When may I see them?"

"Soon. Your condition is still critical. Tonight possibly. Tomorrow morning at the latest."

Quay nodded her understanding then asked, "Harlowe. My Captain. If he is not here, where is he?"

Leucadia was unsure how much Quay needed to know. Without consulting with Ian, she kept her answers simple and brief. "He is on a mission."

"My Captain spoke of you often," Quay said. "You were afraid he would risk his life for you instead of *Millawanda*?"

"Yes, Harlowe can be quite predictable, I'm afraid."

"After seeing you, I know why you sacrificed your bonding. He is very illogical."

Leucadia found no fault in her wisdom. "Yes, illogical. In that he is quite consistent." Before Quay fell asleep again, she wanted to know a little more about the people she had with her. "Who are these beings, Quay? Why have you come to the middle of Cartooga-Thaat? Surely you must know your ship would have never made it across the star desert."

"We were not crossing the great star desert, Leucadia. We were traveling to a new home within Cartooga-Thaat."

"What happened? Your ship was nearly destroyed."

"We don't know. We never saw them. Our ship was programmed with predetermined coordinates. The Tels were being persecuted and killed by their overseers on Patol. I could not allow that to continue; so with all the quantums I had left, I found them a ship and we traveled here, knowing it was a one way journey. It was a risk they were willing to take. They are a peace-loving people, Leucadia. All they wanted was a place to call home and to live free like your America and my father's planet, Tomar."

"You were traveling to a place inside the Thaat?" Leucadia asked.

"Even a desert has islands of life. We journey to Tabilisi. It is an ancient trading center where ships stop before before continuing their journey across the star desert."

"Our sensors have not detected any forms of life or stars for a hundred lightyears in all directions," Leucadia told her.

"Tabilisi is starless. She belongs to no star system and cannot be detected in the usual manner by your sensors. She was created by my ancestors many thousands of passings ago. Tabilisi is there, I assure you, Leucadia."

Leucadia went to the wall of holographs and pulled up a star chart. "Our ship is on an unknown course." She pointed along a straight, blue line on the star chart. "Would your Tabilisi be here?"

Quay's eyes did not bother to look at the map. She already knew. "Yes."

"But why would our ship set course for this destination on her own?"

"Your ship is Gamadin."

"Yes."

"Then that is the reason. All Gamadin ships would come to Tabilisi on their way through Cartooga-thaat."

"Why?"

"Because Tabilisi is a Gamadin outpost," Quay replied.

Leucadia's eyes brightened with hope. "Then *Millawanda* would do the same?"

"Yes, if *Millawanda* traveled this way, Tabilisi would be her stopover. Her navigational systems are failsafe. She would know no other option."

Leucadia felt a sense of optimism. She didn't know how much thermo-grym fuel Harlowe had managed to gather on Nod, but she was almost certain it was not enough to cross the Thaat. According to Quay, even with adequate fuel, Harlowe would have no other option open to him but to stop at Tabilisi.

Her hope suddenly turned to fear when she thought of the one thing that would have kept him from the desert outpost: Harlowe was illogical!

He may have made it to Tabilisi, but she doubted he would have stayed there long unless the Gamadin outpost had the facilities to fix *Millawanda*. Her heart raced. If that were the case, he could still be there. If not, this was still the only course he could have taken. Now she knew why *Forty-four's* guidance control had taken over. She was taking them to Tabilisi as she was programmed to do.

Relieved that her ship's course change was no sinister plot, she had one more question for Quay before she let her rest.

"Would the Gamadin base have a maintenance facility at Tabilisi?" Leucadia asked, extremely hopeful.

Quay was tired from the conversation and laid her head back down on the table. Through closed eyelids her exhausted reply was brief. "Of course."

88

Surwags

At the top of the dam, they found the monument Isara had spoken of. In reality it wasn't a monument at all but electrical towers built to support the power lines from the dam. It seems the Tappers weren't the first to use the river running through the steep gorge to produce energy. The Gamadin had as well and on a massive scale. From the looks of the structural remains of the ancient dam along the sides of the cliffs, the dam had once been several hundred feet higher than it was today, making the reservoir triple the size in the volume of water it held. It would have been enough to power twenty Ragoss-size cities with ease, Harlowe reckoned.

Another quarter mile away, following the ridgeline, were more towers peeking above the trees. Harlowe wondered what city they served, or could they have powered some massive industrial complex or even a military base? Maybe all three. The power generated by such a humungous dam certainly made that a possibility. On another positive note, a secondary line of towers seemed to branch away from the main towers and lead toward the coast. Although Nath had never seen the pass, his ancestors had, that is, before the Surwags occupied the area. Nath described them as heartless crowlings. "Not even Tappers have invaded the Surwags' land," he said, spitting at the ground. His hate ran so deep, he detested even to speak their name as he went on. "They are foul spirits, and when they find you, they roast you and eat your bones."

By the time the Fagans reached the top of the dam by the primitive switchbacks, it was too dark to go on. Their mounts were sweaty and tired. Everyone was exhausted. The wide, grassy area next to the first tower made a good place to bed down for the night. The stop also gave Monday and Harlowe time to study the towers more closely. If they held any clues about Lamille, he was determined to find it.

While everyone rested, Harlowe let Mowgi find his evening meal. The undog needed no urging. He took off, drooling buckets over his first meal. While he was tending to Mowgi, Monday was preparing Bigbob to search the forest ahead for Surwags or anything else that might give them problems. "You're off, big guy," he said, patting the tall robob's head.

"Be home by midnight, or you're grounded," Harlowe added, walking up. Those words, or something similar, came from Harlowe's mother, Tinker, who would often say that to him just before walking out the door with Riverstone. The one time Harlowe tried to protest the early curfew because Riverstone got to stay out as late as he wanted, Buster, Harlowe's dad, pulled him aside with some fatherly advice. "You really want to go there, Harlowe?" The risk of being even one minute late had its consequences. Tinker never told him what the downside would be, but being thrown through a window at the age of nine for not taking out the trash when she told him to had always been his marker buoy. Harlowe rethought his position, "Thanks, Dad," and let the matter slide. Curiously, though, after he and Lu became an item, the curfew was never an issue. His parents never waited up for him when they were out, even if it was way past midnight. But on game nights, Leucadia always made sure he was in bed by nine. And that was also the end of THAT story.

Bigbob's head cocked to one side as if to say, "Huh?"

Harlowe waved him on without explanation. "Go on. Don't let anyone see you." The tall clicker tipped his head and leaped off in loping strides, disappearing into the dense forest in a blink. If Bigbob found anything of interest, or if he ran into any kind of trouble, the big clicker would contact Harlowe immediately, sending back sensory readouts that placed him at the scene in real time. He could even control Bigbob's movements if he wanted, like changing direction, grasping something with his pincers, or visually examining objects with multi-level optics just like he would with his own bugeyes.

With Bigbob scouting the forest ahead and the girls sleeping by their grazing ceffyls, Harlowe and Monday made their way to the small plateau where the first tower was located. The structure was fascinating. Even in its deteriorated state, the tower was still recognizable. Most of its structure was missing, but its support legs were still over a hundred feet high. The fact that there were so many left after hundreds of centuries was remarkable. Even Gamadin dura-metal has its limits. *Millawanda* had survived so long because she was sealed in a tomb away from the elements. Even so, without a routine maintenance schedule programed into the core of her memory banks, she might have disintegrated to rubble eons ago.

"Think they're Gamadin?" Harlowe asked Monday, as they studied the remains of the footings that were once tall structures that carried the power lines.

"Maybe," Monday guessed.

"That's all you have to say is 'maybe'?"

"That's all I know."

"That looks like dura-metal, doesn't it?"

"It's a stretch."

"Think positive, Squid."

Monday shrugged. "Okay, it's Gamadin dura-metal."

Harlowe smiled. "That's the spirit."

Looking along the terraced level leading away from the dam, they saw the second structure a short distance away. "If we head in that direction and through that pass," Harlowe speculated, looking up the side of the far mountains, "I bet we find more towers."

"Or Lamille."

"Yeah, that would make my day." Harlowe tapped his wrist activator, wondering if the big clicker had found anything by now. He was about to check in with the clicker when Mowgi flew in out of the night, doing his prancing thing. With his parabolics twisting and turning like scanning radar dishes, then zeroing in toward the direction Bigbob had gone through the trees, it appeared the undog was onto something. Ever since the river back at Ragoss, Harlowe was sensitive to the undog's gyrations. Harlowe and Monday didn't ask why. They donned their Gamadin hoodies and instantly transported themselves into Bigbob's virtual world, jogging stride for stride along with the robob through the forest.

"Bigbob's on it," Monday commented.

With the robob's super strength, he leaped over thick vines, grabbed a branch like Tarzan, swung across a short ravine, and dropped down next to a pile of rocks. There wasn't much to see. But what got both their attentions was when Bigbob flipped over a large section of the ancient tower and saw what none of the other towers had: a Gamadin symbol, rather part of one, and that part was unmistakeable. Harlowe smiled. "Now that's cool."

Monday kept watching the undog with interest. "He's still torqued, Captain."

"Yeah, not good," Harlowe said as he quickly verified the railroad bed veering away from the lake toward the mountain pass. He was about to break the connection with Bigbob to concentrate more on Mowgi's behavior when the robob's sensors picked up movement coming fast from the easterly mountain pass. The distance was over two miles away, but the beings were unmistakeable. They leaped and jumped like a swarm of locust devouring whatever life form got in their way. Besides powerful legs, they had long arms, and thick, hairy bodies with large heads. What he saw could only be the beings everyone had warned him about . . . the Surwags. One thing was certain. The Surwags weren't out jogging on a Sunday evening. They were headed straight for their campsite. At the speed the mass was traveling, Harlowe figured they would be at Bigbob's position in minutes. That meant they had less than fifteen to book it back to camp and warn the others.

Clank! Thunk!

A metal projectile careened off Bigbob's triangle-shaped head and buried itself in a nearby tree. If the clicker had been a human, the shaft would have passed through his head like warm butter. Not only were the Surwags fast, they were down right killer shots on the run. Harlowe wasn't sure how much abuse the big clicker could take. No doubt the robob's Gamadin metal was tougher than any metal on the planet, but he wasn't going allow Bigbob to stand around and be a target. He signaled his big robob for a fast return while he and Monday split for camp. They had hardly gone a mile when they heard the roar of the Surwag mass coming through the forest. Fifteen minutes was a pipe dream. They had less than five.

Mowgi was his usual self. If Harlowe would have let him, he would have taken on the entire mob by himself. As tough as Mowgi was, he wasn't Robob tough. The thought of the undog turning into a pincushion sent shivers up his spine. "No, Mowgi!"

That was all it took. Itching for a few good heads to eat, the undog reluctantly backed off. With his incisors fully extended, he let out a godawful roar that shook the forest before he fell in line with Harlowe, shaking with seething disappointment the whole way back to camp.

They didn't have time to gather their things. The ceffyls were already alerted by the time Harlowe cried out "Surwags!" coming into the camp. Isara jumped out of her sleeping blanket the moment she heard the ceffyls first snort of alarm. Oea handed Monday his reins as they both mounted like a crack equestrian team. While Monday and Oea charged ahead to scout the pass back down the cliff, Harlowe and Isara stayed behind to cover Nath and his riders, who were all saddled and ready.

"Go, go, go!" Harlowe urged, as he counted the seven riders, making sure no one was left behind.

As the last rider passed by, Isara took off next, followed by Harlowe right on her ceffyls' big toes. Suddenly, Monday's voice came across Harlowe's com in a controlled urgency. "Tappers, Captain."

"Tappers?" Harlowe called back in disbelief, thinking that was quick even for Tappers. They hadn't even waited for daybreak.

"They came up the valley and are closing the gates. Three gerbids are standing by to push giant blocks of granite against the doors. Looks like they intend to seal us in, Captain."

Harlowe galloped to the ledge and saw the bright headlights of the gerbids flooding the gorge. As the Tappers put the finishing touches on the giant blocks against the gates, Harlowe understood a little more about the gates. They weren't there to keep anyone from entering the dam. They were there to keep Surwags from coming out of the gorge.

From what Harlowe could see, there was no escape. When he turned and looked up the gorge, the Surwag torches were lighting up the forest. With Tappers below the dam and the Surwags above the dam, they were sandwiched. The only way open to them was blocked by the fast moving river. If they entered here, no one would survive. They would all go over the spillway and plunge two thousand feet to the rocks below. Neither Tappers nor Surwags took prisoners. Even Mowgi saw the writing. He was breathing deeply, moments away from turning himself into what, no doubt, a Surwag would consider terrifying. Harlowe checked his sidearm. They had brought plenty of ammo but not enough to take down the horde that was coming. Harlowe's eyes met with Monday's as the first Surwags came through the trees. "Ready?"

Monday checked his weapon and nodded. "Aye."

89

Tabilisi

"Forty-four is stopping, Captain," Leucadia announced.

They had been traveling toward the center of Cartooga-Thaat for two days. In all that time, traveling at far beyond the speed of light, they had not seen or passed a single star. It was creepy and unnerving to travel a hundred lightyears with nothing in between.

"We're there, huh?" Ian asked surprised, for as hard as he looked through the forward window, he saw nothing but the black void of space.

"Coordinates verified, Captain," Leucadia confirmed.

Cheesa added, "Sensors indicate structure ahead, Captain." She turned in her chair, her face large with wonder. "Of incredible size, sir!"

To Ian's alarm there was indeed a massive structure on the overhead screen drifting all alone in the blackness, directly ahead of them. It was shaped like two rings, one smaller ring floating inside a much greater outer ring.

"We are here," Quay said with such confidence, she never looked up at the screen to confirm what the sensors showed her. She knew! Standing around her was a small group of Tels that Ian had allowed on the bridge to witness the event.

"You're certain?" Ian asked, unsure the middle of the void is where he wanted to leave eighty-two people and children in the darkness.

"Yes, this is Tabilisi, our new home," Quay assured him.

"All right. Let's take a peek then," Ian nodded toward Dev. "Forward

427

lights, if you please, Dev."

Dev reached across his console and slid his hand across a green, lighted bar. Instantly, bright beacons illuminated the inky void ahead.

"Wow," Ian gasped, marveling at the immense size of the rings. "What are the large holes on the sides of the large ring," he asked, turning to Quay.

"They are the portals to Tabilisi itself. Inside is where we will make our new home," she said.

Ian had extreme doubt about how such a dead structure could be turned into any kind of environmentally safe haven for anyone to survive. "You're expecting to live here?"

The way Quay looked at Ian, unaffected by the impossibility of such an undertaking, there was no doubt in his mind that she at least believed it. "Of course. This is where our freedom begins."

Ian wanted to laugh. If Riverstone or Simon were here, they would be rolling on the floor in hysterics about now. Make a place that had been dead for thousands of years habitable? Ha, ha, ha... yeah, right. He didn't even crack a smirk when he caught an evil eye from Leucadia that said in no uncertain terms, don't even think about jinxing her plan. Coming around to Cheesa for a sympathy vote he got nothing but the same look. They were all ganging up on him. Dev was the only one who had no clue as to what the silent banter was all about.

Lucky him!

"Okay," Ian said, turning back to the overhead closeups of the torus rings. Once Quay saw there was nothing she could do to make Tabilisi livable again, he would find them a nice, new world with an atmosphere and a bright, warm sun to call home where they could live happily ever after. In the meantime, Tabilisi needed a close inspection before they dropped in unannounced. "Let's see what we have to work with. Ahead, slow Chee. Take us around for a tour."

* * *

After several exploratory passes around the rings with no unusual sensor reading that suggested any danger to the ship, Ian gave the go ahead to enter through one of the large access portals. Easing into the bowels of the main torus was unnerving. The silence, the blackness, and the absolute creepiness of flying into a city that had once been the home of millions felt eerie, like they were walking across a graveyard. At least in a graveyard there was a full moon to see the headstones, and owls making creepy noises, and ghosts floating by as they haunted the night. Here it was spookier, making the hairs on his neck stand even straighter.

What would they find upon closer inspection? Bodies? Like the ones Harlowe and Leucadia found on Hitt? Ugh… He hoped not. Why had the Tabilisians abandoned the city in the first place, he wondered? How would the Tels survive if there was no power? How long could *Forty-four* protect them before they had to leave? *Millawanda* needed her crystals now, so remaining long to fix things was out of the question. Where was Harlowe? Had Millie run out of thermo-grym yet? They could already be stranded somewhere in the Thaat. If that were true, then on what course had they taken *Millawanda*? How far away was she now? It was such a huge galaxy. The odds of finding Orixy were off the charts. So many questions, so many decisions to make, yet so little time, and not one hint as to whether his judgments were right or wrong or whether he was taking his new crew on a course to certain death.

Harlowe spoke in Ian's ear. *Sitting in the chair is never easy, Wiz.*

Ian's eyes drifted across the bridge from one station to the next. Dev's eyes were straining at the weapons array while doing double duty watching the sensor screens for threats. Cheesa was no less focused, helping Leucadia with sensors and watching out for any suspicious fluctuations or power surges that could be threats as they cruised slowly toward the main city. This was the first time Dev and Cheesa had been put to the test. So far they were handling their roles dutifully. They had a long way to go before they could be considered part of a real Gamadin crew, but their hours of training were paying off. Maybe one day, he thought, if they survived, they could be one of them.

"All quiet, Captain," Leucadia reported, when they were a good mile inside the main torus ring.

"Very well," Ian acknowledged; then to Cheesa he said, "All stop, Chee, if you please."

"Aye, Captain," she replied. "All stop."

Outside *Forty-four* was total darkness. It was as if they had ventured into a black hole. Except for the little saucer's perimeter, blue light, no light penetrated the torus ring. Although no one could actually see the city ahead, the bridge's upper screen displayed a vast network of tall buildings, rail systems, malls, miles of streets, city parks and lakes. All the physical aspects of a major metropolitan center were there. Only this city wasn't flat. It curved around the torus circle like it was built inside the outer rim of a tire. There was no down, only up. Looking skyward, one would see the tops of other buildings miles above their heads. But nothing fell.

"Why is the ball hanging from the center?" a little girl asked, holding her mother's hand as she stared at the main display above.

Quay bent down to her and kissed her on the head before she answered. "That is Tabilisi's sun, Mei. When the power is restored to our new home, it will glow bright as Patol's sun. It will follow a path along the inner circle to bring day to those who live below it. As it travels along it will disappear, and there will be night. When it returns, it will bring morning and the day-night cycle will begin again."

Ian caressed Molly's silky white neck as she sat next to his command chair studying the darkness. He wondered how far she could see without light. "Time to set light globes, Chee. Let's see what Tabilisi looks like all lit up."

"Yes, Captain," Cheesa said, following Ian's command.

Moments later brilliant globes of light flew out from Forty-four's upper hull to prearranged positions high in the torus sky, illuminating the interior like fifty tiny suns. Bathed in the light like it was high noon everywhere, mouths dropped open at the sight of the gigantic city below them. The architecture was modern and efficient with lots of glass, metal beams, grids, and open balconies. There was no need for protection from the weather because Tabilisi's inner torus controlled it. There was no hot sun, no wind, no rain, no snow or dust storms. Every day was perfect, every day was the same inside the torus.

Quay pointed to a large, open area several thousand feet above their heads. "Can we land there, Ian? It appears to be a good place to begin," she said.

Before giving the go-ahead, Ian glanced over at Leucadia for her opinion. Being in control of the sensors, she was the ultimate authority on where to land or not. "It is near a frozen lake that is surrounded by a large open area. I agree with Quay. It will be a fine place to put down, Captain."

As Ian drifted Forty-four upward, he rolled the saucer over so the buildings were upright for everyone looking through the forward window. He silently went along the main avenue between the tall, glass structures allowing everyone to view the city and hopefully their new home. The near absolute zero temperature and airless interior had been a perfect preservative. Even after thousands of passings, the streets and structures all appeared like they never aged.

Soon they came out to the open area Quay had seen from below. As they drifted over a curious, circular building near the lake, Ian couldn't help but think how this building seemed out of place among the other glass and steel structures of the city across the lake. It was enormous, too, like a great sports arena might look back on Earth. Yet, there were no gates or doorways for people to enter. Cheesa found it fascinating as well, and as they were moving over the building, she pointed to a marking along the outer wall of the building, "Is that symbol not the same as what is above our bridge, Captain?" she asked, looking at the Gamadin symbol above the rear wall of dancing lights.

Both Ian and Leucadia stood frozen in disbelief. There was no doubt about it in both their minds. The symbol on the circular building was indeed Gamadin.

Ian slowly murmured, "Harlowe was here."

90

Nath's Hidy-Hole

*N*ath shouted at Oea to follow him as he and his posse mounted up and headed toward the river. Harlowe and Monday saw no reason to be trapped by the lake. Harlowe would rather stay right here and take his chances. But Isara was having none of that. "Harlowe!" she shouted at him. It wasn't a request. This was no time for heroics. A flying hatchet nearly split her head open, but Harlowe shot it out of the sky. Then Mowgi got into the act, slicing, dicing, and ripping off heads as Harlowe dropped seven more Surwags with his pistol. Even for the undog, the numbers were overwhelming. Harlowe had to do something quick. He mounted his black, called the undog, "We're out of here, Mowg!," and charged after Isara.

Harlowe figured the Fagans knew the area, but a quick scan with his sensors revealed no way out. The reservoir lake blocked their way for miles in both directions. Even if they found a path along the shoreline, they only had a short distance before the vertical cliffs of the ancient valley cut them off.

Was there a choice here?

Harlowe shouted a string of curses as Mowgi scampered to the front of his saddle. While he tried lagging behind to cover Isara and Monday's backs, he couldn't wait long. It was time to scoot when he ducked two spears, blasted another hatchet that nearly struck his black, and saw the dozens of Surwags leaping out of the forest. He charged ahead, following groups of hoof prints that were easy to see, but when he hit the hard rocks, the trail disappeared, and so did everyone else, leaving him all alone with the Surwags.

Fortunately for him, his ceffyl seemed to know the way. Ducking under low-hanging branches, the shoreline suddenly vanished, and he was a couple of hundred feet above it, galloping along a narrow path. With raging, white water below and another hundred feet of rocky cliff above him, all Harlowe could think to do was hold on. How his black managed to stay on the narrow path without slipping he hadn't a clue. There seemed barely enough room for a human to walk. The rocks that broke away and thunked into the water below, never fazed the ceffyl. Mowgi wasn't breaking a sweat, either. Even if the black slipped off the edge, all he had to do was take to the air, and he was cool. For a nanosecond Harlowe thought of deploying his SIBA wings, too, but no, the black and he were pards. They had ridden too far together to watch him fall to a crushing death alone. He was sticking with the black no matter what, just like he would one of his crew.

And on they went, with Harlowe gritting his teeth at various times when he thought for sure they were about to eat it. When he and the black finally broke onto a wider path, Isara and her ceffyl were leaping from the end of the path to another impossible spit of rock that would frighten a mountain goat. Before Harlowe could take a breather from the last trail, his black followed Isara over the side and down the nearly vertical descent.

OMG!

Needless to say, Harlowe's eyes were shut all the way to the bottom of the cliff. When his black leaped out to a horizontal shoreline running next to the river that was only a few feet wide, Harlowe felt like he was driving on Interstate 5, cruising south in Baby headed toward Newport. When he looked back over his shoulder, it was no surprise to see Surwag daks falling off the side of the cliff to a gruesome death as they tried to negotiate the same path he and his ceffyl had miraculously crossed. They were almost to another turn in the river when Harlowe caught sight of long, vine-like ropes being tossed from the top of the cliff. Like a hive of army ants, the Surwags began rappelling down the vines in droves. Looking ahead, Nath and his posse were dismounting where the cliff wall stopped beside a river. This made no sense to Harlowe. There was no more shoreline and no more path for their mounts to run on. The first wave of Surwags was so close it sounded like the bloodthirsty screams and howling were right in his ear.

As Harlowe rode toward the Fagans, all could see was a dead end. Nath was leading his riders around the corner of the cliff onto what had to be a submerged pathway at the river's edge. Sloshing in foot-deep water, he was careful to keep his mount close to the cliff as he went. The other Fagans followed his lead, each in a narrow line. But when one Fagan tried to pass another rider, his mount slipped, falling into the river. Both rider and mount were sucked into the current before anyone could help them. Down river, a swarm of Surwag spears struck them both with rope vines attached to the ends. Like grisly pincushions, they were reeled into shore and were quickly cut into pieces with long knives and hatchets.

Harlowe wanted to throw up. If it weren't for his SIBA controlling his spasms, he would have lost it. Watching one of Nath's riders go down felt like he had lost one of his own crew.

Isara turned him away from the scene. "Come, Harlowe. We must hurry."

Oea went next, then Monday. Isara motioned for Harlowe to go first, but a spear clanking off a nearby rock nixed that idea. Harlowe shot the spear-chucker and four more Surwags before he exchanged an empty ammo clip for a full one. Isara saw his point. As good as she was with her own weapon, she was not in the same league as Harlowe. She grabbed her ceffyl and disappeared around the rock corner. Harlowe plucked off another score of Surwags before he made the black go ahead of him. When the dark, bushy tail disappeared behind the corner, Harlowe jumped in the water, took out two more Surwags, and strode off for the others. Five steps later, he slipped, worrying about what was behind him more than where he was stepping. He fell below the water line and was nearly grabbed by the current when a strong hand snared him, pulling him back to ledge. Heart pounding and feeling like a dweeb, he met Isara's eyes asking him what-were-you-doing?

"I was thirsty," was his lame comeback.

Isara didn't laugh. The embarrassment was enough.

They splashed along for a short distance until they came to an opening in the cliff wall. Behind them, dozens of screaming Surwags were being consumed by the river as they tried to follow them around the corner. Harlowe wondered how high the body count would go before they figured out a workaround. He never doubted for a moment, nor did anyone else, that they were safe for long. They had only bought a little time.

"How did you find this place?" Harlowe asked Nath.

"The river is lower in the dry season. I wounded a *bemarn,* and it came this way to die," Nath replied, holding up the giant claw around his neck.

Harlowe was impressed and patted Nath on the back. In the last thirty minutes, his respect for the Fagan leader had grown ten-fold.

Looking in at the tunnel entrance, Harlowe asked, "Where does it go?"

Nath gave a short shrug. He didn't know. He never ventured farther back than where the daylight penetrated.

Monday touched Harlowe's shoulder to bring his attention back to the cave opening. "It doesn't look natural, Captain."

The entrance was full of broken rocks that had fallen from the cliff above. But there were small sections in the mouth that appeared carved out by machine rather than dug out by flowing water or some other natural force.

There was no time to analyze it further. They had to keep moving. One of Nath's riders stepped up and pointed back to the submerged ledge. Just as Harlowe feared, the Surwag had improvised a workaround. They were pounding their spears into the stone cracks of the cliff and attaching their vine ropes to them for a handrail.

"I'll take it from here," Harlowe said.

"But how will we walk without light?" Nath asked as he stared doubtfully into the blackness of the cave.

Harlowe handed Nath the small flashlight he had shown the group earlier at the dam. He showed him how to turn it on and off and adjust the beam's intensity. Monday switched his on and handed it to Oea.

"What about you? How will you see?" Nath asked.

Monday pointed at his bulbous bugeyes. "With these," he replied.

Harlowe pointed at the cave. "Go with Monday," he told Nath.

The Surwags had reached the halfway point with their guardrail. Now and then a Surwags would lose his footing and be swept away by the river, but for the most part, their vine rail was a success. Surwags were already lined up along the cliff, backside to bellybutton, shouting like frenzied beasts at nearing their prey. Soon their best spear-chuckers would be in range of their mounts. Harlowe or Monday could pluck the horde all day long, but the number of Surwags could outlast their ammo. They needed to conserve what clips they had left for whatever lay ahead.

Harlowe nodded at the undog. "You're up, Mowg. Find us a safe path." If there was anything hostile inside the cave, Harlowe knew Mowgi would handle it. He then turned to find the black, but to his surprise the ceffyl was right behind him, ready to follow him into the darkness like a faithful dog. Harlowe reached up and ran his fingers through his steed's long, silky mane as he touched his head with his like he would another Gamadin. They had only been together for five short days, but already he felt they had been pards all their lives. At that moment Harlowe could not bring himself to harness the black ever again. He removed his bridle, releasing the headstall from around his head and the bit from his mouth. He wound the reins around it all and tossed it into the river. There was no time for any rite of passage. The Surwags were steps away. "You're free . . .ah, ah…" His mind went blank. Black had no name. *How uncool was that?* There was no time for thought. No time to get all teary-eyed about the baptizing. *It's just name him, dude!* And blurted out the first word that popped into his head. "Delamo." Why he had chosen the name of the street where he grew up in Lakewood? He hadn't the slightest idea. It was crazy. But staring at his black eyes all proud, majestic, strong, and devoted, he could think of no other name that felt so right. Delamo it was!

"Go with Mowgi, Delamo," he said, pointing the way into the tunnel.

* * *

When everyone, mounts and all, were a good distance from the opening, Harlowe removed his sidearm and attached an explosive head to the front of the barrel. He ordered everyone to cover their ears as he aimed at the tunnel roof.

KAABLUUUWEY!

The detonation did its work, collapsing the entrance and sealing them in.

Nath, who had his flashlight on high, was stunned like everyone else by the sudden cave in. Harlowe re-holstered his sidearm and walked casually away from the settling dust. "Lets hope there is a back way out of this place," he remarked, as he went on to catch up with Mowgi and Delamo.

91

Big Prints

Parked at the edge of the frozen lake, while standing with Leucadia and Dev a quarter mile away beside the immense, round Gamadin building of glass, golden beams, and doorless walls, Ian admired his new ship. The small, artificial sun, and many others like it, glowed a thousand feet above their heads, spreading light upon a frozen world that had remained in darkness for eons.

"You're so hot," Ian said, beaming with pride at *Forty-four*. Sleek and cool, watching her, all radiant and clean, his heart raced, his chest tightened, honored to be her latest custodian. Shiny upper decks, sloping dome, powerful, she was poised, ready do whatever was asked of her.

With a crowd of Tels around her, Quay, looking purposeful in the SIBA Harlowe had given her, stepped through the forcefield, leaving her followers behind *Forty-four's* protective wall. She switched on her thrusters, rose above the bright globes, then leaned forward, jetting across the frozen lake, the treetops, and the tall buildings, rising higher and higher as she went. "She is very good," Leucadia uttered in a tone that had more meaning behind it than spoken words.

"She had plenty of practice on number 2," Ian said.

"And a good teacher, no doubt."

Ian turned to Leucadia, his posture a little bent, wondering where the conversation was going. "Everyone helped her, Lu. She was a quick study."

"Everyone?"

437

Ian tried to slip by the question. "You should see her hit a baseball."

"Everyone?" she asked again.

"Yeah, everyone," Ian emphasized. "Riverstone and Rerun were falling all over themselves to help her."

"I can imagine." After an uncomfortable silence, Leucadia dropped the other shoe. "And Harlowe? Did he fall all over her, too?"

"No. He didn't have—" Ian stopped short of finishing his thought, knowing he had just stepped in it, big time.

"He didn't have to. Is that what you were going to say, Ian?" On personal matters of this nature, Leucadia dropped the job titles.

"Lu, you were dead, remember? What do you expect a guy like Harlowe to do, become a Tibetan monk or something?"

"No. I just wanted to see who won the prize."

"She's a hot babe. We all wanted her."

"But Harlowe won." It was a statement, not a question.

Ian looked at her sternly. "I need to tell you that?"

"No. I just needed to see how serious it was, and you just told me."

Ian felt like he had been sucker-punched. He stepped away from her, shaking his head. Arguing with her over something out of his control was pointless. Harlowe never did anything wrong. He never went looking for Quay. What happened between them, happened. There was no other way to describe it. Who else was she going to fall for but the guy who saved her life? It was a natural thing, like night and day, Romeo and Juliet…and women and chocolate.

Ian followed Quay as she flew straight for the torus opening. According to her father, Anor Ran, Tabilisi's power core remained intact. All she needed to do was switch it on.

Yeah, he thought, watching her tiny speck pass through an opening. *If she came on to me like she did Harlowe, would I have kissed her? Duh! Who wouldn't!*

After Quay flew out of visual range toward the inner ring, Ian refocused his attention on the Gamadin building. In an effort to patch things up, he started slowly with a little harmless conversation. "The Gamadin built everything to last, didn't they?"

Leucadia made only a short, guttural sound that made no sense. Dev, on the other hand, had no idea what was going on between them. For him, it was business as usual. "How do we get inside, Captain?" he asked, kinking his head up at the hundred foot wide Gamadin symbol emblazoned across the outer wall.

Ian held his answer as he marveled at the structure, wondering how extensive the Gamadin network was throughout the galaxy. They had been its protectors for over a thousand years, which seemed like plenty of time to establish bases and outposts, he figured. The biggest question for him and Leucadia, when she was talking, was where was Harlowe now? Had he found the way to Orixy yet? If he had, what road had he taken? Like traveling from San Diego to New York, the destination was clear but the highway to get there, not so much. Harlowe may have taken *Millawanda* north through North Dakota while he was taking *Forty-four* south through Oklahoma. How would they know? And what if *Millawanda* ran out of fuel between here and Montana, how could they find them unless they traveled the same road? Without direction, the crystals they had were useless.

"The door is here, Dev. It's just not like the ones we're used to," Ian finally replied.

"Will I know it if I see it?" Dev asked.

Ian thought it would speed up the search if they all looked. "Yeah, maybe, but stay in visual range," he cautioned.

This was the first opportunity for Dev to use his SIBA wings. The Prince started out doing short sorties in *Forty-four's* storage area, but now that the area was occupied by the Tels, there was no place to practice before his first real-world flight. His first attempt nearly ended in disaster when instead of yawing, he pitched, and ended up skidding across the frozen lake, embarrassing himself in front of a crowd of Tel onlookers who got a belly laugh at his expense. Before he found himself implanted in a frozen tree, Ian and Leucadia picked him off the ice and carried him to the round building. The reduced gravity was about as easy as walking on Earth's moon, which Ian had done several times. That made carrying the Prince like lifting a pillow instead of a sack of potatoes. Without power, Tabilisi had gradually slowed her rotational speed. The slowdown was constant, enabling Leucadia to calculate within a few decades when the lights actually went dark. Nine thousand four hundred thirty-seven years ago was her calculation.

"The Gamadin round structure has the same circumference as Millie," Leucadia commented, apparently coming out of her Harlowe funk.

A quick thought popped into Ian's head. "The roof could be a landing platform for a Millie-sized saucer."

"It would certainly hold her weight," Leucadia affirmed.

"If Harlowe came this way, you know he would have tried to find a way in," Ian said.

Leucadia turned her attention to the ground. "I see nothing to suggest he was here."

Ian thought out loud. "I can't imagine Harlowe missing Tabilisi if he crossed the Thaat. Millie would have guided him here, for sure."

"Agreed, but where's the evidence, Ian." She looked around a little concerned. "And where's Dev?"

Ian nodded to their right. "He was standing over there a second ago."

"Call him."

Ian switched his com to include the Prince. "Dev?"

Dev answered immediately. *"Captain?"*

"I told you to say in visual."

"Sorry, Captain. I'm around the curve," Dev replied.

"Did you see a way into the Gamadin building?" Ian asked.

"No entry, yet, Captain."

"Something else, Dev?" Leucadia asked. She could hear it in his voice that the young prince was preoccupied.

"Well, a few footprints and some round impressions. Nothing important. They kinda look like one of the clickers, but they're way too big," was Dev's casual reply.

Ian's and Leucadia's SIBA bugeyes met. "Ya think?" Ian said, feeling a jolt of excitement.

Ian took Leucadia by the hand and together they leaped their way around to Dev, who was touching the wall, trying to find the doorway. Ian identified the prints as Harlowe's the moment he saw them. Each Gamadin has his own unique SIBA print to identify him in case he needed to follow the other's trail.

"It's really Harlowe's?" Leucadia asked with a small crack in her voice.

It was the first solid evidence they were looking for. "Yeah, it's his, Lu," Ian replied reassuringly.

She knelt down beside his print and caressed the tiny particles of frozen dust as if she were touching a part of him.

"And those big riverboats are Monday's," Ian added with a snicker.

Leucadia reached over and felt Monday's prints as well. She missed them both terribly.

"And what about these big circles?" Dev asked of the round impressions intermixed with the others on the ground.

Ian looked them over confused. "They're clicker prints, all right. But they're way bigger than any clicker footprint I've ever seen." He turned to Leucadia. "What do you think?"

"Prints that size would make this robob over seven feet tall," Leucadia calculated.

Ian was convinced that this oversized clicker print didn't come from *Millawanda*. "Quincy is the biggest android I've ever seen, and he's got Monday sized feet."

Leucadia stood up and refocused her attention on the Gamadin building. "No doubt they found it here."

"That would mean they found a way inside," Ian surmised.

Leucadia followed the impressions to a portal-like framework in the wall. "The footprints would suggest you're right, Captain."

Dev touched the wall surface. "It's closed up, Captain. How can we get past the glass without breaking it?"

Ian ran his SIBA claws along the portal. "It may look like glass, Dev, but trust me, it's infinitely stronger than any glass or metal you've ever seen. We couldn't break it if we tried."

"They found a way in, Captain," Dev stated, feeling the portal glass with his SIBA claws. "We can, too."

Ian had no doubt in his mind. "I'm sure they did, Dev."

"How did they do it then, Captain?" the Prince asked.

Leucadia pulled the Prince aside, putting a claw to her lips. "Chill a moment, Dev, and let the Captain work his magic."

Ian stepped back from the wall and simply said, "Gamadin requesting entry." At first nothing happened. But the wait was short. A blue light suddenly snapped on over the portal header, scanning the three of them. A few more seconds went by and the glass dissolved in front of them, allowing them entry into the building.

"How did you know it was that simple?" Leucadia asked as they all peered down a long corridor.

Ian took the first step through the portal as he replied, "Remember, I said the same thing to *Forty-four*. It worked then, why not now?"

"After all this time, the security system is still activated. Wow!" Dev exclaimed, amazed.

"Yeah, lucky for us. Let's see what else still works," Ian said, but before going in he held Dev back with a stiff, but firm hand. "You need to stay outside, Dev," he ordered calmly.

Dev wanted to see the Gamadin station as much as they did. "Why can't I go inside? There is no one around to harm us."

"Because I need you here in case something does happen."

"But—"

Ian leaned into the Prince's face. "Dev. Stay put." When he was sure, he was understood, he continued on through the portal.

Leucadia took the Prince's arm. "Don't take it personally, Dev. The Captain would be neglecting his duty if he didn't leave someone guarding the portal," she explained.

Dev nodded, disappointed, but took up his position next to the portal with no more protest. Leucadia then followed Ian into the Gamadin structure. Taking orders from someone not of royal blood was still hard to accept at times. There were moments, like now, he wanted to tell Ian to guard his own portal. But he stayed. He wasn't quite sure why. Maybe it was the way he felt when he wore his SIBA, like he belonged to something bigger than any kingdom. "This is yours, Dev," Ian had said to him two weeks earlier when he handed him his own medallion. "You've earned your place here on *Forty-four*. Wear it with honor, Dev." And he did. He wore his SIBA medallion everyday, even when he didn't have to. He wore it to bed, to workout, to walk about the ship in his off-the-clock hours. He even tried to wear the SIBA on duty until Ian told him he was out of uniform. It's not for the bridge, Dev. Go change. So Dev stood guard over the portal even though he desperately wanted to go inside. He stayed because for the first time in his life he belonged to a team that he knew cared more for him than his title, and if he didn't follow orders, then wearing his SIBA meant nothing. There was no going back for him and no meaning to his life more dear to him than this crew he was now part of.

* * *

After two hours of searching, Ian and Leucadia rejoined Dev at the portal. The Prince's questions continued the moment they stepped through. "What did you find?" he asked.

Ian, head downcast, stepped by the Prince in silence like he was an inert post.

Leucadia came to his side, taking his arm as they stepped away from the portal. "When the Gamadin left, they took everything, Dev."

Suddenly, above their heads tiny lights began to flicker. Then across the lake, streetlights throughout the city went on. Ian nodded at the entry portal of Tabilisi where the intermittent shimmer of the force field flickered and then went steady. "She really did it," Leucadia said with disbelief.

"I found the power center," Quay said over the com, confirming their observations.

92

Bright Sunny Day

From a high bluff, Harlowe and the others gazed for miles upon the wide, crescent bay below them. The sun was hot and high overhead. The windy, warm, and salty, dry air that caressed his face reminded Harlowe of the Santa Ana's that blew in off the SoCal coast in the fall. The water was clear and green, and the waves that rolled across the long, white beach were glassy and perfectly formed, peeling right to left. Then as they broke, the low roar of their frothy, white lines became music to his ears. There was nothing like it in the universe, he thought. Back home, with surf and waves like this, he and Riverstone, more often than not, would miss their morning classes. School for them meant studying the waves at the crack of dawn.

"Not much here, Dog," Monday pronounced in such a way that one could feel the heart-felt regret that he bore for Harlowe's gambit. It appeared this was where his all-in, do or die, against all odds, and the impossibility of success ended, here, right now, on the bluff with nothing to show for his gambit but crumbled rocks, sweat, dirty clothes, new friends, Delamo, and a bright sunny day.

The morning had started with an upbeat air, too. Trekking through thirty miles of tunnel ended well. The far side only required a couple of well placed plas rounds to make an exit large enough to walk through. They found no Surwags at the end to greet them, either. Not yet, anyway. But no one believed they were out of danger. Inside Surwag land, death was but a hatchet or spear throw away. With weapons ready, they came out of the tunnel, slow and easy, listening for movement, vibrations, things that scratched or crawled, clanking spears, and godawful screams, all the while keeping a watchful eye on the ridge line, the shadows in the rocks, or anything that moved like ghosts around them. The Fagans' amazing sense of direction located an ancient road that led them through the narrow gorge, and by noon, they arrived at the bluff overlooking the coast. Incredible! Harlowe thanked Nath for his masterful guidance, knowing that without his help finding the bay they were after might have taken days of searching.

Harlowe gazed at the remnants of pillars in the shallow parts of the bay, a three hundred foot fragment of an archway, the corner of a structure, a broken, stone wall, and other indefinable lumps of things that were so worn, pitted, or broken had nothing to do with quest for aara. What was left of a once thriving city by the sea disappeared altogether a quarter mile out into the bay.

"There's enough, Mr. Platter. This is the place. This is Lamille," Harlowe stated in such a way that even if the crumbled ruins weren't Lamille, his will would make it so. They would look no farther than here for their aara.

"What do you expect to find here, Harlowe?" Nath asked, as he stared pathetically at the scattered, wave-beaten remains.

Harlowe leaped onto Delamo's back. "What we came for," he replied, full of confidence.

The others saddled up as Harlowe led them down the narrow path toward the beach. It was no casual ride, no take off your shirt and get a tan, no eagerness for a dip in the ocean. From the moment they left the tunnel, they saw no animals scurrying about, not a bird in the sky, and no fish in the streams they crossed. Except for the dull rumble of the ocean, an uneasy quiet prevailed. Each step down the path they took seemed inhospitable and chilling, as if Death was behind them the whole way.

According to the Fagans, the Surwags enjoyed the water about as much as the Wicked Witch of the West. For Surwags it was like being doused with battery acid. That was why Ragoss was built on one side of the river. It protected them from the beastly savages. Their "drink of choice" was the blood of creatures big and small, and unlike Bram Stoker's vampires back on Earth, Surwags had no aversion to spiritual crosses, wooden stakes, silver bullets, or daylight…only water. It was said a Surwag could run down a Fagan mount in a crazed thirst for its blood. To Nath and his riders, Surwags were more frightening than Darkn and a squadron of gerbids. As to whether they could outrun a ceffyl, Harlowe had no desire to find out. While he and Monday stayed behind to search the ruins, Isara, Oea, and the Fagans were to cross the nearest river to the north with their horses and ceffyls and wait for them there. No one liked the plan, especially Isara, whose concern for Harlowe was more like a mate than a friend. She insisted on staying with him even if it meant the Surwags sucking the life out of her.

Harlowe felt terrible. But Isara left him no choice. He shot her with a low powered plas round that only stunned her. She collapsed, and Harlowe laid her across her ceffyl with orders to Nath and Oea not to untie her until they were safely across the northern river. They were both so surprised by the swiftness of Harlowe's action that neither questioned his instructions.

Harlowe guided Delamo toward the north. "Now go, that's an order, big guy. And don't stop until you've reached the other side of the river."

Reluctantly, Delamo lumbered away, looking back now and then, in case Harlowe changed his mind. He didn't. The group disappeared around the rocky point at the far end of the bay, and that was that.

"Now what?" Monday wondered, his hands on his hips, eyeing the stacks of ancient rubble with doubt.

Harlowe tossed Bigbob out on the sand and watched the big clicker come to life next to Mowgi. "We start looking."

Monday shrugged. "Looking for what, Dog?" he asked, searching the shoreline for anything that made sense.

"Not here, Squid." Harlowe pointed at the bay. "Out there."

"In the ocean?"

"Lamille is underwater now. That's where we look." Harlowe removed a new power pack from his utility belt and snapped it in. He pointed at Monday's utility belt and added, "Better start with a fresh one. We may be out there awhile."

"You're serious?"

"I am."

Monday followed orders as Harlowe turned to Mowgi with instructions. "No dining on Surwags, Mowg. Get scarce. Kapish?"

Mowgi growled his disappointment.

Harlowe bent down to the yellow eyes. "Lu wouldn't like it if I brought you back lookin' like a pin cushion no would she?"

The undog growled, refusing to answer the question.

Harlowe patted him on the head. "Thatta boy." He energized his SIBA fully, bugeyes and all, made a quick, systems check, ratcheted his sidearm to high, remembering how many underwater beasts had nearly dined on him in the recent past, and then waved Monday and Bigbob toward the the water, hoping that any beasts they did see were shy.

93

Vanished!

"Ahlian!" Naree cried out. "Ahlian!"

Simon felt the shaking, waking him out of a deep sleep. Their transport rattled and shook like it was going to tear itself apart. Disoriented and confused, he had no idea where he was. For a brief instant he wondered who it was shouting in his ear.

"Ahlian, what is happening!" Naree wailed, panicked and frightened over the roar that followed.

"I don't know!" Simon shouted, holding on to anything he could grasp to keep himself from being thrown out of his seat. He looked out the window and saw a massive shadow coming to toward them. He instinctively stepped on the throttle and took off across the plain, oblivious of direction, only knowing that he had to get out of the area or die. The ground was in such a state of upheaval, their transport bounced and thumped in such gyrations it felt like the earth under them was about to explode. Then, just when they thought it could get no worse, a dreadful crack exploded overhead, forcing them sideways with its power. Simon twisted the steering wheel hard right, then an equally hard left, fighting for control. The transport nearly flipped, but somehow it righted itself, coming down flat, the shocks bottoming, screaming in protest as a blast of hot air violently pushed them forward, lifting them for what seemed like an eternity before they landed again, and the tires grabbed.

Through all the dust and mayhem, Simon bent around and saw a dark mass drift high overhead. It was firing great bolts at the plain where *Millawanda* had once parked. Again and again, thick, orange charges struck the impressions like they were trying to kill her anyway.

Simon wasn't waiting around to see if he was next on the list of targets. He slammed the throttle down and drove for miles and miles until thunder, the burst of charged light, and hurricane force winds were behind them, and they had reached the foothills of the mountains. He got out of the car and looked back from where they came. From a hilltop above the swirling clouds of dark dust, he saw the crater-sized blast hole as large as his ship. Then above him, the vibration shaking him to the bone, drew his attention to the immense black ship, slowly rising into the stratosphere like there was no force in the galaxy that would stop it. Simon's lips moved. The shape of the vessel was unmistakeable. "Mysterians…" The beings that had been dogging them the whole way since leaving the Omni Quadrant had crossed Cartooga-Thaat. They had found them at their weakest and were making sure that even her footprints were eradicated from existence.

Simon switched on his com. "Skipper!" he called in a panic as he watched with jaw-dropping awe, the power it had to defy Osset's gravity like it was nothing.

"Rerun?" Harlowe answered, his voice agitated. *"What's a matter? How's Millie?"*

"I don't know, Skipper. It's the Mysterians. They're here."

"They found Millie?"

"No, Skipper. I'm in a car headed back to the coast."

"Did they see you?"

"No, I don't think so. They were too busy shooting up the planet."

"Can you make it to the coast?"

"I can, Skipper."

"You have the abordar?"

"Yes. I still have it."

"Good. Get back to Millie at all costs, Rerun. That could be our last hope."

"Aye, Skipper. I will."

"And Naree?"

"She's here with me."

Then Riverstone broke in. *"Captain, Prigg says we have to go dark. If the Mysterians can cross the Thaat, they can find us all."*

"All right, then. Stay off the com until you need a ride. Harlowe out."

Then silence, like someone had crushed all their communicators with a sledgehammer.

Keeping his eyes on the Mysterians, Simon spoke out the side of his mouth to his open window. "Did you hear that, Naree?"

No one answered.

Simon came back to her, wondering why she was so silent. "Did you hear me? We have to keep driving for the…" He poked his head inside the door, expecting to see Naree in her seat, but she was gone, vanished. He scanned the surrounding country side. There was nothing but short grass and tiny shrubs, nothing large enough to hide anything but a small rabbit. He called out several more times, "Naree, Naree," he stepped around the transport and looked underneath. Nothing. He opened her side of the transport, thinking now about the most absurd places she could have slid into during the blast, like between the seats, or behind them, or who knows where. If there was trunk, he would have looked there. Still, there was no Naree anywhere. It was like someone or something had come along when he wasn't looking and plucked her off the face of the planet.

How does someone vanish into thin air, he asked himself, over and over and over? His focus went back across the plains where they had just driven, thinking she could have somehow fallen out or have been left behind in all the upheaval. But no, all he saw were tire tracks and crushed *Follish Pimars*.

"NAREEEEE!" he shouted so loudly the Mysterians could have heard him. He didn't care. He wanted to find her. After walking for nearly an hour in ever widening circles, his voice exhausted and hoarse, and finding nothing of Naree, not a single trace of clothing, hair, or God forbid, a body part, he returned to his transport and collapsed across the seat, drained of all emotion. "Naree…Naree…" he cried, his hand dropping to the floor where her feet had been. "Naree…" Then, as his hand touched the abordar where it must have fallen from her lap, he touched something angular and faceted. He stared at the object wondering where it had come from. He didn't remember it belonging to her or ever seeing it in her possession since the day they had met. Curious, he sat up, taking the fist-sized object in his hand, turning it around and around, up and down, examining it from every imaginable angle. It was light and grey with many sides, like a finely cut diamond. He tried seeing into it, but it was opaque and smooth like soft skin. He activated his bugeyes and scanned it with his probes. Under the gamma ray beam a rose color light glowed as if something were trying to get out.

"Naree?" he asked the object. "Is that you?"

94

Lamille

They had to hurry. Simon's contact put their mission further into overdrive than than it already was. Whatever sensor capabilities the Mysterian's had was only a guess. Whether they had probes sensitive enough to find his ship at the ocean bottom or not, Harlowe figured; they had to realize eventually they would find them. Riverstone would shut Millie down to a trickle of energy. That would help. Osset's earth-sized mass and even larger ocean was another plus for their side. But if their snooping systems were anything like Millie's...well, Harlowe prayed they weren't.

The sea floor was a gradual decline. A hundred yards out and they were still only hip deep in the small swells. Between the minor troughs, Monday asked Harlowe about tall clicker's swimming abilities. Harlowe chuckled. "Yeah, like a dolphin. Show 'em your breast stroke, Bigbob."

Monday's eyes went round when Bigbob dove forward, cutting his way through the surf, bouncing playfully over one wave to the next in sweeping arm strokes. Turning back to Harlowe, he asked, "How does he do that? He should be sinking like a rock."

Harlowe dove under the next wave beside Monday, continuing their conversation below the surface, moving fast in jet packs. "Prigg figured it out. Bigbob uses his forcefield to pull himself through the water like a caterpillar motor."

"Like in *Red October*? But that was pure fiction," Monday recalled.

"Yeah, but his isn't."

451

"Sweet."

And down they went, deeper and deeper, scooting along the bottom at better than twenty knots. The water was so clear and blue they felt like they were floating in air, allowing them to see for a great distance with their SIBA enhanced vision. The farther out they went, the more remains of the ancient city they found. Whether the ruins were Lamille was unimportant. The fact was they were two hundred feet below the surface and moving along at a good clip through an incredible complex of high towers, buildings, shops and avenues. Harlowe felt certain it was the city he was looking for. The buildings were no longer tall and architecturally modern. Time and the sea had taken their toll, but the streets and byways were still recognizable. They went gliding over what Harlowe called the main drag and followed it for a good way. They propelled by buildings that were empty frameworks, but teemed with brightly colored fish, crawling sea creatures, coral, and plant life growing freely and abundantly, in and out of the doorways and windows. Most of the sea life resembled their earthly cousins, but others, like the snake creatures with large feather-like fins at their sides, were strange to them. Watching the schools of sea life dart in and out of the crags and slits in the ancient ruins, it was difficult to believe the resort city was once the playground for the Gamadin.

"Fishing is good here," Monday observed.

"Stay alert," Harlowe cautioned. "Plenty of food means plenty of predators."

"Like that big boy coming toward us?" Monday questioned, pointing ahead. Something dark and slithery was making its way up the avenue. When it opened its maw to suck in water, its long sharp teeth stuck out like butcher's knives. It could swallow them both and never worry about picking its teeth.

"Yeah, like him," Harlowe concurred, heading for deeper water.

Their sudden change, however, caught the giant creature's attention. If Harlowe and Monday weren't on its menu plans before, they were now. They veered right and jetted between two buildings. The plan was a good one. The slithery thing was too big to fit through the narrow gap, but that didn't seem to matter as it opened its jaws and began sucking volumes of water through its open mouth. Harlowe and Monday tried to fight the current, but their jet packs weren't strong enough to overcome the sucking force. Tossing and tumbling toward a ghastly end, Harlowe tried unholstering his sidearm when it was suddenly ripped away from his grasp. Monday was in no better position to take a shot, even if he could have reached his sidearm. About the time they thought they would be chewed up, Bigbob shot down from above and jolted the creature's snout with a jagged bolt of blue fire, shocking the be-geezus out of the slithery thing. The creature quickly turned and headed off to the depths with its tail between its whatevers.

As Harlowe and Monday performed a systems check on their SIBAs, Monday asked, "What happened to your pistol?"

Harlowe responded unhappily. "The snake swallowed it."

"That was close."

"Yeah, too close."

"What did Bigbob zap it with?"

"Beats me. He's full of surprises." Harlowe then asked, "You okay?"

Monday returned a confident thumbs up as Bigbob swam beside them and gave them a once over of his own. His blue headband flickered and darted from side to side checking for any leaks. Harlowe tapped the big clicker on its chinahat and said, "Thanks." Bigbob nodded a silent okay, and together the three of them went on, picking up where they left off, traveling between structures, looking for anything Gamadin, even if it was an old shoe. Five miles later, they came to the end of the avenue. Farther out there was no more city. Their sensors indicated the ocean floor was flat and sandy and went on for another mile before it dropped off forever into a deep abyss.

Hovering above the ancient shoreline, Harlowe grumbled, "I was expecting to find something by now."

"It's a big city. Maybe we should separate. We could cover twice as much that way," Monday suggested.

The idea made sense, but Harlowe recalled the first rule of diving was always swim with a buddy. And after what happened earlier with the snake-creature, this was no time to separate, even if things weren't going their way. "No. We stay together. What's your power?"

"Over seventy," Monday replied.

"I'm close to that. We'll keep going until one of us hits twenty," Harlowe suggested.

"Roger that. Where's Bigbob?" Monday asked, turning around slowly in his search for the big clicker. He had been like a shadow since the snake.

Harlowe initiated contact with Bigbob through his com. To his startled amazement, Bigbob's visuals put him directly in front of a luxurious, five-star hotel lobby.

Monday saw the same visual. "He's that way a few blocks," he said, flicking his claw along the ancient shoreline.

Harlowe wondered how they could have missed the structure coming in. Unlike all the other buildings among the ruins, it was well preserved. Or maybe they missed it because it lacked the typical modest, blue look of a Gamadin-styled structure. He never imagined a gaudy palace like this was linked to anything Gamadin.

Without questioning Bigbob's motive, they jetted over to the structure and found the clicker standing just outside a shimmering blue force field.

"Looks like Harry's," Monday commented, kinking his head up at the grand marquee on the other side of the shimmering barrier next to Bigbob.

Monday's first impression hit the nail on the head. The structure was by no means as grand as Harry's Hotel and Casino in Las Vegas, but everything else about it was five-star panache. The front entry was extraordinarily opulent, fitting right in with any hotel on the Las Vegas Strip. Harlowe marveled over how it was frozen in time, so clean and polished and new that it looked like it was still open for business, waiting for them to check in. All they had to do was step through the barrier and sign in at the front desk to get a room.

"The barrier is definitely 54th century," Harlowe observed. The idea the force field still functioned after all these thousands of passings was no surprise. If indeed it was a Gamadin establishment, a functioning force field was par for the course. More than that, it was expected.

Harlowe wasted no time putting the first Gamadin test to work. He reached out and slid his SIBA claw through the barrier without resistance. "Come on, Squid," and he went on through as comfortably as stepping through *Millawanda's* force field. Incredibly, no water leaked around his suit as he stepped through the field and onto the portico floor under the marquee. Bigbob came through next, followed by Monday. A short moment later and the lights came on, welcoming them. It was dry as a bone inside as they stepped onto the tiled floors and into the lobby.

"Nice place," Monday said, retracting his SIBA headgear. "The air is okay, too."

Harlowe followed Monday's lead. SIBA headgear is comfortable, but nothing feels better than no headgear at all, and it was a relief to be free again. He sucked in a long breath of sweet air, and sighed, "Nice."

Monday slid his claws along the posh gold and red lobby desk. "Think we'll find anything, Captain?"

"We're due for a break," was Harlowe's droll reply.

There were doorways everywhere, large and small, arched and square, gaudy and plain, some open, but most were closed, leading to other rooms all around the grand foyer. They split up, Harlowe taking one side, Monday the other. If they found something cool, they were to report immediately, and no one was to go in a room without backup.

Harlowe had no luck at all. The rooms were normal enough, like one would expect in a five-star hotel: furniture, sitting lounges, and bars, lots of bars and places to eat. One open door led out to a veranda that overlooked what at one time would have been the ocean. There was a beautiful, dark blue glass bar with barstools and cocktail tables to match. But other than fine furniture and small knick-knacks, Harlowe found nothing that would help *Millawanda*.

Monday was gone for several long minutes. When he returned to the foyer, he was wearing a dark blue beret on his head. It had a stylized Gamadin emblem on the underside of the narrow brim. Harlowe thought the hat was cool, but he hoped there was more for being gone so long. "That's it?"

Monday grinned from ear to ear. "How 'bout these, then," he said, holding two short versions of Gama rifles. "They were in a weapons vault back there."

Harlowe took one to examine it. "They look functional. Any more?"

"Yeah, a whole rack of them, Captain. I found one of these, too," and handed Harlowe a sidearm he had stuck in his utility belt.

Harlowe examined the pistol, feeling its balance and weight. "Better than my old one. Thanks, Squid," he said, placing it in his empty holster.

Monday continued admiring his new rifle. "It looks like a trimmed down version of one of ours."

"That's exactly what it is." Harlowe touched his claw on the power button.

Monday added, "They're dead. I tried them both."

Knowing what he did about Gamadin longevity, Harlowe took a fresh power clip from his belt and snapped it into the magazine well. The weapon lit up like a Christmas tree. "It works now."

Monday snapped a clip of his own into his rifle with the same results. "Good to go here, too, Dog."

By accident they discovered the assault rifles would stick like Velcro to the back of their SIBAs. Harlowe had turned around, looking for the next place to search, when Monday's rifle affixed itself to Harlowe's pack. "Cool," Harlowe commented and nodded with satisfaction as he unstuck the weapon and returned it to Monday. After fastening their new finds in place, they continued on with their survey of the immense lobby.

"There has to be more to this place," Harlowe speculated. "Where are all the guest rooms?"

Monday thought that was odd himself. "Hmm. No elevators, either."

"Yeah, as big as this lobby is, you'd think this hotel would be a hundred stories high." He pointed up. "It's barely five. What's up with that?"

"Damn peculiar," Monday thought, too.

Harlowe spotted two large alcoves, one on each side of the front desk. "Did you check those out?"

Monday's excuse was, "They didn't have doors."

They meandered over to the nearest one to the right of the front desk and spotted a familiar sight on the floor; "A blinker!" they said together.

Harlowe looked down at the ten-foot wide disk. "Ya think it works?"

"The lights and force field do," Monday replied.

"It's big enough for fifty people. Wonder where it goes?"

Monday shrugged. "Try it."

Normally, Harlowe wouldn't have thought twice about stepping on a blinker plate. They used them so often on *Millawanda;* traveling that way from one place to the next was second nature. But on his ship, he knew exactly where he was going. Here, five hundred feet down and ten miles from shore, inside a building he knew nothing about, was a challenging decision. There was no telling where he would end up. He reactivated his SIBA headgear and head-motioned Bigbob to step on the plate. "I'll see what he sees on the other side."

Monday pointed at his noggin. "Good idea."

Bigbob stepped out and blinked away.

What Harlowe saw sent him reeling backwards into Monday's arms. Standing in Bigbob's footpads, he was at the edge of a platform, looking into an unbelievable, vast underground installation of levels, walkways, and elevator platforms that went hundreds of stories down. Looking up, Harlowe saw himself and Monday through the floor.

With jaw-dropping awe, Harlowe said to Monday. "That's insane."

Monday's view was the same as Harlowe's. Feeling queasy, he had to step back to catch his breath. "How will we search that?" he asked, holding on to Harlowe's shoulder.

Harlowe grabbed Monday's hand and together they zapped down to the platform beneath the main floor where Bigbob was patiently waiting for the next command.

Once on the platform, Monday stayed back. There were no guardrails at all. He gulped to keep his butterflies in check. "I hate heights."

Harlowe peered over the side. The dizzy precipice didn't bother him. "You're right. It will take us forever to search this place."

Monday glanced at Bigbob. "Maybe he knows where to look."

Harlowe's gaze went from the vast underground installation to Bigbob. "Yeah, can't hurt." Coming to the robob's side, he asked, "Bigbob. Find us a blue crystal."

Bigbob didn't move or even give any indication that he knew what Harlowe wanted. The blue light around his brim didn't flicker, but remained constant, like his hearing was somehow muted. Harlowe asked the same question several more times but with differing command tones in his voice. No matter what voice he used, Bigbob was unresponsive.

Harlowe faced Monday with a stumped shrug. "Any suggestions?"

Monday had one. "You know when we ask Millie a question we always have to be precise or she clams up. This could be the same deal."

"Bigbob needs a more exact question, huh?"

"That's what I'm thinking."

"What is it about blue crystal that Bigbob doesn't understand?"

Monday lifted his wide shoulders. "Azure crystal? I don't know. What's the Gamadin word for blue?"

A light turned on in Harlowe's head. "Not blue, Squid. Power. It begins with an 'A'. Millie called it…" The word was stuck under a pile of dirty socks inside his brain.

Monday knew the word, too. "Aara?"

The big clicker's blue headband suddenly grew brighter.

Harlowe grinned with satisfaction. "Bingo!"

"I think we did it, Captain," Monday congratulated.

Harlowe went back to the clicker with renewed hope. "Bigbob, find us some aara."

Bigbob went immediately to the center of the platform and passed his hand through a soft blue beam. The gesture produced a holographic console out of thin air. Bigbob's mechanical fingers touched the virtual activators, and suddenly they were all dropping like stones, passing through levels, cross structures, shopping malls, corridors, and other platforms in the hotel where Gamadin guests played and slept their vacations away.

There was no telling how far they traveled downward. The Gamadin numbers looked like a blur on Bigbob's console. Harlowe's SIBA, however, indicated an eleven hundred foot drop in elevation before the platform began to slow. It came to a complete stop inside the hub of five metal walkways that led to five floating round buildings made of glass. Bigbob leaped off the platform and headed for one of the buildings with Harlowe and Monday sticking to him like shadows. How Bigbob knew which building to enter was a mystery. But there was little doubt from the clicker's strong intention that he knew exactly were he was headed. When he arrived at the doorway, he passed his metal hand over the side actuator and was granted entry into a large foyer, no questions asked. Bigbob then moved swiftly through the main doorway and on to another doorway, second on the left.

Harlowe couldn't believe what he saw as he entered the room. "It's a bedroom just like mine." The circular bed, the thick blue carpet, chairs, tables and furnishings were identical to his quarters on *Millawanda*. A picture on the nightstand next to her bed was of a tall, dark, redheaded girl standing on the beach with a handsome, young man in a Gamadin uniform. They were holding each other close, appearing obviously in love.

"She was hot," Monday commented.

"Yeah, he looks pretty studly, too," Harlowe added. He removed the love letter from his utility belt pouch and placed it next to the picture. "Special delivery, brah. Sorry it ain't good news."

They inspected the room, looking in drawers, nooks and shelves, but found nothing. No aara anywhere.

Monday looked at Bigbob standing next to a bank of wall drawers. "Do you think Bigbob got his wires crossed?"

Harlowe thought otherwise. "No. It's here. He doesn't make mistakes. He's a clicker. Whatever he does, it's always right because that's all he knows to do."

Harlowe turned on his link with Bigbob on a whim. "He's staring at the fourth drawer up from the bottom. Didn't you check that one?"

Monday turned a little sheepish. "It was full of women's underwear."

Harlowe rolled his eyes. "They're 17,000 years old, Squid. They won't bite ya." He went to the bank of drawers, pulled open the fourth drawer, and began feeling his way through the girlish undergarments. It wasn't long before he found something solid and removed it from its silky wrappings, revealing a necklace with a large blue crystalline rock about the size of a walnut.

"That's it?" Monday gasped, staring at the blue object in shock. "This is what we've risked everything for, Captain?"

Harlowe held the blue crystal up to the ceiling light as he turned it around with his claw fingers. "Well, what did you expect? Big blue ones lying around for us to pick up?"

"Yeah, something like that. Something bigger than that anyway. How far will that get us?"

"It's not very big, is it?" Harlowe admitted with a long sigh.

"That wouldn't fill one of Rex's cavities," Monday piled on. "Riverstone will have a cow."

"I'm having one now." Harlowe put the aara crystal in his utility pouch as he headed out the bedroom door. "Well, we got what we came for. Maybe it's big enough to get us off this planet and to the next station."

"I hope you're right, Captain."

* * *

They went out the door and made their way back to the center platform. Harlowe felt like he wanted to fight a hundred Surwags barehanded to release the steam that was exploding in his head. After stepping onto the platform, Bigbob hit the up button and away they rose as fast as they'd descended. Harlowe couldn't stop thinking about the hundreds of lightyears they'd traveled to find a treasure chest full of gold, only to come away with a penny.

"Don't beat yourself up, Captain. We didn't have a lot of choices," Monday said, hoping to cool Harlowe's jets. "It was worth the shot."

As they stopped before the portal that led them back to the watery depths outside the building, Harlowe lowered his SIBA headgear revealing an angry, red face. "Was it, Squid? Was it the only choice? Or was it my stupid, thickheaded ego that brought us here? Millie could be at the bottom of the ocean forever because of me!"

Monday wasn't going to let Harlowe take the fall without a fight. "That's right. It was your decision, Captain. But, and this is a big but, Millie would have never made it this far without you. You saved her back on Earth from the Daks and the U.S. Government. In the Omni Quadrant you kept Anor Ran, the Consortium, and the Fhaal from stealing her, and you saved Mrs. M's planet, Nija, as a bonus, completing your promise. Then on Gazz, against all possible odds, you sailed a 16th century galleon half way around the globe and back again to save Lu, your crew, the planet, and Millie. No human being alive could have done what you did, Captain. No one. You made the choice because it was the only choice to make. Win or lose, Prigg, Riverstone, and me are with you, Captain. Even when you're—"

"Even when I'm wrong, huh, Squid?"

"Especially when you're wrong, Captain. But you're never wrong. What seems like it's wrong in the moment, never turns out that way. In the end you're always on top, Dog. That's why you're the head dude and not me, Riverstone, or Wiz."

Harlowe leaned against the wall with his claws above his head, trying to get himself right again. After a few deep breaths, he came back to Monday, tapping him on the shoulder. "I shouldn't worry, then? Sooner or later I'll be right?"

"Aye. Something like that. It's going to work."

Harlowe reactivated his headgear, covering all signs of self-doubt. "I sure hope you're right, Squid."

Then together the three them dove through the portal and began the long swim back to the shoreline. They were just offshore, where the waves began to form. When Harlowe and Monday finally poked their heads above the surface and looked out at the beach, behind them, a wispy line of deep red and pink clouds had spread wide along the horizon. The sun was not far behind, sinking fast, and soon it would be dark. Just ahead, the waves were unchanged. Small sets, two to three feet high continued to peel off along the sandy beach. At any other time Harlowe would be drooling over the thought of snagging a few tubes before catching up with Isara and the others, but the thousands of Surwags bivouacked along the beach nixed the thought of any off-the-clock time.

"Sweet . . ."

95

The Long Farewell

Ian, Quay, and Leucadia walked together along the thawing shoreline. Parked close by, *Forty-four* was ready for liftoff. Their eyes were tired, their bodies exhausted, and their minds were numb from long hours of retro-fitting Tabilisi's power core from thermo-grym to the practically inexhaustible aara power supply. Working three days straight along side their robob mechanics, they had accomplished the impossible. The space city, alone in the center of the vast star desert, would once again become the thriving way station for travelers journeying across Cartooga-Thaat.

Looking up, Ian marveled at Tabilisi coming back to life. *Forty-four's* tiny suns were gone. The light from the central sun was blazing hot and fully functional. Its light was just now peaking by the night shade that gave the illusion of day and night as the torus rotated on its axis. The light was yellowy warm and felt soothing on his face. But he missed the sky. That was also odd to him. He yearned for a blue heaven filled with fluffy white clouds in the day and the stars at night. As the radiant heat spread throughout Tabilisi, Ian envisioned leafy, tree-filled parks, bright marquees, moving transports, pavilions, street lights, farms, and lakes all arching their way up and around the vast interior like they had many eons ago. Seeing the segments of the city already coming to life, he was struck by a sky of structures that did not fall from their foundations or lakes emptying, splashing down in a massive deluge on his head. That would take some getting used to, he thought. He wondered how long it would be before the Tels could step out of the

461

Gamadin building where they had taken up temporary living quarters, and live normal lives again, strolling along the lake or playing catch, or simply vegging on the grass, contemplating life in their new world that Quay had brought them.

Quay smiled at the portal along the outer hull of the torus wall. "The force field is holding."

Leucadia checked her handheld com readouts. "Atmospheric pressure is rising rapidly along with the outside temperature. It is now a balmy minus 200 degrees," she added, whimsically.

That was remarkable. Ian remembered the temperature being minus 350 when they landed three days ago. "You're half way there already," he said, taking her hand.

Leucadia added, "It will take some time for the plants to regenerate, but it will be beautiful, Quay. Tabilisi will be a wonderful home again for the Tels."

"I am so happy for them. This would never have happened without you," Quay said as she gathered Ian and Leucadia in her arms.

When they separated again, Quay asked, "How will you find my Captain?"

Leucadia looked at Quay, who was nearly a head taller than she, and replied, "We know he is very low on fuel. But that's all we know. It's possible he is stranded somewhere. If he is, we must hurry to find him or . . . well . . ." She didn't want to say aloud the worst that could happen to *Millawanda* and her crew.

"I understand," Quay said, feeling the sting in her heart. "Find him. Find him for the sake of our galaxy."

Leucadia smiled confidently. "We will."

"Do you know his course?" Quay asked.

Ian stepped away from the conversation as he repeated the question in a low whisper that had been nagging him the second he saw the Tabilisi torus. "So why did everyone up and leave such a cool place?"

The question may have been a whisper, but it was loud enough for both Quay and Leucadia to hear.

"Disease, loss of thermo-grym supplies, invasion," Leucadia answered. "Any number of things could have been the cause, Ian."

"Yeah, but when Cheesa and I walked the streets, we entered shops, restaurants, and homes. And in every case, food was either left on the tables or left half cooked in pots. We saw transports abandoned in the middle of intersections, their doors flung open like they were deserting a sinking ship. We saw closets full of clothes and pets frozen at the door like they were left behind. Who leaves their pet behind unless . . ."

"Unless they were in a hurry," Leucadia said, finishing Ian's thought.

"That's right. Unless they had to book it outta here big time," Ian said, and then turned to Quay. "We need to know what happened here before we leave you."

"What happened here was a long time ago, Ian. It would be unlike my father to invest so much time and effort to discover Tabilisi unless he knew it was a valuable resource for Tomar," Quay insisted. "If there was something wrong with Tabilisi, my father would never have come here in the first place. Of that, I am certain. You must not worry about the Tels. Our mission is here. Your mission is to find my Captain and fix *Millawanda*. She is what is important to us," she said, pointing at herself then spreading her arms across the torus, "and our new home. The quadrant depends on her presence, Ian. Without *Millawanda*, a healthy, powerful Gamadin ship, the quadrant will die. It is written, *'The Gamadin will cleanse the stars for all, and return peace to the heavens…'* You must not fail that mission, Ian!"

No, he would not fail that mission, not if he could help it. He had the means to save *Millawanda* in *Forty-four's* storage hold. All he had to was find her; yet, he felt like he was missing the bigger picture. Anor Ran had the vision. He would have thoroughly checked out Tabilisi before spending his resources on the desert city. So was the discovery of *Millawanda* the real reason for abandoning Tabilisi, or was it something else? What caused him to reconsider his Tabilisi investment?

Whatever *it* was, and even though the panic that befell Tabilisi a thousand years ago was in the distant past and unresolved, Ian's discomfort persisted. The question of "Why?" would nag him until he found the answer, and leaving Quay and the Tels totally defenseless didn't set well with him. He felt as though he was neglecting his first duty as a Gamadin, to protect the defenseless. As he watched Molly and Rhud striding casually down the ramp for their morning stretch, the idea of leaving them at the doorway to freeze in the near absolute zero temperatures sent a terrifying jolt through his body.

It wouldn't happen, he thought defiantly. No power in the universe would make him do that. Just like Nod, they would never be left behind!

"Did you hear me, Ian?" Quay directed, trying to get Ian's attention. "Ian?"

Ian blinked himself back into the conversation. "Yes, Quay."

"Have you been listening to me? The quadrant's defense is your mission. You cannot fail."

"Yes, but our mission changed when we found you, Quay. Leaving you here unprotected is irresponsible. We can't do that, Quay," Ian replied. "As much as we need to leave here, your safety is now our mission."

Ian turned to Leucadia. "You've been mum on this, Lu."

Leucadia stood quietly, eyeing them both equally. "I know."

"Why?" Ian asked.

"Because it's your decision, Captain."

Ian focused on her passive expression. "That's never stopped you before, Lu. You've always given your opinion, even when I haven't asked for it. What's changed?"

Leucadia was hesitant to answer.

"Come on, Lu; I want your view," he told her straight out.

Quay looked at Leucadia sympathetically. "It is all right, Leucadia. No one will fault you, especially me."

Leucadia was surprised. "You know why I must remain neutral?"

"You are protecting me," Quay replied. "Or I should say, your opinion could sway Ian's decision to stay or go. If you say we must leave to find *Millawanda*, you believe it may look as though you are abandoning us to the danger of what harmed Tabilisi. You feel the love of your Captain, for Harlowe, will interfere with the correct decision to leave Tabilisi in the search for *Millawanda*. If you side with Ian, you may be condemning Harlowe to death."

"Yes, but—"

"You must know my decision is not based on love, Leucadia. It is true, I do love Harlowe more than any being I have ever known. But our paths from the beginning are separate. That is our destiny. It is founded on the greater good of the quadrant. For me to be with Harlowe would mean to give up both our paths. Yours IS with Harlowe. I see that clearly, and I know you do as well. Ian's, too. The Gamadin must survive, Ian. You must leave now. You must find your powerful Gamadin ship and continue the resurrection. There is no other choice." Quay looked into Ian's inner soul and pleaded for his understanding. "Can you not see that? Without the Gamadin, our destinies are insignificant. Tabilisi will cease to exist. It was that day on the planet you call #2, and we were standing near the campfire."

"I remember it like it was yesterday. I showed you the *Declaration of Independence*," Ian interjected, recalling the fun time they had that night cooking hot dogs on a stick, the laughter they shared, and the discussion they had about freedom when he projected a holographic image of the *Declaration of Independence* document above the fire. He remembered seeing her expression change as he read every line to her. He didn't realize it then, but he had changed Quay's life forever. Instead of fleeing the Consortium to save herself, she risked it all; as the *Declaration's* Signers had written over two centuries before, she 'pledged her life, her Fortune, her sacred Honor' for the freedom of the quadrant.

"Yes, that document is my most cherished possession. I have read your planet's history, Ian. The quest for freedom is never easy. It is the most noble cause we can give. You must save *Millawanda*." She pointed back to *Forty-four's* ramp. "Now go. Find our Captain. Find Millawanda. Save our freedom, Captain!"

Leucadia took Ian by the arm. "Thank you, Quay. I understand more than ever why Harlowe cherishes you so highly."

Ian nodded with tears welling up in his eyes. "Alright, Quay. But when we find her, and she is her old self again, we will return to Tabilisi to make sure you are okay."

Quay smiled. "And Tabilisi will welcome you with open arms."

Suddenly, Molly and Rhud leaped through the barrier as Ian, Leucadia, and Quay stood by in horror as they watched the cats touch the thawing surface. They shouldn't have been able to withstand the cold, but Molly and Rhud seemed perfectly fine with their paws splashing in the melting water. Ian looked down at the water's edge and saw the little ripples lapping along the beach. Plants, too, were dripping the frost from their branches and turning green in the artificial light. A quick scan of his SIBA sensors indicated the air was a little above freezing. He stepped past the barrier and took a breath of fresh air. "Nice . . ."

Quay and Leucadia stepped through the barrier together. The air was chilly, like a cool autumn morning, but bearable. Quay knelt down to a small plant already sprouting. "Look, Ian, life!"

Ian smiled back at her joy. "I read somewhere that life always finds a way."

"The Tels will make Tabilisi a wonderful place again for all those who journey across Cartooga-Thaat. They have found many useful things in the storage lockers. There is food enough for many passings."

"I will miss you, Quay," Ian said to her.

The three of them continued to walk along the melting shore. Quay kissed Ian on the cheek. "But don't tell Harlowe just yet."

Ian didn't understand. "Why? He'll want to know."

Quay giggled like a little girl. "Give us a passing so we can have Tabilisi all nice and pretty for him when he arrives."

Ian tried to argue, but Quay's sunlit, dark eyes wouldn't let him deny her wish. "It may be that long before we find him anyway."

"Where will you go next, Ian?" Quay asked.

He had no clear answer as he looked up at *Forty-Four*. "This ship is as old as *Millawanda*. It's nav charts are equally as old. We know nothing of what lies ahead, Quay."

"If my father were here, he could help you, I am sure. He knows all about these matters," Quay said.

Ian's eyes brightened. "He has traveled beyond Cartooga?"

Quay answered as though travel for her father beyond the quadrant was a common practice for him. "Oh, yes. He made many journeys beyond Cartooga-Thaat."

"Where is he? Have you heard from him?" Ian asked.

"Not since Og. But I have heard rumors he was seen on Metis."

"Where is Metis?"

"I'm afraid it is not the direction Harlowe is taking,"

Ian scratched his head. "We're floundering, Quay. It was dumb luck that we found you. Harlowe didn't drop any crumbs for me to follow. He doesn't even know we're looking for him. He still thinks Lu and I are on a planet lightyears from here. There's a thousand star systems between here and there he could have gone to after leaving Tabilisi. If I could find your father, he would be a great help to us, I'm sure."

"Yes, if there is anyone who can help you, it is Anor Ran," Quay admitted of her father.

Ian began to laugh which both Quay and Leucadia found strange. "What do you find so humorous, Ian?" Leucadia asked.

Ian continued laughing as he explained. "The look on Harlowe's face when he sees Anor and me walking down this ramp would stop a T-Rex in his tracks."

Quay joined the laughter. It was an inside joke that Leucadia didn't understand. She had never met Anor Ran.

"Yes, the look on My Captain's face will be, as you say . . . 'rad'. . ."

96

No One Left Behind

Scores of Surwag bonfires burned flaming hot along the shoreline, walling off the horde from the sea. It was like they had marked the beach with caution flags to remind them to stay away from the water. Most were still asleep, save a small number of sentries posted around the perimeter, and a few early risers that sat crosslegged around the fires with their heads and arms reaching to the heavens chanting unintelligible rhythmic sounds to the stars. From the looks of things, the bay around Lamille was a sacred place of prayer and meditation for them. A far cry from a popular beach resort, Harlowe thought, and added with caution that if they were discovered, it would also be a place where Gamadin were breakfast.

Lucky them.

Before taking the next wave in, Harlowe collapsed Bigbob back to a cylinder and returned him to his backpack sleeve next to his new assault rifle. When they started crawling down the beach, he was sure the big, gold stickman with a lighted brim would attract attention crawling with them down the beach.

Using the waves as cover, Harlowe and Monday body surfed quietly to the beach, letting the wave deposit them on the wet sand. Like a pile of seaweed, they remained still until they were sure no one had seen them. After several minutes and no detection, they were about to begin their creep when Monday pointed down the beach at the being hanging from a stake near one of the bonfires. One stack over was a forearm. It was all that was left of a poor soul that had been tied there. Harlowe swallowed the putrid taste in his mouth as he zoomed in on a third stake far down the line of bonfires where loose ropes dangled with nothing in them but charred hands. Movement from the first stake brought Harlowe's attention back to the being tied there. Monday saw the being, too. The conclusion was the same. "Nath," they said together.

Harlowe frantically searched the line of fires. "Anyone else?"

Monday shook his head. "No." But looking farther north toward the rocky point, he added, "I see three Fagan mounts there, Dog."

Harlowe followed Monday's line of sight. "Yeah, three. No ceffyls, though."

"Roger that."

They took their time and carefully scanned everywhere along the beach just to make sure.

Harlowe sighed. "Yeah, no ceffyls."

"Maybe the girls made it," Monday suggested.

"Yeah, the ceffyls are much faster than Nath's mounts," Harlowe knew. "What about Nath?"

"We leave no one behind," Harlowe replied, determined.

Monday agreed. "Aye."

Harlowe and Monday eased back out into the shore break, slithering down the beach until they were in front of Nath's fire. They didn't have much time. The horizon was growing brighter, and soon they would lose their night advantage. Using the same tactic they had earlier, they rode the shore break into the beach. From there, they crawled along the sand until they were within a few yards of the Fagan.

So far. So good.

The seven chanting Surwags sitting around the fire were unaware of their presence. If they were quiet enough and quick enough, they could cut Nath down and carry him away until they were safely back in the water.

With Monday covering his back, Harlowe rose from his prone position when the unthinkable happened. A chanter stood with a large blade in his hand, walked over to Nath, raised his arm, and was about to chop-off a large hunk for breakfast when Harlowe had no choice but to put a plas round through the Surwag's brain.

Harlowe's new sidearm had a silent mode that his other pistol lacked. He put it to good use, dropping the Surwag where he stood. The other chanters apparently heard nothing. A second chanter, however, saw the collapsed body fall, and finding that odd, went to it to see what the problem was. Upon discovering the first chanter was quite dead, another silent round dropped the second chanter before he could utter a sound. Before the bodies piled up any more, Harlowe quickly leaped across the sand and cut Nath's bindings with his black thermo-grym blade. He lifted the weighty Fagan over his shoulder, and then ever so carefully, tip-toed back to the water with hardly a splash. Monday covered their retreat as Harlowe moved with Nath out to deeper water.

"Are we good?" Harlowe asked, keeping Nath's unconscious head out of the water.

"So far," Monday replied as he scanned the beach for any alarmed Surwags.

As the three began floating out to deeper water, Monday asked, "Is he alive?"

Harlowe started to scan Nath's head with his SIBA sensors when he suddenly woke up and began thrashing his arms and legs like he was trying to fend off his Surwag attackers. Harlowe grabbed his arms while Monday held onto his legs.

"Easy, Nath," Harlowe cautioned as he wrapped his upper chest and head with his arms to keep him quiet. They were outside the breakers, but any sound other than the natural sounds of the waves could disturb the Surwags. They had to keep swimming toward the rocky point and hope they could somehow get themselves and Nath past the sentries. It was getting so light out now, Harlowe doubted they would make it ten feet without being seen once they stepped out of the water.

Once Nath stopped his flailing, Harlowe released his grip. Staring at two oversized eyes probably looked to Nath like a giant bo-chee was about to sting him. "It's me, Nath," Harlowe said, keeping his claw over the Fagan's mouth.

"Har . . . Harlowe?" Nath grunted, half consciously.

Harlowe relaxed his grip and let him float beside him. "Yeah, Nath. What happened? Where are Isara and Oea?"

The terror of nearly being eaten was still with him as Nath fumbled through his reply. "We...we separated." Trembling with fear, he added, "They came out of nowhere, Harlowe."

"It's all right, Nath," Harlowe consoled him as they continued drifting toward the rocky point, away from the fires. "What happened to Isara and Oea, Nath? Did you see what happened to them? Did they make it to the river?"

Nath looked like he was about to cry for failing to protect Isara and Oea. "I do not know, Harlowe. The Surwags...they came out at us," he kept repeating.

Monday nudged Harlowe to check out the mounts standing in a makeshift corral. "Nath's horses. Can't leave them, either, Dog."

Harlowe understood. They might make it without the Fagan mounts, but leaving them behind meant they were condemning them to be Surwag Happy Meals when the camp awakened. Besides, Nath was way too weak to move on his own. Stealing back his ride was the answer. But once they rushed the horses, that was it. From then on it was a foot race to the river. And now that the morning was too bright for slyness, a direct assault on the corral was their only option. Being at the fringe of the throngs helped. It meant they would only have to shoot a few dozen sentries instead of thousands.

Harlowe held Nath with one arm around his waist and pulled his sidearm with his free hand. "Go," he said to Monday.

Monday took off straight for the corral. There was no stealth involved. The instant the sentries saw the bug-eyed Gamadin leaping toward them, Monday shot the three before touching the sand for the second time. As Monday was taking care of their mounts, Harlowe put the lights out on the five cliff lookouts above the corral before any one of them could sound the alarm. Another seven Surwags went down behind the corral. Harlowe thought he had every sentry accounted for when a loud alarm blared down the beach from the cliffs. Neither he nor Monday saw the sentry hidden between the crags of the cliff farther down the beach. Harlowe sizzled a plas round through the skull horn from a hundred yards away, but it was too late. The alarm was sounded.

During the mass confusion that followed, Surwags leaped from their sleeping bivouacs without direction. Monday seized the moment of opportunity. He untied the horses, grabbed the reins, and brought them back to Harlowe who threw Nath onto his own mount. Harlowe didn't have time to properly tie Nath to his saddle. He hoped the Fagan had enough horse sense and strength to keep himself from falling off.

Charging ahead toward the rocky point, Monday nailed three spear-chuckers who jumped out in front to cut them off. Then a heart-stopping roar exploded as the earth beneath their feet shook. Scores of Surwags had found guidance and were charging up the beach, brandishing their shining, pointed spears and razor-sharp hatchets, striding, jumping, leaping like a mass of locusts after a field of wheat.

Harlowe had his hands full with Surwags jumping down from the ledges. As fast as the lead Surwags went down, others took take their place. Clicking out one empty clip and snapping in another, he might as well have been trying to stop a tsunami with a finger in the dike. If they were riding ceffyls, they could have beat them to the river, no problem. But as he had witnessed before, the Surwags were as fast as horses. Their strong legs enabled them to leap in great strides, like they were all wearing Gamadin gravs. Even with a fully powered SIBA, Harlowe doubted he could outrun the slowest Surwag. It was ten more miles to the river, and the horde was just getting their stride.

The front Surwags had already cut the lead from two football fields to one. Overhead, a second line of Surwags leaped along the cliffs, where at some point their spears would be in range.

On a dead run, Monday shouted ahead, pointing at a cliff overhang that jutted out over the narrowing beach.

Harlowe spurred his mount to run even faster. They had to beat the horde running across the top of the cliff, or they were screwed. Remembering what had happened in Southern Utah when they first discovered the Gamadin weapons, Harlowe handed Nath's reins to Monday as he reached for his new assault rifle. Back in Utah, they accidentally shot the top off a mountain wondering if the ancient weapons still worked. Here he just needed a fraction of that kind of power to bring the overhang down.

Ratcheting the assault rifle power level to max, Harlowe waited for Monday and Nath to clear the overhang and fired. Unable to see the results, Harlowe urged his mount onward. If the horse had stumbled only a little bit, they would have been squished just like the Surwags that tried to beat the slab that fell on top of them. As it was, the force of the blast was so great, it nearly blew Harlowe off his mount. Like some trick rider in the circus, Harlowe, in one smooth motion, returned his rifle to its sleeve as he touched the sand with both feet, bounced, and landed back on his horse, never losing a step as he galloped on to catch Monday and Nath.

Then tragedy happened. Harlowe's mount faltered for no apparent reason. The courageous steed slowed to a trot as it tried in vain to keep its legs from buckling. Then it stopped, one leg went outward to steady itself then the other. The mount wheezed, fighting for life. But nothing worked. It keeled over and collapsed on its side as Harlowe jumped away before being caught under its weight. He stared dumbfounded as the shore break washed over the inert body. There was nothing Harlowe could do. The steed was already dead. Harlowe saw the blood from the broken arrow sticking from its hindquarter. The shaft was thin, but the poison it had carried was mercifully quick. Harlowe knelt beside the mount, caressing his mane and thanking him for getting him this far.

Suddenly, another arrow sailed out of nowhere, striking the sand at his feet. Harlowe came up firing. Surwags were already climbing over the mound of rubble he had just created; collapsing the cliff had only delayed them. Ahead, Monday had stopped and was about to make a run for Harlowe, when he held up his hand, shouting into his SIBA com, "No, Squid! Get to the river! Millie needs that crystal."

"But Captain—" Monday tried to say before Harlowe cut him off.

Five arrows whizzed past Harlowe's face; two more struck his SIBA, ricocheting harmlessly into the sand. They felt like pestering gnats as he yelled back, "That's an order, Mister Platter!"

97

Metis

*P*lodding his way through the knee-high snow with his escort of two badass cats and six heavily armed robobs, Ian had only one thing to say about his first impression of the planet, Metis: "Whatta dump!" Feeling grateful he was toasty warm in his SIBA, he gave the orange sun straight overhead a cursory look and pronounced, "Useless." Fortunately, the snow was fresh and dry, so walking was easy. Molly and Rhud seemed to enjoy the snow. They jumped around in the powder and playfully dusted one another with slaps of the fluffy, white flakes to the point that Ian twice had to tell them to cool it. "Hey, we're here on business. When we get back home, I'll take you to Park City, and you can play in the powder there all you want."

Rhud grumbled his displeasure, and then he and Molly dutifully fell back into step with the robobs, who didn't care about the snow, or the cold, or tossing a snowball, and never broke formation.

A mile back, *Forty-four* glistened under the sunlight like a plate of gold. There were no landing pads. Ian simply chose to put down at the most convenient spot by the prison, which was outside the small town. He didn't worry about the parking tickets. Let the-powers-that-be try to enforce it, he snorted. Around the outskirts of the prison were dozens of small, two-seater military spacecraft that *Forty-four* had already dusted when the authorities tried to stop him. "Unauthorized visitors are not allowed near the prison," they told him.

Like his parking spot, Ian didn't care about permission. "I'm looking for someone who I'm told resides on your planet," Ian had communicated upon entering high orbit above Metis. Even from a thousand miles away, the planet appeared icy cold and uninviting. He hoped the five-day diversion was worth it.

A hardened military officer dressed in a dark grey uniform and another silly hat asked, "And who would that be?"

"Anor Ran," Ian replied with his best, contrived smile of the day. He was about to describe Anor as a humanoid male with jet black hair, large dark eyes, slightly over six feet tall when he was suddenly cut off. It didn't take Leucadia and Cheesa long to find the reason after probing the planet's computer network.

"Anor is in the high security prison for crimes against the state, Captain," Leucadia reported with a raised right eyebrow. Harlowe always told him to watch the raised eyebrow. The left is pretty harmless, but the right . . . If it's the right, that's when there's trouble. The right eyebrow lifted. "His execution is five hours from now."

Ian released a long breath of what-else-is-new. "Figures."

"You don't act surprised, Captain," Cheesa said.

"If you knew Anor like I do, you wouldn't either."

"Do you have a plan, Captain?" Leucadia asked.

Ian's reply was simple. "Yeah, get him out."

"We're interfering with their laws," Leucadia cautioned.

"No doubt," Ian replied.

"They will be unco-operative," Leucadia said.

"Yep." Ian understood the path he was taking. Without Anor's help, they we're sailing without a rudder. He needed his knowledge of what lay beyond the Thaat. If he didn't get him out, they would be trying to find Harlowe with a blindman's stick.

"So we're going in?" Dev asked.

"No. You're staying here. Just me this time."

Like a good second in command, Leucadia's orders filled in the blanks. "Bring plas cannons to full power, Dev."

"Yes, Ms. Lu," Dev replied, and swiveled his chair to his weapons array, following her orders.

"Let's find that prison, then," Ian ordered.

Cheesa perked up, eager to please. "Already plotted, Captain."

* * *

The prison was a sprawling structure of concrete cell blocks and formidable buildings covering a full square mile. Surrounding it all was a massive, reinforced steel and stone wall a hundred feet high and a third that distance thick. Close by was the town that supported the prison, its employees, and the scum of the planet. There was only one way in, down the wide main street that led to the tall entrance gates of the prison. Narrow alleys and walkways spun off from the main drag, but Ian didn't care about where they led or where he might find a secret entrance to the prison. He was going straight through the front door whether they liked it or not.

Lining both sides of the snow dusted street were old stone buildings with sod roofs that, according to his SIBA readouts, were centuries old and looked it. The bars and bordellos were loud with howls and laughter. The music was harsh and teeth gnawing as musicians played their off-tuned instruments. Inside their hovels, townies were as unclean as the outside. Through the windows, females paraded in skimpy clothes around the hard-faced patrons sitting at tables playing cards. He wondered if it was poker they were playing. Regardless, my Aunt Doris could teach them a lesson or two, whatever the game was. "She'd kick your ass," he said to the players.

Whether the crusty beings were human or not was unimportant. He continued down the street kicking at disgusting rodent-like creatures that came after him. They seemed to have the run of the town. Another beastie with yellow, jagged teeth, tried to bite a robob but with painful results. The dura-metal leg broke a tooth or two in the process. When another rodent went for Molly's leg, Rhud snatched it before it could touch a single white hair, snapping its bones like it was a Dorito. A dozen rodents feasted on the discarded remains, tearing the body to shreds in the middle of the street. The cats and the clickers were left alone after that.

Ian walked up to a sign at the boundary between the town and prison wall. He tried reading the inscription, but the centuries of wind and rain had nearly erased the words from its surface. Even if it was readable, the language was unknown to him. However, it didn't take a passing grade in Farnducky's science class to understand the sign's meaning: "Step beyond this point, and you will be shot," or words to that effect.

Ian felt his sidearm before he motioned for the clickers to ready their weapons and spread themselves out. As strong and lethal as the cats were, bullets could still kill them. Ian held Molly and Rhud behind the line while he and the clickers marched forward. Two steps later a shot from the turret nearest the main gate exploded at Ian's feet. "HALT, OR YOU WILL BE TERMINATED!" the bullhorn roared.

"I'm here for Anor Ran!" Ian called out to the unseen authority.

A second blast from a powerful weapon struck Ian's head. But the projectile was absorbed by the force field that surrounded his SIBA. The sizzling piece of twisted metal fell to the ground in a crackling, molten mess.

Ian spoke into his SIBA com. "Do it now, Dev."

An instant later a hot bolt of blue plasma struck the turret, vaporizing it to a molten pile of of goo. A second later, two more blasts from *Forty-Four* made piles of the other turrets. A fourth shot reduced the foot-thick steel door to a white-hot mass, as an ear-piercing siren blared across the prison. Guards ran along the top of the ramparts, aiming their weapons through narrow slits in the stone. Ian waved his claw at the ramparts. His clicker escort reacted without hesitation, blasting the scores of rifle barrels with utmost precision the instant their muzzles poked out of the stone slits.

"The next rounds will target the main building!" Ian shouted over the screaming sirens.

He wondered if anyone heard him over the wailing alarms, but like a car running out of gas, the sirens soon began to sputter, until finally they lost their scream, and there was nothing but a deathly silence.

Ian marched immediately toward the gaping hole in the stone wall, while the cats, unable to sit for long, bolted out in front taking the lead, their keen, blue eyes scouting ahead for any threats. Several guards tried to take aim at the white targets, but they were quickly dispatched by the clicker backups who never took their blue rims off the walls.

A metal side door in the stone wall opened up fifty yards from the main gate that was now too hot to walk over. Emerging from the doorway, a small contingent of grey clad, heavily armed, two-legged beings came forth. They were taller and much heavier than Ian. Although their shape was human, their skin was scale-like and dark, and their eyes were large and yellow. Whether they had ears or not, was difficult to tell because round, black helmets covered most of their heads. Their noses were flat against their faces, and their lips were mere slits. When they spoke, their underbite jaws stuck out displaying pointy incisors that were common of flesh eaters.

"Who are you?" the guard asked, pointing his sidearm at Ian's belly.

Ian blasted the guard's weapon from his hand before he spoke. "No stupid questions, maggot. Take me to Anor Ran . . . now!"

Molly and Rhud leaped in front of the guards. The lead guard froze in terror as Rhud moved forward, opening his maw of foot-long incisors.

"I should tell you my pets haven't eaten this morning. So be quick about it, if you please, sir," Ian said.

The guards nodded their understanding, and as they were about to lead them away, Ian said, "One is enough. The others will stay here." A nod from Ian and a clicker broke off, covering the other guards with its rifle.

Ian faced the guards, nodding at the robob. "Move from here, and he will kill you."

With that understanding, Ian motioned for the guard to go on. Kicking away rodents from his path, the guard led him through the small entry door to the prison's inner courtyard. Unable to find a clear path between the discarded bones and skulls of rotting beings, Ian had no choice but to step on a few along the way. He wanted to throw up. Not even in the prison planet of Erati had he seen such vile conditions as this.

The guard led him to a large stone building at the far end of the courtyard and stepped through another heavy door. Inside, the guard grabbed a gas lantern from a nearby table and lit it. "This way," he growled, motioning with the lantern.

As they made their way along a dark hallway lined with cells, hands of the barely living clawed at them, begging for food. The guard slapped them away like pestering insects. The lantern's dim glow did not reach into the cell, but Ian's bugeyes saw clearly. The pathetic beings had no beds or waste facilities. A hole in the floor and a bucket was all that he saw. Worse, there were no windows for light or fresh air. Life at the Metis prison was beyond cruel. It was against all life in the universe. Just when he thought the prison could get no worse, they came upon guards feasting hungrily at a long table filled with tall tankards of drink and large platters piled high of legs, arms and ribs, dripping with raw fluids. Five pasty-white beasts with long fangs, red-glowing eyes, thick, six-legged bodies and stubby tails sat patiently to the side like dogs, waiting for a tossed morsel. *My God!* Ian was horrified. He had to puke. He couldn't hold it in any longer. The Metis prison was like nothing he had ever known. Beings that ended up here never left. Their only way out was to be served on a platter.

The instant the sickly beasts saw Molly and Rhud they charged, seeing a meal that required no waiting. The cats reacted swiftly. With a single swipe of her paw, the first beast's head left its body and smashed against a stone wall, splattering body parts over the surprised guards sitting at the table. The four remaining beasts met similar fates: bones crushed, heads torn from their shoulders, backs broken. It was as if the five had been tossed into a meat grinder. Molly and Rhud didn't stop with them, either. The guards at the table, after watching the slaughter, grabbed their long knives and sidearms to kill the creatures that had killed their pets. But like their pets, the cats mauled all of the guards sitting at the table before they could lift a single weapon, thus ending their miserable existence.

Ian turned to the guide and said quite calmly, "Anor Ran, if you please."

The guide was terrified, like he wanted to drop where he stood.

Ian wasn't taking any chances. "You stop now, and you'll never wake up, Turd."

Shaking uncontrollably, the guard led the escort to a stairway that went down to a subterranean level where the walls and floors dripped of a foul ooze with colorless insects as big as a man's hand, and where no life had ever seen the light of day.

How long had Anor been here? How could he have survived a day? Again, Ian's nightmare of Erati rushed back, making him wonder how Riverstone would have felt seeing all this. He had suffered more than him, he knew. Only Ela had saved him back then.

Ian swallowed hard. There was no other choice but to push on. Millie, Harlowe, the Gamadin crew, everyone depended on him keeping it together and finding Anor.

"Hurry up!" Ian snapped, losing every last ounce of patience he had left. "How much farther?"

"Not far, *Dhamaa*," the guide replied. Ian's internal translator didn't recognize the word, but from the tone of the guard's voice, he figured it was a Metis term for "toadface."

At the end of the stone passageway was a heavy, steel door. The guard stopped in front of it. "Anor is here, Toadface," he said, pointing at the door.

"Open it," Ian ordered.

The guard appeared helpless. "I have no key," was his excuse.

Ian drew and fired a searing round at the locking mechanism. "It's open now," and waved the guide in. "You first."

The guard hesitated. He didn't want to go in.

Ian kicked him through the open door. "Move!" The instant he crossed the cell threshold, three long, iron spikes skewered his body from each side. The guard shook for several seconds before going limp.

Ian kicked the dead carcass off the spikes and entered the cell. Like the other cells, the interior was nasty beyond description. A bucket of feces in the corner lay on its side. On the opposite end was a huddled body covered in rags and dirty straw. Ian's SIBA sensors registered a slight heat signature which meant the body was either still alive or recently dead.

Ian prayed for the prior.

Rushing to the body, Ian pulled back the rags, wiping away the slimy fecal matter from his face. It was difficult to tell if the body was really Anor. The Anor he remembered was tall, fit, two hundred pounds, with black hair, and a handsome face. This being was bearded and emaciated. He had lost so much weight his skin drooped from his brittle bones. If this was Anor, life and death were in a tug-of-war, and life was losing by a mile.

Ian immediately removed an enviro-bag from his backpack as the clickers went to work stabilizing the body with their medical globe and Bluestuff hypos. When their emergency care was complete, they placed the near-corpse inside the enviro-bag and sealed it up. That was the best they could do as the clickers made a mad dash back to *Forty-Four*.

*   *   *

When Ian stepped onto the bridge, he clearly wasn't himself.

"Captain on the bridge," Cheesa declared with relief that Ian was back. When she first came onboard, Cheesa didn't understand why the proclamation was necessary. Wasn't it obvious the Captain was on the bridge when everyone saw him. Seeing the flummoxed looked on her face, Leucadia explained the long tradition dating back thousands of years on their planet. Whenever the captain stepped onto the bridge, the announcement was a sign of respect for his position.

Ian made no attempt to greet any of his crew or make eye contact with Cheesa with his usual I-love-you wink. He sat in his command chair like his body was possessed by a sorrowful spirit of melancholy. His vacant stare that looked out the forward window was unblinking, chilling, and filled with death. His crew had never seen him this way. Leucadia, who had know him the longest, trembled. He was not the Ian she knew. Harlowe had told her of the months of tortured suffering through which both Ian and Riverstone had endured on Erati and the many weeks of recovery afterward. It was a seminal moment in both their lives. Their heads were forever altered after the horrifying experience in that underground hell.

Dev said something like, "Welcome back, Captain. Did you find Anor Ran?" But Ian said nothing. His eyes were hostile and brooding. Cheesa wanted to comfort him, but Leucadia stopped her from going near him. A gentle hand on her shoulder said not now, Cheesa, let him be. To the Prince, her troubled, green eyes repeated…let him be.

In the hours that followed, Metis launched sortie after sortie of attack ships at the saucer, her force field absorbing every projectile and explosive that tried to destroy them. Only when *Forty-Four* began to show small signs of weakness in her shields, did Leucadia kneel beside Ian and say softly, "Captain, we need you." She took his hand warmly and squeezed. "Please, Ian, how shall we proceed?"

Finally, when it was fully dark outside, the town quiet, its inhabitants frightened back to their hovels, and as the main gate and the turrets still sizzled hot from *Forty-Four's* blast, Ian tearfully moved from his command chair, nudged Dev aside and turned the entire prison to subatomic dust. The rumble of the blast jolted the saucer, but the shields held firmly. He turned to Leucadia and said with a scratchy hoarseness in his voice, "There was no one alive in there, Lu."

Ian returned to his chair. The pain in his face was heartbreaking. A lesser person might have handed over the ship's responsibilities to the second in command and left his chair. But Ian stayed. Leucadia marveled at his inner strength and his ability to carry on against the obvious emotional battle going on inside him. He stayed at his post because that was his duty. He stayed because that was what was expected of him. He stayed because he was Gamadin. When he was certain Leucadia understood that he was still in charge and still capable of command, he turned to Cheesa and said calmly and without emotion, "Take us out of here, Chee, if you please."

Leucadia stood next to him as he turned his chair toward her. "It was bad, Lu . . .very bad," he said with tears in his eyes. Leucadia just listened. That was all she could do. There was no magic pill for shock. "So much evil .

. ." he went on. His eyes shut hard, blinking the tears away. "They were eating the prisoners, Lu. The guards . . . that is what they lived on. The bodies of the prisoners. They were eating prisoners like they were double-doubles. What would you have done, Lu?"

Projectiles continued to followed *Forty-Four* as she rose. She shook and she shivered, absorbing the hits, but nothing got through, not yet. Through it all, Leucadia kept her cool. "Did you find Anor?"

Ian nodded as he briefly took his eyes from the window and looked at her. "I'm not sure. I think so."

"The body in the bag. Is he alive?" she asked.

"He could be dead," Ian admitted. "I don't know."

"The robobs are doing what they can to keep him alive," she told him.

"Thank you," he nodded, his eyes still unblinking with trauma.

"But now we must save ourselves, Captain. *Forty-Four* is under attack."

Ian inhaled, and as he let go, he seemed to release the horror that had invaded his body. He said to Cheesa, "Set course for the nearest star systems after Tabilisi, Chee."

"Aye, Captain," Cheesa replied.

"Why there, Captain?" Leucadia asked.

Ian's answer was poised and self-assured. "If you had no fuel, where else would you go?"

"Yes," Leucadia agreed, "to the first star system they could find."

"And if they didn't make it?" Cheesa asked.

With Ian still silent in a brooding stare, Leucadia also asked soberly, "Do you think Harlowe is floating in space, Captain?"

Ian locked eyes with them both. "What do you think?"

Leucadia answered for the both of them. "No."

Ian went on. "Not for one second." His eyes returned to the vastness of space. "He wouldn't let fuel stop him. He's out there somewhere. Bet on it. He's left a new set of crumbs to follow. All we have to do is find some."

Leucadia nodded. "Aye."

"Crumbs?" Dev wondered. He was unaware of the reference.

Ian enlightened the Prince. "Yes, crumbs, Dev, and if Anor lives, he'll know how to read them."

"Course calculated, Captain," Cheesa announced, as she waited for Ian's order to proceed.

"Do it, Chee," Ian ordered.

98

Diversion

Harlowe didn't stick around to parley with the Surwags. He bolted in flying leaps down the beach following Monday's hoof prints. As for Monday, he obeyed Harlowe's orders and reluctantly beat it with Nath to the river. Looking back, Harlowe saw the horde stumbling on the crumbling rocks, but once they were back on the sand, they were off to the races. And with their speed, they were all toast unless he could somehow slow them down. The Surwags were tearing up the real estate, and from the looks of things, they were catching up with him fast!

So Harlowe ran for his life.

He leaped past a narrow arroyo, turned in midair, and emptied his pistol at the horde's leaders in the front of the pack. Twenty leaps, turn, and fire. Twenty leaps, turn and fire. That was the routine, and it was getting old fast. The Surwags shot arrows and heaved their spears, all to no avail. Harlowe was still out of range, but the Surwags didn't care. They picked up their spent arrows and spears on the run and fired them again. Harlowe knew his sidearm was useless. It didn't matter. He just wanted to irk them enough to forget Monday and Nath and concentrate on him.

Up ahead, Harlowe found a gap in the beach cliffs and made a beeline for the opening. In their single-minded frenzy, not one Surwag split away from the pack to chase Monday and Nath. Harlowe felt relieved. He had every confidence in Monday's ability to get the aara to *Millawanda*. If he had one regret, he wished the size of the crystal had been larger than a walnut.

When Harlowe reached the mouth of the arroyo, the sides were steep and full of loose sediment. He retrieved his assault rifle from his backpack and shot twice; one time at each side of the cliff. The sides crumbled from the blast, sending tons of rock and debris into the narrow gap and buried the first wave of Surwags under a hundred tons of rock and sand.

"Serves you right, toads!" he shouted at them.

Harlowe wanted to believe he was home free, that all he had to do was run to the cliff and wing his way down to the beach to catch up with the others waiting for him across the river.

Not so!

As Harlowe climbed his way to the top of the arroyo, he got a great view of five thousand more Surwags coming after him down the beach. To make matters worse, behind him where he thought he had slammed the door shut, the second wave Surwags were muscling their way over the debris field and were making progress up the gap. His beach access was now entirely cut off. So now it was Surwags to the right of him, Surwags to the left of him, Surwags behind him. He looked around in desperation for a place to run or hide.

Not so!

Harlowe put away his rifle and took the only path open to him, the arroyo ledge. If he hurried he could make it back to the cliff and push off, spread his wings and glide into the ocean. So with arrows clinking off his SIBA like he was a duck in a shooting gallery, he made a dash for the Lamille side of the cliff. At times the arrows were so thick he could barely see the rocky path ahead of him. Twice he slipped and almost ate it when the crumbly edge of the arroyo broke loose under his feet. With brute determination Harlowe caught himself with an outreached claw and pulled himself back to the ledge and kept running.

With his goal in sight, the ocean was never so beautiful. It was wide and green, stretching all the way to the horizon with clean lines of waves rolling perfectly into shore. One more leap would put him over the side and gliding out on his outstretched wings for a watery touchdown over the heads of the most creepy, disgusting beings he had ever known.

He pushed off and was airborne. He was about to deploy when a spear knocked his hand away from his belt activator and some heavy object struck his head, sending him sideways. The object didn't fracture his skull, but the sudden impact stunned him long enough to lose control of his equilibrium. Tumbling out of control, his arms and legs going this way and that, he fell straight down toward the waiting horde, pointing their spears upward, ready to skewer him before he hit the sand.

Then, as he was about to become the next Surwag meal on a stick, a great, winged creature came swooping down from the glare of the sun and plucked him out of the sky. Stunned by the sudden change of fate, Harlowe looked up at the big, yellow eyes with a heavy sigh of relief.

"You da man, Mowg!" he grunted.

99

Live!

The voice shouted in his ear, "Live, dude!"

Anor wasn't sure who or where the voice was coming from, and all he wanted to do was make the pain go away. Life meant nothing to him anymore. He was through with living. He didn't care about the future, the next business deal, the next anything. There was only one thing he wanted more than death: to be with Sharlon, his wife. He would do anything for one last chance to see her before going on the nether world. He wanted that one last wish in the event there wasn't an afterlife. *Sharlon, Sharlon!* He called to her. *Come to me, my love! Be with me one more time.* He longed to touch her, feel her warmth, run his fingers through her long, black hair, see her kind, thoughtful eyes staring back at him, caress her lips, touch her gentle smile, hear her wit, feel her fresh breath next to him as they rested in their private nook overlooking the valley below their castle. But if he could have none of that, he wished at long last an end to his misery.

"No, Anor, you can't check out now! You have to live! Understand? You have to live!" the voice kept shouting. The voice was closer now.

Go away! Let me die! Go away, go away...

He felt the slap on his face. "Live, Anor, you toad! You're not checking out now!"

No. Everything I had is gone. There is nothing I want more than death, except...

"Live, Anor. I didn't come all this way to save your worthless hide just to bury you. You've got work to do first, then you can sprout wings all you want, and I'll pull the trigger. Now live, I say! LIVE!"

The voice faded and was gone.

100

Dang You!

Flying north a few hundred feet above the waves, Harlowe climbed from Mowgi's claws to his back as they followed the shoreline to the river rendezvous point. The mid-afternoon sun felt good on his shoulders. He reached behind him, making sure Bigbob's cylinder and his assault rifle were still firmly in place after all the recent scrambling he had done with the horde. Touching them both with relief, he glanced to his left. The Surwags were still in hot pursuit. Their bloodthirsty screams and hissing shouts cut through the gentle rumble of the waves like a plas round through stone. The arrows and the spears didn't stop, but Mowgi was out of range so it didn't matter. There seemed to be no getting around it, the flesh eating creatures were with him all the way to the river.

"Squid!" Harlowe called to Monday using his SIBA communicator. For what seemed like an eternity, there was no response. He called two more times before making a systems check. He had plenty of juice still left in his suit's power pack. Monday should be answering, he said to himself. In near panic, Harlowe called again. "Come on, Squid, talk to me!"

"Here, Captain," Monday finally replied. *"Where are you?"*

"Mowg and I are winging it your way. Did you make it to the river okay?" Harlowe asked.

"Made it to the river, Captain, but there's a small problem. There's no river."

"What?"

"It's dried up, Captain. The river's just a trickle. Looks like someone cut the flow

488

because fish are flopping around in shallow pools."

"What about Isara and Oea?" Harlowe asked worriedly.

"Oea's here waiting for us, but Isara and Nath took off to warn Ragoss that the river's down before the Surwags get there. Oea believes it's the Tappers' doing as payback for wrecking their gerbids."

"Makes sense. They're letting the Surwags do their dirty work."

With the Surwags following him, there was now no natural barrier to keep the horde from crossing the river. Not only were Monday and Oea in their direct path, once the Surwags made their way to the river, they would follow the empty riverbed straight up the valley to Ragoss. The Fagans would be overrun in a matter of hours if he didn't get the water turned back on.

"Captain… I see you. Oh, my gawd!" Monday spotted the horde chasing Harlowe up the beach.

"I know, Squid. You can't stay there. You'll be eaten alive. Are the ceffyls with you?" Harlowe knew if Monday had his ceffyl that he and Oea could out run the Surwags.

"That's affirmative, Captain. So is Delamo."

"Take off now, Squid, and take Delamo with you. You and Oea keep heading north. Get the crystal back to Millie. Whatever you do, you have to get Riverstone that crystal. They can't last too much longer down there."

"Aye, Captain. What about you?"

"Don't worry about me. Just get that crystal back to the ship. Understand?"

"Aye, Captain. I'll get it there."

Harlowe had only one choice open to him. He knew that heading north would take Monday and Oea a lot of hard riding to cover the thousand miles to where *Millawanda* was resting offshore in her underwater hiding place. But there was no other way. He needed Mowgi to carry him up the river valley, taking the Surwags with him. If what Oea said was true, he had to figure out a way to turn the water back on to save Ragoss. He had a plan, but first he had to know Isara and Nath were out of harm's way. "Go now, Squid! Dog out!"

* * *

Monday and Oea were already a mile a way, galloping fast down the beach with Delamo running freely right beside them, when Harlowe brought Mowgi around and began following the riverbed up the valley. Like before, the Surwags didn't let Harlowe out of their sight. Circling once to give the

Surwags more to chew on, he urged Mowgi up the valley toward Elrish Dag. While his plan to rescue the Fagans was fluidly taking shape in his head, Monday broke in with a frantic call. *"Captain, Delamo saw you headed up the valley. He's following you and Mowgi, Captain!"*

Harlowe looked back and sure enough, his tall, black ceffyl, all grace on four legs, was charging up the valley ahead of the horde. The Surwags were launching arrows at Delamo by the hundreds, and so far their efforts were falling short. Delamo was starting to pull away from the front line, but one misstep or one lucky shot and he would fall from a poisoned arrow. Harlowe had no choice but to turn back. Diving in like a World War II Spitfire on a strafing run, Harlowe broke out his assault rifle and began firing on the lead Surwags. He managed to take them out, but what he didn't expect was Delamo to slow down when he saw Harlowe coming in to help him.

"Dang you, Delamo! Don't stop!" Harlowe shouted at his mount, now trying to follow him.

In a desperate move, endangering them all, Harlowe put away his rifle again, brought Mowgi around, and at just the right instant, leaped from the undog's back. The airborne jump wasn't exactly fluid. Harlowe overshot, missing Delamo by a body length. He hit the rocky riverbed hard, managed somehow to keep his wits about him without knocking himself out, bounced up, drew his pistol and came up firing an entire twenty-round clip into the horde. While reloading, Delamo swung around from the side; Harlowe reached out, grabbed one horn with his claw, threw himself over Delamo's head and climbed aboard.

"Go Delamo!" Harlowe cried out, firing another clip as he turned back and shot arrowheads on the fly before they hit Delamo. As this was going on, Mowgi covered their escape, slicing through thirty more Surwags, severing heads, arms, and ripping open bodies as he swooped in, strafing the horde's front line. It all happened so fast. Mowgi was out of arrow range before the Surwags knew what hit them. The undog's diversion allowed Harlowe to concentrate on putting distance between them and the horde. Delamo went charging up the riverbed in long, graceful strides, appearing to touch the ground only when he had to, staying an arrow's shot away from the tireless Surwags who screamed and shouted after them by the thousands.

"Where did they all come from?" Harlowe cried out, looking back.

101

Lamillian Brandy

Anor awakened in a world of darkness. Where he was meant nothing. His eyes felt opened yet he saw only an inky void. There was no up or down, angles or lines. Any references of dimension were nonexistent. So he remained still for the longest time, reveling in the fact that wherever he was, there was no pain, no cold, no putrid suffering. His only conclusion was that he had crossed the threshold to the afterlife that he so desperately prayed for over the months of his imprisonment. Too weak to initiate his own demise, he figured the holy spirits had finally granted him his merciful end.

Thank you, he said to them. *Thank you, thank you.*

Yet, the ability to conjure a conscious thought suggested otherwise. Can one think in the afterlife? His question went unanswered when he felt the rhythmic beat of his chest rise and fall as the scent of sweet air filled his lungs. This was not the afterlife he thought existed. And when he wiggled his toes and touched the silky covering with his fingers, regrettably it appeared the afterlife for him, at least for the time being, had been placed on hold.

He reached out searching for the ungodliness of his cubicle. The bitter cold, the rancid odor, and the utter slime he had wallowed in for months had all vanished. The space around him felt clean and wholesome. The air warm and dry. And so again, he surmised that he was either in a dream world, or this place was not his cell.

But how? There was no reprieve from Metis.

He moved to one side, pushing with his right hand to raise himself enough to see the blinking red, blue and yellow lights in the distance.

His hand?

The guard had cut it off some time ago when he tried to reach for more food. He should not have felt anything with his right hand. The stump that was left was seared with a brazen iron. But yet, his hand felt whole again. He could move his fingers. He could clench his fist and feel simple things like his skin and the soft fabric beneath him. His foot, too, had toes. He wiggled them again to make sure. Yes, they were there. They were frozen and had broken off, but somehow they had grown back.

How was this possible?

"You're up, huh?" a voice asked from somewhere inside the room. The blinking lights were not enough to see anything tangible. The voice, however, was familiar. It was the same voice that had shouted at him to live.

Instead of answering the voice, Anor asked, "Why?"

"Why?" the voice answered and replied simply, "Because I need you."

Like most things in life, he knew there was always a price. That was simply business. There were times when the price, however, was too high, and death was a much better choice than living. On Metis, when the venture that he had come to the planet for was compromised, he realized the power he once had meant nothing on a planet of cannibals.

Anor nodded, without words. He thought he was closer to death than that. He thought he had died the day he entered the Metis prison. He thought he would never see Sharlon, his family, or the light of day again.

"I see," Anor said, and then asked, "Do I know you?"

"I'm going to slowly turn up the lights," the voice said. "It may hurt your eyes a little, but then you will know."

"Yes, I would like that."

As the darkness fell to light, Anor saw his savior's face. Yes, he did know this being and all too well. His lips tried to move, but all he could utter was the one word, "Gamadin . . ." in a whispered breath.

"We never met officially."

"I know the uniform."

"I am Ian Wizzixs, sir. I command this ship," Ian explained.

Anor looked around. The walls, the blue carpet, the furnishings, and the doors were all familiar to him. "I don't understand. I thought..."

"Harlowe? No, he's not here. This is not *Millawanda*. You are aboard

Forty-Four."

Ian crossed the room to a lighted wall and touched several screens that suddenly came alive with Anor's internal body scans. As he spoke, he studied the screens. "You'll see in time. But for right now, rest and enjoy the hospitality." He pointed at the largest screen to his right and commented. "You're a very lucky dude, Anor. A few more hours in that piss hole and you would have been history." He touched the screens and added, "You'll be ready for a 10k in a week or so."

"10k?"

"Sorry, bad joke."

"Am I a prisoner?"

Ian smiled. "No. You're our guest. You have the run of the ship. It's not as big as Millie so you won't get lost. Tomorrow, if all your readouts are cool, we'll find you a room of your own." He pointed at a niche on the wall. "You know how to work the food dispenser, right?"

"Of course."

"Good. I'm afraid *Forty-Four* isn't programmed for double-doubles and animal fries yet, but I was able to tweak her enough to make a fair chocolate shake and breakfast burrito. Have at it."

It was Anor's turn to smile. "Thank you." And then he asked, "You call your ship, *Forty-Four*?"

"Yeah," Ian replied as he looked around the room, full of pride. "She may be small, but she's tough as nails."

Anor nodded his understanding. He had experienced the sting of the Gamadin mothership first hand. His Tamoranian fleet, along with the Consortium and the Fhaal Empire fleets were all destroyed singlehandedly by her over the planet, Og. She was the most powerful weapon he had ever seen. And if *Forty-Four* was but a fraction of the mothership's power, she was indeed a force to be reckoned with.

Anor eyed the overstuffed chair in the corner. He rolled over on his side and tried to sit upright, hanging his legs over the med table. Ian saw his difficulty and gave him a hand. As good as the Gamadin medical unit had been to save his life, he was still too weak to walk on his own. Ian lifted Anor's sickly, thin body from the table and sat him down in the chair. A robob brought a small blanket into the room and placed it over Anor's legs up to his chest.

"Better?" Ian asked.

"Yes, thank you," Anor replied gratefully. "Your accommodations are most comfortable."

"Can I get you something?" Ian asked.

"Something to drink. I am quite thirsty."

"Sure." Ian leaned over to the robob and whispered something to its lighted brim. A moment later the mechanical servant returned with a tray of amber shots. Ian held it up to Anor's lips and let him take a sip.

Anor closed his eyes savoring every drop. "Incredible. Lamillian brandy. There are only two bottles known to exist anywhere, and I have them both. Where did you get this?"

Ian gave Anor another sip as he replied, "I found a case of the stuff in *Forty-Four's* storeroom. I don't know how long it's been there, but the clickers gave it a passing grade. My dad would have a small shot when he had a head cold. It worked for him. And you being a man of good taste, I thought you would enjoy it."

"Do you know how much you could get for one bottle on the Gibbian market?" Anor asked.

Ian shrugged. "I haven't a clue."

"Wealth beyond your dreams."

"Cool. Drink it like Kool-aid then. It's all yours. I'll have some guac and chips brought in to go with it," Ian said as he handed the shot glass over to the robob.

"You would give it all to me?"

"Why not? I'm not old enough to drink."

Anor stared at Ian like he was as crazy as a Thorwellian she-beast. But as Ian was about to leave the room, he asked the question of the day. "Why am I here? Metis is a thousand light passings from Omni Prime."

Ian crossed his arms in front of him. "Simple. Like I said, I need your help."

Anor nearly choked on his brandy. "A Gamadin requires my help?"

"I need to find Harlowe."

Anor's face slid into confusion. "Harlowe?"

"I know. Strange turn of events. We were separated. It's a long story, but basically *Millawanda* has a few problems. She's an old ride and needs a tune up. The only place Lu believes we can fix her is a planet called Orixy. Heard of it?"

"Lu?"

"She is a member of my crew."

"No, I've never heard of…"

"Orixy."

Anor knew practically every planetary system for a thousand light passings out from the Omni Prime Quadrant. But he had never heard of a planet called Orixy.

"Understandable. It's far, far away from here," Ian said.

"And you need me because?"

"You know more about what lies beyond the Cartooga-Thaat than anyone we know."

"Cartooga-Thaat? You want to cross Cartooga-Thaat?"

"We're crossing it now. Quay said—"

Anor sat up, visibly troubled. "Quay? Where is she?"

"She's fine. You would be very proud of her. She is leading a group of people to a new home." At Quay's request, he would not divulge her whereabouts to her father.

"Your young captain set her on a new path."

"We're all on a new path. She told us how to find you and that you would know how to cross the Thaat and find Harlowe. We want your assistance."

Anor stared at his glass, stunned. "To cross the star desert?"

"That's just the start."

"And go where?"

Ian cut to the chase. "The Galactic core. We figure Orixy is a star system or a planet…we really don't know which, but it's somewhere near the center of our galaxy."

If Anor was traumatized before, he was even more shocked at the expedition he was being asked to guide. "Do you know what you're asking?"

"I do, but it's a journey we have to make."

"An impossible journey. The fuel alone will take more than my fleet of transport ships could carry."

"The Gamadin ships don't run on thermo-grym. You know that. That is why you were willing to risk everything to steal Millie from us. You know her power requirement are limitless."

"Yes, but the Galactic Core?"

"That's where Harlowe's headed. We have to find him before it's too late. Will you help us or not?"

"Do I have a choice?"

"I could take you back to Metis if you like," Ian suggested.

Anor stared at the young captain wondering if he was serious or bluffing. He played the game well, but he was only half the player Pylott was. The Gamadin captain would have never given him a choice. If he didn't cooperate, he would have been dropped off at the nearest rock of a planet and left to die. Pylott played to win at all costs. Still, the Lamillie brandy was fabulous, and he now had case of it for his own pleasure.

Before he could reply, a young female entered the room taking his breath away. Anor spilled the rest of the precious liquid in his lap. He didn't care. He would have traded an entire case of it to be with her for a night.

"He's awake," she said, looking over Anor like a physician examining a patient. She went to the screens on the wall as Ian had done earlier. "Yes, much better. He will live."

"We were just discussing his service to the cause," Ian said.

She stared at him with her green eyes. "And?"

Anor looked her over carefully, his mouth open in awe. "You are Neejian?"

"My mother was. I am half," she replied. "And will you guide us, sir?" she asked.

"If you tell me your name," Anor said, smiling.

"Leucadia Mars. Will you guide us, sir?" she asked again.

Anor nodded obligingly. The Neejian girl was determined. If Ian lacked the courage to return him to Metis, she would take him back in a heartbeat if he refused her request. "Of course. I am at your service, Leucadia Mars."

"Good, get plenty of rest, Mr. Ran. You're going to need it. Captain," she said to Ian as she turned and left through the sliding doorway.

Ian tapped Anor on the shoulder. "I'd be careful, Anor."

"And why is that?"

"That's Harlowe's squeeze."

Anor grinned sheepishly. "He would kill me if I, shall we say, became too friendly with her."

Ian grinned. "No, Harlowe won't kill you. But I saw the look in your eyes the moment she walked in. I would imagine it was the same look you had when you first laid your greedy, black eyes on *Millawanda*. Well, you know where that got you? A fleet of subatomic dust. Take my advice and forgettabouther."

Anor looked at the doorway Leucadia went through. "She is a remarkable female."

"You don't know the half of it. Let's just say you've been warned and let it go at that." Ian turned and headed out the door with one last comment. "TTFN, Anor."

Giddy with opportunity he saw on the horizon, Anor watched the door slide back in its pocket. Yes, he would help the Gamadin, but... *There's always a catch, huh, Anor? Nothing is ever free for services rendered.*

102

Faux Dam

It was nearly nightfall when Harlowe, riding Delamo and guarded by a giant winged creature overhead, splashed through the pools of still water toward the crumbling city of Ragoss. Behind them, the low hanging clouds from the west were awash with a fiery red glow of thousands of Surwags' torches charging after him and toward the Fagan city. Harlowe figured he had less than an hour to find the reason the river had suddenly stopped running, allowing the hordes to enter the steep gorge from the coast.

When Harlowe reached the outskirts of the city, he found Baago and his clan kneeling along the riverbank, praying for the river to return.

"Baago! Baago!" Harlowe shouted at the elder Fagan.

Baago raised his head. "Harlowe!" he called to the young savior of his people. "The river has left us. What have we done? The gods have forsaken us, Harlowe."

Harlowe dismounted and came to the elder leader. "Baago, listen to me. The Surwags are right behind me." Harlowe pointed to the flaming red sky. "You must get your people to safety. Now!"

Baago stared at the horizon in terror. "Surwags?"

"Yes. They'll be here shortly."

"Where can we go? The river has always protected us."

"Anywhere but here, Baago," Harlowe lifted the other members of the clan to their feet. There was nothing they could do on their knees. The leaders had to rally their people and leave the city before the horde arrived.

Even then, escape in the forest would be doubtful. All he was buying them was a little time.

"Can you help us, Harlowe?" a clansman asked.

"I will do what I can, my friend, but you and your people must leave Ragoss. I cannot defend you against the Surwags."

After some back and forth, the elders reluctantly scurried off to spread the alarm. It would be a tough choice for many Fagans. They were proud and courageous beings. They cared about their city, such as it was, but it was their home. Some would leave, the women and children, he figured, but the men would stay, preferring to stand and fight than leave their home to the Surwags. What would Baago do? Would he lead his people away from the city or fight? He was Nath's father. Harlowe hated the choices.

Harlowe asked the old Fagan as he lifted him onto Delamo's back. "Baago, where are Isara and Nath?"

Baago's eyes were filled with worry. "Nath has ridden west to speak with the river."

"And Isara? Where is she?"

"Isara?"

"Yes, Isara. She came here with Nath."

Baago tried to think through his fog of stress. "She has left. Her family was taken, Harlowe."

"Taken? I don't understand. Taken by whom?"

"By Darkn. His Tappers have taken her family."

Harlowe stared straight through Baago. He couldn't believe what he was hearing. The Tappers had returned with a vengeance. They had not come to Ragoss, after all, but to Fyn's ranch. *What was she doing?* She should have waited for him. A dozen Isaras couldn't help Fyn now. The old rancher was already short-handed. He had no one to help him but Muis. Harlowe could think of no happy ending. Fyn had been lucky the first time against the Tappers. Now he was too far away to help, and he had an empty riverbed to refill before the Surwags overran the city.

Do what you came here for first, a voice told him. "Yeah, right. Nath first." So how would Nath bring back the river by asking it anything? He was one of the bravest beings Harlowe had ever met and definitely Gamadin material. He loved him like a brother. *But dude, that's not the way.* Harlowe didn't have to put two and two together to understand that the Tappers had shut the gates, stopping the flow of water from the dam.

It's not the spirits of the river, Nath. It's the Tappers!

Harlowe shook as he called Monday, wondering how he and Oea were doing. But after several tries, Monday was dark. He tapped his head thinking it was his SIBA. But nothing was wrong. A quick systems check showed his suit was cool. *Was it Monday? Why can't he talk to me?* Gawd, how he wanted to be in ten places at once!

Harlowe led Delamo toward the forest with Baago on his back. Looking down at Harlowe, his mighty horns bowed, waiting for his command. "Take Baago to safety, Delamo."

Reluctantly and with a heavy heart, he let his noble mount go, watching him disappear into the night. He swallowed the lump in his throat, knowing he might never see him again as he ran back to the river where the yelling and screaming of the relentless horde was much closer than he had thought. He whistled for Mowgi, and the giant chenneroth came swooping down out of the night. At the riverbank and with one long leap off the ledge, he landed squarely onto Mowgi's back and flew on toward the dam. It had taken them a whole day to reach the dam before. It would take him less than ten minutes on Mowgi's back to travel the same distance. But before he had covered half that, the crack of Fagan rifles against blasts of gerbid cannons echoed throughout the gorge. The flashes lit up the rock walls like high power strobes as he rounded the last bend in the river before the dam. Sadly, many Fagan riders and their mounts were lying dead near the bottom of the dam. Nath and the rest of his riders were pinned down behind the massive gates. Harlowe didn't know how long they could hold out against the three gerbid tanks shooting down on them from the dam above. As he suspected, the Tappers had closed off the spillway to the dam, allowing only enough water through the penstock to keep their turbines running.

"NATH!" Harlowe cried out, waving and pointing radically toward the upper cliffs. "Get out of there! Get to high ground!"

"Harlowe," Nath shouted back over the gunfire and cannons. "The river! Tappers have stopped the river!"

Harlowe pointed as he fly by the Fagans. "Take the trail to high ground! NOW!" he demanded.

Harlowe had no time to stop and explain why the Fagans had to reach high ground. They just had to do it quickly as Harlowe swished by the Fagans, shouting orders.

Then, whisper silent, Mowgi flew straight up the side of the dam wall. When he breached the parapet he let out the loudest, gut-wrenching scream any Tappers had ever heard. So shocked by the godawful shriek, the Tappers froze in horror as the beast spit blue bolts of fire, plucking off dozens of them were they stood before they even knew what hit them. But before their blistering orange rounds could shoot him down, he dove below the tree line and was gone. They looked everywhere, down in the valley, below the dam, and skyward, but no dragon. Then from out of nowhere, the ear-piercing screech came out of the inky blackness flying low over the lake, spitting more fire. More Tappers fell as they scattered for cover. When a gerbid turret turned on the beast, a bright blast of blue energy exploded from his head, vaporizing the turret before it fired a single round.

Mowgi dipped his wings down, and Harlowe brought his Gamadin assault rifle to bear on the blocked spillway and fired, figuring a couple of well placed shots would do the trick.

But nothing happened.

Incredibly, the hits had no effect, not even a little bit. The blast left no scorch marks or dents in the barrier at all. Even with his new assault rifle ratcheted to high, it had all the punch of a Nerf bullet. The spillway blockage remained intact.

Harlowe shot two more times with the same effect until he realized what he was actually shooting at wasn't real. Like the Cornicen city, the barrier was a fake, held together by an energy field of molecular particles. The only way to take out the dam was to find the energy source and disrupt the bond that held the particles together. Taking a moment to study the problem, Harlowe saw no energy source, except the gerbids. Then that was it. The gerbids parked on each side of the dam were providing the faux barrier with all the energy it needed to keep the water back.

Harlowe shot at the second gerbid closest to him with the same result. His new assault rifle had the power to blow up anything that was real. But molecular-charged particles were a different deal. The Tapper shields required more power than the Gamadin rifle could penetrate. An explosive piton might work, but he had to be closer. This required a change in tactics. As a barrage of Tapper fire clipped Mowgi's wing in three places, Harlowe couldn't risk a forward assault on any of the gerbids. Doing an end over,

Harlowe fell off Mowgi's back and dove into the water. After that, Mowgi flew out over the dam and down the gorge. With the Tappers fully engaged on him, Harlowe made his way underwater, using his SIBA propulsion to cover the distance in the less than a minute. Coming to shore, he didn't try anything stealth. He leaped up out of the water as soon as he touched ground and came up firing. He had no head count on his way to the gerbid, but it was three and half clips worth, and Harlowe didn't miss. Just before the gerbid barrier, he attached his piton to the front of his assault rifle, clicked the explosive head to high, and fired without missing a step.

WHAM!

The explosive force was so violent, it blew Harlowe backwards fifty feet onto his butt. Any Tapper within a hundred yards of the blast was no doubt sprouting wings. Harlowe uncrossed his eyes, shook his head, and climbed to his feet, reminding himself the next time to cutback the power setting a might. He found his assault rifle close by and checked it for damage. It seemed okay. Returning it to his backpack he pulled his sidearm, snapped in a fresh clip, and bolted for the front hatch of the gerbid. He dove through open hatch. To his surprise, everyone inside was either knocked unconscious or was dead. Seeing he had no resistance, he quickly found the power box and killed the switch. Outside, the barrier disintegrated before his eyes. Water once again came gushing over the spillway and out the penstock tubes in a massive torrent. The two gerbids parked on the parapet went over the side and down the cliff, taking what was left of the Tappers with them. Immediately, the raging water flooded the gorge, roaring down the dry riverbed like a massive tsunami. There was no way for him to know if the wall of water had done its job on the Surwags. He just had to believe it would. As for Ragoss, after living for centuries near a river that often flooded, the city was built high enough above the river that the wall of water coming down the gorge would cause little or no damage to it.

As Harlowe stepped out of the gerbid, he was met by Nath, who was just coming over the ledge from the trail. They greeted each other happily as Harlowe scolded the round-faced Fagan for taking on the Tappers without him. "You toadhead, you were almost killed!"

Nath laughed. "Harlowe, we had them in our sights," he said, pointing at his rifle.

Harlowe quickly turned serious. "Where is Isara, Nath. What's happened to her?"

Nath lost his victory face. "Home, Harlowe. Word came that her father and brother were taken. She rode to help them."

"Alone?"

"Yes, alone." Nath pointed east. "Through the mountains was the swiftest way."

Harlowe feared the worst. He felt it was all his fault. Like Ragoss, he didn't realize the Tappers would muster a counterattack so fast. It seemed it was Darkn's turn for payback.

With no time to rest or break bread for saving Ragoss, he had to leave to help Isara and her family. He whistled for Mowgi, but the undog didn't respond. His normal screeching outcry didn't respond to his call. A bolt of heat went up his backbone, adding to the anxiety that was already tying his stomach in knots. One of Nath's riders came charging up from the escarpment trail.

"Nath, Nath!" the rider shouted, pointing back from the trail. "The creature. It is dying."

"Where?" Nath asked, meeting the rider in a panic.

The rider kept pointing. "Down the trail. It hangs on the side of the cliff. I think it will fall."

Harlowe didn't waste a second. He ran faster than any horse would take him, diving off the side of the cliff as he attached a dura-line to the rock. Jumping outward, he saw Mowgi clinging to the side of the cliff face by a single claw. If the undog let go, he doubted he would survive the two mile drop to the bottom of the gorge.

With the dura-line firmly attached to his utility belt, Harlowe leaped out across the rock face to Mowgi, a hundred feet below the cliff. The undog was still large and way too heavy for Harlowe to hold onto if he decided to suddenly let go.

Clinging to the rock face with his claws, Harlowe came to the side of Mowgi's head. Up and down the side of his wings were dozens of plas wounds he had taken during the assault. Sticky green ooze dripped off the wing and onto the rocks below. Harlowe didn't know how much blood Mowgi had lost but to him every drop was precious.

Harlowe cradled the large head in his arm while keeping a firm grip on the rock. "Don't let go, Mowg, okay? Just don't let go, pard."

Harlowe could see the pain in the undog's eyes saying, *I'm trying, Dog.*

"You gotta shrink up, Mowg," Harlowe said to him. He didn't know if there was a place he could touch on the undog's body that would make him get smaller without consciously thinking about it. "I can't hold you when you're Godzilla," Harlowe pleaded. "Shrink, Mowg—"

Suddenly, the unthinkable happened. The rock ledge Mowgi was gripping broke loose. The helplessness in the undog's eyes was like nothing Harlowe had ever seen. Time seemed to stop as Mowgi's claw tore away from his hold, and he began to fall away into the depths of the gorge.

103

Monday's Chair

Monday and Oea rode through the night, stopping only briefly to water and rest their ceffyls. A small number of Surwags had broke away from Harlowe's horde and continued the chase north along the coast. But the ceffyls' speed kept them well ahead of their poisonous arrows. When morning came and they had crossed over two large rivers flowing into the sea, there were no screams or outcries of the devilish beings. They figured it was safe enough to hold up for a spell.

Still, it wasn't until Monday scanned the beach for miles in all directions with his bugeyes that he'd give the okay to dismount. "It's cool," he said to Oea, as the orange light from the Ossetian sun peeked above the ocean horizon. He couldn't remember the last time he closed his eyes. The idea of some good sleep without screaming, bloodthirsty demons' whizzing arrows flying past his head was music to his ears. He wasn't asking for a full eight hours, though. Just ten minutes of peace was all that he wanted.

The high cliffs had given way to rolling, green, grassy hills. At the top of one small hill, they found a good place to rest. They could see in both directions for miles. It also protected them from the brisk wind that had dogged them since crossing the second river.

From his days lying on the beach in front of the Mars beach house, Monday dug a hole in the sand and fashioned a back rest out the pile he created. Looking down at his accomplishment, the makeshift lounge chair looked as comfortable to him as a La-Z-boy at Harry's Casino. He knelt

505

down and rolled into the cavity, sighing like a man who had toiled all day and night and stepped into a hot bath. He closed his eyes and thought to himself, nothing in the world ever felt so good.

Unless…

A warm body lifted up his arm and snuggled close to him. Her soft hair against his chin, the touch of her smooth skin, her warm arms holding him as the scent of leather and cloth and salt and ceffyl filled his senses. It was all wonderful and peaceful and natural. Now the true meaning of feeling good was complete.

"Where are we going, Squid?" Oea asked. She had never heard Harlowe call Monday by any other name, so it was the only name she knew to call him.

Oea's sweetness was intoxicating. He pushed away the strands of her long, dark hair that tickled his nose. "To a place very far north of here."

"I have never been that far north," Oea admitted. "The Clarity. They are evil. How will we defend against them? They have gerbids and flying machines that kill."

The Clarity never entered Monday's mind. His thoughts of getting *Millawanda* off the ocean floor and away from Osset were his only concerns. Explaining to Oea anything more than that would only confuse her, so he kept his answers short. "I know," he replied.

"I am worried about Isara and Harlowe, Squid."

"Me, too."

"How will they escape the Surwags without the river to protect them?"

"The Captain will find a way."

"I pray you are right, Squid."

Monday removed the blue crystal from his pouch. "If I can deliver this," he said, showing her the walnut-sized aara between his thumb and forefinger, "we can make things right again for your people, Oea."

Oea pointed at the crystal. "This stone will save us?" she asked.

"I hope it will save all of us," Monday admitted and returned the aara to its pouch.

"I don't understand."

"It may sound weird, but I don't know either. I just know without it, we are all in deep doo-doo."

She looked at him funny, leaning against his broad chest. "What is doo-doo?"

Monday wrinkled his nose. "You don't want to know."

Suddenly, like she couldn't help herself, Oea kissed him fully on the lips. For a split second he opened his eyes in surprise. She was totally into the passion. Warm and tender, he pulled her close and didn't let go. A minute passed, maybe two. He had no recollection of time. He just let the moment happen, forgetting for a small bit of time why they had come to Osset, Harlowe, the aara, and *Millawanda*. They might have stayed locked that way for the rest of eternity but for the alert vibration coming from his SIBA.

"What's a matter?" Oea asked, wanting more of him.

Monday felt his chest first, then his utility belt power box. "I'm not sure. My power levels are cool." He rose up slightly from his chair, adjusting Oea enough for him to touch the side of his SIBA. He had only felt the sound a few times since becoming a Gamadin. But each time he had, it meant the SIBA was trying to alert him to something he needed to be aware of. The sound had nothing to do with communication. That was a different alert tone. This tone was a burst, three short, one long, three short, one long and repeated until Monday shut it down manually.

He climbed to his feet, taking Oea with him. His gut was telling him the alarm was serious.

Oea became uneasy. "What is it, Squid?"

Monday covered her mouth as he activated his headgear and scanned the sensor readouts inside his suit. "It's a proximity alert. Something's coming our way," he said in a low whisper.

Oea looked around. Except for their ceffyl mounts, she saw nothing but the long, empty beach in both directions.

"Not that way," Monday said. He pointed skyward toward the rising sun. "Up there. Whatever it is, it's coming our way."

Oea saw nothing. She tried to talk, but again he silenced her with a gentle cuff of his claw over her mouth.

"There," he said quietly as a deep hum came toward them. Soon it was easy to see the squadron of ten black, spidery objects flying in V formation a thousand feet above their heads.

Monday didn't know why exactly, but he quickly hit the power activator on his suit, collapsing it to a small coin sized object that fell out of the bottom of his pant leg. He picked it up out of the sand just as two objects broke formation and headed straight for them.

"Mysterians . . ." Monday said softly to himself. "They found us."

104

Bad Boy

Mowgi dropped, but to Harlowe's astonishment, he fell only a few inches. Like he was defying gravity, the undog remained along side the cliff face with Harlowe holding onto him for dear life. His SIBA claw was strong but not that powerful. At this size, Mowgi's weight should have ripped him away from his grip. Loud, exhaustive grunts below were the reason why, as two long horns jutted outward from under Mowgi's body, keeping him up. Sounding like an Olympian weightlifter, Delamo's Herculean effort was keeping the undog from falling. Not wasting a second before he lost both of them to the depths, Harlowe switched on his power winch, and together they shoved and pulled with all their mights, inching Mowgi slowly up the side of the cliff. Even with all their muscle, Harlowe wasn't sure they could make it, until Nath and his riders roped the chenner's wings and hauled him the rest of the way up the cliff. At the top, Delamo was so spent he collapsed next to Mowgi breathing in great heaves. Fearing the worst, Harlowe uncorked a vial of Bluestuff and poured it down the ceffyl's mouth. Delamo lapped it up like it was an In-n-Out chocolate shake. With him coming around, he turned to Mowgi, who was slowly reducing himself in size.

Oh, now you're getting small, Harlowe wanted to say, but the hurt in Mowgi's dull eyes, and the green blood that oozed from his wounds, turned his thoughts of jest to the sobering effort of just keeping him alive. While he popped open another vial of Bluestuff for the Mowg, he tossed Nath a roll of Gamadin gauze. The Fagans knew exactly what to do and began wrapping the undog's midsection, legs, and neck with a tight bandage that stopped the flow of green ooze from his body. When they were done, it wasn't a pretty job, but it did the trick. The color in the undog's bulbous, yellow eyes began to brighten as the red, squiggly veins around his pupils grew thicker and redder.

It was now good news, bad news for Harlowe. The goods news was both of his animals were out of danger. The emergency first aid had worked. The bad news was he needed to be on the road to Fyn's ranch, but with both his rides laid up, he had no speedy way of getting there. Thinking his only choice left was to take off running the two hundred miles back to Fyn's and leaving his animals in the Fagans' capable hands, another choice suddenly popped into his head. And he was staring right at it…a Tapper gerbid.

Harlowe nudged Nath on the arm. "Do you know how to run one of those?"

Nath grunted at Harlowe like he was nutso. "Fagans ride horses, not gerbids."

Of course, Harlowe should have figured a Fagan wouldn't be caught dead on anything without four legs.

Harlowe started for the one remaining gerbid parked at the side of the lake.

"Where are you going, Harlowe?" DaboS, one of Nath's young riders asked.

"I'm going to check out that bad boy over there," Harlowe replied, walking toward the three story high armored truck.

To that DaboS said, "But that is a Tapper's gerbid, Harlowe."

Harlowe began climbing the ramp, eyeing its possibilities. "It's mine now," he replied.

Unlike the other two gerbids, and the ones he had encountered before, this one appeared to be an upgrade. The heavy metal body had few scratches and no dings, like it was just off the assembly line. Its wide tires were taller with much deeper treads. The fore and aft plas cannons were bigger and polished. They lacked the typical dark scorch marks on the bores from overuse. The paint job wasn't the usual drab grey-green color, either but was jet black with cool red striping through the middle and around the wheel wells. Painted on the front was an opened jawed, evil looking beast with long, blood dripping fangs. A Mowgi wannabe, Harlowe thought. He wondered, too, how well it handled and if it had enough gas to get him to Fyn's. That aside, the pluses by far outweighed any negatives he could think of.

Harlowe grunted his satisfaction. However far it got him was that much closer to Fyn's. *Cool,* he thought, as a tinge of regret welled up in his throat that Wiz wasn't here to drool over the beastly truck with him.

He stepped through the open hatch and right away smelled the odorous taint of metal, grease, and a myriad of unexplainable stenches coming from the large cargo bay filled with boxes, crates, and an assortment of things the Tappers had plundered on their raids. Harlowe had no use for any of it. He pulled Bigbob from his backpack and set the clicker to work on gutting the gerbid.

Curious to see inside the metal beast, Nath and his round-faced riders stopped short of the hatchway threshold. They seemed filled with a mixture of fear and awe to go any farther. None of them, not even Nath, had ever set foot inside a gerbid before today.

Harlowe waved them in. "Come on, guys. There's nothing to be afraid of," he said to the five Fagans. He picked up a heavy rod from the floor and tossed it against the interior wall with a loud clank. "See, it won't bite you. It's just a big heap of metal." He picked up the bar again and this time, handed it to Nath. "Nothing to worry about, brah. Ram one home for Ragoss."

Nath held the bar, studying it intently before he slammed it against the wall, following Harlowe's example. When nothing happened, a big cheer exploded from his riders. Nath grabbed the rod off the floor beating the wall like it was Darkn's face. DaboS and the others chimed in next, picking up objects off the floor and slamming them against the wall. This was all great fun for the Fagans, but for Harlowe time was precious. He needed to get the storage room cleared out and be on his way. He picked up a box and tossed it outside. The Fagans got the idea. Soon they were tossing out the plunder right alongside Bigbob. Nath also saw value in the booty and sent one of his riders back to Ragoss to fetch a party of Fagans to haul the cargo back to the city.

While the holds were being cleared, Harlowe and Nath climbed to the upper levels. A gangway encircled the entire cargo bay that led to the outer gun ports. Two more smaller ladders, fore and aft, led to the main cannon turrets. Finally, the forward ladder led to the bridge, where the driver sat just below the high-command chair. Harlowe had no interest in that chair and gave it to Nath while he went to the driver's seat. There was nothing trick about the controls. Everything was within easy reach of the curved console in front of him. He gripped the two steering joysticks and tested each independently, moving them back and forth and side to side. The buttons and switches were all clearly identified but in a language he was unable to decipher. He would have to go by the seat-of-his-pants method of learning what they all meant. Starting from his left, he pressed a large green button on the left side of the console, hoping it was the start button. It seemed the logical choice. When he did, the aft cannon exploded with a fiery round, sending a sharp jolt throughout the gerbid. A rearview video cam showed a two-hundred foot tree cut in half. That sent Nath into a uproarious belly laugh as two of his Fagans scrambled out the hatch.

Harlowe turned back to Nath with an apologetic grin. "Sorry about that."

"You must learn to read Tapper, my friend," Nath said.

"Some other time," Harlowe said, returning to the console of switches and buttons. "Can you read any of this?" he asked Nath.

Still laughing, Nath replied, "Not a word."

Harlowe decided to leave the other activators on that side alone, figuring that they were all armament related. For his second try, he went to the far right side and pressed the large button in the middle. Bingo! The giant motor roared to life. Giddy with success, he pulled a knob below the start button and the engine revved. The noise level was surprisingly quiet, which led Harlowe to believe the motor probably wasn't anything like the diesel engines he was familiar with.

Harlowe felt like he was on a roll. He tried an activator to the left of the start button, turning on the forward lights and lighting up the forest ahead even in broad daylight. Another button turned the cockpit lights on and off, while another lit up the cargo hold below. Next, he tried the right joystick by touching slightly along the axis toward him. The front wheels didn't move, but as he watched the rear screen, the back wheels moved when he brought the joystick back to its original position. The front wheels made the same movement when he applied pressure to the left joystick in the same way.

Harlowe looked back at Nath with a thumbs up. "I think I got it."

Nath tapped Harlowe on the shoulder. "You know Tapper now, huh?"

"Enough," he replied, and then asked, "Is the hold empty?"

Nath twisted around and looked down. He could see it clearly from his command chair behind Harlowe. "Yes, Harlowe. The hold is empty."

Harlowe tapped an activator next to the screen. There were three screens, and, apparently, each could be tuned to one of the many views surrounding the gerbid, including the cargo bay. A knob at the bottom of each screen allowed the operator to zoom the camera as well as position it at the desired angle. After several tries, Harlowe found the angle he was looking for: the one with his animals. Zooming in, he saw Delamo getting up. His ceffyl was a little shaky on his feet, but he willed himself to stand and remain steady on all fours. Mowgi was a different story. He was still lying on his side. Harlowe didn't want anyone but himself handling the undog, so he jumped back down the ladder, ran outside, and picked up his Mowg. With the undog in his arms, he found a soft cushion and laid him on it. He located a blanket for Delamo's back and patted his long nose. "We're going back to Fyn's now. The ride could get a little bumpy, so hold on." He gave each one another vial of Bluestuff. He only had a few left, and all he had would go to them.

Feeling satisfied that his animals were as comfortable as he could make them, he went back to his driver's chair and asked, "Ready, Nath?"

Nath nodded as he gripped the sides of the command chair. "Ready, Harlowe."

"Are your riders inside?"

Nath looked up at the screens. "Yes, Harlowe."

Harlowe touched the side of his neck, activating his SIBA headgear, which was far superior to any gerbid screens he had before him. Using his bugeyes, he not only could see out at a much greater distance, but he could read the terrain ahead more accurately, day or night.

Harlowe grabbed the joysticks, thought briefly about the direction he wanted to go, then moved them to the desired position. Suddenly, the monster truck turned three times around before Harlowe could stop it.

Embarrassed, Harlowe turned to Nath, whose eyes were wide as saucers. "Sorry. *Bad Boy*'s are a little touchy. I've got it, though. No worries."

Nath's expression didn't change as he gave the head nod to just go.

Harlowe sucked in a breath before he gently nudged the steerage sticks. This time the gerbid turned only one-hundred-eighty degrees on its axis. "Sweet." He revived the engine and maneuvered around the still smoking sections of the second gerbid. Comfortable now with the operation, he put pedal to the metal as the tires screamed, smoked, and spun like a dragster taking off from the start line. Rocks and dirt spit backwards as the giant truck roared along the shoreline, blazing its own trail and breaking two-foot thick trees like they were toothpicks.

105

An Unexpected Find

Time was against them. Monday tried to warn Harlowe, but his hail went unanswered. But a voice out of the blue that did respond was music to his ears. *"Yo, Squid, you and Dog been partying while we're swimming with the fishes down here?"*

Riverstone's voice was full of crackle and static. That didn't matter to Monday, he understood every glorious word. "Jester, that you?" It seems he and Oea were finally in range of *Millawanda's* weak communications array.

"You bet it's me. Have you seen Rerun?"

"No. Haven't seen him since we left Cornicen."

"Well, when you do, tell him Pigpo's driving Prigg and me nuts down here. The big dweeb tried to crawl into bed with me last night and wouldn't stop groaning and grunting, or whatever it is with that throat thing he does."

"Does it sound like he's going to puke his guts out?"

"Yeah, that's exactly what it sounds like."

"You didn't let him in your bed?"

"You're joking right? No, he didn't sleep in my bed. He couldn't fit through the door, thank God. I had to sleep with him in the corridor."

"Oh, that's bad."

Riverstone abruptly changed the subject back to the problem at hand. *"Listen, pard, you better have some good news for us, because this ain't no picnic down here."*

Monday hesitated, searching for an answer that made sense. He looked at Oea, gorgeous, all legs, riding in a skin-tight outfit with two pistols and a knife attached to the three-inch wide leather belt she had strapped around her thin waist as she stood holding two of the most beautiful mounts he had ever seen. How was he going to explain to Riverstone that it was all business when he and Prigg were gutting it out at the bottom of the ocean wet nursing Pigpo? "Well, sort of."

That wasn't the reply Riverstone was looking for. He wanted answers, and he wanted them quick. *"SORT OF? What kind of garbage is that? Did Harlowe's gamble pay off or not? Is Millie stuck on the bottom forever, or do you have the crystal to get us off this junk heap of a planet? By the way, where is Harlowe? No offense, Squid, but why am I talking to you?"*

"Harlowe's busy right now," Monday explained. "I'm it."

"Okay, so why the hemming and hawing?"

Monday hesitated again. The last time he saw Harlowe, five thousand Surwags were after him. The question was reasonable, but the answer would take a little finessing. "Well, it's complicated."

"All right, he's in trouble. I get it. That's always a given with him. But he was alive the last time you saw him, right?"

"Oh, yeah, he was alive all right."

"Okay, I'll keep it simple then. You have the crystal, right? Yes?"

"Yes."

"Good. You can bring it to us, right, because there's no way I can bring Millie to you."

"That's the plan."

"Cool. That's the answer I want to hear. How far away are you?"

Monday activated his headgear and zeroed in on Riverstone's transmission. *Millawanda* appeared to be five point two miles, three miles from his position and one thousand one hundred nineteen feet down, below the surface. A little deeper than when he and Harlowe were diving down on Lamille but doable. "Not far."

"All right, I'll stay on the line and guide you in."

"Can't do that, Matt, we have company. Three Mysterian drones just flew past us."

Riverstone's tone changed. *"Really? You're sure?"*

"Sensors ID'd their structure."

"That can't be good. We need to go dark, or they'll find Millie in a hurry."

"Roger that."

"Okay, Squid, just get here any way you can. We'll leave the light on for you. Riverstone out."

The connection with Riverstone winked out like it was never there. Monday scanned the skies again just to make sure the Mysterian drones hadn't zeroed in on his com. He saw nothing unusual. The sky was green and quiet. Birds had even stopped squawking in the nearby trees. Maybe, we got lucky, he told himself, then just as quickly slapped himself for believing such a naïve thought. Of course the drones had clicked on to their coms. *Standard procedure, Squid*, Harlowe's voice reminded him. They would return real soon, too, scanning the area with a vengeance. He was about to go dark when he heard a sickly groan in his ear. His sensors pinpointed the source two point three miles away, and slightly inland from the coast. It wasn't Harlowe, he knew. The Captain was hundreds of miles away. And since no one on the planet was able to communicate with a Gamadin com but another Gamadin, there was only one other person left of the crew unaccounted for: *Rerun!*

Monday snapped the power off his SIBA as he grabbed the reins of his ceffyl from Oea.

"Where are we going, Squidy?" she asked,

Monday saddled up and brought the long horns around, heading north. "To find a Gamadin."

Monday was about to charge down the beach when Oea held him up. A deep hum coming over the coastal hills had caught her attention.

106

Unleash Hell

If Harlowe wasn't in such a hurry to make it to Fyn's ranch, he would have enjoyed driving Bady Boy over the mountainous terrain. As for Nath, he had never been more frightened in his life with Harlowe at the controls. No less than six times did he think he was going to die. So far, because the terrain was filled with hazards, Harlowe found it necessary to keep the throttle between the third and fourth speed marks. He still had three more marks to go for full speed. The real test of the gerbid's power came when it approached an open ravine where a bridge had long ago collapsed. On the approach, Harlowe gunned the engine all the way to the sixth mark, draining every drop of green blood from Nath's face.

"What are you doing, Harlowe? The bridge is gone!" Nath shouted from behind as the sudden g-force slammed his body against the back of his command chair.

"I know," Harlowe replied, nudging the throttle to the seventh mark like it was routine.

"But—"

"We're getting a little air, Nath! Are your seat belts tight?"

Tight? Nath had his seat restraints maxed out from the first screeching of the wheels. He could barely breathe as it was. What did Harlowe mean by "a little air?"

Nath cried out for Harlowe to brake before it was too late. *Bad Boy* went faster. Then suddenly, the rumbling stopped, and there was silence. Nath's face grew dimensionally as he watched the ground separate from the wheels, and his body became weightless. Somewhere high above the gap, the river below looked like a wavy thread as they flew across the thousand feet of open air and landed with a jawbreaking jolt when the 300 ton monster slammed back to the planet.

The metal beast shuddered under the stress as it rocked and swayed on its mighty shocks, but it didn't complain once. It kept rolling along like it was all in a day's ride. Using the outside cams, Harlowe checked the gerbid for damage. From what he could see, it had survived with only a couple of added nicks to the fenders when they kissed the rock walls on the descent. Nothing a little touchup paint couldn't cure. Down in the storage hold, the Fagans were yelling and screaming, shaking off the sudden twists and thumps the four-point landing had done to their bodies. Harlowe wasn't sure, but he thought he heard one of the Fagans say he lost a tooth. Both Delamo and Mowgi came through in good shape. Mowgi seemed his old self again and felt right at home with Harlowe behind the wheel. The undog was standing calmly on the floor, looking normal, with his claws stuck fast to the mat. Delamo, on the other hand, had climbed up the starboard wall and used whatever he could claw onto for gripping posts.

"You okay, Nath?" Harlowe inquired, reducing his speed to a nail biting fourth mark. "Nath?" he asked again.

The Fagan leader seemed unusually quiet. He twisted around to check on his Fagan friend's condition and found him slouched in his chair, out cold. Harlowe smiled and drove on.

* * *

Once down in the valley, the weather turned nasty. The thunder and rain sounded like they were in a war zone. The deluge turned the dirt road to instant mud. The gerbid was too heavy to get stuck as it squished and splashed its way toward Fyn's ranch. When they got to the lower elevations, Harlowe slowed the gerbid to the first notch to avoid hitting the beings walking along the side of the road. They looked half starved in their tattered rags and were wet to the bone. Harlowe wanted to stop and offer them the food that was still left in the holds. But when they saw the gerbid motoring toward them, they took off running into the forest.

"They think we are Tappers," DaboS said. With Nath still suffering from shock, the young Fagan had come to the bridge to assist Harlowe with a second pair of eyes.

Two hours later, when the gerbid rolled into Fyn's valley, the rain had let up, but even the charred odor of burning wood could not mask the unmistakable stench of death.

They were too late.

"Fyn's place?" Nath asked, suddenly coming to life.

All Harlowe could do was nod silently as he brought the gerbid to a dead stop at the edge of the meadow where he and Monday first came upon the Tappers assaulting the ranch. There was nothing left of Fyn's house. The barn, the corral, and the bridge across the river were all smoldering ashes. Someone might as well have taken a bulldozer and leveled every structure to the ground.

Gerbid tracks were everywhere in the meadow. As Harlowe feared, the Tappers had returned with a vengeance. He was sick to his stomach when he climbed down out of the cockpit, lowered the hatch, and ran down the ramp toward the burning pile of ashes. What was left of Fyn's front door was still burning. It was cracked in half and black with soot. Harlowe stepped on the flames, forgetting that he might injure himself in the process. He didn't care. Not one more splinter of wood of Fyn's house would burn if he could help it.

"FYN!" Harlowe shouted, two, three times. "ISARA! MUIS!" he called out. No one answered. He activated his SIBA headgear and scanned the surrounding area for bodies. They were everywhere, Tappers along with ranch hands. From what Harlowe could see, Fyn didn't go without a fight. Of the ranch hands they found, they had all been tortured and their heads cut off. Nath and his Fagans found more bodies in a similar condition. Not one was left alive. But neither Fyn's, Isara's, nor Muis' bodies were among the dead. No ceffyls, either, and Nath knew the reason. "The Tappers have taken the ceffyls for Darkn. That is their way, Harlowe. Fyn and his family are now his slaves."

Harlowe spit on the burnt remains of a Tapper. "That's not going to happen, Nath."

"It is the way, Harlowe."

Harlowe glared at Nath. "It is not my way. I will get them back."

Nath doubted Darkn would take the ceffyls to the Osset capital of Cornicen far to the north. "He will take them for his own, Harlowe."

"If not to Cornicen, then where?" Harlowe asked.

Nath shrugged as if it were common knowledge to everyone. "Elrish Dag. He will take them there. It is his fortress at the foot of the Northern Ozans."

Harlowe walked toward the giant tread marks left behind by the gerbids. Nath already knew what Harlowe had in mind as he ran beside his long, deliberate strides.

"Harlowe, you cannot go to Elrish Dag," Nath warned vehemently.

"It's not up for discussion, Nath. If Darkn's hangout is Elrish Dag, then that's where I'm going," he replied without slowing his pace.

"No, no, Harlowe. You will die. Elrish Dag is a fortress beyond destruction. It cannot be taken."

"I've heard that from a lot of people."

Nath stepped in front of Harlowe, his dark green eyes a mixture of fear and resolve.

"No, Harlowe. You do not understand. You are not from the Ozans. This is not your fight. It is our fight. Our land, our water, our people," he pointed up. "Our air. We know the land. It was good once, but now it is evil. It will kill you. Darkn will kill you. Stay away, or I must stop you."

Harlowe kicked a dirt clod left behind by the gerbid tires digging into the soft ground. The wide trail that was left behind by the Tapper gerbids was enormous. Harlowe pointed in the direction the tracks had taken. "Elrish Dag is that way, right?" he asked Nath.

Nath grabbed Harlowe by the arms and held him fast. "Stop. We are going no farther than where you stand now. If there is a war to be fought, the Fagans will fight Darkn. But not at Elrish Dag. Elrish Dag is certain death. Fagans will fight Darkn here, like we always have, since my father and his father and his father before him."

Harlowe bent down to Nath. "I hear you, Nath. Your people have resisted the Clarity for many passings. The Fagans are the bravest people I have ever met. I'm sure one day you will be victorious over Darkn and his scumbag Tappers. But Fyn and his family can't wait that long. They need our help now. That's it! Darkn is history, Nath. He's going down. You haven't seen me when I'm angry, really angry. Now look at me. What do you see?" He pointed at his eyes. "This is anger, Nath. Do what you want. Stay here, go home, or go with me. It's up to you, but I'm going to Elrish Dag to find

Fyn's family and bring them home." He ended with such intensity that all Nath saw was evil.

Nath took a long, futile breath and said, "Then we will all die together, my friend."

"That's not my plan. It's Darkn who's going down, Nath," Harlowe seethed. "That's a promise!"

They both stood, looking into each other's faces like two fighters about to go to blows. Neither blinked nor backed down. Then Harlowe's white teeth began to show between his lips. Nath couldn't hold it much longer as his yellowed and cracked points appeared between his lips. Harlowe nodded with satisfaction as he grabbed Nath by the back of the neck, and they walked back to *Bad Boy*. Together they would unleash hell on Darkn's world.

107

Slippery Slope

There was little light left of the day as Monday and Oea rode along a dry riverbed, searching for the origin of the Gamadin signal that he hoped was Simon's. Two miles into the gorge leading away from the ocean they found what sensors indicated was the source: a steel grey and brown military vehicle high up on a steep incline. It appeared it to have been there for some time. A small tree was the only thing keeping it from crashing to the bottom of the gorge. The loose rocks on the slope made the going too slippery for the ceffyls. A hundred feet below the vehicle was as far as they could go without bringing down the side of the incline and the vehicle with it. Now they could see the dozens of scorched plasma holes that riddled the vehicle. Monday recognized Simon's gaudy uniform sleeve sticking out of the broken windshield. He wasn't moving.

After a quick search, Monday didn't see or detect anyone in the area. He handed Oea his reins and told her to stay put. She didn't question what he was going to do next. Over the days they had been together she had witnessed the many amazing feats that he and Harlowe had performed together. She had come to trust his judgment and let him work. But like a good pard, she unholstered her weapon in case he needed her backup.

Monday attached a piton head to his pistol and fired at the rock face above the vehicle. The explosive head held fast. After a couple of tugs, he slapped his belt winch to the line and started crawling up the gravel slope. When he reached the height of the vehicle, he sidestepped his way across

521

to the overturned car. It was smooth going until he came within a few yards of the vehicle, and the cliff began to give way. Monday froze knee-deep in gravel looking at the gash along the side of Simon's head. His SIBA hadn't protected him. Apparently he had reverted back to his Julian Starr outfit when he saw the Mysterians. He was so still, Monday wondered if he was even alive.

"Rerun," Monday called out, being careful not to cause anymore disturbance than he already had. He called three more times, each time his voice grew louder. Monday was about to risk lunging for the car when Simon's left hand moved ever so slightly, squeezing a multi-faceted object about the size of a tennis ball.

"Rerun, wake up," Monday urged.

Simon mumbled something unintelligible.

Monday held out his claw hand to warn him. "Don't move, Simon. The cliff under you is about to go."

Simon groaned again. The only word that Monday could make out was a whisper quiet, "Nareeee."

Monday remembered they last saw her with Simon back in Cornicen. From a quick search of the vehicle it was clear Simon was the only one inside.

"Naree," Simon said again as he continued holding the object tightly in his hand. "Naree, Naree," he gasped repeatedly.

Monday was at a loss. He knew if he moved any closer, the vehicle would tumble down into the gorge with Simon in it. But then the worst possible thing happened. Plas rounds began hissing past him, striking the vehicle from above. Monday looked up and saw a drone hovering over the gorge, spitting orange projectiles at their position. Now he had no choice but to activate his SIBA and shields. As he did, the rounds struck the incline, causing unstable ground to give way. Monday reacted with the only choice he had… he leaped out and grabbed Simon by the collar of his uniform as the vehicle started to slide. Holding on with one great heave, Monday pulled him out of the side window as the car dropped away, bouncing and flipping down into the gorge with a loud crash. Locked together in a life and death grip, they rolled together as the rocks broke under their combined weight. They twisted round and round together with the avalanche of loose rock roaring into the gorge. Through it all, the dura-line held. Unaware of all that was going on around him, Simon kept thirstily wheezing for Naree, drifting in and out of consciousness as Monday swung his back around, doing his best to protect Simon against the incoming rounds. Just when he was expecting a sizzling hot round to his head, an ear-popping explosion detonated above the rim of the gorge. When Monday twisted around again, the fiery remains of the drone hit the incline, adding to to the burning pile at the bottom of the gorge.

With Simon tightly in his grasp, he swung away from the slide. Below, Oea waited for him, holding his rifle, as she kept an eye on the sky above. There was no time for thank-yous, nice-shots, or that-a-girls. A quick nod of appreciation was all he had time for. They mounted their ceffyls and rode out of the gorge as fast as they could ride. There were still more drones out there, probably already zeroing in on their position at that very moment. As Harlowe would say, "Count on it!"

108

Eradication

The deep reports of gerbid cannons awakened Harlowe with a start. The orange sun was low on the horizon, and Bigbob was at the controls of *Bad Boy* while he napped. Nath laid a soft hand on Harlowe's shoulder and said, "They are not shooting at us, my friend."

Through the forward window a dark grey skyline of another no-named city lay ahead. A low-hanging, smokey haze hung over the buildings like Death had arrived ahead of them. The tallest structures pushed through the clouds, appearing to grow through a muddy ooze. Like Ragoss, the ity was crumbling in decay. Along the main road, trees and vines grew out of control, cracking the pavement and the foundations of buildings. Like refugees in a war zone, beings were fleeing the city in droves with whatever worldly possessions they could carry. The moment they saw their gerbid, like before, the exiled dropped what little they had and ran screaming into the woods. The Tappers had shown no mercy here, either. Along the road were hundreds of dead bodies of men, women, and children who never made it out of the city. They were shot or mowed down by gerbid tires in a wholesale slaughter.

Harlowe was sickened. Upon their approach to the city, two black gerbids stood watch as Darkn's forces continued their plundering.

"Steady as she goes, Bigbob," Harlowe said, touching the ball shoulder of his clicker.

Nath looked over at Harlowe nervously.

"They won't shoot us," Harlowe said calmly. "They think we're one of them." Then he pointed at the main forward cannon and asked Nath, "Can you handle that?"

Nath smiled back. Of course he could. It was a gun, wasn't it?

The Fagan leader eagerly climbed the short ladder and sat himself down in the main battle canopy like it was second nature. He was about to turn on the weapons array controls when Harlowe cooled his jets. "Not yet, Nath. Let's let them think we're here to join the party."

As they rumbled closer, Harlowe relieved Bigbob at the helm. The big robob was quite capable of handling the gerbid, but when the slop hit the fan, Harlowe wanted the controls. Robobs were unemotional. It was their nature. Where he might hesitate in pulling the trigger, Harlowe, on the other hand, would not. After seeing what Darkn's Tappers had done to Fyn's ranch, his ranch hands, and the cruel butchering of the city's inhabitants, this was a take-no-prisoners moment for him.

When they came to within a hundred yards of the two gerbid sentinels, Harlowe called to the canopy, and ordered, "Do it, Nath!"

Nath grinned with pleasure as he switched on the cannon generators to full power. The green lights on the weapons array console lit up his round face like an Ossetian moon. When all was ready, Nath glanced down at Harlowe for one last okay. Harlowe just nodded, his eyes hard, fixed with the complete and utter annihilation of the Tappers.

BOOM!

The first blast practically tore the first gerbid in half at this range. Then before the second gerbid could react, Nath swung the massive muzzle to the right and—

BOOM!

Two more rapid shots blew it to parts unknown.

Harlowe eased the throttle forward and motored like hungry Death on the prowl. He didn't care how many gerbids there were. All he knew was by the time they were done, the city would be eradicated of Tappers.

109

No Place to Hide

They broke out onto the open beach when Monday's bugeyes picked up a pair of tiny dots on the horizon. Traveling at hypersonic speeds, the drones would be on them in minutes. At the water's edge, Monday hopped off his ceffyl, taking Simon down and laying him face up on the sand. He reached out to Oea, and she tossed him his Gamadin assault rifle. She seemed to know exactly what he wanted without asking, except one thing. Monday handed her the reins of his ceffyl and yelled, "RIDE!"

"No, Monday. I stay with you," Oea pleaded.

"You can't, Oea," he said and pointed at the ocean. "I must go there. I can't take you with me. Please, go, before the drones get here."

"No, Monday!" Oea begged with tears in her eyes. After all they had been through, she couldn't end it this way, even with Death about to descend from the skies. Especially now!

Monday scanned the horizon. Ten more drones had swooped in from the stratosphere right behind the first wave.

"Go, Oea. You must save your ceffyls. They will be killed if you stay. Please, Oea. Let me handle this. If you don't go, we will all die!"

Oea struggled. She couldn't leave Monday's side, but she seemed to sense their was no other choice. Monday was right. Their mounts would be killed. Finally, she galloped over to him and kissed him hard on the lips. When she broke away, her eyes spoke to him. This wasn't goodbye. She was telling him to come back to her or there would be hell to pay.

526

Rifle in the air, he shouted at her galloping away on a dead run, "I WILL!"

She never looked back, not once, as she rode flat out south back to her home.

Monday was heartbroken. In his entire life he had never cared for someone as much as Oea. But what choice did he have? This was not about Oea, or him, the ceffyls, or even saving Simon. They were all expendable. It was about what he had in his pouch. The crystal was everything. It was *Millawanda's* only chance for survival, and without her, they were all dead.

He turned away from Oea and slapped in a fresh mag for his rifle. The blue light glowed hot. That done, and with only seconds left before the drones were on them, he grabbed Simon's SIBA from around his neck and sealed him up. He didn't have time for a complete systems check, just a quick once over to make sure his headgear was tight and he was breathing. That was it! Then lifting him over his shoulder, and with his rifle firmly in the other hand, Monday sloshed his way through the shore break for open water.

By the time he was hip deep, the drones were on him, blasting the water all around him. Monday angled his rifle upward and squeezed off two rounds in succession. At this range, Gamadin don't miss. Two black, spider-like drones went bye-bye, raining shards of hot metal around them. With less than a minute before the others were on him, a wave came out of nowhere, driving him backwards toward the beach with no cover and no Simon. He got up and got off three quick rounds and three kills before he spotted Simon's legs and arms, twisting and flailing in the shallow surf. He got another kill over his shoulder as he managed to grab Simon's ankle. He was pulling him back out to deeper water when a drone struck him in the shoulder, knocking him down. Scrambling to his feet, Monday came up shooting. A dozen rounds later and the sky was clear, but he had run out of ammo. He kept pulling the trigger, but nothing came out. A quick glance at at the power light, and it was dark.

Disoriented from the fog of battle, he turned back to the water, and Simon was gone again. He was no longer nearby but a hundred yards down the beach, floating face down in the water. With his SIBA, Simon could breathe under water. The worry was more drones, and he had no way to save Simon or himself unless they went to deeper water.

High stepping as fast as he could, Monday dashed through the shallow shore break, picked up Simon's dripping body and flung him over his shoulder again. He turned once more and looked out at the long flat shore break he needed to wade through to get back out to deep water. Instead of a quarter mile, it seemed more like a mile. He hadn't figured on the tide retreating so fast. Head down, he lunged forward, making his way back through the surf when a throbbing hum stopped him in his tracks. The drone dropped down out of nowhere and faced him over the ocean. Standing in ankle deep water on a wide-open beach with an empty rifle and no place to hide, Monday laid Simon aside and pulled out his pistol. It was like taking a pea-shooter to a nuclear war.

110

Montevideo

Harlowe looked south and saw the black storm clouds coming their way. SoCal had storms but never like this. The wind and rain outside the gerbid were already gusting over a hundred sixty miles per hour ahead of the front. The rain pelting the gerbid windshield sounded like bullets. Harlowe felt grateful he was inside the biggest, badass tank on the planet as Nath brought the aiming dots together on another Tapper tank. "I have them, Harlowe!" he shouted down to the bridge.

His crew of one tall robob and six Fagan gunners was about to destroy their thirteenth gerbid in the cleansing process. They had to act fast. Darkn's gerbids were still blasting their way across the the city, killing and plundering as they went. There was no way of knowing how many monster tanks were left. The best they could do throughout the night was follow the destruction, crisscrossing the streets and sniffing out every gerbid they could find before they killed more helpless inhabitants.

Unlike Cornicen's manufactured molecules, this unnamed city was real. Its many walls were three-feet thick of reinforced concrete, brick, and stone. No doubt this was to protect the city from the massive storms that blew down from the Orzans, Harlowe thought. As fortress-like as the buildings were, the city had culture and was built with many faces. Old ornate buildings stood next to modern skyscrapers. A once thriving industrial section merged into suburbs of art deco homes and colonial estates of verandas and porches, once beautifully landscaped along a riverfront embarcadero. It reminded

Harlowe a lot of the capital city of Uruguay, Montevideo, where he and Leucadia had gone on a trip to South America. At the time, he was unaware of her purpose, which was to search for *Millawanda's* clues. The trip's motives may have been secret to him, but he never forgot that city and the places they traveled. Especially Montevideo, its beaches, its surf in front of their hotel, and the cozy, little tango bars they discovered along the boardwalks at night under a heaven of bright southern stars.

Harlowe sighed, remembering how the ocean played and the breath of salty air blew warm across their faces, holding her, kissing her often, looking into her green eyes filled with happiness as he caressed her golden hair glistening under the city's lights. No, he couldn't let one more blast destroy another theatre, museum, or beautiful building. Not this city. Not Montevideo!

With surprise on their side, the bulk of Darkn's forces were easy prey. They never suspected one of their own would be out to kill them. The majority of the gerbids were in the open, shooting into buildings for no reason other than destruction. Two smaller gerbid tanks had to be handled differently than the others. They had motored down one alley where the buildings were too close together. One explosive shot from the cannon and the buildings would be destroyed along with the gerbid they were trying to kill. Harlowe solved the problem by tossing a low output thader under each tank.

Varoom!

Nath's Fagan riders then dusted the Tappers as they exited the burning tank.

Every Tapper was a target. No mercy. No escape. And the Tappers that managed to flee without being shot were quickly hunted down like rats by a raging chenneroth.

"No, Nath," Harlowe responded to Nath's call to fire. "I want this one alive."

Nath had the battlewagon clearly in his sights. "The markings. It is their lead gerbid, Harlowe."

Harlowe didn't care about markings. What he did care about was what it was carrying in its hold. "*Bad Boy* needs a resupply of ammo, Nath, before we go to Elrish Dag," he explained.

Nath looked down at his power meters. He had four shots left. He had been so focused on killing Tappers, thinking about what rounds were left in the magazine had slipped his mind.

Nath grunted. Tappers deserved the best shot he had. It was full power, or he would throw himself in the river as Surwag meat.

"Throttle back and target their fuel line," Harlowe ordered.

Nath squinted. The gerbid's armor plate was covering the engine compartment. How would he hit anything at low power?

"It will have to be dead on," Harlowe instructed. "So don't miss."

Grumbling his distaste for the reduced shot, Nath fired once. Missed. Fired three more times and hit all three, but the power settings were set so low, they hardly nicked the outer hull.

Between the second and third shot, the Darkn gerbid turned on them. In a panic, Nath rammed the cannon throttle back to full and fired. This time the plas round was so powerless, it appeared like a bright, fuzzy ball of orange cotton as it hit the battlewagon's armor plate and careened harmlessly into the sky. The spent round went skyward and looked like a 4th of July fireworks rocket when it burst into a million bits of brilliant tiny flashes.

"What happened?" Harlowe asked Nath, more than a little anxious that their main weapon had lost its punch.

Quickly, Nath reloaded and fired again. This time the cannon couldn't even produce a respectable cotton ball. Meanwhile, the Tapper tank's muzzle swung around and zeroed in on their cockpit. Nath kicked and pounded his fist against the control console, but nothing he did could bring the cannon back to full power. With no time to waste, Harlowe popped out of his driver's chair, threw open the upper hatch, and pointed his small assault rifle at the battlewagon.

Now, by the gods, what did Harlowe think he was doing, Nath wondered? Had his new friend lost his mind? If the situation wasn't so serious, Nath might have had a belly laugh over watching Harlowe trying to stop a full-sized gerbid with a rifle shorter than his arm. Even if Harlowe's small rifle could somehow shoot that far with accuracy, the storm was growing stronger by the minute. The rain and wind were so strong, Nath could barely see the outline of the gerbid from his chair. Wanting to help, Nath reached down on the floor and picked up his own rifle that was never too far from his grasp. He couldn't let Harlowe make a fool of himself. His friend should have a real weapon like his Fagan rifle to shoot the gerbid before it sent them to their ancestors.

Holding his rifle with in one hand, Nath grabbed the rim of the hatch with the other and lifted himself up the instant Harlowe pulled the trigger of his toy rifle. The blue flash from the muzzle was so bright, it nearly blinded Nath. Harlowe handed his rifle over to him and commented casually, "There, that should do it."

Nath didn't know exactly what his friend meant until he looked across the distance and saw the black smoke billowing up from the Tapper tank. Harlowe said, "Take a look through the scope. He's down. We should hurry, though, in case he decides to scuttle her."

Nath put his eye up to the lens and was shocked by how clearly he could see through the storm. The Tapper's turret was blown away. His focus then went to the side hatch where a struggle was going on between a Tapper officer and a dark-haired female. Nath quickly handed the tiny rifle back to Harlowe and pointed at the gerbid. "Isara is there, Harlowe."

Harlowe grabbed the weapon and tried to zero in on the hatch. At first the rain was so thick, there was nothing to see.

"You're sure it was her?" Harlowe asked.

"Yes, it was her. It was Isara. The Tapper commander had a gun at her head," Nath replied. "I only saw her for a few seconds, but I know it was her, Harlowe."

Harlowe made sure his rifle was locked and loaded before returning it to his backpack. He was heading for the ladder down to the hatchway when Nath asked, "Where are you going, Harlowe?"

"To get Isara," Harlowe replied sharply.

"No, Harlowe. If the Tappers don't kill you, the *glaw* will," Nath warned.

Harlowe presumed what Nath meant by glaw was the hurricane force winds that were snapping trees and kicking up debris so much he was unable to see but a few yards in front of his face, even with his bugeyes. "I'm going after Isara, and no one is stopping me."

"The glaw will, my friend!" Nath shouted at Harlowe as he took one step out of the partially opened hatch before the blast from the glaw blew him off his feet and slammed him against the side of his gerbid like he was an insect.

111

You're Joking?

Monday faced the drone. Maybe he was dead meat, but he had shots left. The black, engineless mass fired just above the waves. The orange shot streaked over his head and exploded fifty yards behind him. It wasn't even close.

He casually checked his pistol. Four rounds. Humm, he thought, better make them count. He confronted the pilotless thing, its whippy antennas, moving and undulating, zeroing in on his position for a better shot.

Monday raised his hand, waving it closer. The drone's buzzing noise grew louder just before another orange ball of sizzling spit whizzed passed his head and exploded.

"Not even close, butthead!" he shouted and waved at it again with his pistol. "Come on. Is that all ya got?"

The third try zeroed in on his head. Monday ducked. "Another miss, turkey!" Drifting lower by another hundred feet, the drone leveled off, cutting the distance between them by half and fired two successive volleys this time. Monday turned sideways. One round sizzled past his bellybutton while the second nicked the back of his leg, spinning him around to one knee. Looking down at his leg, there wasn't a scratch. His SIBA was tough, but he wondered how it would protect against a direct hit.

Monday grunted as he tried to stand. "Where did you learn to—"

WHAM!

Monday tumbled backwards like he had been hit by a Quincy right cross at level 4. "That's better. That's better," he said, lying flat out, covered with wet sand. Stunned and disoriented and with his pistol still in hand, he rolled over as the surf receded and then squeezed off a round right between its antennae.

BAAHLEWEEY!

With sizzling shards falling into the ocean, Monday groggily got to his feet. "See. That's how it's—"

BOOM, BOOM, BOOM!

Monday went flying, tumbling over and over, and lost his pistol from the blindsided hit. He pulled his face out of the sand in time to see three more drones buzzing toward him. He reached for his pistol. It was gone. His body felt intact, but his head was scrambled eggs. He crawled for his weapon. It was covered with wet sand. It didn't matter. He found the trigger.

Three shots, three kills.

"If you're going to shoot, shoot," he grunted in pain. "I haven't got all day to screw around."

Feeling cranky because his head was throbbing, he wanted a whole bottle of Bluestuff to make the hurt go away. Add to that a kiss from Oea, and he would take on the whole damn Mysterian fleet!

He slumped back on the sand like a beached whale and contemplated his next move. He figured if it wasn't for his SIBA's protective shield, he would have been easily fried. As it was, he was only stunned and shook himself out of the temporary daze as he stared at his sidearm with a whole lot of respect. Getting up was getting tougher. He found Simon not far away. The shore break swirled around his inert body making his head turn one way then the other. Monday checked his vitals. No change. Simon was still among the living but oblivious to all that was going on around him. Amazingly, through it all, he never lost hold of the faceted ball in his hand.

Monday sighed exhausted; the thought of carrying him again didn't set well. Dragging him felt like a better option. Breathing hard, he grabbed the back of Simon's ankle and began towing him out to sea like he was road kill. They were doing well, too, when a fearful vibration came from behind. It was an exact copy of the other drones, only a thousand times bigger and undoubtedly had the fire power to match. The muzzle ends of its guns were large enough for him to crawl through.

Monday slid the aara out of his utility pouch and put it inside Simon's pocket with the medallion he was carrying. Then he let him go to drift into shore, hoping that whatever happened to him, at least Simon and the crystal would survive.

The vibrations grew louder. At any moment its thick, black antenna would find him, and it would be over.

CRACK!

Monday couldn't believe his eyes as the massive drone's face, antennas, and all split in two by a tremendous blast of blue light. Exploding over the beach, fragments of fire scattered everywhere as the main body slammed against the cliffs.

From certain death to salvation, all in a single breath, Monday hurried to catch Simon before he got away again. Dragging him back out to sea was getting old.

"Hey, Squid!" a familiar voice called to him through his com. *"What are you trying to do?"*

He turned around looking for the source of the transmission. High stepping out of the shore break was another SIBA carrying a full size Gamadin rifle. Now that made a lot more sense, he thought. After seeing what a fully charged rifle could do to a mountaintop ten miles away, a drone, even the size of this one, would be like killing a bee with a *Forty-Four* magnum. There was only one person he knew with that kind of swagger in his voice. "Man, am I glad to see you, Jester."

Riverstone slung his rifle over his shoulder and reached out with a helping hand to lift Simon out of the water. With the fiery debris smoldering around them, he asked, "Not a moment too soon, huh?"

"Not a moment."

"What was it?"

"Deadly."

Riverstone scanned the debris field with his bugeyes. "Looks Mysterian."

"It is."

"Anymore around like that?"

"They just appeared. They're homing in on our suits."

Riverstone kept searching the sky. "Yeah, we better make ourselves scarce. Harlowe still AWOL?"

"Long story."

Riverstone didn't like the way the conversation was going. "Where's the crystal?"

Monday retrieved the aara from Simon's pocket. "I've got it right here." He placed it in Riverstone's claw.

Turning it around in the sun like a jeweler, Riverstone asked, "This is what we came here for?"

"Yep."

"This is going to get Millie off the bottom of the ocean and into space?"

"The Captain thinks so."

Riverstone kept looking at the blue stone in disbelief. "You're joking. Tell me you're joking, Squid, or I'm going to let the next drone fry your ass," he threatened, pointing at the fires around them. "Do you know what it's like being down there with Pigpo and Prigg for roommates?"

"It can't be fun," Monday figured.

"No, it's not! It's a long ways from fun. On a scale of one to ten, it's a minus fifty! It's frickin' miserable down there. And all you have to show me is a blue walnut."

"A blue aara," Monday corrected.

"A blue? What does it matter? It's a blue rock."

"Not just an ordinary blue rock. It's Gamadin blue aara." Monday held up the crystal like it was magical. "We found it in the babe's underwear five hundred feet under water. Now how's that for possibilities?"

Riverstone wasn't impressed. His eyes rolled as he glared down at Simon. "What's wrong with Bolt? Is he sprouting wings?" Riverstone asked, bending down to turn Simon over.

"Last I checked he was breathing."

"My sensors say he's still alive . . . but barely. That's a plus."

"I was trying to get him to Millie."

Riverstone replaced Simon's power module with a fresh one. "Millie's not much help. She can hardly keep us alive, Squid."

"We can't let him die."

"Prigg will think of something. We'll stuff him in an enviro-bag if we have to." Riverstone handed him off to Monday. "Better go. We can't stay here, that's for sure. The Mysterians will be back looking for payback."

"Aye."

Riverstone lifted Simon over his shoulder, and together they double-timed it into the surf as fast as their SIBAs could take them.

"What's that buzzing sound?" Riverstone asked, sloshing his way through the surf.

Monday zoomed his bugeyes on dozens of objects on the horizon. The lead drone fired off a bright orange round their way. "We really made them mad this time."

Riverstone ducked under a wave and asked, "Are they big or small ones?"

"They're all big," Monday replied.

Two more shots hit the water around them. The drone's aim was improving, and they had another quarter mile to go before they could dive into deeper water.

Riverstone pointed with his free hand. "Nail the lead suckwad! That should give us some time!"

Monday ripped off three quick rounds while Riverstone continued on with Simon. Even five miles out, Gamadin sights were lethal. The first shot severed the lead drone in half and at the same time cut off the wing of the drone behind it. A twofer! The second and third were direct hits. The rest of the squad scattered, but the other formations behind them kept their speed, bursting through the debris field as if nothing had happened.

"Nice shooting!" Riverstone exclaimed as Monday caught up, and they dove beneath the surface. "Did it slow them down?"

"Not even a little bit!" Monday exclaimed.

112

Crumbs

Ian paced along the riverbank. It was midday. A few pink and bruise-colored clouds drifted overhead like little puffs of cotton, but it was nothing threatening. *Nothing!* That word again. It was all his mind could say to him. *Nothing!* This was the seventh planet they had searched for *Millawanda*, and for the seventh time they found no trace of their ship. *Nothing!* If the planet they were on didn't already have a name, he would call it *"Nothing!"* But it had a name. What was it again? Esco? Grackdoa? No, it was Niz. Yes, that was it. Niz. Normally, Ian would not have put down on a planet unless they found something of interest. But after weeks of travel from planet to planet in search of their mothership, everyone needed some wide open air. Especially the cats. They needed to get out and stretch their legs. On *Millawanda*, Dodger's Place was so large they could roam the artificial habitat and feel like they had never left #2. But *Forty-Four* was too small for artificial environments. A week or ten days was all anyone, human or beast, could stand being cooped up in a ship without putting down somewhere under a warm sun and an open sky…if they could find one, that is. Niz was the first planet in three weeks where they could land and not have to worry about the locals getting their prickly hairs in a bind over an alien ship searching their planet for whatever reason. Ian pointed his face toward the orange sun, allowing the soothing rays to calm his malaise. It only helped a little bit. It was the two arms around him that more than anything else kept him positive. Her flowery freshness, her warmth, and their closeness eased his worries as much as a thousand suns. "You will find them, Ian," Cheesa said in a soft voice.

Ian could only utter a muffled grunted. On the bridge a grunt reply was never questioned. But during off-the-clock time, the strict rules of command were tossed. Ian's garbled mumble wouldn't fly. Cheesa turned him around and stared him down, eye to eye. "You will find your ship and your friends, Ian, and they will be okay. There can be no other answer that has meaning. So don't you dare snip at me, you haapflin beast," she scolded.

Ian stared back, or tried. He found his eyes drifting to one side, unable to match her strength.

"Look at me," Cheesa demanded. "Look at me, Ian."

She shook him, not harshly but lovingly, enough to get his attention. He had never had a "girlfriend" before. Lu was a girlfriend, of course, but she was different than Cheesa. Lu was more like Harlowe and Riverstone. She was a pard. Besides, she was Harlowe's girl and always would be. The way they looked and spoke to each other, the respect, the worry in their eyes when one or the other was in trouble, and the way they finished each other's sentences, they knew their thoughts, their likes and dislikes, how they held hands and kissed. Man, there was no one else whom Harlowe could love . . . except . . .

Before he finished his thought, Cheesa shook him again, forcing him to give her his full and undivided attention. "Where did you go, Ian?"

Ian saw her worry for him and the way he was beating himself up over something out of his control. It was a massive universe out there, and to expect to find a single speck of sand on a beach in a thousand miles of sand was beyond description as to how difficult that was. The edge of Cartooga-thaat had few star systems where life abounded. Harlowe could be anywhere. It was possible he might never have made it across the Thaat at all. But Leucadia thought he had made it, because in the thorough searching she and Cheesa had done, so far they had discovered no sign of Millie's power signature. Not one peep. "Besides," Leucadia said as confidently as anyone can, "it's Harlowe were talking about, Ian. You know he made it, and I know he did. The problem is where did he make it to?"

Yes, where? That was the galactic question. It would take a thousand years of searching to find a ship the size of *Millawanda* with *Forty-Four's* limited resources. Where did Harlowe go? Space was not like traveling on

Earth. Traveling on Earth was two-dimensional. Forward, backward or left or right, traveling on the same plane. In space there was that, but also up and down. Farnducky called it the 'z' dimension. Harlowe might have gone in a zillion different z directions if he had the power. Fortunately, *Millawanda's* power was so low, traveling much farther beyond the edge of the Thaat was out of the question. So that's where they searched; the planets and star systems along the edge of the star desert. Still, to find a crumb, a tiny speck indicating direction was all that he needed. Harlowe would know that, too. That is, if he knew the crumbs would lead them to him. But he didn't know. Harlowe had no idea they had escaped Nod, found a Gamadin ship, and had crossed the Thaat with a half dozen crystals the size of a human. Oh mygawd, to see the look on Harlowe's face the moment he lays eyes on that aara. Where did you find it? he would ask. Ian giggled. He couldn't wait to say. "Just lying around."

"No, no, you were somewhere else," Cheesa barked, interrupting his thoughts again. "You were not with me. I want you with me, Ian Wizzixs."

Ian grinned defensively. "Captain." He didn't deny her observation.

She punched him playfully in the stomach. "Captain, huh? Do you want me to leave you alone?" she asked.

Ian shook his head. "No," he replied, looking away at first, then coming back to her thoughtfully, holding her hands, feeling how natural and warm they felt together.

"You want me to stay then?" she asked.

"Yes. Stay, Chee, don't go."

Her eyes brightened when he said that. Ian went on: "I've never had someone like you in my life before. A girlfriend, I mean. Harlowe and Riverstone always had girls they dated or cared about. Not me." Ian let go a small chuckle. "The way they always complained about their girlfriends and how they caused them so much trouble . . ." He laughed again. "Well, I wanted no part of that noise. I stuck with cars. They never complained. Life was uncomplicated that way. I could go anywhere and do anything I wanted, and my cars were always happy to see me. So I went through life never worrying about anyone but me. Me, me, me. That was me, Chee. Worry only about me, me, me."

"What are you saying, Ian?"

"My life has changed, Chee."

"More complicated. You have told me that."

"I know. I know. I have said that. That's true. It is."

"And you regret it? You wish it was just you and your cars, Ian?"

He looked at her strangely. Her questions were innocent enough, but the meaning behind them ran deep. Her manner was thoughtful, unaggressive, but most of all…sincere. She wanted the best for him, but at the same time she understood it was not for her to say what was right and what was wrong. It was his life to discover. Not hers. She could not give him happiness, but together they could find it. Their differences, their wants, their combined strengths and weaknesses, could unlock a world of happiness that neither ever knew existed before. But it would be complicated, hard, filled with ups and downs, anger, hate, joy, happiness, and love. It was all part of the glorious mix he was now just starting to understand.

He pulled his arms around her. "Yes, but I didn't mean that," he told her.

"You said it."

"I said it, yes, but I didn't mean it that way."

"Tell me what you meant then. I am here. I am listening. Talk to me, Ian. Tell me what frightens you."

He laughed. "You do. And not just a little bit. Loving you frightens me." There he said it. He sighed feeling that a whole world opened up to him. She was there in his arms, all comfy and nice, her eyes giving and happy to be with him.

She smiled. "As much as a haapffin?"

"More. Much more."

They kissed, and when they parted, she asked innocently, "Am I better than a car?"

He thought a moment too long and received a punch on the arm for his non-answer. Finally, he said, "Nearly."

She tried to hit him again, but he caught her before the blow struck, and they kissed again. She snuggled closer, standing along the riverbank. "You will find your Captain," she repeated. There was a confidence in her voice that was real. She was not telling him that to make him feel better. She was telling him because she believed in him, and her words were true. There was no other option. No plan B, as Harlowe often said.

Suddenly, Maa Dev came shouting down the ramp with Molly loping in easy, long strides beside him. "Ian, Ian . . . ah, Captain Ian!" he cried out.

Cheesa and Ian casually separated. It was no secret among the crew that they were an item. From day one, Leucadia saw the change in him when he rescued Cheesa off of the poverty stricken streets of Nod. "What is it, Dev?" Ian asked as Molly put her massive head under his arm. It was her way of saying scratch behind my ears, if you please.

Breathing hard, Dev replied, "Ms. Lu. She and Anor believe they have found something."

Ian grabbed Cheesa's hand and began double-timing it back to the ramp. "What is it, Dev? What did she say it was?"

"She would not say, Captain. She said, 'Find Ian and tell him I found a crumb.' She said you would know what that meant."

Ian put his head down and ran, pulling Cheesa along with him.

113

Dabos & Babos

The yellow Ossetian sun was coming through the gerbid porthole amd awakened Harlowe with a start. He felt his head and wondered if that was a Mack truck that had hit him. The cramped metal room he found himself in smelled of sweat and dirty clothes, like a football locker room after a game. The lower bunk where he slept was hard and lacked bedding and a pillow. He remembered the Clarity faux couch that was equally as hard. Besides realizing he was still alive, the eerie quiet unsettled him. There was no throbbing vibration of the motor, no feet clomping along the metal grates inside the main hold, and not one sound of Nath's gruff voice shouting orders at his riders.

He rolled off the edge in a panic. All he could recall was Isara's swollen, bloody face pleading for someone to help her.

His feet hit the metal floor grates with a clank. He had to find her. His last memory was of her being dragged inside the battlewagon. Stupid toad, he called himself. He should have listened to Nath. He reached for his sidearm and found only air. It wasn't attached to his leg. He checked under and around the other bunks and found nothing but his leather jacket hanging on a wall hook. He rechecked his bed again, searching every nook and cranny in the room, thinking he might have put them somewhere in his sleep. But nothing, no pistols, no holsters anywhere. Knowing he could not go anywhere without them, he expanded his search, lifting up blankets, mattresses, and articles of clothing everywhere inside the bunk room.

No weapons!

Ready to slam his head against the bulkhead, he grabbed his leather jacket from the wall, and there they were hanging beautifully underneath the garment. Staring in disbelief, he said, "How stupid are you, Pylott?" thinking he must have passed them by a dozen times in his search.

He strapped on his weapons and checked to make sure their power levels were up to snuff. He topped them off with two more power mags and sighed. Now he was locked and loaded and ready for bad guys.

The rest his of startup was automatic. SIBA systems check, backpack check, utility pouch check, ammo pouches, all check. If there was one thing the General had taught him, it was never assume your equipment is ready until you *know* it *is* ready. It was a never-to-be-forgotten lesson they all had learned during one particularly grueling training period on Mars.

The General had awakened them before dawn for what they were told was a short training exercise. The five of them, Riverstone, Wiz, Simon, Monday, and himself packed up their gear, and they all piled into the back of the Grannywagon. With the giant android, Quincy, driving and the General riding shotgun, whistling Vivaldi's *Four Seasons, Concerto No. 2 in G minor,* the *Summer* one, they drove at three hundred miles per hour across the Martian plateau, skirting Valles Marinaras for a thousand miles until they arrived at the edge of the Schiaparelli impact crater. The General, in his usual manner, marveled at the view across the vast impact crater. "Beautiful worms," he said to them as they got out and stretched their legs. "Just beautiful." Then while everyone stood enjoying the overlook, the General hopped back in the Grannywagon and took off with Quincy, whistling Vivaldi, leaving them all at the edge of the crater with their jaws on the ground.

Leaving them didn't make sense. They were over a thousand miles from *Millawanda*, with no way back but on foot. No one believed it a first, but after an hour of standing like a mime, reality sank in. The General wasn't coming back. They checked their supplies for the long journey to the Mons and discovered, to their dismay, that all of their survival packs had been shorted. No one had bothered to check their packs before leaving the ship.

Harlowe gritted his teeth, still thinking of the trek that nearly killed them. The trek through Valles Marinaras was particularly harrowing. If Riverstone hadn't stumbled onto Lu's Place by pure luck, Mars would have been their graveyard. But through it all, they survived and learned the one important lesson of a lifetime: never assume anything.

Somewhere in the back of his scrambled brains, a voice told him until Isara, Fyn, and Muis were rescued alive and well, all his nights would be long and sleepless. He straightened the sleeves of his leather jacket and marched through the open doorway looking for Nath.

To his surprise, the gerbid hold was empty of life. So was the bridge. Nath, his riders, and all their horses were gone. Delamo and Mowgi included. It was like everyone had deserted him. He walked out of the main hatch and clambered out onto the ramp. To his relief, Delamo was grazing along the street where Nath had parked their gerbid against a stone building for protection. A squawk at the top of a building brought his attention to a winged dragon eating some coppery-orange thing he had captured for breakfast. The day was clear and bright. The sun was not too far up on the horizon. He could go for a couple of double-doubles, fries, and a chocolate shake himself. Scanning the empty street for eateries, he saw nothing that had been open for a hundred passings.

"No In-n-Outs or taco stands, either? What's up with that?" Harlowe grumbled. He reached into his utility pouch and popped in the usual chalk tasting nourishment cube. "Yum. Fries, animal style," he smirked, like he just ingested a sour grape. When *Millawanda* was right again, he promised himself to have Mother make the cubes with tasty flavors like grape, strawberry, or Reese's Peanut Butter Cups.

A shuffling sound made Harlowe whirl around, locked and loaded, about to shoot whatever was creeping up on him. In that split nano-second between go and no go, Harlowe held his fire. It was Bucky, DaboS' older brother, walking from behind the gerbid tire with his mount. Bucky wasn't his real name. It was the name Harlowe gave him because he had a serious overbite, and his translator inside his head made their Fagan names sound too much alike. He could never keep them straight. Bucky was a better fit than BaboS, his real name, and the little buck-toothed Fagan didn't seem to care what anyone called him.

"Where is everyone?" Harlowe asked Bucky.

"Gone," the young Fagan replied.

"They went looking for broken gerbids," said another voice from behind. Harlowe spun in the opposite direction with gun leveled. It was DaboS, this time with his mount coming around the front of the gerbid. Neither Fagan seemed too concerned that they nearly had their heads blown off. "We have no more fuel modules," he added.

"How long will that take?" Harlowe asked either brother.

"Until they are back," said DaboS.

Bucky shrugged indifference. "Yes, until they are back."

"That could mean what?" Harlowe asked.

DaboS looked up at the sun. "Maybe until the great star reaches the horizon."

"Or when the *Tonus* moon rises," Bucky added, pointing behind them.

For Isara, Fyn, and Muis there was no waiting, only long seconds and minutes of torture. Harlowe whistled and Delamo bolted, his long nails clicking on the pavement as he leaped for Harlowe's voice. Mowgi heard the call, too, and dropped his meal from ten stories high, taking flight.

"Are you leaving, Harlowe?" Bucky asked.

"Yeah. I can't wait for Nath. Tell him to meet me in Elrish Dag."

"You can't go alone, Harlowe," DaboS said, alarmed that anyone would attempt such a ride. "Elrish Dag is very far,s and you are without a guide."

"Yes, Darkn's Tappers are everywhere," Bucky warned.

The mighty, black ceffyl galloped to the foot of the ramp and reared up, pawing its foreclaws above Harlowe's head like a happy dog. When he touched down again, Harlowe grabbed a single horn and swung himself up and onto his bare back in one easy motion.

"I know," Harlowe said to the brothers, "but I must ride to find my friends."

DaboS jumped aboard his horse like he was going along, too.

"What are you doing, DaboS?" Harlowe asked.

"I must go with you, Harlowe," the little rider said as if there was no arguing the matter.

"Yes, DaboS will show you the way," Bucky added.

Harlowe tried arguing with the brothers. His ceffyl was much faster and stronger than the Fagan mounts. DaboS would be unable to keep up. He would fall behind, and they would lose valuable time. But to them the matter was settled. DaboS would go with Harlowe because Nath's orders were clear;

to look after Harlowe while their leader was away. Either Harlowe stayed, which he wouldn't, or DaboS went with him. There was no third choice.

"I will tell Nath of your undertaking," Bucky said.

Harlowe saw no alternative without disgracing the brothers. If he didn't allow DaboS to be his guide and protector, then their family would suffer terrible humiliation. They would never ride with Nath again. For them, it was a fate worse than death, so Harlowe had no choice but to accept his guardianship graciously. "Tell Nath I will see him in Elrish Dag," he said to Bucky.

"I will. We will all see you there," Bucky said proudly. "And put an end to Darkn and his Tappers."

Harlowe flashed Bucky a thumbs up as DaboS pointed his mount down the street that would lead them out of the city. "This way, Harlowe." DaboS motioned. "This is the road to Elrish Dag!"

Bucky waved a final goodbye and said with a broad smile, "Leave us a few Tappers to fight, Harlowe. Do not kill them all."

"I will leave fifty just for you, Bucky," Harlowe shouted back and urged Delamo on with a slight pat to the side of his long mane. Surprisingly, DaboS was already a hundred yards ahead and moving away fast.

Bucky laughed. "It looks like DaboS will beat you to Elrish Dag, Harlowe."

"We'll see about that!" Harlowe cried out. The big ceffyl sprang like a loaded catapult in the air, bolting across the pavement in great leaps to catch up with the little Fagan who had already disappeared around the far corner.

114

Harlowe's Mind

When Ian, Cheesa, and Maa Dev stepped onto the bridge, it was dark except for a three-dimensional holograph in the middle of the room. The projection was a star map containing hundreds of planets and star systems thirty parsecs out from their present location. The upper portion of the map was filled with dozens of systems and nebulas of different intensities and colors. Going down the map, the stars were less dense until there was nothing but the empty space of Cartooga-Thaat at the lower end of the projection. A small, blue light pulsed in a slow, rhythmic beat near the bottom where there were only scattered stars. Not far from the void of stars and the blue light, a thin red line curved around the projection in a half circle.

"What crumb did you find, Lu?" Ian asked, coming right to the point.

"Something. It's not much to go on, but it's more than we had an hour ago," Leucadia replied, upbeat but reserved.

Ian pointed at the blue light. "We're here at the edge of the Thaat?"

"That's right." Leucadia waved her hand at several star systems near the void. "And these stars in red are the systems we've searched since coming out of the star desert."

"Yeah, with no luck at all," Ian grumbled.

"One would think that if Harlow's ship was so low on fuel, he would have come straight to one of these star systems," said Cheesa.

"You're speaking logically, Cheesa," Leucadia said, leading the discussion. "I'm afraid logic is not part of Harlowe's vocabulary."

548

Ian touched Cheesa's hand. "Lu is right, Cheesa. Harlowe never takes the short cut, even when he's low on fuel." He returned to the holograph and asked about the thin red line arcing over their position like a fan. "What is this?"

"The line indicating the maximum distance *Millawanda* should have been able to travel after leaving Tabilisi," she explained.

Dev eyed all the bright dots below the red line and wondered aloud. "We have searched seven star systems already. Must we search all those systems, Ms. Lu?"

"Yes, Dev, all three hundred ninety-two possibilities," she replied.

The Prince's lips thinned. "Is there a way to cut down that number?"

Leucadia crossed her arms in front of her, staring at the map as she went on: "No, Dev. We already eliminated the star systems that cannot support life. Three hundred ninety-two is what's left."

"Dev said you found crumbs, Lu. What are they?" Ian asked, impatient with conversation that had nothing to do with finding *Millawanda*.

"It wasn't me; it was Anor. He's found something. A pattern I had not seen before," Leucadia replied.

Ian looked around the bridge. "Where are you Anor? Are you hiding?"

"I am here, Captain," Anor's deep voice answered from the dark shadows of the bridge. As he stepped closer to the star map's tiny lights, he became visible to everyone in the room. Seeing Anor in a Gamadin blue uniform felt like disloyalty to his fellow crewmen who had worked so hard to earn the right to wear them, but clothes wise, that was all they had. *Forty-Four* was not a Gamadin mothership. She lacked the unlimited wardrobe, so clothing for everyone was limited to Gamadin blue, and that was it.

"You've been holed up in your room practically the whole time you've been aboard," Ian began. "You seem to prefer the darkness than the light of our ship and her crew. I'm beginning to think that rescuing you was a waste of time. Maybe you would prefer your pals on Metis to us, Anor?"

"No, Captain. I assure you. I am eternally grateful for your efforts to save my life," Anor replied.

"Time to earn your keep, then. Tell us what you've found, Anor," Ian ordered, tersely.

Anor smiled defensively. "I do apologize for my aloofness, Captain. Do not take it personally."

Ian scoffed. "Trust me. I don't."

Anor went on, picking up where he left off. "I have been studying the maps, your ship's logs, and all the empirical data collected thus far. I must admit, I am quite impressed that someone so novel to space travel as yourself," he said looking directly at Ian, "has managed to amass such a body of information."

"I had good help," Ian said glumly, touching Leucadia on her sleeve.

"Yes, Miss Lu's knowledge is quite remarkable."

Ian nodded. "Go on then. Tell us what you found."

"Of course, Captain," he said. Anor motioned for increased lighting as he went to a table at the back of the room. A robob stepped over to Anor and handed him a rolled up chart that he spread out on the table. "You'll have to forgive my script. It was the best I could do under the circumstances."

The chart was quite remarkable. When Anor said 'forgive my script,' Ian was half expecting something like the chicken scratch homework assignment Riverstone would turn in for Farnducky's science class. To his astonishment and everyone else's around the table, the star chart Anor produced was a perfectly hand-scribed map so precise one might have thought it was generated by a computer. The star systems aligned as near as he could tell exactly like the star charts projected on *Forty-four's* 3D holographs.

"Is there something wrong, Captain? Do you find my chart wanting?" Anor asked, looking around the table of mesmerized faces, including Leucadia's.

"No, not at all, Anor," Ian replied, losing his impatient edge. "Please continue."

Anor brushed his graying hair back over his head as he returned to the chart. The gesture was more a nervous trait for his hair had always been finely groomed in the past. "As we know, the last reported position of the Gamadin mothership was Tabilisi. Here," he said pointing at the solitary point at very edge of the chart. He continued, "From the Gamadin way station it is assumed Captain Pylott's only course of travel was the shortest route as he searched for another source of thermo-grym. I believe that is correct."

"Yeah, he had no other choice," Ian pointed out.

Anor raised his finger in the air. "Maybe. But as we have discovered in our search, there are sources of thermo-grym on planets much closer to

Tabilisi," he pointed, "here, here, and here, where our young Captain could have landed but chose not to."

Leucadia's eyes brightened. "You believe he may have found an alternate source of power?"

"I do."

"But the only alternate source of power Millie can use is aara, and aara doesn't occur naturally. It's Gamadin," Ian asserted.

Anor agreed. "You are correct, Captain."

"You believe Harlowe has somehow found a source of aara?" Leucadia asked with hope in her manner.

"Yes. I believe he has found another Gamadin station."

"But we haven't found any maps or records at Tabilisi that would lead us to any Gamadin station on this side of the Thaat," Ian stated.

Anor placed a photo on the table. Ian and Leucadia recognized it immediately. It was the star map on the wall Leucadia and Harlowe discovered at the Gamadin station at Hitt. "As you can see, much of the map has been destroyed. But there are fragments remaining that are clear enough to decipher. And if we put these together like so," he said, pushing two photos together. "They seem to connect precisely like a puzzle."

Leucadia twisted her head around as she slid the two pieces together and matched the star clusters with Anor's original chart. "These star groups are a perfect match."

"Exactly," Anor said. "Your Captain is headed this way, not the shortest way, but the way that would find him a source of aara, another Gamadin outpost, I assume."

Ian stared at the map. He saw nothing wrong with Anor's findings, except for one thing. "So how do we know which one?"

Anor nodded at the robob. "If you would turn the lights blue, please."

The robob tilted its head toward Ian. "Do it, Ginger," Ian said to the robob. The girlbob stepped to the sidewall and moved her mechanical fingers across a lighted bar, turning the bright white light to a sky blue light. As the light changed color, the star map from Hitt displayed cuneiform symbols on dozens of stars from the two photos.

"Wow," Dev cooed. "There are a lot of stations."

"Yes, but we need only one to concern our search in this area," Anor said as he redrew the arc of maximum distance *Millawanda* could travel from

Tabilisi on her remaining fuel. "The arc differs somewhat from the distance Ms. Lu calculated, but only by point zero, zero one light passing. That is well within the margin of error."

"If Harlowe had it in his mind to go there, then he would go there, with or without fuel," Ian stated with absolute confidence.

"Of course. The Captain is very resourceful. I have also accounted for a generous six point seven one percent overage. Would you consider that adequate, Captain?"

Ian nodded. "Yeah, sure." He turned to Leucadia for her opinion. "Lu?"

"Acceptable, but even a nine or ten percent overage would not be beyond his thickheadedness," Leucadia said, shaking her head at the thought of Harlowe's ability to go all in on a wild hunch to fix his ship.

Ian agreed. "Bump it up to twelve for good measure, Anor. That should make everyone happy."

"But that is impossible," Anor protested politely. "That is twice my allotted overage."

"Move your distance arc, Anor," Ian ordered.

"But, but . . ."

Ian stood fast. "Humor us, Anor. We can change it later."

Anor brushed his hair back twice before adding six more points to the total as ordered. When he completed the alterations, Ian asked, "So, where does that put Harlowe if he still follows your line of thinking?"

Anor put his finger on the first Gamadin station out of the Cartooga-Thaat. "Here. It's the closest," Anor replied with confidence. "That is where he has taken his ship."

Dev pointed to a small star system above the twelve percent arc. "That one there. What is that, Anor?"

"That is not a station, Dev," Anor replied.

"What is it, then? It has markings that look like the others," Dev pointed out.

Anor read the print with a magnifier. "Its markings are faded, but it appears to be some kind of retreat."

"A Gamadin resort?" Ian asked, amused.

"A place to play," Anor said.

Ian and Leucadia held each other's eyes, having both found the answer at the same time. "He went there," they said together.

"But that is even beyond the twelve," Anor objected.

"We know, Anor," Leucadia said, happily. "But that's where Harlowe has gone."

"That would be suicide."

Ian grinned sheepishly. "That's our Captain."

"That is our next destination, Anor," Leucadia said, nodding at Cheesa to set *Forty-Four's* course. "Because Harlowe knows no boundaries."

Ian added, "I'll bet the farm that there's a wave or two there, too." Ian glanced at Anor. "What's it called?"

Anor shifted the map around and read the glowing letters aloud. "Lamille…"

115

Margrave

Darkn strode along the gravel path, his giant, muscular body and thick orange mane flowing behind him as he held the heavy chain leashes of his three ilodudd pets in check. Their kinky dark hair, massive narrow heads, rows of protruding sharp teeth, drooling for anything meaty, alive or dead, looked like rusty versions of a grogan. Flanking Darkn, leaving plenty of room for his pets, was his entourage of twenty-two elite guards. Between them all, Pox, a personal subordinate, struggled to keep up as the group made their way to the corrals.

"How are my ceffyls today, Pox?" Darkn thundered at his subordinate, who was out of breath. The ceffyl corral was a considerable distance from the palace. Until the new compound was completed on the palace grounds, Darkn made the trip a daily routine since their arrival from the southern Ozans. For many passings he had hunted the majestic beauties for his stables, but they had always eluded his capture. Now he had six of them, including their keeper. He looked out across his fortress city and what it represented, the most powerful force on the planet, his palace of riches, and the vast treasure of Cornicen plunder inside the mountain vaults. Yet, he would give it all to have the black ceffyl he had heard was by far the greatest prize on the planet.

"They are well, Margrave," Pox answered. "Now that his son has been subdued, the ceffyl rancher has been most cooperative. The small herd was eating well and had made no more attempts to breach their enclosure."

"Excellent, Pox. The boy? I want no more trouble from him."

"Yes, Margrave. The boy's appendages have been removed by your order."

"And the Ozan expedition? What is their condition?"

"They were attacked, Margrave."

Darkn halted and faced Pox, his eyes becoming glazed with yellow and dark green jagged lines of hate. "How many gerbids this time?"

"Nine, Margrave," Pox replied, impassively. He knew if he tried to hide any detail at all, he would be whipped. "They say Fagans were behind the losses."

Darkn doubted the explanation. "No. This is not a Fagan's work. They have only small weapons. They are useless against my gerbids. It is the Offworlders, of that I am certain. They are the only ones with the power to destroy my machines."

"For what purpose, Margrave?"

Darkn stared toward the corral. "My ceffyls. They seek my ceffyls," he breathed slowly, speaking mostly to himself. He then suddenly became alarmed. "Cornicen! What have you heard from the capital? Have communications been restored? Have they found the off-world ship?"

"No, Margrave. From our last communication this ship still eluded them," Pox replied.

"And there is still no communication with Cornicen?"

"Yes, Cornicen is still dark, Margrave. We have heard nothing for three days. All requests for assistance have gone unanswered."

"We must have those airships. The Offworlders are destroying my gerbids. What of Commander Fiv?" Darkn demanded.

"He refuses to answer our demands, Margrave," Pox answered.

Darkn made a mental note to have the commander executed. Since the arrival of the Offworlders, his armies had ignored all his requests for assistance.

"And the 10th Mechanized?" Darkn asked.

"No communication, Margrave. They are presumed lost."

"ALL?"

"Their last communiqué said they were being attacked by another gerbid. The commander's report was just coming through when they were cut off, Margrave."

That brought the total to seventeen gerbids confirmed destroyed and another six were presumed lost. Darkn kicked an ilodudd out of the way and then strutted toward the corrals as he spoke.

"The rancher's daughter?"

"The 2ⁿᵈ Mechanized arrived in time. She will be at Elrish Dag by nightfall."

Finally, there was good news. "Bring her to me as soon as they arrive."

"Yes, Margrave."

The entourage came upon the corral where the ceffyls were kept. Darkn's eyes dilated with pride the moment he set eyes upon their arched horns extending above the top of their keep.

116

Elrish Dag

Harlowe and DaboS stood beside their mounts on a hill that overlooked the Tapper stronghold of Elrish Dag as Mowgi, with little interest in the citadel, gnawed on his breakfast he had snagged on the previous hill. Harlowe figured by the size of the carcus had been as large as an earthly antelope. But after five minutes with a ravenous chenner, not even DaboS knew what it was Mowgi was eating.

The fortress city was nestled at the base of a two-mile high wall of black granite. Positioned across the top of the sheer vertical cliffs were ten ginormous plas-cannons that stuck out like giant howitzers protecting Elrish Dag from any aerial or ground assaults. At the base of the mountain behind the city, stood six vault doors, each ten-stories high and half again as wide, that Nath said protected Darkn's vast treasures inside the mountain. Finally, in the front of the city was a massive bulwark of metal walls that were fused to the base of the cliffs to protect the city from a frontal assault. Nine guard towers were positioned at strategic locations along the perimeter, two each, straddled the three gates into the city. From the fortress wall all the way to the horizon, there were no structures or shantytowns just flat, barren ground. The roads to the gates were treeless and open. Anyone or anything straying from the way into the city was shot immediately, no questions asked.

DaboS' round face looked down at certain death. He knew without saying that Nath and all the Fagans were powerless against Darkn's vast number of gerbids kept inside the city walls. As scared as he was, he remained at

Harlowe's side, standing tall with his mount's reins firmly in hand, ready for battle. "Through which gate shall we enter first, Harlowe?" DaboS asked.

"Through the front door, of course," Harlowe answered calmly. He removed a golden cylinder from his backpack and tossed it in the air with a casual flip of his wrist. Before it hit the ground, the cylinder had transformed into a mechanical being that was taller than Harlowe. "Meet Bigbob, DaboS. He's one of us."

He doesn't look like one of us, DaboS thought. Connected to balls and tubes, its arms, legs, and head swiveled easily in all directions. The top of its head was pointed. It had no face, no eyes, and no mouth. He had heard about the golden being from other Fagans who described in great detail how Harlowe's inhuman assistant was quite strong and fearless in battle. Now he had seen him for real, and he was quite shocking to behold.

"He has no mount," DaboS said surprised.

Harlowe tapped the side of Bigbob's leg. The sound was not hollow or fragile but solid like hitting stone. "It's built in."

DaboS turned to Harlowe, wondering if there was something he was missing in the translation. Since Harlowe was not of the Ozans, his meanings and descriptions were often peculiar. Most of the time DaboS simply nodded like he understood his words so as not to offend him. This was one of those times when a nod was all that was required. Instead of asking further clarification he asked, "We will wait until night to assault Elrish Dag?"

Harlowe rested his hand on DaboS's shoulder. "Fyn and his family can't wait, DaboS. This must be done now, little dude."

DaboS turned back to the walls. Whatever it was that Harlowe decided, he was ready to give his life for him.

Harlowe added, "When you wake up, I want you to ride to Nath as fast as you can. Tell him to meet me here where we are now. Understand?"

DaboS kinked his head up at Harlowe. His blue eyes were looking at him sorrowfully. "Wake up, Harlowe? I have no intention of sleeping before we attack Mar—"

117

Visitor at the Gate

A frightening shock wave roared across Elrish Dag. The ceffyls leaped high above the corral walls, nearly escaping. Darkn cried out in anger as the reins he was holding ripped from his hands. Guards surrounding the corrals, cocked their weapons and turned toward the west and the billowing black smoke rising high in the morning sun. "What is responsible for this outrage!" Darkn bellowed. "I shall have his head—" But he was cut off when a second blast brought everyone's attention to the central guard tower.

It was gone!

A third blast immediately blew away another tower to the east. Darkn thought a gerbid carrying explosive supplies into the city had exploded. But upon seeing the towers annihilated, there could be no explanation other than Elrish Dag was under attack. But what entity on the planet could mount such an attack and not be seen? He could think of none, except—. Even he would not attack Elrish Dag. He quickly scanned the cliffs. The plas cannons were quiet. Elrish Dag sensors would have sounded a full alert long before the first explosion if any assault had come from the sky. The massive barrels were as silent as the rock cliffs encasing them. The attack could only be coming from the ground.

But how? Where had the invaders come from?

Guards quickly surrounded him, urging him to leave the corral.

"My ceffyls," Darkn cried out. They could have his treasure but not his ceffyls. "Move them to the vaults!"

A full squad of guards broke away from the pack. "Yes, Margrave!"

"Pox! What does central command say?" Darkn demanded as he fled for the safety of the palace.

Pox listened to the latest update from central command before answering. Turning back to Darkn, his face became a combination of disbelief and fear. "The Offworlder, Margrave. He is at the front gate."

"He?" Darkn was shocked by the revelation. "He has caused this attack on my fortress?"

"Yes, Margrave. He is alone. There are no other forces but him."

"KILL HIM!" Darkn roared.

"He rides the black ceffyl, Margrave." Pox cautioned.

Darkn's eyes flew open. He raised his hand, halting his train of guards along the path. "The black?"

"Yes, Margrave, he rides the fabled black that has eluded you."

Darkn saw his dream come true. The mythical black was now within his grasp. "Allow the Offworlder to pass."

* * *

The thunderous roar from Elrish Dag awakened DaboS from his induced slumber. He closed his eyes in prayer as he recalled Harlowe's last words. Hurriedly, he mounted Ove and prayed, *May the gods be with Harlowe.* His head was a little woozy, but by the time he was off the hill, he was fine as he urged his mount to run to her limits. He drove her hard down a rocky path that led into a narrow gorge. Ove's little hooves, knees, and hocks were but a blur as she darted between prickly bushes and trees, hopped over fallen branches, and splashed through streams that Delamo's twenty-foot strides would have easily crossed.

Bursting out of the woods at the end of the narrow valley, DaboS found the road he was looking for and turned abruptly south until he came face to face with a gerbid lumbering up the road. The gerbid might have run Ove down, if at the last second, she hadn't cut to one side, missing the two-story tires by a fraction.

The giant wheels squealed to a stop. DaboS was expecting a horde of Tappers to leap out from the main hatch and gun him down when, to his surprise, Nath and his fellow Fagans jumped to the ground. Ove reared, running up to Nath, front legs high in the air, then settled to the ground as several Fagans surrounded DaboS with greetings and back slaps.

Nath reached for DaboS, grabbing his forearm and embracing him like a prideful father welcoming his son home. "Where is Harlowe?" Nath asked as he checked DaboS for injuries and found him solid, fit, and unharmed.

"Elrish Dag," DaboS replied, holding his wrists.

Nath's face quickly changed from pride to one of grave disappointment. DaboS was instructed to stay with Harlowe regardless of peril. "Elrish Dag? You left Harlowe at Elrish Dag?"

DaboS bowed his head in shame. With tear-swollen eyes, he answered, "I did, Nath." He did not offer any excuse or explanation as to why he was on the trail without Harlowe but waited instead for his punishment.

A lesser leader might have slain DaboS where he stood for deserting his duty. But Nath knew his riders well. DaboS was no spineless lith. His mount foamed with sweat, and she had been driven to the point of near collapse, something a Fagan rider would never do to his mount unless the life of the tribe was at stake. And DaboS' clothes were torn and filthy, full of thorns and debris from a grueling ride. These were not the mount and dress of a coward or a warrior that had abandoned his post, but someone whose mission had been altered by uncontrollable forces.

"Alone?" Nath asked.

"No. He was accompanied by his Mowgi and a tall, golden man," DaboS replied.

Nath's jowls twisted with defenselessness. He wanted to help his friend but feared by the time he arrived, he would too late. Darkn was powerful. At Elrish Dag, he was invincible.

"What were Harlowe's orders?" Nath asked.

DaboS wiped his nostrils with the back of his sleeve before replying, "He said to meet him at the hilltop overlooking the fortress city."

Nath ordered everyone back to the gerbid. "Then we must hurry before it is too late!"

* * *

Darkn and his entourage charged through gilded doors of the palace the moment the fourth explosion rocked the city. "CLOSE THE ACCESS!" a voice shouted. Upon the command, the massive two-foot thick metal doors pivoted on their hinges and locked into place with a heavy clank, sealing the interior against the outside world. Darkn stomped along the white marble floors and into the ornate hallway covered in crimson and gold velvet tapestries, jade framed mirrors, and rare wooden inlays. Overhead, jeweled crystalline chandeliers hung down from high arched ceiling on heavy gold chains, lighting his path to his throne room. As he approached the seat of power, twelve snarling ilodudd statutes, flanked the stairway to the throne of bones and skulls from the empire's enemies that were all interconnected and overlaid with the finest gold and scores of rubies, thick as a human's fist. Darkn took his place while fifty fully armed guards positioned themselves at the base of power.

An officer knelt in front of the throne with his head bowed. "All is secure, Sire!"

"And what of the Offworlder now?" Darkn barked angrily.

A runner entered the throne chamber and spoke with the guard commander. The commander knelt, holding his helmet under his arm, and reported to Darkn. "The Offworlder is at the palace doors wishing to speak with you of the captured prisoners, Margrave."

Darkn expanded his chest as he yearned for a chance to see the black. "Show him the way, Commander. Bring him yourself. I want no harm to come to the black until I am done with him."

The Commander stood, crossing his forearm in front of his red and yellow uniform. "Yes, Sire. By your leave." Then the officer snapped crisply around and stepped fast, the sound of his boots echoing off the walls toward the opening palace doors.

118

Black of Fables

When he saw the black prancing in his palace lair, Darkn couldn't help himself. He stood in awe before the creature of the gods. The majestic steed, proud, pompous, his head high and mighty, was utterly contemptuous of those around him. Prancing forward, his lofty horns swayed to and fro like twin scepters over his long, silky mane. The marbled floors, too, resonated the tap of his high-stepping dance as the closing doors sealed him in. Still, he trotted on, unafraid, poised for conflict, for there was nothing in the great hall that he feared. His whinny, loud and clear, let all those near and far know this lord of stallions was here to destroy them.

Darkn stumbled uneasily back down onto his throne feeling a sense of foreboding that his rule was evaporating before his eyes.

"Toad! I'm talking to you," the voice shouted at him. "I want Fyn. Where is he?" he demanded.

Eyes unblinking, Darkn had no recollection of anyone speaking to him since the black entered the throne room. But when he finally realized it was the Offworlder, he seethed with hate at the boyish being who had stolen his abordar, destroyed his gerbids, and utterly made a fool of him in front of the Cornicen army. Without the protection of his ship, he seemed common and vulnerable. He had entered his palace with but one small rifle, two pistols, a small, large-eared pet, and one tall droid. It was a foolish miscalculation for him to believe he could leave his throne room alive. "You have your audience, Offworlder. What is it you seek?" Darkn demanded.

"Fyn, his son, and the female, Isara," the he dictated in no uncertain terms. "I want them brought here unharmed, immediately."

Darkn laughed. "You come into my palace, insult my realm, steal my abordar, and expect me to grant you the freedom of my prisoners?"

"I do. And quickly."

"Or what, you will kill me?" Darkn threw his head back and laughed.

"Since you brought it up, Scumbag, that's exactly what will happen unless Fyn and his family are brought before me now." The Offworlder spoke so profoundly and with such confidence, those in the room began questioning their own future.

Darkn sat back on his throne. With a haughty air of distain, he shot back, "Enough of such insolence. I will take the black ceffyl now and be done with you!"

Darkn was about to call his guards to complete his threat when the Offworlder expressed his amusement. "Sir, you misunderstand my offer. I have not come to Elrish Dag to negotiate for my friends' lives with my mount. You must leave Osset now and I will spare you. It is that simple. You are not of this planet. That is obvious. You came here and enslaved the good people of this planet for your own greedy power and plunder. This will not continue. Osset is no longer yours to exploit."

"Who are you to make such threats on my empire?"

"I am Gamadin, toad! And I'm here to put you, your Tappers, and the Clarity, out of business."

Darkn's eyes widened, allowing one to see for the first time the fear behind them. "The Gamadin. Impossible. They are but dust in the wind."

The Offworlder slid off the black and stepped to the center of the room with his tall-eared companion at his side. He touched his wrist, and his clothes dissolved, replaced by dark armor with his head covered by a tough skin and large, faceted eyes like that of a Bo-chee.

"Dust, you say? Do I look like dust to you, Toad? You came to this planet with your highly sophisticated intellect and advanced technology. You could have used it to better the lives of these fine beings, but you didn't. You used your superior knowledge to enslave them and extract their wealth. You sucked them dry. You destroyed cities, raped their land, created poverty by stealing, killing, and pillaging for generations. But worst of all, you have stolen their pursuit of happiness and their freedom to live their lives in peace!

For that you must and will be eradicated from this planet!"

"They are my subjects. I do with them as I see fit," Darkn declared, pounding his fist on this throne arm.

"NO, THEY ARE NOT! You are not a god! You are not their keeper, king, emperor, or ruler. You are nothing but a useless tyrant. You're finished here, Toad. Now bring me Fyn and his family, or I will unleash a hell upon Elrish Dag so destructive there will be nothing left of you, your gerbids, and this fortress but a crumbled heap of rock!"

"And how will you accomplish this Offworlder? With your little pet?"

The Offworlder looked down at his companion with a smile. "Mowgi is my backup."

The entire room broke out in laughter, but Darkn thought of it as no laughing matter. He was finished with the Offworlder. He wanted the black in his possession now! He pointed a plump finger and commanded his guards to, "Kill him!"

Five guards stepped forward with their sidearms drawn. But before they could pulled their triggers, they were summarily dropped by plasma bolts between the eyes. Ten more guards raised their weapons, but in less time than it takes to blink, they were also blown away by the Gamadin.

The guard commander stepped forward only to be stopped by the Gamadin's sidearm pointed at his head. "Do you wish to continue the slaughter, sir?"

"No."

"Leave then, before I change my mind," the Gamadin told him. The commander ordered his guards to drop their weapons and exited the palace. Darkn was aghast. His shouts to return or lose their heads went unheeded as the room emptied of everyone except him and the Gamadin.

"Just you and me now, Toad," the Gamadin snarled.

Darkn lost it. He removed his outer garments and expanded his hairy orange, chest, screaming like a wild dog, "Die, Gamadin!" and released his ilodudds to kill the Gamadin. But before the wild beasts could rip their teeth into him, the long-eared pet grew into a giant beast that tore off the head of the first ilodudd. The second was skewered by twin horns and tossed aside, wiggling and twitching in a quick death. The droid's powerful tubular fists struck the wild dogs' heads, audibly snapping them backwards. They were both still as stone by the time they hit the floor.

The winged monster crawled up the throne stairs, its drooling maw, dripping acid like spit upon the floor from its long, saber teeth. Darkn fell back on his throne holding his sword in a pathetic effort to fend off the beast. When he lunged to slice open his neck, a long, whippy tail snapped, slicing off his hand and the sword with it. Then it hung over Darkn, hissing and snarling as he waited for the command to feast upon his flesh.

"What do you think of my backup now, Toad?" the Gamadin asked.

"Make it go away! Don't eat me. Don't eat me," Darkn begged, holding his bloody stump.

"I want Fyn and his family. Where are they?" the Gamadin demanded.

"Pox! Take him. Take the Gamadin to Fyn. Hurry!"

Pox stepped out of the darkness, shaking in his shoes. He bowed deep. "This way, Offworlder."

Before leaving the throne room, the Gamadin turned to Darkn and warned, "Pray this pencil-neck leads me to Fyn, or you *will* be his next meal."

"Yes, yes, go with Pox," Darkn stuttered, staring up at the crazed, yellow eyes, hovering thirstily over his head. "No tricks. He will lead you to Fyn."

119

Liberation

Pox brought Harlowe, Delamo, and Bigbob to the stables where he found the herd of Fyn's ceffyls. Delamo went crazy with excitement. Harlowe saw the joy in his eyes and gave him the go ahead to join his brothers and sisters. He leaped over the corral wall, jumping and prancing about in a heartfelt reunion. Soon they would all be free.

Pox pointed at a small shed off to the side of the corral. "Fyn. He is in there." Thinking his duty was done, he tried scurrying away when Harlowe fired a round at his feet, stopping the pencil-neck puss-head in his tracks.

"Where do you think you're going, Prick?" Harlowe asked, waving his pistol at Pox's face.

"I was—"

"You're done when I say you're done," Harlowe said, and pointed the barrel at the ground. "Stand right here until I get back." He nodded at Bigbob. "Move, and he'll kill ya."

Pox ran to the indicated spot and remained stiff as a pole while Harlowe went to the shed. He found it locked with a heavy bolt, but one blast from his "fine adjustment tool" and the lock was history. Harlowe pulled the door open and found Fyn lying on the dirt floor that was mired in urine and feces. He quickly checked his vital signs and closed his eyes. Unbelievably, the rancher was still alive. He brought him out in the sun as he called to him, "Fyn...Fyn... Stay with me, Fyn."

Barely able to talk, Fyn uttered, "Mu...is?" and tried crawling back to his shed. He didn't know he was being rescued, nor did he know it was Harlowe who was trying to comfort him. The sun was too bright for his eyes to focus.

Harlowe continued to ease his torment. "Don't talk, Fyn. It's me. Harlowe. I've come to get you out of here."

"Harlowe?" Fyn uttered hoarsely.

"Yeah, Fyn, it's me."

Harlowe reached into his gama-belt and retrieved a vial of Bluestuff, giving it all to Fyn. The rancher's lips were so parched, he couldn't take it without losing some out the side of his mouth. Harlowe tilted his head back slightly to help him swallow. After a second dose, he moved him to the shade of a nearby tree to help his eyes. Within moments, Fyn began to come around.

"Har...lowe?"

"Fyn, yeah, it's me," Harlowe repeated.

Fyn coughed and spit up phlegm as he cried in a raspy voice, "Mu...is..."

Harlowe looked back at the shed. There was no one else there. "I don't see Muis, Fyn. Where is Muis?"

Fyn wheezed and coughed as he tried to breathe the fresh air and said, "Muis..." over and over.

Harlowe continued working on Fyn, injecting him with nutrients and infection fighting Gamadin medicine that would stabilize his tortured condition. "He's not here, Fyn."

"Taken...taken to..." was all Fyn could manage to say in his feeble condition.

Harlowe laid Fyn's head and shoulders on the ground as he turned to Pox. The slimy toad hadn't moved an inch from where Harlowe had told him to stand. If there was anyone who knew where Muis was stuffed away, it was him. "The boy and the girl? Where are they?" Harlowe asked politely, snatching him off the ground by his purple velvet tunic.

Pox's mouth opened with gut-wrenching fear. "If I tell you, you'll kill me."

Harlowe practically spit in the dweeb's face as he came nose to nose with the scumbag. "If you don't, that's guaranteed," he assured him.

Pox heard the ear-piercing scream of the Gamadin's creature coming from the palace. "I will show you if you—"

"No deals," Harlowe said quickly. He turned Pox around while he held him in the air and asked, "Which way, Turd?"

Pox pointed down an alternate path away from the corrals. Harlowe tossed him forward, and said, "Go!"

They crossed a wide courtyard to what appeared to be Tapper living quarters. The barracks was as big as a football field and three levels high. It wasn't too far from the palaces, so Harlowe figured it housed Darkn's elite officer corps. With sirens blaring loudly across the city, Tappers were scurrying about, running to their respective stations to defend against the all out attack on the city. So it wasn't surprising for Harlowe to come face to face with a half dozen officers along the same path as he kicked Pox ahead of him. Donning shiny bronze helmets full of yellow feathers, the officers were as big as Gamadin and ugly as sin. Strapped to their red and yellow uniforms was an assortment of weapons, knives, and ammunition packs. In the distance beyond the barracks, hundreds of red uniforms were scurrying toward the rows of gerbids lined up, ready for battle. It was an armada like nothing Harlowe had ever seen.

The officers stopped. Seeing Darkn's aide manhandled like a Fagan slave, they figured Harlowe was no friendly spirit. There were no Who-are-you's or What-are-you-doing-here introductions. Without a word of welcome, they drew their weapons.

Harlowe had no words for them, either. He shot the five officers outright, dropping them before their sidearms cleared their holsters. The sixth officer was allowed to live because he had seen him before. He shot away his sidearm and stripped away his knives and utility belt with two more shots, and said to him, "You're the zero who took Isara hostage. Where is she?"

"I…I…don't—" the gerbid commander tried to say when Harlowe shot off his left ear.

"Cut the 'I-don'ts'. Where is she?" he asked again.

The commander's head turned from side to side in excruciating pain. "I…I—"

Blam!

It was the right ear this time, along with a thick section of the Tapper's scalp. Green blood flowed down the officer's head and neck as Harlowe continued the questioning. "Where is she?" He would slice the officer into a thousand pieces until he got the answer he wanted.

The Tapper's jaw clenched so hard Harlowe thought he might break his crooked teeth. Unable to talk, the commander nodded at the doorway.

"You better pray that she lives, Butthead," Harlowe warned before he sprang toward the doorway. In no time at all he was up the short stairway and through the door. Several sentries were standing guard and were surprised by Harlowe's sudden entry. They would have shot him had they the time to react, but Harlowe was so swift and forceful, their weapons were useless. He slammed their faces against the walls with such impact, not one guard would ever awaken again.

Harlowe continued through to a small foyer that was the center of two long hallways of rooms. The choice was clear as to which hallway was the correct one. The trail of blue-green blood on the floor led him to a room three doors down on the right. One hard kick and the door blew open. Three of the most loathsome beings he had ever come across hovered over Isara's body like hungry dogs. Her clothes were nearly ripped from her body as she lay unconscious and bleeding, chained against the wall, barely alive.

Harlowe shot the three outright, kicked their bodies aside, and went to Isara, feverishly blasting away the steel shackles that bound her to the wall. Maybe she was breathing, maybe she wasn't. He cupped her head in his arm as he looked down at her blackened, swollen eyes. Her pupils were twitching back and forth uncontrollably under her eyelids. She had a broken arm, two broken wrists, her nose was smashed to one side, all from the fists that had struck her face. Like he had done for Fyn, he gave her a vial of Bluestuff and injected her with life sustaining fluids. But unlike Fyn, Isara's condition was far more critical.

After he had done medically what he could for her, he took a moment to scan her body. Although she was still alive, there was little doubt she was at Death's doorstep. He wished with all his heart for *Millawanda* to be parked outside with a squad of robob medics waiting to carrying her to the nearest med unit. Knowing he could do nothing else for her but remove her from the rat hole, he gathered her in his arms and ran for the corrals where he had left Fyn. On his way down the path, Harlowe came face to face with the gerbid commander and Pox. The huge Tapper, now earless and bleeding all over himself, blocked his way, while Pox looked on at a safe distance, grinning evilly for payback.

"Put the female down, Offworlder," the commander raved. "We will settle this the Tapper way."

The commander was a third larger than Harlowe and two heads taller. His arms were so long, they nearly touched the ground. To say he was as ugly as Quasimodo would be giving him a compliment.

Harlowe made no attempt to stop and confront the commander, nor did he put Isara down or slow his pace even a little bit to avoid the "Tapper way." When he came within reach of the commander's powerful extremities, Harlowe leaped high with Isara still in his arms, pulverizing the commander's face with such a mashing kick that it broke his neck, twisting his head around to the point that when he hit the ground, his face slammed against the gravel first as his body fell chest up.

Pox started to run, but another shot from Harlowe's pistol stopped the toad before he got too far. "Back to the corral, ferret face," Harlowe ordered.

*   *   *

Back at the corral, Bigbob had Pox's neck in his pincers ready to snap it. "Go ahead, stickman, twist it off," Fyn urged. In his mind, death couldn't come soon enough for Darkn's assistant. "Kill him, kill him," he seethed.

"Not yet, Fyn. I still have need for the toad," Harlowe said, laying Isara down beside her father.

Trembling with fear at the sight of his daughter's tortured state, Fyn asked the obvious question. "Is she?"

Harlowe swallowed hard. "I'll not lie to you, Fyn. She's in a bad way."

With heavy tears falling down his ruddy cheeks, Fyn picked her up in his weakened condition and held her head to his chest. "Thank you, Harlowe. Thank you. Thank you." He sniffled, fighting back the tears as he made sure she was comfortable. He brushed her matted hair away from her face and tried to straightened what was left of her garments knowing she would be concerned with her dignity if she were conscious. After he had done all that he could for her, he took Harlowe's arm, his teary gaze full of gratitude, and said, "You are my spirit, Harlowe. There is no one greater than you."

Harlowe nodded his thanks and said, "It's not over, Fyn. We still have Muis to find."

Fyn drew Harlowe's weapon from his holster and pointed it at Pox. "He knows where Muis is."

Pox saw the acidic hate in Fyn's eyes and knew his scummy life was over unless he cooperated. "Yes, yes, I know where the boy is."

Once Fyn and Isara were secure with Bigbob standing guard over them, Harlowe said to Pox, "Lead the way, Zithead."

Harlowe prayed he was wrong, but his gut told him the boy would be the worst of them all.

120

Muis

Pox took off running, veering away from the barracks until they came an area of well-guarded, stone cells. He stopped in the center of the compound and informed Harlowe the boy was held in the second cell.

"Go there. You will find him," Pox instructed.

Harlowe took two steps toward the cell when Pox bolted away screaming, "Kill him! He's after the Fyn boy!"

The idea that Pox had led Harlowe into a trap was predictable. Harlowe would have been surprised if the pusshead had acted otherwise. With no more use for the smarmy being, Harlowe dusted Pox's pathetic life for good, dropping him before he made it out of the compound gate. After that, neutralizing the security force surrounding the compound was swift. Three guards went down with shots to the head; the remaining five saw they were clearly outgunned and dropped their weapons, and fled the scene. The guard holding the keys tossed them at Harlowe in an effort to distract him long enough to make his escape.

Harlowe opened the cell and looked into the inky cavity. What his bugeyes revealed made him lose it before he could step through the door. Even his SIBA internal life support systems couldn't stop him from puking his guts out at the side of the entrance. Fighting off the nausea, he reset his bugeyes' headgear back over his mouth and entered the cell. Muis was naked, bruised, and lying in his own waste. Both feet were gone. Whoever had cut them off had seared the ends of his legs to stop him from bleeding to death. The miracle of miracles was that somehow the boy was alive. Harlowe became so angry, that if Muis had been dead, he would have run back to the Palace and beaten Darkn unrecognizable. Instead, Harlowe's only option was to de-energize his SIBA and use it to keep Muis alive by engulfing him in the Gamadin suit in the hope Monday and the crystal had made it back to *Millawanda* in time. For that to happen, though, he had to get both Isara and Muis back to the coast and find some way to transport them down to his ship. *Millawanda's* med units were the only place on the planet where Muis had an angel's chance of saving his life.

Once the SIBA covered Muis, the life sustaining functions of the suit were immediate. The suit needed no activation button to press, no auto systems to set. All it required was a body in need. The SIBA was fail-safe. It would do its job. Harlowe scooped the boy up in his arms and ran for the corral.

Time was against them. The coast and *Millawanda* were a two day drive at best in a gerbid. There was no time to think about why any plan would save them. All he had was a pipe dream. He had no time to think what would happen if they met Darkn's gerbids along the way, or worse, Cornicen's forces charging in to protect Elrish Dag and its wealth. No time, either, to think if Squid and Oea made it or not. If Monday failed to deliver the aara crystal to Riverstone, even if they did make it to the coast, they were all dead because his ship was stuck on the bottom of the ocean forever!

Damn!

A lot of ifs and only one option.

Stealing a gerbid!

There was no plan B and a slew more ifs.

A fully gassed gerbid could rumble across the plains at top speed and make the coast in two days. If Nath had scrounged the fuel to replenish the gerbid, and if DaboS was successful in finding him rolling fast on the road to Elrish Dag, and if the little Fagan had led them to a hilltop then all he had to do was get to the rendezvous point and pray Nath was there with a fat-faced smile, the hatch wide open, and the engine running!

121

Escape from Elrish Dag

Elrish Dag was a fortress in chaos. Sirens blared loudly, preparing the population for invasion, as fires burned along the fortress walls. The central and north guard towers had crumbled from internal explosions. With no SIBA to protect him and dressed in regular clothes splattered with blue-green blood and mud, Harlowe strapped Isara and Muis to the backs of two ceffyls inside the corral while Fyn hobbled to the gates and opened them. None of the ceffyls would leave the compound until Delamo led the herd out. Fyn could walk, but when he tried to hoist himself on a ceffyl, he didn't have the strength. Already on Delamo, Harlowe galloped across the corral, reached down and grabbed Fyn by the back of his shirt, and placed him onto the ceffyl's back. Harlowe made sure the herd and Fyn, Isara, and Muis were through the gates before he let go an ear-piercing whistle and rode to catch up with the herd.

* * *

Inside the palace Darkn held his bloody stump frozen to his throne, unable to move with the Gamadin beast hovering over his head. Its putrid breath was blowing down on him, inches from his face. Twice the palace guards tried to shoot the beast. The first guard was cut in half by its tail when it whipped around, slicing him clean through his torso. The second was struck in the face by a glob of spit, emulsifying his features into a puddle of acidic ooze. Seeing the result of two failed attempts, no one else wanted to risk that kind of death for the Margrave.

Outside the palace an imperceptible high-pitched sound resonated throughout the great hallway, to everyone but the beast. The beast raised its head, letting go a roar so loud every wall in the palace shook. Darkn slipped to the floor, believing the end was near. When the hot, acidic breath left the room, and he was still alive, he opened his eyes and watched the beast gliding down the long hallway, flapped its wings once as it passed through the giant doors and lifted into the noon-day sky.

With the beast gone, the commander returned to the throne room to check on Darkn.

"Sire, Sire, oh, thank the gods; you have survived the beast!" the commander cried upon seeing Darkn's ashen face. Several guards assisted him back to his throne. Rid of the beast, Darkn's eyes searched for retribution. If he had a weapon in his possession, he would have killed his commander instantly for allowing the beast to torture him. The only thing that saved the officer's life was a runner charging into the throne room with the report that the Margrave's ceffyls had escaped the city.

"Launch the gerbids!" Darkn roared at the top of his lungs. "Dispatch them all!" he screamed. "No one returns to Elrish Dag until my ceffyls are captured! I want them back! Hear me! I want them all, but above all else, I want the black!"

* * *

Harlowe couldn't believe his eyes. As he rode out of the gate, the first thing he saw in the distance was a lone, black and orange gerbid tank on the far hilltop. Without his bugeyes the beings standing beside the giant wheels were tiny specks. They had to be Nath and his Fagan riders, Harlowe told himself as he urged Delamo to fly like the wind. *DaboS did it!* He had found Nath and *Bad Boy*.

As he ascended the hill, he saw the Fagans waving and jumping up and down for him to run faster. "Come on, Harlowe!" the voices shouted.

He had expected to see Nath's round face greeting him like a long lost brother back from the war. But the last hundred yards up the hill, Nath was incredibly distressed. Even as the first ceffyls galloped through the hatchway, the Fagan leader was fit-to-be-tied. "Move, Harlowe, move! Get everyone inside, now!!!" he shouted, slapping ceffyls on their back ends.

Next came Isara, then Muis, and Fyn, followed by the remainder of the herd. Only Harlowe remained outside the hatchway.

"Nath, you are a sight for sore eyes, pard!" Harlowe exclaimed, atop the prancing Delamo.

"Shut up, Harlowe! Get inside!" Nath cried out again.

"Nath, why are you so angry? Where is my little friend, DaboS?"

Nath pointed at the smoking city of Elrish Dag behind him. "Look, Harlowe! The gerbids! THEY'RE COMING!"

When Harlowe turned on Delamo, he couldn't believe his eyes. Hundreds of gerbids were spewing out of the city gates like someone had kicked over a giant mound of fire ants. Nothing could stop them. Their engines violently shook the earth as their stories' high wheels kicked up huge amounts of dust and dirt, killing all who happened to be in the way.

The first salvo of gerbid cannon shots exploded around them, widely missing their marks by some distance. Harlowe put Delamo's head down, and they leaped through the hatch just as another shell exploded at the bottom of the ramp. Harlowe slid down from Delamo and waited for Nath before closing the hatch.

But no Nath.

Through the smoldering dirt and debris, Harlowe found Nath's broken body under the gerbid. Unable to check his condition, with blue-green blood splattered over Nath's face and arms, Harlowe tossed the Fagan over his shoulder and dove for the open hatch the instant before another blast detonated behind them, blowing them inside. DaboS and several other riders slammed the hatch shut and secured the latches as another blast rocked the gerbid.

"GO, BIGBOB!" Harlowe cried out. "GET US OUT OF HERE!"

There was no time to check on Nath's condition. Harlowe handed DaboS a vile of Bluestuff, his last, and said, "Take care of him!" Then he sprinted up the ladder to the bridge.

The giant tank lurched forward with *Bad Boy*'s wheels digging into the earth, rumbling down the backside of the hill, giving them some precious cover. Harlowe brought up the topo map on the screen and pointed out the route he wanted Bigbob to follow. That done, he grabbed his assault rifle and headed for the topside hatch. Slamming open the hatch, he cranked his rifle to full power and blasted three Darkn gerbids coming over the the hill.

BAALEWWWEY!

Next, he zeroed in on the the cliffs above Elrish Dag. Three squeezes later, the face of the black granite mountain exploded, bringing down the escarpment wall and crushed the city beneath with a billion tons of rock and stone.

*   *   *

Darkn heard the explosion, felt the rumble of the aftershock, and the thunderous roar of hurricane force winds that blew open the palace doors which knocked him and his throne of skulls off its pedestal. The avalanche of black boulders crushed the fortress-city, obliterating the palace, the plunder, and Darkn and his evil forever!

122

Race for the Coast

The scores of gerbids that had survived the avalanche spread out, cutting off any chance of escape across the narrow plain. For the first twenty miles, Harlowe's beast drove flat out across the grassy plain with nothing in their way but scattered thorn trees that were easily crushed under its heavy tires. Bigbob drove tirelessly on, allowing Harlowe to pick off rogue gerbids on the fly when they got too close.

"We are coming upon the first gorge, Harlowe!" DaboS shouted up from the bridge. With Nath injured or dead, Harlowe appointed the little Fagan second in command. There was no one Harlowe trusted more. After eating, sleeping, and facing Death together, choosing DaboS was a no-brainer.

"Aye, DaboS!" Harlowe acknowledged. He fired his last two rounds, eliminating two more gerbids, as the hive charged relentlessly after them, their great dust cloud rising thousands of feet in the air. Time and again the lead gerbids took their best shots, trying to slow them down with a lucky shot. But the race was too fast and way too bumpy to get a clear bead on the runaway tank.

Out of ammo, and with the gorge coming up fast, Harlowe had no choice but to take over the controls from Bigbob. Out on the open flats, there was no one better at the controls than the big clicker, but rumbling into a rocky, pitted hole in the middle of the plain, took another kind of driver… someone crazy like Harlowe, who had lost his license the first week he was old enough to drive.

Dropping down to the bridge floor, Harlowe grabbed DaboS' arm as *Bad Boy* took a sharp bounce. "Get below. Make sure your guys and the ceffyls are strapped down. The ride is going to get a lot worse. That includes you, DaboS. Bigbob and I can handle the bridge. You stay in the hold and watch over Isara and Muis for me."

"I will, Harlowe."

DaboS leaped for the ladder and slid down the rails faster than a New York City fireman.

With DaboS dispatched to the hold, Harlowe relieved Bigbob and sent him to the navigation station. Through the forward window, the gorge was already in view.

"Bigbob, find me a path through that gorge ahead!" Harlowe ordered.

Harlowe never had to say, "Hurry!" because robobs only worked one way…fast. Two thumps later, Bigbob displayed several paths on the monitor. The choice was difficult with neither a clear route, so Harlowe chose the nearest one and went for it.

Before he made his turn, a blue-green bloody arm reached past him and touched the monitor screen. "No, Harlowe," a gruff voice said, "take that one."

Harlowe twisted around, surprised by Nath, his face cut and bloody, one arm splinted and held close to his stomach as he hobbled along on one, sort of, good leg. "Why, you're as ugly as ever, Roundface. You need to clean up when you're on my bridge."

Nath snorted. "Like you, Pinkface."

Harlowe glanced at his own arms and clothes covered with blue-green crusty blood and dirt from head to foot. In a contest between him and Nath as to whom was the filthiest, he would have won hands down.

"Yeah, like me. Why aren't you taking it easy?"

"Because without me, you will lose your way, my friend."

Harlowe pointed a finger at the robob. "Right you are, Nath. Take Bigbob's chair and give me a route to ditch these toads."

Nath saluted. "Aye, Captain."

For the second time in less than a minute, Bigbob was relieved of his chair. Harlowe put him in the co-pilot's chair directly behind him, knowing that if anything happened to him, the tall clicker would take the helm without a hitch.

A barrage of shells detonated around them just as they entered the gorge, blowing out three port side windows that injured two Fagan riders with cuts and lacerations from flying glass. The last round, however, lifted the rear right wheel causing Harlowe to briefly lose control, bulldozing his way down the steep grade and into the gorge. Banking the front bumper off the stone face of the starboard cliff, sparks flew as the outside tires nearly went off the path. Nath's face lost its color when the road disappeared. All he could see was two thousand feet of cliff looking down the port side windows.

Bumping and slamming against the rock face, doing his best to keep them from careening off the cliff, Harlowe drove like it was all planned. He found traction again and made it to the bottom of the gorge, where he had no choice but to slow to a crawl as he wound the beastly gerbid around boulders and washed out ruts that could have easily eaten his old Volkswagen, Baby, for lunch.

Along the ridgeline several foolhardy gerbids turned into the gorge chasing Harlowe. The first one never made it beyond the lip. His front end lost it on the first switchback, and he paid the price, bouncing along like a loose beach ball into the ravine, exploding in a ball of fire before he hit bottom. The second and third gerbids had no better luck. By the time Harlowe was motoring up the backside of the ravine, there was a serious pile of wreckage at the bottom of the gorge. Two smaller gerbids managed to make it to the bottom but were swallowed by the washouts. One went head first into the deep rut, resembling an ostrich with its head in the sand and its rear sticking high in the air. The other crossed the rut only to slide backward into a deep hole.

Once he reached the top of the ravine, Harlowe floored it, catching air off the lip. On the return to earth, the wheels spewed dirt as he resumed his blistering pace across the plains. With level ground ahead for the next hundred miles, Harlowe handed the controls back to Bigbob. While they were putting distance between them and the hive, he took care of loose ends, checking on the damage and seeing to the injured. He called DaboS to the bridge and had him relieve Nath at navigation. Harlowe helped Nath back to his bunk and told him if he moved again, he would put him in chains for the rest of the trip. He dressed Nath's wounds, reset his arm and leg and encased them both in Gamadin jell splints that felt like not even having a splint on. Isara and Muis were far worse. Outwardly they were both alive…

maybe. Fyn, on the other hand, was beside himself with the fear that he would lose both of his children. With his head bowed at their bedsides, deep in prayer, he held Isara's hand with one hand and laid his head on the SIBA encapsulating Muis. Harlowe doubted that Fyn ever knew he was standing next to him.

Finished with all he could do, Harlowe went back to the hold to check on the ceffyls. They were all agitated, their eyes bulging from the frightening ride, but they were all unhurt. He found Mowgi stretched out between Delamo's horns, firmly attached for stability. Both were unshaken and cool as ice. Mowgi released his grip when Harlowe walked over and gave each one a thank you pat for the help they had given him at Elrish Dag.

"Nice work, boys," Harlowe congratulated them.

Mowgi yipped twice, and Delamo snorted approvingly.

Suddenly Harlowe felt his stomach growl. He couldn't remember the last time he had eaten. He found the food locker and was about to take his second bite of mystery meat when DaboS called him to the bridge in a frazzle. Harlowe tossed the morsel over to Mowgi, who made short work of the slimy meat. By the time he made it back to the bridge, the problem was evident as he felt the engine sputter beneath his feet.

"Out of gas?" Harlowe questioned with surprise. The tanks were full when they left Elrish Dag. He had checked himself, always remembering the General's never-to-be-forgotten lesson: never assume anything when your life depends on it!

"The starboard tank is empty, Harlowe," DaboS reported.

123

If

Harlowe checked the fuel level, and sure enough, it was riding on E. He hit the fuel indicator twice with his palm. It didn't budge. He had Bigbob pull to a stop so he could inspect the outer hull. The instant the main hatch cracked open, gas fumes poured into the hold. It didn't take an "A" student in Farnducky's class to understand there was a leak. Harlowe knew right where to look. At the exact point where *Bad Boy's* left rear tire hit the ground, thick, black fuel was gushing out of a jagged blast hole on the starboard side of the hull. There was an auxiliary tank, but it was small. Making it to the coast now was out of the question. The rate they were burning fuel they would be lucky to make it to the next ravine.

A Fagan came scrambling around the back wheel. "Harlowe! Look!" He pointed off their port flank. Rising high in the air was another cloud. But it wasn't dust. This time it was billowing plumes of black smoke.

Fire!

If they were caught in the fast moving prairie fire, they would ignite like a bomb from the fuel that had already poured out on the ground around them. Directly behind them Darkn's gerbids had found a way across the first ravine, so going back was not an option. Their commanders were smart. By setting the fire to the east, they had cut down the width of the prairie to a narrow road. They were trapped. If Darkn's gerbids didn't catch them, the fire would.

Harlowe ordered everyone back inside and to strap themselves in. In the next breath he yelled up to Bigbob to floor it and sealed the hatch. The giant tank jerked ahead, slamming Fagans and ceffyls not tied down against the bulkheads. As everyone scrambled for anything to hold onto, Harlowe climbed over the backs of bracing ceffyls on his way to the bridge. DaboS already had the monitors fixed on the fire by the time Harlowe took back the helm from Bigbob. On the rear screen, explosions from gerbid cannons were falling far short of the target. Hitting him wasn't the point. They wanted Harlowe to know his only choice was the death trap they were setting him up for.

Scanning DaboS' maps, he saw no easy way down the next gorge except for the north end. They had planned to take the much flatter south end, but the fire nixed that. The north side was the only choice open, that is, if he could find a way to cross it. Darkn's commanders were looking at the same maps he was, smugly knowing there was no other path but a three thousand foot drop.

Harlowe saw only one way open to them. Maybe there was no path into the gorge, or a bridge to cross it, but there was one place along the cliffs he saw opportunity. If the map was correct, it was where the gap was only a hundred yards wide, maybe less. He had done it before; he could do it again. If he could get up enough speed… If, if, if… he would fly across. Looking at the reserve gauge, he had just enough fuel to make it, too. Once they made it to the other side, they would leave *Bad Boy* behind and ride the ceffyls the rest of the way to the coast. He knew Darkn's gerbids didn't have the *cajones* to try that jump. It would be days waiting out the fire before they could cross the southern end of the ravine. By then Harlowe and his Fagan pals would be at the coast, calling for help. That is, if…if Riverstone could get *Millawanda* off the bottom of the ocean.

Still going with plan A or nothing, Harlowe made the slight course change and headed directly for the narrow gap on the monitor.

124

Taking Flight

Feeling the heat from the prairie fire tickling his backside and his engine starting to sputter, *Bad Boy* was running on fumes. Bulldozing over a rut and a few boulders in his path, Harlowe managed to jerk the fuel tank enough to gather what fumes were left into the gas lines. He felt the push on the back of his seat as the thirsty motor sucked in the remaining energy and raced forward. But even if they made it to the cliff, they would be out of gas by the time they landed on the other side of the ravine.

"Harlowe!" DaboS cried out, pointing up at the forward monitor. "The fire has jumped ahead! We are cut off! The flames have extended across our path!"

Harlowe saw the fire. They were a hundred yards from the edge, and he wasn't stopping. "Forget the fire, DaboS, mark the line!"

"The navigation points are lost. My readouts switched off."

"What?"

"We are driving blind, Harlowe!" DaboS shouted.

Harlowe peered through the upper windows above his command chair. He saw dark objects in the sky swooping down, firing bright yellow pulses above the gorge. What they were, and what they were shooting at was impossible to tell from his chair."

"Harlowe, something is shooting at us from the sky."

"Hold on, DaboS!"

Harlowe couldn't see squat through the flames, and the screen was dark!

But it didn't matter…there was no stopping.

Harlowe locked his arms straight out as he pressed his back against the chair, ready for flight. Then suddenly the engines quit. No sputter, no cough. They just died.

Looking out, the flames in front had disappeared and were replaced by a flood of green sky. Simultaneously, Harlowe felt the buoyancy of weightlessness. They were airborne. The feeling of flight lasted a few seconds before the erosion of forward motion began to lower the front end from up to down. The power loss before liftoff had sealed their fate. Reaching the far edge of the gorge was now a physical impossibility.

It wasn't long before they were headed straight down, staring into the three thousand foot gorge at a bed of jagged rocks. At impact they would be traveling over a hundred miles per hour. If there was any good news at all, the end would be swift and painless.

They picked up speed and passed the one thousand foot mark within seconds. The two thousand foot level was less time after that. At the twenty-five hundred foot mark Harlowe's body suddenly slammed forward hard against his restraints. He let out a breathless grunt believing they should have sucked face with the riverbed by now. He drew in a lungful of air like a free diver coming up for air and looked out the window. Of all things peculiar, the bottom of the gorge was pulling away. They were no longer headed down, but up!

DaboS pushed himself away from his console enough to twist his head around to Harlowe in shock. All the little Fagan could say was, "What happened?"

Harlowe's mouth tried to move as he looked around the bridge. All the monitors were offline. The banks of lights, gauges, and readouts indicating fuel consumption, tire pressure, revs, temperature, and oil pressure were all dark. They may have run out of fuel, but if nothing else, the gerbid's batteries should have kept the lights on. Incredibly, the power was shut down like someone had flicked off the circuit breakers. His focus traveled from the forward windows to the side portals. They were rising above the cliffs like some giant crane was hoisting them from the jaws of Death.

"I…I haven't a clue," Harlowe finally stammered.

As Harlowe's head began to reassert itself from the sudden turn of fate, he focused on the blue lines of bright light slicing across the sky. He knew those lines. There was only one thing in the galaxy that had that much energy, and it belonged to him. With incredible accuracy the blue streaks were vaporizing the flying black objects by the scores. As *Bad Boy* began to right itself in midair over the ravine, the familiar rim of *Millawanda's* golden hull came into view through the upper windows. Harlowe didn't think he had ever seen anything more beautiful.

125

Captain on the Bridge

With *Bad Boy* leveled off, Harlowe released his restraints and climbed through the upper hatch waving at his ship with all the shouts of joy he could muster. "You da babe, Hon!" Harlowe said to Her. If his arms were long enough, he would have reached up and hugged her.

Millawanda had them firmly in her tractor beam, lifting the thousand-ton gerbid into her center foyer as easily as a toy car. The scores of Darkn's gerbids came to a screeching halt on the black and smoldering plain near the edge of the gorge en mass. They lifted their tank muzzles high and fired their explosive shells by the hundreds at the dangling rogue. It was all a futile exercise. A wall of wispy, blue light stopped the murderous rounds cold. Then in the middle of their foray, a barrage of blue bolts reduced every last one of Darkn's gerbids to molten heaps of worthless metal.

"DaboS!" Harlowe called down to the little Fagan from the top hatch. "Get everyone out. There will be someone along shortly to show you where to go. Bigbob! Mowgi! You're with me," he ordered.

Bigbob bolted from his chair, bounding through the hatch a split second before Mowgi's small body flew by with his tail waging like a tuning fork. All three jumped down from the gerbid hatch, touching the fine softness of the blue, carpeted floor. Mowgi rolled on his back, wiggling from side to side, stretching out on the carpet, happy to be home. Harlowe wanted to join him, but his ship was under attack. He needed to be elsewhere. While Mowgi cooed on the carpet, Harlowe and Bigbob stepped on the nearest blinker, and an instant later…

"Captain on the bridge!" Monday called out.

Jewels was already waiting with a fresh uniform the moment Harlowe stepped off the blinker. Stripping down to his underwear, he wasted no time in getting straight to business. "Report, Mr. Riverstone."

"Incoming bad guys, Captain."

"Millie up to speed?"

"Prigg has a handle on her, sir. He's down in the power room as we speak." He rose from the center chair, giving Harlowe his place. Moving one chair to his right, Riverstone added, "Glad to see you, Captain."

"Nice timing, Mr. Riverstone. Thank you," Harlowe said, sliding one leg at a time through his pant legs.

"We figured it was you, sir. No one else in the galaxy can piss off so many toads at one time."

Harlowe cracked a grin, stretching through his dress-blue topcoat. "Right you are, Mr. Riverstone. We have some critical people below. Put the med units on them, stat."

"Aye, Captain, stat!"

Harlowe shot Monday a quick nod of appreciation, buttoning his collar. "Nice work, Mr. Platter."

"Thank you, Captain."

"Everyone aboard?" Harlowe asked, meaning all the crew onboard that came to Osset with them.

Monday answered, "Aye, Captain. *All* aboard."

Harlowe stretched out his neck as he stepped into his shoes and straightened his cuff, brushed his sleeve, and tugged once on the bottom of his coat, putting every crease and stitch in its proper place. He was about to take his position at his center chair when Simon stepped off the blinker. His head was down and sullen as he walked onto the bridge. Before Harlowe could ask why the long face, Riverstone covered for him. "He just came out of sickbay, Captain."

Harlowe studied his First Mate with a caring eye before asking him, "Are you fit for duty, Mr. Bolt?"

Simon straightened to attention and saluted. "Right as rain, Skipper."

Even though it was obvious Simon had issues, Harlowe nodded his approval. After all, he was a Gamadin, and a Gamadin threshold for pain, emotional or physical, was far above normal human beings. Allowing Simon to return to duty was the best medicine he could have. "Very well, Mr. Bolt. Take your station."

"Thank you, Skipper."

Harlowe turned to the tall robob standing patiently behind him. "Take the nav station, if you would, Mr. Bigbob."

Without comment, the robob went to his station and placed their position on the overhead screen. Harlowe studied the numerous blips and asked, "Are these the same Mysterians that have been dogging us since the Omni Quadrant, Mr. Riverstone?"

"Aye, Captain."

"Do we have power for battle?"

Riverstone faced Harlowe with a discouraged look. "The blue crystal you found was too small, Captain."

Harlowe's mouth dropped open. "So what's keeping her up?"

Riverstone cracked a grin. "The other crystals."

"What? What other crystals? That was all we found."

As if right on cue, Jewels clickity-clacked from Harlowe's quarters, carrying a tray in one claw and Riverstone's ornate cane given to him by General Fiv in the other. Riverstone took the cane and removed the abordar from the tray. The top stone from the cane and the center stone of the abordar were missing.

"We lucked out, Captain," Riverstone began, holding up both pieces for hm to see. "This broach Mr. Bolt lifted from the museum had small aara crystals around the center diamond." He pointed the butt of the cane toward Harlowe. "And this had an aara twice the size of the one Mr. Platter had with him."

"Twice?" Harlowe questioned.

Riverstone squinted his face up tight. "Maybe three times."

Harlowe didn't like losing even a little bit. "So that worked, huh?"

"Not until Prigg figured out a way to suspend them all in a matrix. So we have juice, but Prigg's not sure how long it will hold up. The good news is Millie has a second wind, but for how long, we don't know. She could last a week, a month, maybe even a year if we take it easy. Who knows?"

Harlowe saw his First Officer had more to say. "And your point?"

"My point is, Millie is far from sweet, Captain. If we go in blasting away like *The Expendables*, she'll have nothing left to get her to Orixy. Ask Prigg. He'll tell ya. We have to tone it down a might, or we'll end up on another Osset without a love-nut Gamadin letter to show us the way."

Harlowe grunted his dissatisfaction. "We've been down this road before."

"Too many times, Captain."

With his ship taking hits, rising toward the stratosphere, Harlowe came back to the screen, mulling over his options. Through the forward windows, blue bolts of light continued striking out at the incoming drones, destroying them like irritant flies.

Harlowe glanced over at Simon. "How are we doing out there, Mr. Bolt?"

"Like ducks in a shooting gallery, Captain," Simon replied. His hands slid over lighted bars, tapped activators, and twisted knobs like he was thrilled to be back at his weapons station again.

"Give me a read on the mothership, Mr. Platter."

"Aye, Captain." Monday immediately found the source of the drones and placed the positions on the overhead screen. "Plotted, Captain."

"Very well, Mr. Platter." Then to Riverstone, Harlowe said, "Let's pay them a visit."

Riverstone nearly came out of his seat. "Didn't you hear what I said, Captain? Millie's still in recovery, and we've got a long way to go to the galactic core!"

"Objection noted, Mr. Riverstone, but these toads have been following us for a long time. I don't know what their game is, and this is the second time they've hit us. They're scared of us, for sure. The only time they've really attacked Millie head-on is when they thought she was down for the count. We need to show them she still has a lot of bite left in her."

Riverstone reluctantly agreed. "Aye."

Back to Monday, Harlowe requested a visual of the Mysterian ship. "On screen, Mr. Platter."

"She's sitting pretty, Captain, behind that moon," Monday said.

"She's way bigger than we are," Riverstone noted from the readouts.

"Ten plus, Mr. Riverstone," Monday concurred.

The Mysterian ship was ten times the size of *Millawanda;* nevertheless, Harlowe recalled a much bigger ship that assaulted them.

"That's not the mothership," Harlowe pointed out, recalling a much bigger ship that had attacked them when they had to leave Wiz, Lu, and the cats behind on the planet.

Riverstone concurred. "Yeah, it's way smaller."

Harlowe motioned to Monday that he was taking control of the helm. "They're testing us. She's making sure we're too weak to fight back, then she'll pounce. The way she's acting, I don't think she wants to kill us just yet. She wants to scavenge us." Harlowe turned to Riverstone, the light bulb having turned on. "She wants the secret of the most powerful ship in the galaxy."

Riverstone grew angry at the thought. "We'll have something to say about that."

Harlowe went on. "That we will, Mr. Riverstone. She knows Millie's weak, but she doesn't know how weak. She's out of sensor range now, but you can bet she knows exactly where we are at any given time using her stand-ins as relays."

"How do we stop them from following us to Orixy, Captain?" Riverstone asked.

At this point, Harlowe didn't see any alternative. He was sticking with Plan A. "We have no choice. Millie has to survive. It's Orixy or bust for us. We've gotta beat them there, and that's our only option. But once Millie's right, we'll take on every Mysterian mothership in the universe, mano a mano, Mr. Riverstone. Then we'll see who's the king of the hill."

Riverstone was still digesting the idea of leading the Mysterians to Orixy. If the Mysterians discovered the Gamadin home world, it would be the end of them, *Millawanda*, and the Gamadin comeback.

That sucked!

Harlowe slid his hand across the accelerator bar, leaving the drones to wonder where their target had vanished. Breaking into space, the front windows went from emerald green to black with glittering stars lighting the heavens. Harlowe made a one-eighty, bringing the saucer perpendicular to Osset's polar axis as he kept the moon between the Mysterian ship and *Millawanda*. Once they broke behind the far moon, the Mysterian sensors would pick them up and would try to flee.

Surprise!

Millawanda was on them before the Mysterian vessel could react. Just before going to hyperlight, Simon fired a single beam of blue fire at the Mysterian ship's power core. The ship exploded, lighting up the nightside of the moon like a brilliant sun. *Millawanda* didn't stay for the fireworks, winking away, leaving the Osset system far behind.

Harlowe clicked his tongue with satisfaction. "That should give them something chew on for a while." Passing the baton back to Monday, he rose from his command chair and began walking toward the blinker. "The bridge is yours, Mr. Riverstone."

"Where are you going, Captain?" Riverstone asked, noticing Harlowe's haggard appearance. "You could use some rest."

Jewels followed in lock step with Harlowe as he replied, "The foyer, gentlemen. I have some friends to check first before I do anything else."

Monday stepped away from his station. "Can I tag along, Captain?" They were his friends, too.

"Our course, Mr. Platter. They would be happy to see you, Captain."

"Course, Captain?" Riverstone asked. "Where are we headed?"

"Orixy, Mr. Riverstone. Best speed. We don't stop now until we get there. Wherever there is," Harlowe ordered.

"Aye, but how do we know what course to take, Captain. Nobody knows how to get there," Riverstone said, taking over the center command chair.

Harlowe smiled, nodding at Bigbob sitting silently at the navigation console. "Ask Mr. B. He'll show you."

And with that, Harlowe, Monday, and Jewels stepped on the blinker and left the bridge to Riverstone and Simon.

126

Harlowe's Doing

The whole crew, including Anor, was present on the bridge as *Forty-Four* sank into the emerald green atmosphere of Osset. Leucadia was unusually quiet. She stood alone, off to one side of the bridge, a mixture of worry and hope that Harlowe, some way, somehow, was on the planet and alive. Everyone let her be. They saw her arms crossing and uncrossing, her weight shifting, calm one second, then shifting again, doing her best to keep herself together while they drifted lower.

Cheesa looked up from her nav screen. "Where should we begin, Captain?"

Before Ian replied, Anor made a proposal "May I suggest we start with those dark clouds along the coast, Captain. The fires appears recent."

Ian glanced at Leucadia for her analysis. She nodded approvingly. "Yes, it is a logical place to begin, Captain," she said evenly.

Ian looked at Cheesa. "Okay, Chee, take us there, if you please."

Forty-Four leveled off five thousand feet above the planet's surface as she drifted at Mach one toward the coastline. When they were ten miles from the coast, they slowed to a crawl, dropping another four thousand feet for a closer look below the black clouds. What they saw was devastating. The city along the shore had been obliterated. Like a nuclear bomb had gone off in the center of the city, there were no buildings left standing. But what was even more unusual was the fact there was very little debris for a city of millions.

Ian spoke first as they peered down upon the charred remains. "Harlowe would never have done this."

"No, this is not Harlowe," Leucadia concurred.

"I have seen his destruction. He is quite capable of this," Anor said.

Leucadia turned on Anor. "Harlowe is no murderer, Mr. Ran," she snapped. "A fleet, perhaps, or an empire that has invaded a planet," meaning her mother's planet of Neeja by the Fhaal, "or a rogue government in league with a consortium bent on the enslavement of an entire quadrant. Yes, he would have wiped them out to expel that kind of madness, but never a wanton murder of a city of millions, SIR!"

Infuriated, Leucadia's eyes left Anor frozen in his place. He had no response to her explosive retort. Neither Dev nor Cheesa had ever seen her so vexed.

Anor bowed his head contritely. "I am sorry, Ms. Leucadia. You are quite right. This is not the mark of your Captain. I misspoke."

Leucadia returned to the forward window without acknowledging Anor's apology. Ian let the air settle as his crew studied the ruins with their monitors. "The destruction is recent, Captain," Cheesa said, focusing on her screens. "Surface temperatures are quite high."

"I estimate three or four days ago," Ian guessed.

No one disagreed.

"Do we go lower?" Dev asked.

"No. The radiation is too high, Dev," Ian replied. "Hold her here."

* * *

After a thorough search, they found no signs that any Gamadin were in the debris field. Leucadia came to Ian at his command chair and said privately while the others were busy with the hunt, "We should move on." There was an urgency in her eyes as she explained, "I feel him, Ian. Harlowe was here. I know it."

Ian stared off in the distance. "I feel him, too, Lu. But where do we go from here?"

Leucadia's eyes went to Anor. "How far can we trust him?"

"About as much as a Dak."

"He believes there is a Gamadin outpost here," Leucadia said.

It was Ian's turn to eye Anor with suspicion. "For whose benefit? His or ours?"

"If it is here, we need to find it. This is where Harlowe would have searched."

"Aye."

Cheesa apologized for interrupting them. "The Gamadin alarm has tripped, Captain."

"Where?"

"In several locations southwest of here."

Instead of one person watching every sensor readout 24/7 for Gamadin presence, the monitors were set on automatic. If the alarm tripped, it was a sure bet that sometime in the past, whether it be two seconds ago or a year, if a Gamadin ship had landed on the surface, the residual sweet odor of her being there would still linger. Ian had Cheesa recheck her screen as he brought *Forty-four* over a flat valley where they found the first Gamadin traces.

"See anything, Dev?" Ian asked.

"A lot of grass, Captain," Dev replied.

A false alarm was possible, Ian supposed. Visually, there was nothing to see for miles, but past experience taught him one thing: a Gamadin sensor was never wrong. Check it out. "Radiation?"

"Negligible, Captain," Dev replied.

Ian glanced over at Cheesa. "The source?"

"Directly ahead, Captain."

"Take her down for a look-see, Chee."

*   *   *

Hovering two hundred feet off the ground, there was no need to land. *Forty-Four's* sensors guided them to the exact location of the Gamadin emission. "That's pretty clear," Ian stated, ecstatic at seeing the three massive impressions in the grassy plain.

Anor added his own thoughts, pointing at all the other tracks and impressions that encircled the three pods for miles in all directions. "A great force had the mothership surrounded."

Leucadia joined the speculation next. "Of course. If Harlowe was as low on fuel as we believe, he put down wherever he was told."

"Could his crew have been taken prisoner and the ship destroyed?" Dev wondered.

Neither Ian nor Leucadia believed that scenario was possible.

"Not likely, Dev," Ian countered. "There is no evidence of her destruction anywhere. From what we've seen of the planet so far, they haven't the means to destroy or capture Millie. They had space flight, but judging by what was left of their air force, it was limited to their star system. I agree with Lu. Harlowe put down and went out looking for a power source for Millie."

"There is no thermo-grym anywhere on the planet," Anor said.

"Aara, then," Leucadia stated. "Harlowe would not have risked everything on a planet that he knew had no thermo-grym unless it was aara he was after, Mr. Ran."

Cheesa's face brightened. "He could still be here then. I mean, if he did not find power for *Millawanda.*"

"Maybe," Ian replied.

"But the mothership is not here," Dev said.

"That's right, she's not here. She moved," Ian concluded.

"Moved where?" Cheesa asked.

Ian tapped his fingers in thought trying to figure out Harlowe's next move. "Depends on what he found. If he found a cache of aara like we did, then all bets are off. He's outta here."

"And if he didn't?" Anor asked.

"He would hide," Leucadia reasoned.

Ian agreed. "That's my guess, too."

"Where?" Dev asked.

Ian looked out the forward window. "There's a big ocean out there. If I were Harlowe, that's where I would hide her."

"How will we find her if she's hidden?" Cheesa asked.

Ian kept his eyes on the horizon as he ordered the ship to continue on a southwesterly course. "Harlowe leaves a trail wherever he goes. If he's still on this planet, we'll find him sooner or later."

* * *

Forty-Four continued toward second area of radiation at the edge of a mile-deep canyon. For a hundred miles to the east, the grassy plain was a flatland, blackened from a recent fire. Pockets of dark smoke continued to rise high in the skies as they spread wide like an eerie shroud above the prairie. Catching everyone's attention amongst the smoke were the scores of melted globs along the rim of the gorge.

"What are they?" Cheesa asked.

Anor pointed to a pool of metal that was only partly liquefied. "They were weapons, Cheesa," and then added, "The long barrel, the armor plating, the wheels. Yes, they were weapons."

"Their size. They must have been enormous," Ian said in awe.

Leucadia unemotionally studied the piles, almost trance-like; she said, almost too low to hear, "Now this was Harlowe's doing."

127

Mysterian Motive

"That confirms it, then," Ian stated solemnly, after checking the surface measurements. He turned to Anor Ran. "Agreed?"

Anor validated the findings.

Leucadia looked up from her monitors. "Yes, *Millawanda* has left the planet," she stated after studying the debris field.

Cheesa was disappointed. She asked, "How do you know, Captain? You thought it was possible Harlowe was still here."

The overhead screen displayed closeups of the smoldering, black piles. "Those lumps down there were caused by Gamadin plas fire, Chee. The sensors confirmed it."

"That means the mothership has left the planet?" Dev asked.

"It means more than that, Dev. It means Harlowe found the aara he needed to go on," Ian replied. "He couldn't have done this without it."

Anor added, "And if he found aara for *Millawanda*, then he will continue his search for Orixy."

Ian looked over at Leucadia. She plopped down on the nearest chair with tears falling from her cheeks. She didn't even bother to wipe her face; she just let the disappointment flow. If Cheesa was disappointed *Millawanda* had left the planet, Leucadia was crushed. Osset was the closest she had been to him since leaving Nod, and she had only missed him by a few days. Now there was no telling in what direction he was headed. Orixy for sure, but how, and what course had he taken? Did he know where Orixy was? Had

598

he found *Millawanda's* origin? Even if Harlowe found the aara he needed, *Millawanda* was still broken. She wasn't *fixed*. Could she make it all the way to the galactic core on her own? They were still over thirty thousand lightyears away from the center of the galaxy where Orixy was thought to be. They had been so very close to catching up, and now they didn't know where to go. She felt like they had just taken ten steps back and they were starting all over again in their search.

Ian looked over the faces of his crew. No one was talking, but they each had that look of "What now, Captain?" on their faces. Knowing they had just missed *Millawanda* was a big let down for everyone.

Whether Anor was let down or not, nobody could tell. He seemed to take everything in stride, as a being who knew great wealth and power, failure, frustration, and roadblocks were all part of the game for him. It was his ability to persevere that made him the once powerful being he was. If he had chosen an alternate course instead of trying to capture the ultimate prize, life would have been quite different. *But then life is all about choices, huh, Anor?*

Before making a decision on his next course of action, Ian conferred with Anor. "Are we done here, Anor?"

Anor carefully calculated his answer before he spoke. "We continue on to the Gamadin station. That is where your young captain found his aara."

Ian listened. As much as he figured Anor always had a dark motive, he listened anyway. Ulterior motive not withstanding, this was a time of desperation, and he needed all the help he could get, regardless of the source.

"Explain," Ian said to Anor.

Anor went to the forward window to speculate. "Perhaps someone else is after *Millawanda?*"

"The Mysterians, no doubt."

Anor was less concerned over who was trailing Harlowe than their motive. "They won't kill her. They want her."

Ian felt his answer was an honest one. "Go on."

"They will not kill her yet."

"They attacked her here. We have the evidence," Ian said.

Anor smiled. "By design."

"There was Mysterian debris in the atmosphere."

"But not their mothership."

"Good point."

Anor added, "They are watching from a discreet distance."

"Why wait? Why not just jump when she was down?"

"They want the same thing your captain wants. They want her origin."

That surprised Ian. "Orixy?"

"Yes. They want to destroy Orixy and make sure the Gamadin never rise again."

"For what purpose?"

"To protect their ships."

"Invasion?" Ian questioned.

Anor nodded yes.

"That's stupid."

It was Leucadia's turn to wear the power hat that years of running with the wolves of the government and corporate world had taught her. "When Harlowe destroyed the Fhaal and the Consortium, he created a power vacuum, Captain."

"And these suckwads want to fill it?" Ian questioned.

"I could be wrong," Anor admitted.

Leucadia shook her head. "No, you are not wrong, Mr. Ran. 'You have', as my father liked to say, 'hit the nail on the head.' *Millawanda* is their means to an end."

Ian studied Anor's face. "So that's what any invader would do?"

"Destroy their opponent."

Anor nodded yes, again.

"Harlowe is leading them to Orixy?" Ian asked.

"Yes," Anor and Leucadia said together.

"So if that's their motive, then we need to find Harlowe before he finds Orixy," Ian figured.

"I think that's clear, Captain," Leucadia affirmed.

Ian looked over at Dev and Cheesa waiting patiently for his next order. "Okay, where do we go from here?"

"The outpost, Captain," Anor said.

"You're dying to find that place, aren't you, dude?" Ian asked.

"I am. I think it holds the key to finding Orixy," Anor replied confidently.

Ian turned to Leucadia for her input. "I agree," she replied. "Lamille is worth exploring."

"It will take time," Ian said.

"It could also save us time," Leucadia countered.

Anor may have had other motives for wanting to find the Gamadin outpost, but Ian didn't care. The idea of the Mysterians tailing Harlowe to find Orixy was sound enough for him. The game had suddenly changed. It was now a race to the finish. Instead of searching for Harlowe, their focus was now Orixy. Find the point of Gamadin origin, and hopefully, they could warn anyone there that Death was headed their way. Having no idea how powerful the Mysterians were, or even if Orixy still existed after all these thousands of centuries, the only certainty was that the Galaxy's future rested with the Gamadin resurrection. If the Gamadin were defeated and its origin wiped out, they were all doomed.

"Okay, let's find that outpost, Chee," Ian ordered.

She turned back to her controls. "Yes, Captain."

Ian looked at Anor. "You got your wish, Mr. Ran. Let's hope it's a good one."

128

The Station

$f$orty-Four traveled straight for the Gamadin station. They made no diversions or stops crossing over from the daylight side of the planet into night. Since it was a near certainty that *Millawanda* had already left the planet, the consensus was to push on to the station regardless of Harlowe's trail of crumbs that were really more like loaves of bread. Following his path across the continent was like unraveling the Gordian Knot one loop at a time. Whether it was *Millawanda's* beam cannons, or something as small as dirty socks, the sensors were so powerful they could pinpoint a Gamadin's trail because it was comparable to no one else in the Galaxy.

Ian cut through the morass and focused on their one objective: finding the Gamadin station. It was the key. If the planet had anything of value left for them, it was there. It was undeniable that Harlowe had found enough aara to propel *Millawanda* beyond the star system and obliterate a few bad guys along the way. Although how much of a boost he was able to get was impossible to know. At this point, that question was moot. Reaching Orixy before the Mysterians had risen to the top of the list. *Millawanda* was second. If they found Her in the process, great. If they didn't...well, they would continue the search *after* Orixy. Harlowe had gone to the station in search of aara. They were going in search of information.

* * *

"The station is beneath the ocean," Cheesa observed as *Forty-Four* hovered over the shallow ruins at the edge of the ocean. What had once been a flourishing, coastal city thousands of years before, had sunk hundreds of feet below the surface and miles out to sea.

"Impressive," Anor said in awe of the extent of the underwater structures.

While the others looked at the past, Maa Dev focused on the horde of creatures along the beach. "What are they doing?" he wondered aloud pointing at the fires on the beach. Upon closer scrutiny, the gangly creatures were wildly dancing around their blazing fires, feasting on an assortment of dissected things, winged creatures, and four-legged animals. Ian could only wonder how Harlowe had dealt with the dreadful savages.

No diversions, Ian told himself. *Stay on target. Find what Harlowe found.*

"Stay focused, Dev," Ian said calmly

"What do we look for, Captain?" Cheesa asked.

Leucadia came to Cheesa's station, deftly moving her fingers over the lighted bars as she changed the focus of their search to deeper waters. "For any structure not in ruin, Chee," she replied. "There!" she called out, transferring the monitor's display to the overhead screen for everyone to see. "That building there," she indicated, pointing at the out-of-place structure that stood out like a black eye between crumbled structures surrounding it. It appeared untouched by the centuries of lying on the ocean floor, like it was built yesterday.

"Sweet," Ian gasped, continually awed by the superior know-how of the Gamadin engineers.

"That is a Gamadin station?" Dev asked. He didn't quite believe that a structure so grand would be a simple way station. "It looks more like one of my father's palaces."

"They treated their crews well," Ian commented.

"But it is so small," Leucadia said, disappointed. "I would have expected something much bigger, really. Something many stories high."

"That is peculiar," Anor said, surprised himself at the structure's minimalistic size.

"We should check it out, anyway," Ian said, believing that something still so posh after thousands of years had a story to tell. "Harlowe came here for a reason."

Leucadia was of the same opinion.

Anor made it unanimous. "Quite right, Captain. This is no ordinary outpost. I would be curious to learn how something survives this long under the ocean without disintegrating."

A wispy, blue shimmer caught Leucadia's attention. "It has a shield around it."

Ian saw it, too. "A Gamadin barrier."

"Makes sense," Leucadia concurred. "That's why it had longevity, Mr. Ran."

Ian kept shaking his head, looking at Leucadia for the answer. "It's not like any Gamadin structure we've ever seen. Why would Harlowe come here?"

"Don't look at me," Leucadia said, "I have no idea what makes that boy tick."

"He's your boyfriend."

"And you grew up with him," Leucadia countered. "What have you learned?"

Ian returned a sheepish grin. "Yeah, point made."

She made another observation. "If the structure's shield is still operational after all these centuries…"

"Then, there's air inside," Ian stated.

Back at her station, Leucadia probed the interior with her sensors. "Correct. The temperature is chilly but well above freezing."

"Take her down, Dev. Let's find the front door," Ian ordered, still trying to wrap his head around why Harlowe had risked so much to travel this far out of his way.

129

Hotel Gamadin

Whatever the Gamadin structure was, it looked open for business as *Forty-Four* touched down just shy of the force field. The portico and brightly lit pavilion were two-stories tall, reminding Ian a lot of Harry's Las Vegas Hotel and Casino, only on a much smaller scale. The interior lights were still on, and the main street level entry doors were left wide open. The only things missing were the bellmen, luggage, beach towels, and the Gamadin vacationers in their flip-flops.

"Looks like Harlowe left the lights on," Ian quipped.

"It's surprisingly garish for a Gamadin outpost," Leucadia observed.

"You're right. It's over the top," Ian concurred.

"What is it?" Cheesa wondered out loud.

Leucadia took the first stab at defining the structure's purpose. "I think it's a hotel, Chee."

"With only three stories?" Ian questioned. "There's not much room for guests."

"Unless what you see is only a fraction of the establishment," Anor suggested. "I have several places of luxury where most of the activity is below the surface."

Ian glanced at Leucadia. Anor's point had merit. "My father's casino has a convention center, two stadiums, shopping malls, and parking for three thousand automobiles, all underground." She adjusted her sensors to probe below the structure. "And there it is!"

Eyes popped as the vast underground structure materialized on the overhead screen.

Ian leaned back in awe. "Woooow…" he said, practically breathless.

"That is impressive," Anor commented with eyes as wide as everyone else's. Even by his standards, the structure was a sight to behold.

Leucadia smiled with pride. "That's my Harlowe."

*   *   *

After everyone got over the shock, Ian went to Cheesa's station. With his assistance, she guided *Forty-Four* forward ever so slowly. Ian figured, like his SIBA, *Forty-four* could pass through the barrier without resistance. But just in case he was wrong, it was ahead ultra-slow with everyone buckled in the their seats for a sudden impact. As the hull touched the barrier, it slid through the field without a single drop of water leaking out around the penetration.

Ian breathed a sigh of relief. "Nice work, Chee."

She brought *Forty-Four* all the way through the barrier and slid under the massive portal of the hotel until her rim came within a foot of the front door.

Ian headed for blinker. "Ms. Lu, Mr. Ran, you're with me."

"Can I go, too?" Cheesa asked, giving the hurt puppy look of wanting to tag along.

How was he going to tell her no? He glanced at Leucadia for advice. She only giggled. "Sure. Get your stuff, Chee."

"A sidearm, too?"

"Always."

"And me?" Anor asked.

Ian didn't have a ready answer for that one. Anor with a weapon went against the grain. There were too many times in the past the two-faced dweeb had tried to shoot a Gamadin in the back. He had yet to earn the kind of trust that would allow him to hold a weapon while he led the team into the unknown. His gut told him no, but Leucadia thought otherwise.

"Let him have one, Captain," Leucadia said with a silent look that indicated she would have his back.

Ian turned to gather his away things. He couldn't bring himself to say yes.

When Ian had blinked away, Anor asked Leucadia, "Was that a yes, Ms. Lu?"

"He didn't say no." But gave Anor a piece of advice. "Don't give him a reason to shoot you, Mr. Ran. He will, you know."

Anor understood and thanked her for the warning. "I believe you, Ms. Lu."

*   *   *

The plan was to meet at the bottom of the ramp. Everyone wore SIBAs except Anor. Ian refused to give him a suit, believing he hadn't earned the right yet. So his attire was a standard issue, Gamadin blue jumpsuit, the same kind they had as recruits back on Mars.

The moment Ian opened the hatch, Molly and Rhud took off running. Ian tried calling them back, but things seemed to be getting out of control. Everyone wanted to see the Gamadin structure, even the cats.

Tossing caution to the wind, Ian said, "Lu, you're with me." He didn't want to lose sight of the cats. Anor was tardy as usual, but with the cats bounding down the ramp for the entry doors, Ian couldn't wait. "When Anor gets here, meet us inside," Ian said to Cheesa as he and Leucadia took off running.

Cheesa wanted to be with Ian but understood the urgency. She only had time to wave goodbye and say, "Aye, Captain."

*   *   *

Ian and Leucadia followed the cats across the beautiful rose-colored stone floors under the pavilion. When they came to the perimeter edge of the ship, they were surprised by the water that had pushed through the force field, plopping down along the entire line of the hull. "That can't be good," Ian said, concerned. "The force field should be stopping every drop."

"Unless its growing weaker," Leucadia said, as she held out her hand to feel the drops.

Ian hustled along. "We better hurry then and find what we need and get out."

"Aye."

The instant Leucadia stepped through the entry doors, she stopped dead in her tracks and grabbed Ian's arm.

"Problem?" Ian asked, holding her steady.

She took a moment to understand what was affecting her. "Harlowe."

Ian felt something, too, but not in the same way she did. "Okay, we're in the right place. The cats feel him, too. That's why they took off so fast." He then asked her, "Can you walk?"

She crossed her arms in front of her and took a step. "Yeah, I think so."

Inside the lobby, Ian marveled over the tall ceilings and ornate interior decorations. Twice he almost tripped over furniture focusing on what was up instead of what was in front of him. The Gamadin structure was unlike anything he had ever seen. It was showy, pretentious, and very, very rich, not simple, clean, and blue like he was used to.

"I think our guess was right, Captain. It is a hotel," Leucadia declared. "The lobby, front desk, comfortable places to sit, read, and eat," she added, pointing here and there. "And over there through those doors. That looks like a bar on the terrace."

"Hotel Gamadin, huh? Your dad would have loved this place."

She smiled, thinking reverently of her father. "I think he would, too."

A call from Cheesa came in. *"Anor is with me, Captain."*

Ian turned to Leucadia looking for any reason to deny him access. "Let them in," she said. "He's come all this way, Ian."

Ian swallowed his doubt and answered Cheesa, "All right, but don't let him out of your sight for a second, Chee. We don't have much time. The barrier seems to be deteriorating," he informed her.

"Understood, Captain."

Ian said to Leucadia with a sour drawl, "She'll make sure he doesn't break anything."

They went farther into the lobby, looking for the cats. "Where'd they get off to?" she wondered.

Ian checked his sensors. "They're below us," he said surprised. "How?" He began searching the lobby in earnest. "I don't see any stairway or elevator, do you?"

Leucadia spotted one of two alcoves on each side of what they believed was the front desk to the hotel. "Over there!" Upon reaching the ornately decorated gold and white marbled bay, they discovered the way down. "Ah, a blinker. I should have guessed."

"That's humongous!" Ian exclaimed. He had never seen a Gamadin transport disk so large. "You could blink the entire Lakewood football team with that."

Leucadia took hold of Ian's hand. "Let's hope we don't end up in Munchkinland."

"Or on top of the Wicked Witch," Ian grunted as they stepped on the disk together and winked to who-knew-where.

130

Crack in the Ceiling

When Ian and Leucadia materialized, they found themselves overlooking the vast underground facility they had seen from the overhead holograph. It was no Land of Oz, but it was no less awe inspiring. From the platform where they were standing, the open space alone was large enough to swallow the Bellagio, Caesar's Palace, and Harry's Casino, and all of their underground facilities, combined!

"WHOA!" Ian cried out the instant he peered over the edge of the elevator platform.

Molly and Rhud were waiting for them. They couldn't have cared less about the view. They wanted Ian to press the down button, but the problem was the lower floors were already flooded with ocean water, and it was rising fast.

One look and Ian made the decision, "We're outta time."

Leucadia checked her com device. "We have about an hour—" But before she could finish her thought, she pointed to a crack in the ceiling where water was gushing through like a broken water main had burst. "We can't go down. The upper floor is about to give, Ian."

Cheesa's voice broke in. *"Captain, where are you?"*

"We're below you? What's the water situation where you are, Chee?" Ian asked her.

"Water is flowing over Forty-four's hull and into the main entrance, Captain," she replied.

609

"Molly, Rhud, and Anor," Leucadia said alarmed. "They have no suits to protect them. They will drown."

CRACK!

A section of the subfloor suddenly gave way. Instead of an hour, the fill time had shortened to minutes.

"MOLLY! RHUD!" Leucadia screamed, just as another section of the lobby ceiling fell. It was now a cascading event. There was no telling how much time they had before the entire Hotel Gamadin collapsed in on itself.

"CHEESA! GET BACK TO THE SHIP! HAVE DEV PULL US AWAY THE INSTANT WE'RE INSIDE THE HATCH!" Ian had visions of *Forty-Four* being sucked into a vortex of water when the structure collapsed.

Ian, Leucadia, and the cats leaped for the blinker. The instant they appeared on the upper level, they found themselves in knee-deep water. Through the entry doors, water was rising like the tide, cascading off the ship's perimeter hull like a giant waterfall. Together, Molly and Rhud bounded through the surge of flooding water for the exit doors. They didn't need anyone telling them it was survival time. Ian and Leucadia were right behind them, high stepping through the water using their SIBAs to power through the surge.

Molly made it through the wall okay. She was pushed back once, but fought her way through on her second effort. Rhud wasn't so lucky. He hit the wall and was slammed sideways to the floor. He tried getting up, but the wall reached out like a giant hand and slammed him down again. It didn't look like the big cat was going to make it. He was tiring fast.

As Rhud tumbled backwards, Ian grabbed his leg, just as a wall hit them both broadside. Surrounded by three feet of gushing water, he forced Rhud's head above the surface so he could breathe, straining and pushing until the big cat claimed his footing again when another wall hit them. It was all Ian could do to hold onto Rhud and hope for a letup in the surge.

Suddenly, something forced them through the cascading water to the other side. A mass of tangled SIBA limbs, paws, and growling tiger tumbled onto the dry floor. Now safely behind the ship's protective shield, Ian saw Leucadia sprawled out on the pavement next to him. He reached out and pulled her to her feet. "Thanks," he said.

Leucadia had been that extra push they needed. Rhud shook himself off as Molly went to his side and began licking his face. They were all about to ascend the ramp when Cheesa came tumbling through the barrier. Ian couldn't believe his eyes. He thought all along she was safe inside the ship. He rushed to her side and picked her up off the wet floor.

"I thought I told you to get back in the ship," he growled. He was more scared that she had almost perished than being upset for disobeying orders.

Looking up at him, she began sobbing. "I am sorry, Captain, I was trying to find Anor."

"He's still out there?" he asked incredulously.

"Yes. He said he had one more place to search."

Leucadia took Cheesa by the arm as Ian looked at her through his bulbous eyes. "He won't make it."

"As much of a dweeb as he is, I can't let him die, Lu," Ian said.

There was no time to argue. Leucadia shoved Cheesa toward the ramp before she turned to Ian and snapped a dura-line to his utility belt. "Go! I have you."

Ian dove through the barrier; the cascade of water hitting him so hard, he felt like he had been slammed to the floor by a ten-foot wave. By the time he found his bearings and broke the surface, the entry doors to the lobby were completely submerged. Stroking for the entrance, he dove down through the opening asking Cheesa where Anor was.

Leucadia answered instead. *Cheesa passed out, Ian. She said something about a large glass thing. Go to the front desk. It is the only logical place.*

"Got it!"

Ian was no Harlowe or Riverstone in the water, but in a SIBA he was Michael Phelps. He stroked through the twisting surges, his body yanked and pulled every which way as he fought to keep his course for the front desk. It wasn't just water and currents he struggled against; but also all the floating furniture and disintegrating structural debris all around him.

He broke the surface, touching the ceiling of the lobby. "ANOR!" he cried out. "ANOR, WHERE ARE YOU?"

Hearing nothing, Ian dove down into a swirling mass that slammed him against a glass counter.

The front desk!

He grabbed an end with his claw and pulled himself along until he was over the top of the desk. There was no sign of Anor anywhere. He shoved off and broke for the surface.

"ANOR!" he shouted again.

A distant voice called to him. If it weren't for the heightened senses of his SIBA, he never would have heard him. Anor's voice called out again, and from that, his location was back toward the ship. All he could think of was that he had passed him while swimming underwater.

Stroking back, fighting, and pushing off more debris from the currents, Ian spotted Anor hanging from what was left of a chandelier. Under one arm he was holding something that looked like a book.

Ian had only one shot to grab him. The current was too strong for a second chance.

"JUMP, ANOR!" Ian shouted, reaching out.

Anor clumsily let go of the fixture and belly-flopped onto the water. By the sheerest luck, Ian grabbed an ankle and pulled him in.

"NOW, LU!" Ian shouted, wrapping his arms around Anor's waist.

The instant he called out, his utility belt yanked him backwards toward the ship. The two intertwined bodies spun against the debris as they went. When they popped through the surface, Ian caught a glimpse of the lobby crashing through the floor, completely swallowed up.

"HURRY, LU!"

"HOLD ON, IAN. THE HOTEL IS COLLAPSING!" Leucadia shouted. "WE ARE PULLING THE SHIP OUT! WE CANNOT WAIT ANOTHER SECOND!"

Ian's belt was cutting him in half as the water rushed faster and faster around his body. Through it all, he never let go of Anor who was completely limp, unable to breathe. All around him he watched the marquees, portico, and the stone floors collapse through the massive drain hole as he and Anor were being pulled away.

Within moments, *Forty-Four* broke the surface. It was morning on the ocean's surface. Pink and orange clouds stood out against the green sky as he and Anor dangled in the air while they rose into the hold of the ship. When their bruised and banged up bodies touched the floor, Ian finally let go of Anor's chest and said, spitting mad, "What do you think you were doing?"

Anor coughed and threw up a belly-full of water before raising the packet from under his arm. "I found the origin."

131

Vitamin D

Fifty-one days later -- 22,920.94 l.y. from Earth

Where they had put down was like the planet...unknown. The morning sun was warm and yellow. A blue-green ocean twinkled under a scattering of fluffy, white clouds with a canvas of delicious pinks and subtle oranges that spread loosely on the horizon. The Class 5 hurricane that hit them two days ago had moved on. The weather was peaceful now, the waves calm and small, but good enough to ride, Harlowe mused. Feeling the warm offshore breeze, reminded him of a dry Santa Ana day in SoCal. Things might not have been so bad for them if *Millawanda* had survived. Their once beautiful ship was now nose down at a thirty-degree angle with her hind end sticking out of the pile of sand she had created when she plowed into the beach during the storm. The fact that her crew had survived without a scratch was a miracle. Forty-eight hours ago *Millawanda* was powerless and headed straight down. Unlike Gazz, when Harlowe had enough maneuvering capability to skip her across the ocean to a nearby island, he had no control over this landing. Her aara crystals had completely evaporated a million miles out before he could put her in a controlled orbit. So down they went, gravity having its way with them. As they looked outside at the wind-driven rain, Prigg had no scientific answer. Harlowe just shook his head while Riverstone congratulated him on his excellent parking job. Simon said with all the billions of stars around them inside the galactic core, the least he could have done was put down near a real, live city instead of one that died out a "ZILLION YEARS AGO!" The part-time movie star, full-time Gamadin, apologized to Harlowe later for the sudden outburst. No one blamed Harlowe. It was all part of being Gamadin. But kicking sand at the crumbling ruins helped ease the pain. Harlowe was bummed, like everyone else, and could think of nothing useful to say, except, "Does anyone know how to fish?"

Since leaving Osset, they had traveled over fifteen thousand lightyears in less than two months without stopping for off-the-clock breaks. From all the data Prigg could glean from Bigbob's memory, Orixy was somewhere close.

"Close?" Riverstone wondered, staring out at the endless ocean. "What does that mean, Prigg? Close as in it's just over the next hill over there," he said, pointing at the lush-green mound among the ruins, "or close in galactic terms: like ten or twenty lightyears from here? Right now, they both seem far."

Now that their ship was out of commission, off-the-clock monikers were okay.

With clenched fists resting on his hips, Simon replied cynically, "What does it matter, Jester? One mile or one lightyear. Millie couldn't make either one. After 17,000 years, she's finally kaput. Zip, Nadda, the big E, dude! Right, Skipper?"

Harlowe stepped toward the water without answering. It was a useless argument. So his immediate thoughts turned to the waves. Riding some tubes would let his mind work out the details on how they were going to survive this snafu.

If the Mysterians were still following them, there was no sign of them yet. As far as anyone could tell, their evasive action back at Osset had succeeded. Regardless, no one thought they were home free. They felt just like they did when the Daks back in Utah followed them into the box canyon with grogans howling and guns blazing. Problem was they had no canyon trail to help them escape. They were out in the open beach with no place to hide against a Mysterian attack. Their weapons could handle the small drones, but what about the big guys? How long would they last against them?

Harlowe considered Mowgi next, remembering how the undog's big parabolic ears had heard the Daks coming for miles before they even saw their dust clouds. Back then he had yipped to warn them in plenty of time. When he wasn't foraging for food, Mowgi spent the rest of his day curled up on Pigpo's back with his radars down, fast asleep. Obviously, the Mysterians were of no concern to him.

The trip to the core was hardly a smooth one, either. Several times along the way, authoritarian forces made every effort to capture or destroy her. It was the monkey on their back until they crossed through the Near 3-kiloparsec Arm of the Milky Way Galaxy. Like a boat tossed around in a rough sea, and suddenly hitting the smooth waters of a calm harbor, they finally got a break. It took a few hundred lightyears to get comfortable with the idea that no one was out to get them. Encountering friendly, non-hostile ships was now the norm. Some ships were neighborly enough to travel with them for a lightyear or two before veering off to wherever they were going. At no time did anyone ask to see their out-of-date drivers' licenses or expired plates.

But as friendly as the inner core of the galaxy was, not one ship could point the way to Orixy.

Then the inevitable happened. After 51 days of nonstop travel, *Millawanda's* jerry-rigged aara went bye-bye. Harlowe felt the Grim Reaper calling even before Riverstone stepped off the blinker with a teary-eyed Prigg by his side. The look on his First Officer's face said it all.

"We're done, huh?" Harlowe asked.

"Finished," Riverstone replied with a comforting arm around Prigg's shoulders.

"Your Majesty—" Prigg tried to say before Harlowe cut him off.

"It's not your fault, Mr. Prigg. Without you, Millie would have bought it a long time ago. It's a miracle we got this far. No, if it's anyone's fault, I'm to blame." Not only was it heartbreaking for Harlowe to lose his ship, but Isara and Muis were still comatose inside their isolation capsules. *Millawanda's* power problems were so acute, she had nothing left with with to treat them except for life support. Her med rooms were offline and her robob medics dormant. No one, not even a Gamadin, could get treatment for even the smallest cut.

* * *

That was two days ago. They cashed in all their chips on Bigbob's ability to locate a planet where they could survive without *Millawanda* supplying them with the necessities of life. In anticipation of running out of food and water because they were already scraping the bottom of their supplies and yucky nourishment cubes, Harlowe sent Riverstone to wake up Simon on the beach and find some food. Riverstone didn't have far to go. Fully attired in his SIBA and sidearms, he walked down the giant sand hill under *Millawanda's* hull and found Simon lying on a blue beach towel, basking in the sun. He started easy by asking Simon, "Catching up on the tan, brah?"

"Can't dance," Simon replied without opening his eyes. "Looks like we'll be here for a while." He twisted himself around to get better exposure. "Ya think the vitamin D is the same here as on Earth?"

Riverstone squinted up at the sun without his bugeyes activated as yet. "It's a yellow star, isn't it?"

"Yeah."

"Then it's the same. Yellow is yellow. The D is good here. Count on it."

"Did you learn that in Farnducky's class?"

"I did. What of it?"

"What if it's not the same?" Simon argued. "What if it's off a few wavelengths of yellow? I could get the big C, man. My face could end up like Mickey Rouke's. Then what would I do for my next movie?"

"You could play a Dak," Riverstone sallied.

"Not funny."

"Listen putzhead, even if the rays were slightly off, Millie would fix it for you," Riverstone assured.

Simon knew that wasn't right. "Millie's down for the count, brah. She can't even help Fyn's kids."

"Isara is no kid," Riverstone corrected.

Simon's eyes went wide. "You saw her, too, huh?"

Riverstone eyes brightened. "Yeah, I saw her."

"She's hot, all right," Simon agreed with his eyes still closed. "How does Dog do it? I don't care what planet we stumble on, he finds the babes. Every time!"

"He has a knack."

"You think he could search for babes here while we're looking for food?"

"I think his mind is on other things, Rerun," Riverstone replied.

Simon eyed *Millawanda's* precarious position as he acknowledged, 'Yeah, I guess he does." He grabbed a handful of sand and tossed it. "Ya think there's babes here?"

"If there is, he'll find them."

"It's about time we got our share, don't ya think?"

Riverstone looked over the ancient ruins of the dead city. "Got a clue where we could look for our share?"

Simon pressed his lips together with disappointment. "Not a one. We'd stand a better chance on Mimas." Mimas was a tiny, lifeless moon inside Saturn's rings where he and Simon would hit five-mile long drives with golf balls off the side of a giant meteor crater.

Riverstone looked down the beach at Pigpo soaking in a large tidal pool. "Piggy and the Mowg don't seem to care what color the sun is."

Simon twisted around, affectionately looking at his big, lumbering pig-faced pet. "They've been out there all morning, too." Turning back to Riverstone with his eyes open, he finally got a glimpse of Riverstone in his SIBA. "Expecting trouble?"

"We're back on the clock," Riverstone informed him.

Simon's face turned sour. "Now?"

"Harlowe wants us out looking for In-n-Outs ASAP."

Simon knew what he meant. "Platter said we had over a month's supply of food left."

Riverstone stuck out his hand with a SIBA medallion. "We're down to chalk cubes. You want to keep eating those barfy things?"

Simon reluctantly took the medallion as he brushed off some loose sand from his trunks. "A couple of days of R&R would be cool." He glared at Riverstone. "We have come a little ways, you know. I'm just saying we deserve a longer rest than two days is all."

Riverstone could sympathize. It had been a grueling two months. Simon stretched his six-foot seven frame to the sky, and asked, "Got a direction?"

Riverstone lethargically waved his hand down the beach. "That way?"

Simon didn't care one way or another. "Good as any." He activated his SIBA without further protest. He knew the protocol: New planet, unknown environment, possible threats anywhere, anytime. He allowed his suit to engulf every part of his body except his head. It was a vanity thing for him. Until his bugeyes were needed, he didn't like strutting around the neighbor in a Spiderman costume. The bulbous eyes might scare the locals (meaning any potential babes), he figured. Following an internal systems check, he adjusted his sidearm on his hip and checked his ammo clips. When he was all powered up and in order, they set off down the beach where Fyn was tending his herd of ceffyls.

Simon elbowed Riverstone in the arm. "Up for a ride? We can cover a lot more ground with a couple of those," he said, pointing at the ceffyls. He used to ride a lot with Leucadia at her parent's ranch in Aztec, New Mexico. But once Harlowe entered her life, riding alone in the high country hills was never the same.

Riverstone was in.

132

When the Music Stops

Fyn laughed so hard he could barely stand as he watched Simon flying off Delamo's back for the umpteenth time. The movie star had his heart set on riding Harlowe's mount the moment he laid eyes on the black ceffyl. The steed was so magnificent above all the others in the herd, he felt the experience would be like driving a four-legged Aston Martin Vantage. But after getting bucked off one too many times, he got the idea that, like the Skipper's chair, Harlowe's mount was a one-owner ride.

Fyn gave Simon a hand up off the sand. "I warned you, young man. He is an ilodudd, that one."

Simon could only imagine what an ilodudd was. Something like Cujo, no doubt. After extending a stiff middle claw toward the rancher, Simon limped over to Riverstone, who gave him the reins of another mount.

"This is Monday's ride, Josie," Riverstone said. "He swears she's as gentle as a kitten."

Simon spit a few grits from his mouth, and asked, "Whose idea was this, anyway?"

Riverstone snickered. "Yours."

Simon leaped aboard the dark red ceffyl. As promised, she was nothing like Delamo. She crow-hopped a few times at first, showing off her prideful prance. But soon she settled down, and they were running like the wind, looking for resources for their survival.

* * *

A few miles down the beach, Riverstone and Simon discovered a small river that emptied into the ocean. The water was fresh, and according to their coms, it was also fit to drink. They decided to cut inland along the river, figuring if the water was good, then anything that they drank it was good, too.

As they trotted along the river banks, now and then a startled fish leaped out of the stream at the alien trespassers. Although Riverstone wasn't a big fish eater, he saw himself becoming one if the choice were between the yucky chalk bites or the fish.

They kept going for a few more miles, following the river as it meandered through the lush, green foothills along the coast. The ruins of the ancient city never left them. Crumbling foundations, overgrown streets, and piles of rubble were everywhere. As they went along, they followed Harlowe's explicit orders and checked in every thirty minutes. On their first away mission, he didn't want them going too far in case they ran into trouble. Continuing on, the fish remained plentiful, but they found nothing particularly edible like berries or fruit trees, or even an ancient burger stand, so Harlowe ordered them back to the ship. The next day they would try their luck going up the beach instead of down.

On their way back, Simon glimpsed a symbol stamped on a gold, weather-worn column they didn't see the first time.

"Is that what I think it is?" Simon asked, pulling Josie back a step or two to get a better look at the impression.

Riverstone activated his bugeyes and zoomed in. "It's Gamadin, all right. No doubt about it."

Simon twisted around on Josie's back and pointed at the other columns lining the ancient avenue. Some were broken, some had fallen over eons ago, and a few were lying in the dirt this way and that, but a few were still standing like soldiers lining both sides of the avenue for as far as they could see.

"How did we miss this?" Simon wondered aloud.

Riverstone shrugged. He didn't know either. "It's like they just shot up out of the ground."

"Do, do, do, do. Do, do, do, do," Simon hummed the tune of the *Twilight Zone*.

Riverstone was about to contact Harlowe with the news when they heard the giggling of girls' laughter. "Did you hear that?"

Simon's ears perked up like Mowgi's parabolics. "I did."

"We better contact Dog first," Riverstone said, concerned with protocol.

Simon looked at Riverstone like he had a loose nut inside his brain. "If we call Harlowe saying we hear babes laughing up ahead, what do you think he's going to say?"

For a split second Riverstone wasn't buying it until he heard the laughter again, together with musical instruments a lot like a violin and a guitar playing together. "Yeah, we better check it out first before we tell him."

They turned their mounts toward the laughter and crossed the river. Before they came to the top of the rise, they dismounted and left their ceffyls tied to bushes.

"If they look like Pigpo, you can have first choice, Jester," Simon whispered as they approached the playful voices. If they had gone another fifty yards farther, they would have run right into them. Peeking between the tall reeds along the riverbank, they spied two feathery, biped creatures with spindly long legs, thick long necks, sharp beaks, and large eyes. They reminded them a lot like ostriches back on Earth, except here they grew long wings instead of short stubby ones. On Earth, ostriches didn't fly, but these creatures looked like they could if they stretched their wings even a little bit.

They couldn't believe the music could be coming from the ostrich creatures, until they migrated to a fresh patch of grass. "Whoa, pard," Riverstone gasped as his eyes landed on the angelic beauties beyond the birds, playing their instruments. The two females had long hair past their waists. One had dark brown hair; the other was also dark but with sun streaked strands that made her appear more blond than brown. They were both leggy and gorgeously tan, wearing shorts and skimpy white and light green tops.

"We're not telling Harlowe about the babes, right?" Simon suggested earnestly.

They were on the same page with that one, and touched their SIBA claws together to seal the deal.

"Not a word," Riverstone agreed.

Riverstone scooted back down the rise, pulling Simon with him. "So how do we do this? If we go dancing over the rise, we'll scare them in our SIBAs."

"Yeah, and none of that 'take us to your leader' stuff either. That's so fifties," Simon added.

Riverstone was ready for action. "Do you have a plan?"

Simon smiled. "I do."

"Do I need to know what it is?"

They rose together. "No, just follow my lead."

Riverstone stopped him. "We didn't bring extra clothes. All I have is a pair of shorts under my SIBA."

Simon deactivated his SIBA revealing the bathing suit he wore before Riverstone showed up. "Me, too. Less threatening that way."

Riverstone still had issues. "What about our weapons?"

"We'll leave them with the ceffyls."

Riverstone didn't like the plan. He was about ready to tell Simon to go on ahead when the music suddenly stopped.

Simon hurried them along. "Come on. That's our cue."

Against his better judgment, Riverstone deactivated his SIBA down to his loud boxers. "All right, but I have first shot at the blond with the gunnels."

Simon didn't care. They were both tens! "She's yours, pard," and motioned to follow him through the reeds. As a way of introduction, Simon started to clap. "Bravo, ladies!" he said, breaking into the open. He wanted to say more, but looking down the barrels of two high caliber weapons made him lose his voice.

Riverstone glared at Simon. "Really?"

133

The Crab

It was nearly dark and Riverstone and Simon had missed their last three check-in calls. Harlowe was past worry. He was angry that the two had managed to get themselves into trouble again. It wasn't like Riverstone to miss a call, especially since he made five before that without a hitch. There could be a million simple reasons why they missed their check-in, he thought, but right now he couldn't think of one that wasn't bad. Somehow he knew they were in trouble, and he needed to find them, pronto!

Harlowe made sure Monday and Prigg had all the weapons necessary to protect themselves and *Millawanda* from anything other than a full on Mysterian attack. If that happened, they were history anyway, so he ordered them to save themselves.

"How far do you think they went?" Monday asked, holding his Gama rifle pointed skyward.

Harlowe made sure his own rifle was firmly attached to his back before he took Delamo's reins from Fyn and leaped onto his back. "Riding ceffyls there's no telling, Squid. They can go a long ways in a few hours."

"But not out of range of their coms."

"No. They would have to be off the planet for that."

"Do not worry, Harlowe, Delamo will find them," Fyn said confidently as he stroked the great ceffyl's mane like a proud father.

Harlowe leaned forward and patted the side of Delamo's neck. "Between him and the Mowg, we'll find them." Looking at Millawanda, he said to

Monday, "Keep her safe, Squid."

"Understood, Captain."

Harlowe slapped his leg. "Up you go, Mowg."

The undog yipped twice and effortlessly leaped aboard in front of Harlowe. He patted the side of the undog's coarse, reddish fur, feeling whole, and then charged down the beach to find his missing crewmen.

*   *   *

Delamo followed the scent like he was using Harlowe's com. They quickly found the river where the two Gamadin had veered away from the coast. Monday reported in that Fyn and his ceffyls were back in the ship for the night, but Pigpo was being a royal pain because his pals, Simon and Mowgi were gone, and now he had no one to sleep with.

Harlowe suggested Monday stay with the emotional beast until Simon returned. The suggestion brought on a hushed silence at the other end of the com. Animal sitting was not part of his First Officer's job description, but at this point, Monday said painfully, "I'll do anything to stop the moaning."

Harlowe suggested Monday find Simon's stash of coconuts from Gazz. "I'm sure they're in a storage bin near his room. Rerun gives Piggy one right before bedtime, and he's out like a light." Monday was so elated that there was a possible solution to his Pigpo problem, he didn't bother to sign off and just left Harlowe hanging. "You're welcome," Harlowe said to the silence.

He hadn't gone far up the river when when Mowgi and Delamo suddenly began acting crazy. Harlowe nearly went tumbling off Delamo's backside when Mowgi took off, growing his wings. Delamo pranced and whined as the undog circled overhead and screeched and yipped in a continuous tirade. Harlowe had never seen either animal act that way before. Inside his SIBA headgear, his sensors were acting similarly. It seemed the anomaly was growing more powerful as Harlowe made his way toward the ancient city.

Harlowe zoomed in on the horizon, hoping to catch a glimpse at whatever was causing the thunderous noise. The first thing that popped into his mind were the Mysterians. They found them down and broken on the beach and were zeroing in for the kill.

Suddenly, there it was, flying low and coming toward him fast. Whatever it was, it was massive, many times bigger than *Millawanda*. The roar grew louder as the ground violently shook, disturbing the ancient columns so much, the taller ones broke apart and toppled to the ground. As the golden object approached, its long mechanical arms were miles across, moving and stretching outward from its main body like undulating claws of a spindly crab. Its snapping pincers, moved back and forth, clamping and unclamping as if it were probing the night heavens for prey.

Suddenly it dawned on Harlowe where the object was headed. It wasn't the ancient city at all, but "MILLIE!" he shouted over the thunderous hum. "NO, NO, NO, NO! LEAVE MILLIE ALONE!" he kept shouting as Delamo took off in mighty leaps back out to the beach.

Mowgi flew ahead, screeching and cawing in ear shattering pain. Harlowe tried desperately to call him, but he couldn't stop him and flew on. But there was nothing the undog could do against such power. If it caught him in its claws, it would rip him to shreds in a heartbeat.

Harlowe had never felt so helpless as he watched the undog disappear over the horizon and chase after the crab that was after his ship. What would Monday and Prigg do, he wondered? How would they fight something so ungodly?

Delamo ran on with miles left to go.

What choice was there? What would he find? Would his crew be alive? And what of Fyn and his ceffyl herd, and Isara and Muis? What of them? How would they all survive?

Harlowe rode.

He refused to answer his questions. He refused to give up any one of them.

And Harlowe rode.

134

Snort, Snort

The stars at the galactic core were so luminous one could easily read a book by their light. Dejected and heartbroken, Harlowe didn't need the help of ten billion, billion stars to see that *Millawanda* was gone. With Delamo beside him, his worst fear had come true. There was no trace of his crew, Fyn, the ceffyls, or his ship. No Mowgi, either. They were all gone, taken by the giant crab thing. From miles away he had watched the long arms snatch his ship off the mound and reel his ship into its belly like it was eating it whole. There was no power in the galaxy that could stop it from taking all that he loved.

He dismounted and stood on the beach next to the empty mound. There was no point in going anywhere. There was no place to go. The quest to find Orixy was over. His ship was gone. Who or what had taken her seemed superfluous questions at this point, but they were questions he wanted answered. The crab-beast had no markings that he saw, no distinguishing characteristics that he recognized. He didn't believe it was Mysterian, either. It was golden and smooth, not dark and angular. Except for the thunderous vibrations, it flew silently. Mysterian hyperdrives were loud and overbuilt. Still, where did the crab come from, and why had it taken his ship? The obvious answer was the only one he could think of: salvage. The crab had taken *Millawanda* to strip her down and crush her into a solid block of compressed metal. He could think of nothing more painful than she would end up in a junkyard pile of rubble as her final resting place.

Don't give up, babe. Don't give up.

Strange, he thought. Leucadia's voice was talking to him from tens of thousands of lightyears away. He had left her on a planet far, far away, yet she sounded as real as if she were here standing next to him.

He felt lightheaded and exhausted, lost in a wishful dream.

Keep walking, Babe, she told him. *There is a reason.*

He interrupted their chat. *Reason for what, Lu? That my ship is gone? That she's been sent to the scrap yard?* he scowled at her.

She tried to talk to him, but he was in no mood for nonsense. "Stop it, Lu! I don't want to hear any more!"

He slapped the side of his neck, retracting his bugeye mask into his suit. "That's enough noise," he growled.

As he looked over the mound, the sand around it was completely clean of any telltale signs that anyone had been there before. No footprints, no beach chairs, no towels or surfboards were anywhere to be seen. All their gear was gone. He heard a flutter of wings flapping. Unbelievably, Mowgi was sitting at the top of the mound like he was king of the hill.

"Couldn't stop it, huh, Mowg?" Harlowe asked him. Mowgi yipped once. "What good are you?" he said, trying to hide his grief. He sat down in the sand, letting go of Delamo's reins as the undog joined them. It had been a long journey. Thirty-five thousand lightyears, and it had come down to this: sitting in the sand with his dog and his steed, looking out at the ocean, surrounded by a dead city.

"Sweet."

He leaned back, closed his eyes, and was about to dream of what could have been with Leucadia by his side when he heard a snort. Thinking his dream wasn't taking him in the direction he wanted, he reset his brain and tried again to find Leucadia. If this was it, he wanted her with him, even if she was a dream.

Snort, snort.

Harlowe's eyes flew open with annoyance as a giant tongue reached out and licked the side of his face with a smelly wet one.

"WHAT THE... PIGPO! You piece of— Where did you come from?" Harlowe roared, pushing the large pig face away before he licked him again. He wiped the Pigpo slobber from his face and said, "Why are you here? Did the crab reject you or something?"

Pigpo's grief-stricken face was enough to bring Harlowe to tears. He reached out and took his head in his arms and held him. "There, there now. We'll be okay, Piggy. Don't worry."

Snort, snort.

It was more like a sob than a snort, but holding Pigpo in his arms was comforting. Harlowe didn't let go as the tears began to flow together.

Snort, snort.

"I know, Piggy. I feel the same way."

"What way is that, Harlowe?" Fyn's voice asked.

Harlowe wiped his eyes and turned toward the voice. "What rock did you crawl out from, Fyn?"

Fyn pointed at the ruins. "The moment we heard it, Monday told us to run."

Now he saw the herd of ceffyls grazing between the ruins. He didn't know how he had missed them before. His grief had obviously shortened his peripheral vision to a point that was just past his nose.

Harlowe let Pigpo go as he wiped his face. "Monday? Prigg? Where are they?" he asked, still sitting in the sand.

Fyn pressed his lips together. "Still with the ship, Harlowe. What was it?"

"I don't know, Fyn."

"Riverstone and Rerun?"

"I didn't find them."

"Delamo couldn't…"

"No. When I saw the thing, we came back. They're still out there somewhere," Harlowe explained.

Fyn sat down beside Harlowe, dejected as everyone else. His daughter and son were on the ship, too.

"I'm sorry, Fyn."

"What do we do, Harlowe?"

Harlowe had no real answer. "Find Riverstone and Rerun first, then we survive and keep looking."

Fyn nodded in silence. That was the only practical answer. Survive.

Harlowe felt like he should get up, gather wood, make a campfire, go hunting maybe, do something to begin their existence on this unknown planet. But nothing in his bones allowed him to move. After thousands of lightyears across the galaxy, he just wanted to sit with his fellow survivors and contemplate nothing more stressful than his belly-button lint. That was all the energy he could muster, that is, until Mowgi began to yip.

"Now what, Mowg?" Harlowe asked, tossing a handful of sand at the undog's paws to get him to shut up.

A couple ernest yips with his parabolics hyperextended at a shapely blonde walking toward them, caught his attention. He wiped his eyes, wondering if the babe was a mirage or some wishful apparition of a former captain of a Gamadin ship who lost his mind.

He stood, staring at the babe's strut that he would know from half a galaxy away. She wore a soft blue, long flowing, silk dress, that when the breeze blew, it clung to her like a magnet, revealing every curve on her twelve body.

Fyn saw her, too. "Is she real, Harlowe?"

"I'm not sure."

"You know her?"

"I certainly do, Fyn."

She was the only thing in the galaxy that would make him move from his sand chair. Harlowe bolted. He couldn't tell if she was real or not until he touched her.

"LU! LU!" he shouted.

He kept running. And then she ran, too. Together they shorten the distance by half until they were in each other's arms, kissing and touching and falling on the wet sand, never wanting to let go, smothering each other with long kisses, talking little, holding, breathing in gasps, rolling, crying, saying things like, It's really you. Yes, it's me. But how? Kissing more, with no answers, tears, thankfulness and pounding hearts.

With mouth agape, his face covered with wet sand, his chest only partially filled with air, Harlowe finally asked her, "But how?"

She took his face in her hands and kissed him before she answered, "In time, Harlowe. What's important is that we found you at last."

Harlowe turned toward the mound, his face long and sad. "I lost her, Lu. I lost Millie. We never found Orixy."

She smiled gently, turning his face back to her as she told him, "Harlowe, you did make it. This is Orixy."

135

The Greeter

For the longest time, Harlowe sat silent, digesting her long blonde hair, bright green eyes, and flawless skin, half stunned, half blown away, wondering the usual: is this all a dream? There was a better chance of him winning the lotto than for Leucadia to find him here, at this moment of his greatest need.

He stood, letting go of her hand as he rose. A wave slowly built, forming a perfect right as it curled into a glassy tube and broke into a frothy line, coming into the beach. Finally, he spoke to her. "You know, there are a lot of people in this galaxy. A lot of beings that I met coming here. But you're the—"

She stopped him abruptly. "The last person you thought you would ever see?"

Harlowe smiled first, then pressed his lips together as he shook his head slowly back and forth. "That's putting it mildly."

Her face turned sad. "You didn't miss me?"

"Oh, God yes! I missed you every day. It tore my heart out to leave you behind on that planet." He hesitated briefly. "What was its name, anyway?"

A perplexed look came over her. "I forgot. Is it important?"

"No, I guess not."

"Well, I'm here now," she said.

Still, something wasn't right for Harlowe. "Yes, you are. Very convenient."

Had Fate blessed them again? Had It brought them back together and that was all that was necessary to know and be thankful for? No what-ifs to ponder. No more second guessing. Was it really that simple? Was this it? Was the journey over? They were together, and that was all that he needed to know. The past was past. It was time to move on.

"So what about Wiz?" Harlowe asked. "He is with you, right? He's okay?"

"Yes, he is well, Harlowe."

He closed his eyes, thanking someone above his pay grade. "And the rest of my crew?"

"They are safe and well, Harlowe."

"My ship. Whatever it was," he said pointing skyward, "took my ship." He looked at her hard. "What do you know about that?"

She glared back. "Why do you always think I know so much?"

"Because you always do. Sun rises, sun sets. What goes up, comes down. It's a given, Lu."

She tried to take his hand, but Harlowe wasn't in the touchy-feely mood. "I'm here to help you, Harlowe. Is there more that you need to know?"

"Yeah, there is! Tell me what happened to Millie!"

"Alright, alright, that was a salvage narn. Millie was taken to the repair facility."

"See, that wasn't hard, was it?" Before she could answer, Harlowe asked, "So she'll be okay, right?"

"Maybe even better than before."

He looked skyward, his lips muttering silent disbeliefs. "So what happened to Riverstone and Bolt? Where are they?"

Leucadia drew a concerned face with the mention of their names. "I don't know. They were not aboard *Millawanda*, Harlowe."

"No, they're MIA. I sent them looking for food, but they didn't come back. Their coms are dark. I was looking for them when," he said waving his hand in the air, "that crab thing—"

"The narn?"

"Yeah, that gobbled up Millie."

"They must be okay," she said.

"Maybe. There's a lot about this place you're not telling me. I can see that. So who lives on this planet, anyway?"

"It's complicated."

"I can imagine. How long have you been here?"

"A few days before you."

"Have you met the people here? There are people here, right? No disembodied spirits, I hope, looking for another body to replace theirs. I saw that in an old *Star Trek* episode once. It was a yucky life."

"No, nothing like that."

Harlowe sighed. "That's a relief. Are they friendly?"

"Yes."

"That's good. That's good. What about the Old Ones? Are they still around?"

"No, they're gone, Harlowe."

Harlowe clacked his lips with disappointment. "I was hoping to meet one of Kron's relatives. That would have been cool." His thoughts quickly sobered. "Who's in charge here?"

"No one."

"No one? What do you mean, 'no one'?"

"No one. There are no authorities in charge here."

Harlowe stared at her. "No governments, huh? Don't try to brighten my day 'cause that might work." He looked off briefly again, eyeing another small wave do its thing. "So who took Millie?"

"Let me show you, babe."

"Please do."

"Then can we get back to being friends again?"

"When I get my ship back, we'll be bosom buddies, Romeo and Juliet, Mr. & Mrs. Smith, Heckle and Jeckle, take your pick. I want my ship back, Lu!"

"Okay, okay. Follow me."

Leucadia led Harlowe a small ways down the beach before they went inland through a maze of ancient avenues. In a peculiar way it felt secure and warm meandering through a city that wasn't destroyed by war, political greed, or corruption, just time. As they walked along, Harlowe grew more and more skeptical of her. He shied away from taking her hand. Noticed the small things about her that were not quite right. Like Mowgi. The undog never once jumped into her arms or wagged his whippy tail at her. Or the fact she was not chatty at all about the cats. It was as if she didn't know they existed.

By the time they came to an open plaza of time-worn stone, Harlowe had enough pretending and grabbed her arm. "This is nuts. Who are you?"

"I'm Lu, Harlowe. Don't you know me?"

She tried to break free, but Harlowe was holding on until she spilled the beans. Whatever she was selling, he wasn't buying it.

"You don't believe me."

"No, I don't. You're a very good likeness," Harlowe began. "And thanks for the romp back there. I really needed that. But you don't taste like the real Lu."

She looked at him oddly as he let go of her arm. "My lips taste bad?" she asked.

"No, they have no taste at all. Lu's lips are sweet. There's no one who tastes like her. No one in this whole galaxy."

The girl seemed hurt by the disapproval.

Harlowe lifted her chin. "Don't be sad. It's okay. Really, ah… Mowgi didn't believe you, either," he said, nodding toward the undog who seemed bored by the masquerade.

"What is your name, anyway?"

"Name?"

"What do people call you?"

"I am the Greeter," she replied. "I have no name."

Harlowe turned his nose up.

"Does my name offend you, Harlowe?" the Greeter asked.

After a short chuckle, Harlowe replied. "No, your name doesn't offend me. It's just a girl with your…ah…assets, should have a name. What did your parents call you?"

"Parents?"

"Yeah, your mom and…" he hesitated, knowing he made a brain fart. How could she have parents if she wasn't real. She was Leucadia for his benefit and nothing more.

"Look. My fault. Forget about the parents thing. Can I call you Nance? It's short for Nancy. She was my second grade girlfriend. We were going to run away and get married, but Riverstone said his mom was taking us to the beach. Well, so that was that. But no one ever called her Nancy. Everyone called her Nance."

"Nance? You would prefer to call me Nance?"

"Is that cool?"

"I, I guess so," she replied indifferently. "Whatever pleases you, Harlowe."

"Great!" Harlowe took her shoulders and kissed her on the forehead. "From this day forward, you are known as Nance. Now where is my ship, Nance?"

Waving her hand toward the middle of the plaza, "If you will step this way, I will take—"

Suddenly, she stopped mid sentence as her face turned worrisome.

"What's the matter, Nance?" Harlowe asked.

She grabbed his hand and led him toward the center of the plaza. "Hurry, Harlowe. We have no time to lose."

136

The Babes

Riverstone awakened to the fresh, warm scent of pine. From his bed, the morning sun was shining through an open, double-hung window across the room that was decorated with homey, wood furniture, cushiony chairs, and pots of blue flowers that smelled amazingly like the ones at the Mars' beach estate in California and then later in the gorge where they first found *Millawanda*. Physically, he felt unusually fine. Better than normal, he thought. His head was clear and functioning like it should, even after being knocked out by whatever it was the girls stunned them with.

Bare chested, he swung his feet over the edge of the bed and was relieved to see he still had on his trunks. So far, he didn't get the sense he had been captured by bad guys. His room was anything but dark, dungeonous, and smelly. If he didn't know better, he might have thought he was back on Earth. His sheets were fresh and clean like his mother had just changed them.

Yeah, bad guys never made you feel like you just checked in at Harry's, he thought.

Feeling somewhat better about his predicament, he got up and went to the window. Outside, the sky was blue and sunny with a few wispy clouds overhead. Nothing threatening. The grounds were tastefully landscaped with green and yellow bushes, wide manicured lawns, and trimmed hedges. Beyond was a forest of tall evergreens where their ceffyls were casually munching on the high grass in the meadow. They seemed perfectly at peace with their surroundings.

Still, as good as the place looked, he had to find Simon and contact Harlowe, who he knew by now would be going nutso because they hadn't checked in since yesterday.

Walking out in public in just his trunks, didn't seem cool. He picked up a dark purple robe that fit him perfectly. Obviously, their host had anticipated his need.

Now publicly fit to venture out, he found the door unlocked and went out into the hall. His room was at the end so which direction to go was a no brainer. Before he came to the next turn, he heard Simon's voice mixed with the laughter of girls and knew he was on the right path. Two turns later, he came to an open porch where Simon was yucking it up around a white, wooden table with the babes who stunned them.

"Jester!" Simon cried out the moment he saw Riverstone coming toward them. "Sue here makes a mean Denver omelette with a Texas twist to it. Yumm." He motioned toward the second girl. "And this lovely thing is Maggie. Girls, meet Riverstone."

"Hello, Riverstone," they said together.

Riverstone forced a smile and said a cursory hello to the girls, Sue and Maggie. "Rerun. We have to tell Harlowe where we are."

"I tried calling him earlier, but he didn't answer," Simon said defensively.

"Then we have to boogie back to the ship, pronto," Riverstone said.

Then like a switch turned on in their heads, both girls became suddenly alarmed. "Yes, you must go now, Simon," Sue said.

Maggie added, "Yes, you must go to the meadow and wait there. Hurry!"

Riverstone confronted her before leaving. "We need our things, Maggie. Where are they?"

She pointed toward the meadow. "On your mounts." She practically pushed him out the door as Simon gave Sue a quick peck on the lips and thanked her for the wonderful breakfast.

As they ran for the meadow, they saw their weapons and Gamadin clothes folded nicely and strapped to their ceffyls. "What torqued them?" Simon asked. "I was really liking their company. You know they—"

Riverstone interrupted him as they ran. "They weren't real, Rerun. What girls have names like Sue and Maggie thirty-thousand lightyears from Earth?"

"Yeah, I thought that was weird, too. But she sure kissed real," Simon said smiling fondly.

"You kissed her?"

"Yeah, throw me a steak like that, and what would you do?"

Just as they grabbed their ceffyls, Simon spotted the flying platform descending fast toward the meadow. "What is it?"

The object looked like a large airborne blinker. It was dark gold, round, and flat, without any visible means of propulsion. It simply floated down to them like a flying carpet. Standing on top were two people frantically waving at them.

Riverstone didn't know what it was, either, but they sure recognized the babe with Harlowe. "That's Lu! How did she get here?"

Simon's eyes grew round as bugeyes. "Dog is full of surprises."

Riverstone shook his head. "Can't wait to hear the story."

Before the platform touched the ground, Harlowe was barking orders. "Jump on!"

"How did you find us?" Riverstone asked, leading his mount toward the platform. Simon was right behind him.

"Doesn't matter. Get on!" Harlowe barked.

"What about the ceffyls, Skipper?" Simon asked.

"Leave them. They'll be okay. Fyn will get them."

"Lu, what are you doing here?" Simon asked, looking at her up and down in disbelief.

"That's not Lu. It's Nance," Harlowe said.

Simon's eyes turned instantly to lust. "Even better."

"Eyes back in your head, Mr. Bolt," Harlowe ordered.

"Where are we going?" Riverstone asked, hopping aboard the disk.

Harlowe replied, "To pick up, Millie."

"What?" Riverstone shot back. "With her butt sticking out of a sand dune?"

"She was taken by a narn, and we have bad guys coming in fast," Harlowe spelled out as the force field snapped over the platform just before it left the ground at incredible speed.

"Mysterians?" Riverstone asked.

Harlowe wanted everyone on the clock. "Yeah, big time. They've entered the star system."

"What star system is that?" Riverstone wanted to know. He felt like he was getting bits and pieces as the platform raced across the planet due south.

"Orixy. This planet is Orixy. We made it, and we're going to pick up Millie," Harlowe explained.

"Millie's not at the beach?" Simon asked.

"No. She's…she's… I don't know where she is. But that's where Nance is taking us."

Miles below, the land and the oceans were passing by at better than five thousand miles per hour toward an unknown destination.

137

The Facility

At the polar end of Orixy, the platform came upon a massive frozen continent that was covered by thousands of feet of snow pack. It seemed like the last place on the planet they would find *Millawanda*. During the journey, Harlowe caught up Riverstone and Simon with a Cliffs Notes version of what happened to Millie after they disappeared, telling them that he left Mowgi behind to protect Fyn and the herd of ceffyls from predators. Riverstone and Simon told their story, but they left out the part about being caught with their pants down. Harlowe grinned, knowing there was plenty more to the story. He had his crew back, and that was enough. A couple hundred miles farther inland, the platform slowed as they approached a single, snow shrouded pyramid as big as a mountain, jutting three miles above the icepack. There was no apparent reason to be here until the massive structure began to move aside, revealing a five-mile wide cavity below the planet's surface.

Down they went.

Down, down, down, descending into a vast open area of many levels and corridors where miles and miles of golden dura-metal machines were kept. There were gigantic cranes, platforms and machinery of all shapes and sizes. There were even giant robobs standing around patiently that were so big, it looked as though they could pick up *Millawanda* with a single mechanical claw.

They floated on, winding their way through the vast corridors until they came upon an area of bright lights in the distance. As they came closer, three robobs were busy working on a small golden disk lying on a table with blinking lights of many colors all around it. The first clicker turned the disk on its side, touched the undersides, and an electrical discharge arced, sending sparks of hot embers into the air and onto the table and floor.

Nance frowned at seeing the robobs clustered around the disk. "She's not done yet, Harlowe."

Harlowe was confused. "What's not done?"

"Your ship, Harlowe."

He looked everywhere. The only thing he saw was what looked like Wiz's garage, full of old parts left over from broken spaceships. He didn't see Millie anywhere. "Where is she?"

Nance pointed at the disk on the table. "There, Harlowe. That is *Millawanda.*"

Harlowe activated his bugeyes to make sure his own eyes weren't playing tricks on him. Yes, it was Millie. The three forward windows of the bridge were staring right at him. As they came closer, the size of everything grew exponentially until *Millawanda* was her normal size, and they were like tiny ants compared to everything else around them. The robobs were so gargantuan, Millie appeared like a small toy in the palm of their mechanical hands.

"I thought Bigbob was big," Simon quipped.

"I hope they're careful with her," Riverstone added. "That's our ride home."

A second giant clicker touched her on the side, and the lights around her perimeter turned on briefly, flickered, and then went out again. It repeated the process with another instrument with similar results.

"I wish Wiz were here," Harlowe commented.

The third clicker stuck her with a needle-like probe that made her extend her landing struts like she was in pain. When the struts retracted, the robob did it again. Only two struts extended this time. It thumped the side of her hull once, twice, three times before the third strut finally stretched itself out.

None of the Gamadin liked what they were seeing and shouted collectively at the robobs. "YO, STOP THAT! GIVE HER A BREAK, SUCKWADS! THAT'S OUR MILLIE YOU'RE STICKING, TOADS!"

Like someone heard their shouting, the robobs stopped whatever they were doing and placed *Millawanda* on the table with her landing struts extended. The second robob touched her again, and this time her running lights stayed on.

"I want to go aboard," Harlowe said to Nance. It was not a request.

"She is still damaged, Harlowe," Nance cautioned him.

"I know, but my crew is on board. I need to know they're okay."

Realizing he wasn't taking no for an answer, she flew them to the outer hatch that led to Harlowe's quarters. Harlowe jumped from the platform before it touched down and didn't stop until he went through the sliding door to the bridge.

"Captain on the bridge!" Monday's voice boomed.

Harlowe froze. He didn't expect to see anyone aboard the ship, especially with all the tossing and turning the giant robobs had done to it. Monday appeared like they hadn't experienced any discomfort at all. As a matter of fact, he looked healthy and ready for duty like he was just fed a stack of pancakes and eggs for breakfast. The surprises didn't stop there. Stepping off the blinker was Naree. Instead of Clarity grey, she wore a Gamadin blue jumpsuit that fit her like a glove. Harlowe thought Simon was going to pass out. Riverstone caught him before he did a nosedive at her feet. "Steady, Rerun," he said, helping to him to the sunrise observation couch.

"Naree's been a great help to us on the bridge, Captain," Monday said.

Harlowe looked up at the overhead as he and Riverstone made their way to their respective command chairs. "Where's Mr. Prigg?"

"Working with the aara chips, Captain."

"Chips? That doesn't sound like what we came here for," Riverstone pointed out.

"What do we have, Mr. Platter?" Harlowe asked.

"Small pieces are all we found, Captain, so we only have sub-light." Monday replied.

"This is Orixy. What happened to all the big stuff?"

"It was used up, Captain. While the big guys were working on putting Millie back together, Prigg got lucky and found some little ones on the back shelves."

"Great. What about weapons?"

"Some. Plas cannons maybe twenty percent."

Harlowe tapped the sides of his chair in frustration. "Any good news?"

"Prigg has shields up to ninety percent."

"We can work with that. Communications?"

"Not much, but better than before. Sensors are good to go, Captain."

Now it was Riverstone's turn to ask, "So what you're telling us, Mr. Platter, is we're about to face the most powerful bad ass bad guy we've ever come up against, and we don't have squat after traveling a zillion lightyears to the planet that made her?"

"Something like that, Mr. Riverstone," Monday replied in agreement.

Nance made a suggestion. "Let the mechanics continue working on *Millawanda*, Harlowe. While they work, we can use the platform to search the facility for more aara."

Harlowe glanced at the overhead. "How far out are they?"

Monday went to his console. "A day and a half before they reach us, Captain."

"I thought we lost them," Riverstone said.

Harlowe studied the star map. "Someone brought them here."

"Okay," Riverstone said, getting up. "That's a day and a half of breathing room. Let's do it, Nance. I'll frisk the place down, Dog. If there are any rocks out there, we'll find them."

Harlowe raised his hand. "Hold on, Mr. Riverstone." He pointed at the overhead. "What's that blue dot doing?"

Riverstone came back and looked up at the screen. "Attacking the big guy?"

"I think so," Harlowe muttered. "Blue could only mean it's a Gamadin ship."

Nance studied the overhead and concurred. "Correct, Harlowe. That is a Gamadin ship." She went to the sensor console and fine tuned the readouts. "But this is no warship. She is a minor vessel with limited capabilities."

Harlowe turned to Riverstone first and ordered, "Delay that search, Mr. Riverstone." Back to Monday he added, "Contact that ship, Mr. Platter. Tell them to veer off. We'll be there shortly."

"Aye, Captain," Monday replied.

After several tries and a ton of clicks and static, Naree came to Monday's aide, and together they managed to contact the ship but on a limited basis. "Come in, Gamadin ship. Do you read us?" Monday hailed.

"Yes, yes, we do? Is that you, Platter?" Ian's voice said over the ship's com.

The entire bridge suddenly went silent listening to the inconceivable. Harlowe quickly answered back. "Wiz! Is that you?"

"Harlowe! Yeah, yeah, it's me. Lu is here, too. We found a ship and..."

The static crackle and pop severed communications between the two ships.

"Get them back, Mr. Platter. STAT!"

"The Mysterians are jamming us, Captain," Naree said.

Harlowe slammed his fist on the arm of his chair. "Buckle up, everyone. Our day and a half just went to zero." To Nance he said, "Save us a parking place, Nance."

She started to protest, but Harlowe shook his head. They were going regardless. "You must hurry, then. Bring them back to Orixy, Captain."

Harlowe winked at her. "I will. That's a promise," he told her.

She winked away without a blinker. An instant later, she was on the platform, waving goodbye as she sped away down the vast corridor. Harlowe took control, retracting the landing struts as he guided *Millawanda* to the open hold of the facility. Then he turned her up on a near vertical ascent, exiting the great hole as he pushed the throttle to the max, praying they would get there in time.

138

Maw of the Beast

"Ten more drones, Captain," Monday announced.

"Hurry, Mr. Platter! They're after Wiz and Lu," Harlowe urged.

It was like watching paint dry for the Gamadin crew. The trip to the outer star system took a little over a full day to travel three billion miles. Way slower than the seconds they would have normally taken. When they finally reached the Mysterian mothership, they were met by wave after wave of annoying drones.

"Mr. Bolt?"

"I have a lock, Skipper!" Simon replied.

Like pesky gnats, the mothership kept sending its attack drones to intercept them.

"Do it, Mr. Bolt," Harlowe ordered.

Blasting bogies to subatomic dust kept Simon so busy he was able to overcome the fact that Naree had turned back into a faceted hunk of grey molecules the moment they left Orixy's gravitational pull. Instead of falling into a melancholy depression requiring a session or two with his robob therapist, Simon found solace in shooting up drones by the dozens. More than once, Harlowe had to caution him on overshooting his prey when he already had blown them to smithereens.

"Easy, Mr. Bolt. Save some for the mothership," Harlowe cautioned.

Simon turned toward Harlowe with crazed eyes. "Sorry, Skipper," and went back to his weapons array, eager for more bogies.

Riverstone stole a sip of Harlowe's chocolate shake saying to Harlowe. "I don't think he heard ya."

Harlowe grabbed a fry from the food tray beside his chair. Now that they had some power, they could eat real food again and were grabbing small bites whenever they could.

Out of earshot, Harlowe said, "Let him be. He hasn't missed yet." He shot a glance at the overhead when the blue dot winked out. "What happened to Wiz? He just went dark."

Riverstone put the shake back. "You're kidding. It was just there a second ago."

"Look. He's gone now."

"Pull Prigg from the aara drive bay to lend us a hand," Riverstone suggested.

"Do it!"

*   *   *

Less than a minute later, Prigg blinked to the bridge from the engine room, putting his three eyes feverishly to work on the sensors. When he was done with a systems check, he revealed his findings. "The sensor station is operating at top efficiency, Your Majesty."

"So what happened to Wiz, Mr. Prigg? He should be there somewhere on the map."

"That is correct, Your Majesty. His ship should be displayed on the screen."

That left Riverstone with the dreaded question no one wanted to ask. "So did they buy the big one, Mr. Prigg?"

Prigg had been around the Gamadin crew lingo enough to decipher the nuances of SoCal phraseology and replied without asking for an interpretation, "No, Mr. Riverstone, sensors show no Gamadin debris field."

Harlowe went back to the overhead. "So where could they be? There are no moons, planets, or asteroids for a million miles."

Prigg came up with the only logical answer. "The Mysterians have them, Your Majesty."

"That's a stretch, Mr. Prigg. Wiz would have winked out of there in a heartbeat if the Mysterians got too close," Riverstone said.

Prigg's middle eye went to the screen. "I am sorry, Mr. Riverstone, but there is no other conclusion."

"Their ship's been swallowed?" Harlowe asked.

"It doesn't appear to be destroyed, Your Majesty. And since it is no longer there, that is the only place she could be."

Riverstone tapped Harlowe's arm. "The big guy is coming after us now."

On the overhead the big orange blip had altered course and was coming straight for them.

"Give them all ya got, Mr. Bolt!" Harlowe ordered.

Once, twice, three times, Simon fired at the oncoming mothership. But each time, the long range optics showed the reduced power of their plasma hits were unable to penetrate the Mysterian shields.

"Nothing, Skipper. The rounds are bouncing off their force field."

Suddenly, the mothership returned fire, discharging a bright orange bolt past their sunrise perimeter, jolting *Millawanda* like she had been struck with a giant sledge hammer.

"We can't take many more of those, Captain," Monday declared. "That last one reduced our shields by half."

"What now?" Riverstone asked, as another jolt dumped the tray of fries and shakes onto the floor.

"Back to Orixy," Harlowe ordered.

"We don't have the speed to outrun them, Captain," Riverstone said.

Harlowe looked forcefully at Monday. "Do it, Mr. Platter!"

"Aye, Captain!"

Then *Millawanda* flipped over and did a complete one-eighty, heading back to Orixy at the same snail's pace she had left planet. The only problem was that it was going to take another day to get there, and the Mysterians were only thirty seconds from eating them for lunch.

Everyone's eyes were on the overhead as the view screen turned from a star map to the actual sight of the moon-sized mothership racing toward them with its maw of Death opening wide to swallow them whole.

"They are powering up their tractor beam, Your Majesty," Prigg called out from his station.

"Thank you, Mr. Prigg," Harlowe said calmly.

Harlowe bent down to the floor and picked up what was left of his shake. He stuck the straw back in the cup and sucked on what was left.

Riverstone stared at Harlowe like he had lost it. "Should I have Jewels get you another shake, Captain?"

Suddenly, from out of nowhere a blue shimmer of light spread at the same moment the Mysterian tractor beam reached out and grabbed them from behind.

"Give it all you got, Mr. Platter!" Harlowe ordered.

"She's floored now, Captain," Monday shot back.

"Mr. Prigg, how close are we to the field?"

Prigg responded instantly, "Seconds, Your Majesty!"

Harlowe handed his empty cup to Jewels who replaced it with a full one. "Everyone strap in!"

Millawanda screamed as she shuddered and twisted, fighting against the pull of the beam.

"Hang in there, girl," Harlowe said to her. "A little ways farther and..."

The mothership's fangs were practically touching the saucer's outer hull when Harlowe turned another one-eighty and flew into the Mysterian's maw. Now the bridge was looking right down the mouth of the huge ship as they passed through the field. Incredibly, *Millawanda* passed through the blue light like it was nothing, but the Mysterian mothership was breaking up and disintegrating before their eyes. Its powerful protective shields were useless. There were no sparks, no fire, no crackling sound as the giant ship dissolved before their eyes like it was tossed in a vat of acid.

And then it was over. The two-mile long Mysterian mothership faded away into oblivion.

"WOW!" was the only sound Riverstone could utter.

Simon was no less awed by what he had seen, but unlike Riverstone, his voice was good to go. "How did you know, Skipper?"

"It was Nance," Harlowe began. "She said, 'Bring them back here.'"

Monday chimed in, "I thought she was talking about Wiz and Lu."

Simon believed like the others. "Yeah, me, too."

"No, she was talking about the Mysterians."

"Orixy's power reaches this far, Your Majesty?" Prigg asked in wonder.

Harlowe reached out and squeezed Prigg's little shoulder. "Yes, Mr. Prigg, the Gamadin, after all this time, is still someone you don't want to mess with."

"May I steal your Captain, gentlemen?" a woman's voice asked from the back of the bridge.

The crew turned to Leucadia, who was stepping off the blinker in a stunning, blue jumpsuit.

"LU!" everyone cried out.

Harlowe handed Riverstone his shake as he walked to her. "You have the bridge, Mr. Riverstone."

Riverstone had found his voice again. "Aye, Captain."

Harlowe took her in his arms. Was she real, or was she another ruse? His hands felt her warmth as her fragrance filled his senses. There was orchid, bergamot, orris, that hint of vanilla that he always loved, combined with ylang-ylang and tropical grass that drove him crazy. He touched her hair. It was silky smooth and golden against her flawless skin. Her eyes, brilliant and green, glowed with a radiance of happiness that only one woman in the galaxy could truly give him.

"Are you going to just stand there or kiss me?" she asked as her rosy lips parted with a loving smile.

"I was hoping you weren't a dream," he told her.

She pulled him in and kissed him softly. The duration was brief but filled with a loving tenderness that only two people, whose souls are forever linked, can feel.

There were tears forming in both their eyes. Their bodies trembled. They seemed to be the only ones on the bridge at that moment, when he said, "God, how I missed you."

They spoke no more words and kissed again, deeper, longer, shaking as if they would never part for an eternity. They turned round and round, and then they winked away, stepping on the blinker by accident maybe...but probably not.

"Why did his Majesty and Miss Lu leave?" Prigg asked so innocently it brought smiles to the bridge.

As he shifted over to the captain's command chair, Riverstone replied, "There's no kissing on the bridge, Mr. Prigg. Captain's orders."

Prigg's eyes went in several directions as he said, "Oh, I see."

Out the forward window a small golden saucer drifted to within a few feet of the bridge. There were a number of people waving inside. A familiar face sitting in the command chair stood up and saluted, mouthing the words, "Reporting for duty, Mr. Riverstone!"

139

Permission Granted

They found it difficult to believe it was nighttime on Orixy. The three rose colored moons of various sizes were scattered across a heaven filled with a billion,billion stars so bright, they made what was supposed to be the dark side of the planet appear like day. Harlowe and Leucadia stood together overlooking the beach from the bungalow deck that the robobs had built by the time the two saucers had returned to Orixy. The beach house sat peacefully on thick pylons atop the mountain of sand *Millawanda* had piled high upon her arrival. It was their place to sleep, eat, ride, bask in the sun, and surf until Millawanda's overhaul was complete. The bungalow was built of rare tropical woods. The addition of large open doorways, shady overhangs, and wide open decks surrounding it, gave the building a homey appearance that looked like it was transported straight from the beach-front cottages of Hawaii.

The waves, the warm days, and clear nights made the wait bearable. Nance was a gracious hostess and did everything in her formidable power to make the young Gamadin crew stay comfortable. She even altered her appearance when Simon asked if she might change her physical form from that of Leucadia Mars to someone else.

"Is there a problem with my appearance, Mr. Bolt?" Nance asked him.

Simon put his arms around her. "No, no, you look better than hot, Nance. It's just that having more than one Leucadia walking around in a string bikini makes the other ladies a little uncomfortable. They want our full attention if you get my drift."

"Of course," she said, and returned to her natural state which turned out to be a small Quincy with a grey fabric covering, no hair, no nose, ears or mouth, and tiny red eyes that glowed in the dark.

Simon jumped back. "Whoa! Don't do that. That's going too far."

"Is there someone you would like me to be?" Nance asked, eager to please.

"You can be anyone?"

Nance nodded with a smile. "Anyone from your ship's memory cache," she replied.

Simon pondered, focusing on Riverstone riding the ceffyl called Chance with the girls, Maggie, Sue, and now Isara, who along with her brother, Muis, had recovered fully when Nance transported them to their underground medical facility. The robob medics reenergized and returned to duty. Maggie and Sue, who were real, unlike Nance, named their rides Tux and Scratch. "Can you find a Hollywood babe named Phoebe Marlee in Millie's memory?" he asked her.

Nance closed her eyes, and when the transformation was complete, she was an exact copy of the famous movie actress. "Am I to your liking now, Mr. Bolt?"

Simon was stunned. She even pressed her lips together in that sultry way she would to get his attention. "Perfect. Wow!"

"Must I change my name, too? I like the one Harlowe gave me."

"No, no. You can keep that. We like your name."

Changing her to Phoebe Marlee solved the problem. Riverstone practically fell off Chance's back when he laid eyes on the faux starlet for the first time. He had a crush on her since her first film, *Wicked Martian,* was released. It was not like his puppy-dog love with Leucadia's mom, or his heart-breaking loss of Ela, Phoebe was the dream babe that he always knew would never come true.

Until now! Simon chuckled.

* * *

"Any word from Nance on when Millie will be done?" Harlowe asked for the umpteenth time.

Leucadia looked at him pathetically. "I swear, babe, you're worse than a little kid asking, 'Daddy, are we there yet?'"

Harlowe snickered back. "How would you know about riding in a car for very long. If it was too far, Jewels would have dropped you at the nearest heliport, and Martin would fly you there."

Suddenly a kid in blue trunks ran across the sand, tossing a football to Harlowe. "Can we go surfing after I get back, Captain?"

"Sure, Muis. Where are you going?" Harlowe asked.

"With Wiz. He said I can go with him and Nath in the *Bad Boy*," Muis replied, just as the loud engines roared to life. A ways down the beach, the giant orange and black gerbid Harlowe had brought with him from Osset was parked along side *Forty-Four*. *Bad Boy* towered over the smaller saucer like a bully. A cloud of dark smoke blew out the rear of the tank, sounding like a loud cannon. Ever since Harlowe handed Ian the keys, he had barely seen his science officer for over a week. What exactly he was doing, Harlowe didn't know, nor did he care. *Bad Boy* was Ian's baby now, and he knew whatever the changes were, they would be cool and would make it better than before.

Leucadia focused on Muis. Fyn's son was a paragon of courage and heart. The boy had suffered the amputation of both feet, but with his new Gamadin prosthetics, he was running and jumping all over creation, playing Over-the-line, tossing the football, and by the second day, he was taking up surfing under Harlowe's tutelage.

Harlowe cocked his arm and said, "Go long, Muis!" And like he was shot out of plas cannon, Muis took off down the beach, waving for Harlowe to throw the football. Harlowe let loose with a perfect spiral. He was a little rusty from his quarterback days at Lakewood High, but it didn't matter to Muis. He sprang high into the air and pulled it down like he was ten feet tall.

Muis held up the football, danced, and performed a double forward flip before he took off again on his way to *Bad Boy*.

"He is an amazing boy," Leucadia said, watching him run in long graceful steps.

"Yes, he is," Harlowe said. He didn't have much to say. Describing Muis' injuries was still difficult for him to talk about.

"So what now, babe?" Leucadia asked.

"After we get Millie, we go home," he replied.

"That simple?"

"It's our home. Besides, Rerun can't wait to write our story. He says it will be the next summer blockbuster."

She watched him and Naree batting a shuttlecock back and forth on the beach, having the time of their lives.

"Does he know she can never leave Orixy?" Leucadia asked.

"He knows."

"Sadly, I've never seen him this happy since Sizzle left him."

"He'll find another, babe. He always does," Harlowe said dryly.

Leucadia turned around. Behind the bungalow in the grassy meadow that was lined with ancient structures, Fyn and the Fagans were tending the herd of horses and ceffyls that were grazing together. "What about the others?"

Harlowe joined her admiration, especially of the tall black ceffyl standing alone watching over his herd. "We're taking them home, too. They have a planet to rebuild."

"They would have made a fine addition to our crew," she said.

"I trust them all with my life, Lu," Harlowe said. Then he asked, "And what of your Prince? Wiz said he was a handful. Does he want to return to Nod and be king?"

Leucadia paused, as she found the Prince walking alone on the beach. "Someday, maybe. When he's ready. Right now all he wants is for you to accept him."

"He'll have to earn it. No shortcuts. You told him that?"

"Yes."

"Alright. But the first time he steps out of line, he's back to Nod."

"Understood, Captain," she said, with a light peck on the cheek. She then asked, "And what of Anor? Have you spoken with him?"

Harlowe's mouth twisted sourly. "Not yet."

"He helped us find Orixy, babe."

"Yeah," Harlowe said, unenthused by the idea of Anor Ran becoming a permanent member of his crew.

"We owe him."

Harlowe wasn't buying the trade. "I owe him nothing. Wiz saved his ass; that makes us even."

"Where will you take him?"

"Back to Tomar, I suppose. It's the least I can do for Sharlon. If it were me, I'd drop him off at Hitt and be done with him."

"Why don't you like him?"

"Because he's a scumbag."

"Even scumbags can change, Harlowe."

"Not him."

"I trust him."

Harlowe glared at her as the fold in his brow deepened. "Does Wiz trust him?"

Leucadia found herself defenseless. "Not so much."

"Yeah, I thought so. He tried to kill me and my crew, Lu. We'll take him to Tomar. Then that's it. End of story."

"He's a wealth of interstellar knowledge, Harlowe," Leucadia said in Anor's defense. "We could use his experience."

"I don't care if the Pope made him a saint. He's not one of us, and he will never be part of my crew."

Leucadia started to take a different tack, when Harlowe let go a loud whistle. As far as he was concerned, the discussion over. Anor was done. From the meadow, Delamo bolted toward the beach house with DaboS on his small horse right along side him. As Delamo came to the edge of the deck, he leaped upward in a great arc. Then in one fluid motion, Harlowe jumped over the rail and landed squarely on his back, grabbing a handful of thick mane; and when rider and ceffyl returned to earth, he and DaboS tore off down the beach, kicking up sand and splashing in the surf as they flew.

"You can come out now, Mr. Ran," Leucadia said to Anor who was hidden from view inside the doorway.

A tall gentleman with greying hair and dressed in a dark crimson jumpsuit walked out onto the deck and joined her. "Am I to be exiled to some far away planet, Ms. Lu?" Anor asked with a hint of fear in his eyes, watching Harlowe ride away.

"Not yet, Anor, but tread lightly," she warned as she turned and looked at him eye to eye. "Harlowe will take you home. But if you have any thoughts of betrayal, subterfuge, or any devious acts of trickery, there is no rock in this entire galaxy that will hide you from his wrath."

Anor nodded his understanding. "I know my place, Ms. Lu."

"I hope so, Mr. Ran, because if that day ever comes, I will help him find that rock."

* * *

Weeks later, it was late afternoon. Harlowe and Muis were surfing. Simon was giving Naree guitar lessons out on the deck, snacking on fresh guac and chips. Riverstone and Nance had just lifted off in the platform, flying south. The only regulars that were missing were Leucadia, Isara, Sue and Maggie. They were all wandering through the ancient ruins on their ceffyls when a great shadow crawled over the beach, blocking out the sun as it came to a stop over the bungalow.

Silently, and ever so slowly, the golden disk drifted down and extended her long landing struts into the shallow waters in front of the beach house. Harlowe let the waves carry his board into shore without him. Shaking and trying to swallow the knot in his throat, he walked to the nearest landing pod and caressed her warm, smooth surface, saying nothing, only marveling at her beauty, her roundness, her size, dwarfing all that was around her. In his study, he looked for scars, chipped paint, dents, cracks in the windows, or anything broken or out of place, like an owner who just had his car returned from the bodyshop. Harlowe found nothing wrong. *Millawanda* was flawlessly new again from outside.

But how would she be on the inside, he wondered. Would she be whole again? Would she be his Millie? Would her carpets be blue like before? The air clean and sweet like before? Would Mother cook their double-doubles, fries, tacos and pancakes to mouthwatering perfection? Would Dodger's place, the lush trees and tropical palms and the pool still be there? Would the dancing lights greet him on the bridge? And would Jewels be standing in his quarters with his uniform of the day all laid out on his bed when he stepped out of the shower? He thought about all this and more as the wide center ramp drew out from under the hull and touched down in the shallow water at his feet. With the waves lapping against the dura-metal sides, he started to walk up the long incline alone but held up after only going a few steps. He turned around, whistled, and waited. Joining him first was Delamo. The great ceffyl came to the bottom of the ramp, reared up, and then settled down, dipping his head and waving his mane, waiting for Harlowe's next command. Right behind the black were Molly and Rhud, splashing through the water to the end of the ramp. They, too, stood there patiently and waited. Then Mowgi and Pigpo, each excited and nervous like the others, sloshed their way to join the others. Then the being he had been waiting for, the one whom he would never go another step without, came riding in. She, dismounted with her green eyes tearing. Wiping her face, she made her way through the surf, petting, hugging, kissing each animal as she passed them and came to his offered hand.

"Ready?" he asked her.

"Very," she replied, taking his arm.

Harlowe waved for everyone to follow them up the ramp.

Normally, the cats would have bounded up the incline ahead of everyone, but not this time. For whatever reason they allowed Harlowe and Leucadia to lead the way. Next came Mowgi, and the cats followed with Pigpo, Delamo, and Josie climbing together. Shaking the earth and roaring like Mowgi at full dragon, *Bad Boy* came to a stop at the foot of the first landing pod. The hatchway opened, and Ian emerged in a hurry, towing Cheesa with him. They splashed through the shore break, shouting with happy faces, "Wait for us, Captain!"

Harlowe smiled and waved them on. He would not take another step without his crew.

From the side door of *Bad Boy*, Nath, Maa Dev, DaboS, and the other riders all waved their congratulations as Fyn, Isara, Maggie, and Sue came walking around the gerbid, joining the celebration. Coming from the bungalow, Simon and Naree walked hand in hand until they were just short of the water. They kissed, and then Naree turned him gently toward the ramp. "Go," she said. "I will always be here for you, Ahlian."

He kissed her one last time and said, "All my love, all my life, Naree."

He released her hand and hurried to catch up with the other Gamadin. Stepping side by side together, arm in arm, they met the rest of the crew, Riverstone, Monday, and Prigg, at the top of the center hatchway.

The Gamadin came to stick-straight attention and saluted. Harlowe wiped his eyes, and with a crack in his voice from the knot in his throat, asked, "Permission to come aboard, Mr. Riverstone?"

With a grin that would light up a city, Riverstone called out, "Permission granted, Captain. *Millawanda* is yours!"

The Next Gamadin Thriller!

Book VI

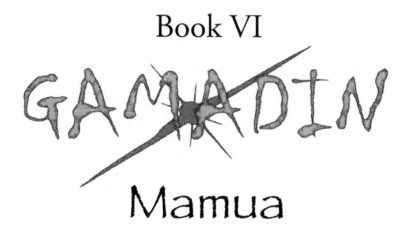

Mamua

Harlow and the Gamadin crew have returned to Earth for much needed R&R with their beautiful, reconditioned ship, *Millawanda*. She is even more powerful and cool than she was 17,000 years ago when she was first built. All is going well. Wiz has installed a new wave maker for the Dodger's place pool, Simon is shooting a new Sci-fi adventure with Riverstone having a bit part, and Tinker, Harlowe's mother, who is now the First Lady of the United States, has arranged for a private high school graduation ceremony for Harlowe, Riverstone, and Wiz. But when an elite mercenary force kidnaps Riverstone and Simon, along with his lovely co-star, Phoebe Marlee, and take over the ship, the graduation is put on hold. The problems mount as the Space Station is sabotaged and Harlowe learns the real name of the Donut, where Quay and her survivors are building a new world, is called Tabilisi. Even if they can retake their ship, the outlook for Quay is grim. The energy hungry Zabits by now have destroyed the Cartooga-Thaat way station and anyone alive inside it. But all of this is small potatoes compared to the Mamua…

Tom Kirkbride grew up in Southern California, where he was a lifeguard on the beaches of LaJolla...thus his Gamadin saga begins. In 2012 his entire Series was selected for the Renaissance Accelerated Reader program for schools nationwide. Tom lives in Oregon with his wife Nancy, their dogs Dolly, Daisy & Jack, three horses, and too many cats.

31354576R00420

Made in the USA
Middletown, DE
28 April 2016